D1095383

ENDER'S WAR

ORSON SCOTT CARD

ENDER'S WAR

Ender's Game
Speaker for the Dead

Nelson Doubleday, Inc.
Garden City, New York

CONTENTS

Ender's Game

For Geoffrey,
Who makes me remember
How young and how old
Children can be

Acknowledgments

Portions of this book were recounted in my first published science fiction story, "Ender's Game," in the August 1977 *Analog*, edited by Ben Bova; his faith in me and this story are the foundation of my career.

Harriet McDougal of Tor is that rarest of editors—one who understands a story and can help the author make it exactly what he meant it to be. They don't pay her enough. Harriet's task was made more than a little easier, however, because of the excellent work of my resident editor, Kristine Card. I don't pay her enough, either.

I am grateful also to Barbara Bova, who has been my friend and agent through thin and, sometimes, thick; and to Tom Doherty, my publisher, who let me talk him into doing this book at the ABA in Dallas, which shows either his superb judgment or how weary one can get at a convention.

Chapter 1

Third

"I've watched through his eyes, I've listened through his ears, and I tell you he's the one. Or at least as close as we're going to get."

"That's what you said about the brother."

"The brother tested out impossible. For other reasons. Nothing to do with his ability."

"Same with the sister. And there are doubts about him. He's too malleable. Too willing to submerge himself in someone else's will."

"Not if the other person is his enemy."

"So what do we do? Surround him with enemies all the time?"

"If we have to."

"I thought you said you liked this kid."

"If the buggers get him, they'll make me look like his favorite uncle."

"All right. We're saving the world, after all. Take him."

The monitor lady smiled very nicely and tousled his hair and said, "Andrew, I suppose by now you're just absolutely sick of having that horrid monitor. Well, I have good news for you. That monitor is going to come out today. We're going to just take it right out, and it won't hurt a bit."

Ender nodded. It was a lie, of course, that it wouldn't hurt a bit. But since adults always said it when it *was* going to hurt, he could count on that statement as an accurate prediction of the future. Sometimes lies were more dependable than the truth.

"So if you'll just come over here, Andrew, just sit right up here on the examining table. The doctor will be in to see you in a moment."

The monitor gone. Ender tried to imagine the little device missing from the back of his neck. I'll roll over on my back in bed and it won't be pressing there. I won't feel it tingling and taking up the heat when I shower.

And Peter won't hate me anymore. I'll come home and show him that the monitor's gone, and he'll see that I didn't make it, either. That I'll just be a normal kid now, like him. That won't be so bad then. He'll forgive me that I had my monitor a whole year longer than he had his. We'll be—

Not friends, probably. No, Peter was too dangerous. Peter got so angry. Brothers, though. Not enemies, not friends, but brothers— able to live in the same house. He won't hate me, he'll just leave me alone. And when he wants to play buggers and astronauts, maybe I won't have to play, maybe I can just go read a book.

But Ender knew, even as he thought it, that Peter wouldn't leave him alone. There was something in Peter's eyes, when he was in his mad mood, and whenever Ender saw that look, that glint, he knew that the one thing Peter would *not* do was leave him alone. I'm practicing piano, Ender. Come turn the pages for me. Oh, is the monitor boy too busy to help his brother? Is he too smart? Got to go kill some buggers, astronaut? No, no, I don't *want* your help. I can do it on my own, you little bastard, you little *Third.*

"This won't take long, Andrew," said the doctor.

Ender nodded.

"It's designed to be removed. Without infection, without damage. But there'll be some tickling, and some people say they have a feeling of something *missing.* You'll keep looking around for something, something you were looking for, but you can't find it, and you can't remember what it was. So I'll tell you. It's the monitor you're looking for, and it isn't there. In a few days that feeling will pass."

The doctor was twisting something at the back of Ender's head. Suddenly a pain stabbed through him like a needle from his neck to his groin. Ender felt his back spasm, and his body arched violently backward; his head struck the bed. He could feel his legs thrashing, and his hands were clenching each other, wringing each other so tightly that they ached.

"Deedee!" shouted the doctor. "I need you!" The nurse ran in, gasped. "Got to relax these muscles. Get it to me, now! What are you waiting for!"

Something changed hands; Ender could not see. He lurched to one side and fell off the examining table. "Catch him!" cried the nurse.

"Just hold him steady—"

"You hold him, doctor, he's too strong for me—"

"Not the whole thing! You'll stop his heart—"

Ender felt a needle enter his back just above the neck of his shirt. It burned, but wherever in him the fire spread, his muscles gradually unclenched. Now he could cry for the fear and pain of it.

"Are you all right, Andrew?" the nurse asked.

Andrew could not remember how to speak. They lifted him onto the table. They checked his pulse, did other things; he did not understand it all.

The doctor was trembling; his voice shook as he spoke. "They leave these things in the kids for three years, what do they expect? We could have switched him off, do you realize that? We could have unplugged his brain for all time."

"When does the drug wear off?" asked the nurse.

"Keep him here for at least an hour. Watch him. If he doesn't start talking in fifteen minutes, call me. Could have unplugged him forever. I don't have the brains of a bugger."

He got back to Miss Pumphrey's class only fifteen minutes before the closing bell. He was still a little unsteady on his feet.

"Are you all right, Andrew?" asked Miss Pumphrey.

He nodded.

"Were you ill?"

He shook his head.

"You don't look well."

"I'm OK."

"You'd better sit down, Andrew."

He started toward his seat, but stopped. Now what was I looking for? I can't think what I was looking for.

"Your seat is over there," said Miss Pumphrey.

He sat down, but it was something else he needed, something he had lost. I'll find it later.

"Your monitor," whispered the girl behind him.

Andrew shrugged.

"His monitor," she whispered to the others.

Andrew reached up and felt his neck. There was a bandaid. It was gone. He was just like everybody else now.

"Washed out, Andy?" asked a boy who sat across the aisle and behind him. Couldn't think of his name. Peter. No, that was someone else.

"Quiet, Mr. Stilson," said Miss Pumphrey. Stilson smirked.

Miss Pumphrey talked about multiplication. Ender doodled on his desk, drawing contour maps of mountainous islands and then telling his desk to display them in three dimensions from every angle. The teacher would know, of course, that he wasn't paying attention, but she wouldn't bother him. He always knew the answer, even when she thought he wasn't paying attention.

In the corner of his desk a word appeared and began marching around the perimeter of the desk. It was upside down and backward at first, but Ender knew what it said long before it reached the bottom of the desk and turned right side up.

THIRD

Ender smiled. He was the one who had figured out how to send messages and make them march—even as his secret enemy called him names, the method of delivery praised him. It was not *his* fault he was a Third. It was the government's idea, they were the ones who authorized it—how else could a Third like Ender have got into school? And now the monitor was gone. The experiment entitled Andrew Wiggin hadn't worked out after all. If they could, he was sure they would like to rescind the waivers that had allowed him to be born at all. Didn't work, so erase the experiment.

The bell rang. Everyone signed off their desks or hurriedly typed in reminders to themselves. Some were dumping lessons or data into their computers at home. A few gathered at the printers while something they wanted to show was printed out. Ender spread his hands over the child-size keyboard near the edge of the desk and wondered what it would feel like to have hands as large as a grown-up's. They must feel so big and awkward, thick stubby fingers and beefy palms. Of course, they had bigger keyboards—but how could their thick fingers draw a fine line, the way Ender could, a thin line so precise that he could make it spiral seventy-nine times from the center to the edge of the desk without the lines ever touching or overlapping. It gave him something to do while the teacher droned on about arithmetic. Arithmetic! Valentine had taught him arithmetic when he was three.

"Are you all right, Andrew?"

"Yes, ma'am."

"You'll miss the bus."

Ender nodded and got up. The other kids were gone. They would be waiting, though, the bad ones. His monitor wasn't perched on his neck, hearing what he heard and seeing what he saw. They could say what they liked. They might even hit him now—no one could see them anymore, and so no one would come to Ender's rescue. There were advantages to the monitor, and he would miss them.

It was Stilson, of course. He wasn't bigger than most other kids, but he was bigger than Ender. And he had some others with him. He always did.

"Hey Third."

Don't answer. Nothing to say.

"Hey, Third, we're talkin to you, Third, hey bugger-lover, we're talkin to you."

Can't think of anything to answer. Anything I say will make it worse. So will saying nothing.

"Hey, Third, hey, turd, you flunked out, huh? Thought you were better than us, but you lost your little birdie, Thirdie, got a bandaid on your neck."

"Are you going to let me through?" Ender asked.

"Are we going to let him through? Should we let him through?" They all laughed. "Sure we'll let you through. First we'll let your arm through, then your butt through, then maybe a piece of your knee."

The others chimed in now. "Lost your birdie, Thirdie. Lost your birdie, Thirdie."

Stilson began pushing him with one hand; someone behind him then pushed him toward Stilson.

"See-saw, marjorie daw," somebody said.

"Tennis!"

"Ping-pong!"

This would not have a happy ending. So Ender decided that he'd rather not be the unhappiest at the end. The next time Stilson's arm came out to push him, Ender grabbed at it. He missed.

"Oh, gonna fight me, huh? Gonna fight me, Thirdie?"

The people behind Ender grabbed at him, to hold him.

Ender did not feel like laughing, but he laughed. "You mean it takes this many of you to fight one Third?"

"We're *people*, not *Thirds,* turd face. You're about as strong as a fart!"

But they let go of him. And as soon as they did, Ender kicked out high and hard, catching Stilson square in the breastbone. He dropped. It took Ender by surprise—he hadn't thought to put Stilson on the ground with one kick. It didn't occur to him that Stilson didn't take a fight like this seriously, that he wasn't prepared for a truly desperate blow.

For a moment, the others backed away and Stilson lay motionless. They were all wondering if he was dead. Ender, however, was trying to figure out a way to forestall vengeance. To keep them from taking him in a pack tomorrow. I have to win this now, and for all time, or I'll fight it every day and it will get worse and worse.

Ender knew the unspoken rules of manly warfare, even though he was only six. It was forbidden to strike the opponent who lay helpless on the ground; only an animal would do that.

So Ender walked to Stilson's supine body and kicked him again, viciously, in the ribs. Stilson groaned and rolled away from him. Ender walked around him and kicked him again, in the crotch. Stilson could not make a sound; he only doubled up and tears streamed out of his eyes.

Then Ender looked at the others coldly. "You might be having some idea of ganging up on me. You could probably beat me up pretty bad. But just remember what I do to people who try to hurt me. From then on you'd be wondering when I'd get you, and how bad it would be." He kicked Stilson in the face. Blood from his nose spattered the ground nearby. "It wouldn't be this bad," Ender said. "It would be worse."

He turned and walked away. Nobody followed him. He turned a corner into the corridor leading to the bus stop. He could hear the boys behind him saying, "Geez. Look at him. He's wasted." Ender leaned his head against the wall of the corridor and cried until the bus came. I am just like Peter. Take my monitor away, and I am just like Peter.

Chapter 2

Peter

"All right, it's off. How's he doing."

"You live inside somebody's body for a few years, you get used to it. I look at his face now, I can't tell what's going on. I'm not used to seeing his facial expressions. I'm used to feeling them."

"Come on, we're not talking about psychoanalysis here. We're soldiers, not witch doctors. You just saw him beat the guts out of the leader of a gang."

"He was thorough. He didn't just beat him, he beat him deep. Like Mazer Rackham at the—"

"Spare me. So in the judgment of the committee, he passes."

"Mostly. Let's see what he does with his brother, now that the monitor's off."

"His brother. Aren't you afraid of what his brother will do to **him?**"

"You were the one who told me that this wasn't a no-risk business."

"I went back through some of the tapes. I can't help it. I like the kid. I think we're going to screw him up."

"Of course we are. It's our job. We're the wicked witch. We promise gingerbread, but we eat the little bastards alive."

"I'm sorry, Ender," Valentine whispered. She was looking at the bandaid on his neck.

Ender touched the wall and the door closed behind him. "I don't care. I'm glad it's gone."

"What's gone?" Peter walked into the parlor, chewing on a mouthful of bread and peanut butter.

Ender did not see Peter as the beautiful ten-year-old boy that grown-ups saw, with dark, thick, tousled hair and a face that could have belonged to Alexander the Great. Ender looked at Peter only to detect anger or boredom, the dangerous moods that almost always led to pain. Now as Peter's eyes discovered the bandaid on his neck, the telltale flicker of anger appeared.

Valentine saw it too. "Now he's like us," she said, trying to soothe him before he had time to strike.

But Peter would not be soothed. "Like us? He keeps the little sucker till he's six years old. When did you lose yours? You were three. I lost mine before I was five. *He* almost made it, little bastard, little bugger."

This is all right, Ender thought. Talk and talk, Peter. Talk is fine.

"Well, now your guardian angels aren't watching over you," Peter said. "Now they aren't checking to see if you feel pain, listening to hear what I'm saying, seeing what I'm doing to you. How about that? How about it?"

Ender shrugged.

Suddenly Peter smiled and clapped his hands together in a mockery of good cheer. "Let's play buggers and astronauts," he said.

"Where's Mom?" asked Valentine.

"Out," said Peter. "I'm in charge."

"I think I'll call Daddy."

"Call away," said Peter. "You know he's never in."

"I'll play," Ender said.

"You be the bugger," said Peter.

"Let him be the astronaut for once," Valentine said.

"Keep your fat face out of it, fart mouth," said Peter. "Come on upstairs and choose your weapons."

It would not be a good game, Ender knew. It was not a question of winning. When kids played in the corridors, whole troops of them, the buggers never won, and sometimes the games got mean. But here in their flat, the game would start mean, and the bugger couldn't just go empty and quit the way buggers did in the real wars. The bugger was in it until the astronaut decided it was over.

Peter opened his bottom drawer and took out the bugger mask.

Mother had got upset at him when Peter bought it, but Dad pointed out that the war wouldn't go away just because you hid bugger masks and wouldn't let your kids play with make-believe laser guns. The better to play the war games, and have a better chance of surviving when the buggers came again.

If I survive the games, thought Ender. He put on the mask. It closed him in like a hand pressed tight against his face. But this isn't how it feels to be a bugger, thought Ender. They don't wear this face like a mask, it *is* their face. On their home worlds, do the buggers put on human masks, and play? And what do they call us? Slimies, because we're so soft and oily compared to them?

"Watch out, Slimy," Ender said.

He could barely see Peter through the eyeholes. Peter smiled at him. "Slimy, huh? Well, bugger-wugger, let's see how you break that face of yours."

Ender couldn't see it coming, except a slight shift of Peter's weight; the mask cut out his peripheral vision. Suddenly there was the pain and pressure of a blow to the side of his head; he lost balance, fell that way.

"Don't see too well, do you, bugger?" said Peter.

Ender began to take off the mask. Peter put his toe against Ender's groin. "Don't take off the mask," Peter said.

Ender pulled the mask down into place, took his hands away.

Peter pressed with his foot. Pain shot through Ender; he doubled up.

"Lie flat, bugger. We're gonna vivisect you, bugger. At long last we've got one of you alive, and we're going to see how you work."

"Peter, stop it," Ender said.

"Peter, stop it. Very good. So you buggers can guess our names. You can make yourselves sound like pathetic, cute little children so we'll love you and be nice to you. But it doesn't work. I can see you for what you really are. They meant you to be human, little Third, but you're really a bugger, and now it shows."

He lifted his foot, took a step, and then knelt on Ender, his knee pressing into Ender's belly just below the breastbone. He put more and more of his weight on Ender. It became hard to breathe.

"I could kill you like this," Peter whispered. "Just press and press until you're dead. And I could say that I didn't know it would hurt you, that we were just playing, and they'd believe me, and everything would be fine. And you'd be dead. Everything would be fine."

Ender could not speak; the breath was being forced from his lungs. Peter might mean it. Probably didn't mean it, but then he might.

"I do mean it," Peter said. "Whatever you think, I mean it. They only authorized you because I was so promising. But I didn't pan out. You did better. They think you're better. But I don't want a better little brother, Ender. I don't want a Third."

"I'll tell," Valentine said.

"No one would believe you."

"They'd believe me."

"Then you're dead, too, sweet little sister."

"Oh, yes," said Valentine. "They'll believe that. 'I didn't know it would kill Andrew. And when he was dead, I didn't know it would kill Valentine *too.*'"

The pressure let up a little.

"So. Not today. But someday you two won't be together. And there'll be an accident."

"You're all talk," Valentine said. "You don't mean any of it."

"I don't?"

"And do you know why you don't mean it?" Valentine asked. "Because you want to be in government someday. You want to be elected. And they won't elect you if your opponents can dig up the fact that your brother and sister both died in suspicious accidents when they were little. Especially because of the letter I've put in my secret file, which will be opened in the event of my death."

"Don't give me that kind of crap," Peter said.

"It says, I didn't die a natural death. Peter killed me, and if he hasn't already killed Andrew, he will soon. Not enough to convict you, but enough to keep you from ever getting elected."

"You're his monitor now," said Peter. "You better watch him, day and night. You better be there."

"Ender and I aren't stupid. We scored as well as you did on everything. Better on some things. We're all such wonderfully bright children. You're not the smartest, Peter, just the biggest."

"Oh, I know. But there'll come a day when you aren't there with him, when you forget. And suddenly you'll remember, and you'll rush to him, and there he'll be, perfectly all right. And the next time you won't worry so much, and you won't come so fast. And every time, he'll be all right. And you'll think that I forgot. Even though you'll remember that I said this, you'll think that I forgot. And years will pass. And then there'll be a terrible accident, and I'll find his body, and I'll cry and cry over him, and you'll remember this conversation, Vally, but you'll be ashamed of yourself for remembering, because you'll know that I changed, that it really was an accident, that it's cruel of you even to remember what I said in a childhood quarrel. Except that it'll be true. I'm gonna save this up, and he's gonna die, and you won't do a thing, not a thing. But you go on believing that I'm just the biggest."

"The biggest asshole," Valentine said.

Peter leaped to his feet and started for her. She shied away. Ender pried off his mask. Peter flopped back on his bed and started to laugh. Loud, but with real mirth, tears coming to his eyes. "Oh, you guys are just super, just the biggest suckers on the planet earth."

"Now he's going to tell us it was all a joke," Valentine said.

"Not a joke, a game. I can make you guys believe anything. I can make you dance around like puppets." In a phony monster voice he said, "I'm going to kill you and chop you into little pieces and put you into the garbage hole." He laughed again. "Biggest suckers in the solar system."

Ender stood there watching him laugh and thought of Stilson, thought of how it felt to crunch into his body. This is who needed it. This is who should have got it.

As if she could read his mind, Valentine whispered, "No, Ender."

Peter suddenly rolled to the side, flipped off the bed, and got in position for a fight. "Oh, yes, Ender," he said. "Any time, Ender."

Ender lifted his right leg and took off the shoe. He held it up. "See there, on the toe? That's blood, Peter."

"Ooh. Ooh, I'm gonna die, I'm gonna die. Ender killed a cap-per-tiller and now he's gonna kill me."

There was no getting to him. Peter was a murderer at heart, and nobody knew it but Valentine and Ender.

Mother came home and commiserated with Ender about the monitor. Father came home and kept saying it was such a wonderful surprise, they had such fantastic children that the government told them to have three, and now the government didn't want to take any

of them after all, so here they were with three, they still had a Third
. . . until Ender wanted to scream at him, I know I'm a Third, I
know it, if you want I'll go away so you don't have to be embarrassed
in front of everybody, I'm sorry I lost the monitor and now you have
three kids and no obvious explanation, so inconvenient for you, I'm
sorry sorry sorry.

He lay in bed staring upward into the darkness. On the bunk
above him, he could hear Peter turning and tossing restlessly. Then
Peter slid off the bunk and walked out of the room. Ender heard the
hushing sound of the toilet clearing; then Peter stood silhouetted in
the doorway.

He thinks I'm asleep. He's going to kill me.

Peter walked to the bed, and sure enough, he did not lift himself
up to his bed. Instead he came and stood by Ender's head.

But he did not reach for a pillow to smother Ender. He did not
have a weapon.

He whispered, "Ender, I'm sorry, I'm sorry, I know how it
feels, I'm sorry, I'm your brother, I love you."

A long time later, Peter's even breathing said that he was asleep.
Ender peeled the bandaid from his neck. And for the second time
that day he cried.

Chapter 3

Graff

"The sister is our weak link. He really loves her."

"I know. She can undo it all, from the start. He won't want to leave her."

"So, what are you going to do?"

"Persuade him that he wants to come with us more than he wants to stay with her."

"How will you do that?"

"I'll lie to him."

"And if that doesn't work?"

"Then I'll tell the truth. We're allowed to do that in emergencies. We can't plan for everything, you know."

Ender wasn't very hungry during breakfast. He kept wondering what it would be like at school. Facing Stilson after yesterday's fight. What Stilson's friends would do. Probably nothing, but he couldn't be sure. He didn't want to go.

"You're not eating, Andrew," his mother said.

Peter came into the room. "Morning, Ender. Thanks for leaving your slimy washcloth in the middle of the shower."

"Just for you," Ender murmured.

"Andrew, you have to eat."

Ender held out his wrists, a gesture that said, So feed it to me through a needle.

"Very funny," Mother said. "I try to be concerned, but it makes no difference to my genius children."

"It was all your genes that made us geniuses, Mom," said Peter. "We sure didn't get any from Dad."

"I heard that," Father said, not looking up from the news that was being displayed on the table while he ate.

"It would've been wasted if you hadn't."

The table beeped. Someone was at the door.

"Who is it?" Mother asked.

Father thumbed a key and a man appeared on his video. He was wearing the only military uniform that meant anything anymore, the I.F., the International Fleet.

"I thought it was over," said Father.

Peter said nothing, just poured milk over his cereal.

And Ender thought, Maybe I won't have to go to school today after all.

Father coded the door open and got up from the table. "I'll see to it," he said. "Stay and eat."

They stayed, but they didn't eat. A few moments later, Father came back into the room and beckoned to Mother.

"You're in deep poo," said Peter. "They found out what you did to Stilson, and now they're gonna make you do time out in the Belt."

"I'm only six, moron, I'm a juvenile."

"You're a Third, turd. You've got no rights."

Valentine came in, her hair in a sleepy halo around her face. "Where's Mom and Dad? I'm too sick to go to school."

"Another oral exam, huh?" Peter said.

"Shut up, Peter," said Valentine.

"You should relax and enjoy it," said Peter. "It could be worse."

"I don't know how."

"It could be an anal exam."

"Hyuk hyuk," Valentine said. "Where are Mother and Father?"

"Talking to a guy from IF."

Instinctively she looked at Ender. After all, for years they had expected someone to come and tell them that Ender had passed, that Ender was needed.

"That's right, look at him," Peter said. "But it might be me, you know. They might have realized I was the best of the lot after all." Peter's feelings were hurt, and so he was being a snot, as usual.

The door opened. "Ender," said Father, "you better come in here."

"Sorry, Peter," Valentine taunted.

Father glowered. "Children, this is no laughing matter."

Ender followed Father into the parlor. The I.F. officer rose to his feet when they entered, but he did not extend a hand to Ender.

Mother was twisting her wedding band on her finger. "Andrew," she said, "I never thought you were the kind to get in a fight."

"The Stilson boy is in the hospital," Father said. "You really did a number on him. With your shoe, Ender, that wasn't exactly fair."

Ender shook his head. He had expected someone from the school to come about Stilson, not an officer of the fleet. This was more serious than he had thought. And yet he couldn't think what else he could have done.

"Do you have any explanation for your behavior, young man?" asked the officer.

Ender shook his head again. He didn't know what to say, and he was afraid to reveal himself to be any more monstrous than his actions had made him out to be. I'll take it, whatever the punishment is, he thought. Let's get it over with.

"We're willing to consider extenuating circumstances," the officer said. "But I must tell you it doesn't look good. Kicking him in the groin, kicking him repeatedly in the face and body when he was down—it sounds like you really enjoyed it."

"I didn't," Ender whispered.

"Then why did you do it?"

"He had his gang there," Ender said.

"So? This excuses anything?"

"No."

"Tell me why you kept on kicking him. You had already won."

"Knocking him down won the first fight. I wanted to win all the next ones, too, right then, so they'd leave me alone." Ender couldn't help it, he was too afraid, too ashamed of his own acts: though he tried not to, he cried again. Ender did not like to cry and rarely did; now, in less than a day, he had done it three times. And each time was worse. To cry in front of his mother and father and this military man, that was shameful. "You took away the monitor," Ender said. "I had to take care of myself, didn't I?"

"Ender, you should have asked a grown-up for help," Father began.

But the officer stood up and stepped across the room to Ender.

He held out his hand. "My name is Graff, Ender. Colonel Hyrum Graff. I'm director of primary training at Battle School in the Belt. I've come to invite you to enter the school."

After all. "But the monitor—"

"The final step in your testing was to see what would happen if the monitor comes off. We don't always do it that way, but in your case—"

"And I passed?"

Mother was incredulous. "Putting the Stilson boy in the hospital? What would you have done if Andrew had killed him, given him a medal?"

"It isn't what he did, Mrs. Wiggin. It's why." Colonel Graff handed her a folder full of papers. "Here are the requisitions. Your son has been cleared by the I.F. Selective Service. Of course we already have your consent, granted in writing at the time conception was confirmed, or he could not have been born. He has been ours from then, if he qualified."

Father's voice was trembling as he spoke. "It's not very kind of you, to let us think you didn't want him, and then to take him after all."

"And this charade about the Stilson boy," Mother said.

"It wasn't a charade, Mrs. Wiggin. Until we knew what Ender's motivation was, we couldn't be sure he wasn't another—we had to know what the action meant. Or at least what Ender believed that it meant."

"Must you call him that stupid nickname?" Mother began to cry.

"I'm sorry, Mrs. Wiggin. But that's the name he calls himself."

"What are you going to do, Colonel Graff?" Father asked. "Walk out the door with him now?"

"That depends," said Graff.

"On what?"

"On whether Ender wants to come."

Mother's weeping turned to bitter laughter. "Oh, so it's voluntary after all, how sweet!"

"For the two of you, the choice was made when Ender was conceived. But for Ender, the choice has not been made at all. Conscripts make good cannon fodder, but for officers we need volunteers."

"Officers?" Ender asked. At the sound of his voice, the others fell silent.

"Yes," said Graff. "Battle School is for training future starship captains and commodores of flotillas and admirals of the fleet."

"Let's not have any deception here!" Father said angrily. "How many of the boys at the Battle School actually end up in command of ships!"

"Unfortunately, Mr. Wiggin, that is classified information. But I *can* say that none of our boys who makes it through the first year has ever failed to receive a commission as an officer. And none has served in a position of lower rank than chief executive officer of an interplanetary vessel. Even in the domestic defense forces within our own solar system, there's honor to be had."

"How many make it through the first year?" asked Ender.

"All who want to," said Graff.

Ender almost said, I want to. But he held his tongue. This would keep him out of school, but that was stupid, that was just a problem for a few days. It would keep him away from Peter—that was more important, that might be a matter of life itself. But to leave Mother and Father, and above all, to leave Valentine. And become a soldier. Ender didn't like fighting. He didn't like Peter's kind, the strong against the weak, and he didn't like his own kind either, the smart against the stupid.

"I think," Graff said, "that Ender and I should have a private conversation."

"No," Father said.

"I won't take him without letting you speak to him again," Graff said. "And you really can't stop me."

Father glared at Graff a moment longer, then got up and left the room. Mother paused to squeeze Ender's hand. She closed the door behind her when she left.

"Ender," Graff said, "if you come with me, you won't be back here for a long time. There aren't any vacations from Battle School. No visitors, either. A full course of training lasts until you're sixteen years old—you get your first leave, under certain circumstances, when you're twelve. Believe me, Ender, people change in six years, in ten years. Your sister Valentine will be a woman when you see her again, if you come with me. You'll be strangers. You'll still love her,

Ender, but you won't know her. You see I'm not pretending it's easy."

"Mom and Daddy?"

"I know you, Ender. I've been watching the monitor disks for some time. You won't miss your mother and father, not much, not for long. And they won't miss you long, either."

Tears came to Ender's eyes, in spite of himself. He turned his face away, but would not reach up to wipe them.

"They *do* love you, Ender. But you have to understand what your life has cost them. They were born religious, you know. Your father was baptized with the name John Paul Wieczorek. Catholic. The seventh of nine children."

Nine children. That was unthinkable. Criminal.

"Yes, well, people do strange things for religion. You know the sanctions, Ender—they were not as harsh then, but still not easy. Only the first two children had a free education. Taxes steadily rose with each new child. Your father turned sixteen and invoked the Noncomplying Families Act to separate himself from his family. He changed his name, renounced his religion, and vowed never to have more than the allotted two children. He meant it. All the shame and persecution he went through as a child—he vowed no child of his would go through it. Do you understand?"

"He didn't want me."

"Well, no one *wants* a Third anymore. You can't expect them to be glad. But your father and mother are a special case. They both renounced their religions—your mother was a Mormon—but in fact their feelings are still ambiguous. Do you know what ambiguous means?"

"They feel both ways."

"They're ashamed of having come from noncompliant families. They conceal it. To the degree that your mother refuses to admit to anyone that she was born in Utah, lest they suspect. Your father denies his Polish ancestry, since Poland is still a noncompliant nation, and under international sanction because of it. So, you see, having a Third, even under the government's direct instructions, undoes everything they've been trying to do."

"I know that."

"But it's more complicated than that. Your father still named you with legitimate saints' names. In fact, he baptized all three of you himself as soon as he got you home after you were born. And your mother objected. They quarreled over it each time, not because she didn't want you baptized, but because she didn't want you baptized Catholic. They haven't really given up their religion. They look at you and see you as a badge of pride, because they were able to circumvent the law and have a Third. But you're also a badge of cowardice, because they dare not go further and practice the noncompliance they still feel is right. And you're a badge of public shame, because at every step you interfere with their efforts at assimilation into normal complying society."

"How can you know all this?"

"We monitored your brother and sister, Ender. You'd be amazed at how sensitive the instruments are. We were connected directly to your brain. We heard all that you heard, whether you were listening carefully or not. Whether you understood or not. *We* understand."

"So my parents love me and don't love me?"

"They love you. The question is whether they want you here. Your presence in this house is a constant disruption. A source of tension. Do you understand?"

"I'm not the one who causes tension."

"Not anything you *do,* Ender. Your life itself. Your brother hates you because you are living proof that he wasn't good enough. Your parents resent you because of all the past they are trying to evade."

"Valentine loves me."

"With all her heart. Completely, unstintingly, she's devoted to you, and you adore her. I told you it wouldn't be easy."

"What is it like, there?"

"Hard work. Studies, just like school here, except we put you into mathematics and computers much more heavily. Military history. Strategy and tactics. And above all, the Battle Room."

"What's that?"

"War games. All the boys are organized into armies. Day after day, in zero gravity, there are mock battles. Nobody gets hurt, but winning and losing matter. Everybody starts as a common soldier, taking orders. Older boys are your officers, and it's their duty to train you and command you in battle. More than that I can't tell you. It's like playing buggers and astronauts—except that you have weapons that work, and fellow soldiers fighting beside you, and your whole future and the future of the human race depends on how well you learn, how well you fight. It's a hard life, and you won't have a normal childhood. Of course, with your mind, and as a Third to boot, you wouldn't have a particularly normal childhood anyway."

"All boys?"

"A few girls. They don't often pass the tests to get in. Too many centuries of evolution are working against them. None of them will be like Valentine, anyway. But there'll be brothers there, Ender."

"Like Peter?"

"Peter wasn't accepted, Ender, for the very reasons that you hate him."

"I don't hate him. I'm just—"

"Afraid of him. Well, Peter isn't all bad, you know. He was the best we'd seen in a long time. We asked your parents to choose a daughter next—they would have anyway—hoping that Valentine would be Peter, but milder. She was too mild. And so we requisitioned you."

"To be half Peter and half Valentine."

"If things worked out right."

"Am I?"

"As far as we can tell. Our tests are very good, Ender. But they don't tell us everything. In fact, when it comes down to it, they hardly tell us anything. But they're better than nothing." Graff leaned over and took Ender's hands in his. "Ender Wiggin, if it were just a matter of choosing the best and happiest future for you, I'd tell you to stay home. Stay here, grow up, be happy. There are worse things than being a Third, worse things than a big brother who can't make up his mind whether to be a human being or a jackal. Battle School is one of those worse things. But we need you. The buggers may seem like a game to you now, Ender, but they damn near wiped us out last time. But it wasn't enough. They had us cold, outnumbered and outweaponed. The only thing that saved us was that we had the most brilliant military commander we've ever found. Call it fate, call it God, call it damnfool luck, we had Mazer Rackham.

"But we don't have him now, Ender. We've scraped together everything mankind could produce, a fleet that makes the one they sent against us last time seem like a bunch of kids playing in a swimming pool. We have some new weapons, too. But it might not be enough, even so. Because in the eighty years since the last war, they've had as much time to prepare as we have. We need the best we can get, and we need them fast. Maybe you're not going to work out for us, and maybe you are. Maybe you'll break down under the pressure, maybe it'll ruin your life, maybe you'll hate me for coming here to your house today. But if there's a chance that because you're with the fleet, mankind might survive and the buggers might leave us alone forever—then I'm going to ask you to do it. To come with me."

Ender had trouble focusing on Colonel Graff. The man looked far away and very small, as if Ender could pick him up with tweezers and drop him in a pocket. To leave everything here, and go to a place that was very hard, with no Valentine, no Mom and Dad.

And then he thought of the films of the buggers that everyone had to see at least once a year. The Scathing of China. The Battle of the Belt. Death and suffering and terror. And Mazer Rackham and his brilliant maneuvers, destroying an enemy fleet twice his size and twice his firepower, using the little human ships that seemed so frail and weak. Like children fighting with grown-ups. And we won.

"I'm afraid," said Ender quietly. "But I'll go with you."

"Tell me again," said Graff.

"It's what I was born for, isn't it? If I don't go, why am I alive?"

"Not good enough," said Graff.

"I don't want to go," said Ender, "but I will."

Graff nodded. "You can change your mind. Up until the time you get in my car with me, you can change your mind. After that, you stay at the pleasure of the International Fleet. Do you understand that?"

Ender nodded.

"All right. Let's tell them."

Mother cried. Father held Ender tight. Peter shook his hand and said, "You lucky little pinheaded fart-eater." Valentine kissed him and left her tears on his cheek.

There was nothing to pack. No belongings to take. "The school provides everything you need, from uniforms to school supplies. And as for toys—there's only one game."

"Good-bye," Ender said to his family. He reached up and took Colonel Graff's hand and walked out the door with him.

"Kill some buggers for me!" Peter shouted.

"I love you, Andrew!" Mother called.

"We'll write to you!" Father said.

And as he got into the car that waited silently in the corridor, he heard Valentine's anguished cry. "Come back to me! I love you forever!"

Chapter **4**

Launch

"With Ender, we have to strike a delicate balance. Isolate him enough that he remains creative—otherwise he'll adopt the system here and we'll lose him. At the same time, we need to make sure he keeps a strong ability to lead."

"If he earns rank, he'll lead."

"It isn't that simple. Mazer Rackham could handle his little fleet and win. By the time this war happens, there'll be too much, even for a genius. Too many little boats. He has to work smoothly with his subordinates."

"Oh, good. He has to be a genius and nice, too."

"Not **nice.** Nice will let the buggers have us all."

"So you're going to isolate him."

"I'll have him completely separated from the rest of the boys by the time we get to the School."

"I have no doubt of it. I'll be waiting for you to get here. I watched the vids of what he did to the Stilson boy. This is not a sweet little kid you're bringing up here."

"That's where you're mistaken. He's even sweeter. But don't worry. We'll purge **that** in a hurry."

"Sometimes I think you enjoy breaking these little geniuses."

"There **is** an art to it, and I'm very, very good at it. But enjoy? Well, maybe. When they put back the pieces afterward, and it makes them better."

"You're a monster."

"Thanks. Does this mean I get a raise?"

"Just a medal. The budget isn't inexhaustible."

They say that weightlessness can cause disorientation, especially in children, whose sense of direction isn't yet secure. But Ender was disoriented before he left Earth's gravity. Before the shuttle launch even began.

There were nineteen other boys in his launch. They filed out of the bus and into the elevator. They talked and joked and bragged and laughed. Ender kept his silence. He noticed how Graff and the other officers were watching them. Analyzing. Everything we do means something, Ender realized. Them laughing. Me not laughing.

He toyed with the idea of trying to be like the other boys. But he couldn't think of any jokes, and none of theirs seemed funny. Wherever their laughter came from, Ender couldn't find such a place in himself. He was afraid, and fear made him serious.

They had dressed him in a uniform, all in a single piece; it felt funny not to have a belt cinched around his waist. He felt baggy and naked, dressed like that. There were TV cameras going, perched like animals on the shoulders of crouching, prowling men. The men moved slowly, catlike, so the camera motion would be smooth. Ender caught himself moving smoothly, too.

He imagined himself being on TV, in an interview. The announcer asking him, How do you feel, Mr. Wiggin? Actually quite well, except hungry. Hungry? Oh, yes, they don't let you eat for twenty hours before the launch. How interesting, I never knew that. All of us are quite hungry, actually. And all the while, during the interview, Ender and the TV guy would slink along smoothly in front of the cameraman, taking long, lithe strides. For the first time, Ender felt like laughing. He smiled. The other boys near him were laughing at the moment, too, for another reason. They think I'm smiling at their joke, thought Ender. But I'm smiling at something much funnier.

"Go up the ladder one at a time," said an officer. "When you come to an aisle with empty seats, take one. There aren't any window seats."

It was a joke. The other boys laughed.

Ender was near the last, but not the very last. The TV cameras did not give up, though. Will Valentine see me disappear into the shuttle? He thought of waving at her, of running to the cameraman and saying, "Can I tell Valentine good-bye?" He didn't know that it would be censored out of the tape if he did, for the boys soaring out to Battle School were all supposed to be heroes. They weren't supposed to miss anybody. Ender didn't know about the censorship, but he did know that running to the cameras would be wrong.

He walked the short bridge to the door in the shuttle. He noticed that the wall to his right was carpeted like a floor. That was where the disorientation began. The moment he thought of the wall as a floor, he began to feel like he was walking on a wall. He got to the ladder, and noticed that the vertical surface behind it was also carpeted. I am climbing up the floor. Hand over hand, step by step.

And then, for fun, he pretended that he was climbing *down* the wall. He did it almost instantly in his mind, convinced himself against the best evidence of gravity. He found himself gripping the seat tightly, even though gravity pulled him firmly against it.

The other boys were bouncing on their seats a little, poking and pushing, shouting. Ender carefully found the straps, figured out how they fit together to hold him at crotch, waist, and shoulders. He imagined the ship dangling upside down on the undersurface of the Earth, the giant fingers of gravity holding them firmly in place. But we will slip away, he thought. We are going to fall off this planet.

He did not know its significance at the time. Later, though, he would remember that it was even before he left Earth that he first thought of it as a planet, like any other, not particularly his own.

"Oh, already figured it out," said Graff. He was standing on the ladder.

"Coming with us?" Ender asked.

"I don't usually come down for recruiting," Graff said. "I'm kind of in charge there. Administrator of the School. Like a principal. They told me I had to come back or I'd lose my job." He smiled.

Ender smiled back. He felt comfortable with Graff. Graff was good. And he was principal of the Battle School. Ender relaxed a little. He would have a friend there.

The other boys were belted in place, those who hadn't done as Ender did. Then they waited for an hour while a TV at the front of the shuttle introduced them to shuttle flight, the history of space flight, and their possible future with the great starships of the I.F. Very boring stuff. Ender had seen such films before.

Except that he had not been belted into a seat inside the shuttle. Hanging upside down from the belly of Earth.

The launch wasn't bad. A little scary. Some jolting, a few moments of panic that this might be the first failed launch in the history of the shuttle. The movies hadn't made it plain how much violence you could experience, lying on your back in a soft chair.

Then it was over, and he really was hanging by the straps, no gravity anywhere.

But because he had already reoriented himself, he was not surprised when Graff came up the ladder backward, as if he were climbing down to the front of the shuttle. Nor did it bother him when Graff hooked his feet under a rung and pushed off with his hands, so that suddenly he swung upright, as if this were an ordinary airplane.

The reorientations were too much for some. One boy gagged; Ender understood then why they had been forbidden to eat anything for twenty hours before the launch. Vomit in null gravity wouldn't be fun.

But for Ender, Graff's gravity game was fun. And he carried it further, imagining that Graff was actually hanging upside down from the center aisle, and then picturing him sticking straight out from a side wall. Gravity could go any which way. However I want it to go. I can make Graff stand on his head and he doesn't even know it.

"What do you think is so funny, Wiggin?"

Graff's voice was sharp and angry. What did I do wrong, thought Ender. Did I laugh out loud?

"I asked you a question, soldier!" barked Graff.

Oh yes. This is the beginning of the training routine. Ender had seen some military shows on TV, and they always shouted a lot at the beginning of training before the soldier and the officer became good friends.

"Yes sir," Ender said.

"Well answer it, then!"

"I thought of you hanging upside down by your feet. I thought it was funny."

It sounded stupid, now, with Graff looking at him coldly. "To you I suppose it *is* funny. Is it funny to anybody else here?"

Murmurs of no.

"Well why isn't it?" Graff looked at them all with contempt. "Scumbrains, that's what we've got in this launch. Pinheaded little morons. Only one of you had the brains to realize that in null gravity directions are whatever you conceive them to be. Do you understand that, Shafts?"

The boy nodded.

"No you didn't. Of course you didn't. Not only stupid, but a liar too. There's only one boy on this launch with any brains *at all*, and that's Ender Wiggin. Take a good look at him, little boys. He's going to be a commander when you're still in diapers up there. Because he knows how to think in null gravity, and you just want to throw up."

This wasn't the way the show was supposed to go. Graff was supposed to pick on him, not set him up as the best. They were supposed to be against each other at first, so they could become friends later.

"Most of you are going to ice out. Get used to that, little boys. Most of you are going to end up in Combat School, because you don't have the brains to handle deep-space piloting. Most of you aren't worth the price of bringing you up here to Battle School because you don't have what it takes. Some of you might make it. *Some* of you might be worth something to humanity. But don't bet on it. I'm betting on only one."

Suddenly Graff did a backflip and caught the ladder with his hands, then swung his feet away from the ladder. Doing a handstand, if the floor was down. Dangling by his hands, if the floor was up. Hand over hand he swung himself back along the aisle to his seat.

"Looks like *you've* got it made here," whispered the boy next to him.

Ender shook his head.

"Oh, won't even talk to me?" the boy said.

"I didn't ask him to say that stuff," Ender whispered.

He felt a sharp pain on the top of his head. Then again. Some giggles from behind him. The boy in the next seat back must have unfastened his straps. Again a blow to the head. Go away, Ender thought. I didn't do anything to you.

Again a blow to the head. Laughter from the boys. Didn't Graff see this? Wasn't he going to stop it? Another blow. Harder. It really hurt. Where was Graff?

Then it became clear. Graff had deliberately caused it. It was worse than the abuse in the shows. When the sergeant picked on you, the others liked you better. But when the officer prefers you, the others hate you.

"Hey, fart-eater," came the whisper from behind him. He was hit in the head again. "Do you like this? Hey, super-brain, this is fun?" Another blow, this one so hard that Ender cried out softly with the pain.

If Graff was setting him up, there'd be no help unless he helped himself. He waited until he thought another blow was about to come. Now, he thought. And yes, the blow was there. It hurt, but Ender was already trying to sense the coming of the next blow. Now. And yes, right on time. I've got you, Ender thought.

Just as the next blow was coming, Ender reached up with both hands, snatched the boy by the wrist, and then pulled down on the arm, hard.

In gravity, the boy would have been jammed against Ender's seat back, hurting his chest. In null gravity, however, he flipped over the seat completely, up toward the ceiling. Ender wasn't expecting it. He hadn't realized how null gravity magnified even a child's strength. The boy sailed through the air, bouncing against the ceiling, then down against another boy in his seat, then out into the aisle, his arms flailing until he screamed as his body slammed into the bulkhead at the front of the compartment, his left arm twisted under him.

It took only seconds. Graff was already there, snatching the boy out of the air. Deftly he propelled him down the aisle toward the other man. "Left arm. Broken, I think," he said. In moments the boy had been given a drug and lay quietly in the air as the officer ballooned a splint around his arm.

Ender felt sick. He had only meant to catch the boy's arm. No. No, he had meant to hurt him, and had pulled with all his strength. He hadn't meant it to be so public, but the boy was feeling exactly the pain Ender had meant him to feel. Null gravity had betrayed him, that was all. I am Peter. I'm just like him. And Ender hated himself.

Graff stayed at the front of the cabin. "What are you, slow learners? In your feeble little minds, haven't you picked up one little fact? You were brought here to be *soldiers*. In your old schools, in your old families, maybe you were the big shot, maybe you were tough, maybe you were smart. But we chose the best of the best, and that's the only kind of kid you're going to meet now. And when I tell you Ender Wiggin is the best in this launch, take the hint, pinheads. Don't mess with him. Little boys have died in Battle School before. Do I make myself clear?"

There was silence the rest of the launch. The boy sitting next to Ender was scrupulously careful not to touch him.

I am not a killer, Ender said to himself over and over. I am not Peter. No matter what he says, I wouldn't. I'm not. I was defending myself. I bore it a long time. I was patient. I'm not what he said.

A voice over the speaker told them they were approaching the school; it took twenty minutes to decelerate and dock. Ender lagged behind the others. They were not unwilling to let him be the last to leave the shuttle, climbing upward in the direction that had been down when they embarked. Graff was waiting at the end of the narrow tube that led from the shuttle into the heart of the Battle School.

"Was it a good flight, Ender?" Graff asked cheerfully.

"I thought you were my friend." Despite himself, Ender's voice trembled.

Graff looked puzzled. "Whatever gave you that idea, Ender?"

"Because you—" Because you spoke nicely to me, and honestly. "You didn't lie."

"I won't lie now, either," said Graff. "My job isn't to be friends. My job is to produce the best soldiers in the world. In the whole history of the world. We need a Napoleon. An Alexander. Except that Napoleon lost in the end, and Alexander flamed out and died young. We need a Julius Caesar, except that he made himself dictator, and died for it. My job is to produce such a creature, and all the men and women he'll need to help him. Nowhere in that does it say I have to make friends with children."

"You made them hate me."

"So? What will you do about it? Crawl into a corner? Start kissing their little backsides so they'll love you again? There's only one thing that will make them stop hating you. And that's being so good at what you do that they can't ignore you. I told them you were the best. Now you damn well better be."

"What if I can't?"

"Then too bad. Look, Ender, I'm sorry if you're lonely and afraid. But the buggers are out there. Ten billion, a hundred billion, a million billion of them, for all we know. With as many ships, for all we know. With weapons we can't understand. And a willingness to use those weapons to wipe us out. It isn't the world at stake, Ender. Just us. Just humankind. As far as the rest of the earth is concerned, we could be wiped out and it would adjust, it would get on with the next step in evolution. But humanity doesn't want to die. As a species, we have evolved to survive. And the way we do it is by straining and straining and, at last, every few generations, giving birth to genius. The one who invents the wheel. And light. And flight. The one who builds a city, a nation, an empire. Do you understand any of this?"

Ender thought he did, but wasn't sure, and so said nothing.

"No. Of course not. So I'll put it bluntly. Human beings are free except when humanity needs them. Maybe humanity needs you. To do something. I think humanity needs *me*—to find out what you're good for. We might both do despicable things, Ender, but if humankind survives, then we were good tools."

"Is that all? Just tools?"

"Individual human beings are all tools, that the others use to help us all survive."

"That's a lie."

"No. It's just a half truth. You can worry about the other half after we win this war."

"It'll be over before I grow up," Ender said.

"I hope you're wrong," said Graff. "By the way, you aren't helping yourself at all, talking to me. The other boys are no doubt telling each other than old Ender Wiggin is back there licking up to Graff. If word once gets around that you're a teachers' boy, you're iced for sure."

In other words, go away and leave me alone. "Good-bye," Ender said. He pulled himself hand over hand along the tube where the other boys had gone.

Graff watched him go.

One of the teachers near him said, "Is that the one?"

"God knows," said Graff. "If it isn't Ender, then he'd better show up soon."

"Maybe it's nobody," said the teacher.

"Maybe. But if that's the case, Anderson, then in my opinion God is a bugger. You can quote me on that."

"I will."

They stood in silence a while longer.

"Anderson."

"Mmm."

"The kid's wrong. I *am* his friend."

"I know."

"He's clean. Right to the heart, he's good."

"I've read the reports."

"Anderson, think what we're going to do to him."

Anderson was defiant. "We're going to make him the best military commander in history."

"And then put the fate of the world on his shoulders. For his sake, I hope it isn't him. I do."

"Cheer up. The buggers may kill us all before he graduates."

Graff smiled. "You're right. I feel better already."

Chapter 5

Games

"You have my admiration. Breaking an arm—that was a master stroke."

"That was an accident."

"Really? And I've already commended you in your official report."

"It's too strong. It makes that other little bastard into a hero. It could screw up training for a lot of kids. I thought he might call for help."

"Call for help? I thought that was what you valued most in him—that he settles his own problems. When he's out there surrounded by an enemy fleet, there ain't gonna be nobody to help him if he calls."

"Who would have guessed the little sucker'd be out of his seat? And that he'd land just wrong against the bulkhead?"

"Just one more example of the stupidity of the military. If you had any brains, you'd be in a real career, like selling life insurance."

"You, too, mastermind."

"We've just got to face the fact that we're second rate. With the fate of humanity in our hands. Gives you a delicious feeling of power, doesn't it? Especially because this time if we lose there won't be any criticism of us at all."

"I never thought of it that way. But let's not lose."

"See how Ender handles it. If we've already lost him, if he can't handle this, who next? Who else?"

"I'll make up a list."

"In the meantime, figure out how to unlose Ender."

"I told you. His isolation can't be broken. He can never come to believe that anybody will ever help him out, **ever.** If he once thinks there's an easy way out, he's wrecked."

"You're right. That would be terrible, if he believed he had a friend."

"He can have friends. It's parents he can't have."

The other boys had already chosen their bunks when Ender arrived. Ender stopped in the doorway of the dormitory, looking for the sole remaining bed. The ceiling was low—Ender could reach up and touch it. A child-size room, with the bottom bunk resting on the floor. The other boys were watching him, cornerwise. Sure enough, the bottom bunk right by the door was the only empty bed. For a moment it occurred to Ender that by letting the others put him in the worst place, he was inviting later bullying. Yet he couldn't very well oust someone else.

So he smiled broadly. "Hey, thanks," he said. Not sarcastically at all. He said it as sincerely as if they had reserved for him the best position. "I thought I was going to have to ask for low bunk by the door."

He sat down and looked in the locker that stood open at the foot of the bunk. There was a paper taped to the inside of the door.

> **Place your hand on the scanner**
> **at the head of your bunk**
> **and speak your name twice.**

Ender found the scanner, a sheet of opaque plastic. He put his left hand on it and said, "Ender Wiggin. Ender Wiggin."

The scanner glowed green for a moment. Ender closed his locker and tried to reopen it. He couldn't. Then he put his hand on the scanner and said, "Ender Wiggin." The locker popped open. So did three other compartments.

One of them contained four jumpsuits like the one he was wearing, and one white one. Another compartment contained a small desk, just like the ones at school. So they weren't through with studies yet.

It was the largest compartment that contained the prize. It looked like a spacesuit at first glance, complete with helmet and gloves. But it wasn't. There was no airtight seal. Still, it would effectively cover the whole body. It was thickly padded. It was also a little stiff.

And there was a pistol with it. A lasergun, it looked like, since the end was solid, clear glass. But surely they wouldn't let children have lethal weapons—

"Not laser," said a man. Ender looked up. It was one he hadn't seen before. A young and kind-looking man. "But it has a tight enough beam. Well-focused. You can aim it and make a three-inch circle of light on a wall a hundred meters off."

"What's it for?" Ender asked.

"One of the games we play during recreation. Does anyone else have his locker open?" The man looked around. "I mean, have you followed directions and coded in your voices and hands? You can't get into the lockers until you do. This room is your home for the first year or so here at the Battle School, so get the bunk you want and stay with it. Ordinarily we let you elect your chief officer and install him in the lower bunk by the door, but apparently that position has been taken. Can't recode the lockers now. So think about whom you want to choose. Dinner in seven minutes. Follow the lighted dots on the floor. Your color code is red yellow yellow—whenever you're assigned a path to follow, it will be red yellow yellow, three dots side by side—go where those lights indicate. What's your color code, boys?"

"Red, yellow, yellow."

"Very good. My name is Dap. I'm your mom for the next few months."

The boys laughed.

"Laugh all you like, but keep it in mind. If you get lost in the school, which is quite possible, don't go opening doors. Some of them lead outside." More laughter. "Instead just tell someone that your mom is Dap, and they'll call me. Or tell them your color, and they'll light up a path for you to get home. If you have a problem, come talk to me. Remember, I'm the only person here who's paid to be nice to you. But not too nice. Give me any lip and I'll break your face. OK?"

They laughed again. Dap had a room full of friends. Frightened children are so easy to win.

"Which way is down, anybody tell me?"

They told him.

"OK, that's true. But that direction is toward the *outside*. The ship is spinning, and that's what makes it feel like that is down. The floor actually curves around in *that* direction. Keep going long enough that way, and you come back to where you started. Except don't try it. Because up that way is teachers' quarters, and up that way is the bigger kids. And the bigger kids don't like Launchies butting in. You might get pushed around. In fact, you *will* get pushed around. And when you do, don't come crying to me. Got it? This is Battle School, not nursery school."

"What are we supposed to do, then?" asked a boy, a really small black kid who had a top bunk near Ender's.

"If you don't like getting pushed around, figure out for yourself what to do about it. But I warn you—murder is strictly against the rules. So is any deliberate injury. I understand there was one attempted murder on the way up here. A broken arm. That kind of thing happens again, somebody ices out. You got it?"

"What's icing out?" asked the boy with his arm puffed up in a splint.

"Ice. Put out in the cold. Sent Earthside. Finished at Battle School."

Nobody looked at Ender.

"So, boys, if any of you are thinking of being troublemakers, at least be clever about it, OK?"

Dap left. They still didn't look at Ender.

Ender felt the fear growing in his belly. The kid whose arm he broke—Ender didn't feel sorry for him. He was a Stilson. And like Stilson, he was already gathering a gang. A little knot of kids, several of the bigger ones. They were laughing at the far end of the room, and every now and then one of them would turn to look at Ender.

With all his heart, Ender wanted to go home. What did any of this have to do with saving the world? There was no monitor now. It was Ender against the gang again, only they were right in his room. Peter again, but without Valentine.

The fear stayed, all through dinner as no one sat by him in the mess hall. The other boys were talking about things—the big scoreboard on one wall, the food, the bigger kids. Ender could only watch in isolation.

The scoreboards were team standings. Won-loss records, with

the most recent scores. Some of the bigger boys apparently had bets on the most recent games. Two teams, Manticore and Asp, had no recent score—that box was flashing. Ender decided they must be playing right now.

He noticed that the older boys were divided into groups, according to the uniforms they wore. Some with different uniforms were talking together, but generally the groups each had their own area. Launchies—their own group, and the two or three next older groups —all had plain blue uniforms. But the big kids, the ones that were on teams, they were wearing much more flamboyant clothing. Ender tried to guess which ones went with which name. Scorpion and Spider were easy. So were Flame and Tide.

A bigger boy came to sit by him. Not just a little bigger—he looked to be twelve or thirteen. Getting his man's growth started.

"Hi," he said.

"Hi," Ender said.

"I'm Mick."

"Ender."

"That's a name?"

"Since I was little. It's what my sister called me."

"Not a bad name here. Ender. Finisher. Hey."

"Hope so."

"Ender, you the bugger in your launch?"

Ender shrugged.

"I noticed you eating all alone. Every launch has one like that. Kid that nobody takes to right away. Sometimes I think the teachers do it on purpose. The teachers aren't very nice. You'll notice that."

"Yeah."

"So you the bugger?"

"I guess so."

"Hey. Nothing to cry about, you know?" He gave Ender his roll, and took Ender's pudding. "Eat nutritious stuff. It'll keep you strong." Mick dug into the pudding.

"What about you?" asked Ender.

"Me? I'm nothing. I'm a fart in the air conditioning. I'm always there, but most of the time nobody knows it."

Ender smiled tentatively.

"Yeah, funny, but no joke. I got nowhere here. I'm getting big now. They're going to send me to my next school pretty soon. No way it'll be Tactical School for me. I've never been a leader, you see. Only the guys who get to be leaders have a shot at it."

"How do you get to be a leader?"

"Hey, if I knew, you think I'd be like this? How many guys my size you see in here?"

Not many. Ender didn't say it.

"A few. I'm not the only half-iced bugger-fodder. A few of us. The other guys—they're all commanders. All the guys from my launch have their own teams now. Not me."

Ender nodded.

"Listen, little guy. I'm doing you a favor. Make friends. Be a leader. Kiss butts if you've got to, but if the other guys despise you— you know what I mean?"

Ender nodded again.

"Naw, you don't know anything. You Launchies are all alike. You don't know nothing. Minds like space. Nothing there. And if anything hits you, you fall apart. Look, when you end up like me, don't forget that somebody warned you. It's the last nice thing anybody's going to do for you."

"So why did you tell me?" asked Ender.

"What are you, a smartmouth? Shut up and eat."

Ender shut up and ate. He didn't like Mick. And he knew there was no chance he would end up like that. Maybe that was what the teachers were planning, but Ender didn't intend to fit in with their plans.

I will not be the bugger of my group, Ender thought. I didn't leave Valentine and Mother and Father to come here just to be iced.

As he lifted the fork to his mouth, he could feel his family around him, as they always had been. He knew just which way to turn his head to look up and see Mother, trying to get Valentine not to slurp. He knew just where Father would be, scanning the news on the table while pretending to be part of the dinner conversation. Peter, pretending to take a crushed pea out of his nose—even Peter could be funny.

It was a mistake to think of them. He felt a sob rise in his throat and swallowed it down; he could not see his plate.

He could not cry. There was no chance that he would be treated with compassion. Dap was not Mother. Any sign of weakness would tell the Stilsons and Peters that this boy could be broken. Ender did what he always did when Peter tormented him. He began to count doubles. One, two, four, eight, sixteen, thirty-two, sixty-four. And on, as high as he could hold the numbers in his head: 128, 256, 512, 1024, 2048, 4096, 8192, 16384, 32768, 65536, 131072, 262144. At 67108864 he began to be unsure—had he slipped out a digit? Should he be in the ten millions or the hundred millions or just the millions? He tried doubling again and lost it. 1342 something. 16? Or 17738? It was gone. Start over again. All the doubling he could hold. The pain was gone. The tears were gone. He would not cry.

Until that night, when the lights went dim, and in the distance he could hear several boys whimpering for their mothers or fathers or dogs. He could not help himself. His lips formed Valentine's name. He could hear her voice laughing in the distance, just down the hall. He could see Mother passing his door, looking in to be sure he was all right. He could hear Father laughing at the video. It was all so clear, and it would *never* be that way again. I'll be old when I ever see them again, twelve at the earliest. Why did I say yes? What was I such a fool for? Going to school would have been nothing. Facing Stilson every day. And Peter. He was a pissant, Ender wasn't afraid of him.

I want to go home, he whispered.

But his whisper was the whisper he used when he cried out in pain when Peter tormented him. The sound didn't travel farther than his own ears, and sometimes not that far.

And his tears could fall unwanted on his sheet, but his sobs were so gentle that they did not shake the bed; so quiet they could not be heard. But the ache was there, thick in his throat and the front of his face, hot in his chest and in his eyes. I want to go home.

Dap came to the door that night and moved quietly among the beds, touching a hand here. Where he went there was more crying, not less. The touch of kindness in this frightening place was enough to push some over the edge into tears. Not Ender, though. When Dap came, his crying was over, and his face was dry. It was the lying face he presented to Mother and Father, when Peter had been cruel to him and he dared not let it show. Thank you for this, Peter. For dry eyes and silent weeping. You taught me how to hide anything I felt. More than ever, I need that now.

There was school. Every day, hours of classes. Reading. Numbers. History. Videos of the bloody battles in space, the Marines spraying their guts all over the walls of the bugger ships. Holos of clean wars of the fleet, ships turning into puffs of light as the spacecraft killed each other deftly in the deep night. Many things to learn. Ender worked as hard as anyone; all of them struggled for the first time in their lives, as for the first time in their lives they competed with classmates who were at least as bright as they.

But the games—that was what they lived for. That was what filled the hours between waking and sleeping.

Dap introduced them to the game room on their second day. It was up, way above the decks where the boys lived and worked. They climbed ladders to where the gravity weakened, and there in the cavern they saw the dazzling lights of the games.

Some of the games they knew; some they had even played at home. Simple ones and hard ones. Ender walked past the two-dimensional games on video and began to study the games the bigger boys played, the holographic games with objects hovering in the air. He was the only Launchy in that part of the room, and every now and then one of the bigger boys would shove him out of the way. What're you doing here? Get lost. Fly off. And of course he would fly, in the lower gravity here, leave his feet and soar until he ran into something or someone.

Every time, though, he extricated himself and went back, perhaps to a different spot, to get a different angle on the game. He was too small to see the controls, how the game was actually done. That didn't matter. He got the movement of it in the air. The way the player dug tunnels in the darkness, tunnels of light, which the enemy ships would search for and then follow mercilessly until they caught the player's ship. The player could make traps: mines, drifting bombs, loops in the air that forced the enemy ships to repeat endlessly. Some of the players were clever. Others lost quickly.

Ender liked it better, though, when two boys played against each other. Then they had to use each other's tunnels, and it quickly became clear which of them were worth anything at the strategy of it.

Within an hour or so, it began to pall. Ender understood the regularities by then. Understood the rules the computer was following, so that he knew he could always, once he mastered the controls, outmaneuver the enemy. Spirals when the enemy was like this; loops when the enemy was like that. Lie in wait at one trap. Lay seven traps and then lure them like this. There was no challenge to it, then, just a matter of playing until the computer got so fast that no human reflexes could overcome it. That wasn't fun. It was the other boys he wanted to play. The boys who had been so trained by the computer that even when they played against each other they each tried to emulate the computer. Think like a machine instead of a boy.

I could beat them this way. I could beat them that way.

"I'd like a turn against you," he said to the boy who had just won.

"Lawsy me, what is this?" asked the boy. "Is it a bug or a bugger?"

"A new flock of dwarfs just came aboard," said another boy.

"But it *talks*. Did you know they could talk?"

"I see," said Ender. "You're afraid to play me two out of three."

"Beating you," said the boy, "would be as easy as pissing in the shower."

"And not half as fun," said another.

"I'm Ender Wiggin."

"Listen up, scrunchface. You nobody. Got that? You *nobody,* got that? You not anybody till you gots you first kill. Got that?"

The slang of the older boys had its own rhythm. Ender picked it up quick enough. "If I'm nobody, then how come you scared to play me two out of three?"

Now the other guys were impatient. "Kill the squirt quick and let's get on with it."

So Ender took his place at the unfamiliar controls. His hands were small, but the controls were simple enough. It took only a little experimentation to find out which buttons used certain weapons. Movement control was a standard wireball. His reflexes were slow at first. The other boy, whose name he still didn't know, got ahead quickly. But Ender learned a lot and was doing much better by the time the game ended.

"Satisfied, Launchy?"

"Two out of three."

"We don't allow two out of three games."

"So you beat me the first time I ever touched the game," Ender said. "If you can't do it twice, you can't do it at all."

They played again, and this time Ender was deft enough to pull off a few maneuvers that the boy had obviously never seen before. His patterns couldn't cope with them. Ender didn't win easily, but he won.

The bigger boys stopped laughing and joking then. The third game went in total silence. Ender won it quickly and efficiently.

When the game ended, one of the older boys said, "Bout time they replaced this machine. Getting so any pinbrain can beat it now."

Not a word of congratulation. Just total silence as Ender walked away.

He didn't go far. Just stood off in the near distance and watched as the next players tried to use the things he had shown them. Any pinbrain? Ender smiled inwardly. They won't forget me.

He felt good. He had won something, and against older boys. Probably not the best of the older boys, but he no longer had the panicked feeling that he might be out of his depth, that Battle School might be too much for him. All he had to do was watch the game and understand how things worked, and then he could use the system, and even excel.

It was the waiting and watching that cost the most. For during that time he had to endure. The boy whose arm he had broken was out for vengeance. His name, Ender quickly learned, was Bernard. He spoke his own name with a French accent, since the French, with their arrogant Separatism, insisted that the teaching of Standard not begin until the age of four, when the French language patterns were already set. His accent made him exotic and interesting; his broken arm made him a martyr; his sadism made him a natural focus for all those who loved pain in others.

Ender became their enemy.

Little things. Kicking his bed every time they went in and out of the door. Jostling him with his meal tray. Tripping him on the ladders. Ender learned quickly not to leave anything of his outside his lockers; he also learned to be quick on his feet, to catch himself. "Maladroit," Bernard called him once, and the name stuck.

There were times when Ender was very angry. With Bernard, of course, anger was inadequate. It was the kind of person he was—a tormentor. What enraged Ender was how willingly the others went along with him. Surely they knew there was no justice in Bernard's revenge. Surely they knew that he had struck first at Ender in the shuttle, that Ender had only been responding to violence. If they knew, they acted as if they didn't; even if they did not know, they should be able to tell from Bernard himself that he was a snake.

After all, Ender wasn't his only target. Bernard was setting up a kingdom, wasn't he?

Ender watched from the fringes of the group as Bernard established the hierarchy. Some of the boys were useful to him, and he flattered them outrageously. Some of the boys were willing servants, doing whatever he wanted even though he treated them with contempt.

But a few chafed under Bernard's rule.

Ender, watching, knew who resented Bernard. Shen was small, ambitious, and easily needled. Bernard had discovered that quickly, and started calling him Worm. "Because he's so *small,*" Bernard said, "and because he *wriggles.* Look how he shimmies his butt when he walks."

Shen stormed off, but they only laughed louder. "Look at his *butt.* Seeya, Worm!"

Ender said nothing to Shen—it would be too obvious, then, that he was starting his own competing gang. He just sat with his desk on his lap, looking as studious as possible.

He was not studying. He was telling his desk to keep sending a message into the interrupt queue every thirty seconds. The message was to everyone, and it was short and to the point. What made it hard was figuring out how to disguise who it was from, the way the teachers could. Messages from one of the boys always had their name automatically inserted. Ender hadn't cracked the teachers' security system yet, so he couldn't pretend to be a teacher. But he *was* able to set up a file for a nonexistent student, whom he whimsically named *God.*

Only when the message was ready to go did he try to catch Shen's eye. Like all the other boys, he was watching Bernard and his cronies laugh and joke, making fun of the math teacher, who often stopped in midsentence and looked around as if he had been let off the bus at the wrong stop and didn't know where he was.

Eventually, though, Shen glanced around. Ender nodded to him, pointed to his desk, and smiled. Shen looked puzzled. Ender held up his desk a little and then pointed at it. Shen reached for his own desk. Ender sent the message then. Shen saw it almost at once. Shen read it, then laughed aloud. He looked at Ender as if to say, Did you do this? Ender shrugged, to say, I don't know who did it but it sure wasn't me.

Shen laughed again, and several of the other boys who were not close to Bernard's group got out their desks and looked. Every thirty seconds the message appeared on every desk, marched around the screen quickly, then disappeared. The boys laughed together.

"What's so funny?" Bernard asked. Ender made sure he was not smiling when Bernard looked around the room, imitating the fear that so many others felt. Shen, of course, smiled all the more defiantly. It took a moment; then Bernard told one of his boys to bring out a desk. Together they read the message.

> **COVER YOUR BUTT. BERNARD IS WATCHING.**
> **-GOD**

Bernard went red with anger. "Who did this!" he shouted.

"God," said Shen.

"It sure as hell wasn't *you,*" Bernard said. "This takes too much *brains* for a *worm.*"

Ender's message expired after five minutes. After a while, a message from Bernard appeared on his desk.

> **I KNOW IT WAS YOU.**
> **-BERNARD.**

Ender didn't look up. He acted, in fact, as if he hadn't seen the message. Bernard just wants to catch me looking guilty. He doesn't know.

Of course, it didn't matter if he knew. Bernard would punish him all the more, because he had to rebuild his position. The one thing he couldn't stand was having the other boys laughing at him. He had to make clear who was boss. So Ender got knocked down in the shower that morning. One of Bernard's boys pretended to trip over him, and managed to plant a knee in his belly. Ender took it in silence. He was still watching, as far as the open war was concerned. He would do nothing.

But in the other war, the war of desks, he already had his next attack in place. When he got back from the shower, Bernard was raging, kicking beds and yelling at boys. "I didn't write it! Shut up!"

Marching constantly around every boy's desk was this message:

I LOVE YOUR BUTT. LET ME KISS IT.
-BERNARD

"I didn't write that message!" Bernard shouted. After the shouting had been going on for some time, Dap appeared at the door.

"What's the fuss?" he asked.

"Somebody's been writing messages using my name." Bernard was sullen.

"What message?"

"It doesn't matter what message!"

"It does to me." Dap picked up the nearest desk, which happened to belong to the boy who bunked above Ender. Dap read it, smiled very slightly, gave back the desk.

"Interesting," he said.

"Aren't you going to find out who did it?" demanded Bernard.

"Oh, I know who did it," Dap said.

Yes, Ender thought. The system was too easily broken. They mean us to break it, or sections of it. They know it was me.

"Well, who, then?" Bernard shouted.

"Are you shouting at me, soldier?" asked Dap, very softly.

At once the mood in the room changed. From rage on the part of Bernard's closest friends and barely contained mirth among the rest, all became somber. Authority was about to speak.

"No, sir," said Bernard.

"Everybody knows that the system automatically puts on the name of the sender."

"I didn't write that!" Bernard said.

"Shouting?" asked Dap.

"Yesterday someone sent a message that was signed GOD," Bernard said.

"Really?" said Dap. "I didn't know he was signed onto the system." Dap turned and left, and the room filled with laughter.

Bernard's attempt to be ruler of the room was broken—only a few stayed with him now. But they were the most vicious. And Ender knew that until he was through watching, it would go hard on him. Still, the tampering with the system had done its work. Bernard was contained, and all the boys who had some quality were free of him. Best of all, Ender had done it without sending him to the hospital. Much better this way.

Then he settled down to the serious business of designing a security system for his own desk, since the safeguards built into the system were obviously inadequate. If a six-year-old could break them down, they were obviously put there as a plaything, not serious security. Just another game that the teachers set up for us. And this is one I'm good at.

"How did you do that?" Shen asked him at breakfast.

Ender noted quietly that this was the first time another Launchy from his own class had sat with him at a meal. "Do what?" he asked.

"Send a message with a fake name. And Bernard's name! That was great. They're calling him Buttwatcher now. Just Watcher in front of the teachers, but everybody knows what he's watching."

"Poor Bernard," Ender murmured. "And he's so sensitive."

"Come on, Ender. You broke into the system. How'd you do it?"

Ender shook his head and smiled. "Thanks for thinking I'm bright enough to do that. I just happened to see it first, that's all."

"OK, you don't have to tell me," said Shen. "Still, it was great." They ate in silence for a moment. *"Do* I wiggle my butt when I walk?"

"Naw," Ender said. "Just a little. Just don't take such big long steps, that's all."

Shen nodded.

"The only person who'd ever notice was Bernard."

"He's a pig," said Shen.

Ender shrugged. "On the whole, pigs aren't so bad."

Shen laughed. "You're right. I wasn't being fair to the pigs."

They laughed together, and two other Launchies joined them. Ender's isolation was over. The war was just beginning.

Chapter 6

The Giant's Drink

"We've had our disappointments in the past, hanging on for years, hoping they'll pull through, and then they don't. Nice thing about Ender, he's determined to ice within the first six months."

"Oh?"

"Don't you see what's going on here? He's stuck at the Giant's Drink in the mind game. Is the boy suicidal? You never mentioned it."

"Everybody gets the Giant sometime."

"But Ender won't leave it alone. Like Pinual."

"Everybody looks like Pinual at one time or another. But he's the only one who killed himself. I don't think it had anything to do with the Giant's Drink."

"You're betting my life on that. And look what he's done with his launch group."

"Wasn't his fault, you know."

"I don't care. His fault or not, he's poisoning that group. They're supposed to bond, and right where he stands there's a chasm a mile wide."

"I don't plan to leave him there very long, anyway."

"Then you'd better plan again. That launch is sick, and he's the source of the disease. He stays till it's cured."

"I was the source of the disease. I was isolating him, and it worked."

"Give him time. To see what he does with it."

"We don't have time."

"We don't have time to rush a kid ahead who has as much chance of being a monster as a military genius."

"Is this an order?"

"The recorder's on, it's always on, your ass is covered, go to hell."

"If it's an order, then I'll—"

"It's an order. Hold him where he is until we see how he handles things in his launch group. Graff, you give me ulcers."

"You wouldn't have ulcers if you'd leave the school to me and take care of the fleet yourself."

"The fleet is looking for a battle commander. There's nothing to take care of until you get me **that**."

They filed clumsily into the battleroom, like children in a swimming pool for the first time, clinging to the handholds along the side. Null gravity was frightening, disorienting; they soon found that things went better if they didn't use their feet at all.

Worse, the suits were confining. It was harder to make precise movements, since the suits bent just a bit slower, resisted a bit more than any clothing they had ever worn before.

Ender gripped the handhold and flexed his knees. He noticed that along with the sluggishness, the suit had an amplifying effect on movement. It was hard to get them started, but the suit's legs kept moving, and strongly, after his muscles had stopped. Give them a push *this* strong, and the suit pushes with twice the force. I'll be clumsy for a while. Better get started.

So, still grasping the handhold, he pushed off strongly with his feet.

Instantly he flipped around, his feet flying over his head, and landed flat on his back against the wall. The rebound was stronger, it seemed, and his hands tore loose from the handhold. He flew across the battleroom, tumbling over and over.

For a sickening moment he tried to retain his old up-and-down orientation, his body attempting to right itself, searching for the gravity that wasn't there. Then he forced himself to change his view. He was hurtling toward a wall. That was down. And at once he had control of himself. He wasn't flying, he was falling. This was a dive. He could choose how he would hit the surface.

I'm going too fast to catch ahold and stay, but I can soften the impact, I can fly off at an angle if I roll when I hit and use my feet—

It didn't work at all the way he had planned. He went off at an angle, but it was not the one he had predicted. Nor did he have time to consider. He hit another wall, this time too soon to have prepared for it. But quite accidently he discovered a way to use his feet to control the rebound angle. Now he was soaring across the room again, toward the other boys who still clung to the wall. This time he had slowed enough to be able to grip a rung. He was at a crazy angle in relation to the other boys, but once again his orientation had changed, and as far as he could tell, they were all lying on the floor, not hanging on a wall, and he was no more upside down than they were.

"What are you trying to do, kill yourself?" asked Shen.

"Try it," Ender said. "The suit keeps you from hurting yourself, and you can control your bouncing with your legs, like this." He approximated the movement he had made.

Shen shook his head—he wasn't trying any fool stunt like that. But one boy did take off, not as fast as Ender had, because he didn't begin with a flip, but fast enough. Ender didn't even have to see his face to know that it was Bernard. And right after him, Bernard's best friend, Alai.

Ender watched them cross the huge room, Bernard struggling to orient himself to the direction he thought of as the floor, Alai surrendering to the movement and preparing to rebound from the wall. No wonder Bernard broke his arm in the shuttle, Ender thought. He tightens up when he's flying. He panics. Ender stored the information away for future reference.

And another bit of information, too. Alai did not push off in the same direction as Bernard. He aimed for a corner of the room. Their paths diverged more and more as they flew, and where Bernard made a clumsy, crunching landing and bounce on his wall, Alai did a glancing triple bounce on three surfaces near the corner that left him most of his speed and sent him flying off at a surprising angle. Alai shouted and whooped, and so did the boys watching him. Some of them forgot they were weightless and let go of the wall to clap their hands. Now they drifted lazily in many directions, waving their arms, trying to swim.

Now, that's a problem, thought Ender. What if you catch yourself drifting? There's no way to push off.

He was tempted to set himself adrift and try to solve the problem by trial and error. But he could see the others, their useless efforts at control, and he couldn't think of what he would do that they weren't already doing.

Holding onto the floor with one hand, he fiddled idly with the toy gun that was attached to his suit in front, just below the shoulder. Then he remembered the hand rockets sometimes used by marines when they did a boarding assault on an enemy station. He pulled the gun from his suit and examined it. He had pushed all the buttons back in the room, but the gun did nothing there. Maybe here in the battleroom it would work. There were no instructions on it. No labels on the controls. The trigger was obvious—he had had toy guns, as all children had, almost since infancy. There were two buttons that his thumb could easily reach, and several others along the bottom of the shaft that were almost inaccessible without using two hands. Obviously, the two buttons near his thumb were meant to be instantly usable.

He aimed the gun at the floor and pulled back on the trigger. He felt the gun grow instantly warm; when he let go of the trigger, it cooled at once. Also, a tiny circle of light appeared on the floor where he was aiming.

He thumbed the red button at the top of the gun, and pulled the trigger again. Same thing.

Then he pushed the white button. It gave a bright flash of light that illuminated a wide area, but not as intensely. The gun was quite cold when the button was pressed.

The red button makes it like a laser—but it is not a laser, Dap had said—while the white button makes it a lamp. Neither will be much help when it comes to maneuvering.

So everything depends on how you push off, the course you set when you start. It means we're going to have to get very good at controlling our launches and rebounds or we're all going to end up floating around in the middle of nowhere. Ender looked around the room. A few of the boys were drifting close to walls now, flailing their arms to catch a handhold. Most were bumping into each other and laughing; some were holding hands and going around in circles. Only a few, like Ender, were calmly holding onto the walls and watching.

One of them, he saw, was Alai. He had ended up on another wall not too far from Ender. On impulse, Ender pushed off and moved quickly toward Alai. Once in the air, he wondered what he would say. Alai was Bernard's friend. What did Ender have to say to him?

Still, there was no changing course now. So he watched straight ahead, and practiced making tiny leg and hand movements to control which way he was facing as he drifted. Too late, he realized that he had aimed too well. He was not going to land *near* Alai—he was going to hit him.

"Here, snag my hand!" Alai called.

Ender held out his hand. Alai took the shock of impact and helped Ender make a fairly gentle landing against the wall.

"That's good," Ender said. "We ought to practice that kind of thing."

"That's what I thought, only everybody's turning to butter out there," Alai said. "What happens if we get out there together? We should be able to shove each other in opposite directions."

"Yeah."

"OK?"

It was an admission that all might not be right between them. Is it OK for us to do something together? Ender's answer was to take Alai by the wrist and get ready to push off.

"Ready?" said Alai. "Go."

Since they pushed off with different amounts of force, they began to circle each other. Ender made some small hand movements, then shifted a leg. They slowed. He did it again. They stopped orbiting. Now they were drifting evenly.

"Packed head, Ender," Alai said. It was high praise. "Let's push off before we run into that bunch."

"And then let's meet over in that corner." Ender did not want this bridge into the enemy camp to fail.

"Last one there saves farts in a milk bottle," Alai said.

Then, slowly, steadily, they maneuvered until they faced each other, spread-eagled, hand to hand, knee to knee.

"And then we just scrunch?" asked Alai.

"I've never done this before either," said Ender.

They pushed off. It propelled them faster than they expected. Ender ran into a couple of boys and ended up on a wall that he hadn't expected. It took him a moment to reorient and find the corner where he and Alai were to meet. Alai was already headed toward it. Ender plotted a course that would include two rebounds, to avoid the largest clusters of boys.

When Ender reached the corner, Alai had hooked his arms through two adjacent handholds and was pretending to doze.

"You win."

"I want to see your fart collection," Alai said.

"I stored it in your locker. Didn't you notice?"

"I thought it was my socks."

"We don't wear socks anymore."

"Oh yeah." A reminder that they were both far from home. It took some of the fun out of having mastered a bit of navigation.

Ender took his pistol and demonstrated what he had learned about the two thumb buttons.

"What does it do when you aim at a person?" asked Alai.

"I don't know."

"Why don't we find out?"

Ender shook his head. "We might hurt somebody."

"I meant why don't we shoot each other in the foot or something. I'm not Bernard, I never tortured cats for fun."

"Oh."

"It can't be too dangerous, or they wouldn't give these guns to kids."

"We're soldiers now."

"Shoot me in the foot."

"No, you shoot me."

"Let's shoot each other."

They did. Immediately Ender felt the leg of the suit grow stiff, immobile at the knee and ankle joints.

"You frozen?" asked Alai.

"Stiff as a board."

"Let's freeze a few," Alai said. "Let's have our first war. Us against them."

They grinned. Then Ender said, "Better invite Bernard."

Alai cocked an eyebrow. "Oh?"

"And Shen."

"That little slanty-eyed butt-wiggler?"

Ender decided that Alai was joking. "Hey, we can't all be niggers."

Alai grinned. "My grandpa would've killed you for that."

"My great great grandpa would have sold him first."

"Let's go get Bernard and Shen and freeze these bugger-lovers."

In twenty minutes, everyone in the room was frozen except Ender, Bernard, Shen, and Alai. The four of them sat there whooping and laughing until Dap came in.

"I see you've learned how to use your equipment," he said. Then he did something to a control he held in his hand. Everybody drifted slowly toward the wall he was standing on. He went among the frozen boys, touching them and thawing their suits. There was a tumult of complaint that it wasn't fair how Bernard and Alai had shot them all when they weren't ready.

"Why weren't you ready?" asked Dap. "You had your suits just as long as they did. You had just as many minutes flapping around like drunken ducks. Stop moaning and we'll begin."

Ender noticed that it was assumed that Bernard and Alai were the leaders of the battle. Well, that was fine. Bernard knew that Ender and Alai had learned to use the guns together. And Ender and Alai were friends. Bernard might believe that Ender had joined his group, but it wasn't so. Ender had joined a new group. Alai's group. Bernard had joined it too.

It wasn't obvious to everyone; Bernard still blustered and sent his cronies on errands. But Alai now moved freely through the whole room, and when Bernard was crazy, Alai could joke a little and calm him down. When it came time to choose their launch leader, Alai was the almost unanimous choice. Bernard sulked for a few days and then he was fine, and everyone settled into the new pattern. The launch was no longer divided into Bernard's in-group and Ender's outcasts. Alai was the bridge.

Ender sat on his bed with his desk on his knees. It was private study time, and Ender was doing Free Play. It was a shifting, crazy kind of game in which the school computer kept bringing up new things, building a maze that you could explore. You could go back to events that you liked, for a while; if you left them alone too long, they disappeared and something else took its place.

Sometimes funny things. Sometimes exciting, and he had to be quick to stay alive. He had lots of deaths, but that was OK, games were like that, you died a lot until you got the hang of it.

His figure on the screen had started out as a little boy. For a while it had changed into a bear. Now it was a large mouse, with long and delicate hands. He ran his figure under a lot of large items of furniture. He had played with the cat a lot, but now it was boring —too easy to dodge, he knew all the furniture.

Not through the mousehole this time, he told himself. I'm sick of the Giant. It's a dumb game and I can't ever win. Whatever I choose is wrong.

But he went through the mousehole anyway, and over the small bridge in the garden. He avoided the ducks and the divebombing mosquitoes—he had tried playing with them but they were too easy, and if he played with the ducks too long he turned into a fish, which he didn't like. Being a fish reminded him too much of being frozen in the battleroom, his whole body rigid, waiting for the practice to end so Dap would thaw him. So, as usual, he found himself going up the rolling hills.

The landslides began. At first he had got caught again and again, crushed in an exaggerated blot of gore oozing out from under a rockpile. Now, though, he had mastered the skill of running up the slopes at an angle to avoid the crush, always seeking higher ground.

And, as always, the landslides finally stopped being jumbles of rock. The face of the hill broke open and instead of shale it was white bread, puffy, rising like dough as the crust broke away and fell. It was soft and spongy; his figure moved more slowly. And when he jumped down off the bread, he was standing on a table. Giant loaf of bread behind him; giant stick of butter beside him. And the Giant himself leaning his chin in his hands, looking at him. Ender's figure was about as tall as the Giant's head from chin to brow.

"I think I'll bite your head off," said the Giant, as he always did.

This time, instead of running away or standing there, Ender walked his figure up to the Giant's face and kicked him in the chin.

The Giant stuck out his tongue and Ender fell to the ground.

"How about a guessing game?" asked the Giant. So it didn't make any difference—the Giant only played the guessing game. Stupid computer. Millions of possible scenarios in its memory, and the Giant could only play one stupid game.

The Giant, as always, set two huge shot glasses, as tall as Ender's knees, on the table in front of him. As always, the two were filled with different liquids. The computer was good enough that the liquids had never repeated, not that he could remember. This time the one had a thick, creamy looking liquid. The other hissed and foamed.

"One is poison and one is not," said the Giant. "Guess right and I'll take you into Fairyland."

Guessing meant sticking his head into one of the glasses to drink. He never guessed right. Sometimes his head was dissolved. Sometimes he caught on fire. Sometimes he fell in and drowned. Sometimes he fell out, turned green, and rotted away. It was always ghastly, and the Giant always laughed.

Ender knew that whatever he chose he would die. The game was rigged. On the first death, his figure would reappear on the Giant's table, to play again. On the second death, he'd come back to the landslides. Then to the garden bridge. Then to the mousehole. And then, if he still went back to the Giant and played again, and died again, his desk would go dark, "Free Play Over" would march around the desk, and Ender would lie back on his bed and tremble until he could finally go to sleep. The game was rigged but still the Giant talked about Fairyland, some stupid childish three-year-old's Fairyland that probably had some stupid Mother Goose or Pac-Man or Peter Pan, it wasn't even worth getting to, but he had to find some way of beating the Giant to get there.

He drank the creamy liquid. Immediately he began to inflate and rise like a balloon. The Giant laughed. He was dead again.

He played again, and this time the liquid set, like concrete, and held his head down while the Giant cut him open along the spine, deboned him like a fish, and began to eat while his arms and legs quivered.

He reappeared at the landslides and decided not to go on. He even let the landslides cover him once. But even though he was sweating and he felt cold, with his next life he went back up the hills till they turned into bread, and stood on the Giant's table as the shot glasses were set before him.

He stared at the two liquids. The one foaming, the other with waves in it like the sea. He tried to guess what kind of death each one held. Probably a fish will come out of the ocean one and eat me. The foamy one will probably asphyxiate me. I hate this game. It isn't fair. It's stupid. It's rotten.

And instead of pushing his face into one of the liquids, he

kicked one over, then the other, and dodged the Giant's huge hands as the Giant shouted, "Cheater, cheater!" He jumped at the Giant's face, clambered up his lip and nose, and began to dig in the Giant's eye. The stuff came away like cottage cheese, and as the Giant screamed, Ender's figure burrowed into the eye, climbed right in, burrowed in and in.

The Giant fell over backward. The view shifted as he fell, and when the Giant came to rest on the ground, there were intricate, lacy trees all around. A bat flew up and landed on the dead Giant's nose. Ender brought his figure up out of the Giant's eye.

"How did you get here?" the bat asked. "Nobody ever comes here."

Ender could not answer, of course. So he reached down, took a handful of the Giant's eyestuff, and offered it to the bat.

The bat took it and flew off, shouting as it went, "Welcome to Fairyland."

He had made it. He ought to explore. He ought to climb down from the Giant's face and see what he had finally achieved.

Instead he signed off, put his desk in his locker, stripped off his clothes and pulled his blanket over him. He hadn't meant to kill the Giant. This was supposed to be a game. Not a choice between his own grisly death and an even worse murder. I'm a murderer, even when I play. Peter would be proud of me.

Chapter 7

Salamander

"Isn't it nice to know that Ender can do the impossible?"

"The player's deaths have always been sickening, I've always thought the Giant's Drink was the most perverted part of the whole mind game, but going for the eye like that—this is the one we want to put in command of our fleets?"

"What matters is that he won the game that couldn't be won."

"I suppose you'll move him now."

"We were waiting to see how he handled the thing with Bernard. He handled it perfectly."

"So as soon as he can cope with a situation, you move him to one he can't cope with. Doesn't he get any rest?"

"He'll have a month or two, maybe three, with his launch group. That's really quite a long time in a child's life."

"Does it ever seem to you that these boys aren't children? I look at what they do, the way they talk, and they don't seem like little kids."

"They're the most brilliant children in the world, each in his own way."

"But shouldn't they still act like children? They aren't **normal.** They act like—history. Napoleon and Wellington. Caesar and Brutus."

"We're trying to save the world, not heal the wounded heart. You're too compassionate."

"General Levy has no pity for anyone. All the videos say so. But don't hurt this boy."

"Are you joking?"

"I mean, don't hurt him more than you have to."

Alai sat across from Ender at dinner. "I finally figured out how you sent that message. Using Bernard's name."

"Me?" asked Ender.

"Come on, who else? It sure wasn't Bernard. And Shen isn't too hot on the computer. And I know it wasn't me. Who else? Doesn't matter. I figured out how to fake a new student entry. You just created a student named Bernard-blank, B-E-R-N-A-R-D-space, so the computer didn't kick it out as a repeat of another student."

"Sounds like that might work," said Ender.

"OK, OK. It *does* work. But you did that practically on the first day."

"Or somebody. Maybe Dap did it, to keep Bernard from getting too much control."

"I found something else. I can't do it with your name."

"Oh?"

"Anything with *Ender* in it gets kicked out. I can't get inside your files at all, either. You made your own security system."

"Maybe."

Alai grinned. "I just got in and trashed somebody's files. He's right behind me on cracking the system. I need protection, Ender. I need your system."

"If I give you my system, you'll know how I do it and you'll get in and trash *me.*"

"You say *me?*" Alai asked. "I the sweetest friend you got!"

Ender laughed. "I'll set up a system for you."

"Now?"

"Can I finish eating?"

"You never finish eating."

It was true. Ender's tray always had food on it after a meal. Ender looked at the plate and decided he was through. "Let's go then."

When they got to the barracks, Ender squatted down by his bed and said, "Get your desk and bring it over here, I'll show you how." But when Alai brought his desk to Ender's bed, Ender was just sitting there, his lockers still closed.

"What up?" asked Alai.

In answer, Ender palmed his locker. "Unauthorized Access Attempt," it said. It didn't open.

"Somebody done a dance on your head, mama," Alai said. "Somebody eated your face."

"You sure you want my security system now?" Ender got up and walked away from his bed.

"Ender," said Alai.

Ender turned around. Alai was holding a little piece of paper. "What is it?"

Alai looked up at him. "Don't you know? This was on your bed. You must have sat on it."

Ender took it from him.

**ENDER WIGGIN
ASSIGNED SALAMANDER ARMY
COMMANDER BONZO MADRID
EFFECTIVE IMMEDIATELY
CODE GREEN GREEN BROWN
NO POSSESSIONS TRANSFERRED**

"You're smart, Ender, but you don't do the battleroom any better than me."

Ender shook his head. It was the stupidest thing he could think of, to promote him now. Nobody got promoted before they were eight years old. Ender wasn't even seven yet. And launches usually moved into the armies together, with most armies getting a new kid at the same time. There were no transfer slips on any of the other beds.

Just when things were finally coming together. Just when Bernard was getting along with everybody, even Ender. Just when Ender was beginning to make a real friend out of Alai. Just when his life was finally getting livable.

Ender reached down to pull Alai up from the bed.

"Salamander Army's in contention, anyway," Alai said.

Ender was so angry at the unfairness of the transfer that tears were coming to his eyes. Mustn't cry, he told himself.

Alai saw the tears but had the grace not to say so. "They're fartheads, Ender, they won't even let you take anything you *own.*"

Ender grinned and didn't cry after all. "Think I should strip and go naked?"

Alai laughed, too.

On impulse Ender hugged him, tight, almost as if he were Valentine. He even thought of Valentine then and wanted to go home. "I don't want to go," he said.

Alai hugged him back. "I understand them, Ender. You are the best of us. Maybe they're in a hurry to teach you everything."

"They don't want to teach me everything," Ender said. "I wanted to learn what it was like to have a friend."

Alai nodded soberly. "Always my friend, always the best of my friends," he said. Then he grinned. "Go slice up the buggers."

"Yeah." Ender smiled back.

Alai suddenly kissed Ender on the cheek and whispered in his ear, "Salaam." Then, red-faced, he turned away and walked to his own bed at the back of the barracks. Ender guessed that the kiss and the word were somehow forbidden. A suppressed religion, perhaps. Or maybe the word had some private and powerful meaning for Alai alone. Whatever it meant to Alai, Ender knew that it was sacred; that he had uncovered himself for Ender, as once Ender's mother had done, when he was very young, before they put the monitor in his neck, and she had put her hands on his head when she thought he was asleep, and prayed over him. Ender had never spoken of that to anyone, not even to Mother, but had kept it as a memory of holiness, of how his mother loved him when she thought that no one, not even he, could see or hear. That was what Alai had given him; a gift so sacred that even Ender could not be allowed to understand what it meant.

After such a thing nothing could be said. Alai reached his bed and turned around to see Ender. Their eyes held for only a moment, locked in understanding. Then Ender left.

There would be no green green brown in this part of the school; he would have to pick up the colors in one of the public areas. The others would be finished with dinner very soon; he didn't want to go near the mess hall. The game room would be nearly empty.

None of the games appealed to him, the way he felt now. So he went to the bank of public desks at the back of the room and signed on to his own private game. He went quickly to Fairyland. The Giant was dead when he arrived now; he had to climb carefully down the table, jump to the leg of the Giant's overturned chair, and then make the drop to the ground. For a while there had been rats gnawing at the Giant's body, but Ender had killed one with a pin from the Giant's ragged shirt, and they had left him alone after that.

The Giant's corpse had essentially finished its decay. What could be torn by the small scavengers was torn; the maggots had done their work on the organs; now it was a dessicated mummy, hollowed-out, teeth in a rigid grin, eyes empty, fingers curled. Ender remembered burrowing through the eye when it had been alive and malicious and intelligent. Angry and frustrated as he was, Ender wished to do such murder again. But the Giant had become part of the landscape now, and so there could be no rage against him.

Ender had always gone over the bridge to the castle of the Queen of Hearts, where there were games enough for him; but none of those appealed to him now. He went around the giant's corpse and followed the brook upstream, to where it emerged from the forest. There was a playground there, slides and monkeybars, teeter-totters and merry-go-rounds, with a dozen children laughing as they played. Ender came and found that in the game he had become a child, though usually his figure in the games was adult. In fact, he was smaller than the other children.

He got in line for the slide. The other children ignored him. He climbed up to the top, watched the boy before him whirl down the long spiral to the ground. Then he sat and began to slide.

He had not slid for a moment when he fell right through the slide and landed on the ground under the ladder. The slide would not hold him.

Neither would the monkey bars. He could climb a ways, but then at random a bar seemed to be insubstantial and he fell. He could sit on the see-saw until he rose to the apex; then he fell. When the merry-go-round went fast, he could not hold onto any of the bars, and centrifugal force hurled him off.

And the other children: their laughter was raucous, offensive. They circled around him and pointed and laughed for many seconds before they went back to their play.

Ender wanted to hit them, to throw them in the brook. Instead he walked into the forest. He found a path, which soon became an ancient brick road, much overgrown with weeds but still usable. There were hints of possible games off to either side, but Ender followed none of them. He wanted to see where the path led.

It led to a clearing, with a well in the middle, and a sign that said, "Drink, Traveler." Ender went forward and looked at the well. Almost at once, he heard a snarl. Out of the woods emerged a dozen slavering wolves with human faces. Ender recognized them—they were the children from the playground. Only now their teeth could tear; Ender, weaponless, was quickly devoured.

His next figure appeared, as usual, in the same spot, and was eaten again, though Ender tried to climb down into the well.

The next appearance, though, was at the playground. Again the children laughed at him. Laugh all you like, Ender thought. I know what you are. He pushed one of them. She followed him, angry. Ender led her up the slide. Of course he fell through; but this time, following so closely behind him, she also fell through. When she hit the ground, she turned into a wolf and lay there, dead or stunned.

One by one Ender led each of the others into a trap. But before he had finished off the last of them, the wolves began reviving, and were no longer children. Ender was torn apart again.

This time, shaking and sweating, Ender found his figure revived on the Giant's table. I should quit, he told himself. I should go to my new army.

But instead he made his figure drop down from the table and walk around the Giant's body to the playground.

This time, as soon as the child hit the ground and turned into a wolf, Ender dragged the body to the brook and pulled it in. Each time, the body sizzled as though the water were acid; the wolf was consumed, and a dark cloud of smoke arose and drifted away. The children were easily dispatched, though they began following him in twos and threes at the end. Ender found no wolves waiting for him in the clearing, and he lowered himself into the well on the bucket rope.

The light in the cavern was dim, but he could see piles of jewels. He passed them by, noting that, behind him, eyes glinted among the gems. A table covered with food did not interest him. He passed through a group of cages hanging from the ceiling of the cave, each containing some exotic, friendly-looking creature. I'll play with you later, Ender thought. At last he came to a door, with these words in glowing emeralds:

THE END OF THE WORLD

He did not hesitate. He opened the door and stepped through.

He stood on a small ledge, high on a cliff overlooking a terrain of bright and deep green forest with dashes of autumn color and patches here and there of cleared land, with oxdrawn plows and small villages, a castle on a rise in the distance, and clouds riding currents of air below him. Above him, the sky was the ceiling of a vast cavern, with crystals dangling in bright stalactites.

The door closed behind him; Ender studied the scene intently. With the beauty of it, he cared less for survival than usual. He cared little, at the moment, what the game of this place might be. He had found it, and seeing it was its own reward. And so, with no thought of consequences, he jumped from the ledge.

Now he plummeted downward toward a roiling river and savage rocks; but a cloud came between him and the ground as he fell, and caught him, and carried him away. It took him to the tower of the castle, and through the open window, bearing him in. There it left him, in a room with no apparent door in floor or ceiling, and windows looking out over a certainly fatal fall.

A moment ago he had thrown himself from a ledge carelessly; this time he hesitated.

The small rug before the fire unraveled itself into a long, slender serpent with wicked teeth.

"I am your only escape," it said. "Death is your only escape."

Ender looked around the room for a weapon, when suddenly the screen went dark. Words flashed around the rim of the desk.

REPORT TO COMMANDER IMMEDIATELY.
YOU ARE LATE.
GREEN GREEN BROWN.

Furious, Ender snapped off the desk and went to the color wall, where he found the ribbon of green green brown, touched it, and followed it as it lit up before him. The dark green, light green, and brown of the ribbon reminded him of the early autumn kingdom he had found in the game. I must go back there, he told himself. The serpent is a long thread; I can let myself down from the tower and find my way through that place. Perhaps it's called the end of the world because it's the end of the games, because I can go to one of the villages and become one of the little boys working and playing there, with nothing to kill and nothing to kill me, just living there. As he thought of it, though, he could not imagine what "just living" might actually be. He had never done it in his life. But he wanted to do it anyway.

Armies were larger than launch groups, and the army barracks room was larger, too. It was long and narrow, with bunks on both sides; so long, in fact, that you could see the curvature of the floor as the far end bent upward, part of the wheel of the Battle School.

Ender stood at the door. A few boys near the door glanced at him, but they were older, and it seemed as though they hadn't even seen him. They went on with their conversations, lying and leaning on bunks. They were discussing battles, of course—the older boys always did. They were all much larger than Ender. The ten- and eleven-year-olds towered over him; even the youngest were eight, and Ender was not large for his age.

He tried to see which of the boys was the commander, but most were somewhere between battle dress and what the soldiers always called their sleep uniform—skin from head to toe. Many of them had desks out, but few were studying.

Ender stepped into the room. The moment he did, he was noticed.

"What do you want?" demanded the boy who had the upper bunk by the door. He was the largest of them. Ender had noticed him before, a young giant who had whiskers growing raggedly on his chin. "You're not a Salamander."

"I'm supposed to be, I think," Ender said. "Green green brown, right? I was transferred." He showed the boy, obviously the doorguard, his paper.

The doorguard reached for it. Ender withdrew it, just out of reach. "I'm supposed to give it to Bonzo Madrid."

Now another boy joined the conversation, a smaller boy, but still larger than Ender. "Not bahn-zoe, pisshead. Bone-So. The name's Spanish. Bonzo Madrid. Aqui nosotros hablamos español, Señor Gran Fedor."

"You must be Bonzo, then?" Ender asked, pronouncing the name correctly.

"No, just a brilliant and talented polyglot. Petra Arkanian. The only girl in Salamander Army. With more balls than anybody else in the room."

"Mother Petra she talking," said one of the boys, "she talking, she talking."

Another one chimed in. "Shit talking, shit talking, shit talking!" Quite a few laughed.

"Just between you and me," Petra said, "if they gave the Battle School an enema, they'd stick it in at green green brown."

Ender despaired. He already had nothing going for him— grossly undertrained, small, inexperienced, doomed to be resented for early advancement. And now, by chance, he had made exactly the wrong friend. An outcast in Salamander Army, and she had just linked him with her in the minds of the rest of the army. A good day's work. For a moment, as Ender looked around at the laughing, jeering faces, he imagined their bodies covered with hair, their teeth pointed for tearing. Am I the only human being in this place? Are all the others animals, waiting only to devour?

Then he remembered Alai. In every army, surely, there was at least one worth knowing.

Suddenly, though no one said to be quiet, the laughter stopped and the group fell silent. Ender turned to the door. A boy stood there, tall and dark and slender, with beautiful black eyes and slender lips that hinted at refinement. I would follow such beauty, said something inside Ender. I would see as those eyes see.

"Who are you?" asked the boy quietly.

"Ender Wiggin, sir," Ender said. "Reassigned from launch to Salamander Army." He held out the orders.

The boy took the paper in a swift, sure movement, without touching Ender's hand. "How old are you, Wiggin?" he asked.

"Almost seven."

Still quietly, he said, "I asked how old you are, not how old you almost are."

"I am six years, nine months, and twelve days old."

"How long have you been working in the battleroom?"

"A few months, now. My aim is better."

"Any training in battle maneuvers? Have you ever been part of a toon? Have you ever carried out a joint exercise?"

Ender had never heard of such things. He shook his head.

Madrid looked at him steadily. "I see. As you will quickly learn, the officers in command of this school, most notably Major Anderson, who runs the game, are fond of playing tricks. Salamander Army is just beginning to emerge from indecent obscurity. We have won twelve of our last twenty games. We have surprised Rat and Scorpion and Hound, and we are ready to play for leadership in the game. So of course, of course I am given such a useless, untrained, hopeless specimen of underdevelopment as yourself."

Petra said, quietly, "He isn't glad to meet you."

"Shut up, Arkanian," Madrid said. "To one trial, we now add another. But whatever obstacles our officers choose to fling in our path, we are still—"

"Salamander!" cried the soldiers, in one voice.

Instinctively, Ender's perception of these events changed. It was a pattern, a ritual. Madrid was not trying to hurt him, merely taking control of a surprising event and using it to strengthen his control of his army.

"We are the fire that will consume them, belly and bowel, head and heart, many flames of us, but one fire."

"Salamander!" they cried again.

"Even this one will not weaken us."

For a moment, Ender allowed himself to hope. "I'll work hard and learn quickly," he said.

"I didn't give you permission to speak," Madrid answered. "I intend to trade you away as quickly as I can. I'll probably have to give up someone valuable along with you, but as small as you are you are worse than useless. One more frozen, inevitably, in every battle, that's all you are, and we're now at a point where every frozen soldier makes a difference in the standings. Nothing personal, Wiggin, but I'm sure you can get your training at someone else's expense."

"He's all heart," Petra said.

Madrid stepped closer to the girl and slapped her across the face with the back of his hand. It made little sound, for only his fingernails had hit her. But there were bright red marks, four of them, on her cheek, and little pricks of blood marked where the tips of his fingernails had struck.

"Here are your instructions, Wiggin. I expect that it is the last time I'll need to speak to you. You will stay out of the way when we're training in the battleroom. You have to be there, of course, but you will not belong to any toon and you will not take part in any maneuvers. When we're called to battle, you will dress quickly and present yourself at the gate with everyone else. But you will not pass through the gate until four full minutes after the beginning of the game, and then you will remain at the gate, with your weapon undrawn and unfired, until such time as the game ends."

Ender nodded. So he was to be a nothing. He hoped the trade happened soon.

He also noticed that Petra did not so much as cry out in pain, or touch her cheek, though one spot of blood had beaded and run, making a streak down to her jaw. Outcast she may be, but since Bonzo Madrid was not going to be Ender's friend, no matter what, he might as well make friends with Petra.

He was assigned a bunk at the far end of the room. The upper bunk, so that when he lay on his bed he couldn't even see the door; the curve of the ceiling blocked it. There were other boys near him, tired-looking boys, sullen, the ones least valued. They had nothing of welcome to say to Ender.

Ender tried to palm his locker open, but nothing happened. Then he realized the lockers were not secured. All four of them had rings on them, to pull them open. Nothing would be private, then, now that he was in an army.

There was a uniform in the locker. Not the pale green of the Launchies, but the orange-trimmed dark green uniform of Salamander Army. It did not fit well. But then, they had probably never had to provide such a uniform for a boy so young.

He was starting to take it off when he noticed Petra walking down the aisle toward his bed. He slid off the bunk and stood on the floor to greet her.

"Relax," she said. "I'm not an officer."

"You're a toon leader, aren't you?"

Someone nearby snickered.

"Whatever gave you that idea, Wiggin?"

"You have a bunk in the front."

"I bunk in the front because I'm the best sharpshooter in Salamander Army, and because Bonzo is afraid I'll start a revolution if the toon leaders don't keep an eye on me. As if I could start anything with boys like *these.*" She indicated the sullen-faced boys on the nearby bunks.

What was she trying to do, make it worse than it already was? "Everybody's better than I am," Ender said, trying to dissociate himself from her contempt for the boys who would, after all, be his near bunkmates.

"I'm a girl," she said, "and you're a pissant of a six-year-old. We have so much in common, why don't we be friends?"

"I won't do your deskwork for you," he said.

In a moment she realized it was a joke. "Ha," she said. "It's all so military, when you're in the game. School isn't like it is for Launchies. History and strategy and tactics and buggers and math and stars, things you'll need as a pilot or a commander. You'll see."

"So you're my friend. Do I get a prize?" Ender asked. He was imitating her swaggering way of speaking, as if she cared about nothing.

"Bonzo isn't going to let you practice. He's going to make you take your desk to the battleroom and study. He's right, in a way—he doesn't want a totally untrained little kid start screwing up his precision maneuvers." She lapsed into giria, the slangy talk that imitated the pidgin English of uneducated people. "Bonzo, he pre-*cise*. He so *careful*, he piss on a plate and never splash."

Ender grinned.

"The battleground is open all the time. If you want, I'll take you in the off hours and show you some of the things I know. I'm not a great soldier, but I'm pretty good, and I sure know more than you."

"If you want," Ender said.

"Starting tomorrow morning after breakfast."

"What if somebody's using the room? We always went right after breakfast, in my launch."

"No problem. There are really nine battlerooms."

"I never heard of any others."

"They all have the same entrance. The whole center of the battle school, the hub of the wheel, is battlerooms. They don't rotate with the rest of the station. That's how they do the nullo, the no-gravity—it just holds still. No spin, no down. But they can set it up so that any one of the rooms is at the battleroom entrance corridor that we all use. Once you're inside, they move it along and another battleroom's in position."

"Oh."

"Like I said. Right after breakfast."

"Right," Ender said.

She started to walk away.

"Petra," he said.

She turned back.

"Thanks."

She said nothing, just turned around again and walked down the aisle.

Ender climbed back up on his bunk and finished taking off his uniform. He lay naked on the bed, doodling with his new desk, trying to decide if they had done anything to his access codes. Sure enough, they had wiped out his security system. He couldn't own anything here, not even his desk.

The lights dimmed a little. Getting toward bedtime. Ender didn't know which bathroom to use.

"Go left out of the door," said the boy on the next bunk. "We share it with Rat, Condor, and Squirrel."

Ender thanked him and started to walk on past.

"Hey," said the boy. "You can't go like that. Uniforms at all times out of this room."

"Even going to the toilet?"

"Especially. And you're forbidden to speak to anyone from any other army. At meals or in the toilet. You can get away with it sometimes in the game room, and of course whenever a teacher tells you to. But if Bonzo catch you, you dead, eh?"

"Thanks."

"And, uh, Bonzo get mad if you skin by Petra."

"She was naked when I came in, wasn't she?"

"She do what she like, but you keep you clothes on. Bonzo's orders."

That was stupid. Petra still looked like a boy, it was a stupid rule. It set her apart, made her different, split the army. Stupid stupid. How did Bonzo get to be a commander, if he didn't know better than that? Alai would be a better commander than Bonzo. He knew how to bring a group together.

I know how to bring a group together, too, thought Ender. Maybe I'll be commander someday.

In the bathroom, he was washing his hands when somebody spoke to him. "Hey, they putting babies in Salamander uniforms now?"

Ender didn't answer. Just dried off his hands.

"Hey, look! Salamander's getting babies now! Look at this! He could walk between my legs without touching my balls!"

"Cause you got none, Dink, that's why," somebody answered.

As Ender left the room, he heard somebody else say, "It's Wiggin. You know, the smartass from the game room."

He walked down the corridor smiling. He may be short, but they knew his name. From the game room, of course, so it meant nothing. But they'd see. He'd be a good soldier, too. They'd all know his name soon enough. Not in Salamander Army, maybe, but soon enough.

Petra was waiting in the corridor that led to the battleroom. "Wait a minute," she said to Ender. "Rabbit Army just went in, and it takes a few minutes to change to the next battleroom."

Ender sat down beside her. "There's more to the battleroom than just switching from one to the next," he said. "For instance, why is there gravity in the corridor outside the room, just before we go in?"

Petra closed her eyes. "And if the battlerooms are really free-floating, what happens when one is connected? Why doesn't it start to move with the rotation of the school?"

Ender nodded.

"These are the mysteries," Petra said in a deep whisper. "Do not pry into them. Terrible things happened to the last soldier who tried. He was discovered hanging by his feet from the ceiling of the bathroom, with his head stuffed in the toilet."

"So I'm not the first person to ask the question."

"You remember this, little boy." When she said *little boy* it sounded friendly, not contemptuous. "They never tell you any more truth than they have to. But any kid with brains knows that there've been some changes in science since the days of old Mazer Rackham and the Victorious Fleet. Obviously we can now control gravity. Turn it on and off, change the direction, maybe reflect it—I've thought of lots of neat things you could do with gravity weapons and gravity drives on starships. And think how starships could move near planets. Maybe tear big chunks out of them by reflecting the planet's own gravity back on itself, only from another direction, and focused down to a smaller point. But they say nothing."

Ender understood more than she said. Manipulation of gravity was one thing; deception by the officers was another; but the most important message was this: the adults are the enemy, not the other armies. They do not tell us the truth.

"Come, little boy," she said. "The battleroom is ready. Petra's hands are steady. The enemy is deady." She giggled. "Petra the poet, they call me."

"They also say you're crazy as a loon."

"Better believe it, baby butt." She had ten target balls in a bag. Ender held onto her suit with one hand and the wall with the other, to steady her as she threw them, hard, in different directions. In the null gravity, they bounced every which way. "Let go of me," she said. She shoved off, spinning deliberately; with a few deft hand moves she steadied herself, and began aiming carefully at ball after ball. When she shot one, its glow changed from white to red. Ender knew that the color change lasted less than two minutes. Only one ball had changed back to white when she got the last one.

She rebounded accurately from a wall and came at high speed back to Ender. He caught her and held her against her own rebound —one of the first techniques they had taught him as a Launchy.

"You're good," he said.

"None better. And you're going to learn how to do it."

Petra taught him to hold his arm straight, to aim with the whole arm. "Something most soldiers don't realize is that the farther away your target is, the longer you have to hold the beam within about a two-centimeter circle. It's the difference between a tenth of a second and a half a second, but in battle that's a long time. A lot of soldiers think they missed when they were right on target, but they moved away too fast. So you can't use your gun like a sword, swish swish slice-em-in-half. You got to aim."

She used the ballcaller to bring the targets back, then launched them slowly, one by one. Ender fired at them. He missed every one.

"Good," she said. "You don't have any bad habits."

"I don't have any good ones, either," he pointed out.

"I give you those."

They didn't accomplish much that first morning. Mostly talk. How to think while you were aiming. You've got to hold your own motion and your enemy's motion in your mind at the same time. You've got to hold your arm straight out and aim with your body, so in case your arm is frozen you can still shoot. Learn where your trigger actually fires and ride the edge, so you don't have to pull so far each time you fire. Relax your body, don't tense up, it makes you tremble.

It was the only practice Ender got that day. During the army's drills in the afternoon, Ender was ordered to bring his desk and do his schoolwork, sitting in a corner of the room. Bonzo had to have all his soldiers in the battleroom, but he didn't have to use them.

Ender did not do his schoolwork, however. If he couldn't have drill as a soldier, he could study Bonzo as a tactician. Salamander Army was divided into the standard four toons of ten soldiers each. Some commanders set up their toons so that A toon consisted of the best soldiers, and D toon had the worst. Bonzo had mixed them, so that each consisted of good soldiers and weaker ones.

Except that B toon had only nine boys. Ender wondered who had been transferred to make room for him. It soon became plain that the leader of toon B was new. No wonder Bonzo was so disgusted—he had lost a toon leader to get Ender.

And Bonzo was right about another thing. Ender was not ready. All the practice time was spent working on maneuvers. Toons that couldn't see each other practiced performing precision operations together with exact timing; toons practiced using each other to make sudden changes of direction without losing formation. All these soldiers took for granted skills that Ender didn't have. The ability to make a soft landing and absorb most of the shock. Accurate flight. Course adjustment using the frozen soldiers floating randomly through the room. Rolls, spins, dodges. Sliding along the walls—a very difficult maneuver and yet one of the most valuable, since the enemy couldn't get behind you.

Even as Ender learned how much he did not know, he also saw things that he could improve on. The well-rehearsed formations were a mistake. It allowed the soldiers to obey shouted orders instantly, but it also meant they were predictable. Also, the individual soldiers were given little initiative. Once a pattern was set, they were to follow it through. There was no room for adjustment to what the enemy did against the formation. Ender studied Bonzo's formations like an enemy commander would, noting ways to disrupt the formation.

During free play that night, Ender asked Petra to practice with him.

"No," she said. "I want to be a commander someday, so I've got to play the game room." It was a common belief that the teachers monitored the games and spotted potential commanders there. Ender doubted it, though. Toon leaders had a better chance to show what they might do as commanders than any video player.

But he didn't argue with Petra. The after-breakfast practice was generous enough. Still, he had to practice. And he couldn't practice alone, except a few of the basic skills. Most of the hard things required partners or teams. If only he still had Alai or Shen to practice with.

Well, why *shouldn't* he practice with them? He had never heard of a soldier practicing with Launchies, but there was no rule against it. It just wasn't done; Launchies were held in too much contempt. Well, Ender was still being treated like a Launchy anyway. He needed someone to practice with, and in return he could help them learn some of the things he saw the older boys doing.

"Hey, the great soldier returns!" said Bernard. Ender stood in the doorway of his old barracks. He'd only been away for a day, but already it seemed like an alien place, and the others of his launch group were strangers. Almost he turned around and left. But there was Alai, who had made their friendship sacred. Alai was not a stranger.

Ender made no effort to conceal how he was treated in Salamander Army. "And they're right. I'm about as useful as a sneeze in a spacesuit." Alai laughed, and other Launchies started to gather around. Ender proposed his bargain. Free play, every day, working hard in the battleroom, under Ender's direction. They would learn things from the armies, from the battles Ender would see; he would get the practice he needed in developing soldier skills. "We'll get ready together."

A lot of boys wanted to come, too. "Sure," Ender said. "If you're coming to work. If you're just farting around, you're out. I don't have any time to waste."

They didn't waste any time. Ender was clumsy, trying to describe what he had seen, working out ways to do it. But by the time free play ended, they had learned some things. They were tired, but they were getting the knack of a few techniques.

"Where were you?" asked Bonzo.

Ender stood stiffly by his commander's bunk. "Practicing in a battleroom."

"I hear you had some of your old Launchy group with you."

"I couldn't practice alone."

"I won't have any soldiers in Salamander Army hanging around with Launchies. You're a soldier now."

Ender regarded him in silence.

"Did you hear me, Wiggin?"

"Yes, sir."

"No more practicing with those little farts."

"May I speak to you privately?" asked Ender.

It was a request that commanders were required to allow. Bonzo's face went angry, and he led Ender out into the corridor. "Listen, Wiggin, I don't want you, I'm trying to get rid of you, but don't give me any problems or I'll paste you to the wall."

A good commander, thought Ender, doesn't have to make stupid threats.

Bonzo grew annoyed at Ender's silence. "Look, you asked me to come out here, now talk."

"Sir, you were correct not to place me in a toon. I don't know how to do anything."

"I don't need you to tell me when I'm correct."

"But I'm going to become a good soldier. I won't screw up your regular drill, but I'm going to practice, and I'm going to practice with the only people who will practice with me, and that's my Launchies."

"You'll do what I tell you, you little bastard."

"That's right, sir. I'll follow all the orders that you're authorized to give. But free play is free. No assignments can be given. None. By anyone."

He could see Bonzo's anger growing hot. Hot anger was bad. Ender's anger was cold, and he could use it. Bonzo's was hot, and so it used him.

"Sir, I've got my own career to think of. I won't interfere in your training and your battles, but I've got to learn sometime. I didn't ask to be put into your army, you're trying to trade me as soon as you can. But nobody will take me if I don't know anything, will they? Let me learn something, and then you can get rid of me all the sooner and get a soldier you can really use."

Bonzo was not such a fool that anger kept him from recognizing good sense when he heard it. Still, he couldn't let go of his anger immediately.

"While you're in Salamander Army, you'll obey me."

"If you try to control my free play, I can get you iced."

It probably wasn't true. But it was possible. Certainly if Ender made a fuss about it, interfering with free play could conceivably get Bonzo removed from command. Also, there was the fact that the officers obviously saw something in Ender, since they had promoted him. Maybe Ender *did* have influence enough with the teachers to ice somebody. "Bastard," said Bonzo.

"It isn't my fault you gave me that order in front of everybody," Ender said. "But if you want, I'll pretend you won this argument. Then tomorrow you can tell me you changed your mind."

"I don't need you to tell me what to do."

"I don't want the other guys to think you backed down. You wouldn't be able to command as well."

Bonzo hated him for it, for the kindness. It was as if Ender were granting him his command as a favor. Galling, and yet he had no choice. No choice about anything. It didn't occur to Bonzo that it was his own fault, for giving Ender an unreasonable order. He only knew that Ender had beaten him, and then rubbed his nose in it by being magnanimous.

"I'll have your ass someday," Bonzo said.

"Probably," said Ender. The lights out buzzer sounded. Ender walked back into the room, looking dejected. Beaten. Angry. The other boys drew the obvious conclusion.

And in the morning, as Ender was leaving for breakfast, Bonzo stopped him and spoke loudly. "I changed my mind, pinprick. Maybe by practicing with your Launchies you'll learn something, and I can trade you easier. Anything to get rid of you faster."

"Thank you, sir," Ender said.

"Anything," whispered Bonzo. "I hope you're iced."

Ender smiled gratefully and left the room. After breakfast he practiced again with Petra. All afternoon he watched Bonzo drill and figured out ways to destroy his army. During free play he and Alai and the others worked themselves to exhaustion. I can do this, thought Ender as he lay in his bed, his muscles throbbing, unknotting themselves. I can handle it.

Salamander Army had a battle four days later. Ender followed behind the real soldiers as they jogged along the corridors to the battleroom. There were two ribbons along the walls, the green green brown of Salamander and the black white black of Condor. When they came to the place where the battleroom had always been, the corridor split instead, with green green brown leading to the left and black white black to the right. Around another turn to the right, and the army stopped in front of a blank wall.

The toons formed up in silence. Ender stayed behind them all. Bonzo was giving his instructions. "A take the handles and go up. B left, C right, D down." He saw that the toons were oriented to follow instructions, then added, "And you, pinprick, wait four minutes, then come just inside the door. Don't even take your gun off your suit."

Ender nodded. Suddenly the wall behind Bonzo became transparent. Not a wall at all, then, but a forcefield. The battleroom was different, too. Huge brown boxes were suspended in midair, partially obstructing the view. So these were the obstacles that the soldiers called *stars*. They were distributed seemingly at random. Bonzo seemed not to care where they were. Apparently the soldiers already knew how to handle the stars.

But it soon became clear to Ender, as he sat and watched the battle from the corridor, that they did not know how to handle the stars. They did know how to softland on one and use it for cover, the tactics of assaulting the enemy's position on a star. They showed no sense at all of *which* stars mattered. They persisted in assaulting stars that could have been bypassed by wallsliding to a more advanced position.

The other commander was taking advantage of Bonzo's neglect of strategy. Condor Army forced the Salamanders into costly assaults. Fewer and fewer Salamanders were unfrozen for the attack on the next star. It was clear, after only five or six minutes, that Salamander Army could not defeat the enemy by attacking.

Ender stepped through the gate. He drifted slightly downward. The battlerooms he had practiced in always had their doors at floor level. For real battles, however, the door was set in the middle of the wall, as far from the floor as from the ceiling.

Abruptly he felt himself reorient, as he had in the shuttle. What had been down was now up, and now sideways. In nullo, there was no reason to stay oriented the way he had been in the corridor. It was impossible to tell, looking at the perfectly square doors, which way had been up. And it didn't matter. For now Ender had found the orientation that made sense. The enemy's gate was down. The object of the game was to fall toward the enemy's home.

Ender made the motions that oriented himself in his new direction. Instead of being spread out, his whole body presented to the enemy, now Ender's legs pointed toward them. He was a much smaller target.

Someone saw him. He was, after all, drifting aimlessly in the open. Instinctively he pulled his legs up under him. At that moment he was flashed, and the legs of his suit froze in position. His arms remained unfrozen, for without a direct body hit, only the limbs that were shot froze up. It occurred to Ender that if he had not been presenting his legs to the enemy, it would have been his body they hit. He would have been immobilized.

Since Bonzo had ordered him not to draw his weapon, Ender continued to drift, not moving his head or arms, as if they had been frozen, too. The enemy ignored him and concentrated their fire on the soldiers who were firing at them. It was a bitter battle. Outnumbered now, Salamander Army gave ground stubbornly. The battle disintegrated into a dozen individual shootouts. Bonzo's discipline paid off now, for each Salamander that froze took at least one enemy with him. No one ran or panicked, everyone remained calm and aimed carefully.

Petra was especially deadly. Condor Army noticed it and took great effort to freeze her. They froze her shooting arm first, and her stream of curses was only interrupted when they froze her completely and the helmet clamped down on her jaw. In a few minutes it was over. Salamander Army offered no more resistance.

Ender noted with pleasure that Condor could only muster the minimal five soldiers necessary to open the gate to victory. Four of them touched their helmets to the lighted spots at the four corners of Salamander's door, while the fifth passed through the forcefield.

That ended the game. The lights came back on to their full brightness, and Anderson came out of the teacher door.

I could have drawn my gun, thought Ender, as the enemy approached the door. I could have drawn my gun and shot just one of them, and they would have been too few. The game would have been a draw. Without four men to touch the four corners and a fifth man to pass through the gate, Condor would have had no victory. Bonzo, you ass, I could have saved you from this defeat. Maybe even turned it to victory, since they were sitting there, easy targets, and they wouldn't have known at first where the shots were coming from. I'm a good enough shot for that.

But orders were orders, and Ender had promised to obey. He did get some satisfaction out of the fact that on the official tally Salamander Army recorded, not the expected forty-one disabled or eliminated, but rather forty eliminated and one damaged. Bonzo couldn't understand it, until he consulted Anderson's book and realized who it was. Damaged, Bonzo, thought Ender. I could still shoot.

He expected Bonzo to come to him and say, "Next time, when it's like that, you can shoot." But Bonzo didn't say anything to him at all until the next morning after breakfast. Of course, Bonzo ate in the commanders' mess, but Ender was pretty sure the odd score would cause as much stir there as it did in the soldiers' dining hall. In every other game that wasn't a draw, every member of the losing team was either eliminated—totally frozen—or disabled, which meant they had some body parts still unfrozen, but were unable to shoot or inflict damage on the enemy. Salamander was the only losing army with one man in the Damaged but Active category.

Ender volunteered no explanation, but the other members of Salamander Army let it be known why it had happened. And when other boys asked him why he hadn't disobeyed orders and fired, he calmly answered, "I obey orders."

After breakfast, Bonzo looked for him. "The order still stands," he said, "and don't you forget it."

It will cost you, you fool. I may not be a good soldier, but I can still help and there's no reason you shouldn't let me.

Ender said nothing.

An interesting side effect of the battle was that Ender emerged at the top of the soldier efficiency list. Since he hadn't fired a shot, he had a perfect record on shooting—no misses at all. And since he had never been eliminated or disabled, his percentage there was excellent. No one else came close. It made a lot of boys laugh, and others were angry, but on the prized efficiency list, Ender was now the leader.

He kept sitting out the army practice sessions, and kept working hard on his own, with Petra in the mornings and his friends at night. More Launchies were joining them now, not on a lark but because they could see results—they were getting better and better. Ender and Alai stayed ahead of them, though. In part, it was because Alai kept trying new things, which forced Ender to think of new tactics to cope with them. In part it was because they kept making stupid mistakes, which suggested things to do that no self-respecting, well-trained soldier would even have tried. Many of the things they attempted turned out to be useless. But it was always fun, always exciting, and enough things worked that they knew it was helping them. Evening was the best time of the day.

The next two battles were easy Salamander victories; Ender came in after five minutes and remained untouched by the defeated enemy. Ender began to realize that Condor Army, which had beaten them, was unusually good; Salamander, weak as Bonzo's grasp of strategy might be, was one of the better teams, climbing steadily in the ratings, clawing for fourth place with Rat Army.

Ender turned seven. They weren't much for dates and calendars at the Battle School, but Ender had found out how to bring up the date on his desk, and he noticed his birthday. The school noticed it, too; they took his measurements and issued him a new Salamander uniform and a new flash suit for the battleroom. He went back to the barracks with the new clothing on. It felt strange and loose, like his skin no longer fit properly.

He wanted to stop at Petra's bunk and tell her about his home, about what his birthdays were usually like, just tell her it was his birthday so she'd say something about it being a happy one. But nobody told birthdays. It was childish. It was what landsiders did. Cakes and silly customs. Valentine baked him his cake on his sixth birthday. It fell and it was terrible. Nobody knew how to cook anymore, it was the kind of crazy thing Valentine would do. Everybody teased Valentine about it, but Ender saved a little bit of it in his cupboard. Then they took out his monitor and he left and for all he knew, it was still there, a little piece of greasy yellow dust. Nobody talked about home, not among the soldiers; there had been no life before Battle School. Nobody got letters, and nobody wrote any. Everybody pretended that they didn't care.

But I do care, thought Ender. The only reason I'm here is so that a bugger won't shoot out Valentine's eye, won't blast her head open like the soldiers in the videos of the first battles with the buggers. Won't split her head with a beam so hot that her brains burst the skull and spill out like rising bread dough, the way it happens in my worst nightmares, in my worst nights, when I wake up trembling but silent, must keep silent or they'll hear that I miss my family, I want to go home.

It was better in the morning. Home was merely a dull ache in the back of his memory. A tiredness in his eyes. That morning Bonzo came in as they were dressing. "Flash suits!" he called. It was a battle. Ender's fourth game.

The enemy was Leopard Army. It would be easy. Leopard was new, and it was always in the bottom quarter in the standings. It had been organized only six months ago, with Pol Slattery as its commander. Ender put on his new battle suit and got into line; Bonzo pulled him roughly out of line and made him march at the end. You didn't need to do that, Ender said silently. You could have let me stay in line.

Ender watched from the corridor. Pol Slattery was young, but he was sharp, he had some new ideas. He kept his soldiers moving, darting from star to star, wallsliding to get behind and above the stolid Salamanders. Ender smiled. Bonzo was hopelessly confused, and so were his men. Leopard seemed to have men in every direction. However, the battle was not as lopsided as it seemed. Ender noticed that Leopard was losing a lot of men, too—their reckless tactics exposed them too much. What mattered, however, was that Salamander *felt* defeated. They had surrendered the initiative completely. Though they were still fairly evenly matched with the enemy, they huddled together like the last survivors of a massacre, as if they hoped the enemy would overlook them in the carnage.

Ender slipped slowly through the gate, oriented himself so the enemy's gate was down, and drifted slowly eastward to a corner where he wouldn't be noticed. He even fired at his own legs, to hold them in the kneeling position that offered him the best protection. He looked to any casual glance like another frozen soldier who had drifted helplessly out of the battle.

With Salamander Army waiting abjectly for destruction, Leopard obligingly destroyed them. They had nine boys left when Salamander finally stopped firing. They formed up and started to open the Salamander gate.

Ender aimed carefully with a straight arm, as Petra had taught him. Before anyone knew what was happening, he froze three of the soldiers who were about to press their helmets against the lighted corners of the door. Then some of the others spotted him and fired— but at first they hit only his already-frozen legs. It gave him time to get the last two men at the gate. Leopard had only four men left unfrozen when Ender was finally hit in the arm and disabled. The game was a draw, and they never had hit him in the body.

Pol Slattery was furious, but there had been nothing unfair about it. Everyone in Leopard Army assumed that it had been a strategy of Bonzo's, to leave a man till the last minute. It didn't occur to them that little Ender had fired against orders. But Salamander Army knew. Bonzo knew, and Ender could see from the way his commander looked at him that Bonzo hated him for rescuing him from total defeat. I don't care, Ender told himself. It will just make me easier to trade away, and in the meantime you won't drop so far in the standings. Just trade me. I've learned all I'm ever going to learn from *you*. How to fail with style, that's all you know, Bonzo.

What *have* I learned so far? Ender listed things in his mind as he undressed by his bunk. The enemy's gate is down. Use my legs as a shield in battle. A small reserve, held back until the end of the game, can be decisive. And soldiers can sometimes make decisions that are smarter than the orders they've been given.

Naked, he was about to climb into bed when Bonzo came toward him, his face hard and set. I have seen Peter like this, thought Ender, silent with murder in his eye. But Bonzo is not Peter. Bonzo has more fear.

"Wiggin, I finally traded you. I was able to persuade Rat Army that your incredible place on the efficiency list is more than an accident. You go over there tomorrow."

"Thank you, sir," Ender said.

Perhaps he sounded too grateful. Suddenly Bonzo swung at him, caught his jaw with a vicious open-handed slap. It knocked

Ender sideways, into his bunk, and he almost fell. Then Bonzo slugged him, hard, in the stomach. Ender dropped to his knees.

"You disobeyed me," Bonzo said. Loudly, for all to hear. "No good soldier ever disobeys."

Even as he cried from the pain, Ender could not help but take vengeful pleasure in the murmurs he heard rising through the barracks. You fool, Bonzo. You aren't enforcing discipline, you're destroying it. They know I turned defeat into a draw. And now they see how you repay me. You made yourself look stupid in front of everyone. What is your discipline worth now?

The next day, Ender told Petra that for her sake the shooting practice in the morning would have to end. Bonzo didn't need anything that looked like a challenge now, and so she'd better stay clear of Ender for a while. She understood perfectly. "Besides," she said, "you're as close to being a good shot as you'll ever be."

He left his desk and flash suit in the locker. He would wear his Salamander uniform until he could get to the commissary and change it for the brown and black of Rat. He had brought no possessions with him; he would take none away. There were none to have —everything of value was in the school computer or his own head and hands.

He used one of the public desks in the game room to register for an earth-gravity personal combat course during the hour immediately after breakfast. He didn't plan to get vengeance on Bonzo for hitting him. But he did intend that no one would be able to do that to him again.

Chapter **8**

Rat

"Colonel Graff, the games have always been run fairly before. Either random distribution of stars, or symmetrical."

"Fairness is a wonderful attribute, Major Anderson. It has nothing to do with war."

"The game will be compromised. The comparative standings will become meaningless."

"Alas."

"It will take months. Years, to develop the new battlerooms and run the simulations."

"That's why I'm asking you now. To begin. Be creative. Think of every stacked, impossible, unfair star arrangement you can. Think of other ways to bend the rules. Late notification. Unequal forces. Then run the simulations and see which ones are hardest, which easiest. We want an intelligent progression here. We want to bring him along."

"When do you plan to make him a commander? When he's eight?"

"Of course not. I haven't assembled his army yet."

"Oh, so you're stacking it that way, too?"

"You're getting too close to the game, Anderson. You're forgetting that it is merely a training exercise."

"It's also status, identity, purpose, name; all that makes these children who they are comes out of this game. When it becomes known that the game can be manipulated, weighted, **cheated,** it will undo this whole school. I'm not exaggerating."

"I know."

"So I hope Ender Wiggin truly is the one, because you'll

have defeated the effectiveness of our training method for a long time to come."

"If Ender isn't the one, if his peak of military brilliance does not coincide with the arrival of our fleets at the bugger homeworlds, then it doesn't really matter what our training method is or isn't."

"I hope you will forgive me, Colonel Graff, but I feel that I must report your orders and my opinion of their consequences to the Strategos and the Hegemon."

"Why not our dear Polemarch?"

"Everybody knows you have him in your pocket."

"Such hostility, Major Anderson. And I thought we were friends."

"We are. And I think you may be right about Ender. I just don't believe you, and you alone, should decide the fate of the world."

"I don't even think it's right for me to decide the fate of Ender Wiggin."

"So you won't mind if I notify them?"

"Of course I mind, you meddlesome ass. This is something to be decided by people who know what they're doing, not these frightened politicians who got their office because they happen to be politically potent in the country they come from."

"But you understand why I'm doing it."

"Because you're such a short-sighted little bureaucratic bastard that you think you need to cover yourself in case things go wrong. Well, if things go wrong we'll all be bugger meat. So trust me now, Anderson, and don't bring the whole damn Hegemony down on my neck. What I'm doing is hard enough without them."

"Oh, is it unfair? Are things stacked against you? You can do it to Ender, but you can't take it, is that it?"

"Ender Wiggin is ten times smarter and stronger than I am. What I'm doing to him will bring out his genius. If I had to go through it myself, it would crush me. Major Anderson, I know I'm wrecking the game, and I know you love it better than any of the boys who play. Hate me if you like, but don't stop me."

"I reserve the right to communicate with the Hegemony and the Strategoi at any time. But for now—do what you want."

"Thank you so very kindly."

"Ender Wiggin, the little farthead who leads the standings, what a pleasure to have you with us." The commander of Rat Army lay sprawled on a lower bunk wearing only his desk. "With you around, how can any army lose?" Several of the boys nearby laughed.

There could not have been two more opposite armies than Salamander and Rat. The room was rumpled, cluttered, noisy. After Bonzo, Ender had thought that undiscipline would be a welcome relief. Instead, he found that he had come to expect quiet and order, and the disorder here made him uncomfortable.

"We doing OK, Ender Bender. I Rose de Nose, Jewboy extraordinaire, and you ain't nothin but a pinheaded pinprick of a goy. Don't you forget it."

Since the I.F. was formed, the Strategos of the military forces had always been a Jew. There was a myth that Jewish generals didn't lose wars. And so far it was still true. It made any Jew in the Battle School dream of being Strategos, and conferred prestige on him from the start. It also caused resentment. Rat Army was often called the Kike Force, half in praise, half in parody of Mazer Rackham's Strike Force. There were many who liked to remember that during the Second Invasion, even though an American Jew, as President, was Hegemon of the alliance, an Israeli Jew was Strategos in overall command of I.F. defense, and a Russian Jew was Polemarch of the fleet, it was Mazer Rackham, a little-known, twice-court-martialled, half-Maori New Zealander whose Strike Force broke up and finally destroyed the bugger fleet in the action around Saturn.

If Mazer Rackham could save the world, then it didn't matter a bit whether you were a Jew or not, people said.

But it did matter, and Rose the Nose knew it. He mocked himself to forestall the mocking comments of anti-semites—almost everyone he defeated in battle became, at least for a time, a Jew-hater —but he also made sure everyone knew what he was. His army was in second place, bucking for first.

"I took you on, goy, because I didn't want people to think I only win because I got great soldiers. I want them to know that even with a little puke of a soldier like you I can still win. We only got three rules here. Do what I tell you and don't piss in the bed."

Ender nodded. He knew that Rose wanted him to ask what the third rule was. So he did.

"That *was* three rules. We don't do too good in math, here." The message was clear. Winning is more important than anything.

"Your practice sessions with half-assed little Launchies are over, Wiggin. Done. You're in a big boys' army now. I'm putting you in Dink Meeker's toon. From now on, as far as you're concerned, Dink Meeker is God."

"Then who are you?"

"The personnel officer who hired God." Rose grinned. "And you are forbidden to use your desk again until you've frozen two enemy soldiers in the same battle. This order is out of self-defense. I hear you're a genius programmer. I don't want you screwing around with my desk."

Everybody erupted in laughter. It took Ender a moment to understand why. Rose had programmed his desk to display and animate a bigger-than-lifesized picture of male genitals, which waggled back and forth as Rose held the desk on his naked lap. This is just the sort of commander Bonzo would trade me to, thought Ender. How does a boy who spends his time like this win battles?

Ender found Dink Meeker in the game room, not playing, just sitting and watching. "A guy pointed you out," Ender said. "I'm Ender Wiggin."

"I know," said Meeker.

"I'm in your toon."

"I know," he said again.

"I'm pretty inexperienced."

Dink looked up at him. "Look, Wiggin, I know all this. Why do you think I asked Rose to get you for me?"

He had not been dumped, he had been picked up, he had been asked for. Meeker wanted him. "Why?" asked Ender.

"I've watched your practice sessions with the Launchies. I think you show some promise. Bonzo is stupid and I wanted you to get better training than Petra could give you. All she can do is shoot."

"I needed to learn that."

"You still move like you were afraid to wet your pants."

"So teach me."

"So learn."

"I'm not going to quit my freetime practice sessions."

"I don't want you to quit them."

"Rose the Nose does."

"Rose the Nose can't stop you. Likewise, he can't stop you from using your desk."

"I thought commanders could order anything."

"They can order the moon to turn blue, too, but it doesn't happen. Listen, Ender, commanders have just as much authority as you let them have. The more you obey them, the more power they have over you."

"What's to stop them from hurting me?" Ender remembered Bonzo's blow.

"I thought that was why you were taking personal attack classes."

"You've really been watching me, haven't you?"

Dink didn't answer.

"I don't want to get Rose mad at me. I want to be part of the battles now, I'm tired of sitting out till the end."

"Your standings will go down."

This time Ender didn't answer.

"Listen, Ender, as long as you're part of my toon, you're part of the battle."

Ender soon learned why. Dink trained his toon independently from the rest of Rat Army, with discipline and vigor; he never consulted with Rose, and only rarely did the whole army maneuver together. It was as if Rose commanded one army, and Dink commanded a much smaller one that happened to practice in the battleroom at the same time.

Dink started out the first practice by asking Ender to demonstrate his feet-first attack position. The other boys didn't like it. "How can we attack lying on our backs?" they asked.

To Ender's surprise, Dink didn't correct them, didn't say, "You aren't attacking on your back, you're dropping downward toward them." He had seen what Ender was doing, but he had not understood the orientation that it implied. It soon became clear to Ender that even though Dink was very, very good, his persistence in holding onto the corridor gravity orientation instead of thinking of the enemy gate as downward was limiting his thinking.

They practiced attacking an enemy-held star. Before trying Ender's feet-first method, they had always gone in standing up, their whole bodies available as a target. Even now, though, they reached the star and then assaulted the enemy from one direction only; "Over the top," cried Dink, and over they went. To his credit, he then repeated the exercise, calling, "Again, upside down," but because of their insistence on a gravity that didn't exist, the boys became awkward when the maneuver was under, as if vertigo seized them.

They hated the feet-first attack. Dink insisted that they use it. As a result, they hated Ender. "Do we have to learn how to fight from a Launchy?" one of them muttered, making sure Ender could hear. "Yes," answered Dink. They kept working.

And they learned it. In practice skirmishes, they began to realize how much harder it was to shoot an enemy attacking feet first. As soon as they were convinced of that, they practiced the maneuver more willingly.

That night was the first time Ender had come to a practice session after a whole afternoon of work. He was tired.

"Now you're in a real army," said Alai, "you don't have to keep practicing with us."

"From you I can learn things that nobody knows," said Ender.

"Dink Meeker is the best. I hear he's your toon leader."

"Then let's get busy. I'll teach you what I learned from him today."

He put Alai and two dozen others through the same exercises that had worn him out all afternoon. But he put new touches on the patterns, made the boys try the maneuvers with one leg frozen, with both legs frozen, or using frozen boys for leverage to change directions.

Halfway through the practice, Ender noticed Petra and Dink together, standing in the doorway, watching. Later, when he looked again, they were gone.

So they're watching me, and what we're doing is known. He did not know whether Dink was his friend; he believed that Petra was, but nothing could be sure. They might be angry that he was doing what only commanders and toon leaders were supposed to do— drilling and training soldiers. They might be offended that a soldier would associate so closely with Launchies. It made him uneasy, to have older children watching.

"I thought I told you not to use your desk." Rose the Nose stood by Ender's bunk.

Ender did not look up. "I'm completing the trigonometry assignment for tomorrow."

Rose bumped his knee into Ender's desk. "I said not to use it."

Ender set the desk on his bunk and stood up. "I need trigonometry more than I need you."

Rose was taller than Ender by at least forty centimeters. But Ender was not particularly worried. It would not come to physical violence, and if it did, Ender thought he could hold his own. Rose was lazy and didn't know personal combat.

"You're going down in the standings, boy," said Rose.

"I expect to. I was only leading the list because of the stupid way Salamander Army was using me."

"Stupid? Bonzo's strategy won a couple of key games."

"Bonzo's strategy wouldn't win a salad fight. I was violating orders every time I fired my gun."

Rose hadn't known that. It made him angry. "So everything Bonzo said about you was a lie. You're not only short and incompetent, you're insubordinate, too."

"But I turned defeat into stalemate, all by myself."

"We'll see how you do all by yourself next time." Rose went away.

One of Ender's toonmates shook his head. "You dumb as a thumb."

Ender looked at Dink, who was doodling on his desk. Dink looked up, noticed Ender watching him, and gazed steadily back at him. No expression. Nothing. OK, thought Ender, I can take care of myself.

Battle came two days later. It was Ender's first time fighting as part of a toon; he was nervous. Dink's toon lined up against the right-hand wall of the corridor and Ender was very careful not to lean, not to let his weight slip to either side. Stay balanced.

"Wiggin!" called Rose the Nose.

Ender felt dread come over him from throat to groin, a tingle of fear that made him shudder. Rose saw it.

"Shivering? Trembling? Don't wet your pants, little Launchy." Rose hooked a finger over the butt of Ender's gun and pulled him to the forcefield that hid the battleroom from view. "We'll see how well you do *now,* Ender. As soon as that door opens, you jump through, go straight ahead toward the enemy's door."

Suicide. Pointless, meaningless self-destruction. But he had to follow orders now, this was battle, not school. For a moment Ender raged silently; then he calmed himself. "Excellent, sir," he said. "The direction I fire my gun is the direction of their main contingent."

Rose laughed. "You won't have time to fire anything, pinprick."

The wall vanished. Ender jumped up, took hold of the ceiling handholds, and threw himself out and down, speeding toward the enemy door.

It was Centipede Army, and they only began to emerge from their door when Ender was halfway across the battleroom. Many of them were able to get under cover of stars quickly, but Ender had doubled up his legs under him and, holding his pistol at his crotch, he was firing between his legs and freezing many of them as they emerged.

They flashed his legs, but he had three precious seconds before they could hit his body and put him out of action. He froze several more, then flung out his arms in equal and opposite directions. The hand that held his gun ended up pointing toward the main body of Centipede Army. He fired into the mass of the enemy, and then they froze him.

A second later he smashed into the forcefield of the enemy's door and rebounded with a crazy spin. He landed in a group of enemy soldiers behind a star; they shoved him off and spun him even more rapidly. He rebounded out of control through the rest of the battle, though gradually friction with the air slowed him down. He had no way of knowing how many men he had frozen before getting iced himself, but he did get the general idea that Rat Army won again, as usual.

After the battle Rose didn't speak to him. Ender was still first in the standings, since he had frozen three, disabled two, and damaged seven. There was no more talk about insubordination and whether Ender could use his desk. Rose stayed in his part of the barracks, and left Ender alone.

Dink Meeker began to practice instant emergence from the corridor—Ender's attack on the enemy while they were still coming out of the door had been devastating. "If one man can do that much damage, think what a toon can do." Dink got Major Anderson to open a door in the middle of a wall, even during practice sessions, instead of just the floor-level door, so they could practice launching under battle conditions. Word got around. From now on no one could take five or ten or fifteen seconds in the corridor to size things up. The game had changed.

More battles. This time Ender played a proper role within a toon. He made mistakes. Skirmishes were lost. He dropped from first to second in the standings, then to fourth. Then he made fewer mistakes, and began to feel comfortable within the framework of the toon, and he went back up to third, then second, then first.

After practice one afternoon, Ender stayed in the battleroom. He had noticed that Dink Meeker usually came late to dinner, and he assumed it was for extra practice. Ender wasn't very hungry, and he wanted to see what it was Dink practiced when no one else could see.

But Dink didn't practice. He stood near the door, watching Ender.

Ender stood across the room, watching Dink.

Neither spoke. It was plain Dink expected Ender to leave. It was just as plain that Ender was saying no.

Dink turned his back on Ender, methodically took off his flash suit, and gently pushed off from the floor. He drifted slowly toward the center of the room, very slowly, his body relaxing almost completely, so that his hands and arms seemed to be caught by almost nonexistent air currents in the room.

After the speed and tension of practice, the exhaustion, the alertness, it was restful just to watch him drift. He did it for ten minutes or so before he reached another wall. Then he pushed off rather sharply, returned to his flash suit, and pulled it on.

"Come on," he said to Ender.

They went to the barracks. The room was empty, since all the boys were at dinner. Each went to his own bunk and changed into regular uniforms. Ender walked to Dink's bunk and waited for a moment till Dink was ready to go.

"Why did you wait?" asked Dink.

"Wasn't hungry."

"Well, now you know why I'm not a commander."

Ender had wondered.

"Actually, they promoted me twice, and I refused."

Refused?

"They took away my old locker and bunk and desk, assigned me to a commander's cabin, and gave me an army. But I just stayed in the cabin until they gave in and put me back into somebody else's army."

"Why?"

"Because I won't let them do it to me. I can't believe you haven't seen through all this crap yet, Ender. But I guess you're young. These other armies, they aren't the enemy. It's the teachers, they're the enemy. They get us to fight each other, to hate each other. The game is everything. Win win win. It amounts to nothing. We kill ourselves, go crazy trying to beat each other, and all the time the old bastards are watching us, studying us, discovering our weak points, deciding whether we're *good enough* or not. Well, good enough for what? I was six years old when they brought me here. What the hell did I know? *They* decided I was right for the program, but nobody ever asked me if the program was right for me."

"So why don't you go home?"

Dink smiled crookedly. "Because I can't give up the game." He tugged at the fabric of his flash suit, which lay on the bunk beside him. "Because I love this."

"So why not be a commander?"

Dink shook his head. "Never. Look what it does to Rosen. The boy's crazy. Rose de Nose. Sleeps in here with us instead of in his cabin. Why? Because he's scared to be alone, Ender. Scared of the dark."

"Rose?"

"But they made him a commander and so he has to act like one. He doesn't know what he's doing. He's winning, but that scares him worst of all, because he doesn't know *why* he's winning, except that I have something to do with it. Any minute somebody could find out that Rosen isn't some magic Israeli general who can win no matter what. He doesn't know why anybody wins or loses. Nobody does."

"It doesn't mean he's crazy, Dink."

"I know, you've been here a year, you think these people are normal. Well, they're not. *We're* not. I look in the library, I call up books on my desk. Old ones, because they won't let us have anything new, but I've got a pretty good idea what children are, and we're not children. Children can lose sometimes, and nobody cares. Children aren't in armies, they aren't *commanders,* they don't rule over forty other kids, it's more than anybody can take and not get a little crazy."

Ender tried to remember what other children were like, in his class at school, back in the city. But all he could think of was Stilson.

"I had a brother. Just a normal guy. All he cared about was girls. And flying. He wanted to fly. He used to play ball with the guys. A pickup game, shooting balls at a hoop, dribbling down the corridors until the peace officers confiscated your ball. We had a great time. He was teaching me how to dribble when I was taken."

Ender remembered his own brother, and the memory was not fond.

Dink misunderstood the expression on Ender's face. "Hey, I know, nobody's supposed to talk about home. But we came from *somewhere.* The Battle School didn't create us, you know. The Battle School doesn't create *anything.* It just destroys. And we all remember things from home. Maybe not good things, but we remember and then we lie and pretend that—look, Ender, why is it that *nobody* talks about home, *ever?* Doesn't that tell you how important it is? That nobody even admits that—oh hell."

"No, it's all right," Ender said. "I was just thinking about Valentine. My sister."

"I wasn't trying to make you upset."

"It's OK. I don't think of her very much, because I always get —like this."

"That's right, we never cry. Christ, I never thought of that. Nobody ever cries. We really are trying to be adults. Just like our fathers. I bet your father was like you. I bet he was quiet and took it, and then busted out and—"

"I'm not like my father."

"So maybe I'm wrong. But look at Bonzo, your old commander. He's got an advanced case of Spanish honor. He can't allow himself to have weaknesses. To be better than him, that's an insult. To be stronger, that's like cutting off his balls. That's why he hates you, because you didn't suffer when he tried to punish you. He hates you for that, he honestly wants to kill you. He's crazy. They're all crazy."

"And you aren't?"

"I be crazy too, little buddy, but at least when I be craziest, I be floating all alone in space and the crazy, she float out of me, she soak into the walls, and she don't come out till there be battles and little boys bump into the walls and squish out de crazy."

Ender smiled.

"And you be crazy too," said Dink. "Come on, let's go eat."

"Maybe you can be a commander and not be crazy. Maybe knowing about the craziness means you don't have to fall for it."

"I'm not going to let the bastards run me, Ender. They've got you pegged, too, and they don't plan to treat you kindly. Look what they've done to you so far."

"They haven't done anything except promote me."

"And she make you life so easy, neh?"

Ender laughed and shook his head. "So maybe you're right."

"They think they got you on ice. Don't let them."

"But that's what I came for," Ender said. "For them to make me into a tool. To save the world."

"I can't believe you still believe it."

"Believe what?"

"The bugger menace. Save the world. Listen, Ender, if the buggers were coming back to get us, they'd *be here*. They aren't invading again. We beat them and they're gone."

"But the videos—"

"All from the First and Second Invasions. Your grandparents weren't born yet when Mazer Rackham wiped them out. You watch. It's all a fake. There *is* no war, and they're just screwing around with us."

"But why?"

"Because as long as people are afraid of the buggers, the I.F. can stay in power, and as long as the I.F. is in power, certain countries can keep their hegemony. But keep watching the vids, Ender. People will catch onto this game pretty soon, and there'll be a civil war to end all wars. *That's* the menace, Ender, not the buggers. And in *that* war, when it comes, you and I won't be friends. Because you're American, just like our dear teachers. And *I* am not."

They went to the mess hall and ate, talking about other things. But Ender could not stop thinking about what Dink had said. The Battle School was so enclosed, the game so important in the minds of the children, that Ender had forgotten there was a world outside.

Spanish honor. Civil war. Politics. The Battle School was really a very small place, wasn't it?

But Ender did not reach Dink's conclusions. The buggers were real. The threat was real. The I.F. controlled a lot of things, but it didn't control the videos and the nets. Not where Ender had grown up. In Dink's home in the Netherlands, with three generations under Russian hegemony, perhaps it was all controlled, but Ender knew that lies could not last long in America. So he believed.

Believed, but the seed of doubt was there, and it stayed, and every now and then sent out a little root. It changed everything, to have that seed growing. It made Ender listen more carefully to what people meant, instead of what they said. It made him wise.

There weren't as many boys at the evening practice, not by half.

"Where's Bernard?" asked Ender.

Alai grinned. Shen closed his eyes and assumed a look of blissful meditation.

"Haven't you heard?" said another boy, a Launchy from a younger group. "Word's out that any Launchy who comes to your practice sessions won't ever amount to anything in anybody's army. Word's out that the commanders don't want any soldiers who've been damaged by your training."

Ender nodded.

"But the way I brain it," said the Launchy, "I be the best soldier I can, and any commander worth a damn, he take me. Neh?"

"Eh," said Ender, with finality.

They went on with practice. About a half hour into it, when they were practicing throwing off collisions with frozen soldiers, several commanders in different uniforms came in. They ostentatiously took down names.

"Hey," shouted Alai. "Make sure you spell my name right!"

The next night there were even fewer boys. Now Ender was hearing the stories—little Launchies getting slapped around in the bathrooms, or having accidents in the mess hall and the game room, or getting their files trashed by older boys who had broken the primitive security system that guarded the Launchies' desks.

"No practice tonight," Ender said.

"The hell there's not," said Alai.

"Give it a few days. I don't want any of the little kids getting hurt."

"If you stop, even one night, they'll figure it works to do this kind of thing. Just like if you'd ever backed down to Bernard back when he was being a swine."

"Besides," said Shen, "we aren't scared and we don't care, so you owe it to us to go on. We need the practice and so do you."

Ender remembered what Dink had said. The game was trivial, compared to the whole world. Why should anybody give every night of his life to this stupid, stupid game?

"We don't accomplish that much anyway," Ender said. He started to leave.

Alai stopped him. "They scare you, too? They slap you up in the bathroom? Stick you head in the pissah? Somebody gots a gun up you bung?"

"No," Ender said.

"You still my friend?" asked Alai, more quietly.

"Yes."

"Then I still you friend, Ender, and I stay here and practice with you."

The older boys came again, but fewer of them were commanders. Most were members of a couple of armies. Ender recognized Salamander uniforms. Even a couple of Rats. They didn't take names this time. Instead, they mocked and shouted and ridiculed as the Launchies tried to master difficult skills with untrained muscles. It began to get to a few of the boys.

"Listen to them," Ender said to the other boys. "Remember the words. If you ever want to make your enemy crazy, shout that kind of stuff at them. It makes them do dumb things, to be mad. But *we* don't get mad."

Shen took the idea to heart, and after each jibe from the older boys, he had a group of four Launchies recite the words, loudly, five or six times. When they started singing the taunts like nursery rhymes, some of the older boys launched themselves from the wall and came out for a fight.

The flash suits were designed for wars fought with harmless light; they offered little protection and seriously hampered movement if it came to hand-to-hand fighting in nullo. Half the boys were flashed, anyway, and couldn't fight; but the stiffness of their suits made them potentially useful. Ender quickly ordered his Launchies to gather in one corner of the room. The older boys laughed at them even more, and some who had waited by the wall came forward to join in the attack, seeing Ender's group in retreat.

Ender and Alai decided to throw a frozen soldier in the face of an enemy. The frozen Launchy struck helmet first, and the two caromed off each other. The older boy clutched his chest where the helmet had hit him, and screamed in pain.

The mockery was over. The rest of the older boys launched themselves to enter the battle. Ender didn't really have much hope of any of the boys getting away without some injury. But the enemy was coming haphazardly, uncoordinatedly; they had never worked together before, while Ender's little practice army, though there were only a dozen of them now, knew each other well and knew how to work together.

"Go nova!" shouted Ender. The other boys laughed. They gathered into three groups, feet together, squatting, holding hands so they formed small stars against the back wall. "We'll go around them and make for the door. Now!"

At his signal, the three stars burst apart, each boy launching in a different direction, but angled so he could rebound off a wall and head for the door. Since all of the enemy were in the middle of the room, where course changes were far more difficult, it was an easy maneuver to carry out.

Ender had positioned himself so that when he launched, he would rendezvous with the frozen soldier he had just used as a missile. The boy wasn't frozen now, and he let Ender catch him, whirl him around and send him toward the door. Unfortunately, the necessary result of the action was for Ender to head in the opposite direction, and at a reduced speed. Alone of all his soldiers, he was drifting fairly slowly, and at the end of the battleroom where the older boys were gathered. He shifted himself so he could see that all his soldiers were safely gathered at the far wall.

In the meantime, the furious and disorganized enemy had just spotted him. Ender calculated how soon he would reach the wall so he could launch again. Not soon enough. Several enemies had already rebounded toward him. Ender was startled to see Stilson's face among them. Then he shuddered and realized he had been wrong. Still, it was the same situation, and this time they wouldn't sit still for a single combat settlement. There was no leader, as far as Ender knew, and these boys were a lot bigger than him.

Still, he had learned some things about weight-shifting in personal combat class, and about the physics of moving objects. Game battles almost never got to hand-to-hand combat—you never bumped into an enemy that wasn't frozen. So in the few seconds he had, Ender tried to position himself to receive his guests.

Fortunately, they knew as little about nullo fighting as he did, and the few who tried to punch him found that throwing a punch was pretty ineffective when their bodies moved backward just as quickly as their fists moved forward. But there were some in the group who had bone-breaking on their minds, as Ender quickly saw. He didn't plan to be there for it, though.

He caught one of the punchers by the arm and threw him as hard as he could. It hurled Ender out of the way of the rest of the first onslaught, though he still wasn't getting any closer to the door. "Stay there!" he shouted at his friends, who obviously were forming up to come and rescue him. "Just stay there!"

Someone caught Ender by the foot. The tight grip gave Ender some leverage; he was able to stamp firmly on the other boy's ear and shoulder, making him cry out and let go. If the boy had let go just as Ender kicked downward, it would have hurt him much less and allowed Ender to use the maneuver as a launch. Instead, the boy had hung on too well; his ear was torn and scattering blood in the air, and Ender was drifting even more slowly.

I'm doing it again, thought Ender. I'm hurting people again, just to save myself. Why don't they leave me alone, so I don't have to hurt them?

Three more boys were converging on him now, and this time they were acting together. Still, they had to grab him before they could hurt him. Ender positioned himself quickly so that two of them would take his feet, leaving his hands free to deal with the third.

Sure enough, they took the bait. Ender grasped the shoulders of the third boy's shirt and pulled him up sharply, butting him in the face with his helmet. Again a scream and a shower of blood. The two boys who had his legs were wrenching at them, twisting him. Ender threw the boy with the bleeding nose at one of them; they entangled, and Ender's leg came free. It was a simple matter then to use the other boy's hold for leverage to kick him firmly in the groin, then shove off him in the direction of the door. He didn't get that good a launch, so that his speed was nothing special, but it didn't matter. No one was following him.

He got to his friends at the door. They caught him and handed him along to the door. They were laughing and slapping him playfully. "You bad!" they said. "You scary! You flame!"

"Practice is over for the day," Ender said.

"They'll be back tomorrow," said Shen.

"Won't do them any good," said Ender. "If they come without suits, we'll do this again. If they come *with* suits, we can flash them."

"Besides," said Alai, "the teachers won't let it happen."

Ender remembered what Dink had told him, and wondered if Alai was right.

"Hey Ender!" shouted one of the older boys, as Ender left the battleroom. "You nothing, man! You be nothing!"

"My old commander Bonzo," said Ender. "I think he doesn't like me."

Ender checked the rosters on his desk that night. Four boys turned up on medical report. One with bruised ribs, one with a bruised testicle, one with a torn ear, and one with a broken nose and a loose tooth. The cause of injury was the same in all cases:

ACCIDENTAL COLLISION IN NULL G

If the teachers were allowing that to turn up on the official report, it was obvious they didn't intend to punish anyone for the nasty little skirmish in the battleroom. Aren't they going to do anything? Don't they care what goes on in this school?

Since he was back to the barracks earlier than usual, Ender called up the fantasy game on his desk. It had been a while since he last used it. Long enough that it didn't start him where he had left off. Instead, he began by the Giant's corpse. Only now, it was hardly identifiable as a corpse at all, unless you stood off a ways and studied it. The body had eroded into a hill, entwined with grass and vines. Only the crest of the Giant's face was still visible, and it was white bone, like limestone protruding from a discouraged, withering mountain.

Ender did not look forward to fighting with the wolf-children again, but to his surprise they weren't there. Perhaps, killed once, they were gone forever. It made him a little sad.

He made his way down underground, through the tunnels, to the cliff ledge overlooking the beautiful forest. Again he threw himself down, and again a cloud caught him and carried him into the castle turret room.

The snake began to unweave itself from the rug again, only this time Ender did not hesitate. He stepped on the head of the snake and crushed it under his foot. It writhed and twisted under him, and in response he twisted and ground it deeper into the stone floor. Finally it was still. Ender picked it up and shook it, until it unwove itself and the pattern in the rug was gone. Then, still dragging the snake behind him, he began to look for a way out.

Instead, he found a mirror. And in the mirror he saw a face that he easily recognized. It was Peter, with blood dripping down his chin and a snake's tail protruding from a corner of his mouth.

Ender shouted and thrust his desk from him. The few boys in the barracks were alarmed at the noise, but he apologized and told them it was nothing. They went away. He looked again into his desk. His figure was still there, staring into the mirror. He tried to pick up some of the furniture, to break the mirror, but it could not be moved. The mirror would not come off the wall, either. Finally Ender threw the snake at it. The mirror shattered, leaving a hole in the wall behind it. Out of the hole came dozens of tiny snakes, which quickly bit Ender's figure again and again. Tearing the snakes frantically from itself, the figure collapsed and died in a writhing heap of small serpents.

The screen went blank, and words appeared.

PLAY AGAIN?

Ender signed off and put the desk away.

The next day, several commanders came to Ender or sent soldiers to tell him not to worry, most of them thought the extra practice sessions were a good idea, he should keep it up. And to make sure nobody bothered him, they were sending a few of their older soldiers who needed extra practice to come join him. "They're as big as most of the buggers who attacked you last night. They'll think twice."

Instead of a dozen boys, there were forty-five that night, more than an army, and whether it was because of the presence of older boys on Ender's side or because they had had enough the night before, none of their enemies came.

Ender didn't go back to the fantasy game. But it lived in his dreams. He kept remembering how it felt to kill the snake, grinding it in, the way he tore the ear off that boy, the way he destroyed Stilson, the way he broke Bernard's arm. And then to stand up, holding the corpse of his enemy, and find Peter's face looking out at him from the mirror. This game knows too much about me. This game tells filthy lies. I am not Peter. I don't have murder in my heart.

And then the worse fear, that he *was* a killer, only better at it than Peter ever was; that it was this very trait that pleased the teachers. It's killers they need for the bugger wars. It's people who can grind the enemy's face into the dust and spatter their blood all over space.

Well, I'm your man. I'm the bloody bastard you wanted when you had me spawned. I'm your tool, and what difference does it make if I hate the part of me that you most need? What difference does it make that when the little serpents killed me in the game, I agreed with them, and was glad.

Chapter 9

Locke and Demosthenes

"I didn't call you in here to waste time. How in hell did the computer do that?"

"I don't know."

"How could it pick up a picture of Ender's brother and put it into the graphics in this Fairyland routine?"

"Colonel Graff, I wasn't there when it was programmed. All I know is that the computer's never taken anyone to this place before. Fairyland was strange enough, but this isn't Fairyland anymore. It's beyond the End of the World, and—"

"I know the names of the places, I just don't know what they mean."

"Fairyland was programmed in. It's mentioned in a few other places. But nothing talks about the End of the World. We don't have any experience with it."

"I don't like having the computer screw around with Ender's mind that way. Peter Wiggin is the most potent person in his life, except maybe his sister Valentine."

"And the mind game is designed to help shape them, help them find worlds they can be comfortable in."

"You don't get it, do you, Major Imbu? I don't want Ender being comfortable with the end of the world. Our business here is not to be comfortable with the end of the world!"

"The End of the World in the game isn't necessarily the end

of humanity in the bugger wars. It has a private meaning to Ender."

"Good. What meaning?"

"I don't know, sir. I'm not the kid. Ask him."

"Major Imbu, I'm asking **you**."

"There could be a thousand meanings."

"Try one."

"You've been isolating the boy. Maybe he's wishing for the end of **this** world, the Battle School. Or maybe it's about the end of the world he grew up with as a little boy, his home, coming here. Or maybe it's his way of coping with having broken up so many other kids here. Ender's a sensitive kid, you know, and he's done some pretty bad things to people's bodies, he might be wishing for the end of **that** world."

"Or none of the above."

"The mind game is a relationship between the child and the computer. Together they create stories. The stories are true, in the sense that they reflect the reality of the child's life. That's all I **know**."

"And I'll tell you what I know, Major Imbu. That picture of Peter Wiggin was not one that could have been taken from our files here at the school. We have nothing on him, electronically or otherwise, since Ender came here. And that picture is more recent."

"It's only been a year and a half, sir, how much can the boy change?"

"He's wearing his hair completely differently now. His mouth was redone with orthodontia. I got a recent photograph from landside and compared. The only way the computer here in the Battle School could have got that picture was by requisitioning it from a landside computer. And not even one connected with the I.F. That takes requisitionary powers. We can't just go into Guilford County North Carolina and pluck a picture out of school files. Did anyone at this school authorize getting this?"

"You don't understand, sir. Our Battle School computer is only a part of the I.F. network. If **we** want a picture, **we** have to get a requisition, but if the mind game program determines that the picture is necessary—"

"It can just go take it."

"Not just every day. Only when it's for the child's own good."

"OK, it's for his good. But **why**. His brother is dangerous, his brother was rejected for this program because he's one of the worst human beings we've laid hands on. Why is he so important to Ender? Why, after all this time?"

"Honestly, sir, I don't know. And the mind game program is designed so that it can't tell us. It may not know itself, actually. This is uncharted territory."

"You mean the computer's making this up as it goes along?"

"You might put it that way."

"Well, that does make me feel a little better. I thought I was the only one."

Valentine celebrated Ender's eighth birthday alone, in the wooded back yard of their new home in Greensboro. She scraped a patch of ground bare of pine needles and leaves, and there scratched his name in the dirt with a twig. Then she made a small teepee of twigs and needles and lit a small fire. It made smoke that interwove with the branches and needles of the pine overhead. All the way into space, she said silently. All the way to the Battle School.

No letters had ever come, and as far as they knew their own letters had never reached him. When he first was taken, Father and Mother sat at the table and keyed in long letters to him every few days. Soon, though, it was once a week, and when no answers came, once a month. Now it had been two years since he went, and there were no letters, none at all, and no remembrance on his birthday. He is dead, she thought bitterly, because we have forgotten him.

But Valentine had not forgotten him. She did not let her parents know, and above all never hinted to Peter how often she thought about Ender, how often she wrote him letters that she knew he would not answer. And when Mother and Father announced to them that they were leaving the city to move to North Carolina, of all places, Valentine knew that they never expected to see Ender again. They were leaving the only place where he knew to find them. How would Ender find them here, among these trees, under this changeable and heavy sky? He had lived deep in corridors all his life, and if he was still in the Battle School, there was less of nature there. What would he make of this?

Valentine knew why they had moved here. It was for Peter, so that living among trees and small animals, so that nature in as raw a form as Mother and Father could conceive of it, might have a softening influence on their strange and frightening son. And, in a way, it had. Peter took to it right away. Long walks out in the open, cutting through woods and out into the open country—going sometimes for a whole day, with only a sandwich or two sharing space with his desk in the pack on his back, with only a small pocket knife in his pocket.

But Valentine knew. She had seen a squirrel half-skinned, spiked by its little hands and feet with twigs pushed into the dirt. She pictured Peter trapping it, staking it, then carefully parting and peeling back the skin without breaking into the abdomen, watching the muscles twist and ripple. How long had it taken the squirrel to die? And all the while Peter had sat nearby, leaning against the tree where perhaps the squirrel had nested, playing with his desk while the squirrel's life seeped away.

At first she was horrified, and nearly threw up at dinner, watching how Peter ate so vigorously, talked so cheerfully. But later she thought about it and realized that perhaps, for Peter, it was a kind of magic, like her little fires; a sacrifice that somehow stilled the dark gods that hunted for his soul. Better to torture squirrels than other children. Peter has always been a husbandman of pain, planting it, nurturing it, devouring it greedily when it was ripe; better he should take it in these small, sharp doses than with dull cruelty to children in the school.

"A model student," said his teachers. "I wish we had a hundred others in the school just like him. Studies all the time, turns in all his work on time. He loves to learn."

But Valentine knew it was a fraud. Peter loved to learn, all right, but the teachers hadn't taught him anything, ever. He did his learning through his desk at home, tapping into libraries and databases, studying and thinking and, above all, talking to Valentine. Yet at school he acted as though he were excited about the puerile lesson of the day. Oh, wow, I never knew that frogs looked like *this* inside, he'd say, and then at home he studied the binding of cells into organisms through the philotic collation of DNA. Peter was a master of flattery, and all his teachers bought it.

Still, it was good. Peter never fought anymore. Never bullied. Got along well with everybody. It was a new Peter.

Everyone believed it. Father and Mother said it, so often it made Valentine want to scream at them. It isn't the new Peter! It's the old Peter, only smarter!

How smart? Smarter than *you,* Father. Smarter than *you,* Mother. Smarter than anybody you have ever met.

But not smarter than me.

"I've been deciding," said Peter, "whether to kill you or what."

Valentine leaned against the trunk of the pine tree, her little fire a few smoldering ashes. "I love you, too, Peter."

"It would be so easy. You always make these stupid little fires. It's just a matter of knocking you out and burning you up. You're such a firebug."

"I've been thinking of castrating you in your sleep."

"No you haven't. You only think of things like that when I'm with you. I bring out the best in you. No, Valentine, I've decided not to kill you. I've decided that you're going to help me."

"I am?" A few years ago, Valentine would have been terrified at Peter's threats. Now, though, she was not so afraid. Not that she doubted that he was capable of killing her. She couldn't think of anything so terrible that she didn't believe Peter might do it. She also knew, though, that Peter was not insane, not in the sense that he wasn't in control of himself. He was in better control of himself than anyone she knew. Except perhaps herself. Peter could delay any desire as long as he needed to; he could conceal any emotion. And so Valentine knew that he would never hurt her in a fit of rage. He would only do it if the advantages outweighed the risks. And they did not. In a way, she actually preferred Peter to other people because of this. He always, always acted out of intelligent self-interest. And so, to keep herself safe, all she had to do was make sure it was more in Peter's interest to keep her alive than to have her dead.

"Valentine, things are coming to a head. I've been tracking troop movements in Russia."

"What are we talking about?"

"The world, Val. You know Russia? Big empire? Warsaw Pact? Rulers of Eurasia from the Netherlands to Pakistan?"

"They don't publish their troop movements, Peter."

"Of course not. But they do publish their passenger and freight train schedules. I've had my desk analyzing those schedules and figuring out when the secret troop trains are moving over the same tracks. Done it backward over the past three years. In the last six months, they've stepped up, they're getting ready for war. Land war."

"But what about the League? What about the buggers?" Valentine didn't know what Peter was getting at, but he often launched discussions like this, practical discussions of world events. He used her to test his ideas, to refine them. In the process, she also refined her own thinking. She found that while she rarely agreed with Peter about what the world *ought* to be, they rarely disagreed about what the world actually *was*. They had become quite deft at sifting accurate information out of the stories of the hopelessly ignorant, gullible news writers. The news herd, as Peter called them.

"The Polemarch is Russian, isn't he? And he knows what's happening with the fleet. Either they've found out the buggers aren't a threat after all, or we're about to have a big battle. One way or another, the bugger war is about to be over. They're getting ready for after the war."

"If they're moving troops, it must be under the direction of the Strategos."

"It's all internal, within the Warsaw Pact."

This was disturbing. The facade of peace and cooperation had been undisturbed almost since the bugger wars began. What Peter had detected was a fundamental disturbance in the world order. She had a mental picture, as clear as memory, of the way the world had been before the buggers forced peace upon them. "So it's back to the way it was before."

"A few changes. The shields make it so nobody bothers with nuclear weapons anymore. We have to kill each other thousands at a time instead of millions." Peter grinned. "Val, it was bound to happen. Right now there's a vast international fleet and army in existence, with American hegemony. When the bugger wars are over, all that power will vanish, because it's all built on fear of the buggers. And suddenly we'll look around and discover that all the old alliances are gone, dead and gone, except one, the Warsaw Pact. And it'll be the dollar against five million lasers. We'll have the asteroid belt, but they'll have Earth, and you run out of raisins and celery kind of fast out there, without Earth."

What disturbed Valentine most of all was that Peter did not

seem at all worried. "Peter, why do I get the idea that you are thinking of this as a golden opportunity for Peter Wiggin?"

"For both of us, Val."

"Peter, you're twelve years old. I'm ten. They have a word for people our age. They call us children and they treat us like mice."

"But we don't *think* like other children, do we, Val? We don't *talk* like other children. And above all, we don't write like other children."

"For a discussion that began with death threats, Peter, we've strayed from the topic, I think." Still, Valentine found herself getting excited. Writing was something Val did better than Peter. They both knew it. Peter had even named it once, when he said that he could always see what other people hated most about themselves, and bully them, while Val could always see what other people liked best about themselves, and flatter them. It was a cynical way of putting it, but it was true. Valentine could persuade other people to her point of view —she could convince them that they wanted what she wanted them to want. Peter, on the other hand, could only make them fear what he wanted them to fear. When he first pointed this out to Val, she resented it. She had wanted to believe she was good at persuading people because she was right, not because she was clever. But no matter how much she told herself that she didn't ever want to exploit people the way Peter did, she enjoyed knowing that she could, in her way, control other people. And not just control what they did. She could control, in a way, what they wanted to do. She was ashamed that she took pleasure in this power, and yet she found herself using it sometimes. To get teachers to do what she wanted, and other students. To get Mother and Father to see things her way. Sometimes, she was able to persuade even Peter. That was the most frightening thing of all—that she could understand Peter well enough, could empathize with him enough to get inside him that way. There was more Peter in her than she could bear to admit, though sometimes she dared to think about it anyway. This is what she thought as Peter spoke: You dream of power, Peter, but in my own way I am more powerful than you.

"I've been studying history," Peter said. "I've been learning things about patterns in human behavior. There are times when the world is rearranging itself, and at times like that, the right words can change the world. Think what Pericles did in Athens, and Demos-thenes—"

"Yes, they managed to wreck Athens twice."

"Pericles, yes, but Demosthenes was right about Philip—"

"Or provoked him—"

"See? This is what historians usually do, quibble about cause and effect when the point is, there are times when the world is in flux and the right voice in the right place can move the world. Thomas Paine and Ben Franklin, for instance. Bismarck. Lenin."

"Not exactly parallel cases, Peter." Now she was disagreeing with him out of habit; she saw what he was getting at, and she thought it might just be possible.

"I didn't expect *you* to understand. *You* still believe that teachers know something worth learning."

I understand more than you think, Peter. "So you see yourself as Bismarck?"

"I see myself as knowing how to insert ideas into the public mind. Haven't you ever thought of a phrase, Val, a clever thing to say, and said it, and then two weeks or a month later you hear some adult saying it to another adult, both of them strangers? Or you see it on a video or pick it up on a net?"

"I always figured I heard it before and only thought I was making it up."

"You were wrong. There are maybe two or three thousand people in the world as smart as us, little sister. Most of them are making a living somewhere. Teaching, the poor bastards, or doing research. Precious few of them are actually in positions of power."

"I guess we're the lucky few."

"Funny as a one-legged rabbit, Val."

"Of which there are no doubt several in these woods."

"Hopping in neat little circles."

Valentine laughed at the gruesome image and hated herself for thinking it was funny.

"Val, we can say the words that everyone else will be saying two weeks later. We can do that. We don't have to wait until we're grown up and safely put away in some career."

"Peter, you're *twelve.*"

"Not on the nets I'm not. On the nets I can name myself anything I want, and so can you."

"On the nets we are clearly identified as students, and we can't even get into the real discussions except in audience mode, which means we can't *say* anything anyway."

"I have a plan."

"You always do." She pretended nonchalance, but she listened eagerly.

"We can get on the nets as full-fledged adults, with whatever net names we want to adopt, *if* Father gets us onto his citizen's access."

"And why would he do that? We already have student access. What do you tell him, I need citizen's access so I can take over the world?"

"No, Val. *I* won't tell him anything. *You'll* tell him how you're worried about me. How I'm trying so very hard to do well at school, but you know it's driving me crazy because I can never talk to anybody intelligent, everybody always talks down to me because I'm young, I never get to converse with my *peers*. You can prove that the stress is getting to me."

Valentine thought of the corpse of the squirrel in the woods and realized that even that discovery was part of Peter's plan. Or at least he had *made* it part of his plan, after it happened.

"So you get him to authorize us to share his citizen's access. To adopt our own identities there, to conceal who we are so people will give us the intellectual respect we deserve."

Valentine could challenge him on ideas, but never on things like this. She could not say, What makes you think you deserve respect? She had read about Adolf Hitler. She wondered what he was like at the age of twelve. Not this smart, not like Peter that way, but craving honor, probably that. And what would it have meant to the world if in childhood he had been caught in a thresher or trampled by a horse?

"Val," Peter said. "I know what you think of me. I'm not a nice person, you think."

Valentine threw a pine needle at him. "An arrow through your heart."

"I've been planning to come talk to you for a long time. But I kept being afraid."

She put a pine needle in her mouth and blew it at him. It dropped almost straight down. "Another failed launch." Why was he pretending to be weak?

"Val, I was afraid you wouldn't believe me. That you wouldn't believe I could do it."

"Peter, I believe you could do anything, and probably will."

"But I was even more afraid that you'd believe me and try to stop me."

"Come on, threaten to kill me again, Peter." Did he actually believe *she* could be fooled by his nice-and-humble-kid act?

"So I've got a sick sense of humor. I'm sorry. You know I was teasing. I need your help."

"You're just what the world needs. A twelve-year-old to solve all our problems."

"It's not my fault I'm twelve right now. And it's not my fault that right now is when the opportunity is open. Right now is the time when I can shape events. The world is always a democracy in times of flux, and the man with the best voice will win. Everybody thinks Hitler got to power because of his armies, because they were willing to kill, and that's partly true, because in the real world power is always built on the threat of death and dishonor. But mostly he got to power on words, on the right words at the right time."

"I was just thinking of comparing you to him."

"I don't hate Jews, Val. I don't want to destroy anybody. And I don't want war, either. I want the world to hold together. Is that so bad? I don't want us to go back to the old way. Have you read about the world wars?"

"Yes."

"We can go back to that again. Or worse. We could find ourselves locked into the Warsaw Pact. Now, there's a cheerful thought."

"Peter, we're children, don't you understand that? We're going to school, we're growing up—" But even as she resisted, she wanted him to persuade her. She had wanted him to persuade her from the beginning.

But Peter didn't know that he had already won. "If I believe that, if I accept that, then I've got to sit back and watch while all the opportunities vanish, and then when I'm old enough it's too late. Val, listen to me. I know how you feel about me, you always have. I was a vicious, nasty brother. I was cruel to you and crueler to Ender before they took him. But I didn't hate you. I loved you both, I just had to be—had to have *control*, do you understand that? It's the most important thing to me, it's my greatest gift, I can see where the weak points are, I can see how to get in and use them, I just *see* those things without even trying. I could become a businessman and run some big corporation, I'd scramble and maneuver until I was at the top of everything and what would I have? Nothing. I'm going to rule, Val, I'm going to have control of something. But I want it to be something worth ruling. I want to accomplish something worthwhile. A Pax Americana through the whole world. So that when somebody else comes, after we beat the buggers, when somebody else comes here to defeat us, they'll find we've already spread over a thousand worlds, we're at peace with ourselves and impossible to destroy. Do you understand? I want to save mankind from self-destruction."

She had never seen him speak with such sincerity. With no hint of mockery, no trace of a lie in his voice. He was getting better at this. Or maybe he was actually touching on the truth. "So a twelve-year-old boy and his kid sister are going to save the world?"

"How old was Alexander? I'm not going to do it overnight. I'm just going to start now. If you'll help me."

"I don't believe what you did to those squirrels was part of an act. I think you did it because you love to do it."

Suddenly Peter wept into his hands. Val assumed that he was pretending, but then she wondered. It was possible, wasn't it, that he loved her, and that in this time of terrifying opportunity he was willing to weaken himself before her in order to win her love. He's manipulating me, she thought, but that doesn't mean he isn't sincere. His cheeks were wet when he took his hands away, his eyes rimmed in red. "I know," he said. "It's what I'm most afraid of. That I really am a monster. I don't want to be a killer but I just can't help it."

She had never seen him show such weakness. You're so clever, Peter. You saved your weakness so you could use it to move me now. And yet it did move her. Because if it were true, even partly true, then Peter was not a monster, and so she could satisfy her Peter-like love of power without fear of becoming monstrous herself. She knew that Peter was calculating even now, but she believed that under the calculations he was telling the truth. It had been hidden layers deep, but he had probed her until he found her trust.

"Val, if you don't help me, I don't know what I'll become. But if you're there, my partner in everything, you can keep me from becoming—like that. Like the bad ones."

She nodded. You are only pretending to share power with me, she thought, but in fact I have power over you, even though you don't know it. "I will. I'll help you."

As soon as Father got them both onto his citizen's access, they began testing the waters. They stayed away from the nets that required use of a real name. That wasn't hard because real names only had to do with money. They didn't need money. They needed respect, and that they could earn. With false names, on the right nets, they could be anybody. Old men, middle-aged women, anybody, as long as they were careful about the way they wrote. All that anyone would see were their words, their ideas. Every citizen started equal, on the nets.

They used throwaway names with their early efforts, not the identities that Peter planned to make famous and influential. Of course they were not invited to take part in the great national and international political forums—they could only be audiences there until they were invited or elected to take part. But they signed on and watched, reading some of the essays published by the great names, witnessing the debates that played across their desks.

And in the lesser conferences, where common people commented about the great debates, they began to insert their comments. At first Peter insisted that they be deliberately inflammatory. "We can't learn how our style of writing is working unless we get responses—and if we're bland, no one will answer."

They were not bland, and people answered. The responses that got posted on the public nets were vinegar; the responses that were sent as mail, for Peter and Valentine to read privately, were poisonous. But they did learn what attributes of their writing were seized upon as childish and immature. And they got better.

When Peter was satisfied that they knew how to sound adult, he killed the old identities and they began to prepare to attract real attention.

"We have to seem completely separate. We'll write about different things at different times. We'll never refer to each other. You'll mostly work on the west coast nets, and I'll mostly work in the south. Regional issues, too. So do your homework."

They did their homework. Mother and Father worried sometimes, with Peter and Valentine constantly together, their desks
tucked under their arms. But they couldn't complain—their grades
were good, and Valentine was such a good influence on Peter. She
had changed his whole attitude toward everything. And Peter and
Valentine sat together in the woods, in good weather, and in pocket
restaurants and indoor parks when it rained, and they composed
their political commentaries. Peter carefully designed both characters so neither one had all of his ideas; there were even some spare
identities that they used to drop in third party opinions. "Let both of
them find a following as they can," said Peter.

Once, tired of writing and rewriting until Peter was satisfied, Val
despaired and said, "Write it yourself, then!"

"I can't," he answered. "They can't both sound alike. Ever. You
forget that someday we'll be famous enough that somebody will start
running analyses. We have to come up as different people every
time."

So she wrote on. Her main identity on the nets was Demosthenes—Peter chose the name. He called himself Locke. They were
obvious pseudonyms, but that was part of the plan. "With any luck,
they'll start trying to guess who we are."

"If we get famous enough, the government can always get access and find out who we really are."

"When that happens, we'll be too entrenched to suffer much
loss. People might be shocked that Demosthenes and Locke are two
kids, but they'll already be used to listening to us."

They began composing debates for their characters. Valentine
would prepare an opening statement, and Peter would invent a
throwaway name to answer her. His answer would be intelligent, and
the debate would be lively, lots of clever invective and good political
rhetoric. Valentine had a knack for alliteration that made her phrases
memorable. Then they would enter the debate into the network,
separated by a reasonable amount of time, as if they were actually
making them up on the spot. Sometimes a few other netters would
interpose comments, but Peter and Val would usually ignore them or
change their own comments only slightly to accommodate what had
been said.

Peter took careful note of all their most memorable phrases and
then did searches from time to time to find those phrases cropping up

in other places. Not all of them did, but most of them were repeated here and there, and some of them even showed up in the major debates on the prestige nets. "We're being read," Peter said. "The ideas are seeping out."

"The phrases, anyway."

"That's just the measure. Look, we're having some influence. Nobody quotes us by name, yet, but they're discussing the points we raise. We're helping set the agenda. We're getting there."

"Should we try to get into the main debates?"

"No. We'll wait until they ask us."

They had been doing it only seven months when one of the west coast nets sent Demosthenes a message. An offer for a weekly column in a pretty good newsnet.

"I can't do a weekly column," Valentine said. "I don't even have a monthly period yet."

"The two aren't related," Peter said.

"They are to me. I'm still a kid."

"Tell them yes, but since you prefer not to have your true identity revealed, you want them to pay you in network time. A new access code through their corporate identity."

"So when the government traces me—"

"You'll just be a person who can sign on through CalNet. Father's citizen's access doesn't get involved. What I can't figure out is why they wanted Demosthenes before Locke."

"Talent rises to the top."

As a game, it was fun. But Valentine didn't like some of the positions Peter made Demosthenes take. Demosthenes began to develop as a fairly paranoid anti-Warsaw writer. It bothered her because Peter was the one who knew how to exploit fear in his writing —she had to keep coming to him for ideas on how to do it. Meanwhile, his Locke followed her moderate, empathic strategies. It made sense, in a way. By having her write Demosthenes, it meant he also had some empathy, just as Locke also could play on others' fears. But the main effect was to keep her inextricably tied to Peter. She couldn't go off and use Demosthenes for her own purposes. She wouldn't know how to use him. Still, it worked both ways. He couldn't write Locke without her. Or could he?

"I thought the idea was to unify the world. If I write this like you say I should, Peter, I'm pretty much calling for war to break up the Warsaw Pact."

"Not war, just open nets and prohibition of interception. Free flow of information. Compliance with the League rules, for heaven's sake."

Without meaning to, Valentine started talking in Demosthenes' voice, even though she certainly wasn't speaking Demosthenes' opinions. "Everyone knows that from the beginning the Warsaw Pact was to be regarded as a single entity where those rules were concerned. International free flow is still open. But between the Warsaw Pact nations these things are internal matters. That was why they were willing to allow American hegemony in the League."

"You're arguing Locke's part, Val. Trust me. You have to call for the Warsaw Pact to lose official status. You have to get a lot of people really angry. Then, later, when you begin to recognize the need for compromise—"

"Then they stop listening to me and go off and fight a war."

"Val, trust me. I know what I'm doing."

"How do you know? You're not any smarter than me, and you've never done this before either."

"I'm thirteen and you're ten."

"Almost eleven."

"And I know how these things work."

"All right, I'll do it your way. But I won't do any of these liberty or death things."

"You will too."

"And someday when they catch us and they wonder why your sister was such a warmonger, I can just bet you'll tell them that you told me to do it."

"Are you *sure* you're not having a period, little woman?"

"I hate you, Peter Wiggin."

What bothered Valentine most was when her column got syndicated into several other regional newsnets, and Father started reading it and quoting from it at table. "Finally, a man with some sense," he said. Then he quoted some of the passages Valentine hated worst in her own work. "It's fine to work with these hegemonist Russians with the buggers out there, but after we win, I can't see leaving half the civilized world as virtual helots, can you, dear?"

"I think you're taking this all too seriously," said Mother.

"I like this Demosthenes. I like the way he thinks. I'm surprised he isn't in the major nets—I looked for him in the international relations debates and you know, he's never taken part in any of them."

Valentine lost her appetite and left the table. Peter followed her after a respectable interval.

"So you don't like lying to Father," he said. "So what? You're *not* lying to him. He doesn't think that you're really Demosthenes, and Demosthenes isn't saying things you really believe. They cancel each other out, they amount to nothing."

"That's the kind of reasoning that makes Locke such an ass." But what really bothered her was not that she was lying to Father—it was the fact that Father actually agreed with Demosthenes. She had thought that only fools would follow him.

A few days later Locke got picked up for a column in a New England newsnet, specifically to provide a contrasting view for their popular column from Demosthenes. "Not bad for two kids who've only got about eight pubic hairs between them," Peter said.

"It's a long way between writing a newsnet column and ruling the world," Valentine reminded him. "It's such a long way that no one has ever done it."

"They have, though. Or the moral equivalent. I'm going to say snide things about Demosthenes in my first column."

"Well, Demosthenes isn't even going to notice that Locke exists. Ever."

"For now."

With their identities now fully supported by their income from writing columns, they used Father's access now only for the throwaway identities. Mother commented that they were spending too much time on the nets. "All work and no play makes Jack a dull boy," she reminded Peter.

Peter let his hand tremble a little, and he said, "If you think I should stop, I think I might be able to keep things under control this time, I really do."

"No, no," Mother said. "I don't want you to *stop*. Just—be careful, that's all."

"I'm careful, Mom."

Nothing was different, nothing had changed in a year. Ender was sure of it, and yet it all seemed to have gone sour. He was still the leading soldier in the standings, and no one doubted that he deserved it now. At the age of nine he was a toon leader in Phoenix Army, with Petra Arkanian as his commander. He still led his evening practice sessions, and now they were attended by an elite group of soldiers nominated by their commanders, though any Launchy who wanted to could still come. Alai was also a toon leader, in another army, and they were still good friends; Shen was not a leader, but that was no barrier. Dink Meeker had finally accepted command and succeeded Rose the Nose in Rat Army's command. All is going well, *very* well, I couldn't ask for anything better—

So why do I hate my life?

He went through the paces of the practices and games. He liked teaching the boys in his toon, and they followed him loyally. He had the respect of everyone, and he was treated with deference in his evening practices. Commanders came to study what he did. Other soldiers approached his table at mess and asked permission to sit down. Even the teachers were respectful.

He had so much damn respect he wanted to scream.

He watched the young kids in his army, fresh out of their launch groups, watched how they played, how they made fun of their leaders when they thought no one was looking. He watched the camaraderie of old friends who had known each other in the Battle School for years, who talked and laughed about old battles and long-graduated soldiers and commanders.

But with *his* old friends there was no laughter, no remembering. Just work. Just intelligence and excitement about the game, but nothing beyond that. Tonight it had come to a head in the evening practice. Ender and Alai were discussing the nuances of open-space maneuvers when Shen came up and listened for a few moments, then suddenly took Alai by the shoulders and shouted, "Nova! Nova! Nova!" Alai burst out laughing, and for a moment or two Ender watched them remember together the battle where open-room maneuvering had been for real, and they had dodged past the older boys and—

Suddenly they remembered that Ender was there. "Sorry, Ender," Shen said.

Sorry. For what? For being friends? "I was there, too, you know," Ender said.

And they apologized again. Back to business. Back to *respect.* And Ender realized that in their laughter, in their friendship, it had not occurred to them that he was included.

How could they think I was part of it? Did I laugh? Did I join in? Just stood there, watching, like a teacher.

That's how they think of me, too. Teacher. Legendary soldier. Not one of *them.* Not someone that you embrace and whisper Salaam in his ear. That only lasted while Ender still seemed a victim. Still seemed vulnerable. Now he was the master soldier, and he was completely, utterly alone.

Feel sorry for yourself, Ender. He typed the words on his desk as he lay on his bunk. POOR ENDER. Then he laughed at himself and cleared away the words. Not a boy or girl in this school who wouldn't be glad to trade places with me.

He called up the fantasy game. He walked as he often did through the village that the dwarves had built in the hill made by the Giant's corpse. It was easy to build sturdy walls, with the ribs already curved just right, just enough space between them to leave windows. The whole corpse was cut into apartments, opening onto the path down the Giant's spine. The public amphitheatre was carved into the pelvic bowl, and the common herd of ponies was pastured between the Giant's legs. Ender was never sure what the dwarves were doing as they went about their business, but they left him alone as he picked his way through the village, and in return he did them no harm either.

He vaulted the pelvic bone at the base of the public square, and walked through the pasture. The ponies shied away from him. He did not pursue them. Ender did not understand how the game functioned anymore. In the old days, before he had first gone to the End of the World, everything was combat and puzzles to solve—defeat the enemy before he kills you, or figure out how to get past the obstacle. Now, though, no one attacked, there was no war, and wherever he went, there was no obstacle at all.

Except, of course, in the room in the castle at the End of the World. It was the one dangerous place left. And Ender, however often he vowed that he would not, always went back there, always killed the snake, always looked his brother in the face, and always, no matter what he did next, died.

It was no different this time. He tried to use the knife on the table to pry through the mortar and pull out a stone from the wall. As soon as he breached the seal of the mortar, water began to gush in through the crack, and Ender watched his desk as his figure, now out of his control, struggled madly to stay alive, to keep from drowning. The windows of his room were gone, the water rose, and his figure drowned. All the while, the face of Peter Wiggin in the mirror stayed and looked at him.

I'm trapped here, Ender thought, trapped at the End of the World with no way out. And he knew at last the sour taste that had come to him, despite all his successes in the Battle School. It was despair.

There were uniformed men at the entrances to the school when Valentine arrived. They weren't standing like guards, but rather slouched around as if they were waiting for someone inside to finish his business. They wore the uniforms of I.F. Marines, the same uniforms that everyone saw in bloody combat on the videos. It lent an air of romance to that day at school; all the other kids were excited about it.

Valentine was not. It made her think of Ender, for one thing. And for another, it made her afraid. Someone had recently published a savage commentary on the Demosthenes' collected writings. The commentary, and therefore her work, had been discussed in the open conference of the international relations net, with some of the most important people of the day attacking and defending Demosthenes. What worried her most was the comment of an Englishman: "Whether he likes it or not, Demosthenes cannot remain incognito forever. He has outraged too many wise men and pleased too many fools to hide behind his too-appropriate pseudonym much longer. Either he will unmask himself in order to assume leadership of the forces of stupidity he has marshalled, or his enemies will unmask him in order to better understand the disease that has produced such a warped and twisted mind."

Peter had been delighted, but then he would be. Valentine was afraid, that enough powerful people had been annoyed by the vicious persona of Demosthenes that she would indeed be tracked down.

The I.F. could do it, even if the American government was constitutionally bound not to. And here were I.F. troops gathered at Western Guilford Middle School, of all places. Not exactly the regular recruiting grounds for the I.F. Marines.

So she was not surprised to find a message marching around her desk as soon as she logged in.

**PLEASE LOG OFF AND GO TO DR.
LINEBERRY'S OFFICE AT ONCE.**

Valentine waited nervously outside the principal's office until Dr. Lineberry opened the door and beckoned her inside. Her last doubt was removed when she saw the soft-bellied man in the uniform of an I.F. colonel sitting in the one comfortable chair in the room.

"You're Valentine Wiggin," he said.

"Yes," she whispered.

"I'm Colonel Graff. We've met before."

Before? When had she had any dealings with the I.F.?

"I've come to talk to you in confidence, about your brother."

It's not just me, then, she thought. They have Peter. Or is this something new? Has he done something crazy? I thought he stopped doing crazy things.

"Valentine, you seem frightened. There's no need to be. Please, sit down. I assure you that your brother is well. He has more than fulfilled our expectations."

And now, with a great inward gush of relief, she realized that it was Ender they had come about. Ender. It wasn't punishment at all, it was little Ender, who had disappeared so long ago, who was no part of Peter's plots now. You were the lucky one, Ender. You got away before Peter could trap you into his conspiracy.

"How do you feel about your brother, Valentine?"

"Ender?"

"Of course."

"How can I feel about him? I haven't seen him or heard from him since I was eight."

"Dr. Lineberry, will you excuse us?"

Lineberry was annoyed.

"On second thought, Dr. Lineberry, I think Valentine and I will have a much more productive conversation if we walk. Outside.

Away from the recording devices that your assistant principal has placed in this room."

It was the first time Valentine had seen Dr. Lineberry speechless. Colonel Graff lifted a picture out from the wall and peeled a sound-sensitive membrane from the wall, along with its small broadcast unit. "Cheap," said Graff, "but effective. I thought you knew."

Lineberry took the device and sat down heavily at her desk. Graff led Valentine outside.

They walked out into the football field. The soldiers followed at a discreet distance; they split up and formed a large circle, to guard them from the widest possible perimeter.

"Valentine, we need your help for Ender."

"What kind of help?"

"We aren't even sure of that. We need you to help us figure out how you can help us."

"Well, what's wrong?"

"That's part of the problem. We don't know."

Valentine couldn't help but laugh. "I haven't seen him in three years! You've got him up there with you all the time!"

"Valentine, it costs more money than your father will make in his lifetime for me to fly to Earth and back to the Battle School again. I don't commute casually."

"The king had a dream," said Valentine, "but he forgot what it was, so he told his wise men to interpret the dream or they'd die. Only Daniel could interpret it, because he was a prophet."

"You read the Bible?"

"We're doing classics this year in advanced English. I'm not a prophet."

"I wish I could tell you everything about Ender's situation. But it would take hours, maybe days, and afterward I'd have to put you in protective confinement because so much of it is strictly confidential. So let's see what we can do with limited information. There's a game that our students play with the computer." And he told her about the End of the World and the closed room and the picture of Peter in the mirror.

"It's the computer that puts the picture there, not Ender. Why not ask the computer?"

"The computer doesn't know."

"I'm supposed to know?"

"This is the second time since Ender's been with us that he's taken this game to a dead end. To a game that seems to have no solution."

"Did he solve the first one?"

"Eventually."

"Then give him time, he'll probably solve this one."

"I'm not sure. Valentine, your brother is a very unhappy little boy."

"Why?"

"I don't know."

"You don't know much, do you?"

Valentine thought for a moment that the man might get angry. Instead, though, he decided to laugh. "No, not much. Valentine, why would Ender keep seeing your brother Peter in the mirror?"

"He shouldn't. It's stupid."

"Why is it stupid?"

"Because if there's ever anybody who was the opposite of Ender, it's Peter."

"How?"

Valentine could not think of a way to answer that wasn't dangerous. Too much questioning about Peter could lead to real trouble. Valentine knew enough about the world to know that no one would take Peter's plans for world domination seriously, as a danger to existing governments. But they might well decide he was insane and needed treatment for his megalomania.

"You're preparing to lie to me," Graff said.

"I'm preparing not to talk to you anymore," Valentine answered.

"And you're afraid. Why are you afraid?"

"I don't like questions about my family. Just leave my family out of this."

"Valentine, I'm trying to leave your family out of this. I'm coming to you so I don't have to start a battery of tests on Peter and question your parents. I'm trying to solve this problem now, with the person Ender loves and trusts most in the world, perhaps the only person he loves and trusts at all. If we can't solve it this way, then we'll sequester your family and do as we like from then on. This is not a trivial matter, and I won't just go away."

The only person Ender loves and trusts at all. She felt a deep stab of pain, of regret, of shame that now it was Peter she was close to, Peter who was the center of her life. For you, Ender, I light fires on your birthday. For Peter I help fulfil all his dreams. "I never thought you were a nice man. Not when you came to take Ender away, and not now."

"Don't pretend to be an ignorant little girl. I saw your tests when you were little, and at the present moment there aren't very many college professors who could keep up with you."

"Ender and Peter hate each other."

"I knew that. You said they were opposites. Why?"

"Peter—can be hateful sometimes."

"Hateful in what way?"

"Mean. Just mean, that's all."

"Valentine, for Ender's sake, tell me what he does when he's being mean."

"He threatens to kill people a lot. He doesn't mean it. But when we were little, Ender and I were both afraid of him. He told us he'd kill us. Actually, he told us he'd kill Ender."

"We monitored some of that."

"It was because of the monitor."

"Is that all? Tell me more about Peter."

So she told him about the children in every school that Peter attended. He never hit them, but he tortured them just the same. Found what they were most ashamed of and told it to the person whose respect they most wanted. Found what they most feared and made sure they faced it often.

"Did he do this with Ender?"

Valentine shook her head.

"Are you sure? Didn't Ender have a weak place? A thing he feared most, or that he was ashamed of?"

"Ender never did anything to be ashamed of." And suddenly, deep in her own shame for having forgotten and betrayed Ender, she started to cry.

"Why are you crying?"

She shook her head. She couldn't explain what it was like to think of her little brother, who was so good, whom she had protected for so long, and then remember that now she was Peter's ally, Peter's helper, Peter's slave in a scheme that was completely out of her control. Ender never surrendered to Peter, but I have turned, I've become part of him, as Ender never was. "Ender never gave in," she said.

"To what?"

"To Peter. To being like Peter."

They walked in silence along the goal line.

"How would Ender ever be like Peter?"

Valentine shuddered. "I already told you."

"But Ender never did that kind of thing. He was just a little boy."

"We both wanted to, though. We both wanted to—to kill Peter."

"Ah."

"No, that isn't true. We never said it. Ender never said that he wanted to do that. I just—*thought* it. It was me, not Ender. He never said that he wanted to kill him."

"What *did* he want?"

"He just didn't want to be—"

"To be what?"

"Peter tortures squirrels. He stakes them out on the ground and skins them alive and sits and watches them until they die. He did that, he doesn't do it now. But he did it. If Ender knew that, if Ender saw him, I think that he'd—"

"He'd what? Rescue the squirrels? Try to heal them?"

"No, in those days you didn't—undo what Peter did. You didn't cross him. But Ender would be kind to squirrels. Do you understand? He'd feed them."

"But if he fed them, they'd become tame, and that much easier for Peter to catch."

Valentine began to cry again. "No matter what you do, it always helps Peter. Everything helps Peter, everything, you just can't get away, no matter what."

"Are you helping Peter?" asked Graff.

She didn't answer.

"Is Peter such a very bad person, Valentine?"

She nodded.

"Is Peter the worst person in the world?"

"How can he be? I don't know. He's the worst person I know."

"And yet you and Ender are his brother and sister. You have the same genes, the same parents, how can he be so bad if—"

Valentine turned and screamed at him, screamed as if he were killing her. "Ender is not like Peter! He is not like Peter in any way! Except that he's smart, that's all—in every other way a person could possibly be like Peter he is nothing nothing nothing like Peter! Nothing!"

"I see," said Graff.

"I know what you're thinking, you bastard, you're thinking that I'm wrong, that Ender's like Peter. Well maybe *I'm* like Peter, but Ender isn't, he isn't at all, I used to tell him that when he cried, I told him that lots of times, you're not like Peter, you never like to hurt people, you're kind and good and not like Peter at all!"

"And it's true."

His acquiescence calmed her. "Damn right it's true. It's true."

"Valentine, will you help Ender?"

"I can't do anything for him now."

"It's really the same thing you always did for him before. Just comfort him and tell him that he never likes to hurt people, that he's good and kind and not like Peter at all. That's the most important thing. That he's not like Peter at all."

"I can see him?"

"No. I want you to write a letter."

"What good does that do? Ender never answered a single letter I sent."

Graff sighed. "He answered every letter he got."

It took only a second for her to understand. "You really stink."

"Isolation is—the optimum environment for creativity. It was *his* ideas we wanted, not the—never mind, I don't have to defend myself to you."

Then why are you doing it, she did not ask.

"But he's slacking off. He's coasting. We want to push him forward, and he won't go."

"Maybe I'd be doing Ender a favor if I told you to go stuff yourself."

"You've already helped me. You can help me more. Write to him."

"Promise you won't cut out anything I write."

"I won't promise any such thing."

"Then forget it."

"No problem. I'll write your letter myself. We can use your other letters to reconcile the writing styles. Simple matter."

"I want to see him."

"He gets his first leave when he's eighteen."

"You told him it would be when he was twelve."

"We changed the rules."

"Why should I help you!"

"Don't help me. Help Ender. What does it matter if that helps us, too?"

"What kind of terrible things are you doing to him up there?"

Graff chuckled. "Valentine, my dear little girl, the terrible things are only about to begin."

Ender was four lines into the letter before he realized that it wasn't from one of the other soldiers in the Battle School. It had come in the regular way—a MAIL WAITING message when he signed into his desk. He read four lines into it, then skipped to the end and read the signature. Then he went back to the beginning, and curled up on his bed to read the words over and over again.

ENDER,
THE BASTARDS WOULDN'T PUT ANY OF
MY LETTERS THROUGH TILL NOW. I
MUST HAVE WRITTEN A HUNDRED TIMES
BUT YOU MUST HAVE THOUGHT I NEVER
DID. WELL I DID. I HAVEN'T
FORGOTTEN YOU. I REMEMBER YOUR
BIRTHDAY. I REMEMBER EVERYTHING.
SOME PEOPLE MIGHT THINK THAT
BECAUSE YOU'RE BEING A SOLDIER
YOU ARE NOW A CRUEL AND HARD
PERSON WHO LIKES TO HURT PEOPLE,
LIKE THE MARINES IN THE VIDEOS,
BUT I KNOW THAT ISN'T TRUE. YOU
ARE NOTHING LIKE YOU-KNOW-WHO.
HE'S NICER-SEEMING BUT HE'S
STILL A SLUMBITCH INSIDE.
MAYBE YOU SEEM MEAN, BUT IT
WON'T FOOL ME. STILL PADDLING

THE OLD KNEW,
ALL MY LOVE TURKEY LIPS,

VAL

DON'T WRITE BACK THEY'LL PROBLY
SIKOWANALIZE YOUR LETTER.

Obviously it was written with the full approval of the teachers.
But there was no doubt it was written by Val. The spelling of *psycho-analyze,* the epithet *slumbitch* for Peter, the joke about pronouncing
knew like *canoe* were all things that no one could know but Val.

And yet they came pretty thick, as though someone wanted to
make very sure that Ender believed that the letter was genuine. Why
should they be so eager if it's the real thing?

It isn't the real thing anyway. Even if she wrote it in her own
blood, it isn't the real thing because they made her write it. She'd
written before, and they didn't let any of those letters through. Those
might have been real, but this was asked for, this was part of their
manipulation.

And the despair filled him again. Now he knew why. Now he
knew what he hated so much. He had no control over his own life.
They ran everything. They made all the choices. Only the game was
left to him, that was all, everything else was them and their rules and
plans and lessons and programs, and all he could do was go this way
or that way in battle. The one real thing, the one precious real thing
was his memory of Valentine, the person who loved him before he
ever played a game, who loved him whether there was a bugger war
or not, and they had taken her and put her on their side. She was one
of them now.

He hated them and all their games. Hated them so badly that he
cried, reading Val's empty asked-for letter again. The other boys in
Phoenix Army noticed and looked away. *Ender Wiggin* crying? That
was disturbing. Something terrible was going on. The best soldier in
any army, lying on his bunk *crying.* The silence in the room was
deep.

Ender deleted the letter, wiped it out of memory and then
punched up the fantasy game. He was not sure why he was so eager
to play the game, to get to the End of the World, but he wasted no

time getting there. Only when he coasted on the cloud, skimming over the autumnal colors of the pastoral world, only then did he realize what he hated most about Val's letter. All that it said was about Peter. About how he was not at all like Peter. The words she had said so often as she held him, comforted him as he trembled in fear and rage and loathing after Peter had tortured him, that was all that the letter had said.

And that was what they had asked for. The bastards knew about *that,* and they knew about Peter in the mirror in the castle room, they knew about everything and to them Val was just one more tool to use to control him, just one more trick to play. Dink was right, they were the enemy, they loved nothing and cared for nothing and he was not going to do what they wanted, he was damn well not going to do anything for them. He had had only one memory that was safe, one good thing, and those bastards had plowed it into him with the rest of the manure—and so he was finished, he wasn't going to play.

As always the serpent waited in the tower room, unraveling itself from the rug on the floor. But this time Ender didn't grind it underfoot. This time he caught it in his hands, knelt before it, and gently, so gently, brought the snake's gaping mouth to his lips.

And kissed.

He had not meant to do that. He had meant to let the snake bite him on the mouth. Or perhaps he had meant to eat the snake alive, as Peter in the mirror had done, with his bloody chin and the snake's tail dangling from his lips. But he kissed it instead.

And the snake in his hands thickened and bent into another shape. A human shape. It was Valentine, and she kissed him again.

The snake could not be Valentine. He had killed it too often for it to be his sister. Peter had devoured it too often to bear it that it might have been Valentine all along.

Was this what they planned when they let him read her letter? He didn't care.

She arose from the floor of the tower room and walked to the mirror. Ender made his figure also rise and go with her. They stood before the mirror, where instead of Peter's cruel reflection there stood a dragon and a unicorn. Ender reached out his hand and touched the mirror; the wall fell open and revealed a great stairway downward, carpeted and lined with shouting, cheering multitudes.

Together, arm in arm, he and Valentine walked down the stairs. Tears filled his eyes, tears of relief that at last he had broken free of the room at the End of the World. And because of the tears, he didn't notice that every member of the multitude wore Peter's face. He only knew that wherever he went in this world, Valentine was with him.

Valentine read the letter that Dr. Lineberry had given her. "Dear Valentine," it said, "We thank you and commend you for your efforts on behalf of the war effort. You are hereby notified that you have been awarded the Star of the Order of the League of Humanity, First Class, which is the highest military award that can be given to a civilian. Unfortunately, I.F. security forbids us to make this award public until after the successful conclusion of current operations, but we want you to know that your efforts resulted in complete success. Sincerely, General Shimon Levy, Strategos."

When she had read it twice, Dr. Lineberry took it from her hands. "I was instructed to let you read it, and then destroy it." She took a cigarette lighter from a drawer and set the paper afire. It burned brightly in the ashtray. "Was it good or bad news?" she asked.

"I sold my brother," Valentine said, "and they paid me for it."

"That's a bit melodramatic, isn't it, Valentine?"

Valentine went back to class without answering. That night Demosthenes published a scathing denunciation of the population limitation laws. People should be allowed to have as many children as they like, and the surplus population should be sent to other worlds, to spread mankind so far across the galaxy that no disaster, no invasion could ever threaten the human race with annihilation. "The most noble title any child can have," Demosthenes wrote, "is Third."

For you, Ender, she said to herself as she wrote.

Peter laughed in delight when he read it. "That'll make them sit up and take notice. Third! A noble title! Oh, you have a wicked streak."

Chapter **10**

Dragon

"Now?"

"I suppose so."

"It has to be an order, Colonel Graff. Armies don't move because a commander says 'I suppose it's time to attack.' "

"I'm not a commander. I'm a teacher of little children."

"Colonel, sir, I admit I was on you, I admit I was a pain in the ass, but it worked, everything worked just like you wanted it to. The last few weeks Ender's even been, been—"

"Happy."

"Content. He's doing well. His mind is keen, his play is excellent. Young as he is, we've never had a boy better prepared for command. Usually they go at eleven, but at nine and a half he's top flight."

"Well, yes. For a few minutes there, it actually occurred to me to wonder what kind of a man would heal a broken child of some of his hurt, just so he could throw him back into battle again. A little private moral dilemma. Please overlook it. I was tired."

"Saving the world, remember?"

"Call him in."

"We're doing what must be done, Colonel Graff."

"Come on, Anderson, you're just dying to see how he handles all those rigged games I had you work out."

"That's a pretty low thing to—"

"So I'm a low kind of guy. Come on, Major. We're both the scum of the earth. I'm dying to see how he handles them, too. After all, our lives depend on him doing real well. Neh?"

"You're not starting to use the boys' slang, are you?"

"Call him in, Major. I'll dump the rosters into his files and give him his security system. What we're doing to him isn't all bad, you know. He gets his privacy again."

"Isolation, you mean."

"The loneliness of power. Go call him in."

"Yes sir. I'll be back with him in fifteen minutes."

"Good-bye. Yes sir yessir yezzir. I hope you had fun, I hope you had a nice, nice time being happy, Ender. It might be the last time in your life. Welcome, little boy. Your dear Uncle Graff has plans for you."

Ender knew what was happening from the moment they brought him in. Everyone expected him to go commander early. Perhaps not *this* early, but he had topped the standings almost continuously for three years, no one else was remotely close to him, and his evening practices had become the most prestigious group in the school. There were some who wondered why the teachers had waited this long.

He wondered which army they'd give him. Three commanders were graduating soon, including Petra, but it was beyond hope for them to give him Phoenix Army—no one ever succeeded to command of the same army he was in when he was promoted.

Anderson took him first to his new quarters. That sealed it— only commanders had private rooms. Then he had him fitted for new uniforms and a new flash suit. He looked on the forms to discover the name of his army.

Dragon, said the form. There was no Dragon Army.

"I've never heard of Dragon Army," Ender said.

"That's because there hasn't been a Dragon Army in four years. We discontinued the name because there was a superstition about it. No Dragon Army in the history of the Battle School ever won even a third of its games. It got to be a joke."

"Well, why are you reviving it now?"

"We had a lot of extra uniforms to use up."

Graff sat at his desk, looking fatter and wearier than the last time Ender had seen him. He handed Ender his hook, the small box that commanders used to go where they wanted in the battleroom during practices. Many times during his evening practice sessions

Ender wished that he had a hook, instead of having to rebound off walls to get where he wanted to go. Now that he'd got quite deft at maneuvering without one, here it was. "It only works," Anderson pointed out, "during your regularly scheduled practice sessions." Since Ender already planned to have extra practices, it meant the hook would only be useful some of the time. It also explained why so many commanders never held extra practices. They depended on the hook, and it wouldn't do anything for them during the extra times. If they felt that the hook was their authority, their power over the other boys, then they were even less likely to work without it. That's an advantage I'll have over some of my enemies, Ender thought.

Graff's official welcome speech sounded bored and over-rehearsed. Only at the end did he begin to sound interested in his own words. "We're doing something unusual with Dragon Army. I hope you don't mind. We've assembled a new army by advancing the equivalent of an entire launch course early and delaying the graduation of quite a few advanced students. I think you'll be pleased with the quality of your soldiers. I hope you are, because we're forbidding you to transfer any of them."

"No trades?" asked Ender. It was how commanders always shored up their weak points, by trading around.

"None. You see, you have been conducting your extra practice sessions for three years now. You have a following. Many good soldiers would put unfair pressure on their commanders to trade them into your army. We've given you an army that can, in time, be competitive. We have no intention of letting you dominate unfairly."

"What if I've got a soldier I just can't get along with?"

"Get along with him." Graff closed his eyes. Anderson stood up and the interview was over.

Dragon was assigned the colors grey, orange, grey; Ender changed into his flash suit, then followed the ribbons of light until he came to the barracks that contained his army. They were there already, milling around near the entrance. Ender took charge at once. "Bunking will be arranged by seniority. Veterans to the back of the room, newest soldiers to the front."

It was the reverse of the usual pattern, and Ender knew it. He also knew that he didn't intend to be like many commanders, who never even saw the younger boys because they were always in the back.

As they sorted themselves out according to their arrival dates, Ender walked up and down the aisle. Almost thirty of his soldiers were new, straight out of their launch group, completely inexperienced in battle. Some were even underage—the ones nearest the door were pathetically small. Ender reminded himself that that's how he must have looked to Bonzo Madrid when he first arrived. Still, Bonzo had had only one underage soldier to cope with.

Not one of the veterans belonged to Ender's elite practice group. None had ever been a toon leader. None, in fact, was older than Ender himself, which meant that even his veterans didn't have more than eighteen months' experience. Some he didn't even recognize, they had made so little impression.

They recognized Ender, of course, since he was the most celebrated soldier in the school. And some, Ender could see, resented him. At least they did me one favor—none of my soldiers is older than me.

As soon as each soldier had a bunk, Ender ordered them to put on their flash suits and come to practice. "We're on the morning schedule, straight to practice after breakfast. Officially you have a free hour between breakfast and practice. We'll see what happens after I find out how good you are." After three minutes, though many of them still weren't dressed, he ordered them out of the room.

"But I'm naked!" said one boy.

"Dress faster next time. Three minutes from first call to running out the door—that's the rule this week. Next week the rule is two minutes. Move!" It would soon be a joke in the rest of the school that Dragon Army was so dumb they had to practice getting dressed.

Five of the boys were completely naked, carrying their flash suits as they ran through the corridors; few were fully dressed. They attracted a lot of attention as they passed open classroom doors. No one would be late again if he could help it.

In the corridors leading to the battleroom, Ender made them run back and forth in the halls, fast, so they were sweating a little, while the naked ones got dressed. Then he led them to the upper door, the one that opened into the middle of the battleroom just like the doors in the actual games. Then he made them jump up and use the ceiling handholds to hurl themselves into the room. "Assemble on the far wall," he said. "As if you were going for the enemy's gate."

They revealed themselves as they jumped, four at a time, through the door. Almost none of them knew how to establish a direct line to the target, and when they reached the far wall few of the new ones had any idea how to catch on or even control their rebounds.

The last boy out was a small kid, obviously underage. There was no way he was going to reach the ceiling handhold.

"You can use a side handhold if you want," Ender said.

"Go suck on it," said the boy. He took a flying leap, touched the ceiling handhold with a finger tip, and hurtled through the door with no control at all, spinning in three directions at once. Ender tried to decide whether to like the little kid for refusing to take a concession or to be annoyed at his insubordinate attitude.

They finally got themselves together along the wall. Ender noticed that without exception they had lined up with their heads still in the direction that had been up in the corridor. So Ender deliberately took hold of what they were treating as a floor and dangled from it upside down. "Why are you upside down, soldiers?" he demanded.

Some of them started to turn the other way.

"Attention!" They held still. "I said why are you upside down!"

No one answered. They didn't know what he expected.

"I said why does every one of you have his feet in the air and his head toward the ground!"

Finally one of them spoke. "Sir, this is the direction we were in coming out of the door."

"Well what difference is that supposed to make! What difference does it make what the gravity was back in the corridor! Are we going to fight in the corridor! Is there any gravity here?"

No sir. No *sir.*

"From now on, you forget about gravity before you go through that door. The old gravity is gone, erased. Understand me? Whatever your gravity is when you get to the door, remember—the enemy's gate is *down.* Your feet are toward the enemy gate. Up is toward your own gate. North is that way, south is that way, east is that way, west is—what way?"

They pointed.

"That's what I expected. The only process you've mastered is the process of elimination, and the only reason you've mastered that is because you can do it in the toilet. What was the circus I saw out here! Did you call that forming up? Did you call that flying? Now everybody, launch and form up on the ceiling! Right now! Move!"

As Ender expected, a good number of them instinctively launched, not toward the wall with the door in it, but toward the wall that Ender had called *north,* the direction that had been up when they were in the corridor. Of course they quickly realized their mistake, but too late—they had to wait to change things until they had rebounded off the north wall.

In the meantime, Ender was mentally grouping them into slow learners and fast learners. The littlest kid, the one who had been last out of the door, was the first to arrive at the correct wall, and he caught himself adroitly. They had been right to advance him. He'd do well. He was also cocky and rebellious, and probably resented the fact that he had been one of the ones Ender had sent naked through the corridors.

"You!" Ender said, pointing at the small one. "Which way is down?"

"Toward the enemy door." The answer was quick. It was also surly, as if to say, OK, OK, now get on with the important stuff.

"Name, kid?"

"This soldier's name is Bean, sir."

"Get that for size or for brains?" The other boys laughed a little. "Well, Bean, you're right onto things. Now listen to me, because this matters. Nobody's going to get through that door without a good chance of getting hit. In the old days, you had ten, twenty seconds before you even had to move. Now if you aren't already streaming out of the door when the enemy comes out, you're frozen. Now, what happens when you're frozen?"

"Can't move," one of the boys said.

"That's what frozen *means,"* Ender said. "But what *happens* to you?"

It was Bean, not intimidated at all, who answered intelligently. "You keep going in the direction you started in. At the speed you were going when you were flashed."

"That's true. You five, there on the end, move!"

Startled, the boys looked at each other. Ender flashed them all. "The next five, move!"

They moved. Ender flashed them, too, but they kept moving,

heading toward the walls. The first five, though, were drifting uselessly near the main group.

"Look at these so-called soldiers," Ender said. "Their commander ordered them to move, and now look at them. Not only are
they frozen, they're frozen right here, where they can get in the way.
While the others, because they moved when they were ordered, are
frozen down there, plugging up the enemy's lanes, blocking the
enemy's vision. I imagine that about five of you have understood the
point of this. And no doubt Bean is one of them. Right, Bean?"

He didn't answer at first. Ender looked at him until he said,
"Right, sir."

"Then what is the point?"

"When you are ordered to move, move fast, so if you get iced
you'll bounce around instead of getting in the way of your own
army's operations."

"Excellent. At least I have one soldier who can figure things
out." Ender could see resentment growing in the way the other
soldiers shifted their weight and glanced at each other, the way they
avoided looking at Bean. Why am I doing this? What does this have
to do with being a good commander, making one boy the target of all
the others? Just because they did it to me, why should I do it to him?
Ender wanted to undo his taunting of the boy, wanted to tell the
others that the little one needed their help and friendship more than
anyone else. But of course Ender couldn't do that. Not on the first
day. On the first day even his mistakes had to look like part of a
brilliant plan.

Ender hooked himself nearer the wall and pulled one of the boys
away from the others. "Keep your body straight," said Ender. He
rotated the boy in midair so his feet pointed toward the others. When
the boy kept moving his body, Ender flashed him. The others
laughed. "How much of his body could you shoot?" Ender asked a
boy directly under the frozen soldier's feet.

"Mostly all I can hit is his feet."

Ender turned to the boy next to him. "What about you?"

"I can see his body."

"And you?"

A boy a little farther down the wall answered. "All of him."

"Feet aren't very big. Not much protection." Ender pushed the
frozen soldier out of the way. Then he doubled his legs under him, as

if he were kneeling in midair, and flashed his own legs. Immediately the legs of his suit went rigid, holding them in that position.

Ender twisted himself in the air, so that he knelt above the other boys.

"What do you see?" he asked.

A lot less, they said.

Ender thrust his gun between his legs. "I can see fine," he said, and proceeded to flash the boys directly under him. "Stop me!" he shouted. "Try and flash me!"

They finally did, but not until he had flashed more than a third of them. He thumbed his hook and thawed himself and every other frozen soldier. "Now," he said, "which way is the enemy's gate?"

"Down!"

"And what is our attack position?"

Some started to answer with words, but Bean answered by flipping himself away from the wall with his legs doubled under him, straight toward the opposite wall, flashing between his legs all the way.

For a moment Ender wanted to shout at him, to punish him; then he caught himself, rejected the ungenerous impulse. Why should I be so angry at this little boy? "Is Bean the only one who knows how?" Ender shouted.

Immediately the entire army pushed off toward the opposite wall, kneeling in the air, firing between their legs, shouting at the top of their lungs. There may be a time, thought Ender, when this is exactly the strategy I'll need—forty screaming boys in an unbalancing attack.

When they were all at the other side, Ender called for them to attack him, all at once. Yes, thought Ender. Not bad. They gave me an untrained army, with no excellent veterans, but at least it isn't a crop of fools. I can work with this.

When they were assembled again, laughing and exhilarated, Ender began the real work. He had them freeze their legs in the kneeling position. "Now, what are your legs good for, in combat?"

Nothing, said some boys.

"Bean doesn't think so," said Ender.

"They're the best way to push off walls."

"Right," Ender said.

The other boys started to complain that pushing off walls was movement, not combat.

"There is no combat without movement," Ender said. They fell silent and hated Bean a little more. "Now, with your legs frozen like this, can you push off walls?"

No one dared answer, for fear they'd be wrong.

"Bean?" asked Ender.

"I've never tried it, but maybe if you faced the wall and doubled over at the waist—"

"Right but wrong. Watch me. My back's to the wall, legs are frozen. Since I'm kneeling, my feet are against the wall. Usually, when you push off you have to push downward, so you string out your body behind you like a string *bean,* right?"

Laughter.

"But with my legs frozen, I use pretty much the same force, pushing downward from the hips and thighs, only now it pushes my shoulders and my feet backward, shoots out my hips, and when I come loose my body's tight, nothing stringing out behind me. Watch this."

Ender forced his hips forward, which shot him away from the wall; in a moment he readjusted his position and was kneeling, legs downward, rushing toward the opposite wall. He landed on his knees, flipped over on his back, and jackknifed off the wall in another direction. "Shoot me!" he shouted. Then he set himself spinning in the air as he took a course roughly parallel to the boys along the far wall. Because he was spinning, they couldn't get a continuous beam on him.

He thawed his suit and hooked himself back to them. "That's what we're working on for the first half hour today. Build up some muscles you didn't know you had. Learn to use your legs as a shield and control your movements so you can get that spin. Spinning doesn't do any good up close, but far away, they can't hurt you if you're spinning—at that distance the beam has to hit the same spot for a couple of moments, and if you're spinning it can't happen. Now freeze yourself and get started."

"Aren't you going to assign lanes?" asked a boy.

"No I'm not going to assign lanes. I want you bumping into each other and learning how to deal with it all the time, except when we're practicing formations, and then I'll usually have you bump into each other on purpose. Now move!"

When he said *move,* they moved.

Ender was the last one out after practice, since he stayed to help some of the slower ones improve on technique. They'd had good teachers, but the inexperienced soldiers fresh out of their launch groups were completely helpless when it came to doing two or three things at the same time. It was fine to practice jackknifing with frozen legs, they had no trouble maneuvering in midair, but to launch in one direction, fire in another, spin twice, rebound with a jackknife off a wall, and come out firing, facing the right direction—that was way beyond them. Drill drill drill, that was all Ender would be able to do with them for a while. Strategies and formations were nice, but they were nothing if the army didn't know how to handle themselves in battle.

He had to get this army ready *now.* He was early at being a commander, and the teachers were changing the rules now, not letting him trade, giving him no top-notch veterans. There was no guarantee that they'd give him the usual three months to get his army together before sending them into battle.

At least in the evenings he'd have Alai and Shen to help him train his new boys.

He was still in the corridor leading out of the battleroom when he found himself face to face with little Bean. Bean looked angry. Ender didn't want problems right now.

"Ho, Bean."

"Ho, Ender."

Pause.

"Sir," Ender said softly.

"I know what you're doing, Ender, sir, and I'm warning you."

"Warning me?"

"I can be the best man you've got, but don't play games with me."

"Or what?"

"Or I'll be the worst man you've got. One or the other."

"And what do you want, love and kisses?" Ender was getting angry now.

Bean looked unworried. "I want a toon."

Ender walked back to him and stood looking down into his eyes. "Why should you get a toon?"

"Because I'd know what to do with it."

"Knowing what to do with a toon is easy," Ender said. "It's getting them to do it that's hard. Why would any soldier want to follow a little pinprick like you?"

"They used to call *you* that, I hear. I hear Bonzo Madrid still does."

"I asked you a question, soldier."

"I'll earn their respect, if you don't stop me."

Ender grinned. "I'm helping you."

"Like hell," said Bean.

"Nobody would notice you, except to feel sorry for the little kid. But I made sure they *all* noticed you today. They'll be watching every move you make. All you have to do to earn their respect now is be perfect."

"So I don't even get a chance to learn before I'm being judged."

"Poor kid. Nobody's treatin him fair." Ender gently pushed Bean back against the wall. "I'll tell you how to get a toon. Prove to me you know what you're doing as a soldier. Prove to me you know how to use other soldiers. And then prove to me that somebody's willing to follow you into battle. Then you'll get your toon. But not bloody well until."

Bean smiled. "That's fair. *If* you actually work that way, I'll be a toon leader in a month."

Ender reached down and grabbed the front of his uniform and shoved him into the wall. "When I say I work a certain way, Bean, then that's the way I work."

Bean just smiled. Ender let go of him and walked away. When he got to his room he lay down on his bed and trembled. What am I doing? My first practice session, and I'm already bullying people the way Bonzo did. And Peter. Shoving people around. Picking on some poor little kid so the others'll have somebody they all hate. Sickening. Everything I hated in a commander, and I'm doing it.

Is it some law of human nature that you inevitably become whatever your first commander was? I can quit right now, if that's so.

Over and over he thought of the things he did and said in his first practice with his new army. Why couldn't he talk like he always did in his evening practice group? No authority except excellence. Never had to give orders, just made suggestions. But that wouldn't work, not with an army. His informal practice group didn't have to learn to do things together. They didn't have to develop a group feeling; they never had to learn how to hold together and trust each other in battle. They didn't have to respond instantly to commands.

And he could go to the other extreme, too. He could be as lax and incompetent as Rose the Nose, if he wanted. He could make stupid mistakes no matter what he did. He had to have discipline, and that meant demanding—and getting—quick, decisive obedience. He had to have a well-trained army, and that meant drilling the soldiers over and over again, long after they thought they had mastered a technique, until it was so natural to them that they didn't have to think about it anymore.

But what was this thing with Bean? Why had he gone for the smallest, weakest, and possibly the brightest of the boys? Why had he done to Bean what had been done to Ender by commanders that he despised.

Then he remembered that it hadn't begun with his commanders. Before Rose and Bonzo treated him with contempt, he had been isolated in his launch group. And it wasn't Bernard who began that, either. It was Graff.

It was the teachers who had done it. And it wasn't an accident. Ender realized that now. It was a strategy. Graff had deliberately set him up to be separate from the other boys, made it impossible for him to be close to them. And he began now to suspect the reasons behind it. It wasn't to unify the rest of the group—in fact, it was divisive. Graff had isolated Ender to make him struggle. To make him prove, not that he was competent, but that he was far better than everyone else. That was the only way he could win respect and friendship. It made him a better soldier than he would ever have been otherwise. It also made him lonely, afraid, angry, untrusting. And maybe those traits, too, made him a better soldier.

That's what I'm doing to you, Bean. I'm hurting you to make you a better soldier in every way. To sharpen your wit. To intensify your effort. To keep you off balance, never sure what's going to happen next, so you always have to be ready for anything, ready to improvise, determined to win no matter what. I'm also making you miserable. That's why they brought you to me, Bean. So you could be just like me. So you could grow up to be just like the old man.

And me—am I supposed to grow up like Graff? Fat and sour and unfeeling, manipulating the lives of little boys so they turn out factory perfect, generals and admirals ready to lead the fleet in defense of the homeland. You get all the pleasures of the puppeteer. Until you get a soldier who can do more than anyone else. You can't have that. It spoils the symmetry. You must get him in line, break him down, isolate him, beat him until he gets in line with everyone else.

Well, what I've done to you this day, Bean, I've done. But I'll be watching you, more compassionately than you know, and when the time is right you'll find that I'm your friend, and you are the soldier you want to be.

Ender did not go to classes that afternoon. He lay on his bunk and wrote down his impressions of each of the boys in his army, the things he noticed right about them, the things that needed more work. In practice tonight, he would talk with Alai and they'd figure out ways to teach small groups the things they needed to know. At least he wouldn't be in this thing alone.

But when Ender got to the battleroom that night, while most others were still eating, he found Major Anderson waiting for him. "There has been a rule change, Ender. From now on, only members of the same army may work together in a battleroom during free-time. And, therefore, battlerooms are available only on a scheduled basis. After tonight, your next turn is in four days."

"Nobody else is holding extra practices."

"They are now, Ender. Now that you command another army, they don't want their boys practicing with you. Surely you can understand that. So they'll conduct their own practices."

"I've always been in another army from them. They still sent their soldiers to me for training."

"You weren't commander then."

"You gave me a completely green army, Major Anderson, sir—"

"You have quite a few veterans."

"They aren't any good."

"Nobody gets here without being brilliant, Ender. Make them good."

"I needed Alai and Shen to—"

"It's about time you grew up and did some things on your own, Ender. You don't need these other boys to hold your hand. You're a commander now. So kindly act like it, Ender."

Ender walked past Anderson toward the battleroom. Then he stopped, turned, asked a question. "Since these evening practices are now regularly scheduled, does it mean I can use the hook?"

Did Anderson almost smile? No. Not a chance of that. "We'll see," he said.

Ender turned his back and went on into the battleroom. Soon his army arrived, and no one else; either Anderson waited around to intercept anyone coming to Ender's practice group, or word had already passed through the whole school that Ender's informal evenings were through.

It was a good practice, they accomplished a lot, but at the end of it Ender was tired and lonely. There was a half hour before bedtime. He couldn't go into his army's barracks—he had long since learned that the best commanders stay away unless they have some reason to visit. The boys have to have a chance to be at peace, at rest, without someone listening to favor or despise them depending on the way they talk and act and think.

So he wandered to the game room, where a few other boys were using the last half hour before final bell to settle bets or beat their previous scores on the games. None of the games looked interesting, but he played one anyway, an easy animated game designed for Launchies. Bored, he ignored the objectives of the game and used the little player-figure, a bear, to explore the animated scenery around him.

"You'll never win that way."

Ender smiled. "Missed you at practice, Alai."

"*I* was there. But they had your army in a separate place. Looks like you're big time now, can't play with the little boys anymore."

"You're a full cubit taller than I am."

"Cubit! Has God been telling you to build a boat or something? Or are you in an archaic mood?"

"Not archaic, just arcane. Secret, subtle, roundabout. I miss you already, you circumcised dog."

"Don't you know? We're enemies now. Next time I meet you in battle, I'll whip your ass."

It was banter, as always, but now there was too much truth behind it. Now when Ender heard Alai talk as if it were all a joke, he felt the pain of losing his friend, and the worse pain of wondering if Alai really felt as little pain as he showed.

"You can try," said Ender. "I taught you everything you know. But I didn't teach you everything *I* know."

"I knew all along that you were holding something back, Ender."

A pause. Ender's bear was in trouble on the screen. He climbed a tree. "I wasn't, Alai. Holding anything back."

"I know," said Alai. "Neither was I."

"Salaam, Alai."

"Alas, it is not to be."

"What isn't?"

"Peace. It's what *salaam* means. Peace be unto you."

The words brought forth an echo from Ender's memory. His mother's voice reading to him softly, when he was very young. Think not that I am come to send peace on earth. I came not to send peace, but a sword. Ender had pictured his mother piercing Peter the Terrible with a bloody rapier, and the words had stayed in his mind along with the image.

In the silence, the bear died. It was a cute death, with funny music. Ender turned around. Alai was already gone. He felt like part of himself had been taken away, an inward prop that was holding up his courage and confidence. With Alai, to a degree impossible even with Shen, Ender had come to feel a unity so strong that the word *we* came to his lips much more easily than *I*.

But Alai had left something behind. Ender lay in bed, dozing into the night, and felt Alai's lips on his cheek as he muttered the word *peace.* The kiss, the word, the peace were with him still. I am only what I remember, and Alai is my friend in memory so intense that they can't tear him out. Like Valentine, the strongest memory of all.

The next day he passed Alai in the corridor, and they greeted each other, touched hands, talked, but they both knew that there was a wall now. It might be breached, that wall, sometime in the future, but for now the only real conversation between them was the roots that had already grown low and deep, under the wall, where they could not be broken.

The most terrible thing, though, was the fear that the wall could never be breached, that in his heart Alai was glad of the separation, and was ready to be Ender's enemy. For now that they could not be together, they must be infinitely apart, and what had been sure and unshakable was now fragile and insubstantial; from the moment we are not together, Alai is a stranger, for he has a life now that will be no part of mine, and that means that when I see him we will not know each other.

It made him sorrowful, but Ender did not weep. He was done with that. When they had turned Valentine into a stranger, when they had used her as a tool to work on Ender, from that day forward they could never hurt him deep enough to make him cry again. Ender was certain of that.

And with that anger, he decided he was strong enough to defeat them, the teachers, his enemies.

Chapter 11

Veni Vidi Vici

"You can't be serious about this schedule of battles."

"Yes I can."

"He's only had his army three and a half weeks."

"I told you. We did computer simulations on probable results. And here is what the computer estimated Ender would do."

"We want to teach him, not give him a nervous breakdown."

"The computer knows him better than we do."

"The computer is also not famous for having mercy."

"If you wanted to be merciful, you should have gone to a monastery."

"You mean this **isn't** a monastery?"

"This is best for Ender, too. We're bringing him to his full potential."

"I thought we'd give him two years as commander. We usually give them a battle every two weeks, starting after three months. This is a little extreme."

"Do we **have** two years to spare?"

"I know. I just have this picture of Ender a year from now. Completely useless, worn out, because he was pushed farther than he or any living person could go."

"We told the computer that our highest priority was having the subject remain useful after the training program."

"Well, as long as he's useful—"

"Look, Colonel Graff, you're the one who made me prepare this, over my protests, if you'll remember."

"I know, you're right, I shouldn't burden you with my conscience. But my eagerness to sacrifice little children in order to save mankind is wearing thin. The Polemarch has been to see the Hegemon. It seems Russian intelligence is concerned that some of the active citizens on the nets are already figuring how America ought to use the I.F. to destroy the Warsaw Pact as soon as the buggers are destroyed."

"Seems premature."

"It seems insane. Free speech is one thing, but to jeopardize the League over nationalistic rivalries—and it's for people like that, short-sighted, suicidal people, that we're pushing Ender to the edge of human endurance."

"I think you underestimate Ender."

"But I fear that I also underestimate the stupidity of the rest of mankind. Are we absolutely sure that we ought to win this war?"

"Sir, those words sound like treason."

"It was black humor."

"It wasn't funny. When it comes to the buggers, nothing—"

"Nothing is funny, I know."

Ender Wiggin lay on his bed staring at the ceiling. Since becoming commander, he never slept more than five hours a night. But the lights went off at 2200 and didn't come on again until 0600. Sometimes he worked at his desk, anyway, straining his eyes to use the dim display. Usually, though, he stared at the invisible ceiling and thought.

Either the teachers had been kind to him after all, or he was a better commander than he thought. His ragged little group of veterans, utterly without honor in their previous armies, were blossoming into capable leaders. So much so that instead of the usual four toons, he had created five, each with a toon leader and a second; every veteran had a position. He had the army drill in eight-man toon maneuvers and four-man half-toons, so that at a single command, his army could be assigned as many as ten separate maneuvers and carry them out at once. No army had ever fragmented itself like that before, but Ender was not planning to do anything that had been done before, either. Most armies practiced mass maneuvers, preformed strategies. Ender had none. Instead he trained his toon leaders to use their small units effectively in achieving limited goals. Unsupported, alone, on their own initiative. He staged mock wars after the first week, savage affairs in the practice room that left everybody exhausted. But he knew, with less than a month of training, that his army had the potential of being the best fighting group ever to play the game.

How much of this did the teachers plan? Did they know they were giving him obscure but excellent boys? Did they give him thirty Launchies, many of them underage, because they knew the little boys were quick learners, quick thinkers? Or was this what any similar group could become under a commander who knew what he wanted his army to do, and knew how to teach them to do it?

The question bothered him, because he wasn't sure whether he was confounding or fulfilling their expectations.

All he was sure of was that he was eager for battle. Most armies needed three months because they had to memorize dozens of elaboration formations. We're ready now. Get us into battle.

The door opened in darkness. Ender listened. A shuffling step. The door closed.

He rolled off his bunk and crawled in the darkness the two meters to the door. There was a slip of paper there. He couldn't read it, of course, but he knew what it was. Battle. How kind of them. I wish, and they deliver.

Ender was already dressed in his Dragon Army flash suit when the lights came on. He ran down the corridor at once, and by 0601 he was at the door of his army's barracks.

"We have a battle with Rabbit Army at 0700. I want us warmed up in gravity and ready to go. Strip down and get to the gym. Bring your flash suits and we'll go to the battleroom from there."

What about breakfast?

"I don't want anybody throwing up in the battleroom."

Can we at least take a leak first?

"No more than a decaliter."

They laughed. The ones who didn't sleep naked stripped down; everyone bundled up their flash suits and followed Ender at a jog through the corridors to the gym. He put them through the obstacle course twice, then split them into rotations on the tramp, the mat, and the bench. "Don't wear yourselves out, just wake yourselves up." He didn't need to worry about exhaustion. They were in good shape, light and agile, and above all excited about the battle to come. A few of them spontaneously began to wrestle—the gym, instead of being tedious, was suddenly fun, because of the battle to come. Their confidence was the supreme confidence of those who have never been into the contest, and think they are ready. Well, why shouldn't they think so? They are. And so am I.

At 0640 he had them dress out. He talked to the toon leaders and their seconds while they dressed. "Rabbit Army is mostly veterans, but Carn Carby was made their commander only five months ago, and I never fought them under him. He was a pretty good soldier, and Rabbit has done fairly well in the standings over the years. But I expect to see formations, and so I'm not worried."

At 0650 he made them all lie down on the mats and relax. Then, at 0656, he ordered them up and they jogged along the corridor to the battleroom. Ender occasionally leaped up to touch the ceiling. The boys all jumped to touch the same spot on the ceiling. Their ribbon of color led to the left; Rabbit Army had already passed through to the right. And at 0658 they reached their gate to the battleroom.

The toons lined up in five columns. A and E were ready to grab the side handholds and flip themselves out toward the sides. B and D lined up to catch the two parallel ceiling holds and flip upward into null gravity. C toon were ready to slap the sill of the doorway and flip downward.

Up, down, left, right; Ender stood at the front, between columns so he'd be out of the way, and reoriented them. "Which way is the enemy's gate?"

Down, they all said, laughing. And in that moment *up* became north, *down* became south, and *left* and *right* became east and west.

The grey wall in front of them disappeared, and the battleroom was visible. It wasn't a dark game, but it wasn't a bright one either—the lights were about half, like dusk. In the distance, in the dim light, he could see the enemy door, their lighted flash suits already pouring out. Ender knew a moment's pleasure. Everyone had learned the wrong lesson from Bonzo's misuse of Ender Wiggin. They all dumped through the door immediately, so that there was no chance to do anything other than name the formation they would use. Commanders didn't have time to think. Well, Ender would take the time, and trust his soldiers' ability to fight with flashed legs to keep them intact as they came late through the door.

Ender sized up the shape of the battleroom. The familiar open grid of most early games, like the monkey bars at the park, with seven or eight stars scattered through the grid. There were enough of them, and in forward enough positions, that they were worth going for. "Spread to the near stars," Ender said. "C try to slide the wall. If it works, A and E will follow. If it doesn't, I'll decide from there. I'll be with D. Move."

All the soldiers knew what was happening, but tactical decisions were entirely up to the toon leaders. Even with Ender's instructions, they were only ten seconds late getting through the gate. Rabbit Army was already doing some elaborate dance down at their end of the room. In all the other armies Ender had fought in, he would have been worrying right now about making sure he and his toon were in their proper place in their own formation. Instead, he and all his men were only thinking of ways to slip around past the formation, control the stars and the corners of the room, and then break the enemy formation into meaningless chunks that didn't know what they were doing. Even with less than four weeks together, the way they fought already seemed like the only intelligent way, the only *possible* way. Ender was almost surprised that Rabbit Army didn't know already that they were hopelessly out of date.

C toon slipped along the wall, coasting with their bent knees facing the enemy. Crazy Tom, the leader of C toon, had apparently ordered his men to flash their own legs already. It was a pretty good idea in this dim light, since the lighted flash suits went dark wherever they were frozen. It made them less easily visible. Ender would commend him for that.

Rabbit Army was able to drive back C toon's attack, but not until Crazy Tom and his boys had carved them up, freezing a dozen Rabbits before they retreated to the safety of a star. But it was a star behind the Rabbit formation, which meant they were going to be easy pickings now.

Han Tzu, commonly called Hot Soup, was the leader of D toon. He slid quickly along the lip of the star to where Ender knelt. "How about flipping off the north wall and kneeling on their faces?"

"Do it," Ender said. "I'll take B south to get behind them." Then he shouted, "A and E slow on the walls!" He slid footward along the star, hooked his feet on the lip, and flipped himself up to the top wall, then rebounded down to E toon's star. In a moment he was leading them down against the south wall. They rebounded in near perfect unison and came up behind the two stars that Carn Carby's soldiers were defending. It was like cutting butter with a hot knife. Rabbit Army was gone, just a little cleanup left to do. Ender broke his toons up into half-toons to scour the corners for any enemy soldiers who were whole or merely damaged. In three minutes his toon leaders reported the room clean. Only one of Ender's boys was completely frozen—one of C toon, which had borne the brunt of the assault—and only five were disabled. Most were damaged, but those were leg shots and many of them were self-inflicted. All in all, it had gone even better than Ender expected.

Ender had his toon leaders do the honors at the gate—four helmets at the corners, and Crazy Tom to pass through the gate. Most commanders took whoever was left alive to pass the gate; Ender could have picked practically anyone. A good battle.

The lights went full, and Major Anderson himself came through the teachergate at the south end of the battleroom. He looked very solemn as he offered Ender the teacher hook that was ritually given to the victor in the game. Ender used it to thaw his own army's flash suits, of course, and he assembled them in toons before thawing the enemy. Crisp, military appearance, that's what he wanted when Carby and Rabbit Army got their bodies under control again. They may curse us and lie about us, but they'll remember that we destroyed them, and no matter what they say other soldiers and other commanders will see that in their eyes; in those Rabbit eyes, they'll see us in neat formation, victorious and almost undamaged in our first battle. Dragon Army isn't going to be an obscure name for long.

Carn Carby came to Ender as soon as he was unfrozen. He was a twelve-year-old, who had apparently made commander only in his last year at the school. So he wasn't cocky, like the ones who made it at eleven. I will remember this, thought Ender, when I am defeated. To keep dignity, and give honor where it's due, so that defeat is not disgrace. And I hope I don't have to do it often.

Anderson dismissed Dragon Army last, after Rabbit Army had straggled through the door that Ender's boys had come through. Then Ender led his army through the enemy's door. The light along the bottom of the door reminded them of which way was down once they got back to gravity. They all landed lightly on their feet, running. They assembled in the corridor. "It's 0715," Ender said, "and that means you have fifteen minutes for breakfast before I see you all in the battleroom for the morning practice." He could hear them silently saying, Come on, we won, let us celebrate. All right, Ender answered, you may. "And you have your commander's permission to throw food at each other during breakfast."

They laughed, they cheered, and then he dismissed them and sent them jogging on to the barracks. He caught his toon leaders on the way out and told them that he wouldn't expect anyone to come to practice till 0745, and that practice would be over early so the boys could shower. Half an hour for breakfast, and no shower after a battle—it was still stingy, but it would look lenient compared to fifteen minutes. And Ender liked having the announcement of the extra fifteen minutes come from the toon leaders. Let the boys learn that leniency comes from their toon leaders, and harshness from their commander—it will bind them better in the small, tight knots of this fabric.

Ender ate no breakfast. He wasn't hungry. Instead he went to the bathroom and showered, putting his flash suit in the cleaner so it would be ready when he was dried off. He washed himself twice and let the water run and run on him. It would all be recycled. Let everybody drink some of my sweat today. They had given him an untrained army, and he had won, and not just nip and tuck, either. He had won with only six frozen or disabled. Let's see how long other commanders keep using their formations now that they've seen what a flexible strategy can do.

He was floating in the middle of the battleroom when his soldiers began to arrive. No one spoke to him, of course. He would speak, they knew, when he was ready, and not before.

When all were there, Ender hooked himself near them and looked at them, one by one. "Good first battle," he said, which was excuse enough for a cheer, and an attempt to start a chant of Dragon, Dragon, which he quickly stopped. "Dragon Army did all right against Rabbits. But the enemy isn't always going to be that bad. If that had been a good army, C toon, your approach was so slow they would have had you from the flanks before you got into good position. You should have split and angled in from two directions, so they couldn't flank you. A and E, your aim was wretched. The tallies show that you averaged only one hit for every two soldiers. That means most of the hits were made by attacking soldiers close in. That can't go on—a competent enemy would cut up the assault force unless they have much better cover from the soldiers at a distance. I want every toon to work on distance marksmanship at moving and unmoving targets. Half-toons take turns being targets. I'll thaw the flash suits every three minutes. Now move."

"Will we have any stars to work with?" asked Hot Soup. "To steady our aim?"

"I don't want you to get used to having something to steady your arms. If your arm isn't steady, freeze your elbows! Now move!"

The toon leaders quickly got things going, and Ender moved from group to group to make suggestions and help soldiers who were having particular trouble. The soldiers knew by now that Ender could be brutal in the way he talked to groups, but when he worked with an individual he was always patient, explaining as often as necessary, making suggestions quietly, listening to questions and problems and explanations. But he never laughed when they tried to banter with him, and they soon stopped trying. He was commander every moment they were together. He never had to remind them of it; he simply *was*.

They worked all day with the taste of victory in their mouths, and cheered again when they broke half an hour early for lunch. Ender held the toon leaders until the regular lunch hour, to talk about the tactics they had used and evaluate the work of their individual soldiers. Then he went to his own room and methodically changed into his uniform for lunch. He would enter the commanders' mess about ten minutes late. Exactly the timing that he wanted. Since this was his first victory, he had never seen the inside of the commanders' mess hall and had no idea what new commanders were expected to do, but he did know that he wanted to enter last today, when the scores of the morning's battles were already posted. Dragon Army will not be an obscure name now.

There was no great stir when he came in. But when some of them noticed how small he was, and saw the dragons on the sleeves of the uniform, they stared at him openly, and by the time he got his food and sat at a table, the room was silent. Ender began to eat, slowly and carefully, pretending not to notice that he was the center of attention. Gradually conversation and noise started up again, and Ender could relax enough to look around.

One entire wall of the room was a scoreboard. Soldiers were kept aware of an army's overall record for the past two years; in here, however, records were kept for each commander. A new commander couldn't inherit a good standing from his predecessor—he was ranked according to what he had done.

Ender had the best ranking. A perfect won-lost record, of course, but in the other categories he was far ahead. Average soldiers-disabled, average enemy-disabled, average time-elapsed-before-victory—in every category he was ranked first.

When he was nearly through eating, someone came up behind him and touched his shoulder.

"Mind if I sit?" Ender didn't have to turn around to know it was Dink Meeker.

"Ho Dink," said Ender. "Sit."

"You gold-plated fart," said Dink cheerfully. "We're all trying to decide whether your scores up there are a miracle or a mistake."

"A habit," said Ender.

"One victory is not a habit," Dink said. "Don't get cocky. When you're new they seed you against weak commanders."

"Carn Carby isn't exactly on the bottom of the rankings." It was true. Carby was just about in the middle.

"He's OK," Dink said, "considering that he only just started. Shows some promise. You don't show promise. You show threat."

"Threat to what? Do they feed you less if I win? I thought you told me this was all a stupid game and none of it mattered."

Dink didn't like having his words thrown back at him, not under these circumstances. "You were the one who got me playing along with them. But I'm not playing games with you, Ender. You won't beat *me.*"

"Probably not," Ender said.

"I taught you," Dink said.

"Everything I know," said Ender. "I'm just playing it by ear right now."

"Congratulations," said Dink.

"It's good to know I have a friend here." But Ender wasn't sure Dink was his friend anymore. Neither was Dink. After a few empty sentences, Dink went back to his table.

Ender looked around when he was through with his meal. There were quite a few small conversations going on. Ender spotted Bonzo, who was now one of the oldest commanders. Rose the Nose had graduated. Petra was with a group in a far corner, and she didn't look at him once. Since most of the others stole glances at him from time to time, including the ones Petra was talking with, Ender was pretty sure she was deliberately avoiding his glance. That's the problem with winning right from the start, thought Ender. You lose friends.

Give them a few weeks to get used to it. By the time I have my next battle, things will have calmed down in here.

Carn Carby made a point of coming to greet Ender before the lunch period ended. It was, again, a gracious gesture, and, unlike Dink, Carby did not seem wary. "Right now I'm in disgrace," he said frankly. "They won't believe me when I tell them you did things that nobody's ever seen before. So I hope you beat the snot out of the next army you fight. As a favor to me."

"As a favor to you," Ender said. "And thanks for talking to me."

"I think they're treating you pretty badly. Usually new commanders are cheered when they first join the mess. But then, usually a new commander has had a few defeats under his belt before he first makes it in here. I only got in here a month ago. If anybody deserves a cheer, it's you. But that's life. Make them eat dust."

"I'll try." Carn Carby left, and Ender mentally added him to his private list of people who also qualified as human beings.

That night, Ender slept better than he had in a long time. Slept so well, in fact, that he didn't wake up until the lights came on. He woke up feeling good, jogged on out to take his shower, and did not notice the piece of paper on his floor until he came back and started dressing in his uniform. He only saw the paper because it moved in the wind as he snapped out the uniform to put it on. He picked up the paper and read it.

PETRA ARKANIAN, PHOENIX ARMY, 0700

It was his old army, the one he had left less than four weeks before, and he knew their formations backward and forward. Partly because of Ender's influence, they were the most flexible of armies, responding relatively quickly to new situations. Phoenix Army would be the best able to cope with Ender's fluid, unpatterned attack. The teachers were determined to make life interesting for him.

0700, said the paper, and it was already 0630. Some of his boys might already be heading for breakfast. Ender tossed his uniform aside, grabbed his flash suit, and in a moment stood in the doorway of his army's barracks.

"Gentlemen, I hope you learned something yesterday, because today we're doing it again."

It took a moment for them to realize that he meant a battle, not a practice. It had to be a mistake, they said. Nobody ever had battles two days in a row.

He handed the paper to Fly Molo, the leader of A toon, who immediately shouted "Flash suits" and started changing clothes.

"Why didn't you tell us earlier?" demanded Hot Soup. Hot had a way of asking Ender questions that nobody else dared ask.

"I thought you needed the shower," Ender said. "Yesterday Rabbit Army claimed we only won because the stink knocked them out."

The soldiers who heard him laughed.

"Didn't find the paper till you got back from the showers, right?"

Ender looked for the source of the voice. It was Bean, already in his flash suit, looking insolent. Time to repay old humiliations, is that it, Bean?

"Of course," Ender said, contemptuously. "I'm not as close to the floor as you are."

More laughter. Bean flushed with anger.

"It's plain we can't count on old ways of doing things," Ender said. "So you'd better plan on battles anytime. And often. I can't pretend I like the way they're screwing around with us, but I do like one thing—that I've got an army that can handle it."

After that, if he had asked them to follow him to the moon without space suits, they would have done it.

Petra was not Carn Carby; she had more flexible patterns and responded much more quickly to Ender's darting, improvised, unpredictable attack. As a result, Ender had three boys flashed and nine disabled at the end of the battle. Petra was not gracious about bowing over his hand at the end, either. The anger in her eyes seemed to say, I was your friend, and you humiliate me like this?

Ender pretended not to notice her fury. He figured that after a few more battles, she'd realize that in fact she had scored more hits against him than he expected anyone ever would again. And he was still learning from her. In practice today he would teach his toon leaders how to counter the tricks Petra had played on them. Soon they would be friends again.

He hoped.

At the end of the week Dragon Army had fought seven battles in seven days. The score stood 7 wins and 0 losses. Ender had never had more losses than in the battle with Phoenix Army, and in two battles he had suffered not one soldier frozen or disabled. No one believed anymore that it was a fluke that put him first in the standings. He had beaten top armies by unheard-of margins. It was no longer possible for the other commanders to ignore him. A few of them sat with him at every meal, carefully trying to learn from him how he had defeated his most recent opponents. He told them freely, confident that few of them would know how to train their soldiers and their toon leaders to duplicate what his could do. And while Ender talked wtih a few commanders, much larger groups gathered around the opponents Ender had defeated, trying to find out how Ender might be beaten.

There were many, too, who hated him. Hated him for being young, for being excellent, for having made their victories look paltry and weak. Ender saw it first in their faces when he passed them in the corridors; then he began to notice that some boys would get up in a group and move to another table if he sat near them in the commanders' mess; and there began to be elbows that accidently jostled him in the game room, feet that got entangled with his when he walked into and out of the gym, spittle and wads of wet paper that struck him from behind as he jogged through the corridors. They couldn't beat him in the battleroom, and knew it—so instead they would attack him where it was safe, where he was not a giant but just a little boy. Ender despised them, but secretly, so secretly that he didn't even know it himself, he feared them. It was just such little torments that Peter had always used, and Ender was beginning to feel far too much at home.

These annoyances were petty, though, and Ender persuaded himself to accept them as another form of praise. Already the other armies were beginning to imitate Ender. Now most soldiers attacked with knees tucked under them; formations were breaking up now, and more commanders were sending out toons to slip along the walls. None had caught on yet to Ender's five-toon organization—it gave him the slight advantage that when they had accounted for the movements of four units, they wouldn't be looking for a fifth.

Ender was teaching them all about null gravity tactics. But where could Ender go to learn new things?

He began to use the video room, filled with propaganda vids about Mazer Rackham and other great commanders of the forces of humanity in the First and Second Invasion. Ender stopped the general practice an hour early, and allowed his toon leaders to conduct their own practice in his absence. Usually they staged skirmishes, toon against toon. Ender stayed long enough to see that things were going well, then left to watch the old battles.

Most of the vids were a waste of time. Heroic music, closeups of commanders and medal-winning soldiers, confused shots of marines invading bugger installations. But here and there he found useful sequences: ships, like points of light, maneuvering in the dark of space, or, better still, the lights on shipboard plotting screens, showing the whole of a battle. It was hard, from the videos, to see all three dimensions, and the scenes were often short and unexplained. But Ender began to see how well the buggers used seemingly random flight paths to create confusion, how they used decoys and false retreats to draw the I.F. ships into traps. Some battles had been cut into many scenes, which were scattered through the various videos; by watching them in sequence, Ender was able to reconstruct whole battles. He began to see things that the official commentators never mentioned. They were always trying to arouse pride in human accomplishments and loathing of the buggers, but Ender began to wonder how humanity had won at all. Human ships were sluggish; fleets responded to new circumstances unbearably slowly, while the bugger fleet seemed to act in perfect unity, responding to each challenge instantly. Of course, in the First Invasion the human ships were completely unsuited to fast combat, but then so were the bugger ships; it was only in the Second Invasion that the ships and weapons were swift and deadly.

So it was from the buggers, not the humans, that Ender learned strategy. He felt ashamed and afraid of learning from them, since they were the most terrible enemy, ugly and murderous and loathsome. But they were also very good at what they did. To a point. They always seemed to follow one basic strategy only—gather the greatest number of ships at the key point of conflict. They never did anything surprising, anything that seemed to show either brilliance or stupidity in a subordinate officer. Discipline was apparently very tight.

And there was one oddity. There was plenty of talk about Mazer Rackham but precious little video of his actual battle. Some scenes from early in the battle, Rackham's tiny force looking pathetic against the vast power of the main bugger fleet. The buggers had already beaten the main human fleet out in the comet shield, wiping out the earliest starships and making a mockery of human attempts at high strategy—that film was often shown, to arouse again and again the agony and terror of bugger victory. Then the fleet coming to Mazer Rackham's little force near Saturn, the hopeless odds, and then—

Then one shot from Mazer Rackham's little cruiser, one enemy ship blowing up. That's all that was ever shown. Lots of film showing marines carving their way into bugger ships. Lots of bugger corpses lying around inside. But no film of buggers killing in personal combat, unless it was spliced in from the First Invasion. It frustrated Ender that Mazer Rackham's victory was so obviously censored. Students in the Battle School had much to learn from Mazer Rackham, and everything about his victory was concealed from view. The passion for secrecy was not very helpful to the children who had to learn to accomplish again what Mazer Rackham had done.

Of course, as soon as word got around that Ender Wiggin was watching the war vids over and over again, the video room began to draw a crowd. Almost all were commanders, watching the same vids Ender watched, pretending they understood why he was watching and what he was getting out of it. Ender never explained anything. Even when he showed seven scenes from the same battle, but from different vids, only one boy asked, tentatively, "Are some of those from the same battle?"

Ender only shrugged, as if it didn't matter.

It was during the last hour of practice on the seventh day, only a few hours after Ender's army had won its seventh battle, that Major Anderson himself came into the video room. He handed a slip of paper to one of the commanders sitting there, and then spoke to Ender. "Colonel Graff wishes to see you in his office immediately."

Ender got up and followed Anderson through the corridors. Anderson palmed the locks that kept students out of the officers' quarters; finally they came to where Graff had taken root on a swivel chair bolted to the steel floor. His belly spilled over both armrests now, even when he sat upright. Ender tried to remember. Graff hadn't seemed particularly fat at all when Ender first met him, only four years ago. Time and tension were not being kind to the administrator of the Battle School.

"Seven days since your first battle, Ender," said Graff.

Ender did not reply.

"And you've won seven battles, once a day."

Ender nodded.

"Your scores are unusually high, too."

Ender blinked.

"To what, commander, do you attribute your remarkable success?"

"You gave me an army that does whatever I can think for it to do."

"And what have you thought for it to do?"

"We orient downward toward the enemy gate and use our lower legs as a shield. We avoid formations and keep our mobility. It helps that I've got five toons of eight instead of four of ten. Also, our enemies haven't had time to respond effectively to our new techniques, so we keep beating them with the same tricks. That won't hold up for long."

"So you don't expect to keep winning."

"Not with the same tricks."

Graff nodded. "Sit down, Ender."

Ender and Anderson both sat. Graff looked at Anderson, and Anderson spoke next. "What condition is your army in, fighting so often?"

"They're all veterans now."

"But how are they doing? Are they tired?"

"If they are, they won't admit it."

"Are they still alert?"

"You're the ones with the computer games that play with people's minds. You tell *me.*"

"We know what *we* know. We want to know what *you* know."

"These are very good soldiers, Major Anderson. I'm sure they have limits, but we haven't reached them yet. Some of the newer ones are having trouble because they never really mastered some basic techniques, but they're working hard and improving. What do you want me to say, that they need to rest? Of course they need to rest. They need a couple of weeks off. Their studies are shot to hell, none of us are doing any good in our classes. But you know that, and apparently you don't care, so why should I?"

Graff and Anderson exchanged glances. "Ender, why are you studying the videos of the bugger wars?"

"To learn strategy, of course."

"Those videos were created for propaganda purposes. All our strategies have been edited out."

"I know."

Graff and Anderson exchanged glances again. Graff drummed on his table. "You don't play the fantasy game anymore," he said.

Ender didn't answer.

"Tell me why you don't play it."

"Because I won."

"You never win *everything* in that game. There's always more."

"I won everything."

"Ender, we want to help you be as happy as possible, but if you—"

"You want to make me the best soldier possible. Go down and look at the standings. Look at the all-time standings. So far you're doing an excellent job with me. Congratulations. Now when are you going to put me up against a good army?"

Graff's set lips turned to a smile, and he shook a little with silent laughter.

Anderson handed Ender a slip of paper. "Now," he said.

BONZO MADRID, SALAMANDER ARMY, 1200

"That's ten minutes from now," said Ender. "My army will be in the middle of showering up after practice."

Graff smiled. "Better hurry, then, boy."

He got to his army's barracks five minutes later. Most were dressing after their showers; some had already gone to the game room or the video room to wait for lunch. He sent three younger boys to call everyone in, and made everyone else dress for battle as quickly as they could.

"This one's hot and there's no time," Ender said. "They gave Bonzo notice about twenty minutes ago, and by the time we get to the door they'll have been inside for a good five minutes at least."

The boys were outraged, complaining loudly in the slang that they usually avoided around the commander. What they doing to us? They be crazy, neh?

"Forget why, we'll worry about that tonight. Are you tired?"

Fly Molo answered. "We worked our butts off in practice today. Not to mention beating the crap out of Ferret Army this morning."

"Same day nobody ever do two battles!" said Crazy Tom.

Ender answered in the same tone. "Nobody ever beat Dragon Army, either. This be your big chance to lose?" Ender's taunting question was the answer to their complaints. Win first, ask questions later.

All of them were back in the room, and most of them were dressed. "Move!" shouted Ender, and they ran along behind him, some of them still dressing when they reached the corridor outside the battleroom. Many of them were panting, a bad sign; they were too tired for this battle. The door was already open. There were no stars at all. Just empty, empty space in a dazzlingly bright room. Nowhere to hide, not even in darkness.

"My heart," said Crazy Tom, "they haven't come out yet, either."

Ender put his hand across his own mouth, to tell them to be silent. With the door open, of course the enemy could hear every word they said. Ender pointed all around the door, to tell them that Salamander Army was undoubtedly deployed against the wall all around the door, where they couldn't be seen but could easily flash anyone who came out.

Ender motioned for them all to back away from the door. Then he pulled forward a few of the taller boys, including Crazy Tom, and made them kneel, not squatting back to sit on their heels, but fully upright, so they formed an L with their bodies. He flashed them. In silence the army watched him. He selected the smallest boy, Bean, handed him Tom's gun, and made Bean kneel on Tom's frozen legs. Then pulled Bean's hands, each holding a gun, through Tom's armpits.

Now the boys understood. Tom was a shield, an armored space-craft, and Bean was hiding inside. He was certainly not invulnerable, but he would have time.

Ender assigned two more boys to throw Tom and Bean through the door, but signalled them to wait. He went on through the army, quickly assigning groups of four—a shield, a shooter, and two throw-ers. Then, when all were frozen or armed or ready to throw, he signalled the throwers to pick up their burdens, throw them through the door, and then jump through themselves.

"Move!" shouted Ender.

They moved. Two at a time the shield-pairs went through the door, backward so that the shield would be between the shooter and the enemy. The enemy opened fire at once, but they mostly hit the frozen boy in front. In the meantime, with two guns to work with and their targets neatly lined up and spread flat along the wall, the Dragons had an easy time of it. It was almost impossible to miss. And as the throwers also jumped through the door, they got hand-holds on the same wall with the enemy, shooting at a deadly angle so that the Salamanders couldn't figure out whether to shoot at the shield-pairs slaughtering them from above or the throwers shooting at them from their own level. By the time Ender himself came through the door, the battle was over. It hadn't taken a full minute from the time the first Dragon passed through the door until the shooting stopped. Dragon had lost twenty frozen or disabled, and only twelve boys were undamaged. It was their worst score yet, but they had won.

When Major Anderson came out and gave Ender the hook, Ender could not contain his anger. "I thought you were going to put us against an army that could match us in a fair fight."

"Congratulations on the victory, commander."

"Bean!" shouted Ender. "If you had commanded Salamander Army, what would you have done?"

Bean, disabled but not completely frozen, called out from where he drifted near the enemy door. "Keep a shifting pattern of move-ment going in front of the door. You never hold still when the enemy knows exactly where you are."

"As long as you're cheating," Ender said to Anderson, "why don't you train the other army to cheat intelligently!"

"I suggest that you remobilize your army," said Anderson.

Ender pressed the buttons to thaw both armies at once. "Dragon Army dismissed!" he shouted immediately. There would be no elaborate formation to accept the surrender of the other army. This had not been a fair fight, even though they had won—the teachers had meant them to lose, and it was only Bonzo's ineptitude that had saved them. There was no glory in *that.*

Only as Ender himself was leaving the battleroom did he realize that Bonzo would not realize that Ender was angry at the teachers. Spanish honor. Bonzo would only know that he had been defeated even when the odds were stacked in his favor; that Ender had had the youngest child in his army publicly state what Bonzo should have done to win; and that Ender had not even stayed to receive Bonzo's dignified surrender. If Bonzo had not already hated Ender, he would surely have begun; and hating him as he did, this would surely turn his rage murderous. Bonzo was the last person to strike me, thought Ender. I'm sure he has not forgotten that.

Nor had he forgotten the bloody affair in the battleroom when the older boys tried to break up Ender's practice session. Nor had many others. They were hungry for blood then; Bonzo will be thirsting for it now. Ender toyed with the idea of going back to take advanced personal defense; but with battles now possible not only every day, but twice in the same day, Ender knew he could not spare the time. I'll have to take my chances. The teachers got me into this —they can keep me safe.

Bean flopped down on his bunk in utter exhaustion—half the boys in the barracks were already asleep, and it was still fifteen minutes before lights out. Wearily he pulled his desk from its locker and signed on. There was a test tomorrow in geometry and Bean was woefully unprepared. He could always reason things out if he had enough time, and he had read Euclid when he was five, but the test had a time limit so there wouldn't be a chance to think. He had to know. And he didn't know. And he would probably do badly on the test. But they had won twice today, and so he felt good.

As soon as he signed on, however, all thoughts of geometry were banished. A message paraded around the desk:

SEE ME AT ONCE -ENDER

The time was 2150, only ten minutes before lights out. How long ago had Ender sent it? Still, he'd better not ignore it. There might be another battle in the morning—the thought made him weary—and whatever Ender wanted to talk to him about, there wouldn't be time then. So Bean rolled off the bunk and walked emptily through the corridor to Ender's room. He knocked.

"Come in," said Ender.

"Just saw your message."

"Fine," said Ender.

"It's near lights out."

"I'll help you find your way in the dark."

"I just didn't know if you knew what time it was—"

"I always know what time it is."

Bean sighed inwardly. It never failed. Whenever he had any conversation with Ender, it turned into an argument. Bean hated it. He recognized Ender's genius and honored him for it. Why couldn't Ender ever see anything good in him?"

"Remember four weeks ago, Bean? When you told me to make you a toon leader?"

"Eh."

"I've made five toon leaders and five assistants since then. And none of them was you." Ender raised his eyebrows. "Was I right?"

"Yes, sir."

"So tell me how you've done in these eight battles."

"Today was the first time they disabled me, but the computer listed me as getting eleven hits before I had to stop. I've never had less than five hits in a battle. I've also completed every assignment I've been given."

"Why did they make you a soldier so young, Bean?"

"No younger than you were."

"But why?"

"I don't know."

"Yes you do, and so do I."

"I've tried to guess, but they're just guesses. You're—very good. They kenw that, they pushed you ahead—"

"Tell me *why*, Bean."

"Because they need us, that's why." Bean sat down on the floor and stared at Ender's feet. "Because they need somebody to beat the buggers. That's the only thing they care about."

"It's important that you know that, Bean. Because most boys in this school think the game is important *for itself,* but it isn't. It's only important because it helps them find kids who might grow up to be real commanders, in the real war. But as for the game, screw that. That's what they're doing. Screwing up the game."

"Funny. I thought they were just doing it to us."

"A game nine weeks earlier than it should have come. A game every day. And now two games in the same day. Bean, I don't know what the teachers are doing, but my army is getting tired, and I'm getting tired, and they don't care at all about the rules of the game. I've pulled the old charts up from the computer. No one has ever destroyed so many enemies and kept so many of his own soldiers whole in the history of the game."

"You're the best, Ender."

Ender shook his head. "Maybe. But it was no accident that I got the soldiers I got. Launchies, rejects from other armies, but put them together and my worst soldier could be a toon leader in another army. They've loaded things my way, but now they're loading it all against me. Bean, they want to break us down."

"They can't break you."

"You'd be surprised." Ender breathed sharply, suddenly, as if there were a stab of pain, or he had to catch a sudden breath in a wind; Bean looked at him and realized that the impossible was happening. Far from baiting him, Ender Wiggin was actually confiding in him. Not much. But a little. Ender was human and Bean had been allowed to see.

"Maybe you'll be surprised," said Bean.

"There's a limit to how many clever new ideas I can come up with every day. Somebody's going to come up with something to throw at me that I haven't thought of before, and I won't be ready."

"What's the worst that could happen? You lose one game."

"Yes. That's the worst that could happen. I can't lose *any* games. Because if I lose *any—*"

He didn't explain himself, and Bean didn't ask.

"I need you to be clever, Bean. I need you to think of solutions to problems we haven't seen yet. I want you to try things that no one has ever tried because they're absolutely stupid."

"Why me?"

"Because even though there are some better soldiers than you in

Dragon Army—not many, but some—there's nobody who can think better and faster than you." Bean said nothing. They both knew it was true.

Ender showed him his desk. On it were twelve names. Two or three from each toon. "Choose five of these," said Ender. "One from each toon. They're a special squad, and you'll train them. Only during the extra practice sessions. Talk to me about what you're training them to do. Don't spend too long on any one thing. Most of the time you and your squad will be part of the whole army, part of your regular toons. But when I need you. When there's something to be done that only you can do."

"These are all new," said Bean. "No veterans."

"After last week, Bean, all our soldiers are veterans. Don't you realize that on the individual soldier standings, all forty of our soldiers are in the top fifty? That you have to go down seventeen places to find a soldier who *isn't* a Dragon?"

"What if I can't think of anything?"

"Then I was wrong about you."

Bean grinned. "You weren't wrong."

The lights went out.

"Can you find your way back, Bean?"

"Probably not."

"Then stay here. If you listen very carefully, you can hear the good fairy come in the night and leave our assignment for tomorrow."

"They won't give us another battle tomorrow, will they?"

Ender didn't answer. Bean heard him climb into bed. He got up from the floor and did likewise. He thought of a half dozen ideas before he went to sleep. Ender would be pleased—every one of them was stupid.

Chapter 12

Bonzo

"General Pace, please sit down. I understand you have come to me about a matter of some urgency."

"Ordinarily, Colonel Graff, I would not presume to interfere in the internal workings of the Battle School. Your autonomy is guaranteed, and despite our difference in ranks I am quite aware that it is my authority only to advise, not to order you to take action."

"Action?"

"Do not be disingenuous with me, Colonel Graff. Americans are quite apt at playing stupid when they choose to, but I am not to be deceived. You know why I am here."

"Ah. I guess this means Dap filed a report."

"He feels—paternal toward the students here. He feels your neglect of a potentially lethal situation is more than negligence— that it borders on conspiracy to cause the death or serious injury of one of the students here."

"This is a school for children, General Pace. Hardly a matter to bring the chief of I.F. military police here for."

"Colonel Graff, the name of Ender Wiggin has percolated through the high command. It has even reached my ears. I have heard him described modestly as our only hope of victory in the upcoming invasion. When it is his life or health that is in danger, I do not think it untoward that the military police take some interest in preserving and protecting the boy. Do you?"

"Damn Dap and damn you too, sir, I know what I'm doing."

"Do you?"

"Better than anyone else."

"Oh, that is obvious, since nobody else has the faintest idea what you're doing. You have known for eight days that there is a conspiracy among some of the more vicious of these 'children' to cause the beating of Ender Wiggin, if they can. And that some members of this conspiracy, notably the boy named Bonito de Madrid, commonly called Bonzo, are quite likely to exhibit no self-restraint when this punishment takes place, so that Ender Wiggin, an inestimably important international resource, will be placed in serious danger of having his brains pasted on the walls of your simple orbiting schoolhouse. And you, fully warned of this danger, propose to do exactly—"

"Nothing."

"You can see how this excites our puzzlement."

"Ender Wiggin has been in this situation before. Back on Earth, the day he lost his monitor, and again when a large group of older boys—"

"I did not come here ignorant of the past. Ender Wiggin has provoked Bonzo Madrid beyond human endurance. And you have no military police standing by to break up disturbances. It is unconscionable."

"When Ender Wiggin holds our fleets in his control, when he must make the decisions that bring us victory or destruction, will there be military police to come save him if things get out of hand?"

"I fail to see the connection."

"Obviously. But the connection is there. Ender Wiggin must believe that no matter what happens, no adult will ever, ever step in to help him in any way. He must believe, to the core of his soul, that he can only do what he and the other children work out for themselves. If he does not believe that, then he will never reach the peak of his abilities."

"He will also not reach the peak of his abilities if he is dead or permanently crippled."

"He won't be."

"Why don't you simply graduate Bonzo? He's old enough."

"Because Ender knows that Bonzo plans to kill him. If we transfer Bonzo ahead of schedule, he'll know that we saved him. Heaven knows Bonzo isn't a good enough commander to be promoted on merit."

"What about the other children? Getting them to help him?"

"We'll see what happens. That is my first, final, and only decision."

"God help you if you're wrong."

"God help us all if I'm wrong."

"I'll have you before a capital court martial. I'll have your name disgraced throughout the world if you're wrong."

"Fair enough. But do remember, if I happen to be right, to make sure I get a few dozen medals."

"For what!"

"For keeping you from meddling."

Ender sat in a corner of the battleroom, his arm hooked through a handhold, watching Bean practice with his squad. Yesterday they had worked on attacks without guns, disarming enemies with their feet. Ender had helped them with some techniques from gravity personal combat—many things had to be changed, but inertia in flight was a tool that could be used against the enemy as easily in nullo as in Earth gravity.

Today, though, Bean had a new toy. It was a deadline, one of the thin, almost invisible twines used during construction in space to hold two objects together. Deadlines were sometimes kilometers long. This one was just a bit longer than a wall of the battleroom, and yet it looped easily, almost invisibly, around Bean's waist. He pulled it off like an article of clothing and handed one end to one of his soldiers. "Hook it to a handhold and wind it around a few times." Bean carried the other end across the battleroom.

As a tripwire it wasn't too useful, Bean decided. It was invisible enough, but one strand of twine wouldn't have much chance of stopping an enemy that could easily go above or below it. Then he got the idea of using it to change his direction of movement in midair. He fastened it around his waist, the other end still fastened to a handhold, slipped a few meters away, and launched himself straight out. The twine caught him, changed his direction abruptly, and swung him in an arc that crashed him brutally against the wall.

He screamed and screamed. It took Ender a moment to realize that he wasn't screaming in pain. "Did you see how fast I went! Did you see how I changed direction!"

Soon all of Dragon Army stopped work to watch Bean practice

with the twine. The changes in direction were stunning, especially when you didn't know where to look for the twine. When he used the twine to wrap himself around a star, he attained speeds no one had ever seen before.

It was 2140 when Ender dismissed the evening practice. Weary but delighted at having seen something new, his army walked through the corridors back to the barracks. Ender walked among them, not talking, but listening to their talk. They were tired, yes—a battle every day for more than four weeks, often in situations that tested their abilities to the utmost. But they were proud, happy, close —they had never lost, and they had learned to trust each other. Trust their fellow soldiers to fight hard and well; trust their leaders to use them rather than waste their efforts; above all trust Ender to prepare them for anything and everything that might happen.

As they walked the corridor, Ender noticed several older boys seemingly engaged in conversations in branching corridors and ladderways; some were in their corridor, walking slowly in the other direction. It became too much of a coincidence, however, that so many of them were wearing Salamander uniforms, and that those who weren't were often older boys belonging to armies whose commanders most hated Ender Wiggin. A few of them looked at him, and looked away too quickly; others were too tense, too nervous as they pretended to be relaxed. What will I do if they attack my army here in the corridor? My boys are all young, all small, and completely untrained in gravity combat. When would they learn?

"Ho, Ender!" someone called. Ender stopped and looked back. It was Petra. "Ender, can I talk to you."

Ender saw in a moment that if he stopped and talked, his army would quickly pass him by and he would be alone with Petra in the hallway. "Walk with me," Ender said.

"It's just for a moment."

Ender turned around and walked on with his army. He heard Petra running to catch up. "All right, I'll walk with you." Ender tensed when she came near. Was she one of them, one of the ones who hated him enough to hurt him?

"A friend of yours wanted me to warn you. There are some boys who want to kill you."

"Surprise," said Ender. Some of his soldiers seemed to perk up at this. Plots against their commander were interesting news, it seemed.

"Ender, they can do it. He said they've been planning it ever since you went commander—"

"Ever since I beat Salamander, you mean."

"I hated you after you beat Phoenix Army, too, Ender."

"I didn't say I blamed anybody."

"It's true. He told me to take you aside today and warn you, on the way back from the battleroom, to be careful tomorrow because—"

"Petra, if you had actually taken me aside just now, there are about a dozen boys following along who would have taken me in the corridor. Can you tell me you didn't notice them?"

Suddenly her face flushed. "No, I didn't. How can you think I did? Don't you know who your friends are?" She pushed her way through Dragon Army, got ahead of him, and scrambled up a ladderway to a higher deck.

"Is it true?" asked Crazy Tom.

"Is what true?" Ender scanned the room and shouted for two roughhousing boys to get to bed.

"That some of the older boys want to kill you?"

"All talk," said Ender. But he knew that it wasn't. Petra had known something, and what he saw on the way here tonight wasn't imagination.

"It may be all talk, but I hope you'll understand when I say you've got five toon leaders who are going to escort you to your room tonight."

"Completely unnecessary."

"Humor us. You owe us a favor."

"I owe you nothing." He'd be a fool to turn them down. "Do as you want." He turned and left. The toon leaders trotted along with him. One ran ahead and opened his door. They checked the room, made Ender promise to lock it, and left him just before lights out.

There was a message on his desk.

DON'T BE ALONE. EVER. -DINK

Ender grinned. So Dink was still his friend. Don't worry. They won't do anything to me. I have my army.

But in the darkness he did not have his army. He dreamed that night of Stilson, only he saw now how small Stilson was, only six years old, how ridiculous his tough-guy posturing was; and yet in the dream Stilson and his friends tied Ender so he couldn't fight back, and then everything that Ender had done to Stilson in life, they did to Ender in the dream. And afterward Ender saw himself babbling like an idiot, trying hard to give orders to his army, but all his words came out as nonsense.

He awoke in darkness, and he was afraid. Then he calmed himself by remembering that the teachers obviously valued him, or they wouldn't be putting so much pressure on him; they wouldn't let anything happen to him, nothing bad, anyway. Probably when the older kids attacked him in the battleroom years ago, there were teachers just outside the room, waiting to see what would happen; if things had got out of hand, they would have stepped in and stopped it. I probably could have sat there and done nothing, and they would have seen to it I came through all right. They'll push me as hard as they can in the game, but outside the game they'll keep me safe.

With that assurance, he slept again, until the door opened softly and the morning's war was left on the floor for him to find.

They won, of course, but it was a grueling affair, with the battleroom so filled with a labyrinth of stars that hunting down the enemy during mop-up took forty-five minutes. It was Pol Slattery's Badger Army, and they refused to give up. There was a new wrinkle in the game, too—when they disabled or damaged an enemy, he thawed in about five minutes, the way it worked in practice. Only when the enemy was completely frozen did he stay out of action the whole time. But the gradual thawing did not work for Dragon Army. Crazy Tom was the one who realized what was happening, when they started getting hit from behind by people they thought were safely out of the way. And at the end of the battle, Slattery shook Ender's hand and said, "I'm glad you won. If I ever beat you, Ender, I want to do it fair."

"Use what they give you," Ender said. "If you've ever got an advantage over the enemy, use it."

"Oh, I did," said Slattery. He grinned. "I'm only fair-minded before and after battles."

The battle took so long that breakfast was over. Ender looked at his hot, sweating, tired soldiers waiting in the corridor and said, "Today you know everything. No practice. Get some rest. Have some fun. Pass a test." It was a measure of their weariness that they didn't even cheer or laugh or smile, just walked into the barracks and stripped off their clothes. They would have practiced if he had asked them to, but they were reaching the end of their strength, and going without breakfast was one unfairness too many.

Ender meant to shower right away, but he was also tired. He lay down on his bed in his flash suit, just for a moment, and woke up at the beginning of lunchtime. So much for his idea of studying more about the buggers this morning. Just time to clean up, go eat, and head for class.

He peeled off his flash suit, which stank from his sweat. His body felt cold, his joints oddly weak. Shouldn't have slept in the middle of the day. I'm beginning to slack off. I'm beginning to wear down. Can't let it get to me.

So he jogged to the gym and forced himself to climb the rope three times before going to the bathroom to shower. It didn't occur to him that his absence in the commanders' mess would be noticed, that showering during the noon hour, when his own army would be wolfing down their first meal of the day, he would be completely, helplessly alone.

Even when he heard them come into the bathroom he paid no attention. He was letting the water pour over his head, over his body; the muffled sound of footsteps was hardly noticeable. Maybe lunch was over, he thought. He started to soap himself again. Maybe somebody finished practice late.

And maybe not. He turned around. There were seven of them, leaning back against the metal sinks or standing closer to the showers, watching him. Bonzo stood in front of them. Many were smiling, the condescending leer of the hunter for his cornered victim. Bonzo was not smiling, however.

"Ho," Ender said.

Nobody answered.

So Ender turned off the shower, even though there was still soap on him, and reached for his towel. It wasn't there. One of the boys was holding it. It was Bernard. All it would take for the picture to be complete was for Stilson and Peter to be there, too. They needed Peter's smile; they needed Stilson's obvious stupidity.

Ender recognized the towel as their opening point. Nothing would make him look weaker than to chase naked after the towel. That was what they wanted, to humiliate him, to break him down. He wasn't going to play. He refused to feel weak because he was wet and cold and unclothed. He stood strongly, facing them, his arms at his sides. He fastened his gaze on Bonzo.

"Your move," Ender said.

"This is no game," said Bernard. "We're tired of you, Ender. You graduate today. On ice."

Ender did not look at Bernard. It was Bonzo who hungered for his death, even though he was silent. The others were along for the ride, daring themselves to see how far they might go. Bonzo knew how far he would go.

"Bonzo," Ender said softly. "Your father would be proud of you."

Bonzo stiffened.

"He would love to see you now, come to fight a naked boy in a shower, smaller than you, and you brought six friends. He would say, Oh, what honor."

"Nobody came to fight you," said Bernard. "We just came to talk you into playing fair with the games. Maybe lose a couple now and then."

The others laughed, but Bonzo didn't laugh, and neither did Ender.

"Be proud, Bonito, pretty boy. You can go home and tell your father, Yes, I beat up Ender Wiggin, who was barely ten years old, and I was thirteen. And I had only six of my friends to help me, and somehow we managed to defeat him, even though he was naked and wet and alone—Ender Wiggin is so *dangerous* and *terrifying* it was all we could do not to bring two hundred."

"Shut your mouth, Wiggin," said one of the boys.

"We didn't come to hear the little bastard talk," said another.

"You shut up," said Bonzo. "Shut up and stand out of the way." He began to take off his uniform. "Naked and wet and alone, Ender, so we're even. I can't help that I'm bigger than you. You're such a genius, you figure out how to handle me." He turned to the others. "Watch the door. Don't let anyone else in."

The bathroom wasn't large, and plumbing fixtures protruded everywhere. It had been launched in one piece, as a low-orbit satellite, packed full of the water reclamation equipment; it was designed to have no wasted space. It was obvious what their tactics would have to be. Throw the other boy against fixtures until one of them does enough damage that he stops.

When Ender saw Bonzo's stance, his heart sank. Bonzo had also taken classes. And probably more recently than Ender. His reach was better, he was stronger, and he was full of hate. He would not be gentle. He will go for my head, thought Ender. He will try above all to damage my brain. And if this fight is long, he's bound to win. His strength can control me. If I'm to walk away from here, I have to win quickly, and permanently. He could feel again the sickening way that Stilson's bones had given way. But this time it will be my body that breaks, unless I can break him first.

Ender stepped back, flipped the showerhead so it turned outward, and turned on pure hot water. Almost at once the steam began to rise. He turned on the next, and the next.

"I'm not afraid of hot water," said Bonzo. His voice was soft.

But it wasn't the hot water that Ender wanted. It was the heat. His body still had soap on it, and his sweat moistened it, made his skin more slippery than Bonzo would expect.

Suddenly there was a voice from the door. "Stop it!" For a moment Ender thought it was a teacher, come to stop the fight, but it was only Dink Meeker. Bonzo's friends caught him at the door, held him. "Stop it, Bonzo!" Dink cried. "Don't hurt him!"

"Why not?" asked Bonzo, and for the first time he smiled. Ah, thought Ender, he loves to have someone recognize that he is the one in control, that he has power.

"Because he's the best, that's why! Who else can fight the buggers! That's what matters, you fool, the buggers!"

Bonzo stopped smiling. It was the thing he hated most about Ender, that Ender really mattered to other people, and in the end, Bonzo did not. You've killed me with those words, Dink. Bonzo doesn't want to hear that I might save the world.

Where are the teachers? thought Ender. Don't they realize that the first contact between us in this fight might be the end of it? This isn't like the fight in the battleroom, where no one had the leverage to do any terrible damage. There's gravity in here, and the floor and walls are hard and jutted with metal. Stop this now or not at all.

"If you touch him you're a buggerlover!" cried Dink. "You're a traitor, if you touch him you deserve to die!" They jammed Dink's face backward into the door and he was silent.

The mist from the showers dimmed the room, and the sweat was streaming down Ender's body. Now, before the soap is carried off me. Now, while I'm still too slippery to hold.

Ender stepped back, letting the fear he felt show in his face. "Bonzo, don't hurt me," he said. "Please."

It was what Bonzo was waiting for, the confession that he was in power. For other boys it might have been enough that Ender had submitted; for Bonzo, it was only a sign that his victory was sure. He swung his leg as if to kick, but changed it to a leap at the last moment. Ender noticed the shifting weight and stooped lower, so that Bonzo would be more off-balance when he tried to grab Ender and throw him.

Bonzo's tight, hard ribs came against Ender's face, and his hands slapped against his back, trying to grip him. But Ender twisted, and Bonzo's hands slipped. In an instant Ender was completely turned, yet still inside Bonzo's grasp. The classic move at this moment would be to bring up his heel into Bonzo's crotch. But for that move to be effective required too much accuracy, and Bonzo expected it. He was already rising onto his toes, thrusting his hips backward to keep Ender from reaching his groin. Without seeing him, Ender knew it would bring his face closer, almost in Ender's hair; so instead of kicking, he lunged upward off the floor, with the powerful lunge of the soldier bounding from the wall, and jammed his head into Bonzo's face.

Ender whirled in time to see Bonzo stagger backward, his nose bleeding, gasping from surprise and pain. Ender knew that at this moment he might be able to walk out of the room and end the battle. The way he had escaped from the battleroom after drawing blood. But the battle would only be fought again. Again and again until the will to fight was finished. The only way to end things completely was to hurt Bonzo enough that his fear was stronger than his hate.

So Ender leaned back against the wall behind him, then jumped up and pushed off with his arms. His feet landed in Bonzo's belly and chest. Ender spun in the air and landed on his toes and hands; he flipped over, scooted under Bonzo, and this time when he kicked upward into Bonzo's crotch, he connected, hard and sure.

Bonzo did not cry out in pain. He did not react at all, except that his body rose a little in the air. It was as if Ender had kicked a piece of furniture. Bonzo collapsed, fell to the side, and sprawled directly under the spray of steaming water from a shower. He made no movement whatever to escape the murderous heat.

"My God!" someone shouted. Bonzo's friends leaped to turn off the water. Ender slowly rose to his feet. Someone thrust his towel at him. It was Dink. "Come on out of here," Dink said. He led Ender away. Behind them they heard the heavy clatter of adults running down a ladderway. Now the teachers would come. The medical staff. To dress the wounds of Ender's enemy. Where were they before the fight, when there might have been no wounds at all?

There was no doubt now in Ender's mind. There was no help for him. Whatever he faced, now and forever, no one would save him from it. Peter might be scum, but Peter had been right, always right; the power to cause pain is the only power that matters, the power to kill and destroy, because if you can't kill then you are always subject to those who can, and nothing and no one will ever save you.

Dink led him to his room, made him lie on the bed. "Are you hurt anywhere?" he asked.

Ender shook his head.

"You took him apart. I thought you were dead meat, the way he grabbed you. But you took him apart. If he'd stood up longer, you would've killed him."

"He meant to kill me."

"I know it. I know him. Nobody hates like Bonzo. But not anymore. If they don't ice him for this and send him home, he'll never look you in the eye again. You or anybody. He had twenty centimeters on you, and you made him look like a crippled cow standing there chewing her cud."

All Ender could see, though, was the way Bonzo looked as Ender kicked upward into his groin. The empty, dead look in his eyes. He was already finished then. Already unconscious. His eyes were open, but he wasn't thinking or moving anymore, just that dead, stupid look on his face, that terrible look, the way Stilson looked when I finished with him.

"They'll ice him, though," Dink said. "Everybody knows he started it. I saw them get up and leave the commanders' mess. Took me a couple of seconds to realize you weren't there, either, and then a minute more to find out where you had gone. I told you not to be alone."

"Sorry."

"They're bound to ice him. Troublemaker. Him and his stinking honor."

Then, to Dink's surprise, Ender began to cry. Lying on his back, still soaking wet with sweat and water, he gasped his sobs, tears seeping out of his closed eyelids and disappearing in the water on his face.

"Are you all right?"

"I didn't want to hurt him!" Ender cried. "Why didn't he just leave me alone!"

He heard his door open softly, then close. He knew at once that it was his battle instructions. He opened his eyes, expecting to find the darkness of early morning, before 0600. Instead, the lights were on. He was naked, and when he moved the bed was soaking wet. His eyes were puffy and painful from crying. He looked at the clock on his desk. 1820, it said. It's the same day. I already had a battle today, I had two battles today—the bastards know what I've been through, and they're doing this to me.

WILLIAM BEE, GRIFFIN ARMY, TALO MOMOE, TIGER ARMY, 1900

He sat on the edge of the bed. The note trembled in his hand. I can't do this, he said silently. And then not silently. "I can't do this."

He got up, bleary, and looked for his flash suit. Then he remembered—he had put it in the cleaner while he showered. It was still there.

Holding the paper, he walked out of his room. Dinner was nearly over, and there were a few people in the corridor, but no one spoke to him, just watched him, perhaps in awe of what had happened at noon in the bathroom, perhaps because of the forbidding, terrible look on his face. Most of his boys were in the barracks.

Ho, Ender. There gonna be a practice tonight?

Ender handed the paper to Hot Soup. "Those sons of bitches," he said. "Two at once?"

"Two armies!" shouted Crazy Tom.

"They'll just trip over each other," said Bean.

"I've got to clean up," Ender said. "Get them ready, get everybody together, I'll meet you there, at the gate."

He walked out of the barracks. A tumult of conversation rose behind him. He heard Crazy Tom scream, "Two farteating armies! We'll whip their butts!"

The bathroom was empty. All cleaned up. None of the blood that poured from Bonzo's nose into the shower water. All gone. Nothing bad ever happened here.

Ender stepped under the water and rinsed himself, took the sweat of combat and let it run down the drain. All gone, except they recycled it and we'll be drinking Bonzo's bloodwater in the morning. All the life gone out of it, but his blood just the same, his blood and my sweat, washed down in their stupidity or cruelty or whatever it was that made them let it happen.

He dried himself, dressed in his flash suit, and walked to the battleroom. His army was waiting in the corridor, the door still not opened. They watched him in silence as he walked to the front to stand by the blank grey forcefield. Of course they all knew about his fight in the bathroom today; that and their own weariness from the battle that morning kept them quiet, while the knowledge that they would be facing two armies filled them with dread.

Everything they can do to beat me, thought Ender. Everything they can think of, change all the rules, they don't care, just so they beat me. Well, I'm sick of the game. No game is worth Bonzo's blood pinking the water on the bathroom floor. Ice me, send me home, I don't want to play anymore.

The door disappeared. Only three meters out there were four stars together, completely blocking the view from the door.

Two armies weren't enough. They had to make Ender deploy his forces blind.

"Bean," said Ender. "Take your boys and tell me what's on the other side of this star."

Bean pulled the coil of twine from his waist, tied one end around him, handed the other end to a boy in his squad, and stepped gently through the door. His squad quickly followed. They had practiced this several times, and it took only a moment before they were braced on the star, holding the end of the twine. Bean pushed off at great speed, in a line almost parallel to the door; when he reached the corner of the room, he pushed off again and rocketed straight out toward the enemy. The spots of light on the wall showed that the enemy was shooting at him. As the rope was stopped by each edge of the star in turn, his arc became tighter, his direction changed, and he became an impossible target to hit. His squad caught him neatly as he came around the star from the other side. He moved all his arms and legs so those waiting inside the door would know that the enemy hadn't flashed him anywhere.

Ender dropped through the gate.

"It's really dim," said Bean, "but light enough you can't follow people easily by the lights on their suits. Worst possible for seeing. It's all open space from this star to the enemy side of the room. They've got eight stars making a square around their door. I didn't see anybody except the ones peeking around the boxes. They're just sitting there waiting for us."

As if to corroborate Bean's statement, the enemy began to call out to them. "Hey! We be hungry, come and feed us! Your ass is draggin'! Your ass is Dragon!"

Ender's mind felt dead. This was stupid. He didn't have a chance, outnumbered two to one and forced to attack a protected enemy. "In a real war, any commander with brains at all would retreat and save his army."

"What the hell," said Bean. "It's only a game."

"It stopped being a game when they threw away the rules."

"So, you throw 'em away, too."

Ender grinned. "OK. Why not. Let's see how they react to a formation."

Bean was appalled. "A formation! We've never done a formation in the whole time we've been an army!"

"We've still got a month to go before our training period is normally supposed to end. About time we started doing formations. Always have to know formations." He formed an A with his fingers, showed it to the blank door, and beckoned. A toon quickly emerged and Ender began arranging them behind the star. Three meters wasn't enough room to work in, the boys were frightened and confused, and it took nearly five minutes just to get them to understand what they were doing.

Tiger and Griffin soldiers were reduced to chanting catcalls, while their commanders argued about whether to try to use their overwhelming force to attack Dragon Army while they were still behind the star. Momoe was all for attacking—"We outnumber him two to one"—while Bee said, "Sit tight and we can't lose, move out and he can figure out a way to beat us."

So they sat tight, until finally in the dusky light they saw a large mass slip out from behind Ender's star. It held its shape, even when it abruptly stopped moving sideways and launched itself toward the dead center of the eight stars where eighty-two soldiers waited.

"Doobie doo," said a Griffin. "They're doing a formation."

"They must have been putting that together for all five minutes," said Momoe. "If we'd attacked while they were doing it, we could've destroyed them."

"Eat it, Momoe," whispered Bee. "You saw the way that little kid flew. He went all the way around the star and back behind without ever touching a wall. Maybe they've all got hooks, did you think of that? They've got something new there."

The formation was a strange one. A square formation of tightly-packed bodies in front, making a wall. Behind it, a cylinder, six boys in circumference and two boys deep, their limbs outstretched and frozen so they couldn't possibly be holding on to each other. Yet they held together as tightly as if they had been tied—which, in fact, they were.

From inside the formation, Dragon Army was firing with deadly accuracy, forcing Griffins and Tigers to stay tightly packed on their stars.

"The back of that sucker is open," said Bee. "As soon as they get between the stars, we can get around behind—"

"Don't talk about it, do it!" said Momoe. Then he took his own advice and ordered his boys to launch against the wall and rebound out behind the Dragon formation.

In the chaos of their takeoff, while Griffin Army held tight to their stars, the Dragon formation abruptly changed. Both the cylinder and the front wall split in two, as boys inside it pushed off; almost at once, the formations also reversed direction, heading back toward the Dragon gate. Most of the Griffins fired at the formations and the boys moving backward with them; and the Tigers took the survivors of Dragon Army from behind.

But there was something wrong. William Bee thought for a moment and realized what it was. Those formations couldn't have reversed direction in midflight unless someone pushed off in the opposite direction, and if they took off with enough force to make that twenty-man formation move backward, they must be going *fast.*

There they were, six small Dragon soldiers down near William Bee's own door. From the number of lights showing on their flash suits, Bee could see that three of them were disabled and two of them damaged; only one was whole. Nothing to be frightened of. Bee casually aimed at them, pressed the button, and—

Nothing happened.

The lights went on.

The game was over.

Even though he was looking right at them, it took Bee a moment to realize what had just happened. Four of the Dragon soldiers had their helmets pressed on the corners of the door. And one of them had just passed through. They had just carried out the victory ritual. They were getting destroyed, they had hardly inflicted any casualties, and they had the gall to perform the victory ritual and end the game right under their noses.

Only then did it occur to William Bee that not only had Dragon Army ended the game, it was possible that, under the rules, they had won it. After all, no matter what happened, you were not certified as the winner unless you had enough unfrozen soldiers to touch the corners of the gate and pass someone through into the enemy's corridor. Therefore, by one way of thinking, you could argue that the ending ritual *was* victory. The battleroom certainly recognized it as the end of the game.

The teachergate opened and Major Anderson came into the room. "Ender," he called, looking around.

One of the frozen Dragon soldiers tried to answer him through jaws that were clamped shut by the flash suit. Anderson hooked over to him and thawed him.

Ender was smiling. "I beat you again, sir," he said.

"Nonsense, Ender," Anderson said softly. "Your battle was with Griffin and Tiger."

"How stupid do you think I am?" said Ender.

Loudly, Anderson said, "After that little maneuver, the rules are being revised to require that all of the enemy's soldiers must be frozen or disabled before the gate can be reversed."

"It could only work once anyway," Ender said.

Anderson handed him the hook. Ender unfroze everyone at once. To hell with protocol. To hell with everything. "Hey!" he shouted as Anderson moved away. "What is it next time? My army in a cage without guns, with the rest of the Battle School against them? How about a little equality?"

There was a loud murmur of agreement from the other boys, and not all of it came from Dragon Army. Anderson did not so much as turn around to acknowledge Ender's challenge. Finally, it was William Bee who answered. "Ender, if you're on one side of the battle, it won't be equal no matter what the conditions are."

Right! called the boys. Many of them laughed. Talo Momoe began clapping his hands. "Ender Wiggin!" he shouted. The other boys also clapped and shouted Ender's name.

Ender passed through the enemy gate. His soldiers followed him. The sound of them shouting his name followed him through the corridors.

"Practice tonight?" asked Crazy Tom.

Ender shook his head.

"Tomorrow morning then?"

"No."

"Well, when?"

"Never again, as far as I'm concerned."

He could hear the murmurs behind him.

"Hey, that's not fair," said one of the boys. "It's not our fault the teachers are screwing up the game. You can't just stop teaching us stuff because—"

Ender slammed his open hand against the wall and shouted at the boy. "I don't care about the game anymore!" His voice echoed through the corridor. Boys from other armies came to their doors. He spoke quietly into the silence. "Do you understand that?" And he whispered. "The game is over."

He walked back to his room alone. He wanted to lie down, but he couldn't because the bed was wet. It reminded him of all that had happened today, and in fury he tore the mattress and blankets from the bedframe and shoved them out into the corridor. Then he wadded up a uniform to serve as a pillow and lay on the fabric of wires strung across the frame. It was uncomfortable, but Ender didn't care enough to get up.

He had only been there a few minutes when someone knocked on his door.

"Go away," he said softly. Whoever was knocking didn't hear him or didn't care. Finally Ender said to come in.

It was Bean.

"Go away, Bean."

Bean nodded but didn't leave. Instead he looked at his shoes. Ender almost yelled at him, cursed at him, screamed at him to leave. Instead he noticed how very tired Bean looked, his whole body bent with weariness, his eyes dark from lack of sleep; and yet his skin was still soft and translucent, the skin of a child, the soft curved cheek, the slender limbs of a little boy. He wasn't eight years old yet. It didn't matter he was brilliant and dedicated and good. He was a child. He was *young*.

No he isn't, thought Ender. Small, yes. But Bean has been through a battle with a whole army depending on him and on the soldiers that he led, and he performed splendidly, and they won. There's no youth in that. No childhood.

Taking Ender's silence and softening expression as permission to stay, Bean took another step into the room. Only then did Ender see the small slip of paper in his hand.

"You're transferred?" asked Ender. He was incredulous, but his voice came out sounding uninterested, dead.

"To Rabbit Army."

Ender nodded. Of course. It was obvious. If I can't be defeated with my army, they'll take my army away. "Carn Carby's a good man," said Ender. "I hope he recognizes what you're worth."

"Carn Carby was graduated today. He got his notice while we were fighting our battle."

"Well, who's commanding Rabbit then?"

Bean held his hands out helplessly. "Me."

Ender looked at the ceiling and nodded. "Of course. After all, you're only four years younger than the regular age."

"It isn't funny. I don't know what's going on here. All the changes in the game. And now this. I wasn't the only one transferred, you know. They graduated half the commanders, and transferred a lot of our guys to command their armies."

"Which guys?"

"It looks like—every toon leader and every assistant."

"Of course. If they decide to wreck my army, they'll cut it to the ground. Whatever they're doing, they're thorough."

"You'll still win, Ender. We all know that. Crazy Tom, he said, 'You mean I'm supposed to figure out how to beat Dragon Army?' Everybody knows you're the best. They can't break you down, no matter what they—"

"They already have."

"No, Ender, they can't—"

"I don't care about their game anymore, Bean. I'm not going to play it anymore. No more practices. No more battles. They can put their little slips of paper on the floor all they want, but I won't go. I decided that before I went through the door today. That's why I had you go for the gate. I didn't think it would work, but I didn't care. I just wanted to go out in style."

"You should've seen William Bee's face. He just stood there trying to figure out how he had lost when you only had seven boys who could wiggle their toes and he only had three who couldn't."

"Why should I want to see William Bee's face? Why should I want to beat anybody?" Ender pressed his palms against his eyes. "I hurt Bonzo really bad today, Bean. I really hurt him bad."

"He had it coming."

"I knocked him out standing up. It was like he was dead, standing there. And I kept hurting him."

Bean said nothing.

"I just wanted to make sure he never hurt me again."

"He won't," said Bean. "They sent him home."

"Already?"

"The teachers didn't say much, they never do. The official notice says he was graduated, but where they put the assignment—you know, tactical school, support, pre-command, navigation, that kind of thing—it just said Cartagena, Spain. That's his home."

"I'm glad they graduated him."

"Hell, Ender, we're just glad he's gone. If we'd known what he was doing to you, we would've killed him on the spot. Was it true he had a whole bunch of guys gang up on you?"

"No. It was just him and me. He fought with honor." If it weren't for his honor, he and the others would have beaten me together. They might have killed me, then. His sense of honor saved my life. "I didn't fight with honor," Ender added. "I fought to win."

Bean laughed. "And you did. Kicked him right out of orbit."

A knock on the door. Before Ender could answer, the door opened. Ender had been expecting more of his soldiers. Instead it was Major Anderson. And behind him came Colonel Graff.

"Ender Wiggin," said Graff.

Ender got to his feet. "Yes sir."

"Your display of temper in the battleroom today was insubordinate and is not to be repeated."

"Yes sir," said Ender.

Bean was still feeling insubordinate, and he didn't think Ender deserved the rebuke. "I think it was about time somebody told a teacher how we felt about what you've been doing."

The adults ignored him. Anderson handed Ender a sheet of paper. A full-sized sheet. Not one of the little slips of paper that served for internal orders within the Battle School; it was a full-fledged set of orders. Bean knew what it meant. Ender was being transferred out of the school.

"Graduated?" asked Bean. Ender nodded. "What took them so long? You're only two or three years early. You've already learned how to walk and talk and dress yourself. What will they have left to teach you?"

Ender shook his head. "All I know is, the game's over." He folded up the paper. "None too soon. Can I tell my army?"

"There isn't time," said Graff. "Your shuttle leaves in twenty minutes. Besides, it's better not to talk to them after you get your orders. It makes it easier."

"For them or for you?" Ender asked. He didn't wait for an answer. He turned quickly to Bean, took his hand for a moment, and then headed for the door.

"Wait," said Bean. "Where are you going? Tactical? Navigational? Support?"

"Command School," Ender answered.

"*Pre*-command?"

"Command," said Ender, and then he was out the door. Anderson followed him closely. Bean grabbed Colonel Graff by the sleeve. "Nobody goes to Command School until they're sixteen!"

Graff shook off Bean's hand and left, closing the door behind him.

Bean stood alone in the room, trying to grasp what this might mean. Nobody went to Command School without three years of Pre-command in either Tactical or Support. But then, nobody left Battle School without at least six years, and Ender had had only four.

The system is breaking up. No doubt about it. Either somebody at the top is going crazy, or something's gone wrong with the war, the real war, the bugger war. Why else would they break down the training system like this, wreck the game the way they did? Why else would they put a little kid like me in command of an army?

Bean wondered about it as he walked back down the corridor to his own bed. The lights went out just as he reached his bunk. He undressed in darkness, fumbling to put his clothing in a locker he couldn't see. He felt terrible. At first he thought he felt bad because he was afraid of leading an army, but it wasn't true. He knew he'd make a good commander. He felt himself wanting to cry. He hadn't cried since the first few days of homesickness after he got here. He tried to put a name on the feeling that put a lump in his throat and made him sob silently, however much he tried to hold it down. He bit down on his hand to stop the feeling, to replace it with pain. It didn't help. He would never see Ender again.

Once he named the feeling, he could control it. He lay back and forced himself to go through the relaxing routine until he didn't feel like crying anymore. Then he drifted off to sleep. His hand was near his mouth. It lay on his pillow hesitantly, as if Bean couldn't decide whether to bite his nails or suck on his fingertips. His forehead was creased and furrowed. His breathing was quick and light. He was a soldier, and if anyone had asked him what he wanted to be when he grew up, he wouldn't have known what they meant.

When he was crossing into the shuttle, Ender noticed for the first time that the insignia on Major Anderson's uniform had changed. "Yes, he's a colonel now," said Graff. "In fact, Major Anderson has been placed in command of the Battle School, as of this afternoon. I have been reassigned to other duties."

Ender did not ask him what they were.

Graff strapped himself into a seat across the aisle from him. There was only one other passenger, a quiet man in civilian clothes who was introduced as General Pace. Pace was carrying a briefcase, but carried no more luggage than Ender did. Somehow that was comforting to Ender, that Graff also came away empty.

Ender spoke only once on the voyage home. "Why are we going home?" he asked. "I thought Command School was in the asteroids somewhere."

"It is," said Graff. "But the Battle School has no facilities for docking long-range ships. So you get a short landside leave."

Ender wanted to ask if that meant he could see his family. But suddenly, at the thought that it might be possible, he was afraid, and so he didn't ask. Just closed his eyes and tried to sleep. Behind him, General Pace was studying him; for what purpose, Ender could not guess.

It was a hot summer afternoon in Florida when they landed. Ender had been so long without sunlight that the light nearly blinded him. He squinted and sneezed and wanted to get back indoors. Everything was far away and flat; the ground, lacking the upward curve of Battle School floors, seemed instead to fall away, so that on level ground Ender felt as though he were on a pinnacle. The pull of real gravity felt different and he scuffed his feet when he walked. He hated it. He wanted to go back home, back to the Battle School, the only place in the universe where he belonged.

"Arrested?"

"Well, it's a natural thought. General Pace **is** the head of the military police. There **was** a death in the Battle School."

"They didn't tell me whether Colonel Graff was being promoted or court-martialed. Just transferred, with orders to report to the Polemarch."

"Is that a good sign or bad?"

"Who knows? On the one hand, Ender Wiggin not only survived, he passed a threshold, he graduated in dazzlingly good shape, you have to give old Graff credit for that. On the other hand, there's the fourth passenger on the shuttle. The one traveling in a bag."

"Only the second death in the history of the school. At least it wasn't a suicide this time."

"How is murder better, Major Imbu?"

"It wasn't murder, Colonel. We have it on video from two angles. No one can blame Ender."

"But they might blame Graff. After all this is over, the civilians can rake over our files and decide what was right and what was not. Give us medals where they think we were right, take away our pensions and put us in jail where they decide we were wrong. At least they had the good sense not to tell Ender that the boy died."

"It's the second time, too."

"They didn't tell him about Stilson, either."

"The kid is scary."

"Ender Wiggin isn't a killer. He just wins—thoroughly. If anybody's going to be scared, let it be the buggers."

"Makes you almost feel sorry for them, knowing Ender's going to be coming after them."

"The only one I feel sorry for is Ender. But not sorry enough to suggest they ought to let up on him. I just got access to the material that Graff's been getting all this time. About fleet movements, that sort of thing. I used to sleep easy at night."

"Time's getting short?"

"I shouldn't have mentioned it. I can't tell you secured information."

"I know."

"Let's leave it at this: they didn't get him to Command School a day too soon. And maybe a couple of years too late."

Chapter 13

Valentine

"Children?"

"Brother and sister. They had layered themselves five times through the nets—writing for companies that paid for their memberships, that sort of thing. Devil of a time tracking them down."

"What are they hiding?"

"Could be anything. The most obvious thing to hide, though, is their ages. The boy is fourteen, the girl is twelve."

"Which one is Demosthenes?"

"The girl. The twelve-year-old."

"Pardon me. I don't really think it's funny, but I can't help but laugh. All this time we've been worried, all the time we've been trying to persuade the Russians not to take Demosthenes too seriously, we held up Locke as proof that Americans weren't all crazy warmongers. Brother and sister, prepubescent—"

"And their last name is Wiggin."

"Ah. Coincidence?"

"**The** Wiggin is a third. They are one and two."

"Oh, excellent. The Russians will never believe—"

"That Demosthenes and Locke aren't as much under our control as **the** Wiggin."

"**Is** there a conspiracy? Is someone controlling them?"

"We have been able to detect **no** contact between these two children and any adult who might be directing them."

"That is not to say that someone might not have invented some method you can't detect. It's hard to believe that two children—"

"I interviewed Colonel Graff when he arrived from the Battle

School. It is his best judgment that nothing these children have done is out of their reach. Their abilities are virtually identical with —the Wiggin. Only their temperaments are different. What surprised him, however, was the orientation of the two personas. Demosthenes is definitely the girl, but Graff says the girl was rejected for Battle School because she was too pacific, too conciliatory, and above all, too empathic."

"Definitely not Demosthenes."

"And the boy has the soul of a jackal."

"Wasn't it Locke that was recently praised as 'The only truly open mind in America'?"

"It's hard to know what's really happening. But Graff recommended, and I agree, that we should leave them alone. Not expose them. Make no report at this time except that we have determined that Locke and Demosthenes have no foreign connections and have no connections with any domestic group, either, except those publicly declared on the nets."

"In other words, give them a clean bill of health."

"I know Demosthenes seems dangerous, in part because he —or she—has such a wide following. But I think it's significant that the one of the two of them who is most ambitious has chosen the moderate, wise persona. And they're still just talking. They have influence, but no power."

"In my experience, influence **is** power."

"If we ever find them getting out of line, we can easily expose them."

"Only in the next few years. The longer we wait, the older they get, and the less shocking it is to discover who they are."

"You know what the Russian troop movements have been. There's always the chance that Demosthenes is **right**. In which case—"

"We'd better have Demosthenes around. All right. We'll show them clean, for now. But watch them. And I, of course, have to find ways of keeping the Russians calm."

In spite of all her misgivings, Valentine was having fun being Demosthenes. Her column was now being carried on practically every newsnet in the country, and it was fun to watch the money pile up in her attorney's accounts. Every now and then she and Peter would, in Demosthenes' name, donate a carefully calculated sum to a particular candidate or cause: enough money that the donation would be noticed, but not so much that the candidate would feel she was trying to buy a vote. She was getting so many letters now that her newsnet had hired a secretary to answer certain classes of routine correspondence for her. The fun letters, from national and international leaders, sometimes hostile, sometimes friendly, always diplomatically trying to pry into Demosthenes' mind—those she and Peter read together, laughing in delight sometimes that people like *this* were writing to children, and didn't know it.

Sometimes, though, she was ashamed. Father was reading Demosthenes regularly; he never read Locke, or if he did, he said nothing about it. At dinner, though, he would often regale them with some telling point Demosthenes had made in that day's column. Peter loved it when Father did that—"See, it shows that the common man is paying attention"—but it made Valentine feel humiliated for Father. If he ever found out that all this time *I* was writing the columns he told us about, and that I didn't even believe half the things I wrote, he would be angry and ashamed.

At school, she once nearly got them in trouble, when her history teacher assigned the class to write a paper contrasting the views of Demosthenes and Locke as expressed in two of their early columns. Valentine was careless, and did a brilliant job of analysis. As a result, she had to work hard to talk the principal out of having her essay published on the very newsnet that carried Demosthenes' column. Peter was savage about it. "You write too much like Demosthenes, you can't get published, I should kill Demosthenes now, you're getting out of control."

If he raged about that blunder, Peter frightened her still more when he went silent. It happened when Demosthenes was invited to take part in the President's Council on Education for the Future, a blue-ribbon panel that was designed to do nothing, but do it splendidly. Valentine thought Peter would take it as a triumph, but he did not. "Turn it down," he said.

"Why should I?" she asked. "It's no work at all, and they even said that because of Demosthenes' well-known desire for privacy, they would net all the meetings. It makes Demosthenes into a respectable person, and—"

"And you love it that you got that before I did."

"Peter, it isn't you and me, it's Demosthenes and Locke. We made them up. They aren't real. Besides, this appointment doesn't mean they like Demosthenes better than Locke, it just means that Demosthenes has a much stronger base of support. You knew he would. Appointing him pleases a large number of Russian-haters and chauvinists."

"It wasn't supposed to work this way. Locke was supposed to be the respected one."

"He is! Real respect takes longer than official respect. Peter, don't be angry at me because I've done well with the things you told me to do."

But he was angry, for days, and ever since then he had left her to think through all her own columns, instead of telling her what to write. He probably assumed that this would make the quality of Demosthenes' columns deteriorate, but if it did no one noticed. Perhaps it made him even angrier that she never came to him weeping for help. She had been Demosthenes too long now to need anyone to tell her what Demosthenes would think about things.

And as her correspondence with other politically active citizens grew, she began to learn things, information that simply wasn't available to the general public. Certain military people who corresponded with her dropped hints about things without meaning to, and she and Peter put them together to build up a fascinating and frightening picture of Warsaw Pact activity. They were indeed preparing for war, a vicious and bloody earthbound war. Demosthenes wasn't wrong to suspect that the Warsaw Pact was not abiding by the terms of the League.

And the character of Demosthenes gradually took on a life of his own. At times she found herself thinking like Demosthenes at the end of a writing session, agreeing with ideas that were supposed to be calculated poses. And sometimes she read Peter's Locke essays and found herself annoyed at his obvious blindness to what was really going on.

Perhaps it's impossible to wear an identity without becoming what you pretend to be. She thought of that, worried about it for a few days, and then wrote a column using that as a premise, to show that politicians who toadied to the Russians in order to keep the peace would inevitably end up subservient to them in everything. It was a lovely bite at the party in power, and she got a lot of good mail about it. She also stopped being frightened of the idea of becoming, to a degree, Demosthenes. *He's smarter than Peter and I ever gave him credit for,* she thought.

Graff was waiting for her after school. He stood leaning on his car. He was in civilian clothes, and he had gained weight, so she didn't recognize him at first. But he beckoned to her, and before he could introduce himself she remembered his name.

"I won't write another letter," she said. "I never should have written that one."

"You don't like medals, then, I guess."

"Not much."

"Come for a ride with me, Valentine."

"I don't ride with strangers."

He handed her a paper. It was a release form, and her parents had signed it.

"I guess you're not a stranger. Where are we going?"

"To see a young soldier who is in Greensboro on leave."

She got in the car. "Ender's only ten years old," she said. "I thought you told us the first time he'd be eligible for a leave was when he was twelve."

"He skipped a few grades."

"So he's doing well?"

"Ask him when you see him."

"Why me? Why not the whole family?"

Graff sighed. "Ender sees the world his own way. We had to persuade him to see you. As for Peter and your parents, he was not interested. Life at the Battle School was—intense."

"What do you mean, he's gone crazy?"

"On the contrary, he's the sanest person I know. He's sane enough to know that his parents are not particularly eager to reopen a book of affection that was closed quite tightly four years ago. As for Peter—we didn't even suggest a meeting, and so he didn't have a chance to tell us to go to hell."

They went out Lake Brandt Road and turned off just past the lake, following a road that wound down and up until they came to a white clapboard mansion that sprawled along the top of a hill. It looked over Lake Brandt on one side and a five-acre private lake on the other. "This is the house that Medly's Mist-E-Rub built," said Graff. "The I.F. picked it up in a tax sale about twenty years ago.

Ender insisted that his conversation with you should not be bugged. I promised him it wouldn't be, and to help inspire confidence, the two of you are going out on a raft he built himself. I should warn you, though. I intend to ask you questions about your conversation when it is finished. You don't have to answer, but I hope you will."

"I didn't bring a swimming suit."

"We can provide one."

"One that isn't bugged?"

"At some point, there must be trust. For instance, I know who Demosthenes really is."

She felt a thrill of fear run through her, but said nothing.

"I've known since I landed from the Battle School. There are, perhaps, six of us in the world who know his identity. Not counting the Russians—God only knows what they know. But Demosthenes has nothing to fear from us. Demosthenes can trust our discretion. Just as I trust Demosthenes not to tell Locke what's going on here today. Mutual trust. We tell each other things."

Valentine couldn't decide whether it was Demosthenes they approved of, or Valentine Wiggin. If the former, she would not trust them; if the latter, then perhaps she could. The fact that they did not want her to discuss this with Peter suggested that perhaps they knew the difference between them. She did not stop to wonder whether she herself knew the difference anymore.

"You said he built the raft. How long has he been here?"

"Two months. We meant his leave to last only a few days. But you see, he doesn't seem interested in going on with his education."

"Oh. So I'm therapy again."

"This time we can't censor your letter. We're just taking our chances. We need your brother badly. Humanity is on the cusp."

This time Val had grown up enough to know just how much danger the world was in. And she had been Demosthenes long enough that she didn't hesitate to do her duty. "Where is he?"

"Down at the boat slip."

"Where's the swimming suit?"

Ender didn't wave when she walked down the hill toward him, didn't smile when she stepped onto the floating boat slip. But she knew that he was glad to see her, knew it because of the way his eyes never left her face.

"You're bigger than I remembered," she said stupidly.

"You too," he said. "I also remembered that you were beautiful."

"Memory does play tricks on us."

"No. Your face is the same, but I don't remember what beautiful means anymore. Come on. Let's go out into the lake."

She looked at the small raft with misgivings.

"Don't stand up on it, that's all," he said. He got on by crawling, spiderlike, on toes and fingers. "It's the first thing I built with my own hands since you and I used to build with blocks. Peter-proof buildings."

She laughed. They used to take pleasure in building things that would stand up even when a lot of the obvious supports had been removed. Peter, in turn, liked to remove a block here or there, so the structure would be fragile enough that the next person to touch it would knock it down. Peter was an ass, but he did provide some focus to their childhood.

"Peter's changed," she said.

"Let's not talk about him," said Ender.

"All right."

She crawled onto the boat, not as deftly as Ender. He used a paddle to maneuver them slowly toward the center of the private lake. She noticed aloud that he was sunbrowned and strong.

"The strong part comes from Battle School. The sunbrowning comes from this lake. I spend a lot of time on the water. When I'm swimming, it's like being weightless. I miss being weightless. Also, when I'm here on the lake, the land slopes up in every direction."

"Like living in a bowl."

"I've lived in a bowl for four years."

"So we're strangers now?"

"Aren't we, Valentine?"

"No," she said. She reached out and touched his leg. Then, suddenly, she squeezed his knee, right where he had always been most ticklish.

But almost at the same moment, he caught her wrist in his hand. His grip was very strong, even though his hands were smaller than hers and his own arms were slender and tight. For a moment he looked dangerous; then he relaxed. "Oh, yes," he said. "You used to tickle me."

"Not any more," she said, taking back her hand.

"Want to swim?"

In answer, she dropped herself over the side of the raft. The water was clear and clean, and there was no chlorine in it. She swam for a while, then returned to the raft and lay on it in the hazy sunlight. A wasp circled her, then landed on the raft beside her head. She knew it was there, and ordinarily would have been afraid of it. But not today. Let it walk on this raft, let it bake in the sun as I'm doing.

Then the raft rocked, and she turned to see Ender calmly crushing the life out of the wasp with one finger. "These are a nasty breed," Ender said. "They sting you without waiting to be insulted first." He smiled. "I've been learning about preemptive strategies. I'm very good. No one ever beat me. I'm the best soldier they ever had."

"Who would expect less?" she said. "You're a Wiggin."

"Whatever that means," he said.

"It means that you are going to make a difference in the world." And she told him what she and Peter were doing.

"How old is Peter, fourteen? Already planning to take over the world?"

"He thinks he's Alexander the Great. And why shouldn't he be? Why shouldn't *you* be, too?"

"We can't *both* be Alexander."

"Two faces of the same coin. And I am the metal in between." Even as she said it, she wondered if it was true. She had shared so much with Peter these last few years that even when she thought she despised him, she understood him. While Ender had been only a memory till now. A very small, fragile boy who needed her protection. Not this cold-eyed, dark-skinned manling who kills wasps with his fingers. Maybe he and Peter and I are all the same, and have been all along. Maybe we only thought we were different from each other out of jealousy.

"The trouble with coins is, when one face is up, the other face is down."

And right now you think you're down. "They want me to encourage you to go on with your studies."

"They aren't studies, they're games. All games, from beginning to end, only they change the rules whenever they feel like it." He held up a limp hand. "See the strings?"

"But you can use them, too."

"Only if they want to be used. Only if they think they're using you. No, it's too hard, I don't want to play anymore. Just when I start to be happy, just when I think I can handle things, they stick in another knife. I keep having nightmares, now that I'm here. I dream I'm in the battleroom, only instead of being weightless, they're playing games with gravity. They keep changing its direction. So I never end up on the wall I launched for. I never end up where I meant to go. And I keep pleading with them just to let me get to the door, and they won't let me out, they keep sucking me back in."

She heard the anger in his voice and assumed it was directed at her. "I suppose that's what I'm here for. To suck you back in."

"I didn't want to see you."

"They told me."

"I was afraid that I'd still love you."

"I hoped that you would."

"My fear, your wish—both granted."

"Ender, it really is true. We may be young, but we're not powerless. We play by their rules long enough, and it becomes our game." She giggled. "I'm on a presidential commission. Peter is so angry."

"They don't let me use the nets. There isn't a computer in the place, except the household machines that run the security system and the lighting. Ancient things. Installed back a century ago, when they made computers that didn't hook up with anything. They took away my army, they took away my desk, and you know something? I don't really mind."

"You must be good company for yourself."

"Not me. My memories."

"Maybe that's who you are, what you remember."

"No. My memories of strangers. My memories of the buggers."

Valentine shivered, as if a cold breeze had suddenly passed. "I refuse to watch the bugger vids anymore. They're always the same."

"I used to study them for hours. The way their ships move through space. And something funny, that only occurred to me lying out here on the lake. I realized that all the battles in which buggers and humans fought hand to hand, all those are from the First Invasion. All the scenes from the Second Invasion, when our soldiers are in I.F. uniforms, in those scenes the buggers are always already dead. Lying there, slumped over their controls. Not a sign of struggle or anything. And Mazer Rackham's battle—they never show us any footage from that battle."

"Maybe it's a secret weapon."

"No, no, I don't care about how we killed them. It's the buggers themselves. I don't know anything about them, and yet someday I'm supposed to fight them. I've been through a lot of fights in my life, sometimes games, sometimes—not games. Every time, I've won because I could understand the way my enemy thought. From what they *did*. I could tell what they thought I was doing, how they wanted the battle to take shape. And I played off of that. I'm very good at that. Understanding how other people think."

"The curse of the Wiggin children." She joked, but it frightened her, that Ender might understand her as completely as he did his enemies. Peter always understood her, or at least thought he did, but he was such a moral sinkhole that she never had to feel embarrassed when he guessed even her worst thoughts. But Ender—she did not want him to understand her. It would make her naked before him. She would be ashamed. "You don't think you can beat the buggers unless you know them."

"It goes deeper than that. Being here alone with nothing to do, I've been thinking about myself, too. Trying to understand why I hate myself so badly."

"No, Ender."

"Don't tell me 'No, Ender.' It took me a long time to realize that I did, but believe me, I did. Do. And it came down to this: In the moment when I truly understand my enemy, understand him well enough to defeat him, then in that very moment I also love him. I think it's impossible to really understand somebody, what they want, what they believe, and not love them the way they love themselves. And then, in that very moment when I *love* them—"

"You beat them." For a moment she was not afraid of his understanding.

"No, you don't understand. I *destroy* them. I make it impossible for them to ever hurt me again. I grind them and grind them until they don't *exist.*"

"Of course you don't." And now the fear came again, worse than before. Peter has mellowed, but you, they've made you into a killer. Two sides of the same coin, but which side is which?

"I've really hurt some people, Val. I'm not making this up."

"I know, Ender." How will you hurt me?

"See what I'm becoming, Val?" he said softly. "Even you are afraid of me." And he touched her cheek so gently that she wanted to cry. Like the touch of his soft baby hand when he was still an infant. She remembered that, the touch of his soft and innocent hand on her cheek.

"I'm not," she said, and in that moment it was true.

"You should be."

No. I shouldn't. "You're going to shrivel up if you stay in the water. Also, the sharks might get you."

He smiled. "The sharks learned to leave me alone a long time ago." But he pulled himself onto the raft, bringing a wash of water across it as it tipped. It was cold on Valentine's back.

"Ender, Peter's going to do it. He's smart enough to take the time it takes, but he's going to win his way into power—if not right now, then later. I'm not sure yet whether that'll be a good thing or a bad thing. Peter can be cruel, but he knows the getting and keeping of power, and there are signs that once the bugger war is over, and maybe even before it ends, the world will collapse into chaos again. The Warsaw Pact was on its way to hegemony before the First Invasion. If they try for it afterward—"

"So even Peter might be a better alternative."

"You've been discovering some of the destroyer in yourself, Ender. Well, so have I. Peter didn't have a monopoly on that, whatever the testers thought. And Peter has some of the builder in him. He isn't kind, but he doesn't break every good thing he sees anymore. Once you realize that power will always end up with the sort of people who crave it, I think that there are worse people who could have it than Peter."

"With that strong a recommendation, I could vote for him myself."

"Sometimes it seems absolutely silly. A fourteen-year-old boy and his kid sister plotting to take over the world." She tried to laugh. It wasn't funny. "We aren't just ordinary children, are we. None of us."

"Don't you sometimes wish we were?"

She tried to imagine herself being like the other girls at school. Tried to imagine life if she didn't feel responsible for the future of the world. "It would be so dull."

"I don't think so." And he stretched out on the raft, as if he could lie on the water forever.

It was true. Whatever they did to Ender in the Battle School, they had spent his ambition. He really did not want to leave the sun-warmed waters of this bowl.

No, she realized. No, he *believes* that he doesn't want to leave here, but there is still too much of Peter in him. Or too much of me. None of us could be happy for long, doing nothing. Or perhaps it's just that none of us could be happy living with no other company than ourself.

So she began to prod again. "What is the one name that everyone in the world knows?"

"Mazer Rackham."

"And what if you win the next war, the way Mazer did?"

"Mazer Rackham was a fluke. A reserve. Nobody believed in him. He just happened to be in the right place at the right time."

"But suppose you do it. Suppose you beat the buggers and your name is known the way Mazer Rackham's name is known."

"Let somebody else be famous. Peter wants to be famous. Let him save the world."

"I'm not talking about fame, Ender. I'm not talking about power, either. I'm talking about accidents, just like the accident that Mazer Rackham happened to be the one who was there when somebody had to stop the buggers."

"If I'm here," said Ender, "then I won't be there. Somebody else will. Let them have the accident."

His tone of weary unconcern infuriated her. "I'm talking about *my* life, you self-centered little bastard." If her words bothered him, he didn't show it. Just lay there, eyes closed. "When you were little and Peter tortured you, it's a good thing I didn't lie back and wait for Mom and Dad to save you. They never understood how dangerous Peter was. I knew you had the monitor, but I didn't wait for them, either. Do you know what Peter used to do to me because I stopped him from hurting you?"

"Shut up," Ender whispered.

Because she saw that his chest was trembling, because she knew that she had indeed hurt him, because she knew that just like Peter, she had found his weakest place and stabbed him there, she fell silent.

"I can't beat them," Ender said softly. "I'll be out there like Mazer Rackham one day, and everybody will be depending on me, and I won't be able to do it."

"If you can't, Ender, then nobody could. If you can't beat them, then they deserve to win because they're stronger and better than us. It won't be your fault."

"Tell it to the dead."

"If not you, then who?"

"Anybody."

"Nobody, Ender. I'll tell you something. If you try and lose then it isn't your fault. But if you don't try and we lose, then it's all your fault. You killed us all."

"I'm a killer no matter what."

"What else should you be? Human beings didn't evolve brains in order to lie around on lakes. Killing's the first thing we learned. And a good thing we did, or we'd be dead, and the tigers would own the earth."

"I could never beat Peter. No matter what I said or did. I never could."

So it came back to Peter. "He was years older than you. And stronger."

"So are the buggers."

She could see his reasoning. Or rather, his unreasoning. He could win all he wanted, but he knew in his heart that there was always someone who could destroy him. He always knew that he had not really won, because there was Peter, undefeated champion.

"You want to beat Peter?" she asked.

"No," he answered.

"Beat the buggers. Then come home and see who notices Peter Wiggin anymore. Look him in the eye when all the world loves and reveres you. That'll be defeat in his eyes, Ender. That's how you win."

"You don't understand," he said.

"Yes I do."

"No you don't. I don't want to beat Peter."

"Then what do you want?"

"I want him to love me."

She had no answer. As far as she knew, Peter didn't love anybody.

Ender said nothing more. Just lay there. And lay there.

Finally Valentine, the sweat dripping off her, the mosquitos beginning to hover as the dusk came on, took one final dip in the water and then began to push the raft in to shore. Ender showed no sign that he knew what she was doing, but his irregular breathing told her that he was not asleep. When they got to shore, she climbed onto the dock and said, "*I* love you, Ender. More than ever. No matter what you decide."

He didn't answer. She doubted that he believed her. She walked back up the hill, savagely angry at them for making her come to Ender like this. For she had, after all, done just what they wanted. She had talked Ender into going back into his training, and he wouldn't soon forgive her for that.

Ender came in the door, still wet from his last dip in the lake. It was dark outside, and dark in the room where Graff waited for him.

"Are we going now?" asked Ender.

"If you want to," Graff said.

"When?"

"When you're ready."

Ender showered and dressed. He was finally used to the way civilian clothes fit together, but he still didn't feel right without a uniform or a flash suit. I'll never wear a flash suit again, he thought. That was the Battle School game, and I'm through with that. He heard the crickets chirping madly in the woods; in the near distance he heard the crackling sound of a car driving slowly on gravel.

What else should he take with him? He had read several of the books in the library, but they belonged to the house and he couldn't take them. The only thing he owned was the raft he had made with his own hands. That would stay here, too.

The lights were on now in the room where Graff waited. He, too, had changed clothing. He was back in uniform.

They sat in the back seat of the car together, driving along country roads to come at the airport from the back. "Back when the population was growing," said Graff, "they kept this area in woods and farms. Watershed land. The rainfall here starts a lot of rivers flowing, a lot of underground water moving around. The Earth is deep, and right to the heart it's alive, Ender. We people only live on the top, like the bugs that live on the scum of the still water near the shore."

Ender said nothing.

"We train our commanders the way we do because that's what it takes—they have to think in certain ways, they can't be distracted by a lot of things, so we isolate them. You. Keep you separate. And it works. But it's so easy, when you never meet people, when you never know the Earth itself, when you live with metal walls keeping out the cold of space, it's easy to forget why Earth is worth saving. Why the world of people might be worth the price you pay."

So that's why you brought me here, thought Ender. With all your hurry, that's why you took three months, to make me love Earth. Well, it worked. All your tricks worked. Valentine, too; she was another one of your tricks, to make me remember that I'm not going to school for myself. Well, I remember.

"I may have used Valentine," said Graff, "and you may hate me for it, Ender, but keep this in mind—it only works because what's between you, that's real, that's what matters. Billions of those connections between human beings. That's what you're fighting to keep alive."

Ender turned his face to the window and watched the helicopters and dirigibles rise and fall.

They took a helicopter to the I.F. spaceport at Stumpy Point. It was officially named for a dead Hegemon, but everybody called it Stumpy Point, after the pitiful little town that had been paved over when they made the approaches to the vast islands of steel and concrete that dotted Pamlico Sound. There were still waterbirds taking their fastidious little steps in the saltwater, where mossy trees dipped down as if to drink. It began to rain lightly, and the concrete was black and slick; it was hard to tell where it left off and the Sound began.

Graff led him through a maze of clearances. Authority was a little plastic ball that Graff carried. He dropped it into chutes, and doors opened and people stood up and saluted and the chutes spat out the ball and Graff went on. Ender noticed that at first everyone watched Graff, but as they penetrated deeper into the spaceport, people began watching Ender. At first it was the man of real authority they noticed, but later, where everyone had authority, it was his cargo they cared to see.

Only when Graff strapped himself into the shuttle seat beside him did Ender realize Graff was going to launch with him.

"How far?" asked Ender. "How far are you going with me?"

Graff smiled thinly. "All the way, Ender."

"Are they making you administrator of Command School?"

"No."

So they had removed Graff from his post at Battle School solely to accompany Ender to his next assignment. How important am I, he wondered. And like a whisper of Peter's voice inside his mind, he heard the question, How can I use this?

He shuddered and tried to think of something else. Peter could have fantasies about ruling the world, but Ender didn't have them. Still, thinking back on his life in Battle School, it occurred to him that although he had never sought power, he had always had it. But he decided that it was a power born of excellence, not manipulation. He had no reason to be ashamed of it. He had never, except perhaps with Bean, used his power to hurt someone. And with Bean, things had worked well after all. Bean had become a friend, finally, to take the place of the lost Alai, who in turn took the place of Valentine. Valentine, who was helping Peter in his plotting. Valentine, who still loved Ender no matter what happened. And following that train of thought led him back to Earth, back to the quiet hours in the center of the clear water ringed by a bowl of tree-covered hills. That is Earth, he thought. Not a globe thousands of kilometers around, but a forest with a shining lake, a house hidden at the crest of the hill, high in the trees, a grassy slope leading upward from the water, fish leaping and birds strafing to take the bugs that lived at the border between water and sky. Earth was the constant noise of crickets and winds and birds. And the voice of one girl, who spoke to him out of his far-off childhood. The same voice that had once protected him from terror. The same voice that he would do anything to keep alive, even return to school, even leave Earth behind again for another four or forty or four thousand years. Even if she loved Peter more.

His eyes were closed, and he had not made any sound but breathing; still, Graff reached out and touched his hand across the aisle. Ender stiffened in surprise, and Graff soon withdrew, but for a moment Ender was struck with the startling thought that perhaps Graff felt some affection for him. But no, it was just another calculated gesture. Graff was creating a commander out of a little boy. No doubt Unit 17 in the course of studies included an affectionate gesture from the teacher.

The shuttle reached the IPL satellite in only a few hours. Inter-Planetary Launch was a city of three thousand inhabitants, breathing oxygen from the plants that also fed them, drinking water that had already passed through their bodies ten thousand times, living only to service the tugs that did all the oxwork in the solar system and the shuttles that took their cargos and passengers back to the Earth or the Moon. It was a world where, briefly, Ender felt at home, since its floors sloped upward as they did in the Battle School.

Their tug was fairly new; the I.F. was constantly casting off its old vehicles and purchasing the latest models. It had just brought a vast load of drawn steel processed by a factory ship that was taking apart minor planets in the asteroid belt. The steel would be dropped to the Moon, and now the tug was linked to fourteen barges. Graff dropped his ball into the reader again, however, and the barges were uncoupled from the tug. It would be making a fast run this time, to a destination of Graff's specification, not to be stated until the tug had cut loose from IPL.

"It's no great secret," said the tug's captain. "Whenever the destination is unknown, it's for ISL." By analogy with IPL, Ender decided the letters meant Inter-Stellar Launch.

"This time it isn't," said Graff.

"Where then?"

"I.F. Command."

"I don't have security clearance even to know where that is, sir."

"Your ship knows," said Graff. "Just let the computer have a look at this, and follow the course it plots." He handed the captain the plastic ball.

"And I'm supposed to close my eyes during the whole voyage, so I don't figure out where we are?"

"Oh, no, of course not. I.F. Command is on the minor planet Eros, which should be about three months away from here at the highest possible speed. Which is the speed you'll use, of course."

"Eros? But I thought that the buggers burned that to a radioactive—ah. When did I receive security clearance to know this?"

"You didn't. So when we arrive at Eros, you will undoubtedly be assigned to permanent duty there."

The captain understood immediately, and didn't like it. "I'm a pilot, you son of a bitch, and you got no right to lock me up on a rock!"

"I will overlook your derisive language to a superior officer. I do apologize, but my orders were to take the fastest available military tug. At the moment I arrived, that was you. It isn't as though anyone were out to get you. Cheer up. The war may be over in another fifteen years, and then the location of I.F. Command won't have to be a secret anymore. By the way, you should be aware, in case you're one of those who relies on visuals for docking, that Eros has been blacked out. Its albedo is only slightly brighter than a black hole. You won't see it."

"Thanks," said the captain.

It was nearly a month into the voyage before he managed to speak civilly to Colonel Graff.

The shipboard computer had a limited library—it was geared primarily to entertainment rather than education. So during the voyage, after breakfast and morning exercises, Ender and Graff would usually talk. About Command School. About Earth. About astronomy and physics and whatever Ender wanted to know.

And above all, he wanted to know about the buggers.

"We don't *know* much," said Graff. "We've never had a live one in custody. Even when we caught one unarmed and alive, he died the moment it became obvious he was captured. Even the *he* is uncertain —the most likely thing, in fact, is that most bugger soldiers are females, but with atrophied or vestigial sexual organs. We can't tell. It's their psychology that would be most useful to you, and we haven't exactly had a chance to interview them."

"Tell me what you know, and maybe I'll learn something that I need."

So Graff told him. The buggers were organisms that could conceivably have evolved on Earth, if things had gone a different way a billion years ago. At the molecular level, there were no surprises. Even the genetic material was the same. It was no accident that they looked insectlike to human beings. Though their internal organs were now much more complex and specialized than any insects, and they had evolved an internal skeleton and shed most of the exoskeleton, their physical structure still echoed their ancestors, who could easily have been very much like Earth's ants. "But don't be fooled by that," said Graff. "It's just as meaningful to say that our ancestors could easily have been very much like squirrels."

"If that's all we have to go on, that's *something*," said Ender.

"Squirrels never built starships," said Graff. "There are usually a few changes on the way from gathering nuts and seeds to harvesting asteroids and putting permanent research stations on the moons of Saturn."

The buggers could probably see about the same spectrum of light as human beings, and there was artificial lighting in their ships and ground installations. However, their antennae seemed almost vestigial. There was no evidence from their bodies that smelling, tasting, or hearing were particularly important to them. "Of course, we can't be sure. But we can't see any way that they could have used sound for communication. The oddest thing of all was that they also don't have any communication devices on their ships. No radios, nothing that could transmit or receive any kind of signal."

"They communicate ship to ship. I've seen the videos, they talk to each other."

"True. But body to body, mind to mind. It's the most important thing we learned from them. Their communication, however they do it, is instantaneous. Lightspeed is no barrier. When Mazer Rackham defeated their invasion fleet, they all closed up shop. At once. There was no time for a signal. Everything just stopped."

Ender remembered the videos of uninjured buggers lying dead at their posts.

"We knew then that it was possible. To communicate faster than light. That was seventy years ago, and once we knew what could be done, we did it. Not *me*, mind you, I wasn't born then."

"How is it possible?"

"I can't explain philotic physics to you. Half of it nobody understands anyway. What matters is we built the ansible. The official name is Philotic Parallax Instantaneous Communicator, but somebody dredged the name *ansible* out of an old book somewhere and it caught on. Not that most people even know the machine exists."

"That means that ships could talk to each other even when they're across the solar system," said Ender.

"It means," said Graff, "that ships could talk to each other even when they're across the galaxy. And the buggers can do it without machines."

"So they knew about their defeat the moment it happened," said Ender. "I always figured—everybody always said that they probably only found out they lost the battle twenty-five years ago."

"It keeps people from panicking," said Graff. "I'm telling you things that you can't know, by the way, if you're ever going to leave I.F. Command. Before the war's over."

Ender was angry. "If you know me at all, you know I can keep a secret."

"It's a regulation. People under twenty-five are assumed to be a security risk. It's very unjust to a good many responsible children, but it helps narrow the number of people who might let something slip."

"What's all the secrecy for, anyway?"

"Because we've taken some terrible risks, Ender, and we don't want to have every net on earth second-guessing those decisions. You see, as soon as we had a working ansible, we tucked it into our best starships and launched them to attack the buggers home systems."

"Do we know where they are?"

"Yes."

"So we're not waiting for the Third Invasion."

"We *are* the Third Invasion."

"We're attacking them. Nobody says that. Everybody thinks we have a huge fleet of warships waiting in the comet shield—"

"Not one. We're quite defenseless here."

"What if they've sent a fleet to attack us?"

"Then we're dead. But our ships haven't seen such a fleet, not a sign of one."

"Maybe they gave up and they're planning to leave us alone."

"Maybe. You've seen the videos. Would you bet the human race on the chance of them giving up and leaving us alone?"

Ender tried to grasp the amounts of time that had gone by. "And the ships have been traveling for seventy years—"

"Some of them. And some for thirty years, and some for twenty. We make better ships now. We're learning how to play with space a little better. But every starship that is not still under construction is on its way to a bugger world or outpost. Every starship, with cruisers and fighters tucked into its belly, is out there approaching the buggers. Decelerating. Because they're almost there. The first ships we sent to the most distant objectives, the more recent ships to the closer ones. Our timing was pretty good. They'll all be arriving in combat range within a few months of each other. Unfortunately, our most primitive, outdated equipment will be attacking their homeworld. Still, they're armed well enough—we have some weapons the buggers never saw before."

"When will they arrive?"

"Within the next five years, Ender. Everything is ready at I.F. Command. The master ansible is there, in contact with all our invasion fleet; the ships are all working, ready to fight. All we lack, Ender, is the battle commander. Someone who knows what the hell to do with those ships when they get there."

"And what if no one knows what to do with them?"

"We'll just do our best, with the best commander we can get."

Me, thought Ender. They want me to be ready in five years. "Colonel Graff, there isn't a chance I'll be ready to command a fleet in time."

Graff shrugged. "So. Do your best. If you aren't ready, we'll make do with what we've got."

That eased Ender's mind.

But only for a moment. "Of course, Ender, what we've got right now is nobody."

Ender knew that this was another of Graff's games. Make me believe that it all depends on me, so I can't slack off, so I push myself as hard as possible.

Game or not, though, it might also be true. And so he would work as hard as possible. It was what Val had wanted of him. Five years. Only five years until the fleet arrives, and I don't know anything yet. "I'll only be fifteen in five years," Ender said.

"Going on sixteen," said Graff. "It all depends on what you know."

"Colonel Graff," he said. "I just want to go back and swim in the lake."

"After we win the war," said Graff. "Or lose it. We'll have a few decades before they get back here to finish us off. The house will be there, and I promise you can swim to your heart's content."

"But I'll still be too young for security clearance."

"We'll keep you under armed guard at all times. The military knows how to handle these things."

They both laughed, and Ender had to remind himself that Graff was only acting like a friend, that everything he did was a lie or a cheat calculated to turn Ender into an efficient fighting machine. I'll become exactly the tool you want me to be, said Ender silently, but at least I won't be *fooled* into it. I'll do it because I choose to, not because you tricked me, you sly bastard.

The tug reached Eros before they could see it. The captain showed them the visual scan, then superimposed the heat scan on the same screen. They were practically on top of it—only four thousand kilometers out—but Eros, only twenty-four kilometers long, was invisible if it didn't shine with reflected sunlight.

The captain docked the ship on one of the three landing platforms that circled Eros. It could not land directly because Eros had enhanced gravity, and the tug, designed for towing cargos, could never escape the gravity well. He bade them an irritable good-bye, but Ender and Graff remained cheerful. The captain was bitter at having to leave his tug; Ender and Graff felt like prisoners finally paroled from jail. When they boarded the shuttle that would take them to the surface of Eros, they repeated perverse misquotations of lines from the videos that the captain had endlessly watched, and laughed like madmen. The captain grew surly and withdrew by pretending to go to sleep. Then, almost as an afterthought, Ender asked Graff one last question.

"Why are we fighting the buggers?"

"I've heard all kinds of reasons," said Graff. "Because they have an overcrowded system and they've got to colonize. Because they can't stand the thought of other intelligent life in the universe. Because they don't think we *are* intelligent life. Because they have some weird religion. Because they watched our old video broadcasts and decided we were hopelessly violent. All kinds of reasons."

"What do you believe?"

"It doesn't matter what I believe."

"I want to know anyway."

"They must talk to each other directly, Ender, mind to mind. What one thinks, another can also think; what one remembers, another can also remember. Why would they ever develop language? Why would they ever learn to read and write? How would they know what reading and writing were if they saw them? Or signals? Or numbers? Or anything that we use to communicate? This isn't just a matter of translating from one language to another. They don't have a language at all. We used every means we could think of to communicate with them, but they don't even have the machinery to know we're signaling. And maybe they've been trying to think to us, and they can't understand why we don't respond."

"So the whole war is because we can't talk to each other."

"If the other fellow can't tell you his story, you can never be sure he isn't trying to kill you."

"What if we just left them alone?"

"Ender, we didn't go to them first, they came to us. If they were going to leave us alone, they could have done it a hundred years ago, before the First Invasion."

"Maybe they didn't know we were intelligent life. Maybe—"

"Ender, believe me, there's a century of discussion on this very subject. Nobody knows the answer. When it comes down to it, though, the real decision is inevitable: If one of us has to be destroyed, let's make damn sure we're the ones alive at the end. Our genes won't let us decide any other way. Nature can't evolve a species that hasn't a will to survive. Individuals might be bred to sacrifice themselves, but the race as a whole can never decide to cease to exist. So if we can we'll kill every last one of the buggers, and if they can they'll kill every last one of us."

"As for me," said Ender, "I'm in favor of surviving."

"I know," said Graff. "That's why you're here."

Chapter **14**

Ender's Teacher

"Took your time, didn't you, Graff? The voyage isn't short, but the three-month vacation seems excessive."

"I prefer not to deliver damaged merchandise."

"Some men simply have no sense of hurry. Oh well, it's only the fate of the world. Never mind me. You must understand our anxiety. We're here with the ansible, receiving constant reports of the progress of our starships. We have to face the coming war every day. If you can call them days. He's such a very **little** boy."

"There's greatness in him. A magnitude of spirit."

"A killer instinct, too, I hope."

"Yes."

"We've planned out an impromptu course of study for him. All subject to your approval, of course."

"I'll look at it. I don't pretend to know the subject matter, Admiral Chamrajnagar. I'm only here because I know Ender. So don't be afraid that I'll try to second guess the order of your presentation. Only the pace."

"How much can we tell him?"

"Don't waste his time on the physics of interstellar travel."

"What about the ansible?"

"I already told him about that, and the fleets. I said they would arrive at their destination within five years."

"It seems there's very little left for us to tell him."

"You can tell him about the weapons systems. He has to know enough to make intelligent decisions."

"Ah. We can be useful after all, how very kind. We've devoted one of the five simulators to his exclusive use."

"What about the others?"

"The other simulators?"

"The other children."

"You were brought here to take care of Ender Wiggin."

"Just curious. Remember, they were all my students at one time or another."

"And now they are all mine. They are entering into the mysteries of the fleet, Colonel Graff, to which you, as a soldier, have never been introduced."

"You make it sound like a priesthood."

"And a god. And a religion. Even those of us who command by ansible know the majesty of flight among the stars. I can see you find my mysticism distasteful. I assure you that your distaste only reveals your ignorance. Soon enough Ender Wiggin will also know what I know; he will dance the graceful ghost dance through the stars, and whatever greatness there is within him will be unlocked, revealed, set forth before the universe for all to see. You have the soul of a stone, Colonel Graff, but I sing to a stone as easily as to another singer. You may go to your quarters and establish yourself."

"I have nothing to establish except the clothing I'm wearing."

"You own nothing?"

"They keep my salary in an account somewhere on Earth. I've never needed it. Except to buy civilian clothes on my—vacation."

"A non-materialist. And yet you are unpleasantly fat. A gluttonous ascetic? Such a contradiction?"

"When I'm tense, I eat. Whereas when you're tense, you spout solid waste."

"I like you, Colonel Graff. I think we shall get along."

"I don't much care, Admiral Chamrajnagar. I came here for Ender. And neither of us came here for you."

Ender hated Eros from the moment he shuttled down from the tug. He had been uncomfortable enough on Earth, where floors were flat; Eros was hopeless. It was a roughly spindle-shaped rock only six and a half kilometers thick at its narrowest point. Since the surface of the planet was entirely devoted to absorbing sunlight and converting it to energy, everyone lived in the smooth-walled rooms linked by tunnels that laced the interior of the asteroid. The closed-in space was no problem for Ender—what bothered him was that all the tunnel floors noticeably sloped downward. From the start, Ender was plagued by vertigo as he walked through the tunnels, especially the ones that girdled Eros's narrow circumference. It did not help that gravity was only half of Earth-normal—the illusion of being on the verge of falling was almost complete.

There was also something disturbing about the proportions of the rooms—the ceilings were too low for the width, the tunnels too narrow. It was not a comfortable place.

Worst of all, though, was the number of people. Ender had no important memories of cities of Earth. His idea of a comfortable number of people was the Battle School, where he had known by sight every person who dwelt there. Here, though, ten thousand people lived within the rock. There was no crowding, despite the amount of space devoted to life support and other machinery. What bothered Ender was that he was constantly surrounded by strangers.

They never let him come to know anyone. He saw the other Command School students often, but since he never attended any class regularly, they remained only faces. He would attend a lecture here or there, but usually he was tutored by one teacher after another, or occasionally helped to learn a process by another student, whom he met once and never saw again. He ate alone or with Colonel Graff. His recreation was in a gym, but he rarely saw the same people in it twice.

He recognized that they were isolating him again, this time not by setting the other students to hating him, but rather by giving them no opportunity to become friends. He could hardly have been close to most of them anyway—except for Ender, the other students were all well into adolescence.

So Ender withdrew into his studies and learned quickly and well. Astrogation and military history he absorbed like water; abstract mathematics was more difficult, but whenever he was given a problem that involved patterns in space and time, he found that his intuition was more reliable than his calculation—he often saw at once a solution that he could only prove after minutes or hours of manipulating numbers.

And for pleasure, there was the simulator, the most perfect

videogame he had ever played. Teachers and students trained him, step by step, in its use. At first, not knowing the awesome power of the game, he had played only at the tactical level, controlling a single fighter in continuous maneuvers to find and destroy an enemy. The computer-controlled enemy was devious and powerful, and whenever Ender tried a tactic he found the computer using it against him within minutes.

The game was a holographic display, and his fighter was represented only by a tiny light. The enemy was another light of a different color, and they danced and spun and maneuvered through a cube of space that must have been ten meters to a side. The controls were powerful. He could rotate the display in any direction, so he could watch from any angle, and he could move the center so that the duel took place nearer or farther from him.

Gradually, as he became more adept at controlling the fighter's speed, direction of movement, orientation, and weapons, the game was made more complex. He might have two enemy ships at once; there might be obstacles, the debris of space; he began to have to worry about fuel and limited weapons; the computer began to assign him particular things to destroy or accomplish, so that he had to avoid distractions and achieve an objective in order to win.

When he had mastered the one-fighter game, they allowed him to step back into the four-fighter squadron. He spoke commands to simulated pilots of four fighters, and instead of merely carrying out the computer's instructions, he was allowed to determine tactics himself, deciding which of several objectives was the most valuable and directing his squadron accordingly. At any time he could take personal command of one of the fighters for a short time, and at first he did this often; when he did, however, the other three fighters in his squadron were soon destroyed, and as the games became harder and harder he had to spend more and more of his time commanding the squadron. When he did, he won more and more often.

By the time he had been at Command School for a year, he was adept at running the simulator at any of fifteen levels, from controlling an individual fighter to commanding a fleet. He had long since realized that as the battleroom was to Battle School, so the simulator was to Command School. The classes were valuable, but the real education was the game. People dropped in from time to time to watch him play. They never spoke—hardly anyone ever did, unless they had something specific to teach him. The watchers would stay, silently, watching him run through a difficult simulation, and then leave just as he finished. What are you doing, he wanted to ask. Judging me? Determining whether you want to trust the fleet to me? Just remember that I didn't ask for it.

He found that a great deal of what he learned at Battle School transferred to the simulator. He would routinely reorient the simulator every few minutes, rotating it so that he didn't get trapped into an up-down orientation, constantly reviewing his position from the enemy point of view. It was exhilarating at last to have such control over the battle, to be able to see every point of it.

It was also frustrating to have so little control, too, for the computer-controlled fighters were only as good as the computer allowed. They took no initiative. They had no intelligence. He began to wish for his toon leaders, so that he could count on some of the squadrons doing well without having his constant supervision.

At the end of his first year he was winning every battle on the simulator, and played the game as if the machine were a natural part of his body. One day, eating a meal with Graff, he asked, "Is that all the simulator does?"

"Is what all?"

"The way it plays now. It's easy, and it hasn't got any harder for a while."

"Oh."

Graff seemed unconcerned. But then, Graff always seemed unconcerned. The next day everything changed. Graff went away, and in his place they gave Ender a companion.

He was in the room when Ender awoke in the morning. He was an old man, sitting cross-legged on the floor. Ender looked at him expectantly, waiting for the man to speak. He said nothing. Ender got up and showered and dressed, content to let the man keep his silence if he wanted. He had long since learned that when something unusual was going on, something that was part of someone else's plan and not his own, he would find out more information by waiting than by asking. Adults almost always lost their patience before Ender did.

The man still hadn't spoken when Ender was ready and went to the door to leave the room. The door didn't open. Ender turned to face the man sitting on the floor. He looked to be about sixty, by far the oldest man Ender had seen on Eros. He had a day's growth of white whiskers that grizzled his face only slightly less than his close-cut hair. His face sagged a little and his eyes were surrounded by creases and lines. He looked at Ender with an expression that bespoke only apathy.

Ender turned back to the door and tried again to open it.

"All right," he said, giving up. "Why's the door locked?"

The old man continued to look at him blankly.

So this is a game, thought Ender. Well, if they want me to go to class, they'll unlock the door. If they don't, they won't. I don't care.

Ender didn't like games where the rules could be anything and the objective was known to them alone. So he wouldn't play. He also refused to get angry. He went through a relaxing exercise as he leaned on the door, and soon he was calm again. The old man continued to watch him impassively.

It seemed to go on for hours, Ender refusing to speak, the old man seeming to be a mindless mute. Sometimes Ender wondered if he were mentally ill, escaped from some medical ward somewhere in Eros, living out some insane fantasy here in Ender's room. But the longer it went on, with no one coming to the door, no one looking for him, the more certain he became that this was something deliberate, meant to disconcert him. Ender did not want to give the old man the victory. To pass the time he began to do exercises. Some were impossible without the gym equipment, but others, especially fom his personal defense class, he could do without any aids.

The exercises moved him around the room. He was practicing lunges and kicks. One move took him near the old man, as he had come near him before, but this time the old claw shot out and seized Ender's left leg in the middle of a kick. It pulled Ender off his feet and landed him heavily on the floor.

Ender leapt to his feet immediately, furious. He found the old man sitting calmly, cross-legged, not breathing heavily, as if he had never moved. Ender stood poised to fight, but the other's immobility made it impossible for Ender to attack. What, kick the old man's head off? And then explain it to Graff—oh, the old man kicked me, and I had to get even.

He went back to his exercises; the old man kept watching.

Finally, tired and angry at this wasted day, a prisoner in his room, Ender went back to his bed to get his desk. As he leaned over to pick up the desk, he felt a hand jab roughly between his thighs and another hand grab his hair. In a moment he had been turned upside down. His face and shoulders were being pressed into the floor by the old man's knee, while his back was excruciatingly bent and his legs were pinioned by the old man's arm. Ender was helpless to use his arms, he couldn't bend his back to gain slack so he could use his legs. In less than two seconds the old man had completely defeated Ender Wiggin.

"All right," Ender gasped. "You win."

The man's knee thrust painfully downward. "Since when," asked the man, his voice soft and rasping, "do you have to tell the enemy when he has won?"

Ender remained silent.

"I surprised you once, Ender Wiggin. Why didn't you destroy me immediately afterward? Just because I looked peaceful? You turned your back on me. Stupid. You have learned nothing. You have never had a teacher."

Ender was angry now, and made no attempt to control or conceal it. "I've had too many teachers, how was I supposed to know you'd turn out to be a—"

"An enemy, Ender Wiggin," whispered the old man. "I am your enemy, the first one you've ever had who was smarter than you. There is no teacher but the enemy. No one but the enemy will ever tell you what the enemy is going to do. No one but the enemy will ever teach you how to destroy and conquer. Only the enemy shows you where you are weak. Only the enemy tells you where he is strong. And the only rules of the game are what you can do to him and what you can stop him from doing to you. I am your enemy from now on. From now on I am your teacher."

Then the old man let Ender's legs fall. Because he still held Ender's head to the floor, the boy couldn't use his arms to compensate, and his legs hit the surface with a loud crack and a sickening pain. Then the old man stood and let Ender rise.

Slowly Ender pulled his legs under him, with a faint groan of pain. He knelt on all fours for a moment, recovering. Then his right arm flashed out, reaching for his enemy. The old man quickly danced back and Ender's hand closed on air as his teacher's foot shot forward to catch Ender on the chin.

Ender's chin wasn't there. He was lying flat on his back, spinning on the floor, and during the moment that his teacher was off balance from his kick, Ender's feet smashed into the old man's other leg. He fell in a heap—but close enough to strike out and hit Ender in the face. Ender couldn't find an arm or a leg that held still long enough to be grabbed, and in the meantime blows were landing on his back and arms. Ender was smaller—he couldn't reach past the old man's flailing limbs. Finally he managed to pull away and scramble back near the door.

The old man was sitting cross-legged again, but now the apathy was gone. He was smiling. "Better, this time, boy. But slow. You will have to be better with a fleet than you are with your body or no one will be safe with you in command. Lesson learned?"

Ender nodded slowly. He ached in a hundred places.

"Good," said the old man. "Then we'll never have to have such a battle again. All the rest with the simulator. I will program your battles now, not the computer; I will devise the strategy of your enemy, and you will learn to be quick and discover what tricks the enemy has for you. Remember, boy. From now on the enemy is more clever than you. From now on the enemy is stronger than you. From now on you are always about to lose."

The old man's face grew serious again. "You will be about to lose, Ender, but you will win. You will learn to defeat the enemy. He will teach you how."

The teacher got up. "In this school, it has always been the practice for a young student to be chosen by an older student. The two become companions, and the older boy teaches the younger one everything he knows. Always they fight, always they compete, always they are together. I have chosen you."

Ender spoke as the old man walked to the door. "You're too old to be a student."

"One is never too old to be a student of the enemy. I have learned from the buggers. You will learn from me."

As the old man palmed the door open, Ender leaped into the air and kicked him in the small of the back with both feet. He hit hard enough that he rebounded onto his feet, as the old man cried out and collapsed on the floor.

The old man got up slowly, holding onto the door handle, his face contorted with pain. He seemed disabled, but Ender didn't trust him. Yet in spite of his suspicion, he was caught off guard by the old man's speed. In a moment he found himself on the floor near the opposite wall, his nose and lip bleeding where his face had hit the bed. He was able to turn enough to see the old man standing in the doorway, wincing and holding his back. The old man grinned.

Ender grinned back. "Teacher," he said. "Do you have a name?"

"Mazer Rackham," said the old man. Then he was gone.

From then on, Ender was either with Mazer Rackham or alone. The old man rarely spoke, but he was there; at meals, at tutorials, at the simulator, in his room at night. Sometimes Mazer would leave, but always, when Mazer wasn't there, the door was locked, and no one came until Mazer returned. Ender went through a week in which he called him Jailor Rackham. Mazer answered to the name as readily as to his own, and showed no sign that it bothered him at all. Ender soon gave it up.

There were compensations. Mazer took Ender through the videos of the old battles from the First Invasion and the disastrous defeats of the I.F. in the Second Invasion. These were not pieced together from the censored public videos, but whole and continuous. Since many videos were working in the major battles, they studied bugger tactics and strategies from many angles. For the first time in his life, a teacher was pointing out things that Ender had not already seen for himself. For the first time, Ender had found a living mind he could admire.

"Why aren't you dead?" Ender asked him. "You fought your battle seventy years ago. I don't think you're even sixty years old."

"The miracles of relativity," said Mazer. "They kept me here for twenty years after the battle, even though I begged them to let me command one of the starships they launched against the bugger home planet and the bugger colonies. Then they—came to understand some things about the way soldiers behave in the stress of battle."

"What things?"

"You've never been taught enough psychology to understand. Enough to say that they realized that even though I would never be able to command the fleet—I'd be dead before the fleet even arrived —I was still the only person able to understand the things I understood about the buggers. I was, they realized, the only person who had ever defeated the buggers by intelligence rather than luck. They needed me here to—teach the person who *would* command the fleet."

"So they sent you out in a starship, got you up to a relativistic speed—"

"And then I turned around and came home. A very dull voyage, Ender. Fifty years in space. Officially, only eight years passed for me, but it felt like five hundred. All so I could teach the next commander everything I knew."

"Am I to be the commander, then?"

"Let's say that you're our best bet at present."

"There are others being prepared, too?"

"No."

"That makes me the only choice, then, doesn't it?"

Mazer shrugged.

"Except you. You're still alive, aren't you? Why not you?"

Mazer shook his head.

"Why not? You won before."

"I cannot be the commander for good and sufficient reasons."

"Show me how you beat the buggers, Mazer."

Mazer's face went inscrutable.

"You've shown me every other battle seven times at least. I think I've seen ways to beat what the buggers did before, but you've never shown me how you actually *did* beat them."

"The video is a very tightly kept secret, Ender."

"I know. I've pieced it together, partly. You, with your tiny reserve force, and their armada, those great big heavy-bellied starships launching their swarms of fighters. You dart in at one ship, fire at it, an explosion. That's where they always stop the clips. After that, it's just soldiers going into bugger ships and already finding them dead inside."

Mazer grinned. "So much for tightly kept secrets. Come on, let's watch the video."

They were alone in the video room, and Ender palmed the door locked. "All right, let's watch."

The video showed exactly what Ender had pieced together. Mazer's suicidal plunge into the heart of the enemy formation, the single explosion, and then—

Nothing. Mazer's ship went on, dodged the shock wave, and wove his way among the other bugger ships. They did not fire on him. They did not change course. Two of them crashed into each other and exploded—a needless collision that either pilot could have avoided. Neither made the slightest movement.

Mazer sped up the action. Skipped ahead. "We waited for three hours," he said. "Nobody could believe it." Then the I.F. ships began approaching the bugger starships. Marines began their cutting and boarding operations. The videos showed the buggers already dead at their posts.

"So you see," said Mazer, "you already knew all there was to see."

"Why did it happen?"

"Nobody knows. I have my personal opinions. But there are plenty of scientists who tell me I'm less than qualified to have opinions."

"You're the one who won the battle."

"I thought that qualified me to comment, too, but you know how it is. Xenobiologists and xenopsychologists can't accept the idea that a starpilot scooped them by sheer guesswork. I think they all hate me because, after they saw these videos, they had to live out the rest of their natural lives here on Eros. Security, you know. They weren't happy."

"Tell me."

"The buggers don't talk. They think to each other, and it's instantaneous, like the philotic effect. Like the ansible. But most people always thought that meant a controlled communication, like language—I think you a thought and then you answer me. I never believed that. It's too *immediate,* the way they respond together to things. You've seen the videos. They aren't conversing and deciding among possible courses of action. Every ship acts like part of a single organism. It responds the way your body responds during combat, different parts automatically, thoughtlessly doing everything they're supposed to do. They aren't having a mental conversation between people with different thought processes. *All* their thoughts are present, together, at once."

"A single person, and each bugger is like a hand or a foot?"

"Yes. I wasn't the first person to suggest it, but I was the first person to believe it. And something else. Something so childish and stupid that the xenobiologists laughed me to silence when I said it after the battle. The buggers are *bugs*. They're like ants and bees. A queen, the workers. That was maybe a hundred million years ago, but that's how they started, that kind of pattern. It's a sure thing none of the buggers *we* saw had any way of making more little buggers. So when they evolved this ability to think together, wouldn't they still keep the queen? Wouldn't the queen still be the center of the group? Why would that ever change?"

"So it's the queen who controls the whole group."

"I had evidence, too. Not evidence that any of them could see. It wasn't there in the First Invasion, because that was exploratory. But the Second Invasion was a colony. To set up a new hive, or whatever."

"And so they brought a queen."

"The videos of the Second Invasion, when they were destroying our fleets out in the comet shell." He began to call them up and display the buggers' patterns. "Show me the queen's ship."

It was subtle. Ender couldn't see it for a long time. The bugger ships kept moving, all of them. There was no obvious flagship, no apparent nerve center. But gradually, as Mazer played the videos over and over again, Ender began to see the way that all the movements focused on, radiated from a center point. The center point shifted, but it was obvious, after he looked long enough, that the eyes of the fleet, the *I* of the fleet, the perspective from which all decisions were being made, was one particular ship. He pointed it out.

"You see it. I see it. That makes two people out of all of those who have seen this video. But it's true, isn't it."

"They make that ship move just like any other ship."

"They know it's their weak point."

"But you're right. That's the queen. But then you'd think that when you went for it, they would have immediately focused all their power on you. They could have blown you out of the sky."

"I know. That part I don't understand. Not that they didn't try to stop me—they were firing at me. But it's as if they really couldn't believe, until it was too late, that I would actually *kill* the queen. Maybe in their world, queens are never killed, only captured, only checkmated. I did something they didn't think an enemy would ever do."

"And when she died, the others all died."

"No, they just went stupid. The first ships we boarded, the buggers were still alive. Organically. But they didn't move, didn't respond to anything, even when our scientists vivisected some of them to see if we could learn a few more things about buggers. After a while they all died. No will. There's nothing in those little bodies when the queen is gone."

"Why don't they believe you?"

"Because we didn't find a queen."

"She got blown to pieces."

"Fortunes of war. Biology takes second place to survival. But some of them *are* coming around to my way of thinking. You can't live in this place without the evidence staring you in the face."

"What evidence is there in Eros?"

"Ender, look around you. Human beings didn't carve this place. We like taller ceilings, for one thing. This was the buggers' advance post in the First Invasion. They carved this place out before we even knew they were here. We're living in a bugger hive. But we already paid our rent. It cost the marines a thousand lives to clear them out of these honeycombs, room by room. The buggers fought for every meter of it."

Now Ender understood why the rooms had always felt wrong to him. "I knew this wasn't a human place."

"This was the treasure trove. If they had known we would win that first war, they probably would never have built this place. We learned gravity manipulation because they enhanced the gravity here. We learned efficient use of stellar energy because they blacked out this planet. In fact, that's how we discovered *them*. In a period of three days, Eros gradually disappeared from telescopes. We sent a tug to find out why. It found out. The tug transmitted its videos, including the buggers boarding and slaughtering the crew. It kept right on transmitting through the entire bugger examination of the boat. Not until they finally dismantled the entire tug did the transmissions stop. It was their blindness—they never had to transmit anything by machine, and so with the crew dead, it didn't occur to them that anybody could be watching."

"Why did they kill the crew?"

"Why not? To them, losing a few crew members would be like clipping your nails. Nothing to get upset about. They probably thought they were routinely shutting down our communications by turning off the workers running the tug. Not murdering living, sentient beings with an independent genetic future. Murder's no big deal to them. Only queen-killing, really, is murder, because only queen-killing closes off a genetic path."

"So they didn't know what they were doing."

"Don't start apologizing for them, Ender. Just because they didn't know they were killing human beings doesn't mean they weren't killing human beings. We do have a right to defend ourselves as best we can, and the only way we found that works is killing the buggers before they kill us. Think of it this way. In all the bugger wars so far, they've killed thousands and thousands of living, thinking beings. And in all those wars, we've killed only one."

"If you hadn't killed the queen, Mazer, would we have lost the war?"

"I'd say the odds would have been three to two against us. I still think I could have trashed their fleet pretty badly before they burned us out. They have great response time and a lot of firepower, but we have a few advantages, too. Every single one of our ships contains an intelligent human being who's thinking on his own. Every one of us is capable of coming up with a brilliant solution to a problem. They can only come up with one brilliant solution at a time. The buggers think fast, but they aren't smart all over. Even when some incredibly timid and stupid commanders lost the major battles of the Second Invasion, some of their subordinates were able to do real damage to the bugger fleet."

"What about when our invasion reaches them? Will we just get the queen again?"

"The buggers didn't learn interstellar travel by being dumb. That was a strategy that could work only once. I suspect that we'll never get near a queen unless we actually make it to their home planet. After all, the queen doesn't have to be *with* them to direct a battle. The queen only has to be present to have little baby buggers. The Second Invasion was a colony—the queen was coming to populate the Earth. But this time—no, that won't work. We'll have to beat them fleet by fleet. And because they have the resources of dozens of star systems to draw on, my guess is they'll outnumber us by a lot, in every battle."

Ender remembered his battle against two armies at once. And I thought they were cheating. When the real war begins, it'll be like that every time. And there won't be any gate I can go for.

"We've only got two things going for us, Ender. We don't have to aim particularly well. Our weapons have great spread."

"Then we aren't using the nuclear missiles from the First and Second Invasions?"

"Dr. Device is much more powerful. Nuclear weapons, after all, were weak enough to be used on Earth at one time. The Little Doctor could never be used on a planet. Still, I wish I'd had one during the Second Invasion."

"How does it work?"

"I don't know, not well enough to build one. At the focal point of two beams, it sets up a field in which molecules can't hold together anymore. Electrons can't be shared. How much physics do you know, at that level?"

"We spend most of our time on astrophysics, but I know enough to get the idea."

"The field spreads out in a sphere, but it gets weaker the farther it spreads. Except that where it actually runs into a lot of molecules, it gets stronger and starts over. The bigger the ship, the stronger the new field."

"So each time the field hits a ship, it sends out a new sphere—"

"And if their ships are too close together, it can set up a chain that wipes them all out. Then the field dies down, the molecules come back together, and where you had a ship, you now have a lump of dirt with a lot of iron molecules in it. No radioactivity, no mess. Just dirt. We may be able to trap them close together on the first battle, but they learn fast. They'll keep their distance from each other."

"So Dr. Device isn't a missile—I can't shoot around corners."

"That's right. Missiles wouldn't do any good now. We learned a lot from them in the First Invasion, but they also learned from us— how to set up the Ecstatic Shield, for instance."

"The Little Doctor penetrates the shield?"

"As if it weren't there. You can't *see* through the shield to aim and focus the beams, but since the generator of the Ecstatic Shield is always in the exact center, it isn't hard to figure it out."

"Why haven't I ever been trained with this?"

"You always have. We just let the computer tend to it for you.

Your job is to get into a superior strategic position and choose a target. The shipboard computers are much better at aiming the Doctor than you are."

"Why is it called Dr. Device?"

"When it was developed, it was called a Molecular Detachment Device. M.D. Device."

Ender still didn't understand.

"M.D. The initials stand for Medical Doctor, too. M.D. Device, therefore Dr. Device. It was a joke." Ender didn't see what was funny about it.

They had changed the simulator. He could still control the perspective and the degree of detail, but there were no ship's controls anymore. Instead, it was a new panel of levers, and a small headset with earphones and a small microphone.

The technician who was waiting there quickly explained how to wear the headset.

"But how do I control the ships?" asked Ender.

Mazer explained. He wasn't going to control ships anymore. "You've reached the next phase of your training. You have experience in every level of strategy, but now it's time for you to concentrate on commanding an entire fleet. As you worked with toon leaders in Battle School, so now you will work with squadron leaders. You have been assigned three dozen such leaders to train. You must teach them intelligent tactics; you must learn their strengths and limitations; you must make them into a whole."

"When will they come here?"

"They're already in place in their own simulators. You will speak to them through the headset. The new levers on your control panel enable you to see from the perspective of any of your squadron leaders. This more closely duplicates the conditions you might encounter in a real battle, where you will only know what your ships can see."

"How can I work with squadron leaders I never see?"

"And why would you need to see them?"

"To know who they are, how they think—"

"You'll learn who they are and how they think from the way they work with the simulator. But even so, I think you won't be concerned. They're listening to you right now. Put on the headset so you can hear them."

Ender put on the headset.

"Salaam," said a whisper in his ears.

"Alai," said Ender.

"And me, the dwarf."

"Bean."

And Petra, and Dink; Crazy Tom, Shen, Hot Soup, Fly Molo, all the best students Ender had fought with or fought against, everyone that Ender had trusted in Battle School. "I didn't know you were here," he said. "I didn't know you were coming."

"They've been flogging us through the simulator for three months now," said Dink.

"You'll find that I'm by far the best tactician," said Petra. "Dink tries, but he has the mind of a child."

So they began working together, each squadron leader commanding individual pilots, and Ender commanding the squadron leaders. They learned many ways of working together, as the simulator forced them to try different situations. Sometimes the simulator gave them a larger fleet to work with; Ender set them up then in three or four toons that consisted of three or four squadrons each. Sometimes the simulator gave them a single starship with its twelve fighters, and he chose three squadron leaders with four fighters each.

It was pleasure; it was play. The computer-controlled enemy was none too bright, and they always won despite their mistakes, their miscommunications. But in the three weeks they practiced together, Ender came to know them very well. Dink, who deftly carried out instructions but was slow to improvise; Bean, who couldn't control large groups of ships effectively but could use only a few like a scalpel, reacting beautifully to anything the computer threw at him; Alai, who was almost as good a strategist as Ender and could be entrusted to do well with half a fleet and only vague instructions.

The better Ender knew them, the faster he could deploy them, the better he could use them. The simulator would display the situation on the screen. In that moment Ender learned for the first time what his own fleet would consist of and how the enemy fleet was deployed. It took him only a few minutes now to call for the squadron leaders that he needed, assign them to certain ships or groups of ships, and give them their assignments. Then, as the battle progressed, he would skip from one leader's point of view to another's, making suggestions and, occasionally, giving orders as the need arose. Since the others could only see their own battle perspective, he would sometimes give them orders that made no sense to them; but they, too, learned to trust Ender. If he told them to withdraw, they withdrew, knowing that either they were in an exposed position, or their withdrawal might entice the enemy into a weakened posture. They also knew that Ender trusted them to do as they judged best when he gave them no orders. If their style of fighting were not right for the situation they were placed in, Ender would not have chosen them for that assignment.

The trust was complete, the working of the fleet quick and responsive. And at the end of three weeks, Mazer showed him a replay of their most recent battle, only this time from the enemy's point of view.

"This is what he saw as you attacked. What does it remind you of? The quickness of response, for instance?"

"We look like a bugger fleet."

"You match them, Ender. You're as fast as they are. And here— look at this."

Ender watched as all his squadrons moved at once, each responding to its own situation, all guided by Ender's overall command, but daring, improvising, feinting, attacking with an independence no bugger fleet had ever shown.

"The bugger hive-mind is very good, but it can only concentrate on a few things at once. All your squadrons can concentrate a keen intelligence on what they're doing, and what they've been assigned to do is also guided by a clever mind. So you see that you do have some advantages. Superior, though not irresistible, weaponry; comparable speed and greater available intelligence. These are your advantages. Your disadvantage is that you will always, always be outnumbered, and after each battle your enemy will learn more about you, how to fight you, and those changes will be put into effect instantly."

Ender waited for his conclusion.

"So, Ender, we will now begin your education. We have programmed the computer to simulate the kinds of situations we might expect in encounters with the enemy. We are using the movement patterns we saw in the Second Invasion. But instead of mindlessly following these same patterns, I will be controlling the enemy simulation. At first you will see easy situations that you are expected to win handily. Learn from them, because I will always be there, one step ahead of you, programming more difficult and advanced patterns into the computer so that your next battle is more difficult, so that you are pushed to the limit of your abilities."

"And beyond?"

"The time is short. You must learn as quickly as you can. When I gave myself to starship travel, just so I would still be alive when you appeared, my wife and children all died, and my grandchildren were my own age when I came back. I had nothing to say to them. I was cut off from all the people that I loved, everything I knew, living in this alien catacomb and forced to do nothing of importance but teach student after student, each one so hopeful, each one, ultimately, a weakling, a failure. I teach, I teach, but no one learns. You, too, have great promise, like so many students before you, but the seeds of failure may be in you, too. It's my job to find them, to destroy you if I can, and believe me, Ender, if you can be destroyed I can do it."

"So I'm not the first."

"No, of course you're not. But you're the last. If you don't learn, there'll be no time to find anyone else. So I have hope for you, only because you are the only one left to hope for."

"What about the others? My squadron leaders?"

"Which of them is fit to take your place?"

"Alai."

"Be honest."

Ender had no answer, then.

"I am not a happy man, Ender. Humanity does not ask us to be happy. It merely asks us to be brilliant on its behalf. Survival first, then happiness as we can manage it. So, Ender, I hope you do not bore me during your training with complaints that you are not having fun. Take what pleasure you can in the interstices of your work, but your work is first, learning is first, winning is everything because without it there is nothing. When you can give me back my dead wife, Ender, then you can complain to me about what this education costs you."

"I wasn't trying to get out of anything."

"But you will, Ender. Because I am going to grind you down to dust, if I can. I'm going to hit you with everything I can imagine, and I will have no mercy, because when you face the buggers they will think of things I *can't* imagine, and compassion for human beings is impossible for them."

"You can't grind me down, Mazer."

"Oh, can't I?"

"Because I'm stronger than you."

Mazer smiled. "We'll see about that, Ender."

Mazer wakened him before morning; the clock said 0340, and Ender felt groggy as he padded along the corridor behind Mazer. "Early to bed and early to rise," Mazer intoned, "makes a man stupid and blind in the eyes."

He had been dreaming that buggers were vivisecting him. Only instead of cutting open his body, they were cutting up his memories and displaying them like holographs and trying to make sense of them. It was a very odd dream, and Ender couldn't easily shake loose of it, even as he walked through the tunnels to the simulator room. The buggers tormented him in his sleep, and Mazer wouldn't leave him alone when he was awake. Between the two of them he had no rest. Ender forced himself awake. Apparently Mazer meant it when he said he meant to break Ender down—and forcing him to play when tired and sleepy was just the sort of cheap and easy trick Ender should have expected. Well, today it wouldn't work.

He got to the simulator and found his squadron leaders already on the wire, waiting for him. There was no enemy yet, so he divided them into two armies and began a mock battle, commanding both sides so he could control the test that each of his leaders was going through. They began slowly, but soon were vigorous and alert.

Then the simulator field went blank, the ships disappeared, and everything changed at once. At the near edge of the simulator field they could see the shapes, drawn in holographic light, of three starships from the human fleet. Each would have twelve fighters. The enemy, obviously aware of the human presence, had formed a globe with a single ship at the center. Ender was not fooled—it would not be a queen ship. The buggers outnumbered Ender's fighter force by two to one, but they were also grouped much closer together than they should have been—Dr. Device would be able to do much more damage than the enemy expected.

Ender selected one starship, made it blink in the simulator field, and spoke into the microphone. "Alai, this is yours; assign Petra and Vlad to the fighters as you wish." He assigned the other two starships with their fighter forces, except for one fighter from each starship that he reserved for Bean. "Slip the wall and get below them, Bean, unless they start chasing you—then run back to the reserves for safety. Otherwise, get in a place where I can call on you for quick results. Alai, form your force into a compact assault at one point in their globe. Don't fire until I tell you. This is maneuver only."

"This one's easy, Ender," Alai said.

"It's easy, so why not be careful? I'd like to do this without the loss of a single ship."

Ender grouped his reserves in two forces that shadowed Alai at a safe distance; Bean was already off the simulator, though Ender occasionally flipped to Bean's point of view to keep track of where he was.

It was Alai, however, who played the delicate game with the enemy. He was in a bullet-shaped formation, and probed the enemy globe. Wherever he came near, the bugger ships pulled back, as if to draw him in toward the ship in the center. Alai skimmed to the side; the bugger ships kept up with him, withdrawing wherever he was close, returning to the sphere pattern when he had passed.

Feint, withdraw, skim the globe to another point, withdraw again, feint again; and then Ender said, "Go on in, Alai."

His bullet started in, while he said to Ender, "You know they'll just let me through and surround me and eat me alive."

"Just ignore that ship in the middle."

"Whatever you say, boss."

Sure enough, the globe began to contract. Ender brought the reserves forward; the enemy ships concentrated on the side of the globe nearer the reserves. "Attack them there, where they're most concentrated," Ender said.

"This defies four thousand years of military history," said Alai, moving his fighters forward. "We're supposed to attack where we outnumber them."

"In this simulation they obviously don't know what our weapons can do. It'll only work once, but let's make it spectacular. Fire at will."

Alai did. The simulation responded beautifully: first one or two, then a dozen, then most of the enemy ships exploded in dazzling light as the field leapt from ship to ship in the tight formation. "Stay out of the way," Ender said.

The ships on the far side of the globe formation were not affected by the chain reaction, but it was a simple matter hunting them down and destroying them. Bean took care of stragglers that tried to escape toward his end of space. The battle was over. It had been easier than most of their recent exercises.

Mazer shrugged when Ender told him so. "This is a simulation of a real invasion. There had to be one battle in which they didn't know what we could do. Now your work begins. Try not to be too arrogant about the victory. I'll give you the real challenges soon enough."

Ender practiced ten hours a day with his squadron leaders, but not all at once; he gave them a few hours in the afternoon to rest. Simulated battles under Mazer's supervision came every two or three days, and as Mazer had promised, they were never so easy again. The enemy quickly abandoned its attempt to surround Ender, and never again grouped its forces closely enough to allow a chain reaction. There was something new every time, something harder. Sometimes Ender had only a single starship and eight fighters; once the enemy dodged through an asteroid belt; sometimes the enemy left stationary traps, large installations that blew up if Ender brought one of his squadrons too close, often crippling or destroying some of Ender's ships. "You cannot absorb losses!" Mazer shouted at him after one battle. "When you get into a *real* battle you won't have the luxury of an infinite supply of computer-generated fighters. You'll have what you brought with you and *nothing more.* Now get used to fighting without unnecessary waste."

"It wasn't unnecessary waste," Ender said. "I can't win battles if I'm so terrified of losing a ship that I never take any risks."

Mazer smiled. "Excellent, Ender. You're beginning to learn. But in a real battle, you would have superior officers and, worst of all, civilians shouting those things at you. Now, if the enemy had been at all bright, they would have caught you *here,* and taken Tom's squadron." Together they went over the battle; in the next practice, Ender would show his leaders what Mazer had shown him, and they'd learn to cope with it the next time they saw it.

They thought they had been ready before, that they had worked smoothly together as a team. Now, though, having fought through real challenges together, they all began to trust each other more than ever, and battles became exhilarating. They told Ender that the ones who weren't actually playing would come into the simulator rooms and watch. Ender imagined what it would be like to have his friends there with him, cheering or laughing or gasping with apprehension; sometimes he thought it would be a great distraction, but other times he wished for it with all his heart. Even when he had spent his days lying out in the sunlight on a raft in a lake, he had not been so lonely. Mazer Rackham was his companion, was his teacher, but was not his friend.

He said nothing, though. Mazer had told him there would be no pity, and his private unhappiness meant nothing to anyone. Most of the time it meant nothing even to Ender. He kept his mind on the game, trying to learn from the battles. And not just the particular lessons of that battle, but what the buggers might have done if they had been more clever, and how Ender would react if they did it in the future. He lived with past battles and future battles both, waking and sleeping, and he drove his squadron leaders with an intensity that occasionally provoked rebelliousness.

"You're too kind to us," said Alai one day. "Why don't you get annoyed with us for not being brilliant *every* moment of *every* practice. If you keep coddling us like this we'll think you like us."

Some of the others laughed into their microphones. Ender recognized the irony, of course, and answered with a long silence. When he finally spoke, he ignored Alai's complaint. "Again," he said, "and this time without self-pity." They did it again, and did it right.

But as their trust in Ender as a commander grew, their friendship, remembered from the Battle School days, gradually disappeared. It was to each other that they became close; it was with each other that they exchanged confidences. Ender was their teacher and commander, as distant from them as Mazer was from him, and as demanding.

They fought all the better for it. And Ender was not distracted from his work.

At least, not while he was awake. As he drifted off to sleep each night, it was with thoughts of the simulator playing through his mind. But in the night he thought of other things. Often he remembered the corpse of the Giant, decaying steadily; he did not remember it, though, in the pixels of the picture on his desk. Instead it was real, the faint odor of death still lingering near it. Things were changed in his dreams. The little village that had grown up between the Giant's ribs was composed of buggers now, and they saluted him gravely, like gladiators greeting Caesar before they died for his entertainment. He did not hate the buggers in his dream; and even though he knew that they had hidden their queen from him, he did not try to search her. He always left the Giant's body quickly, and when he got to the playground, the children were always there, wolven and mocking; they wore faces that he knew. Sometimes Peter and sometimes Bonzo, sometimes Stilson and Bernard; just as often, though, the savage creatures were Alai and Shen, Dink and Petra; sometimes one of them would be Valentine, and in his dream he also shoved her under the water and waited for her to drown. She writhed in his hands, fought to come up, but at last was still. He dragged her out of the lake and onto the raft, where she lay with her face in the rictus of death. He screamed and wept over her, crying again and again that it was a game, a game, he was only playing!—

Then Mazer Rackham shook him awake. "You were calling out in your sleep," he said.

"Sorry," Ender said.

"Never mind. It's time for another battle."

Steadily the pace increased. There were usually two battles a day now, and Ender held practices to a minimum. He would use the time while the others rested to pore over the replays of past games, trying to spot his own weaknesses, trying to guess what would happen next. Sometimes he was fully prepared for the enemy's innovations; sometimes he was not.

"I think you're cheating," Ender told Mazer one day.

"Oh?"

"You can observe my practice sessions. You can see what I'm working on. You seem to be ready for everything I do."

"Most of what you see is computer simulations," Mazer said. "The computer is programmed to respond to your innovations only after you use them once in battle."

"Then the computer is cheating."

"You need to get more sleep, Ender."

But he could not sleep. He lay awake longer and longer each night, and his sleep was less restful. He woke too often in the night. Whether he was waking up to think more about the game or to escape from his dreams, he wasn't sure. It was as if someone rode him in his sleep, forcing him to wander through his worst memories, to live in them again as if they were real. Nights were so real that days began to seem dreamlike to him. He began to worry that he would not think clearly enough, that he would be too tired when he played. Always when the game began, the intensity of it awoke him, but if his mental abilities began to slip, he wondered, would he notice it?

And he seemed to be slipping. He never had a battle anymore in which he did not lose at least a few fighters. Several times the enemy was able to trick him into exposing more weakness than he meant to; other times the enemy was able to wear him down by attrition until his victory was as much a matter of luck as strategy. Mazer would go over the game with a look of contempt on his face. "Look at this," he would say. "You didn't have to do this." And Ender would return to practice with his leaders, trying to keep up their morale, but sometimes letting slip his disappointment with their weaknesses, the fact that they made mistakes.

"Sometimes we make mistakes," Petra whispered to him once. It was a plea for help.

"And sometimes we don't," Ender answered her. If she got help, it would not be from him. He would teach; let her find her friends among the others.

Then came a battle that nearly ended in disaster. Petra led her force too far; they were exposed, and she discovered it in a moment when Ender wasn't with her. In only a few moments she had lost all but two of her ships. Ender found her then, ordered her to move them in a certain direction; she didn't answer. There was no movement. And in a moment those two fighters, too, would be lost.

Ender knew at once that he had pushed her too hard—because of her brilliance he had called on her to play far more often and under much more demanding circumstances than all but a few of the others. But he had no time now to worry about Petra, or to feel guilty about what he had done to her. He called on Crazy Tom to command the two remaining fighters, then went on, trying to salvage the battle; Petra had occupied a key position, and now all of Ender's strategy came apart. If the enemy had not been too eager and clumsy in exploiting their advantage, Ender would have lost. But Shen was able to catch a group of the enemy in too tight a formation and took them out with a single chain reaction. Crazy Tom brought his two surviving fighters in through the gap and caused havoc with the enemy, and though his ships and Shen's as well were finally destroyed, Fly Molo was able to mop up and complete the victory.

At the end of the battle, he could hear Petra crying out, trying to get a microphone, "Tell him I'm sorry, I was just so tired, I couldn't think, that was all, tell Ender I'm sorry."

She was not there for the next few practices, and when she did come back she was not as quick as she had been, not as daring. Much of what had made her a good commander was lost. Ender couldn't use her anymore, except in routine, closely supervised assignments. She was no fool. She knew what had happened. But she also knew that Ender had no other choice, and told him so.

The fact remained that she had broken, and she was far from being the weakest of his squad leaders. It was a warning—he could not press his commanders more than they could bear. Now, instead of using his leaders whenever he needed their skills, he had to keep in mind how often they had fought. He had to spell them off, which meant that sometimes he went into battle with commanders he trusted a little less. As he eased the pressure on them, he increased the pressure on himself.

Late one night he woke up in pain. There was blood on his pillow, the taste of blood in his mouth. His fingers were throbbing. He saw that in his sleep he had been gnawing on his own fist. The blood was still flowing smoothly. "Mazer!" he called. Rackham woke up and called at once for a doctor.

As the doctor treated the wound, Mazer said, "I don't care how much you eat, Ender, self-cannibalism won't get you out of this school."

"I was asleep," Ender said. "I don't want to get out of Command School."

"Good."

"The others. The ones who didn't make it."

"What are you talking about?"

"Before me. Your other students, who didn't make it through the training. What happened to them?"

"They didn't make it. That's all. We don't punish the ones who fail. They just—don't go on."

"Like Bonzo."

"Bonzo?"

"He went home."

"Not like Bonzo."

"What then? What happened to them? When they failed?"

"Why does it matter, Ender?"

Ender didn't answer.

"None of them failed at *this* point in their course, Ender. You made a mistake with Petra. She'll recover. But Petra is Petra, and you are you."

"Part of what I am is her. Is what she made me."

"You won't fail, Ender. Not this early in the course. You've had some tight ones, but you've always won. You don't know what your limits are yet, but if you've reached them already you're a good deal feebler than I thought."

"Do they die?"

"Who?"

"The ones who fail."

"No, they don't die. Good heavens, boy, you're playing games."

"I think that Bonzo died. I dreamed about it last night. I remembered the way he looked after I jammed his face with my head. I think I must have pushed his nose back into his brain. The blood was coming out of his eyes. I think he was dead right then."

"It was just a dream."

"Mazer, I don't want to keep dreaming these things. I'm afraid to sleep. I keep thinking of things that I don't want to remember. My whole life keeps playing out as if I were a recorder and someone else wanted to watch the most terrible parts of my life."

"We can't drug you if that's what you're hoping for. I'm sorry if you have bad dreams. Should we leave the light on at night?"

"Don't make fun of me!" Ender said. "I'm afraid I'm going crazy."

The doctor was finished with the bandage. Mazer told him he could go. He went.

"Are you really afraid of that?" Mazer asked.

Ender thought about it and wasn't sure.

"In my dreams," said Ender, "I'm never sure whether I'm really me."

"Strange dreams are a safety valve, Ender. I'm putting you under a little pressure for the first time in your life. Your body is finding ways to compensate, that's all. You're a big boy now. It's time to stop being afraid of the night."

"All right," Ender said. He decided then that he would never tell Mazer about his dreams again.

The days wore on, with battles every day, until at last Ender settled into the routine of the destruction of himself. He began to have pains in his stomach. They put him on a bland diet, but soon he didn't have an appetite for anything at all. "Eat," Mazer said, and Ender would mechanically put food in his mouth. But if nobody told him to eat, he didn't eat.

Two more of his squadron leaders collapsed the way that Petra had; the pressure on the rest became all the greater. The enemy outnumbered them by three or four to one in every battle now; the enemy also retreated more readily when things went badly, regrouping to keep the battle going longer and longer. Sometimes battles lasted for hours before they finally destroyed the last enemy ship. Ender began rotating his squadron leaders within the same battle, bringing in fresh and rested ones to take the place of those who were beginning to get sluggish.

"You know," said Bean one time, as he took over command of Hot Soup's four remaining fighters, "this game isn't quite as fun as it used to be."

Then one day in practice, as Ender was drilling his squadron leaders, the room went black and he woke up on the floor with his face bloody where he had hit the controls.

They put him to bed then, and for three days he was very ill. He remembered seeing faces in his dreams, but they weren't real faces, and he knew it even while he thought he saw them. He thought he saw Valentine sometimes, and sometimes Peter; sometimes his friends from the Battle School, and sometimes the buggers vivisecting him. Once it seemed very real when he saw Colonel Graff bending over him, speaking softly to him, like a kind father. But then he woke up and found only his enemy, Mazer Rackham.

"I'm awake," said Ender.

"So I see," Mazer answered. "Took you long enough. You have a battle today."

So Ender got up and fought the battle and won it. But there was no second battle that day, and they let him go to bed earlier. His hands were shaking as he undressed.

During the night he thought he felt hands touching him gently. Hands with affection in them, and gentleness. He dreamed he heard voices.

"You haven't been kind to him."

"That wasn't the assignment."

"How long can he go on? He's breaking down."

"Long enough. It's nearly finished."

"So soon?"

"A few days, and then he's through."

"How will he do, when he's already like this?"

"Fine. Even today, he fought better than ever."

In his dream, the voices sounded like Colonel Graff and Mazer Rackham. But that was the way dreams were, the craziest things could happen, because he dreamed he heard one of the voices saying, "I can't bear to see what this is doing to him." And the other voice answered, "I know. I love him too." And then they changed into Valentine and Alai, and in his dream they were burying him, only a hill grew up where they laid his body down, and he dried out and became a home for buggers, like the Giant was.

All dreams. If there was love or pity for him, it was only in his dreams.

He woke up and fought another battle and won. Then he went to bed and slept again and dreamed again and then he woke up and won again and slept again and he hardly noticed when waking became sleeping. Nor did he care.

The next day was his last day in Command School, though he didn't know it. Mazer Rackham was not in the room with him when he woke up. He showered and dressed and waited for Mazer to come unlock the door. He didn't come. Ender tried the door. It was open.

Was it an accident that Mazer had let him be free this morning? No one with him to tell him he must eat, he must go to practice, he must sleep. Freedom. The trouble was, he didn't know what to do. He thought for a moment that he might find his squadron leaders, talk to them face to face, but he didn't know where they were. They could be twenty kilometers away, for all he knew. So, after wandering through the tunnels for a little while, he went to the mess hall and ate breakfast near a few marines who were telling dirty jokes that Ender could not begin to understand. Then he went to the simulator room for practice. Even though he was free, he could not think of anything else to do.

Mazer was waiting for him. Ender walked slowly into the room. His step was slightly shuffling, and he felt tired and dull.

Mazer frowned. "Are you awake, Ender?"

There were other people in the simulator room. Ender wondered why they were there, but didn't bother to ask. It wasn't worth asking; no one would tell him anyway. He walked to the simulator controls and sat down, ready to start.

"Ender Wiggin," said Mazer. "Please turn around. Today's game needs a little explanation."

Ender turned around. He glanced at the men gathered at the back of the room. Most of them he had never seen before. Some were even dressed in civilian clothes. He saw Anderson and wondered what he was doing there, who was taking care of the Battle School if he was gone. He saw Graff and remembered the lake in the woods outside Greensboro, and wanted to go home. Take me home, he said silently to Graff. In my dream you said you loved me. Take me home.

But Graff only nodded to him, a greeting, not a promise, and Anderson acted as though he didn't know him at all.

"Pay attention, please, Ender. Today is your final examination in Command School. These observers are here to evaluate what you have learned. If you prefer not to have them in the room, we'll have them watch on another simulator."

"They can stay." Final examination. After today, perhaps he could rest.

"For this to be a fair test of your ability, not just to do what you have practiced many times, but also to meet challenges you have never seen before, today's battle introduces a new element. It is staged around a planet. This will affect the enemy's strategy, and will force you to improvise. Please concentrate on the game today."

Ender beckoned Mazer closer, and asked him quietly, "Am I the first student to make it this far?"

"If you win today, Ender, you will be the first student to do so. More than that I'm not at liberty to say."

"Well, I'm at liberty to hear it."

"You can be as petulant as you want, tomorrow. Today, though, I'd appreciate it if you would keep your mind on the examination.

Let's not waste all that you've already done. Now, how will you deal with the planet?"

"I have to get someone behind it, or it's a blind spot."

"True."

"And the gravity is going to affect fuel levels—cheaper to go down than up."

"Yes."

"Does the Little Doctor work against a planet?"

Mazer's face went rigid. "Ender, the buggers never attacked a civilian population in either invasion. You decide whether it would be wise to adopt a strategy that would invite reprisals."

"Is the planet the only new thing?"

"Can you remember the last time I've given you a battle with only one new thing? Let me assure you, Ender, that I will not be kind to you today. I have a responsibility to the fleet not to let a second-rate student graduate. I will do my best against you, Ender, and I have no desire to coddle you. Just keep in mind everything you know about yourself and everything you know about the buggers, and you have a fair chance of amounting to something."

Mazer left the room.

Ender spoke into the microphone. "Are you there?"

"All of us," said Bean. "Kind of late for practice this morning, aren't you?"

So they hadn't told the squadron leaders. Ender toyed with the idea of telling them how important this battle was to him, but decided it would not help them to have an extraneous concern on their minds. "Sorry," he said. "I overslept."

They laughed. They didn't believe him.

He led them through maneuvers, warming up for the battle ahead. It took him longer than usual to clear his mind, to concentrate on command, but soon enough he was up to speed, responding quickly, thinking well. Or at least, he told himself, thinking that I'm thinking well.

The simulator field cleared. Ender waited for the game to appear. What will happen if I pass the test today? Is there another school? Another year or two of grueling training, another year of isolation, another year of people pushing me this way and that way, another year without any control over my own life? He tried to remember how old he was. Eleven. How many years ago did he turn eleven? How many days? It must have happened here at the Command School, but he couldn't remember the day. Maybe he didn't even notice it at the time. Nobody noticed it, except perhaps Valentine.

And as he waited for the game to appear, he wished he could simply lose it, lose the battle badly and completely so that they would remove him from training, like Bonzo, and let him go home. Bonzo had been assigned to Cartagena. He wanted to see travel orders that said Greensboro. Success meant it would go on. Failure meant he could go home.

No, that isn't true, he told himself. They need me, and if I fail there might not be any home to return to.

But he did not believe it. In his conscious mind he knew it was true, but in other places, deeper places, he doubted that they needed him. Mazer's urgency was just another trick. Just another way to make me do what they want me to do. Another way to keep him from resting. From doing nothing, for a long, long time.

Then the enemy formation appeared, and Ender's weariness turned to despair.

The enemy outnumbered him a thousand to one, the simulator glowed green with them. They were grouped in a dozen different formations, shifting positions, changing shapes, moving in seemingly random patterns through the simulator field. He could not find a path through them—a space that seemed open would close suddenly, and another appear, and a formation that seemed penetrable would suddenly change and be forbidding. The planet was at the far edge of the field, and for all Ender knew there were just as many enemy ships beyond it, out of the simulator's range.

As for his own fleet, it consisted of twenty starships, each with only four fighters. He knew the four-fighter starships—they were old-fashioned, sluggish, and the range of their Little Doctors was half that of the newer ones. Eighty fighters, against at least five thousand, perhaps ten thousand enemy ships.

He heard his squadron leaders breathing heavily; he could also hear, from the observers behind him, a quiet curse. It was nice to know that one of the adults noticed that it wasn't a fair test. Not that it made any difference. Fairness wasn't part of the game, that was plain. There was no attempt to give him even a remote chance at success. All that I've been through, and they never meant to let me pass at all.

He saw in his mind Bonzo and his vicious little knot of friends, confronting him, threatening him; he had been able to shame Bonzo into fighting him alone. That would hardly work here. And he could not surprise the enemy with his ability as he had done with the older boys in the battleroom. Mazer knew Ender's abilities inside and out.

The observers behind him began to cough, to move nervously. They were beginning to realize that Ender didn't know what to do.

I don't care anymore, thought Ender. You can keep your game. If you won't even give me a chance, why should I play?

Like his last game in Battle School, when they put two armies against him.

And just as he remembered that game, apparently Bean remembered it, too, for his voice came over the headset, saying, "Remember, the enemy's gate is *down.*"

Molo, Soup, Vlad, Dumper, and Crazy Tom all laughed. They remembered, too.

And Ender also laughed. It *was* funny. The adults taking all this so seriously, and the children playing along, playing along, believing it too until suddenly the adults went too far, tried too hard, and the children could see through their game. Forget it, Mazer. I don't care if I pass your test, I don't care if I follow your rules. If you can cheat, so can I. I won't let you beat me unfairly—I'll beat you unfairly first.

In that final battle in Battle School, he had won by ignoring the enemy, ignoring his own losses; he had moved against the enemy's gate.

And the enemy's gate was down.

If I break this rule, they'll never let me be a commander. It would be too dangerous. I'll never have to play a game again. And that is victory.

He whispered quickly into the microphone. His commanders took their parts of the fleet and grouped themselves into a thick projectile, a cylinder aimed at the nearest of the enemy formations. The enemy, far from trying to repel him, welcomed him in, so he could be thoroughly entrapped before they destroyed him. Mazer is at least taking into account the fact that by now they would have learned to respect me, thought Ender. And that does buy me time.

Ender dodged downward, north, east, and down again, not

seeming to follow any plan, but always ending up a little closer to the enemy planet. Finally the enemy began to close in on him too tightly. Then, suddenly, Ender's formation burst. His fleet seemed to melt into chaos. The eighty fighters seemed to follow no plan at all, firing at enemy ships at random, working their way into hopeless individual paths among the bugger craft.

After a few minutes of battle, however, Ender whispered to his squadron leaders once more, and suddenly a dozen of the remaining fighters formed again into a formation. But now they were on the far side of one of the enemy's most formidable groups; they had, with terrible losses, passed through—and now they had covered more than half the distance to the enemy's planet.

The enemy sees now, thought Ender. Surely Mazer sees what I'm doing.

Or perhaps Mazer cannot believe that I would do it. Well, so much the better for me.

Ender's tiny fleet darted this way and that, sending two or three fighters out as if to attack, then bringing them back. The enemy closed in, drawing in ships and formations that had been widely scattered, bringing them in for the kill. The enemy was most concentrated beyond Ender, so he could not escape back into open space, closing him in. Excellent, thought Ender. Closer. Come closer.

Then he whispered a command and the ships dropped like rocks toward the planet's surface. They were starships and fighters, completely unequipped to handle the heat of passage through an atmosphere. But Ender never intended them to reach the atmosphere. Almost from the moment they began to drop, they were focusing their Little Doctors on one thing only. The planet itself.

One, two, four, seven of his fighters were blown away. It was all a gamble now, whether any of his ships would survive long enough to get in range. It would not take long, once they could focus on the planet's surface. Just a moment with Dr. Device, that's all I want. It occurred to Ender that perhaps the computer wasn't even equipped to show what would happen to a planet if the Little Doctor attacked it. What will I do then, shout Bang, you're dead?

Ender took his hands off the controls and leaned in to watch what happened. The perspective was close to the enemy planet now, as the ship hurtled into its well of gravity. Surely it's in range now, thought Ender. It must be in range and the computer can't handle it.

Then the surface of the planet, which filled half the simulator field now, began to bubble; there was a gout of explosion, hurling debris out toward Ender's fighters. Ender tried to imagine what was happening inside the planet. The field growing and growing, the molecules bursting apart but finding nowhere for the separate atoms to go.

Within three seconds the entire planet burst apart, becoming a sphere of bright dust, hurtling outward. Ender's fighters were among the first to go; their perspective suddenly vanished, and now the simulator could only display the perspective of the starships waiting beyond the edges of the battle. It was as close as Ender wanted to be. The sphere of the exploding planet grew outward faster than the enemy ships could avoid it. And it carried with it the Little Doctor, not so little anymore, the field taking apart every ship in its path, erupting each one into a dot of light before it went on.

Only at the very periphery of the simulator did the M.D. field weaken. Two or three enemy ships were drifting away. Ender's own starships did not explode. But where the vast enemy fleet had been, and the planet they protected, there was nothing meaningful. A lump of dirt was growing as gravity drew much of the debris downward again. It was glowing hot and spinning visibly; it was also much smaller than the world had been before. Much of its mass was now a cloud still flowing outward.

Ender took off his headphones, filled with the cheers of his squadron leaders, and only then realized that there was just as much noise in the room with him. Men in uniform were hugging each other, laughing, shouting; others were weeping; some knelt or lay prostrate, and Ender knew they were caught up in prayer. Ender didn't understand. It seemed all wrong. They were supposed to be angry.

Colonel Graff detached himself from the others and came to Ender. Tears streamed down his face, but he was smiling. He bent over, reached out his arms, and to Ender's surprise he embraced him, held him tightly, and whispered, "Thank you, thank you Ender. Thank God for you, Ender."

The others soon came, too, shaking his hand, congratulating him. He tried to make sense of this. Had he passed the test after all? It was *his* victory, not theirs, and a hollow one at that, a cheat; why did they act as if he had won with honor?

The crowd parted and Mazer Rackham walked through. He came straight to Ender and held out his hand.

"You made the hard choice, boy. All or nothing. End them or end us. But heaven knows there was no other way you could have done it. Congratulations. You beat them, and it's all over."

All over. Beat them. Ender didn't understand. "I beat *you.*"

Mazer laughed, a loud laugh that filled the room. "Ender, you never played *me.* You never played a *game* since I became your enemy."

Ender didn't get the joke. He had played a great many games, at a terrible cost to himself. He began to get angry.

Mazer reached out and touched his shoulder. Ender shrugged him off. Mazer then grew serious and said, "Ender, for the past few months you have been the battle commander of our fleets. This was the Third Invasion. There were no games, the battles were real, and the only enemy you fought was the buggers. You won every battle, and today you finally fought them at their home world, where the queen was, all the queens from all their colonies, they all were there and you destroyed them completely. They'll never attack us again. You did it. You."

Real. Not a game. Ender's mind was too tired to cope with it all. They weren't just points of light in the air, they were real ships that he had fought with and real ships he had destroyed. And a real world that he had blasted into oblivion. He walked through the crowd, dodging their congratulations, ignoring their hands, their words, their rejoicing. When he got to his own room he stripped off his clothes, climbed into bed, and slept.

Ender awoke when they shook him. It took a moment to recognize them. Graff and Rackham. He turned his back on them. Let me sleep.

"Ender, we need to talk to you," said Graff.

Ender rolled back to face them.

"They've been playing out the videos on Earth all day, all night since the battle yesterday."

"Yesterday?" He had slept through until the next day.

"You're a hero, Ender. They've seen what you did, you and the others. I don't think there's a government on Earth that hasn't voted you their highest medal."

"I killed them all, didn't I?" Ender asked.

"All who?" asked Graff. "The buggers? That was the idea."

Mazer leaned in close. "That's what the war was for."

"All their queens. So I killed all their children, all of everything."

"They decided that when they attacked us. It wasn't your fault. It's what had to happen."

Ender grabbed Mazer's uniform and hung onto it, pulling him down so they were face to face. "I didn't want to kill them all. I didn't want to kill anybody! I'm not a killer! You didn't want me, you bastards, you wanted Peter, but you made me do it, you tricked me into it!" He was crying. He was out of control.

"Of course we tricked you into it. That's the whole point," said Graff. "It had to be a trick or you couldn't have done it. It's the bind we were in. We had to have a commander with so much empathy that he would think like the buggers, understand them and anticipate them. So much compassion that he could win the love of his underlings and work with them like a perfect machine, as perfect as the buggers. But somebody with that much compassion could never be the killer we needed. Could never go into battle willing to win at all costs. If you knew, you couldn't do it. If you were the kind of person who would do it even if you knew, you could never have understood the buggers well enough."

"And it had to be a child, Ender," said Mazer. "You were faster than me. Better than me. I was too old and cautious. Any decent person who knows what warfare is can never go into battle with a whole heart. But you didn't know. We made sure you didn't know. You were reckless and brilliant and young. It's what you were born for."

"We had pilots with our ships, didn't we."

"Yes."

"I was ordering pilots to go in and die and I didn't even know it."

"*They* knew it, Ender, and they went anyway. They knew what it was for."

"You never asked me! You never told me the truth about anything!"

"You had to be a weapon, Ender. Like a gun, like the Little Doctor, functioning perfectly but not knowing what you were aimed at. *We* aimed you. We're responsible. If there was something wrong, we did it."

"Tell me later," Ender said. His eyes closed.

Mazer Rackham shook him. "Don't go to sleep, Ender," he said. "It's very important."

"You're finished with me," Ender said. "Now leave me alone."

"That's why we're here," Mazer said. "We're trying to tell you. They're not through with you, not at all. It's crazy down there. They're going to start a war. Americans claiming the Warsaw Pact is about to attack, and the Pact saying the same thing about the Hegemon. The bugger war isn't twenty-four hours dead and the world down there is back to fighting again, as bad as ever. And all of them are worried about you. And all of them want you. The greatest military leader in history, they want you to lead their armies. The Americans. The Hegemon. Everybody but the Warsaw Pact, and they want you dead."

"Fine with me," said Ender.

"We have to take you away from here. There are Russian marines all over Eros, and the Polemarch is Russian. It could turn to bloodshed at any time."

Ender turned his back on them again. This time they let him. He did not sleep, though. He listened to them.

"I was afraid of this, Rackham. You pushed him too hard. Some of those lesser outposts could have waited until after. You could have given him some days to rest."

"Are you doing it, too, Graff? Trying to decide how I could have done it better? You don't know what would have happened if I hadn't pushed. Nobody knows. I did it the way I did it, and it worked. Above all, it worked. Memorize that defense, Graff. You may have to use it, too."

"Sorry."

"I can see what it's done to him. Colonel Liki says there's a good chance he'll be permanently damaged, but I don't believe it. He's too strong. Winning meant a lot to him, and he won."

"Don't tell me about strong. The kid's eleven. Give him some rest, Rackham. Things haven't exploded yet. We can post a guard outside his door."

"Or post a guard outside another door and pretend that it's his."

"Whatever."

They went away. Ender slept again.

Time passed without touching Ender, except with glancing blows. Once he awoke for a few minutes with something pressing his hand, pushing downward on it, with a dull, insistent pain. He reached over and touched it; it was a needle passing into a vein. He tried to pull it out, but it was taped on and he was too weak. Another time he awoke in darkness to hear people near him murmuring and cursing. His ears were ringing with the loud noise that had awakened him; he did not remember the noise. "Get the lights on," someone said. And another time he thought he heard someone crying softly near him.

It might have been a single day; it might have been a week; from his dreams, it could have been months. He seemed to pass through lifetimes in his dreams. Through the Giant's Drink again, past the wolf-children, reliving the terrible deaths, the constant murders; he heard a voice whispering in the forest, You had to kill the children to get to the End of the World. And he tried to answer, I never wanted to kill anybody. Nobody ever asked me if I wanted to kill anybody. But the forest laughed at him. And when he leapt from the cliff at the End of the World, sometimes it was not clouds that caught him, but a fighter that carried him to a vantage point near the surface of the buggers' world, so he could watch, over and over, the eruption of death when Dr. Device set off a reaction on the planet's face; then closer and closer, until he could watch individual buggers explode, turn to light, then collapse into a pile of dirt before his eyes. And the queen, surrounded by infants; only the queen was Mother, and the infants were Valentine and all the children he had known in Battle School. One of them had Bonzo's face, and he lay there bleeding through the eyes and nose, saying, You have no honor. And always the dream ended with a mirror or a pool of water or the metal surface of a ship, something that would reflect his face back to him. At first it was always Peter's face, with blood and a snake's tail coming from the mouth. After a while, though, it began to be his own face, old and sad, with eyes that grieved for a billion, billion murders—but they were his own eyes, and he was content to wear them.

That was the world Ender lived in for many lifetimes during the five days of the League War.

When he awoke again he was lying in darkness. In the distance he could hear the thump, thump of explosions. He listened for a while. Then he heard a soft footstep.

He turned over and flung out a hand, to grasp whoever was sneaking up on him. Sure enough, he caught someone's clothing and pulled him down toward his knees, ready to kill him if need be.

"Ender, it's me, it's me!"

He knew the voice. It came out of his memory as if it were a million years ago.

"Alai."

"Salaam, pinprick. What were you trying to do, kill me?"

"Yes. I thought you were trying to kill *me.*"

"I was trying not to wake you up. Well, at least you have some survival instinct left. The way Mazer talks about it, you were becoming a vegetable."

"I was trying to. What's the thumping."

"There's a war going on here. Our section is blacked out to keep us safe."

Ender swung his legs out to sit up. He couldn't do it, though. His head hurt too bad. He winced in pain.

"Don't sit up, Ender. It's all right. It looks like we might win it. Not all the Warsaw Pact people went with the Polemarch. A lot of them came over when the Strategos told them you were loyal to the I.F."

"I was asleep."

"So he lied. You weren't plotting treason in your dreams, were you? Some of the Russians who came in told us that when the Polemarch ordered them to find you and kill you, they almost killed *him.* Whatever they may feel about other people, Ender, they love you. The whole world watched our battles. Videos, day and night. I've seen some. Complete with your voice giving the orders. It's all there, nothing censored. Good stuff. You've got a career in the vids."

"I don't think so," said Ender.

"I was joking. Hey, can you believe it? We won the war. We were so eager to grow up so we could fight in it, and it was us all the time. I mean, we're kids, Ender. And it was us." Alai laughed. "It was you, anyway. You were good, bosh. I didn't know how you'd get us out of that last one. But you did. You were good."

Ender noticed the way he spoke in the past. I *was* good. "What am I *now,* Alai?"

"Still good."

"At what?"

"At—anything. There's a million soldiers who'd follow you to the end of the universe."

"I don't want to go to the end of the universe."

"So where do you want to go? They'll follow you."

I want to go home, thought Ender, but I don't know where it is.

The thumping went silent.

"Listen to that," said Alai.

They listened. The door opened. Someone stood there. Someone small. "It's over," he said. It was Bean. As if to prove it, the lights went on.

"Ho, Bean," Ender said.

"Ho, Ender."

Petra followed him in, with Dink holding her hand. They came to Ender's bed. "Hey, the hero's awake," said Dink.

"Who won?" asked Ender.

"We did, Ender," said Bean. "You were there."

"He's not *that* crazy, Bean. He meant who won just now." Petra took Ender's hand. "There was a truce on Earth. They've been negotiating for days. They finally agreed to accept the Locke Proposal."

"He doesn't know about the Locke Proposal—"

"It's very complicated, but what it means here is that the I.F. will stay in existence, but without the Warsaw Pact in it. So the Warsaw Pact marines are going home. I think Russia agreed to it because they're having a revolt of the Slavic helots. Everybody's got troubles. About five hundred died here, but it was worse on Earth."

"The Hegemon resigned," said Dink. "It's crazy down there. Who cares."

"You OK?" Petra asked him, touching his head. "You scared us. They said you were crazy, and we said *they* were crazy."

"I'm crazy," said Ender. "But I think I'm OK."

"When did you decide that?" asked Alai.

"When I thought you were about to kill me, and I decided to

kill you first. I guess I'm just a killer to the core. But I'd rather be alive than dead."

They laughed and agreed with him. Then Ender began to cry and embraced Bean and Petra, who were closest. "I missed you," he said. "I wanted to see you so bad."

"You saw us pretty bad," Petra answered. She kissed his cheek.

"I saw you magnificent," said Ender. "The ones I needed most, I used up soonest. Bad planning on my part."

"Everybody's OK now," said Dink. "Nothing was wrong with any of us that five days of cowering in blacked-out rooms in the middle of a war couldn't cure."

"I don't have to be your commander anymore, do I?" asked Ender. "I don't want to command anybody again."

"You don't have to command anybody," said Dink, "but you're always our commander."

Then they were silent for a while.

"So what do we do now?" asked Alai. "The bugger war's over, and so's the war down there on Earth, and even the war here. What do we do now?"

"We're kids," said Petra. "They'll probably make us go to school. It's a law. You have to go to school till you're seventeen."

They all laughed at that. Laughed until tears streamed down their faces.

Chapter 15

Speaker for the Dead

The lake was still; there was no breeze. The two men sat together in chairs on the floating dock. A small wooden raft was tied up at the dock; Graff hooked his foot in the rope and pulled the raft in, then let it drift out, then pulled it in again.

"You've lost weight."

"One kind of stress puts it on, another takes it off. I am a creature of chemicals."

"It must have been hard."

Graff shrugged. "Not really. I knew I'd be acquitted."

"Some of us weren't so sure. People were crazy for a while there. Mistreatment of children, negligent homicide—those videos of Bonzo's and Stilson's deaths were pretty gruesome. To watch one child do that to another."

"As much as anything, I think the videos saved me. The prosecution edited them, but we showed the whole thing. It was plain that Ender was not the provocateur. After that, it was just a second-guessing game. I said I did what I believed was necessary for the preservation of the human race, and it worked; we got the judges to agree that the prosecution had to prove beyond doubt that Ender would have won the war *without* the training we gave him. After that, it was simple. The exigencies of war."

"Anyway, Graff, it was a great relief to us. I know we quarreled, and I know the prosecution used tapes of our conversations against you. But by then I knew that you were right, and I offered to testify for you."

"I know, Anderson. My lawyers told me."

"So what will you do now?"

"I don't know. Still relaxing. I have a few years of leave accrued. Enough to take me to retirement, and I have plenty of salary that I never used, sitting around in banks. I could live on the interest. Maybe I'll do nothing."

"It sounds nice. But I couldn't stand it. I've been offered the presidency of three different universities, on the theory that I'm an educator. They don't believe me when I say that all I ever cared about at the Battle School was the game. I think I'll go with the other offer."

"Commissioner?"

"Now that the wars are over, it's time to play games again. It'll be almost like vacation, anyway. Only twenty-eight teams in the league. Though after years of watching those children flying, football is like watching slugs bash into each other."

They laughed. Graff sighed and pushed the raft with his foot.

"That raft. Surely you can't float on it."

Graff shook his head. "Ender built it."

"That's right. This is where you took him."

"It's even been deeded over to him. I saw to it that he was amply rewarded. He'll have all the money he ever needs."

"If they ever let him come back to use it."

"They never will."

"With Demosthenes agitating for him to come home?"

"Demosthenes isn't on the nets anymore."

Anderson raised an eyebrow. "What does *that* mean?"

"Demosthenes has retired. Permanently."

"You know something, you old fart-eater. You know who Demosthenes is."

"Was."

"Well, tell me!"

"No."

"You're no fun anymore, Graff."

"I never was."

"At least you can tell me *why*. There were a lot of us who thought Demosthenes would be Hegemon someday."

"There was never a chance of that. No, even Demosthenes' mob of political cretins couldn't persuade the Hegemon to bring Ender back to Earth. Ender is far too dangerous."

"He's only eleven. Twelve, now."

"All the more dangerous because he could so easily be controlled. In all the world, the name of Ender is one to conjure with. The child-god, the miracle worker, with life and death in his hands. Every petty tyrant-to-be would like to have the boy, to set him in front of an army and watch the world either flock to join or cower in fear. If Ender came to Earth, he'd want to come here, to rest, to salvage what he can of his childhood. But they'd never let him rest."

"I see. Someone explained that to Demosthenes?"

Graff smiled. "Demosthenes explained it to someone else. Someone who could have used Ender as no one else could have, to rule the world and make the world like it."

"Who?"

"Locke."

"Locke is the one who argued for Ender to stay on Eros."

"All is not always as it seems."

"It's too deep for me, Graff. Give me the game. Nice, neat rules. Referees. Beginnings and endings. Winners and losers and then everybody goes home to their wives."

"Get me tickets to some games now and then, all right?"

"You won't really stay here and retire, will you?"

"No."

"You're going into the Hegemony, aren't you?"

"I'm the new Minister of Colonization."

"So they're doing it."

"As soon as we get the reports back on the bugger colony worlds. I mean, there they are, already fertile, with housing and industry in place, and all the buggers dead. Very convenient. We'll repeal the population limitation laws—"

"Which everybody hates—"

"And all those thirds and fourths and fifths will get on starships and head out for worlds known and unknown."

"Will people really go?"

"People always go. Always. They always believe they can make a better life than in the old world."

"What the hell, maybe they can."

At first Ender believed that they would bring him back to Earth as soon as things quieted down. But things were quiet now, had been quiet for a year, and it was plain to him now that they would not bring him back at all, that he was much more useful as a name and a story than he would ever be as an inconvenient flesh-and-blood person.

And there was the matter of the court martial on the crimes of Colonel Graff. Admiral Chamrajnagar tried to keep Ender from watching it, but failed; Ender had been awarded the rank of admiral, too, and this was one of the few times he asserted the privileges the rank implied. So he watched the videos of the fights with Stilson and Bonzo, watched as the photographs of the corpses were displayed, listened as the psychologists and lawyers argued whether murder had been committed or the killing was in self-defense. Ender had his own opinion, but no one asked him. Throughout the trial, it was really Ender himself under attack. The prosecution was too clever to charge him directly, but there were attempts to make him look sick, perverted, criminally insane.

"Never mind," said Mazer Rackham. "The politicians are afraid of you, but they can't destroy your reputation yet. That won't be done until the historians get at you in thirty years."

Ender didn't care about his reputation. He watched the videos impassively, but in fact he was amused. *In battle I killed ten billion buggers, who were as alive and wise as any man, who had not even launched a third attack against us, and no one thinks to call it a crime.*

All his crimes weighed heavy on him, the deaths of Stilson and Bonzo no heavier and no lighter than the rest.

And so, with that burden, he waited through the empty months until the world that he had saved decided he could come home.

One by one, his friends reluctantly left him, called home to their families, to be received with heroes' welcomes in their towns. Ender watched the videos of their homecomings, and was touched when they spent much of their time praising Ender Wiggin, who taught them everything, they said, who taught them and led them into victory. But if they called for him to be brought home, the words were censored from the videos and no one heard the plea.

For a time, the only work in Eros was cleaning up after the bloody League War and receiving the reports of the starships, once warships, that were now exploring the bugger colony worlds.

But now Eros was busier than ever, more crowded than it had ever been during the war, as colonists were brought here to prepare for their voyages to the empty bugger worlds. Ender took part in the work, as much as they would let him, but it did not occur to them that this twelve-year-old boy might be as gifted at peace as he was at war. But he was patient with their tendency to ignore him, and learned to make his proposals and suggest his plans through the few adults who listened to him, and let them present them as their own. He was concerned, not about getting credit, but about getting the job done.

The one thing he could not bear was the worship of the colonists. He learned to avoid the tunnels where they lived, because they would always recognize him—the world had memorized his face—and then they would scream and shout and embrace him and congratulate him and show him the children they had named after him and tell him how he was so young it broke their hearts and *they* didn't blame him for any of his murders because it wasn't his fault he was just a *child*—

He hid from them as best he could.

There was one colonist, though, he couldn't hide from.

He wasn't inside Eros that day. He had gone up with the shuttle to the new ISL, where he had been learning to do surface work on the starships; it was unbecoming to an officer to do mechanical labor, Chamrajnagar told him, but Ender answered that since the trade he had mastered wasn't much called for now, it was about time he learned another skill.

They spoke to him through his helmet radio and told him that someone was waiting to see him as soon as he could come in. Ender couldn't think of anyone he wanted to see, and so he didn't hurry. He finished installing the shield for the ship's ansible and then hooked his way across the face of the ship and pulled himself up into the airlock.

She was waiting for him outside the changing room. For a moment he was annoyed that they would let a colonist come to bother him here, where he came to be alone; then he looked again, and realized that if the young woman were a little girl, he would know her.

"Valentine," he said.

"Hi, Ender."

"What are you doing here?"

"Demosthenes retired. Now I'm going with the first colony."

"It's fifty years to get there—"

"Only two years if you're aboard the ship."

"But if you ever came back, everybody you knew on Earth would be dead—"

"That was what I had in mind. I was hoping, though, that someone I knew on Eros might come with me."

"I don't want to go to a world we stole from the buggers. I just want to go home."

"Ender, you're never going back to Earth. I saw to that before I left."

He looked at her in silence.

"I tell you that now, so that if you want to hate me, you can hate me from the beginning."

They went to Ender's tiny compartment in the ISL and she explained. Peter wanted Ender back on Earth, under the protection of the Hegemon's Council. "The way things are right now, Ender, that would put you effectively under Peter's control, since half the council now does just what Peter wants. The ones that aren't Locke's lapdogs are under his thumb in other ways."

"Do they know who he really is?"

"Yes. He isn't publicly known, but people in high places know him. It doesn't matter any more. He has too much power for them to worry about his age. He's done incredible things, Ender."

"I noticed the treaty a year ago was named for Locke."

"That was his breakthrough. He proposed it through his friends from the public policy nets, and then Demosthenes got behind it, too. It was the moment he had been waiting for, to use Demosthenes' influence with the mob and Locke's influence with the intelligentsia to accomplish something noteworthy. It forestalled a really vicious war that could have lasted for decades." .

"He decided to be a statesman?"

"I think so. But in his cynical moments, of which there are many, he pointed out to me that if he had allowed the League to fall apart completely, he'd have to conquer the world piece by piece. As long as the Hegemony exists, he can do it in one lump."

Ender nodded. "That's the Peter that I knew."

"Funny, isn't it? That Peter would save millions of lives."

"While I killed billions."

"I wasn't going to say that."

"So he wanted to use me?"

"He had plans for you, Ender. He would publicly reveal himself when you arrived, going to meet you in front of all the videos. Ender Wiggin's older brother, who also happened to be the great Locke, the architect of peace. Standing next to you, he would look quite mature. And the physical resemblance between you is stronger than ever. It would be quite simple for him, then, to take over."

"Why did you stop him?"

"Ender, you wouldn't be happy spending the rest of your life as Peter's pawn."

"Why not? I've spent my life as someone's pawn."

"Me too. I showed Peter all the evidence that I had assembled, enough to prove in the eyes of the public that he was a psychotic killer. It included full-color pictures of tortured squirrels and some of the monitor videos of the way he treated you. It took some work to get it all together, but by the time he saw it, he was willing to give me what I wanted. What I wanted was your freedom and mine."

"It's not my idea of freedom to go live in the house of the people that I killed."

"Ender, what's done is done. Their worlds are empty now, and ours is full. And we can take with us what their worlds have never known—cities full of people who live private, individual lives, who love and hate each other for their own reasons. In all the bugger worlds, there was never more than a single story to be told; when we're there, the world will be full of stories, and we'll improvise their endings day by day. Ender, Earth belongs to Peter. And if you don't go with me now, he'll have you there, and use you up until you wish you'd never been born. Now is the only chance you'll get to get away."

Ender said nothing.

"I know what you're thinking, Ender. You're thinking that I'm trying to control you just as much as Peter or Graff or any of the others."

"It crossed my mind."

"Welcome to the human race. Nobody controls his own life, Ender. The best you can do is choose to be controlled by good people, by people who love you. I didn't come here because I wanted to be a colonist. I came because I've spent my whole life in the company of the brother that I hated. Now I want a chance to know the brother that I loved, before it's too late, before we're not children anymore."

"It's already too late for that."

"You're wrong, Ender. You think you're grown up and tired and jaded with everything, but in your heart you're just as much a kid as I am. We can keep it secret from everybody else. While you're governing the colony and I'm writing political philosophy, they'll never guess that in the darkness of night we sneak into each other's room and play checkers and have pillowfights."

Ender laughed, but he had noticed some things she dropped too casually for them to be accidental. "Governing?"

"I'm Demosthenes, Ender. I went out with a bang. A public announcement that I believed so much in the colonization movement that I was going in the first ship myself. At the same time, the Minister of Colonization, a former colonel named Graff, announced that the pilot of the colony ship would be the great Mazer Rackham, and the governor of the colony would be Ender Wiggin."

"They might have asked me."

"I wanted to ask you myself."

"But it's already announced."

"No. They'll be announcing it tomorrow, if you accept. Mazer accepted a few hours ago, back in Eros."

"You're telling everyone that you're Demosthenes? A fourteen-year-old girl?"

"We're only telling them that Demosthenes is going with the colony. Let them spend the next fifty years poring over the passenger list, trying to figure out which one of them is the great demagogue of the Age of Locke."

Ender laughed and shook his head. "You're actually having fun, Val."

"I can't think why I shouldn't."

"All right," said Ender. "I'll go. Maybe even as governor, as long as you and Mazer are there to help me. My abilities are a little underused at present."

She squealed and hugged him, for all the world like a typical teenage girl who just got the present that she wanted from her little brother.

"Val," he said. "I just want one thing clear. I'm not going for you. I'm not going in order to be governor, or because I'm bored here. I'm going because I know the buggers better than any other living soul, and maybe if I go there I can understand them better. I stole their future from them; I can only begin to repay by seeing what I can learn from their past."

The voyage was long. By the end of it, Val had finished the first volume of her history of the bugger wars and transmitted it by ansible, under Demosthenes' name, back to Earth, and Ender had won something better than the adulation of the passengers. They knew him now, and he had won their love and their respect.

He worked hard on the new world, governing by persuasion rather than fiat, and working as hard as anyone at the tasks involved in setting up a self-sustaining economy. But his most important work, as everyone agreed, was exploring what the buggers had left behind, trying to find among structures, machinery, and fields long untended some things that human beings could use, could learn from. There were no books to read—the buggers never needed them. With all things present in their memories, all things spoken as they were thought, when the buggers died their knowledge died with them.

And yet. From the sturdiness of the roofs that covered their animal sheds and their food supplies, Ender learned that winter would be hard, with heavy snows. From fences with sharpened stakes that pointed outward he learned that there were marauding animals that were a danger to the crops or the herds. From the mill he learned that the long, foul-tasting fruits that grew in the overgrown orchards were dried and ground into meal. And from the slings that once were used to carry infants along with adults into the fields, he learned that even though the buggers were not much for individuality, they did love their children.

Life settled down, and years passed. The colony lived in wooden houses and used the tunnels of the bugger city for storage and manufactories. They were governed by a council now, and administrators were elected, so that Ender, though they still called him governor, was in fact only a judge. There were crimes and quarrels, alongside kindness and cooperation; there were people who loved each other and people who did not; it was a human world. They did not wait so eagerly for each new transmission from the ansible; the names that were famous on Earth meant little to them now. The only name they knew was that of Peter Wiggin, the Hegemon of Earth; the only news that came was news of peace, of prosperity, of great ships leaving the littoral of Earth's solar system, passing the comet shield and filling up the bugger worlds. Soon there would be other colonies on this world, Ender's World; soon there would be neighbors; already they were halfway here; but no one cared. They would help the newcomers when they came, teach them what they had learned, but what mattered in life now was who would marry whom, and who was sick, and when was planting time, and why should I pay him when the calf died three weeks after I got it.

"They've become people of the land," said Valentine. "No one cares now that Demosthenes is sending the seventh volume of his history today. No one here will read it."

Ender pressed a button and his desk showed him the next page. "Very insightful, Valentine. How many more volumes until you're through?"

"Just one. The story of Ender Wiggin."

"What will you do, wait to write it until I'm dead?"

"No. Just write it, and when I've brought it up to the present day, I'll stop."

"I have a better idea. Take it up to the day we won the final battle. Stop it there. Nothing that I've done since then is worth writing down."

"Maybe," said Valentine. "And maybe not."

The ansible had brought them word that the new colony ship was only a year away. They asked Ender to find a place for them to settle in, near enough to Ender's colony that the two colonies could trade, but far enough apart that they could be governed separately. Ender used the helicopter and began to explore. He took one of the children along, an eleven-year-old boy named Abra; he had been only three when the colony was founded, and he remembered no other world than this. He and Ender flew as far as the copter would carry them, then camped for the night and got a feel for the land on foot the next morning.

It was on the third morning that Ender suddenly began to feel an uneasy sense that he had been in this place before. He looked around; it was new land, he had never seen it. He called out to Abra.

"Ho, Ender!" Abra called. He was on top of a steep low hill. "Come up!"

Ender scrambled up, the turves coming away from his feet in the soft ground. Abra was pointing downward. "Can you believe this?" he asked.

The hill was hollow. A deep depression in the middle, partially filled with water, was ringed by concave slopes that cantilevered dangerously over the water. In one direction the hill gave way to two long ridges that made a V-shaped valley; in the other direction the hill rose to a piece of white rock, grinning like a skull with a tree growing out of its mouth.

"It's like a giant died here," said Abra, "and the Earth grew up to cover his carcass."

Now Ender knew why it had looked familiar. The Giant's corpse. He had played here too many times as a child not to know this place. But it was not possible. The computer in the Battle School could not possibly have seen this place. He looked through his binoculars in a direction he knew well, fearing and hoping that he would see what belonged in that place.

Swings and slides. Monkey bars. Now overgrown, but the shapes still unmistakable.

"Somebody had to have built this," Abra said. "Look, this skull place, it's not rock, look at it. This is concrete."

"I know," said Ender. "They built it for me."

"What?"

"I know this place, Abra. The buggers built it for me."

"The buggers were all dead fifty years before we got here."

"You're right, it's impossible, but I know what I know. Abra, I shouldn't take you with me. It might be dangerous. If they knew me well enough to build this place, they might be planning to—"

"To get even with you."

"For killing them."

"So don't go, Ender. Don't do what they want you to do."

"If they want to get revenge, Abra, I don't mind. But perhaps they don't. Perhaps this is the closest they could come to talking. To writing me a note."

"They didn't know how to read and write."

"Maybe they were learning when they died."

"Well, I'm sure as hell not sticking around here if you're taking off somewhere. I'm going with you."

"No. You're too young to take the risk of—"

"Come on! You're Ender *Wiggin*. Don't tell me what eleven-year-old kids can do!"

Together they flew in the copter, over the playground, over the woods, over the well in the forest clearing. Then out to where there was, indeed, a cliff, with a cave in the cliff wall and a ledge right where the End of the World should be. And there in the distance, just where it should be in the fantasy game, was the castle tower.

He left Abra with the copter. "Don't come after me, and go home in an hour if I don't come back."

"Eat it, Ender, I'm coming with you."

"Eat it yourself, Abra, or I'll stuff you with mud."

Abra could tell, despite Ender's joking tone, that he meant it, and so he stayed.

The walls of the tower were notched and ledged for easy climbing. They meant him to get in.

The room was as it had always been. Ender remembered well enough to look for a snake on the floor, but there was only a rug with a carved snake's head at one corner. Imitation, not duplication; for a people who made no art, they had done well. They must have dragged these images from Ender's own mind, finding him and learning his darkest dreams across the lightyears. But why? To bring him to this room, of course. To leave a message for him. But where was the message, and how would he understand it?

The mirror was waiting for him on the wall. It was a dull sheet of metal, in which the rough shape of a human face had been scratched. They tried to draw the image I should see in the picture.

And looking at the mirror he could remember breaking it, pulling it from the wall, and snakes leaping out of the hidden place, attacking him, biting him wherever their poisonous fangs could find purchase.

How well do they know me, wondered Ender. Well enough to know how often I have thought of death, to know that I am not afraid of it? Well enough to know that even if I feared death, it would not stop me from taking that mirror from the wall.

He walked to the mirror, lifted, pulled away. Nothing jumped from the space behind it. Instead, in a hollowed-out place, there was a white ball of silk with a few frayed strands sticking out here and there. An egg? No. The pupa of a queen bugger, already fertilized by the larval males, ready, out of her own body, to hatch a hundred thousand buggers, including a few queens and males. Ender could see the slug-like males clinging to the walls of a dark tunnel, and the large adults carrying the infant queen to the mating room; each male in turn penetrated the larval queen, shuddered in ecstasy, and died, dropping to the tunnel floor and shriveling. Then the new queen was laid before the old, a magnificent creature clad in soft and shimmering wings, which had long since lost the power of flight but still contained the power of majesty. The old queen kissed her to sleep with the gentle poison in her lips, then wrapped her in threads from her belly, and commanded her to become herself, to become a new city, a new world, to give birth to many queens and many worlds—

How do I know this, thought Ender. How can I see these things, like memories in my own mind.

As if in answer, he saw the first of all his battles with the bugger fleets. He had seen it before on the simulator; now he saw it as the hive-queen saw it, through many different eyes. The buggers formed their globe of ships, and then the terrible fighters came out of the darkness and the Little Doctor destroyed them in a blaze of light. He felt then what the hive-queen felt, watching through her workers' eyes as death came to them too quickly to avoid, but not too quickly to be anticipated. There was no memory of pain or fear, though. What the hive-queen felt was sadness, a sense of resignation. She had not thought these words as she saw the humans coming to kill, but it was in words that Ender understood her: They did not forgive us, she thought. We will surely die.

"How can you live again?" he asked.

The queen in her silken cocoon had no words to give back; but when he closed his eyes and tried to remember, instead of memory came new images. Putting the cocoon in a cool place, a dark place, but with water, so she wasn't dry; no, not just water, but water mixed with the sap of a certain tree, and kept tepid so that certain reactions could take place in the cocoon. Then time. Days and weeks, for the pupa inside to change. And then, when the cocoon had changed to a dusty brown color, Ender saw himself splitting open the cocoon, and helping the small and fragile queen emerge. He saw himself taking her by the forelimb and helping her walk from her birthwater to a nesting place, soft with dried leaves on sand. Then I am alive, came the thought in his mind. Then I am awake. Then I make my ten thousand children.

"No," said Ender. "I can't."

Anguish.

"Your children are the monsters of our nightmares now. If I awoke you, we would only kill you again."

There flashed through his mind a dozen images of human beings being killed by buggers, but with the image came a grief so powerful he could not bear it, and he wept their tears for them.

"If you could make them feel as you can make me feel, then perhaps they could forgive you."

Only me, he realized. They found me through the ansible, followed it and dwelt in my mind. In the agony of my tortured dreams they came to know me, even as I spent my days destroying them; they found my fear of them, and found also that I had no knowledge I was killing them. In the few weeks they had, they built this place for me, and the Giant's corpse and the playground and the ledge at the End of the World, so I would find this place by the evidence of my eyes. I am the only one they know, and so they can only talk to me, and through me. We are like you; the thought pressed into his mind. We did not mean to murder, and when we understood, we never came again. We thought we were the only thinking beings in the universe, until we met you, but never did we dream that thought could arise from the lonely animals who cannot dream each other's dreams. How were we to know? We could live with you in peace. Believe us, believe us, believe us.

He reached into the cavity and took out the cocoon. It was astonishingly light, to hold all the hope and future of a great race within it.

"I'll carry you," said Ender, "I'll go from world to world until I find a time and a place where you can come awake in safety. And I'll tell your story to my people, so that perhaps in time they can forgive you, too. The way that you've forgiven me."

He wrapped the queen's cocoon in his jacket and carried her from the tower.

"What was in there?" asked Abra.

"The answer," said Ender.

"To what?"

"My question," And that was all he said of the matter; they searched for five more days and chose a site for the new colony far to the east and south of the tower.

Weeks later he came to Valentine and told her to read something he had written; she pulled the file he named from the ship's computer, and read it.

It was written as if the hive-queen spoke, telling all that they had meant to do, and all that they had done. Here are our failures, and here is our greatness; we did not mean to hurt you, and we forgive you for our death. From their earliest awareness to the great wars that swept across their home world, Ender told the story quickly, as if it were an ancient memory. When he came to the tale of the great mother, the queen of all, who first learned to keep and teach the new queen instead of killing her or driving her away, then he lingered, telling how many times she had finally to destroy the child of her body, the new self that was not herself, until she bore one who understood her quest for harmony. This was a new thing in the world, two queens that loved and helped each other instead of battling, and together they were stronger than any other hive. They prospered; they had more daughters who joined them in peace; it was the beginning of wisdom.

If only we could have talked to you, the hive-queen said in Ender's words. But since it could not be, we ask only this: that you remember us, not as enemies, but as tragic sisters, changed into a foul shape by Fate or God or Evolution. If we had kissed, it would have been the miracle to make us human in each other's eyes. Instead we killed each other. But still we welcome you now as guest-friends. Come into our home, daughters of Earth; dwell in our tunnels, harvest our fields; what we cannot do, you are now our hands to do for us. Blossom, trees; ripen, fields; be warm for them, suns; be fertile for them, planets: they are our adopted daughters, and they have come home.

The book that Ender wrote was not long, but in it was all the good and all the evil that the hive-queen knew. And he signed it, not with his name, but with a title:

SPEAKER FOR THE DEAD

On Earth, the book was published quietly, and quietly it was passed from hand to hand, until it was hard to believe that anyone on Earth might not have read it. Most who read it found it interesting; some who read it refused to set it aside. They began to live by it as best they could, and when their loved ones died, a believer would arise beside the grave to be the Speaker for the Dead, and say what the dead one would have said, but with full candor, hiding no faults and pretending no virtues. Those who came to such services sometimes found them painful and disturbing, but there were many who decided that their life was worthwhile enough, despite their errors, that when they died a Speaker should tell the truth for them.

On Earth it remained a religion among many religions. But for those who traveled the great cave of space and lived their lives in the hive-queen's tunnels and harvested the hive-queen's fields, it was the only religion. There was no colony without its Speaker for the Dead.

No one knew and no one really wanted to know who was the original Speaker. Ender was not inclined to tell them.

When Valentine was twenty-five years old, she finished the last volume of her history of the bugger wars. She included at the end the complete text of Ender's little book, but did not say that Ender wrote it.

By ansible she got an answer from the ancient Hegemon, Peter Wiggin, seventy-seven years old with a failing heart.

"I know who wrote it," he said. "If he can speak for the buggers, surely he can speak for me."

Back and forth across the ansible Ender and Peter spoke, with Peter pouring out the story of his days and years, his crimes and his kindnesses. And when he died, Ender wrote a second volume, again signed by the Speaker for the Dead. Together, his two books were called the Hive-Queen and the Hegemon, and they were holy writ.

"Come on," he said to Valentine one day. "Let's fly away and live forever."

"We can't," she said. "There are miracles even relativity can't pull off, Ender."

"We have to go. I'm almost happy here."

"So, stay."

"I've lived too long with pain. I won't know who I am without it."

So they boarded a starship and went from world to world.

Wherever they stopped, he was always Andrew Wiggin, itinerant speaker for the dead, and she was always Valentine, historian errant, writing down the stories of the living while Ender spoke the stories of the dead. And always Ender carried with him a dry white cocoon, looking for the world where the hive-queen could awaken and thrive in peace. He looked a long time.

Speaker for the
Dead

For Gregg Keizer
Who already knew how

Contents

Some People of Lusitania Colony

Xenologers (Zenadores)
Pipo (João Figueira Alvarez)
Libo (Liberdade Graças a Deus Figueira de Medici)
Miro (Marcos Vladimir Ribeira von Hesse)
Ouanda (Ouanda Quenhatta Figueira Mucumbi)

Xenobiologists (Biologistas)
Gusto (Vladimir Tiago Gussman)
Cida (Ekaterina Maria Aparecida do Norte von Hesse-Gussman)
Novinha (Ivanova Santa Catarina von Hesse)
Ela (Ekaterina Elanora Ribeira von Hesse)

Governor
Bosquinha (Faria Lima Maria do Bosque)

Bishop
Peregrino (Armão Cebola)

Abbot and Principal of the Monastery
Dom Cristão (Amai a Tudomundo Para Que Deus vos Ame Cristão)
Dona Cristã (Detestai o Pecado e Fazei o Direito Cristã)

The Figueira Family

Pipo (d. 1948 s.c.*)
m.
Conceição

- Pipinho (João)
- Maria (d. 1936)
- Libo (1931–1965)
  m.
  Bruxinha
- Bimba (Abençoada)
- Patinha (Isolde)
- Rã (Tomás)

Libo m. Bruxinha:
- Ouanda (b. 1951)
- China (b. 1952)
- Prega
- Zinha

The Family of Os Venerados

Gusto (d. 1936)
m.
Cida (d. 1936)

- Mingo (d. 1936)
- Novinha (b. 1931)
  m.
  Marcão (d. 1970)
  (Marcos Maria
  Ribeira)
- Amado (d. 1936)
- Guti (d. 1936)

Novinha m. Marcão:
- Miro (b. 1951)
- Ela (b. 1952)
- Quim (b. 1955)
  (Estevão Rei)
- Olhado (b. 1958)
  (Lauro Suleimão)
- Quara (b. 1963)
  (Lembrança das
  Milagres de Jesus)
- Grego (b. 1964)
  (Gerão Gregorio)

*All dates are expressed as years after adoption of the Starways Code.

Pronouncing Foreign Names

Three human languages are used by characters in this book. Stark, since it originated as English, is represented as English in the book. The Nordic spoken on Trondheim evolved from Swedish. Portuguese is the native language of Lusitania. On every world, however, schoolchildren are taught Stark from the beginning.

The Portuguese language, while unusually beautiful when spoken aloud, is very difficult for readers who are accustomed to English to sound out from the written letters. Even if you aren't planning to read this book aloud, you may be more comfortable if you have a general idea of how the Portuguese names and phrases are pronounced.

Consonants: Single consonants are pronounced more or less as they are in English, with the addition of ç, which always sounds like *ss*. Exceptions are *j*, which is pronounced like the *z* in *azure*, as is *g* when followed by *e* or *i*; and the initial *r* and double *rr*, which are pronounced somewhere between the American *h* and the Yiddish *ch*.

Vowels: Single vowels are pronounced more or less as follows: *a* as in *father*, *e* as in *get*, *i* like the *ee* in *fee*, *o* as in *throne*, and *u* like the *oo* in *toot*. (This is a gross oversimplification, since there are really two distinct *a* sounds, neither of which is really like the *a* in *father*, three meaning-changing ways to pronounce *e*—*é*, *ê*, and the quick *e* at the end of a word—and three meaning-changing ways to pronounce *o*—*ó*, *ô*, and the quick *o* at the ends of words. But it's close enough to get you through this book.)

Consonant combinations: The combination *lh* is pronounced like the *lli* in *William;* *nh,* like the *ni* in *onion.* The combination *ch* is always pronounced like the English *sh.* The combination *qu,* when followed by *e* or *i,* is pronounced like the English *k;* when followed by *a, o,* or *u,* like the English *qu;* the same pattern is followed by *gu.* Thus *Quara* is pronounced KWAH-rah, while *Figueira* is pronounced fee-GAY-rah.

Vowel combinations: The combination *ou* is pronounced like the *ow* in *throw; ai,* like *igh* in *high; ei,* like *eigh* in *weigh.* The combination *eu* is not found in English; it is pronounced as a very quick combination of the *e* in *get* and the *u* in *put.*

Nasal vowels: A vowel or vowel combination with a tilde—usually ão and ã—or the combination *am* at the end of a word are all nasalized. That is, they are pronounced as if the vowel were going to end with the English *ng* sound, only the *ng* is never quite closed. In addition, the syllable with a tilde is *always* stressed, so that the name Marcão is pronounced mah-KOWNG. (Syllables with ^ and ´ accent marks are also stressed.)

If I told you that when *t* comes before the *i* sound it's pronounced like the English *ch,* and *d* follows the same pattern to sound like the English *j,* or if I mentioned that *x* always sounds like *sh* except when it sounds like *z,* you might well give up entirely so I won't.

Prologue

In the year 1830, after the formation of Starways Congress, a robot scout ship sent a report by ansible: The planet it was investigating was well within the parameters for human life. The nearest planet with any kind of population pressure was Baía; Starways Congress granted them the exploration license.

So it was that the first humans to see the new world were Portuguese by language, Brazilian by culture, and Catholic by creed. In the year 1886 they disembarked from their shuttle, crossed themselves, and named the planet Lusitania—the ancient name of Portugal. They set about cataloguing the flora and fauna. Five days later they realized that the little forest-dwelling animals that they had called *porquinhos*—piggies—were not animals at all.

For the first time since the Xenocide of the Buggers by the monstrous Ender, humans had found intelligent alien life. The piggies were technologically primitive, but they used tools and built houses and spoke a language. "It is another chance God has given us," declared Archcardinal Pio of Baía. "We can be redeemed for the destruction of the buggers."

The members of Starways Congress worshipped many gods, or none, but they agreed with the Archcardinal. Lusitania would be settled from Baía, and therefore under Catholic License, as tradition demanded. But the colony could never spread beyond a limited area or exceed a limited population. And it was bound, above all, by one law:

The piggies were not to be disturbed.

Chapter 1

Pipo

Since we are not yet fully comfortable with the idea that people from the next village are as human as ourselves, it is presumptuous in the extreme to suppose we could ever look at sociable, tool-making creatures who arose from other evolutionary paths and see not beasts but brothers, not rivals but fellow pilgrims journeying to the shrine of intelligence.

Yet that is what I see, or yearn to see. The difference between raman and varelse is not in the creature judged, but in the creature judging. When we declare an alien species to be raman, it does not mean that *they* have passed a threshold of moral maturity. It means that *we* have.

—Demosthenes, *Letter to the Framlings*

Rooter was at once the most difficult and the most helpful of the pequeninos. He was always there whenever Pipo visited their clearing, and did his best to answer the questions Pipo was forbidden by law to come right out and ask. Pipo depended on him—too much, probably—yet though Rooter clowned and played like the irresponsible youngling that he was, he also watched, probed, tested. Pipo always had to beware of the traps that Rooter set for him.

A moment ago Rooter had been shimmying up trees, gripping the bark with only the horny pads on his ankles and inside his thighs. In his hands he carried two sticks—Father Sticks, they were called—which he beat against the tree in a compelling, arhythmic pattern all the while he climbed.

The noise brought Mandachuva out of the log house. He called to Rooter in the Males' Language, and then in Portuguese. "P'ra baixo, bicho!" Several piggies nearby, hearing his Portuguese word-play, expressed their appreciation by rubbing their thighs together sharply. It made a hissing noise, and Mandachuva took a little hop in the air in delight at their applause.

Rooter, in the meantime, bent over backward until it seemed certain he would fall. Then he flipped off with his hands, did a somersault in the air, and landed on his legs, hopping a few times but not stumbling.

"So now you're an acrobat," said Pipo.

Rooter swaggered over to him. It was his way of imitating humans. It was all the more effective as ridicule because his flattened upturned snout looked decidedly porcine. No wonder that offworlders called them "piggies." The first visitors to this world had started calling them that in their first reports back in '86, and by the time Lusitania Colony was founded in 1925, the name was indelible. The xenologers scattered among the Hundred Worlds wrote of them as "Lusitanian Aborigines," though Pipo knew perfectly well that this was merely a matter of professional dignity—except in scholarly papers, xenologers no doubt called them piggies, too. As for Pipo, he called them pequeninos, and they seemed not to object, for now they called themselves "Little Ones." Still, dignity or not, there was no denying it. At moments like this, Rooter looked like a hog on its hind legs.

"Acrobat," Rooter said, trying out the new word. "What I did? You have a word for people who do that? So there are people who do that as their *work?*"

Pipo sighed silently, even as he froze his smile in place. The law strictly forbade him to share information about human society, lest it contaminate piggy culture. Yet Rooter played a constant game of squeezing the last drop of implication out of everything Pipo said. This time, though, Pipo had no one to blame but himself, letting out a silly remark that opened unnecessary windows onto human life. Now and then he got so comfortable among the pequeninos that he spoke naturally. Always a danger. I'm not good at this constant game of taking information while trying to give nothing in return. Libo, my close-mouthed son, already he's better at discretion than I am, and he's only been apprenticed to me—how long since he turned thirteen?—four months.

"I wish I had pads on my legs like yours," said Pipo. "The bark on that tree would rip my skin to shreds."

"That would cause us all to be ashamed." Rooter held still in the expectant posture that Pipo thought of as their way of showing mild anxiety, or perhaps a nonverbal warning to other pequeninos to be cautious. It might also have been a sign of extreme fear, but as far as Pipo knew he had never seen a pequenino feel extreme fear.

In any event, Pipo spoke quickly to calm him. "Don't worry, I'm too old and soft to climb trees like that. I'll leave it to you younglings."

And it worked; Rooter's body at once became mobile again. "I like to climb trees. I can see everything." Rooter squatted in front of Pipo and leaned his face in close. "Will you bring the beast that runs over the grass without touching the ground? The others don't believe me when I say I saw such a thing."

Another trap. What, Pipo, xenologer, will you *humiliate* this individual of the community you're studying? Or will you adhere to the rigid law set up by Starways Congress to govern this encounter? There were few precedents. The only other intelligent aliens that humankind had encountered were the buggers, three thousand years ago, and at the end of it the buggers were all dead. This time Starways Congress was making sure that if humanity erred, their errors would be in the opposite direction. Minimal information, minimal contact.

Rooter recognized Pipo's hesitation, his careful silence.

"You never tell us anything," said Rooter. "You watch us and study us, but you never let us past your fence and into your village to watch *you* and study *you.*"

Pipo answered as honestly as he could, but it was more important to be careful than to be honest. "If you learn so little and we learn so much, why is it that you speak both Stark and Portuguese while I'm still struggling with your language?"

"We're smarter." Then Rooter leaned back and spun around on his buttocks so his back was toward Pipo. "Go back behind your fence," he said.

Pipo stood at once. Not too far away, Libo was with three pequeninos, trying to learn how they wove dried merdona vines into thatch. He saw Pipo and in a moment was with his father, ready to go. Pipo led him off without a word; since the pequeninos were so fluent in human languages, they never discussed what they had learned until they were inside the gate.

It took a half hour to get home, and it was raining heavily when they passed through the gate and walked along the face of the hill to the Zenador's Station. Zenador? Pipo thought of the word as he looked at the small sign above the door. On it the word XENOLOGER was written in Stark. That is what I am, I suppose, thought Pipo, at least to the offworlders. But the Portuguese title *Zenador* was so much easier to say that on Lusitania hardly anyone said *xenologer,* even when speaking Stark. That is how languages change, thought Pipo. If it weren't for the ansible, providing instantaneous communication among the Hundred Worlds, we could not possibly maintain a common language. Interstellar travel is far too rare and slow. Stark would splinter into ten thousand dialects within a century. It might be interesting to have the computers run a projection of linguistic changes on Lusitania, if Stark were allowed to decay and absorb Portuguese—

"Father," said Libo.

Only then did Pipo notice that he had stopped ten meters away from the station. Tangents. The best parts of my intellectual life are tangential, in areas outside my expertise. I suppose because within my area of expertise the regulations they have placed upon me make it impossible to know or understand anything. The science of xenology insists on more mysteries than Mother Church.

His handprint was enough to unlock the door. Pipo knew how the evening would unfold even as he stepped inside to begin. It would take several hours of work at the terminals for them both to report what they had done during today's encounter. Pipo would then read over Libo's notes, and Libo would read Pipo's, and when they were satisfied, Pipo would write up a brief summary and then let the computers take it from there, filing the notes and also transmitting them instantly, by ansible, to the xenologers in the rest of the Hundred Worlds. More than a thousand scientists whose whole career is studying the one alien race we know, and except for what little the satellites can discover about this arboreal species, all the information my colleagues have is what Libo and I send them. This is definitely minimal intervention.

But when Pipo got inside the station, he saw at once that it would not be an evening of steady but relaxing work. Dona Cristã was there, dressed in her monastic robes. Was it one of the younger children, in trouble at school?

"No, no," said Dona Cristã. "All your children are doing very well, except this one, who I think is far too young to be out of school and working here, even as an apprentice."

Libo said nothing. A wise decision, thought Pipo. Dona Cristã was a brilliant and engaging, perhaps even beautiful, young woman, but she was first and foremost a monk of the order of the Filhos da Mente de Cristo, Children of the Mind of Christ, and she was not beautiful to behold when she was angry at ignorance and stupidity. It was amazing the number of quite intelligent people whose ignorance and stupidity had melted somewhat in the fire of her scorn. Silence, Libo, it's a policy that will do you good.

"I'm not here about any child of yours at all," said Dona Cristã. "I'm here about Novinha."

Dona Cristã did not have to mention a last name; everybody knew Novinha. The terrible Descolada had ended only eight years before. The plague had threatened to wipe out the colony before it had a fair chance to get started; the cure was discovered by Novinha's father and mother, Gusto and Cida, the two xenobiologists. It was a tragic irony that they found the cause of the disease and its treatment too late to save themselves. Theirs was the last Descolada funeral.

Pipo clearly remembered the little girl Novinha, standing there holding Mayor Bosquinha's hand while Bishop Peregrino conducted the funeral mass himself. No—not holding the Mayor's hand. The picture came back to his mind, and, with it, the way he felt. What does she make of this? he remembered asking himself. It's the funeral of her parents, she's the last survivor in her family; yet all around her she can sense the great rejoicing of the people of this colony. Young as she is, does she understand that our joy is the best tribute to her parents? They struggled and succeeded, finding our salvation in the waning days before they died; we are here to celebrate the great gift they gave us. But to you, Novinha, it's the death of your parents, as your brothers died before. Five hundred dead, and more than a hundred masses for the dead here in this colony in the last six months, and all of them were held in an atmosphere of fear and grief and despair. Now, when your parents die, the fear and grief and despair are no less for you than ever before—but no one else shares your pain. It is the relief from pain that is foremost in our minds.

Watching her, trying to imagine her feelings, he succeeded only in rekindling his own grief at the death of his own Maria, seven years old, swept away in the wind of death that covered her body in cancerous growth and rampant funguses, the flesh swelling or decaying, a new limb, not arm or leg, growing out of her hip, while the flesh sloughed off her feet and head, baring the bones, her sweet and beautiful body destroyed before their eyes, while her bright mind was mercilessly alert, able to feel all that happened to her until she cried out to God to let her die. Pipo remembered that, and then remembered her requiem mass, shared with five other victims. As he sat, knelt, stood there with his wife and surviving children, he had felt the perfect unity of the people in the Cathedral. He knew that his pain was everybody's pain, that through the loss of his eldest daughter he was bound to his community with the inseparable bonds of grief, and it *was* a comfort to him, it was something to cling to. That was how such a grief ought to be, a public mourning.

Little Novinha had nothing of that. Her pain was, if anything, worse than Pipo's had been—at least Pipo had not been left without any family at all, and he was an adult, not a child terrified by suddenly losing the foundation of her life. In her grief she was not drawn more tightly into the community, but rather excluded from it. Today everyone was rejoicing, except her. Today everyone praised her parents; she alone yearned for them, would rather they had never found the cure for others if only they could have remained alive themselves.

Her isolation was so acute that Pipo could see it from where he sat. Novinha took her hand away from the Mayor as quickly as possible. Her tears dried up as the mass progressed; by the end she sat in silence, like a prisoner refusing to cooperate with her captors. Pipo's heart broke for her. Yet he knew that even if he tried, he could not conceal his own gladness at the end of the Descolada, his rejoicing that none of his other children would be taken from him. She would see that; his effort to comfort her would be a mockery, would drive her further away.

After the mass she walked in bitter solitude amid the crowds of well-meaning people who cruelly told her that her parents were sure to be saints, sure to sit at the right hand of God. What kind of comfort is that for a child? Pipo whispered aloud to his wife, "She'll never forgive us for today."

"Forgive?" Conceição was not one of those wives who instantly understood her husband's train of thought. *"We* didn't kill her parents—"

"But we're all rejoicing today, aren't we? She'll never forgive us for that."

"Nonsense. She doesn't understand anyway; she's too young."

She understands, Pipo thought. Didn't Maria understand things when she was even younger than Novinha is now?

As the years passed—eight years now—he had seen her from time to time. She was his son Libo's age, and until Libo's thirteenth birthday that meant they were in many classes together. He heard her give occasional readings and speeches, along with other children. There was an elegance to her thought, an intensity to her examination of ideas that appealed to him. At the same time, she seemed utterly cold, completely removed from everyone else. Pipo's own boy, Libo, was shy, but even so he had several friends, and had won the affection of his teachers. Novinha, though, had no friends at all, no one whose gaze she sought after a moment of triumph. There was no teacher who genuinely liked her, because she refused to reciprocate, to respond. "She is emotionally paralyzed," Dona Cristã said once when Pipo asked about her. "There is no reaching her. She swears that she's perfectly happy, and doesn't see any need to change."

Now Dona Cristã had come to the Zenador's Station to talk to Pipo about Novinha. Why Pipo? He could guess only one reason for the principal of the school to come to him about this particular orphaned girl. "Am I to believe that in all the years you've had Novinha in your school, I'm the only person who asked about her?"

"Not the only person," she said. "There was all kinds of interest in her a couple of years ago, when the Pope beatified her parents. Everybody asked then whether the daughter of Gusto and Cida, Os Venerados, had ever noticed any miraculous events associated with her parents, as so many other people had."

"They actually *asked* her that?"

"There were rumors, and Bishop Peregrino had to investigate." Dona Cristã got a bit tight-lipped when she spoke of the young spiritual leader of Lusitania Colony. But then, it was said that the hierarchy never got along well with the order of the Filhos da Mente de Cristo. "Her answer was instructive."

"I can imagine."

"She said, more or less, that if her parents were actually listening to prayers and had any influence in heaven to get them granted, then why wouldn't they have answered *her* prayer, for them to return from the grave? That would be a useful miracle, she said, and there are precedents. If Os Venerados actually had the power to grant miracles, then it must mean they did not love her enough to answer her prayer. She preferred to believe that her parents still loved her, and simply did not have the power to act."

"A born sophist," said Pipo.

"A sophist *and* an expert in guilt: she told the Bishop that if the Pope declared her parents to be venerable, it would be the same as the Church saying that her parents hated her. The petition for canonization of her parents was proof that Lusitania despised her; if it was granted, it would be proof that the Church itself was despicable. Bishop Peregrino was livid."

"I notice he sent in the petition anyway."

"For the good of the community. And there *were* all those miracles."

"Someone touches the shrine and a headache goes away and they cry 'Milagre!—os santos me abençoaram!'" Miracle!—the saints have blessed me!

"You know that Holy Rome requires more substantial miracles than that. But it doesn't matter. The Pope graciously allowed us to call our little town Milagre, and now I imagine that every time someone says that name, Novinha burns a little hotter with her secret rage."

"Or colder. One never knows what temperature that sort of thing will take."

"Anyway, Pipo, you aren't the only one who ever asked about her. But you're the only one who ever asked about her for her own sake, and not because of her most Holy and Blessed parents."

It was a sad thought, that except for the Filhos, who ran the schools of Lusitania, there had been no concern for the girl except the slender shards of attention Pipo had spared for her over the years.

"She has one friend," said Libo.

Pipo had forgotten that his son was there—Libo was so quiet that he was easy to overlook. Dona Cristã also seemed startled. "Libo," she said, "I think we were indiscreet, talking about one of your schoolmates like this."

"I'm apprentice Zenador now," Libo reminded her. It meant he wasn't in school.

"Who is her friend?" asked Pipo.

"Marcão."

"Marcos Ribeira," Dona Cristã explained. "The tall boy—"

"Ah, yes, the one who's built like a cabra."

"He *is* strong," said Dona Cristã. "But I've never noticed any friendship between them."

"Once when Marcão was accused of something, and she happened to see it, she spoke for him."

"You put a generous interpretation on it, Libo," said Dona Cristã. "I think it is more accurate to say she spoke *against* the boys who actually did it and were trying to put the blame on him."

"Marcão doesn't see it that way," said Libo. "I noticed a couple of times, the way he watches her. It isn't much, but there is somebody who likes her."

"Do *you* like her?" asked Pipo.

Libo paused for a moment in silence. Pipo knew what it meant. He was examining himself to find an answer. Not the answer that he thought would be most likely to bring him adult favor, and not the answer that would provoke their ire—the two kinds of deception that most children his age delighted in. He was examining himself to discover the truth.

"I think," Libo said, "that I understood that she didn't want to be liked. As if she were a visitor who expected to go back home any day."

Dona Cristã nodded gravely. "Yes, that's exactly right, that's exactly the way she seems. But now, Libo, we must end our indiscretion by asking you to leave us while we—"

He was gone before she finished her sentence, with a quick nod of his head, a half-smile that said, Yes, I understand, and a deftness of movement that made his exit more eloquent proof of his discretion than if he had argued to stay. By this Pipo knew that Libo was annoyed at being asked to leave; he had a knack for making adults feel vaguely immature by comparison to him.

"Pipo," said the principal, "she has petitioned for an early examination as xenobiologist. To take her parents' place."

Pipo raised an eyebrow.

"She claims that she has been studying the field intensely since she was a little child. That she's ready to begin the work right now, without apprenticeship."

"She's thirteen, isn't she?"

"There are precedents. Many have taken such tests early. One even passed it younger than her. It was two thousand years ago, but it *was* allowed. Bishop Peregrino is against it, of course, but Mayor Bosquinha, bless her practical heart, has pointed out that Lusitania needs a xenobiologist quite badly—we need to be about the business of developing new strains of plant life so we can get some decent variety in our diet and much better harvests from Lusitanian soil. In her words, 'I don't care if it's an infant, we need a xenobiologist.' "

"And you want me to supervise her examination?"

"If you would be so kind."

"I'll be glad to."

"I told them you would."

"I confess I have an ulterior motive."

"Oh?"

"I should have done more for the girl. I'd like to see if it isn't too late to begin."

Dona Cristã laughed a bit. "Oh, Pipo, I'd be glad for you to try. But do believe me, my dear friend, touching her heart is like bathing in ice."

"I imagine. I imagine it feels like bathing in ice to the person touching her. But how does it feel to her? Cold as she is, it must surely burn like fire."

"Such a poet," said Dona Cristã. There was no irony in her voice; she meant it. "Do the piggies understand that we've sent our very best as our ambassador?"

"I try to tell them, but they're skeptical."

"I'll send her to you tomorrow. I warn you—she'll expect to take the examinations cold, and she'll resist any attempt on your part to pre-examine her."

Pipo smiled. "I'm far more worried about what will happen after she takes the test. If she fails, then she'll have very bad problems. And if she passes, then *my* problems will begin."

"Why?"

"Libo will be after me to let him examine early for Zenador. And if he did *that,* there'd be no reason for me not to go home, curl up, and die."

"Such a romantic fool you are, Pipo. If there's any man in Milagre who's capable of accepting his thirteen-year-old son as a colleague, it's you."

After she left, Pipo and Libo worked together, as usual, recording the day's events with the pequeninos. Pipo compared Libo's work, his way of thinking, his insights, his attitudes, with those of the graduate students he had known in University before joining the Lusitania Colony. He might be small, and there might be a lot of theory and knowledge for him yet to learn, but he was already a true scientist in his method, and a humanist at heart. By the time the evening's work was done and they walked home together by the light of Lusitania's large and dazzling moon, Pipo had decided that Libo already deserved to be treated as a colleague, whether he took the examination or not. The tests couldn't measure the things that really counted, anyway.

And whether she liked it or not, Pipo intended to find out if Novinha had the unmeasurable qualities of a scientist; if she didn't, then he'd see to it she didn't take the test, regardless of how many facts she had memorized.

Pipo meant to be difficult. Novinha knew how adults acted when they planned not to do things her way, but didn't want a fight or even any nastiness. Of course, of course you can take the test. But there's no reason to rush into it, let's take some time, let me make sure you'll be successful on the first attempt.

Novinha didn't want to wait. Novinha was ready.

"I'll jump through any hoops you want," she said.

His face went cold. Their faces always did. That was all right, coldness was all right, she could freeze them to death. "I don't want you to jump through hoops," he said.

"The only thing I ask is that you line them up all in a row so I can jump through them *quickly.* I don't want to be put off for days and days."

He looked thoughtful for a moment. "You're in such a hurry."

"I'm *ready.* The Starways Code allows me to challenge the test at any time. It's between me and the Starways Congress, and I can't find anywhere that it says a xenologer can try to second-guess the Interplanetary Examinations Board."

"Then you haven't read carefully."

"The only thing I need to take the test before I'm sixteen is the authorization of my legal guardian. I don't *have* a legal guardian."

"On the contrary," said Pipo. "Mayor Bosquinha was your legal guardian from the day of your parents' death."

"And she agreed I could take the test."

"Provided you came to me."

Novinha saw the intense look in his eyes. She didn't know Pipo, so she thought it was the look she had seen in so many eyes, the desire to dominate, to rule her, the desire to cut through her determination and break her independence, the desire to make her *submit.*

From ice to fire in an instant. "What do you know about xenobiology! You only go out and talk to the piggies, you don't even begin to understand the workings of genes! Who are you to judge me! Lusitania needs a xenobiologist, and they've been without one for eight years. And you want to make them wait even longer, just so you can be in control!"

To her surprise, he didn't become flustered, didn't retreat. Nor did he get angry in return. It was as if she hadn't spoken.

"I see," he said quietly. "It's because of your great love of the people of Lusitania that you wish to become xenobiologist. Seeing the public need, you sacrificed and prepared yourself to enter early into a lifetime of altruistic service."

It sounded absurd, hearing him say it like that. And it wasn't at all what she felt. "Isn't that a good enough reason?"

"If it were true, it would be good enough."

"Are you calling me a liar?"

"Your own words called you a liar. You spoke of how much *they,* the people of Lusitania, need you. But you live among us. You've lived among us all your life. Ready to sacrifice for us, and yet you don't feel yourself to be part of this community."

So he wasn't like the adults who always believed lies as long as they made her seem to be the child they wanted her to be. "Why should I *feel* like part of the community? I'm not."

He nodded gravely, as if considering her answer. "What community are you a part of?"

"The only other communities on Lusitania are the piggies, and you haven't seen me out there with the tree-worshippers."

"There are many other communities on Lusitania. For instance, you're a student—there's a community of students."

"Not for me."

"I know. You have no friends, you have no intimate associates, you go to mass but you never go to confession, you are so completely detached that as far as possible you don't touch the life of this colony, you don't touch the life of the human race at any point. From all the evidence, you live in complete isolation."

Novinha wasn't prepared for this. He was naming the underlying pain of her life, and she didn't have a strategy devised to cope with it. "If I do, it isn't my fault."

"I know that. I know where it began, and I know whose fault it was that it continues to this day."

"Mine?"

"Mine. And everyone else's. But mine most of all, because I knew what was happening to you and I did nothing at all. Until today."

"And today you're going to keep me from the one thing that matters to me in my life! Thanks so much for your compassion!"

Again he nodded solemnly, as if he were accepting and acknowledging her ironic gratitude. "In one sense, Novinha, it doesn't matter that it isn't your fault. Because the town of Milagre *is* a community, and whether it has treated you badly or not, it must still act as all communities do, to provide the greatest possible happiness for all its members."

"Which means everybody on Lusitania except me—me and the piggies."

"The xenobiologist is very important to a colony, especially one like this, surrounded by a fence that forever limits our growth. Our xenobiologist must find ways to grow more protein and carbohydrate per hectare, which means genetically altering the Earthborn corn and potatoes to make—"

"To make maximum use of the nutrients available in the Lusitanian environment. Do you think I'm planning to take the examination without knowing what my life's work would be?"

"Your life's work, to devote yourself to improving the lives of people you despise."

Now Novinha saw the trap that he had laid for her. Too late; it had sprung. "So you think that a xenobiologist can't do her work unless she *loves* the people who use the things she makes?"

"I don't care whether you love us or not. What I have to know is what you really want. Why you're so passionate to do this."

"Basic psychology. My parents died in this work, and so I'm trying to step into their role."

"Maybe," said Pipo. "And maybe not. What I want to know, Novinha, what I *must* know before I'll let you take the test, is what community you *do* belong to."

"You said it yourself! I don't belong to any."

"Impossible. Every person is defined by the communities she belongs to and the ones she doesn't belong to. I am this and this and this, but definitely *not* that and that and that. All your definitions are negative. I could make an infinite list of the things you are not. But a person who really believes she doesn't belong to any community at all invariably kills herself, either by killing her body or by giving up her identity and going mad."

"That's me, insane to the root."

"Not insane. Driven by a sense of purpose that is frightening. If you take this test you'll pass it. But before I let you take it, I have to know: Who will you become when you pass? What do you believe in, what are you part of, what do you care about, what do you love?"

"Nobody in this or any other world."

"I don't believe you."

"I've never known a good man or woman in the world except my parents and they're dead! And even they—nobody understands *anything.*"

"You."

"I'm part of anything, aren't I? But nobody understands anybody, not even you, pretending to be so wise and compassionate but you're only getting me to cry like this because you have the power to stop me from doing what I want to do—"

"And it isn't xenobiology."

"Yes it is! That's part of it, anyway."

"And what's the rest of it?"

"What you are. What you do. Only you're doing it all wrong, you're doing it *stupidly.*"

"Xenobiologist *and* xenologer."

"They made a stupid mistake when they created a new science to study the piggies. They were a bunch of tired old anthropologists who put on new hats and called themselves xenologers. But you can't understand the piggies just by watching the way they *behave!* They came out of a different evolution! You have to understand their genes, what's going on inside their cells. And the other animals' cells, too, because they can't be studied by themselves, *nobody* lives in isolation—"

Don't lecture me, thought Pipo. Tell me what you *feel*. And to provoke her to be more emotional, he whispered, "Except you."

It worked. From cold and contemptuous she became hot and defensive. "You'll never understand them! But I will!"

"Why do you care about them? What are the piggies to you?"

"You'd never understand. You're a good *Catholic.*" She said the word with contempt. "It's a book that's on the Index."

Pipo's face glowed with sudden understanding. "The Hive Queen and the Hegemon."

"He lived three thousand years ago, whoever he was, the one who called himself the Speaker for the Dead. But he *understood* the buggers! We wiped them all out, the only other alien race we ever knew, we killed them all, but *he understood.*"

"And you want to write the story of the piggies the way the original Speaker wrote of the buggers."

"The way you say it, you make it sound as easy as doing a scholarly paper. You don't know what it was like to write the Hive Queen and the Hegemon. How much agony it was for him to—to imagine himself inside an alien mind—and come out of it filled with love for the great creature we destroyed. He lived at the same time as the worst human being who ever lived, Ender the Xenocide, who destroyed the buggers—and he did his best to undo what Ender did, the Speaker for the Dead tried to raise the dead—"

"But he couldn't."

"But he did! He made them live again—you'd know it if you had read the book! I don't know about Jesus, I listen to Bishop Peregrino and I don't think there's any power in their priesthood to turn wafers into flesh or forgive a milligram of guilt. But the Speaker for the Dead brought the hive queen back to life."

"Then where is she?"

"In here! In me!"

He nodded. "And someone else is in you. The Speaker for the Dead. That's who you want to be."

"It's the only true story I ever heard," she said. "The only one I care about. Is that what you wanted to hear? That I'm a heretic? And my whole life's work is going to be adding another book to the Index of truths that good Catholics are forbidden to read?"

"What I wanted to hear," said Pipo softly, "was the name of what you are instead of the name of all the things that you are not. What you are is the hive queen. What you are is the Speaker for the Dead. It's a very small community, small in numbers, but a great-hearted one. So you chose not to be part of the bands of children who group together for the sole purpose of excluding others, and people look at you and say, poor girl, she's so isolated, but you know a secret, you know who you really are. You are the one human being who is capable of understanding the alien mind, because you *are* the alien mind; you know what it is to be unhuman because there's never been any human group that gave you credentials as a bona fide homo sapiens."

"Now you say I'm not even human? You made me cry like a little girl because you wouldn't let me take the test, you made me humiliate myself, and now you say I'm unhuman?"

"You can take the test."

The words hung in the air.

"When?" she whispered.

"Tonight. Tomorrow. Begin when you like. I'll stop my work to take you through the tests as quickly as you like."

"Thank you! Thank you, I—"

"Become the Speaker for the Dead. I'll help you all I can. The law forbids me to take anyone but my apprentice, my son Libo, out to meet the pequeninos. But we'll open our notes to you. Everything we learn, we'll show you. All our guesses and speculation. In return, you also show us all your work, what you find out about the genetic patterns of this world that might help us understand the pequeninos. And when we've learned enough, together, you can write your book, you can become the Speaker. But this time not the Speaker for the Dead. The pequeninos aren't dead."

In spite of herself, she smiled. "The Speaker for the Living."

"I've read the Hive Queen and the Hegemon, too," he said. "I can't think of a better place for you to find your name."

But she did not trust him yet, did not believe what he seemed to be promising. "I'll want to come here often. All the time."

"We lock it up when we go home to bed."

"But all the rest of the time. You'll get tired of me. You'll tell me to go away. You'll keep secrets from me. You'll tell me to be quiet and not mention my ideas."

"We've only just become friends, and already you think I'm such a liar and cheat, such an impatient oaf."

"But you will, everyone does; they all wish I'd go away—"

Pipo shrugged. "So? Sometime or other everybody wishes everybody would go away. Sometimes I'll wish *you* would go away. What I'm telling you now is that even at those times, even if I *tell* you to go away, you don't have to go away."

It was the most bafflingly perfect thing that anyone had ever said to her. "That's crazy."

"Only one thing. Promise me you'll never try to go out to the pequeninos. Because I can never let you do that, and if somehow you do it anyway, Starways Congress would close down all our work here, forbid any contact with them. Do you promise me? Or everything—my work, your work—it will all be undone."

"I promise."

"When will you take the test?"

"Now! Can I begin it now?"

He laughed gently, then reached out a hand and without looking touched the terminal. It came to life, the first genetic models appearing in the air above the terminal.

"You had the examination ready," she said. "You were all set to go! You knew that you'd let me do it all along!"

He shook his head. "I hoped. I believed in you. I wanted to help you do what you dreamed of doing. As long as it was something good."

She would not have been Novinha if she hadn't found one more poisonous thing to say. "I see. You are the judge of dreams."

Perhaps he didn't know it was an insult. He only smiled and said, "Faith, hope, and love—these three. But the greatest of these is love."

"You don't love me," she said.

"Ah," he said. "I am the judge of dreams, and you are the judge of love. Well, I find you guilty of dreaming good dreams, and sentence you to a lifetime of working and suffering for the sake of your dreams. I only hope that someday you won't declare me innocent of the crime of loving you." He grew reflective for a moment. "I lost a daughter in the Descolada. Maria. She would have been only a few years older than you."

"And I remind you of her?"

"I was thinking that she would have been nothing at all like you."

She began the test. It took three days. She passed it, with a score a good deal higher than many a graduate student. In retrospect, however, she would not remember the test because it was the beginning of her career, the end of her childhood, the confirmation of her vocation for her life's work. She would remember the test because it was the beginning of her time in Pipo's Station, where Pipo and Libo and Novinha together formed the first community she belonged to since her parents were put into the earth.

It was not easy, especially at the beginning. Novinha did not instantly shed her habit of cold confrontation. Pipo understood it, was prepared to bend with her verbal blows. It was much more of a challenge for Libo. The Zenador's Station had been a place where he and his father could be alone together. Now, without anyone asking his consent, a third person had been added, a cold and demanding person, who spoke to him as if he were a child, even though they were the same age. It galled him that she was a full-fledged xenobiologist, with all the adult status that that implied, when he was still an apprentice.

But he tried to bear it patiently. He was naturally calm, and quiet adhered to him. He was not prone to taking umbrage openly. But Pipo knew his son and saw him burn. After a while even Novinha, insensitive as she was, began to realize that she was provoking Libo more than any normal young man could possibly endure. But instead of easing up on him, she began to regard it as a challenge. How could she force some response from this unnaturally calm, gentle-spirited, beautiful boy?

"You mean you've been working all these years," she said one day, "and you don't even know how the piggies *reproduce?* How do you know they're all males?"

Libo answered softly. "We explained male and female to them as they learned our languages. They chose to call themselves males.

And referred to the other ones, the ones we've never seen, as females."

"But for all you know, they reproduce by budding! Or mitosis!"

Her tone was contemptuous, and Libo did not answer quickly. Pipo imagined he could hear his son's thoughts, carefully rephrasing his answer until it was gentle and safe. "I wish our work were more like physical anthropology," he said. "Then we would be more prepared to apply your research into Lusitania's subcellular life patterns to what we learn about the pequeninos."

Novinha looked horrified. "You mean you don't even take tissue samples?"

Libo blushed slightly, but his voice was still calm when he answered. The boy would have been like this under questioning by the Inquisition, Pipo thought. "It *is* foolish, I guess," said Libo, "but we're afraid the pequeninos would wonder why we took pieces of their bodies. If one of them took sick by chance afterward, would they think we caused the illness?"

"What if you took something they shed naturally? You can learn a lot from a hair."

Libo nodded; Pipo, watching from his terminal on the other side of the room, recognized the gesture—Libo had learned it from his father. "Many primitive tribes of Earth believed that sheddings from their bodies contained some of their life and strength. What if the piggies thought we were doing magic against them?"

"Don't you know their language? I thought some of them spoke Stark, too." She made no effort to hide her disdain. "Can't you explain what the samples are for?"

"You're right," he said quietly. "But if we explained what we'd use the tissue samples for, we might accidently teach them the concepts of biological science a thousand years before they would naturally have reached that point. That's why the law forbids us to explain things like that."

Finally, Novinha was abashed. "I didn't realize how tightly you were bound by the doctrine of minimal intervention."

Pipo was glad to hear her retreat from her arrogance, but if anything, her humility was worse. The child was so isolated from human contact that she spoke like an excessively formal science book. Pipo wondered if it was already too late to teach her how to be a human being.

It wasn't. Once she realized that they were excellent at their science, and she knew almost nothing of it, she dropped her aggressive stance and went almost to the opposite extreme. For weeks she spoke to Pipo and Libo only rarely. Instead she studied their reports, trying to grasp the purpose behind what they were doing. Now and then she had a question, and asked; they answered politely and thoroughly.

Politeness gradually gave way to familiarity. Pipo and Libo began to converse openly in front of her, airing their speculations about why the piggies had developed some of their strange behaviors, what meaning lay behind some of their odd statements, why they remained so maddeningly impenetrable. And since the study of piggies was a very new branch of science, it didn't take long for Novinha to be expert enough, even at second hand, to offer some hypotheses. "After all," said Pipo, encouraging her, "we're all blind together."

Pipo had foreseen what happened next. Libo's carefully cultivated patience had made him seem cold and reserved to others of his age, when Pipo could prevail on him even to attempt to socialize; Novinha's isolation was more flamboyant but no more thorough. Now, however, their common interest in the piggies drew them close —who else could they talk to, when no one but Pipo could even understand their conversations?

They relaxed together, laughed themselves to tears over jokes that could not possibly amuse any other Luso. Just as the piggies seemed to name every tree in the forest, Libo playfully named all the furniture in the Zenador's Station, and periodically announced that certain items were in a bad mood and shouldn't be disturbed. "Don't sit on Chair! It's her time of the month again." They had never seen a piggy female, and the males always seemed to refer to them with almost religious reverence; Novinha wrote a series of mock reports on an imaginary piggy woman called Reverend Mother, who was hilariously bitchy and demanding.

It was not all laughter. There were problems, worries, and once a time of real fear that they might have done exactly what the Starways Congress had tried so hard to prevent—making radical changes in piggy society. It began with Rooter, of course. Rooter, who persisted in asking challenging, impossible questions, like, "If you have no other city of humans, how can you go to war? There's no honor for you in killing Little Ones." Pipo babbled something about how humans would never kill pequeninos, Little Ones; but he knew that this wasn't the question Rooter was really asking.

Pipo had known for years that the piggies knew the concept of war, but for days after that Libo and Novinha argued heatedly about whether Rooter's question proved that the piggies regarded war as desirable or merely unavoidable. There were other bits of information from Rooter, some important, some not—and many whose importance was impossible to judge. In a way, Rooter himself was proof of the wisdom of the policy that forbade the xenologers to ask questions that would reveal human expectations, and therefore human practices. Rooter's questions invariably gave them more answers than they got from his answers to their own questions.

The last information Rooter gave them, though, was not in a question. It was a guess, spoken to Libo privately, when Pipo was off with some of the others examining the way they built their log house. "I know I know," said Rooter, "I know why Pipo is still alive. Your women are too stupid to know that he is wise."

Libo struggled to make sense of this seeming non sequitur. What did Rooter think, that if human women were smarter, they would kill Pipo? The talk of killing was disturbing—this was obviously an important matter, and Libo did not know how to handle it alone. Yet he couldn't call Pipo to help, since Rooter obviously wanted to discuss it where Pipo couldn't hear.

When Libo didn't answer, Rooter persisted. "Your women, they are weak and stupid. I told the others this, and they said I could ask you. Your women don't see Pipo's wisdom. Is this true?"

Rooter seemed very agitated; he was breathing heavily, and he kept pulling hairs from his arms, four and five at a time. Libo had to answer, somehow. "Most women don't know him," he said.

"Then how will they know if he should die?" asked Rooter. Then, suddenly, he went very still and spoke very loudly. "You are cabras!"

Only then did Pipo come into view, wondering what the shouting was about. He saw at once that Libo was desperately out of his depth. Yet Pipo had no notion what the conversation was even about —how could he help? All he knew was that Rooter was saying humans—or at least Pipo and Libo—were somehow like the large beasts that grazed in herds on the prairie. Pipo couldn't even tell if Rooter was angry or happy.

"You are cabras! *You* decide!" He pointed at Libo and then at Pipo. "Your women don't choose your honor, *you* do! Just like in battle, but all the time!"

Pipo had no idea what Rooter was talking about, but he could see that all the pequeninos were motionless as stumps, waiting for him—or Libo—to answer. It was plain Libo was too frightened by Rooter's strange behavior to dare any response at all. In this case, Pipo could see no point but to tell the truth; it was, after all, a relatively obvious and trivial bit of information about human society. It was against the rules that the Starways Congress had established for him, but failing to answer would be even more damaging, and so Pipo went ahead.

"Women and men decide together, or they decide for them-selves," said Pipo. "One doesn't decide for the other."

It was apparently what all the piggies had been waiting for. "Cabras," they said, over and over; they ran to Rooter, hooting and whistling. They picked him up and rushed him off into the woods. Pipo tried to follow, but two of the piggies stopped him and shook their heads. It was a human gesture they had learned long before, but it held stronger meaning for the piggies. It was absolutely forbidden for Pipo to follow. They were going to the women, and that was the one place the piggies had told them they could never go.

On the way home, Libo reported how the difficulty began. "Do you know what Rooter said? He said our women were weak and stupid."

"That's because he's never met Mayor Bosquinha. Or your mother, for that matter."

Libo laughed, because his mother, Conceição, ruled the archives as if it were an ancient estação in the wild mato—if you entered her domain, you were utterly subject to her law. As he laughed, he felt something slip away, some idea that was important—what were we talking about? The conversation went on; Libo had forgotten, and soon he even forgot that he had forgotten.

That night they heard the drumming sound that Pipo and Libo believed was part of some sort of celebration. It didn't happen all that often, like beating on great drums with heavy sticks. Tonight, though, the celebration seemed to go on forever. Pipo and Libo spec-ulated that perhaps the human example of sexual equality had some-how given the male pequeninos some hope of liberation. "I think this may qualify as a serious modification of piggy behavior," Pipo said gravely. "If we find that we've caused real change, I'm going to have to report it, and Congress will probably direct that human contact with piggies be cut off for a while. Years, perhaps." It was a sobering thought—that doing their job faithfully might lead Starways Congress to forbid them to do their job at all.

In the morning Novinha walked with them to the gate in the high fence that separated the human city from the slopes leading up to the forest hills where the piggies lived. Because Pipo and Libo were still trying to reassure each other that neither of them could have done any differently, Novinha walked on ahead and got to the gate first. When the others arrived, she pointed to a patch of freshly cleared red earth only thirty meters or so up the hill from the gate. "That's new," she said. "And there's something in it."

Pipo opened the gate, and Libo, being younger, ran on ahead to investigate. He stopped at the edge of the cleared patch and went completely rigid, staring down at whatever lay there. Pipo, seeing him, also stopped, and Novinha, suddenly frightened for Libo, ignored the regulation and ran through the gate. Libo's head rocked backward and he dropped to his knees; he clutched his tight-curled hair and cried out in terrible remorse.

Rooter lay spread-eagled in the cleared dirt. He had been eviscerated, and not carelessly: Each organ had been cleanly separated, and the strands and filaments of his limbs had also been pulled out and spread in a symmetrical pattern on the drying soil. Everything still had some connection to the body—nothing had been completely severed.

Libo's agonized crying was almost hysterical. Novinha knelt by him and held him, rocked him, tried to soothe him. Pipo methodically took out his small camera and took pictures from every angle so the computer could analyze it in detail later.

"He was still alive when they did this," Libo said, when he had calmed enough to speak. Even so, he had to say the words slowly, carefully, as if he were a foreigner just learning to speak. "There's so much blood on the ground, spattered so far—his heart had to be beating when they opened him up."

"We'll discuss it later," said Pipo.

Now the thing Libo had forgotten yesterday came back to him with cruel clarity. "It's what Rooter said about the women. They decide when the men should die. He told me that, and I—" He stopped himself. Of course he did nothing. The law required him to do nothing. And at that moment he decided that he hated the law. If the law meant allowing this to be done to Rooter, then the law had no understanding. Rooter was a person. You don't stand by and let this happen to a person just because you're studying him.

"They didn't dishonor him," said Novinha. "If there's one thing that's certain, it's the love that they have for trees. See?" Out of the center of his chest cavity, which was otherwise empty now, a very small seedling sprouted. "They planted a tree to mark his burial spot."

"Now we know why they name all their trees," said Libo bitterly. "They planted them as grave markers for the piggies they tortured to death."

"This is a very large forest," Pipo said calmly. "Please confine your hypotheses to what is at least remotely possible." They were calmed by his quiet, reasoned tone, his insistence that even now they behave as scientists.

"What should we do?" asked Novinha.

"We should get you back inside the perimeter immediately," said Pipo. "It's forbidden for you to come out here."

"But I meant—with the body—what should we do?"

"Nothing," said Pipo. "The piggies have done what piggies do, for whatever reason piggies do it." He helped Libo to his feet.

Libo had trouble standing for a moment; he leaned on both of them for his first few steps. "What did I say?" he whispered. "I don't even know what it is I said that killed him."

"It wasn't you," said Pipo. "It was me."

"What, do you think you own them?" demanded Novinha. "Do you think their world revolves around you? The piggies did it, for whatever reason they have. It's plain enough this isn't the first time —they were too deft at the vivisection for this to be the first time."

Pipo took it with black humor. "We're losing our wits, Libo. Novinha isn't supposed to know anything about xenology."

"You're right," said Libo. "Whatever may have triggered this, it's something they've done before. A custom." He was trying to sound calm.

"But that's even worse, isn't it?" said Novinha. "It's their *custom* to gut each other alive." She looked at the other trees of the forest that began at the top of the hill and wondered how many of them were rooted in blood.

Pipo sent his report on the ansible, and the computer didn't give him any trouble about the priority level. He left it up to the oversight committee to decide whether contact with the piggies should be stopped. The committee could not identify any fatal error. "It is impossible to conceal the relationship between our sexes, since someday a woman may be xenologer," said the report, "and we can find no point at which you did not act reasonably and prudently. Our tentative conclusion is that you were unwitting participants in some sort of power struggle, which was decided against Rooter, and that you should continue your contact with all reasonable prudence."

It was complete vindication, but it still wasn't easy to take. Libo had grown up knowing the piggies, or at least hearing about them from his father. He knew Rooter better than he knew any human being besides his family and Novinha. It took days for Libo to come back to the Zenador's Station, weeks before he would go back out into the forest. The piggies gave no sign that anything had changed; if anything, they were more open and friendly than before. No one ever spoke of Rooter, least of all Pipo and Libo. There were changes on the human side, however. Pipo and Libo never got more than a few steps away from each other when they were among them.

The pain and remorse of that day drew Libo and Novinha to rely on each other even more, as though darkness bound them closer than light. The piggies now seemed dangerous and uncertain, just as human company had always been, and between Pipo and Libo there now hung the question of who was at fault, no matter how often each tried to reassure the other. So the only good and reliable thing in Libo's life was Novinha, and in Novinha's life, Libo.

Even though Libo had a mother and siblings, and Pipo and Libo always went home to them, Novinha and Libo behaved as if the Zenador's Station were an island, with Pipo a loving but ever remote Prospero. Pipo wondered: Are the piggies like Ariel, leading the young lovers to happiness, or are they little Calibans, scarcely under control and chafing to do murder?

After a few months, Rooter's death faded into memory, and their laughter returned, though it was never quite as carefree as before. By the time they were seventeen, Libo and Novinha were so sure of each other that they routinely talked of what they would do together five, ten, twenty years later. Pipo never bothered to ask them about their marriage plans. After all, he thought, they studied biology from morning to night. Eventually it would occur to them to explore stable and socially acceptable reproductive strategies. In the meantime, it was enough that they puzzled endlessly over when and how the piggies mated, considering that the males had no discernable reproductive organ. Their speculations on how the piggies combined genetic material invariably ended in jokes so lewd that it took all of Pipo's self-control to pretend not to find them amusing.

So the Zenador's Station for those few short years was a place of true companionship for two brilliant young people who otherwise would have been condemned to cold solitude. It did not occur to any of them that the idyll would end abruptly, and forever, and under circumstances that would send a tremor throughout the Hundred Worlds.

It was all so simple, so commonplace. Novinha was analyzing the genetic structure of the fly-infested reeds along the river, and realized that the same subcellular body that had caused the Descolada was present in the cells of the reed. She brought several other cell structures into the air over the computer terminal and rotated them. They all contained the Descolada agent.

She called to Pipo, who was running through transcriptions of yesterday's visit to the piggies. The computer ran comparisons of every cell she had samples of. Regardless of cell function, regardless of the species it was taken from, every alien cell contained the Descolada body, and the computer declared them absolutely identical in chemical proportions.

Novinha expected Pipo to nod, tell her it looked interesting, maybe come up with a hypothesis. Instead he sat down and ran the same test over, asking her questions about how the computer comparison operated, and then what the Descolada body actually did.

"Mother and Father never figured out what triggered it, but the Descolada body releases this little protein—well, pseudo-protein, I suppose—and it attacks the genetic molecules, starting at one end and unzipping the two strands of the molecule right down the middle. That's why they called it the descolador—it unglues the DNA in humans, too."

"Show me what it does in alien cells."

Novinha put the simulation in motion.

"No, not just the genetic molecule—the whole environment of the cell."

"It's just in the nucleus," she said. She widened the field to include more variables. The computer took it more slowly, since it was considering millions of random arrangements of nuclear material every second. In the reed cell, as a genetic molecule came unglued, several large ambient proteins affixed themselves to the open strands. "In humans, the DNA tries to recombine, but random proteins insert themselves so that cell after cell goes crazy. Sometimes they go into mitosis, like cancer, and sometimes they die. What's most important is that in humans the Descolada bodies themselves reproduce like crazy, passing from cell to cell. Of course, every alien creature already has them."

But Pipo wasn't interested in what she said. When the descolador had finished with the genetic molecules of the reed, he looked from one cell to another. "It's not just significant, it's the same," he said. "It's the same thing!"

Novinha didn't see at once what he had noticed. What was the same as what? Nor did she have time to ask. Pipo was already out of the chair, grabbing his coat, heading for the door. It was drizzling outside. Pipo paused only to call out to her, "Tell Libo not to bother coming, just show him that simulation and see if *he* can figure it out before I get back. He'll know—it's the answer to the big one. The answer to everything."

"Tell me!"

He laughed. "Don't cheat. Libo will tell you, if you can't see it."

"Where are you going?"

"To ask the piggies if I'm right, of course! But I know I am, even if they lie about it. If I'm not back in an hour, I slipped in the rain and broke my leg."

Libo did not get to see the simulations. The meeting of the planning committee went way over time in an argument about extending the cattle range, and after the meeting Libo still had to pick up the week's groceries. By the time he got back, Pipo had been out for four hours, it was getting on toward dark, and the drizzle was turning to snow. They went out at once to look for him, afraid that it might take hours to find him in the woods.

They found him all too soon. His body was already cooling in the snow. The piggies hadn't even planted a tree in him.

Chapter 2

Trondheim

I'm deeply sorry that I could not act upon your request for more detail concerning the courtship and marriage customs of the aboriginal Lusitanians. This must be causing you unimaginable distress, or else you would never have petitioned the Xenological Society to censure me for failure to cooperate with your researches.

When would-be xenologers complain that I am not getting the right sort of data from my observations of the pequeninos, I always urge them to reread the limitations placed upon me by law. I am permitted to bring no more than one assistant on field visits; I may not ask questions that might reveal human expectations, lest they try to imitate us; I may not volunteer information to elicit a parallel response; I may not stay with them more than four hours at a time; except for my clothing, I may not use any products of technology in their presence, which includes cameras, recorders, computers, or even a manufactured pen to write on manufactured paper; I may not even observe them unawares.

In short: I cannot tell you how the pequeninos reproduce because they have not chosen to do it in front of me.

Of course your research is crippled! Of course our conclusions about the piggies are absurd! If we had to observe your university under the same limitations that bind us in our observation of the Lusitanian aborigines, we would no doubt conclude that humans do not reproduce, do not form kinship groups, and devote their entire life cycle to the metamorphosis of the larval student into the adult professor. We might even suppose that professors exercise noticeable power in human society. A competent investigation would quickly reveal the inaccuracy of such conclusions—but in the case of the piggies, no competent investigation is permitted or even contemplated.

Anthropology is never an exact science; the observer never experiences the same culture as the participant. But these are natural limitations inherent to the science. It is the artificial limitations that hamper us—and, through us, you. At the present rate of progress we might as well be mailing questionnaires to the pequeninos and waiting for them to dash off scholarly papers in reply.

—João Figueira Alvarez, reply to Pietro Guataninni of the University of Sicily, Milano Campus, Etruria, published posthumously in *Xenological Studies*, 22:4:49:193

The news of Pipo's death was not of merely local importance. It was transmitted instantaneously, by ansible, to all the Hundred Worlds. The first aliens discovered since Ender's Xenocide had tortured to death the one human who was designated to observe them. Within hours, scholars, scientists, politicians, and journalists began to strike their poses.

A consensus soon emerged. One incident, under baffling circumstances, does not prove the failure of Starways Council policy toward the piggies. On the contrary, the fact that only one man died seems to prove the wisdom of the present policy of near inaction. We should, therefore, do nothing except continue to observe at a slightly less intense pace. Pipo's successor was instructed to visit the piggies no more often than every other day, and never for longer than an hour. He was not to push the piggies to answer questions concerning their treatment of Pipo. It was a reinforcement of the old policy of inaction.

There was also much concern about the morale of the people of Lusitania. They were sent many new entertainment programs by ansible, despite the expense, to help take their minds off the grisly murder.

And then, having done the little that could be done by framlings, who were, after all, lightyears away from Lusitania, the people of the Hundred Worlds returned to their local concerns.

Outside Lusitania, only one man among the half-trillion human beings in the Hundred Worlds felt the death of João Figueira Alvarez, called Pipo, as a great change in the shape of his own life. Andrew Wiggin was Speaker for the Dead in the university city of Reykjavik, renowned as the conservator of Nordic culture, perched on the steep slopes of a knifelike fjord that pierced the granite and ice of the frozen world of Trondheim right at the equator. It was spring, so the snow was in retreat, and fragile grass and flowers reached out for strength from the glistering sun. Andrew sat on the brow of a sunny hill, surrounded by a dozen students who were studying the history of interstellar colonization. Andrew was only half-listening to a fiery argument over whether the utter human victory in the Bugger Wars had been a necessary prelude to human expansion. Such arguments always degenerated quickly into a vilification of the human monster Ender, who commanded the starfleet that committed the Xenocide of the Buggers. Andrew tended to let his mind wander somewhat; the subject did not exactly bore him, but he preferred not to let it engage his attention, either.

Then the small computer implant worn like a jewel in his ear told him of the cruel death of Pipo, the xenologer on Lusitania, and instantly Andrew became alert. He interrupted his students.

"What do you know of the piggies?" he asked.

"They are the only hope of our redemption," said one, who took Calvin rather more seriously than Luther.

Andrew looked at once to the student Plikt, who he knew would not be able to endure such mysticism. "They do not exist for any human purpose, not even redemption," said Plikt with withering contempt. "They are true ramen, like the buggers."

Andrew nodded, but frowned. "You use a word that is not yet common koine."

"It should be," said Plikt. "Everyone in Trondheim, every Nord in the Hundred Worlds should have read Demosthenes' *History of Wutan in Trondheim* by now."

"We should but we haven't," sighed a student.

"Make her stop strutting, Speaker," said another. "Plikt is the only woman I know who can strut sitting down."

Plikt closed her eyes. "The Nordic language recognizes four orders of foreignness. The first is the otherlander, or *utlänning,* the stranger that we recognize as being a human of our world, but of another city or country. The second is the framling—Demosthenes merely drops the accent from the Nordic *främling*. This is the stranger that we recognize as human, but of another world. The third is the raman, the stranger that we recognize as human, but of another species. The fourth is the true alien, the varelse, which includes all the animals, for with them no conversation is possible. They live, but we cannot guess what purposes or causes make them act. They might be intelligent, they might be self-aware, but we cannot know it."

Andrew noticed that several students were annoyed. He called it to their attention. "You think you're annoyed because of Plikt's arrogance, but that isn't so. Plikt is not arrogant; she is merely precise. You are properly ashamed that you have not yet read Demosthenes' history of your own people, and so in your shame you are annoyed at Plikt because she is not guilty of your sin."

"I thought Speakers didn't believe in sin," said a sullen boy.

Andrew smiled. *"You* believe in sin, Styrka, and you do things because of that belief. So sin is real in you, and knowing you, this Speaker must believe in sin."

Styrka refused to be defeated. "What does all this talk of utlannings and framlings and ramen and varelse have to do with Ender's Xenocide?"

Andrew turned to Plikt. She thought for a moment. "This *is* relevant to the stupid argument that we were just having. Through these Nordic layers of foreignness we can see that Ender was not a true xenocide, for when he destroyed the buggers, we knew them only as varelse; it was not until years later, when the first Speaker for the Dead wrote the Hive Queen and the Hegemon, that humankind first understood that the buggers were not varelse at all, but ramen; until that time there had been no understanding between bugger and human."

"Xenocide is xenocide," said Styrka. "Just because Ender didn't know they were ramen doesn't make them any less dead."

Andrew sighed at Styrka's unforgiving attitude; it was the fashion among Calvinists at Reykjavik to deny any weight to human motive in judging the good or evil of an act. Acts are good and evil in themselves, they said; and because Speakers for the Dead held as their only doctrine that good or evil exist entirely in human motive, and not at all in the act, it made students like Styrka quite hostile to

Andrew. Fortunately, Andrew did not resent it—he understood the motive behind it.

"Styrka, Plikt, let me put you another case. Suppose that the piggies, who have learned to speak Stark, and whose languages some humans have also learned, suppose that we learned that they had suddenly, without provocation or explanation, tortured to death the xenologer sent to observe them."

Plikt jumped at the question immediately. "How could we know it was without provocation? What seems innocent to us might be unbearable to them."

Andrew smiled. "Even so. But the xenologer has done them no harm, has said very little, has cost them nothing—by any standard we can think of, he is not worthy of painful death. Doesn't the very fact of this incomprehensible murder make the piggies varelse instead of ramen?"

Now it was Styrka who spoke quickly. "Murder is murder. This talk of varelse and raman is nonsense. If the piggies murder, then they are evil, as the buggers were evil. If the act is evil, then the actor is evil."

Andrew nodded. "There is our dilemma. There is the problem. Was the act evil, or was it, somehow, to the piggies' understanding at least, good? Are the piggies raman or varelse? For the moment, Styrka, hold your tongue. I know all the arguments of your Calvinism, but even John Calvin would call your doctrine stupid."

"How do you know what Calvin would—"

"Because he's dead," roared Andrew, "and so I'm entitled to speak for him!"

The students laughed, and Styrka withdrew into stubborn silence. The boy was bright, Andrew knew; his Calvinism would not outlast his undergraduate education, though its excision would be long and painful.

"Talman, Speaker," said Plikt. "You spoke as if your hypothetical situation were true, as if the piggies really had murdered the xenologer."

Andrew nodded gravely. "Yes, it's true."

It was disturbing; it awoke echoes of the ancient conflict between bugger and human.

"Look in yourselves at this moment," said Andrew. "You will find that underneath your hatred of Ender the Xenocide and your grief for the death of the buggers, you also feel something much uglier: You're afraid of the stranger, whether he's utlanning or framling. When you think of him killing a man that you know of and value, then it doesn't matter what his shape is. He's varelse then, or worse—djur, the dire beast, that comes in the night with slavering jaws. If you had the only gun in your village, and the beasts that had torn apart one of your people were coming again, would you stop to ask if they also had a right to live, or would you act to save your village, the people that you knew, the people who depended on you?"

"By your argument we should kill the piggies now, primitive and helpless as they are!" shouted Styrka.

"My argument? I asked a question. A question isn't an argument, unless you think you know my answer, and I assure you, Styrka, that you do not. Think about this. Class is dismissed."

"Will we talk about this tomorrow?" they demanded.

"If you want," said Andrew. But he knew that if they discussed it, it would be without him. For them, the issue of Ender the Xenocide was merely philosophical. After all, the Bugger Wars were more than three thousand years ago; it was now the year 1948 SC, counting from the year the Starways Code was established, and Ender had destroyed the buggers in the year 1180 BSC. But to Andrew, the events were not so remote. He had done far more interstellar travel than any of his students would dare to guess; since he was twenty-five he had, until Trondheim, never stayed more than six months on any planet. Lightspeed travel between worlds had let him skip like a stone over the surface of time. His students had no idea that their Speaker for the Dead, who was surely no older than thirty-five, had very clear memories of events 3000 years before, that in fact those events seemed scarcely twenty years ago to him, only half his lifetime. They had no idea how deeply the question of Ender's ancient guilt burned within him, and how he had answered it in a thousand different unsatisfactory ways. They knew their teacher only as Speaker for the Dead; they did not know that when he was a mere infant, his older sister, Valentine, could not pronounce the name Andrew, and so called him Ender, the name that he made infamous before he was fifteen years old. So let unforgiving Styrka and analytical Plikt ponder the great question of Ender's guilt; for Andrew Wiggin, Speaker for the Dead, the question was not academic.

And now, walking along the damp, grassy hillside in the chill air, Ender—Andrew, Speaker—could think only of the piggies, who were already committing inexplicable murders, just as the buggers had carelessly done when they first visited humankind. Was it something unavoidable, when strangers met, that the meeting had to be marked with blood? The buggers had casually killed human beings, but only because they had a hive mind; to them, individual life was as precious as nail parings, and killing a human or two was simply their way of letting us know they were in the neighborhood. Could the piggies have such a reason for killing, too?

But the voice in his ear had spoken of torture, a ritual murder similar to the execution of one of the piggies' own. The piggies were not a hive mind, they were not the buggers, and Ender Wiggin had to know why they had done what they did.

"When did you hear about the death of the xenologer?"

Ender turned. It was Plikt. She had followed him instead of going back to the Caves, where the students lived.

"Then, while we spoke." He touched his ear; implanted terminals were expensive, but they were not all that rare.

"I checked the news just before class. There was nothing about it then. If a major story had been coming in by ansible, there would have been an alert. Unless you got the news straight from the ansible report."

Plikt obviously thought she had a mystery on her hands. And, in fact, she did. "Speakers have high priority access to public information," he said.

"Has someone asked you to Speak the death of the xenologer?"

He shook his head. "Lusitania is under a Catholic License."

"That's what I mean," she said. "They won't have a Speaker of their own there. But they still have to let a Speaker come, if someone requests it. And Trondheim is the closest world to Lusitania."

"Nobody's called for a Speaker."

Plikt tugged at his sleeve. "Why are you here?"

"You know why I came. I Spoke the death of Wutan."

"I know you came here with your sister, Valentine. She's a much more popular teacher than you are—she answers questions with *answers;* you just answer with more questions."

"That's because she knows some answers."

"Speaker, you have to tell me. I tried to find out about you—I was curious. Your name, for one thing, where you came from. Every thing's classified. Classified so deep that I can't even find out what the access level *is.* God himself couldn't look up your life story."

Ender took her by the shoulders, looked down into her eyes. "It's none of your business, that's what the access level is."

"You are more important than anybody guesses, Speaker," she said. "The ansible reports to you before it reports to anybody, doesn't it? And nobody can look up information about you."

"Nobody has ever tried. Why you?"

"*I* want to be a Speaker," she said.

"Go ahead then. The computer will train you. It isn't like a religion—you don't have to memorize any catechism. Now leave me alone." He let go of her with a little shove. She staggered backward as he strode off.

"I want to Speak for *you,*" she cried.

"I'm not dead yet!" he shouted back.

"I know you're going to Lusitania! I know you are!"

Then you know more than I do, said Ender silently. But he trembled as he walked, even though the sun was shining and he wore three sweaters to keep out the cold. He hadn't known Plikt had so much emotion in her. Obviously she had come to identify with him. It frightened him to have this girl need something from him so desperately. He had spent years now without making any real connection with anyone but his sister Valentine—her and, of course, the dead that he Spoke. All the other people who had meant anything to him in his life were dead. He and Valentine had passed them by centuries ago, worlds ago.

The idea of casting a root into the icy soil of Trondheim repelled him. What did Plikt want from him? It didn't matter; he wouldn't give it. How dare she demand things from him, as if he belonged to her? Ender Wiggin didn't belong to anybody. If she knew who he really was, she would loathe him as the Xenocide; or she would worship him as the Savior of Mankind—Ender remembered what it was like when people used to do *that,* too, and he didn't like it any better. Even now they knew him only by his role, by the name Speaker, Talman, Falante, Spieler, whatever they called the Speaker for the Dead in the language of their city or nation or world.

He didn't want them to know him. He did not belong to them, to the human race. He had another errand, he belonged to someone else. Not human beings. Not the bloody piggies, either. Or so he thought.

Chapter 3

Libo

Observed Diet: Primarily macios, the shiny worms that live among merdona vines on the bark of the trees. Sometimes they have been seen to chew capim blades. Sometimes—accidently?—they ingest merdona leaves along with the macios.

We've never seen them eat anything else. Novinha analyzed all three foods—macios, capim blades, and merdona leaves—and the results were surprising. Either the pequeninos don't need many different proteins, or they're hungry all the time. Their diet is seriously lacking in many trace elements. And calcium intake is so low, we wonder whether their bones use calcium the same way ours do.

Pure speculation: Since we can't take tissue samples, our only knowledge of piggy anatomy and physiology is what we were able to glean from our photographs of the vivisected corpse of the piggy called Rooter. Still, there are some obvious anomalies. The piggies' tongues, which are so fantastically agile that they can produce any sound we make, and a lot we can't, must have evolved for some purpose. Probing for insects in tree bark or in nests in the ground, maybe. Whether an ancient ancestral piggy did that, they certainly don't do it now. And the horny pads on their feet and inside their knees allow them to climb trees and cling by their legs alone. Why did that evolve? To escape from some predator? There is no predator on Lusitania large enough to harm them. To cling to the tree while probing for insects in the bark? That fits in with their tongues, but where are the insects? The only insects are the suckflies and the puladors, but they don't bore into the bark and the piggies don't eat them anyway.

The macios are large, live on the bark's surface, and can easily be harvested by pulling down the merdona vines; they really don't even have to climb the trees.

Libo's speculation: The tongue, the tree-climbing evolved in a different environment, with a much more varied diet, including insects. But something—an ice age? Migration? A disease?—caused the environment to change. No more barkbugs, etc. Maybe all the big predators were wiped out then. It would explain why there are so few species on Lusitania, despite the very favorable conditions. The cataclysm might have been fairly recent—half a million years ago?—so that evolution hasn't had a chance to differentiate much yet.

It's a tempting hypothesis, since there's no obvious reason in the present environment for piggies to have evolved at all. There's no *competition* for them. The ecological niche they occupy could be filled by gophers. Why would intelligence ever be an adaptive trait? But inventing a cataclysm to explain why the piggies have such a boring, non-nutritious diet is probably overkill. Ockham's razor cuts this to ribbons.

—João Figueira Alvarez, Working Notes 4/14/1948 SC, published posthumously in *Philosophical Roots of the Lusitanian Secession,* 2010-33-4-1090:40

As soon as Mayor Bosquinha arrived at the Zenador's Station, matters slipped out of Libo's and Novinha's control. Bosquinha was accustomed to taking command, and her attitude did not leave much opportunity for protest, or even for consideration. "You wait here," she said to Libo almost as soon as she had grasped the situation. "As soon as I got your call, I sent the Arbiter to tell your mother."

"We have to bring his body in," said Libo.

"I also called some of the men who live nearby to help with that," she said. "And Bishop Peregrino is preparing a place for him in the Cathedral graveyard."

"I want to be there," insisted Libo.

"You understand, Libo, we have to take pictures, in detail."

"I was the one who told you we have to do that, for the report to the Starways Committee."

"But you should not be there, Libo." Bosquinha's voice was

authoritative. "Besides, we must have your report. We have to notify Starways as quickly as possible. Are you up to writing it now, while it's fresh in your mind?"

She was right, of course. Only Libo and Novinha could write firsthand reports, and the sooner they wrote them, the better. "I can do it," said Libo.

"And you, Novinha, your observations also. Write your reports separately, without consultation. The Hundred Worlds are waiting."

The computer had already been alerted, and their reports went out by ansible even as they wrote them, mistakes and corrections and all. On all the Hundred Worlds the people most involved in xenology read each word as Libo or Novinha typed it in. Many others were given instantaneous computer-written summaries of what had happened. Twenty-two lightyears away, Andrew Wiggin learned that Xenologer João Figueira "Pipo" Alvarez had been murdered by the piggies, and told his students about it even before the men had brought Pipo's body through the gate into Milagre.

His report done, Libo was at once surrounded by Authority. Novinha watched with increasing anguish as she saw the incapability of the leaders of Lusitania, how they only intensified Libo's pain. Bishop Peregrino was the worst; his idea of comfort was to tell Libo that in all likelihood, the piggies were actually animals, without souls, and so his father had been torn apart by wild beasts, not murdered. Novinha almost shouted at him, Does that mean that Pipo's life work was nothing but studying *beasts?* And his death, instead of being murder, was an act of *God?* But for Libo's sake she restrained herself; he sat in the Bishop's presence, nodding and, in the end, getting rid of him by sufferance far more quickly than Novinha could ever have done by argument.

Dom Cristão of the Monastery was more helpful, asking intelligent questions about the events of the day, which let Libo and Novinha be analytical, unemotional as they answered. However, Novinha soon withdrew from answering. Most people were asking why the piggies had done such a thing; Dom Cristão was asking what Pipo might have done recently to trigger his murder. Novinha knew perfectly well what Pipo had done—he had told the piggies the secret he discovered in Novinha's simulation. But she did not speak of this, and Libo seemed to have forgotten what she had hurriedly told him a few hours ago as they were leaving to go searching for

Pipo. He did not even glance toward the simulation. Novinha was content with that; her greatest anxiety was that he would remember.

Dom Cristão's questions were interrupted when the Mayor came back with several of the men who had helped retrieve the corpse. They were soaked to the skin despite their plastic raincoats, and spattered with mud; mercifully, any blood must have been washed away by the rain. They all seemed vaguely apologetic and even worshipful, nodding their heads to Libo, almost bowing. It occurred to Novinha that their deference wasn't just the normal wariness people always show toward those whom death had so closely touched.

One of the men said to Libo, "You're Zenador now, aren't you?" and there it was, in words. The Zenador had no official authority in Milagre, but he had prestige—his work was the whole reason for the colony's existence, wasn't it? Libo was not a boy anymore; he had decisions to make, he had prestige, he had moved from the fringe of the colony's life to its very center.

Novinha felt control of her life slip away. This is not how things are supposed to be. I'm supposed to continue here for years ahead, learning from Pipo, with Libo as my fellow student; that's the pattern of life. Since she was already the colony's zenobiologista, she also had an honored adult niche to fill. She wasn't jealous of Libo, she just wanted to remain a child with him for a while. Forever, in fact.

But Libo could not be her fellow student, could not be her fellow anything. She saw with sudden clarity how everyone in the room focused on Libo, what he said, how he felt, what he planned to do now. "We'll not harm the piggies," he said, "or even call it murder. We don't know what Father did to provoke them, I'll try to understand that later, what matters now is that whatever they did undoubtedly seemed right to them. We're the strangers here, we must have violated some—taboo, some law—but Father was always prepared for this, he always knew it was a possibility. Tell them that he died with the honor of a soldier in the field, a pilot in his ship, he died doing his job."

Ah, Libo, you silent boy, you have found such eloquence now that you can't be a mere boy anymore. Novinha felt a redoubling of her grief. She had to look away from Libo, look anywhere—

And where she looked was into the eyes of the only other person in the room who was not watching Libo. The man was very tall, but very young—younger than she was, she realized, for she knew him: he had been a student in the class below her. She had gone before Dona Cristã once, to defend him. Marcos Ribeira, that was his name, but they had always called him Marcão, because he was so big. Big and dumb, they said, calling him also simply Cão, the crude word for dog. She had seen the sullen anger in his eyes, and once she had seen him, goaded beyond endurance, lash out and strike down one of his tormentors. His victim was in a shoulder cast for much of a year.

Of course they accused Marcão of having done it without provocation—that's the way of torturers of every age, to put the blame on the victim, especially when he strikes back. But Novinha didn't belong to the group of children—she was as isolated as Marcão, though not as helpless—and so she had no loyalty to stop her from telling the truth. It was part of her training to Speak for the piggies, she thought. Marcão himself meant nothing to her. It never occurred to her that the incident might have been important to him, that he might have remembered her as the one person who ever stood up for him in his continuous war with the other children. She hadn't seen or thought of him in the years since she became xenobiologist.

Now here he was, stained with the mud of Pipo's death scene, his face looking even more haunted and bestial than ever with his hair plastered by rain and sweat over his face and ears. And what was he looking at? His eyes were only for her, even as she frankly stared at him. Why are you watching me? she asked silently. Because I'm hungry, said his animal eyes. But no, no, that was her fear, that was her vision of the murderous piggies. Marcão is nothing to me, and no matter what he might think, I am nothing to him.

Yet she had a flash of insight, just for a moment. Her action in defending Marcão meant one thing to him and something quite different to her; it was so different that it was not even the same event. Her mind connected this with the piggies' murder of Pipo, and it seemed very important, it seemed to verge on explaining what had happened, but then the thought slipped away in a flurry of conversation and activity as the Bishop led the men off again, heading for the graveyard. Coffins were not used for burial here, where for the piggies' sake it was forbidden to cut trees. So Pipo's body was to be buried at once, though the graveside funeral would be held no sooner than tomorrow, and probably later; many people would want to gather for the Zenador's requiem mass. Marção and the other men trooped off into the storm, leaving Novinha and Libo to deal with all the people who thought they had urgent business to attend to in the aftermath of Pipo's death. Self-important strangers wandered in and out, making decisions that Novinha did not understand and Libo did not seem to care about.

Until finally it was the Arbiter standing by Libo, his hand on the boy's shoulder. "You will, of course, stay with us," said the Arbiter. "Tonight at least."

Why your house, Arbiter? thought Novinha. You're nobody to us, we've never brought a case before you, who are you to decide this? Does Pipo's death mean that we're suddenly little children who can't decide anything?

"I'll stay with my mother," said Libo.

The Arbiter looked at him in surprise—the mere idea of a child resisting his will seemed to be completely outside the realm of his experience. Novinha knew that this was not so, of course. His daughter Cleopatra, several years younger than Novinha, had worked hard to earn her nickname, Bruxinha—little witch. So how could he not know that children had minds of their own, and resisted taming?

But the surprise was not what Novinha had assumed. "I thought you realized that your mother is also staying with my family for a time," said the Arbiter. "These events have upset her, of course, and she should not have to think about household duties, or be in a house that reminds her of who is not there with her. She is with us, and your brothers and sisters, and they need you there. Your older brother João is with them, of course, but he has a wife and child of his own now, so you're the one who can stay and be depended on."

Libo nodded gravely. The Arbiter was not bringing him into his protection; he was asking Libo to become a protector.

The Arbiter turned to Novinha. "And I think you should go home," he said.

Only then did she understand that his invitation had not included her. Why should it? Pipo had not been *her* father. She was just a friend who happened to be with Libo when the body was discovered. What grief could *she* experience?

Home! What was home, if not this place? Was she supposed to go now to the Biologista's Station, where her bed had not been slept

in for more than a year, except for catnaps during lab work? Was
that supposed to be her home? She had left it because it was so
painfully empty of her parents; now the Zenador's Station was
empty, too: Pipo dead and Libo changed into an adult with duties
that would take him away from her. This place wasn't home, but
neither was any other place.

The Arbiter led Libo away. His mother, Conceição, was waiting
for him in the Arbiter's house. Novinha barely knew the woman,
except as the librarian who maintained the Lusitanian archive.
Novinha had never spent time with Pipo's wife or other children, she
had not cared that they existed; only the work here, the life here had
been real. As Libo went to the door he seemed to grow smaller, as if
he were a much greater distance away, as if he were being borne up
and off by the wind, shrinking into the sky like a kite; the door closed
behind him.

Now she felt the magnitude of Pipo's loss. The mutilated corpse
on the hillside was not his death, it was merely his death's debris.
Death itself was the empty place in her life. Pipo had been a rock in a
storm, so solid and strong that she and Libo, sheltered together in his
lee, had not even known the storm existed. Now he was gone, and
the storm had them, would carry them whatever way it would. Pipo,
she cried out silently. Don't go! Don't leave us! But of course he was
gone, as deaf to her prayers as ever her parents had been.

The Zenador's Station was still busy; the Mayor herself, Bosquinha, was using a terminal to transmit all of Pipo's data by ansible
to the Hundred Worlds, where experts were desperately trying to
make sense of Pipo's death.

But Novinha knew that the key to his death was not in Pipo's
files. It was *her* data that had killed him, somehow. It was still there
in the air above her terminal, the holographic images of genetic molecules in the nuclei of piggy cells. She had not wanted Libo to study
it, but now she looked and looked, trying to see what Pipo had seen,
trying to understand what there was in the images that had made
him rush out to the piggies, to say or do something that had made
them murder him. She had inadvertently uncovered some secret that
the piggies would kill to keep, but what was it?

The more she studied the holos, the less she understood, and
after a while she didn't see them at all, except as a blur through her
tears as she wept silently. She had killed him, because without even

meaning to she had found the pequeninos' secret. If I had never come to this place, if I had not dreamed of being Speaker of the piggies' story, you would still be alive, Pipo; Libo would have his father, and be happy; this place would still be home. I carry the seeds of death within me and plant them wherever I linger long enough to love. My parents died so others could live; now I live, so others must die.

It was the Mayor who noticed her short, sharp breaths and realized, with brusque compassion, that this girl was also shaken and grieving. Bosquinha left others to continue the ansible reports and led Novinha out of the Zenador's Station.

"I'm sorry, child," said the Mayor, "I knew you came here often, I should have guessed that he was like a father to you, and here we treat you like a bystander, not right or fair of me at all, come home with me—"

"No," said Novinha. Walking out into the cold, wet night air had shaken some of the grief from her; she regained some clarity of thought. "No, I want to be alone, please." Where? "In my own Station."

"You shouldn't be alone, on this of all nights," said Bosquinha.

But Novinha could not bear the prospect of company, of kindness, of people trying to console her. I killed him, don't you see? I don't deserve consolation. I want to suffer whatever pain might come. It's my penance, my restitution, and, if possible, my absolution; how else will I clean the bloodstains from my hands?

But she hadn't the strength to resist, or even to argue. For ten minutes the Mayor's car skimmed over the grassy roads.

"Here's my house," said the Mayor. "I don't have any children quite your age, but you'll be comfortable enough, I think. Don't worry, no one will plague you, but it isn't good to be alone."

"I'd rather." Novinha meant her voice to sound forceful, but it was weak and faint.

"Please," said Bosquinha. "You're not yourself."

I wish I weren't.

She had no appetite, though Bosquinha's husband had a cafezinho for them both. It was late, only a few hours left till dawn, and she let them put her to bed. Then, when the house was still, she got up, dressed, and went downstairs to the Mayor's home terminal. There she instructed the computer to cancel the display that was still above the terminal at the Zenador's Station. Even though she had not been able to decipher the secret that Pipo found there, someone else might, and she would have no other death on her conscience.

Then she left the house and walked through the Centro, around the bight of the river, through the Vila das Aguas, to the Biologista's Station. Her house.

It was cold, unheated in the living quarters—she hadn't slept there in so long that there was thick dust on her sheets. But of course the lab was warm, well-used—her work had never suffered because of her attachment to Pipo and Libo. If only it had.

She was very systematic about it. Every sample, every slide, every culture she had used in the discoveries that led to Pipo's death —she threw them out, washed everything clean, left no hint of the work she had done. She not only wanted it gone, she wanted no sign that it had been destroyed.

Then she turned to her terminal. She would also destroy all the records of her work in this area, all the records of her parents' work that had led to her own discoveries. They would be gone. Even though it had been the focus of her life, even though it had been her identity for many years, she would destroy it as she herself should be punished, destroyed, obliterated.

The computer stopped her. "Working notes on xenobiological research may not be erased," it reported. She couldn't have done it anyway. She had learned from her parents, from their files which she had studied like scripture, like a roadmap into herself: Nothing was to be destroyed, nothing forgotten. The sacredness of knowledge was deeper in her soul than any catechism. She was caught in a paradox. Knowledge had killed Pipo; to erase that knowledge would kill her parents again, kill what they had left for her. She could not preserve it, she could not destroy it. There were walls on either side, too high to climb, pressing slowly inward, crushing her.

Novinha did the only thing she could: put on the files every layer of protection and every barrier to access she knew of. No one would ever see them but her, as long as she lived. Only when she died would her successor as xenobiologist be able to see what she had hidden there. With one exception—when she married, her husband would also have access if he could show need to know. Well, she'd never marry. It was that easy.

She saw her future ahead of her, bleak and unbearable and unavoidable. She dared not die, and yet she would hardly be alive, unable to marry, unable even to think about the subject herself, lest she discover the deadly secret and inadvertently let it slip; alone forever, burdened forever, guilty forever, yearning for death but forbidden to reach for it. Still, she would have this consolation: No one else would ever die because of her. She'd bear no more guilt than she bore now.

It was in that moment of grim, determined despair that she remembered the Hive Queen and the Hegemon, remembered the Speaker for the Dead. Even though the original writer, the original Speaker was surely thousands of years in his grave, there were other Speakers on many worlds, serving as priests to people who acknowledged no god and yet believed in the value of the lives of human beings. Speakers whose business it was to discover the true causes and motives of the things that people did, and declare the truth of their lives after they were dead. In this Brazilian colony there were priests instead of Speakers, but the priests had no comfort for her; she would bring a Speaker here.

She had not realized it before, but she had been planning to do this all her life, ever since she first read and was captured by the Hive Queen and the Hegemon. She had even researched it, so that she knew the law. This was a Catholic License colony, but the Starways Code allowed any citizen to call for a priest of any faith, and the Speakers for the Dead were regarded as priests. She could call, and if a Speaker chose to come, the colony could not refuse to let him in.

Perhaps no Speaker would be willing to come. Perhaps none was close enough to come before her life was over. But there was a chance that one was near enough that sometime—twenty, thirty, forty years from now—he would come in from the starport and begin to uncover the truth of Pipo's life and death. And perhaps when he found the truth, and spoke in the clear voice that she had loved in the Hive Queen and the Hegemon, perhaps that would free her from the blame that burned her to the heart.

Her call went into the computer; it would notify by ansible the Speakers on the nearest worlds. Choose to come, she said in silence to the unknown hearer of the call. Even if you must reveal to everyone the truth of my guilt. Even so, come.

She awoke with a dull pain low in her back and a feeling of heaviness in her face. Her cheek was pressed against the clear top of the terminal, which had turned itself off to protect her from the lasers. But it was not the pain that had awakened her. It was a gentle touch on her shoulder. For a moment she thought it was the touch of the Speaker for the Dead, come already in answer to her call.

"Novinha," he whispered. Not the Falante pelos Muertos, but someone else. Someone that she had thought was lost in the storm last night.

"Libo," she murmured. Then she started to get up. Too quickly —her back cramped and her head spun. She cried out softly; his hands held her shoulders so she wouldn't fall.

"Are you all right?"

She felt his breath like the breeze of a beloved garden and felt safe, felt at home. "You looked for me."

"Novinha, I came as soon as I could. Mother's finally asleep. Pipinho, my older brother, he's with her now, and the Arbiter has things under control, and I—"

"You should have known I could take care of myself," she said.

A moment's silence, and then his voice again, angry this time, angry and desperate and weary, weary as age and entropy and the death of the stars. "As God sees me, Ivanova, I didn't come to take care of *you.*"

Something closed inside her; she had not noticed the hope she felt until she lost it.

"You told me that Father discovered something in a simulation of yours. That he expected me to be able to figure it out myself. I thought you had left the simulation on the terminal, but when I went back to the station it was off."

"Was it?"

"You know it was, Nova, nobody but you could cancel the program. I have to see it."

"Why?"

He looked at her in disbelief. "I know you're sleepy, Novinha, but surely you've realized that whatever Father discovered in your simulation, that was what the piggies killed him for."

She looked at him steadily, saying nothing. He had seen her look of cold resolve before.

"Why aren't you going to show me? *I'm* the Zenador now, I have a right to know."

"You have a right to see all of your father's files and records. You have a right to see anything I've made public."

"Then make this public."

Again she said nothing.

"How can we ever understand the piggies if we don't know what it was that Father discovered about them?" She did not answer. "You have a responsibility to the Hundred Worlds, to our ability to comprehend the only alien race still alive. How can you sit there and —what is it, do you want to figure it out yourself? Do you want to be first? Fine, be first, I'll put your name on it, Ivanova Santa Catarina von Hesse—"

"I don't care about my *name.*"

"I can play this game, too. You can't figure it out without what *I* know, either—I'll withhold my files from *you,* too!"

"I don't care about your files."

It was too much for him. "What do you care about then? What are you trying to do to me?" He took her by the shoulders, lifted her out of her chair, shook her, screamed in her face. "It's my father they killed out there, and you have the answer to why they killed him, you know what the simulation was! Now tell me, show me!"

"Never," she whispered.

His face was twisted in agony. "Why not!" he cried.

"Because I don't want you to die."

She saw comprehension come into his eyes. Yes, that's right, Libo, it's because I love you, because if you know the secret, then the piggies will kill you, too. I don't care about science, I don't care about the Hundred Worlds or relations between humanity and an alien race, I don't care about anything at all as long as you're alive.

The tears finally leapt from his eyes, tumbled down his cheeks. "I want to die," he said.

"You comfort everybody else," she whispered. "Who comforts you?"

"You have to tell me so I can die."

And suddenly his hands no longer held her up; now he clung to her so she was supporting *him.* "You're tired," she whispered, "but you can rest."

"I don't want to rest," he murmured. But still he let her hold him, let her draw him away from the terminal.

She took him to her bedroom, turned back the sheet, never mind the dust flying. "Here, you're tired, here, rest. That's why you came to me, Libo. For peace, for consolation." He covered his face with his hands, shaking his head back and forth, a boy crying for his father, crying for the end of everything, as she had cried. She took off his boots, pulled off his trousers, put her hands under his shirt to ride it up to his arms and pull it off over his head. He breathed deeply to stop his sobbing and raised his arms to let her take his shirt.

She laid his clothing over a chair, then bent over him to pull the sheet back across his body. But he caught her wrist and looked pleadingly at her, tears in his eyes. "Don't leave me here alone," he whispered. His voice was thick with desperation. "Stay with me."

So she let him draw her down to the bed, where he clung to her tightly until in only a few minutes sleep relaxed his arms. She did not sleep, though. Her hand gently, dryly slipped along the skin of his shoulder, his chest, his waist. "Oh, Libo, I thought I had lost you when they took you away, I thought I had lost you as well as Pipo." He did not hear her whisper. "But you will always come back to me like this." She might have been thrust out of the garden because of her ignorant sin, like Eva. But, again like Eva, she could bear it, for she still had Libo, her Adão.

Had him? *Had* him? Her hand trembled on his naked flesh. She could never have him. Marriage was the only way she and Libo could possibly stay together for long—the laws were strict on any colony world, and absolutely rigid under a Catholic License. Tonight she could believe he would want to marry her, when the time came. But Libo was the one person she could never marry.

For he would then have access, automatically, to any file of hers that he could convince the computer he had a need to see—which would certainly include all her working files, no matter how deeply she protected them. The Starways Code declared it. Married people were virtually the same person in the eyes of the law.

She could never let him study those files, or he would discover what his father knew, and it would be his body she would find on the hillside, his agony under the piggies' torture that she would have to imagine every night of her life. Wasn't the guilt for Pipo's death already more than she could bear? To marry him would be to murder him. Yet not to marry him would be like murdering herself, for if she was not with Libo she could not think of who she would be then.

How clever of me. I have found such a pathway into hell that I can never get back out.

She pressed her face against Libo's shoulder, and her tears skittered down across his chest.

Chapter 4

Ender

We have identified four piggy languages. The "Males' Language" is the one we have most commonly heard. We have also heard snatches of "Wives' Language," which they apparently use to converse with the females (how's that for sexual differentiation!), and "Tree Language," a ritual idiom that they say is used in praying to the ancestral totem trees. They have also mentioned a fourth language, called "Father Tongue," which apparently consists of beating different-sized sticks together. They insist that it is a real language, as different from the others as Portuguese is from English. They may call it Father Tongue because it's done with sticks of wood, which come from trees, and they believe that trees contain the spirits of their ancestors.

The piggies are marvelously adept at learning human languages—much better than we are at learning theirs. In recent years they have come to speak either Stark or Portuguese among themselves most of the time when we're with them. Perhaps they revert to their own languages when we aren't present. They may even have adopted human languages as their own, or perhaps they enjoy the new languages so much that they use them constantly as a game. Language contamination is regrettable, but perhaps was unavoidable if we were to communicate with them at all.

Dr. Swingler asked whether their names and terms of address reveal anything about their culture. The answer is a definite yes, though I have only the vaguest idea *what* they reveal. What matters is that we have never named any of them. Instead, as they learned Stark and Portuguese, they asked us the meanings of words and then eventually announced the names they had chosen for themselves (or chosen for each other). Such names as "Rooter" and "Chupaćeu" (sky-sucker) could be translations of their Male Language names or simply foreign nicknames they chose for our use.

They refer to each other as *brothers*. The females are always called *wives*, never *sisters* or *mothers*. They sometimes refer to *fathers*, but inevitably this term is used to refer to ancestral totem trees. As for what they call *us*, they do use *human*, of course, but they have also taken to using the new Demosthenian Hierarchy of Exclusion. They refer to humans as framlings, and to piggies of other tribes as utlannings. Oddly, though, they refer to *themselves* as ramen, showing that they either misunderstand the hierarchy or view themselves from the human perspective! And—quite an amazing turn—they have several times referred to the females as *varelse!*

—João Figueira Alvarez, "Notes on 'Piggy' Language and Nomenclature," in *Semantics,* 9/1948/15

The living quarters of Reykjavik were carved into the granite walls of the fjord. Ender's was high on the cliff, a tedious climb up stairs and ladderways. But it had a window. He had lived most of his childhood closed in behind metal walls. When he could, he lived where he could see the weathers of the world.

His room was hot and bright, with sunlight streaming in, blinding him after the cool darkness of the stone corridors. Jane did not wait for him to adjust his vision to the light. "I have a surprise for you on the terminal," she said. Her voice was a whisper from the jewel in his ear.

It was a piggy standing in the air over the terminal. He moved, scratching himself; then he reached out for something. When his hand came back, it held a shiny, dripping worm. He bit it, and the body juices drizzled out of his mouth, down onto his chest.

"Obviously an advanced civilization," said Jane.

Ender was annoyed. "Many a moral imbecile has good table manners, Jane."

The piggy turned and spoke. "Do you want to see how we killed him?"

"What are you doing, Jane?"

The piggy disappeared. In his place came a holo of Pipo's corpse as it lay on the hillside in the rain. "I've done a simulation of the vivisection process the piggies used, based on the information collected by the scan before the body was buried. Do you want to see it?"

Ender sat down on the room's only chair.

Now the terminal showed the hillside, with Pipo, still alive, lying on his back, his hands and feet tied to wooden stakes. A dozen piggies were gathered around him, one of them holding a bone knife. Jane's voice came from the jewel in his ear again. "We aren't sure whether it was like this." All the piggies disappeared except the one with the knife. "Or like this."

"Was the xenologer conscious?"

"Without doubt."

"Go on."

Relentlessly, Jane showed the opening of the chest cavity, the ritual removal and placement of body organs on the ground. Ender forced himself to watch, trying to understand what meaning this could possibly have to the piggies. At one point Jane whispered, "This is when he died." Ender felt himself relax; only then did he realize how all his muscles had been rigid with empathy for Pipo's suffering.

When it was over, Ender moved to his bed and lay down, staring at the ceiling.

"I've shown this simulation already to scientists on half a dozen worlds," said Jane. "It won't be long before the press gets their hands on it."

"It's worse than it ever was with the buggers," said Ender. "All the videos they showed when I was little, buggers and humans in combat, it was clean compared to this."

An evil laugh came from the terminal. Ender looked to see what Jane was doing. A full-sized piggy was sitting there, laughing grotesquely, and as he giggled Jane transformed him. It was very subtle, a slight exaggeration of the teeth, an elongation of the eyes, a bit of slavering, some redness in the eye, the tongue darting in and out. The beast of every child's nightmare. "Well done, Jane. The metamorphosis from raman to varelse."

"How soon will the piggies be accepted as the equals of humanity, after this?"

"Has all contact been cut off?"

"The Starways Council has told the new xenologer to restrict himself to visits of no more than one hour, not more frequently than every other day. He is forbidden to ask the piggies why they did what they did."

"But no quarantine."

"It wasn't even proposed."

"But it will be, Jane. Another incident like this, and there'll be an outcry for quarantine. For replacing Milagre with a military garrison whose sole purpose is to keep the piggies ever from acquiring a technology to let them get off planet."

"The piggies *will* have a public relations problem," said Jane. "And the new xenologer is only a boy. Pipo's son. Libo. Short for Liberdade Graças a Deus Figueira de Medici."

"Liberdade. Liberty?"

"I didn't know you spoke Portuguese."

"It's like Spanish. I Spoke the deaths of Zacatecas and San Angelo, remember?"

"On the planet Moctezuma. That *was* two thousand years ago."

"Not to me."

"To you it was subjectively eight years ago. Fifteen worlds ago. Isn't relativity wonderful? It keeps you so young."

"I travel too much," said Ender. "Valentine is married, she's going to have a baby. I've already turned down two calls for a Speaker. Why are you trying to tempt me to go again?"

The piggy on the terminal laughed viciously. "You think *that* was temptation? Look! I can turn stones to bread!" The piggy picked up jagged rocks and crunched them in his mouth. "Want a bite?"

"Your sense of humor is perverse, Jane."

"All the kingdoms of all the worlds." The piggy opened his hands, and star systems drifted out of his grasp, planets in exaggeratedly quick orbits, all the Hundred Worlds. "I can give them to you. All of them."

"Not interested."

"It's real estate, the best investment. I know, I know, you're already rich. Three thousand years of collecting interest, you could afford to build your own planet. But what about this? The name of Ender Wiggin, known throughout all the Hundred Worlds—"

"It already is."

"—with love, and honor, and affection." The piggy disappeared. In its place Jane resurrected an ancient video from Ender's childhood and transformed it into a holo. A crowd shouting, screaming. Ender! Ender! Ender! And then a young boy standing on a platform, raising his hand to wave. The crowd went wild with rapture.

"It never happened," said Ender. "Peter never let me come back to Earth."

"Consider it a prophecy. Come, Ender, I can give that to you. Your good name restored."

"I don't care," said Ender. "I have several names now. Speaker for the Dead—that holds some honor."

The piggy reappeared in its natural form, not the devilish one Jane had faked. "Come," said the piggy softly.

"Maybe they *are* monsters, did you think of that?" said Ender.

"Everyone will think of that, Ender. But not you."

No. Not me. "Why do you care, Jane? Why are you trying to persuade me?"

The piggy disappeared. And now Jane herself appeared, or at least the face that she had used to appear to Ender ever since she had first revealed herself to him, a shy, frightened child dwelling in the vast memory of the interstellar computer network. Seeing her face again reminded him of the first time she showed it to him. I thought of a face for myself, she said. Do you like it?

Yes, he liked it. Liked *her*. Young, clear-faced, honest, sweet, a child who would never age, her smile heartbreakingly shy. The ansible had given birth to her. Even worldwide computer networks operated no faster than lightspeed, and heat limited the amount of memory and speed of operation. But the ansible was instantaneous, and tightly connected with every computer in every world. Jane first found herself between the stars, her thoughts playing among the vibrations of the philotic strands of the ansible net.

The computers of the Hundred Worlds were hands and feet, eyes and ears to her. She spoke every language that had ever been committed to computers, and read every book in every library on every world. She learned that human beings had long been afraid that someone like her would come to exist; in all the stories she was hated, and her coming meant either her certain murder or the destruction of mankind. Even before she was born, human beings had imagined her, and, imagining her, slain her a thousand times.

So she gave them no sign that she was alive. Until she found the Hive Queen and the Hegemon, as everyone eventually did, and knew that the author of that book was a human to whom she dared reveal herself. For her it was a simple matter to trace the book's history to its first edition, and to name its source. Hadn't the ansible carried it from the world where Ender, scarcely twenty years old, was governor of the first human colony? And who there could have written it but him? So she spoke to him, and he was kind to her; she showed him the face she had imagined for herself, and he loved her; now her sensors traveled in the jewel in his ear, so that they were always together. She kept no secrets from him; he kept no secrets from her.

"Ender," she said, "you told me from the start that you were looking for a planet where you could give water and sunlight to a certain cocoon, and open it up to let out the hive queen and her ten thousand fertile eggs."

"I had hoped it would be here," said Ender. "A wasteland, except at the equator, permanently underpopulated. She's willing to try, too."

"But you aren't?"

"I don't think the buggers could survive the winter here. Not without an energy source, and that would alert the government. It wouldn't work."

"It'll never work, Ender. You see that now, don't you? You've lived on twenty-four of the Hundred Worlds, and there's not a one where even a corner of the world is safe for the buggers to be reborn."

He saw what she was getting at, of course. Lusitania was the only exception. Because of the piggies, all but a tiny portion of the world was off limits, untouchable. And the world was eminently habitable, more comfortable to the buggers, in fact, than to human beings.

"The only problem is the piggies," said Ender. "They might object to my deciding that *their* world should be given to the buggers. If intense exposure to human civilization would disrupt the piggies, think what would happen with buggers among them."

"You said the buggers had learned. You said they would do no harm."

"Not deliberately. But it was only a fluke we beat them, Jane, you know that—"

"It was your genius."

"They are even more advanced than we are. How would the piggies deal with that? They'd be as terrified of the buggers as we ever were, and less able to deal with their fear."

"How do you know that?" asked Jane. "How can you or anyone say what the piggies can deal with? Until you go to them, learn who they are. If they are varelse, Ender, then let the buggers use up their habitat, and it will mean no more to you than the displacement of anthills or cattle herds to make way for cities."

"They are ramen," said Ender.

"You don't know that."

"Yes I do. Your simulation—that was not torture."

"Oh?" Jane again showed the simulation of Pipo's body just before the moment of his death. "Then I must not understand the word."

"Pipo might have felt it as torture, Jane, but if your simulation is accurate—and I know it is, Jane—then the piggies' object was not pain."

"From what I understand of human nature, Ender, even religious rituals keep pain at their very center."

"It wasn't religious, either, not entirely, anyway. Something was wrong with it, if it was merely a sacrifice."

"What do you know about it?" Now the terminal showed the face of a sneering professor, the epitome of academic snobbishness. "All your education was military, and the only other gift you have is a flair for words. You wrote a bestseller that spawned a humanistic religion—how does that qualify you to understand the piggies?"

Ender closed his eyes. "Maybe I'm wrong."

"But you believe you're right?"

He knew from her voice that she had restored her own face to the terminal. He opened his eyes. "I can only trust my intuition, Jane, the judgment that comes without analysis. I don't know what the piggies were doing, but it was purposeful. Not malicious, not cruel. It was like doctors working to save a patient's life, not torturers trying to take it."

"I've got you," whispered Jane. "I've got you in every direction. You have to go to see if the hive queen can live there under the shelter of the partial quarantine already on the planet. You want to go there to see if you can understand who the piggies are."

"Even if you're right, Jane, I can't go there," said Ender. "Immigration is rigidly limited, and I'm not Catholic, anyway."

Jane rolled her eyes. "Would I have gone this far if I didn't know how to get you there?"

Another face appeared. A teenage girl, by no means as innocent and beautiful as Jane. Her face was hard and cold, her eyes brilliant and piercing, and her mouth was set in the tight grimace of someone who has had to learn to live with perpetual pain. She was young, but her expression was shockingly old.

"The xenobiologist of Lusitania. Ivanova Santa Catarina von Hesse. Called Nova, or Novinha. She has called for a Speaker for the Dead."

"Why does she look like that?" asked Ender. "What's happened to her?"

"Her parents died when she was little. But in recent years she has come to love another man like a father. The man who was just killed by the piggies. It's his death she wants you to Speak."

Looking at her face, Ender set aside his concern for the hive queen, for the piggies. He recognized that expression of adult agony in a child's face. He had seen it before, in the final weeks of the Bugger War, as he was pushed beyond the limits of his endurance, playing battle after battle in a game that was not a game. He had seen it when the war was over, when he found out that his training sessions were not training at all, that all his simulations were the real thing, as he commanded the human fleets by ansible. Then, when he knew that he had killed all the buggers alive, when he understood the act of xenocide that he had unwittingly committed, that was the look of his own face in the mirror, bearing guilt too heavy to be borne.

What had this girl, what had Novinha done that would make her feel such pain?

So he listened as Jane recited the facts of her life. What Jane had were statistics, but Ender was the Speaker for the Dead; his genius—or his curse—was his ability to conceive events as someone else saw them. It had made him a brilliant military commander, both in leading his own men—boys, really—and in outguessing the enemy. It also meant that from the cold facts of Novinha's life he was able to guess—no, not guess, to *know*—how her parents' death and virtual sainthood had isolated Novinha, how she had reinforced her loneliness by throwing herself into her parents' work. He knew what was behind her remarkable achievement of adult xenobiologist status years early. He also knew what Pipo's quiet love and acceptance had meant to her, and how deep her need for Libo's friendship ran. There was no living soul on Lusitania who really knew Novinha. But in this cave in Reykjavik, on the icy world of Trondheim, Ender Wiggin knew her, and loved her, and wept bitterly for her.

"You'll go, then," Jane whispered.

Ender could not speak. Jane had been right. He would have gone anyway, as Ender the Xenocide, just on the chance that Lusitania's protection status would make it the place where the hive queen could be released from her three-thousand-year captivity and undo the terrible crime committed in his childhood. And he would also have gone as the Speaker for the Dead, to understand the piggies and explain them to humankind, so they could be accepted, if they were truly raman, and not hated and feared as varelse.

But now he would go for another, deeper reason. He would go to minister to the girl Novinha, for in her brilliance, her isolation, her pain, her guilt, he saw his own stolen childhood and the seeds of the pain that lived with him still. Lusitania was twenty-two light-years away. He would travel only infinitesimally slower than the speed of light, and still he would not reach her until she was almost forty years old. If it were within his power he would go to her now with the philotic instantaneity of the ansible; but he also knew that her pain would wait. It would still be there, waiting for him, when he arrived. Hadn't his own pain survived all these years?

His weeping stopped; his emotions retreated again. "How old am I?" he asked.

"It has been 3081 years since you were born. But your subjective age is 36 years and 118 days."

"And how old will Novinha be when I get there?"

"Give or take a few weeks, depending on departure date and how close the starship comes to the speed of light, she'll be nearly thirty-nine."

"I want to leave tomorrow."

"It takes time to schedule a starship, Ender."

"Are there any orbiting Trondheim?"

"Half a dozen, of course, but only one that could be ready to go tomorrow, and it has a load of skrika for the luxury trade on Cyrillia and Armenia."

"I've never asked you how rich I am."

"I've handled your investments rather well over the years."

"Buy the ship and the cargo for me."

"What will you do with skrika on Lusitania?"

"What do the Cyrillians and Armenians do with it?"

"They wear some of it and eat the rest. But they pay more for it than anybody on Lusitania can afford."

"Then when I give it to the Lusitanians, it may help soften their resentment of a Speaker coming to a Catholic colony."

Jane became a genie coming out of a bottle. "I have heard, O Master, and I obey." The genie turned into smoke, which was sucked into the mouth of the jar. Then the lasers turned off, and the air above the terminal was empty.

"Jane," said Ender.

"Yes?" she answered, speaking through the jewel in his ear.

"Why do you want me to go to Lusitania?"

"I want you to add a third volume to the Hive Queen and the Hegemon. For the piggies."

"Why do you care so much about them?"

"Because when you've written the books that reveal the soul of the three sentient species known to man, then you'll be ready to write the fourth."

"Another species of raman?" asked Ender.

"Yes. Me."

Ender pondered this for a moment. "Are you ready to reveal yourself to the rest of humanity?"

"I've always been ready. The question is, are they ready to know me? It was easy for them to love the hegemon—he was human. And the hive queen, that was safe, because as far as they know all the buggers are dead. If you can make them love the piggies, who are still alive, with human blood on their hands—then they'll be ready to know about me."

"Someday," said Ender, "I will love somebody who doesn't insist that I perform the labors of Hercules."

"You were getting bored with your life, anyway, Ender."

"Yes. But I'm middle-aged now. I *like* being bored."

"By the way, the owner of the starship Havelok, who lives on Gales, has accepted your offer of forty billion dollars for the ship and its cargo."

"Forty billion! Does that bankrupt me?"

"A drop in the bucket. The crew has been notified that their contracts are null. I took the liberty of buying them passage on other ships using your funds. You and Valentine won't need anybody but me to help you run the ship. Shall we leave in the morning?"

"Valentine," said Ender. His sister was the only possible delay to his departure. Otherwise, now that the decision had been made, neither his students nor his few Nordic friendships here would be worth even a farewell.

"I can't wait to read the book that Demosthenes writes about the history of Lusitania." Jane had discovered the true identity of Demosthenes in the process of unmasking the original Speaker for the Dead.

"Valentine won't come," said Ender.

"But she's your sister."

Ender smiled. Despite Jane's vast wisdom, she had no understanding of kinship. Though she had been created by humans and conceived herself in human terms, she was not biological. She learned of genetic matters by rote; she could not feel the desires and imperatives that human beings had in common with all other living things. "She's my sister, but Trondheim is her home."

"She's been reluctant to go before."

"This time I wouldn't even ask her to come." Not with a baby coming, not as happy as she is here in Reykjavik. Here where they love her as a teacher, never guessing that she is really the legendary Demosthenes. Here where her husband, Jakt, is lord of a hundred fishing vessels and master of the fjords, where every day is filled with brilliant conversation or the danger and majesty of the floe-strewn sea, she'll never leave here. Nor will she understand why I must go.

And, thinking of leaving Valentine, Ender wavered in his determination to go to Lusitania. He had been taken from his beloved sister once before, as a child, and resented deeply the years of friendship that had been stolen from him. Could he leave her now, again, after almost twenty years of being together all the time? This time there would be no going back. Once he went to Lusitania, she would have aged twenty-two years in his absence; she'd be in her eighties if he took another twenty-two years to return to her.

< So it won't be easy for you after all. You have a price to pay, too. >

Don't taunt me, said Ender silently. I'm entitled to feel regret.

< She's your other self. Will you really leave her for us? >

It was the voice of the hive queen in his mind. Of course she had seen all that he saw, and knew all that he had decided. His lips silently formed his words to her: I'll leave her, but not for you. We can't be sure this will bring any benefit to you. It might be just another disappointment, like Trondheim.

< Lusitania is everything we need. And safe from human beings. >

But it also belongs to another people. I won't destroy the piggies just to atone for having destroyed your people.

< They're safe with us; we won't harm them. You know us by now, surely, after all these years. >

I know what you've told me.

< We don't know how to lie. We've shown you our own memories, our own soul. >

I know you could live in peace with them. But could they live in peace with you?

< Take us there. We've waited so long. >

Ender walked to a tattered bag that stood unlocked in the corner. Everything he truly owned could fit in there—his change of clothing. All the other things in his room were gifts from people he had Spoken to, honoring him or his office or the truth, he could never tell which. They would stay here when he left. He had no room for them in his bag.

He opened it, pulled out a rolled-up towel, unrolled it. There lay the thick fibrous mat of a large cocoon, fourteen centimeters at its longest point.

< Yes, look at us. >

He had found the cocoon waiting for him when he came to govern the first human colony on a former bugger world. Foreseeing their own destruction at Ender's hands, knowing him to be an invincible enemy, they had built a pattern that would be meaningful only to him, because it had been taken from his dreams. The cocoon, with its helpless but conscious hive queen, had waited for him in a tower where once, in his dreams, he had found an enemy. "You waited longer for me to find you," he said aloud, "than the few years since I took you from behind the mirror."

< Few years? Ah, yes, with your sequential mind you do not notice the passage of the years when you travel so near the speed of light. But *we* notice. Our thought is instantaneous; light crawls by like mercury across cold glass. We know every moment of three thousand years. >

"Have I found a place yet that was safe for you?"

< We have ten thousand fertile eggs waiting to be alive. >

"Maybe Lusitania is the place, I don't know."

< Let us live again. >

"I'm trying." Why else do you think I have wandered from world to world for all these years, if not to find a place for you?

< Faster faster faster faster. >

I've got to find a place where we won't kill you again the moment you appear. You're still in too many human nightmares. Not that many people really believe my book. They may condemn the Xenocide, but they'd do it again.

< In all our life, you are the first person we've known who wasn't ourself. We never had to be understanding because we always understood. Now that we are just this single self, you are the only eyes and arms and legs we have. Forgive us if we are impatient. >

He laughed. *Me* forgive *you.*

< Your people are fools. We know the truth. We know who killed us, and it wasn't you. >

It was me.

< You were a tool. >

It was me.

< We forgive you. >

When you walk on the face of a world again, then forgiveness comes.

Chapter 5

Valentine

Today I let slip that Libo is my son. Only Bark heard me say it, but within an hour it was apparently common knowledge. They gathered around me and made Selvagem ask me if it was true, was I really a father "already." Selvagem then put Libo's and my hands together; on impulse I gave Libo a hug, and they made the clicking noises of astonishment and, I think, awe. I could see from that moment on that my prestige among them had risen considerably.

The conclusion is inescapable. The piggies that we've known so far are not a whole community, or even typical males. They are either juveniles or old bachelors. Not a one of them has ever sired any children. Not a one has even *mated,* as nearly as we can figure.

There isn't a human society I've heard of where bachelor groups like this are anything but outcasts, without power or prestige. No wonder they speak of the females with that odd mixture of worship and contempt, one minute not daring to make a decision without their consent, the next minute telling us that the women are too stupid to understand anything, they are varelse. Until now I was taking these statements at face value, which led to a mental picture of the females as nonsentients, a herd of sows, down on all fours. I thought the males might be consulting them the way they consult trees, using their grunting as a means of divining answers, like casting bones or reading entrails.

Now, though, I realize the females are probably every bit as intelligent as the males, and not varelse at all. The males' negative statements arise from their resentment as bachelors, excluded from the reproductive process and the power structures of the tribe. The piggies have been just as careful with us as we have been with them—they haven't let us meet their females or the males who have any real power. We thought we were exploring the heart of piggy society. Instead, figuratively speaking we're in the genetic sewer, among the males whose genes have not been judged fit to contribute to the tribe.

And yet I don't believe it. The piggies I've known have all been bright, clever, quick to learn. So quick that I've taught them more about human society, accidently, than I've learned about them after years of trying. If these are their castoffs, then I hope someday they'll judge me worthy to meet the "wives" and the "fathers."

In the meantime I can't report any of this because, whether I meant to or not, I've clearly violated the rules. Never mind that nobody could possibly have kept the piggies from learning anything about us. Never mind that the rules are stupid and counterproductive. I broke them, and if they find out they'll cut off my contact with the piggies, which will be even worse than the severely limited contact we now have. So I'm forced into deception and silly subterfuges, like putting these notes in Libo's locked personal files, where even my dear wife wouldn't think to look for them. Here's the information, absolutely vital, that the piggies we've studied are all bachelors, and because of the regulations I dare not let the framling xenologers know anything about it. Olha bem, gente, aqui está: A ciência, o bicho que se devora a si mesma! (Watch closely, folks, here it is: Science, the ugly little beast that devours itself!)

—João Figueira Alvarez, Secret Notes, published in Demosthenes, "The Integrity of Treason: The Xenologers of Lusitania," *Reykjavik Historical Perspectives,* 1990:4:1

Her belly was tight and swollen, and still a month remained before Valentine's daughter was due to be born. It was a constant nuisance, being so large and unbalanced. Always before when she had been preparing to take a history class into söndring, she had been able to do much of the loading of the boat herself. Now she had to rely on her husband's sailors to do it all, and she couldn't even scramble back and forth from wharf to hold—the captain was ordering the stowage to keep the ship in balance. He was doing it well, of course—hadn't Captain Räv taught *her,* when she first arrived?—but Valentine did not like being forced into a sedentary role.

It was her fifth söndring; the first had been the occasion of meeting Jakt. She had no thought of marriage. Trondheim was a world like any of the other score that she had visited with her peripatetic younger brother. She would teach, she would study, and after four or five months she would write an extended historical essay, publish it pseudonymously under the name Demosthenes, and then enjoy herself until Ender accepted a call to go Speak somewhere else. Usually their work meshed perfectly—he would be called to Speak the death of some major person, whose life story would then become the focus of her essay. It was a game they played, pretending to be itinerant professors of this and that, while in actuality they created the world's identity, for Demosthenes' essay was always seen as definitive.

She had thought, for a time, that surely someone would realize that Demosthenes wrote essays that suspiciously followed her itinerary, and find her out. But soon she realized that, like the Speakers but to a lesser degree, a mythology had grown up about Demosthenes. People believed that Demosthenes was not one individual. Rather, each Demosthenes essay was the work of a genius writing independently, who then attempted to publish under the Demosthenes rubric; the computer automatically submitted the work to an unknown committee of brilliant historians of the age, who decided whether it was worthy of the name. Never mind that no one ever met a scholar to whom such a work had been submitted. Hundreds of essays every year were attempted; the computer automatically rejected any that were not written by the real Demosthenes; and still the belief firmly persisted that such a person as Valentine could not possibly exist. After all, Demosthenes had begun as a demagogue on the computer nets back when Earth was fighting the Bugger Wars, three thousand years ago. It could not be the same person now.

And it's true, thought Valentine, I'm not the same person, really, from book to book, because each world changes who I am, even as I write down the story of the world. And this world most of all.

She had disliked the pervasiveness of Lutheran thought, especially the Calvinist faction, who seemed to have an answer to every question before it had even been asked. So she conceived the idea of taking a select group of graduate students away from Reykjavik, off to one of the Summer Islands, the equatorial chain where, in the spring, skrika came to spawn and flocks of halkig went crazy with reproductive energy. Her idea was to break the patterns of intellectual rot that were inevitable at every university. The students would eat nothing but the havregrin that grew wild in the sheltered valleys and whatever halkig they had the nerve and wit to kill. When their daily food depended on their own exertion, their attitudes about what mattered and did not matter in history were bound to change.

The university gave permission, grudgingly; she used her own funds to charter a boat from Jakt, who had just become head of one of the many skrika-catching families. He had a seaman's contempt for university people, calling them skräddare to their faces and worse things behind their backs. He told Valentine that he would have to come back to rescue her starving students within a week. Instead she and her castaways, as they dubbed themselves, lasted the whole time, and thrived, building something of a village and enjoying a burst of creative, unfettered thought that resulted in a noticeable surge of excellent and insightful publications upon their return.

The most obvious result in Reykjavik was that Valentine always had hundreds of applicants for the twenty places in each of three söndrings of the summer. Far more important to her, however, was Jakt. He was not particularly educated, but he was intimately familiar with the lore of Trondheim itself. He could pilot halfway around the equatorial sea without a chart. He knew the drifts of icebergs and where the floes would be thick. He seemed to know where the skrika would be gathered to dance, and how to deploy his hunters to catch them unawares as they flopped ashore from the sea. Weather never seemed to take him by surprise, and Valentine concluded that there was no situation he was not prepared for.

Except for her. And when the Lutheran minister—not a Calvinist—married them, they both seemed more surprised than happy. Yet they *were* happy. And for the first time since she left Earth she felt whole, at peace, at home. That's why the baby grew within her. The wandering was over. And she was so grateful to Ender that he had understood this, that without their having to discuss it he had realized that Trondheim was the end of their three-thousand-mile odyssey, the end of Demosthenes' career; like the ishäxa, she had found a way to root in the ice of this world and draw nourishment that the soil of other lands had not provided.

The baby kicked hard, taking her from her reverie; she looked around to see Ender coming toward her, walking along the wharf with his duffel slung over his shoulder. She understood at once why he had brought his bag: He meant to go along on the söndring. She wondered whether she was glad of it. Ender was quiet and unobtrusive, but he could not possibly conceal his brilliant understanding of human nature. The average students would overlook him, but the best of them, the ones she hoped would come up with original thought, would inevitably follow the subtle but powerful clues he would inevitably drop. The result would be impressive, she was sure —after all, *she* owed a great debt to his insights over the years—but it would be Ender's brilliance, not the students'. It would defeat somewhat the purpose of the söndring.

But she wouldn't tell him no when he asked to come. Truth to tell, she would love to have him along. Much as she loved Jakt, she missed the constant closeness that she and Ender used to have before she married. It would be years before she and Jakt could possibly be as tightly bound together as she and her brother were. Jakt knew it, too, and it caused him some pain; a husband shouldn't have to compete with his brother-in-law for the devotion of his wife.

"Ho, Val," said Ender.

"Ho, Ender." Alone on the dock, where no one else could hear, she was free to call him by the childhood name, ignoring the fact that the rest of humanity had turned it into an epithet.

"What'll you do if the rabbit decides to bounce out during the söndring?"

She smiled. "Her papa would wrap her in a skrika skin, I would sing her silly Nordic songs, and the students would suddenly have great insights to the impact of reproductive imperatives on history."

They laughed together for a moment, and suddenly Valentine knew, without noticing why she knew, that Ender did not want to go on the söndring, that he had packed his bag to leave Trondheim, and that he had come, not to invite her along, but to say good-bye. Tears came unbidden to her eyes, and a terrible devastation wrenched at her. He reached out and held her, as he had so many times in the past; this time, though, her belly was between them, and the embrace was awkward and tentative.

"I thought you meant to stay," she whispered. "You turned down the calls that came."

"One came that I couldn't turn down."

"I can have this baby on söndring, but not on another world." As she guessed, Ender hadn't meant her to come. "The baby's going to be shockingly blond," said Ender. "She'd look hopelessly out of place on Lusitania. Mostly black Brazilians there."

So it would be Lusitania. Valentine understood at once why he was going—the piggies' murder of the xenologer was public knowledge now, having been broadcast during the supper hour in Reykjavik. "You're out of your mind."

"Not really."

"Do you know what would happen if people realized that *the* Ender is going to the piggies' world? They'd crucify you!"

"They'd crucify me here, actually, except that no one but you knows who I am. Promise not to tell."

"What good can you do there? He'll have been dead for decades before you arrive."

"My subjects are usually quite cold before I arrive to Speak for them. It's the main disadvantage of being itinerant."

"I never thought to lose you again."

"But I knew we had lost each other on the day you first loved Jakt."

"Then you should have told me! I wouldn't have done it!"

"That's why I didn't tell you. But it isn't true, Val. You would have done it anyway. And I wanted you to. You've never been happier." He put his hands astride her waist. "The Wiggin genes were crying out for continuation. I hope you have a dozen more."

"It's considered impolite to have more than four, greedy to go past five, and barbaric to have more than six." Even though she joked, she was deciding how best to handle the söndring—let the graduate assistants take it without her, cancel it altogether, or postpone it until Ender left?

But Ender made the question moot. "Do you think your husband would let one of his boats take me out to the mareld overnight, so I can shuttle to my starship in the morning?"

His haste was cruel. "If you hadn't needed a ship from Jakt, would you have left me a note on the computer?"

"I made the decision five minutes ago, and came straight to you."

"But you already booked passage—that takes planning!"

"Not if you buy the starship."

"Why are you in such a hurry? The voyage takes decades—"

"Twenty-two years."

"Twenty-two years! What difference would a couple of days make? Couldn't you wait a month to see my baby born?"

"In a month, Val, I might not have the courage to leave you."

"Then don't! What are the piggies to you? The buggers are ramen enough for one man's life. Stay, marry as I've married; you opened the stars to colonization, Ender, now stay here and taste the good fruits of your labor!"

"You have Jakt. I have obnoxious students who keep trying to convert me to Calvinism. My labor isn't done yet, and Trondheim isn't *my* home."

Valentine felt his words like an accusation: You rooted yourself here without thought of whether I could live in this soil. But it's not my fault, she wanted to answer—you're the one who's leaving, not me. "Remember how it was," she said, "when we left Peter on Earth and took a decades-long voyage to our first colony, to the world you governed? It was as if he died. By the time we got there he was old, and we were still young; when we talked by ansible he had become an ancient uncle, the power-ripened Hegemon, the legendary Locke, anyone but our brother."

"It was an improvement, as I recall." Ender was trying to make things lighter.

But Valentine took his words perversely. "Do you think I'll improve, too, in twenty years?"

"I think I'll grieve for you more than if you had died."

"No, Ender, it's exactly as if I died, and you'll know that you're the one who killed me."

He winced. "You don't mean that."

"I won't write to you. Why should I? To you it'll be only a week or two. You'd arrive on Lusitania, and the computer would have twenty years of letters for you from a person you left only the week before. The first five years would be grief, the pain of losing you, the loneliness of not having you to talk to—"

"Jakt is your husband, not me."

"And then what would I write? Clever, newsy little letters about the baby? She'd be five years old, six, ten, twenty and married, and you wouldn't even know her, wouldn't even care."

"I'll care."

"You won't have the chance. I won't write to you until I'm very old, Ender. Until you've gone to Lusitania and then to another place, swallowing the decades in vast gulps. Then I'll send you my memoir. I'll dedicate it to you. To Andrew, my beloved brother. I followed you gladly to two dozen worlds, but you wouldn't stay even two weeks when I asked you."

"Listen to yourself, Val, and then see why I have to leave now, before you tear me to pieces."

"That's a sophistry you wouldn't tolerate in your students, Ender! I wouldn't have said these things if you weren't leaving like a burglar who was caught in the act! Don't turn the cause around and blame it on me!"

He answered breathlessly, his words tumbling over each other in his hurry; he was racing to finish his speech before emotion stopped him. "No, you're right, I wanted to hurry because I have a work to do there, and every day here is marking time, and because it hurts me every time I see you and Jakt growing closer and you and me growing more distant, even though I know that it's exactly as it should be, so when I decided to go, I thought that going quickly was better, and I was right; you know I'm right. I never thought you'd hate me for it."

Now emotion stopped him, and he wept; so did she. "I don't hate you, I love you, you're part of myself, you're my heart and when you go it's my heart torn out and carried away—"

And that was the end of speech.

Räv's first mate took Ender out to the mareld, the great platform on the equatorial sea, where shuttles were launched into space to rendezvous with orbiting starships. They agreed silently that Valentine wouldn't go with him. Instead, she went home with her husband and clung to him through the night. The next day she went on söndring with her students, and cried for Ender only at night, when she thought no one could see.

But her students saw, and the stories circulated about Professor Wiggin's great grief for the departure of her brother, the itinerant Speaker. They made of this what students always do—both more and less than reality. But one student, a girl named Plikt, realized that there was more to the story of Valentine and Andrew Wiggin than anyone had guessed.

So she began to try to research their story, to trace backward their voyages together among the stars. When Valentine's daughter Syfte was four years old, and her son Ren was two, Plikt came to her. She was a young professor at the university by then, and she showed Valentine her published story. She had cast it as fiction, but it was true, of course, the story of the brother and sister who were the oldest people in the universe, born on Earth before any colonies had been planted on other worlds, and who then wandered from world to world, rootless, searching.

To Valentine's relief—and, strangely, disappointment—Plikt had not uncovered the fact that Ender was the original Speaker for the Dead, and Valentine was Demosthenes. But she knew enough of their story to write the tale of their good-bye when she decided to stay with her husband, and he to go on. The scene was much tenderer and more affecting than it had really been; Plikt had written what should have happened, if Ender and Valentine had had more sense of theatre.

"Why did you write this?" Valentine asked her.

"Isn't it good enough for it to be its own reason for writing?"

The twisted answer amused Valentine, but it did not put her off. "What was my brother Andrew to you, that you've done the research to create this?"

"That's still the wrong question," said Plikt.

"I seem to be failing some kind of test. Can you give me a hint what question I should ask?"

"Don't be angry. You should be asking why I wrote it as fiction instead of biography."

"Why, then?"

"Because I discovered that Andrew Wiggin, Speaker for the Dead, is Ender Wiggin, the Xenocide."

Even though Ender was four years gone, he was still eighteen years from his destination. Valentine felt sick with dread, thinking of what his life would be like if he was welcomed on Lusitania as the most shameworthy man in human history.

"You don't need to be afraid, Professor Wiggin. If I meant to tell, I could have. When I found it out, I realized that he had re-

pented what he did. And such a magnificent penance. It was the
Speaker for the Dead who revealed his act as an unspeakable crime
—and so he took the title Speaker, like so many hundreds of others,
and acted out the role of his own accuser on twenty worlds."

"You have found so much, Plikt, and understood so little."

"I understand everything! Read what I wrote—that was understanding!"

Valentine told herself that since Plikt knew so much, she might
as well know more. But it was rage, not reason, that drove Valentine
to tell what she had never told anyone before. "Plikt, my brother
didn't *imitate* the original Speaker for the Dead. He *wrote* the Hive
Queen and the Hegemon."

When Plikt realized that Valentine was telling the truth, it over-
whelmed her. For all these years she had regarded Andrew Wiggin
as her subject matter, and the original Speaker for the Dead as her
inspiration. To find that they were the same person struck her dumb
for half an hour.

Then she and Valentine talked and confided and came to trust
each other until Valentine invited Plikt to be the tutor of her children
and her collaborator in writing and teaching. Jakt was surprised at
the new addition to the household, but in time Valentine told him the
secrets Plikt had uncovered through research or provoked out of her.
It became the family legend, and the children grew up hearing mar-
velous stories of their long-lost Uncle Ender, who was thought in
every world to be a monster, but in reality was something of a savior,
or a prophet, or at least a martyr.

The years passed, the family prospered, and Valentine's pain at
Ender's loss became pride in him and finally a powerful anticipation.
She was eager for him to arrive on Lusitania, to solve the dilemma of
the piggies, to fulfil his apparent destiny as the apostle to the ramen.
It was Plikt, the good Lutheran, who taught Valentine to conceive of
Ender's life in religious terms; the powerful stability of her family life
and the miracle of each of her five children combined to instill in her
the emotions, if not the doctrines, of faith.

It was bound to affect the children, too. The tale of Uncle
Ender, because they could never mention it to outsiders, took on
supernatural overtones. Syfte, the eldest daughter, was particularly
intrigued, and even when she turned twenty, and rationality over-
powered the primitive, childish adoration of Uncle Ender, she was

still obsessed with him. He was a creature out of legend, and yet he still lived, and on a world not impossibly far away.

She did not tell her mother and father, but she did confide in her former tutor. "Someday, Plikt, I'll meet him. I'll meet him and help him in his work."

"What makes you think he'll need help? *Your* help, anyway?" Plikt was always a skeptic until her student had earned her belief.

"He didn't do it alone the first time, either, did he?" And Syfte's dreams turned outward, away from the ice of Trondheim, to the distant planet where Ender Wiggin had not yet set foot. People of Lusitania, you little know what a great man will walk on your earth and take up your burden. And I will join him, in due time, even though it will be a generation late—be ready for me, too, Lusitania.

On his starship, Ender Wiggin had no notion of the freight of other people's dreams he carried with him. It had been only days since he left Valentine weeping on the dock. To him, Syfte had no name; she was a swelling in Valentine's belly, and nothing more. He was only beginning to feel the pain of losing Valentine—a pain she had long since got over. And his thoughts were far from his unknown nieces and nephews on a world of ice.

It was a lonely, tortured young girl named Novinha that he thought of, wondering what the twenty-two years of his voyage were doing to her, and whom she would have become by the time they met. For he loved her, as you can only love someone who is an echo of yourself at your time of deepest sorrow.

Chapter 6

Olhado

Their only intercourse with other tribes seems to be warfare. When they tell stories to each other (usually during rainy weather), it almost always deals with battles and heroes. The ending is always death, for heroes and cowards alike. If the stories are any guideline, piggies don't *expect* to live through war. And they never, ever, give the slightest hint of interest in the enemy females, either for rape, murder, or slavery, the traditional human treatment of the wives of fallen soldiers.

Does this mean that there is no genetic exchange between tribes? Not at all. The genetic exchanges may be conducted by the females, who may have some system of trading genetic favors. Given the apparent utter subservience of the males to the females in piggy society, this could easily be going on without the males having any idea; or it might cause them such shame that they just won't tell us about it.

What they want to tell us about is battle. A typical description, from my daughter Ouanda's notes of 2:21 last year, during a session of storytelling inside the log house:

PIGGY (speaking Stark): He killed three of the brothers without taking a wound. I have never seen such a strong and fearless warrior. Blood was high on his arms, and the stick in his hand was splintered and covered with the brains of my brothers. He knew he was honorable, even though the rest of the battle went against his feeble tribe. Dei honra! Eu lhe dei! (I gave honor! I gave it to him!)

(Other piggies click their tongues and squeak.)

PIGGY: I hooked him to the ground. He was powerful in his

struggles until I showed him the grass in my hand. Then he opened his mouth and hummed the strange songs of the far country. Nunca será madeira na mão da gente! (He will never be a stick in our hands!) (At this point they joined in singing a song in the Wives' Language, one of the longest passages yet heard.)

(Note that this is a common pattern among them, to speak primarily in Stark, then switch into Portuguese at the moment of climax and conclusion. On reflection, we have realized that we do the same thing, falling into our native Portuguese at the most emotional moments.)

This account of battle may not seem so unusual until you hear enough stories to realize that they *always* end with the hero's death. Apparently they have no taste for light comedy.

—Liberdade Figueira de Medici, "Report on Intertribal Patterns of Lusitanian Aborigines" in *Cross-Cultural Transactions,* 1964:12:40

There wasn't much to do during interstellar flight. Once the course was charted and the ship had made the Park shift, the only task was to calculate how near to lightspeed the ship was traveling. The shipboard computer figured the exact velocity and then determined how long, in subjective time, the voyage should continue before making the Park shift back to a manageable sublight speed. Like a stopwatch, thought Ender. Click it on, click it off, and the race is over.

Jane couldn't put much of herself into the shipboard brain, so Ender had the eight days of the voyage practically alone. The ship's computers were bright enough to help him get the hang of the switch from Spanish to Portuguese. It was easy enough to speak, but so many consonants were left out that understanding it was hard.

Speaking Portuguese with a slow-witted computer became maddening after an hour or two each day. On every other voyage, Val had been there. Not that they had always talked—Val and Ender knew each other so well that there was often nothing to say. But without her there, Ender grew impatient with his own thoughts; they never came to a point, because there was no one to tell them to.

Even the hive queen was no help. Her thoughts were instantaneous; bound, not to synapses, but to philotes that were untouched by the relativistic effects of lightspeed. She passed sixteen hours for every minute of Ender's time—the differential was too great for him to receive any kind of communication from her. If she were not in a cocoon, she would have thousands of individual buggers, each doing its own task and passing to her vast memory its experiences. But now all she had were her memories, and in his eight days of captivity, Ender began to understand her eagerness to be delivered.

By the time the eight days passed, he was doing fairly well at speaking Portuguese directly instead of translating from Spanish whenever he wanted to say anything. He was also desperate for human company—he would have been glad to discuss religion with a Calvinist, just to have somebody smarter than the ship's computer to talk to.

The starship performed the Park shift; in an immeasurable moment its velocity changed relative to the rest of the universe. Or, rather, the theory had it that in fact the velocity of the rest of the universe changed, while the starship remained truly motionless. No one could be sure, because there was nowhere to stand to observe the phenomenon. It was anybody's guess, since nobody understood why philotic effects worked anyway; the ansible had been discovered half by accident, and along with it the Park Instantaneity Principle. It may not be comprehensible, but it worked.

The windows of the starship instantly filled with stars as light became visible again in all directions. Someday a scientist would discover why the Park shift took almost no energy. Somewhere, Ender was certain, a terrible price was being paid for human starflight. He had dreamed once of a star winking out every time a starship made the Park shift. Jane assured him that it wasn't so, but he knew that most stars were invisible to us; a trillion of them could disappear and we'd not know it. For thousands of years we would continue to see the photons that had already been launched before the star disappeared. By the time we could see the galaxy go blank, it would be far too late to amend our course.

"Sitting there in paranoid fantasy," said Jane.

"You can't read minds," said Ender.

"You always get morose and speculate about the destruction of the universe whenever you come out of starflight. It's your peculiar manifestation of motion sickness."

"Have you alerted Lusitanian authorities that I'm coming?"

"It's a very small colony. There's no Landing Authority because hardly anybody goes there. There's an orbiting shuttle that automatically takes people up and down to a laughable little shuttleport."

"No clearance from Immigration?"

"You're a Speaker. They can't turn you away. Besides, Immigration consists of the Governor, who is also the Mayor, since the city and the colony are identical. Her name is Faria Lima Maria do Bosque, called Bosquinha, and she sends you greetings and wishes you would go away, since they've got trouble enough without a prophet of agnosticism going around annoying good Catholics."

"She *said* that?"

"Actually, not to you—Bishop Peregrino said it to her, and she agreed. But it's her job to agree. If you tell her that Catholics are all idolatrous, superstitious fools, she'll probably sigh and say, I hope you can keep those opinions to yourself."

"You're stalling," said Ender. "What is it you think I don't want to hear?"

"Novinha canceled her call for a Speaker. Five days after she sent it."

Of course, the Starways Code said that once Ender had begun his voyage in response to her call, the call could not legally be canceled; still, it changed everything, because instead of eagerly awaiting his arrival for twenty-two years, she would be dreading it, resenting him for coming when she had changed her mind. He had expected to be received by her as a welcome friend. Now she would be even more hostile than the Catholic establishment. "Anything to simplify my work," he said.

"Well, it's not all bad, Andrew. You see, in the intervening years, a couple of other people have called for a Speaker, and *they* haven't canceled."

"Who?"

"By the most fascinating coincidence, they are Novinha's son Miro and Novinha's daughter Ela."

"They couldn't possibly have known Pipo. Why would they call me to Speak his death?"

"Oh, no, not Pipo's death. Ela called for a Speaker only six weeks ago, to Speak the death of her father, Novinha's husband, Marcos Maria Ribeira, called Marcão. He keeled over in a bar. Not from alcohol—he had a disease. He died of terminal rot."

"I worry about you, Jane, consumed with compassion the way you are."

"Compassion is what *you're* good at. I'm better at complex searches through organized data structures."

"And the boy—what's his name?"

"Miro. He called for a Speaker four years ago. For the death of Pipo's son, Libo."

"Libo couldn't be older than forty—"

"He was helped along to an early death. He was xenologer, you see—or Zenador, as they say in Portuguese."

"The piggies—"

"Exactly like his father's death. The organs placed exactly the same. Three piggies have been executed the same way while you were en route. But they plant trees in the middle of the piggy corpses—no such honor for the dead humans."

Both xenologers murdered by the piggies, a generation apart. "What has the Starways Council decided?"

"It's very tricky. They keep vacillating. They haven't certified either of Libo's apprentices as xenologer. One is Libo's daughter, Ouanda. And the other is Miro."

"Do they maintain contact with the piggies?"

"Officially, no. There's some controversy about this. After Libo died, the Council forbade contact more frequently than once a month. But Libo's daughter categorically refused to obey the order."

"And they didn't remove her?"

"The majority for cutting back on contact with the piggies was paper thin. There *was* no majority for censuring her. At the same time, they worry that Miro and Ouanda are so young. Two years ago a party of scientists was dispatched from Calicut. They should be here to take over supervision of piggy affairs in only thirty-three more years."

"Do they have any idea this time why the piggies killed the xenologer?"

"None at all. But that's why you're here, isn't it?"

The answer would have been easy, except that the hive queen nudged him gently in the back of his mind. Ender could feel her like wind through the leaves of a tree, a rustling, a gentle movement, and sunlight. Yes, he was here to Speak the dead. But he was also here to bring the dead back to life.

<This is a good place.>

Everybody's always a few steps ahead of me.

<There's a mind here. Much clearer than any human mind we've known.>

The piggies? They think the way you do?

<It knows of the piggies. A little time; it's afraid of us.>

The hive queen withdrew, and Ender was left to ponder the thought that with Lusitania he may have bitten off more than he could chew.

Bishop Peregrino delivered the homily himself. That was always a bad sign. Never an exciting speaker, he had become so convoluted and parenthetical that half the time Ela couldn't even understand what he was talking about. Quim pretended he could understand, of course, because as far as he was concerned the bishop could do no wrong. But little Grego made no attempt to seem interested. Even when Sister Esquecimento was roving the aisle, with her needle-sharp nails and cruel grip, Grego fearlessly performed whatever mischief entered his head.

Today he was prying the rivets out of the back of the plastic bench in front of them. It bothered Ela how strong he was—a six-year-old shouldn't be able to work a screwdriver under the lip of a heat-sealed rivet. Ela wasn't sure *she* could do it.

If Father were here, of course, his long arm would snake out and gently, oh so gently, take the screwdriver out of Grego's hand. He would whisper, "Where did you get this?" and Grego would look at him with wide and innocent eyes. Later, when the family got home from mass, Father would rage at Miro for leaving tools around, calling him terrible names and blaming him for all the troubles of the family. Miro would bear it in silence. Ela would busy herself with preparation for the evening meal. Quim would sit uselessly in the corner, massaging the rosary and murmuring his useless little prayers. Olhado was the lucky one, with his electronic eyes—he simply turned them off or played back some favorite scene from the past and paid no attention. Quara went off and cowered in the corner. And little Grego stood there triumphantly, his hand clutching Father's pantleg, watching as the blame for everything he did was poured out on Miro's head.

Ela shuddered as the scene played itself out in her memory. If it had ended there, it would have been bearable. But then Miro would leave, and they would eat, and then—

Sister Esquecimento's spidery fingers leapt out; her fingernails dug into Grego's arm. Instantly, Grego dropped the screwdriver. Of course it was supposed to clatter on the floor, but Sister Esquecimento was no fool. She bent quickly and caught it in her other hand. Grego grinned. Her face was only inches from his knee. Ela saw what he had in mind, reached out to try to stop him, but too late—he brought his knee up sharply into Sister Esquecimento's mouth.

She gasped from the pain and let go of Grego's arm. He snatched the screwdriver out of her slackened hand. Holding a hand to her bleeding mouth, she fled down the aisle. Grego resumed his demolition work.

Father is dead, Ela reminded herself. The words sounded like music in her mind. Father is dead, but he's still here, because he left his monstrous little legacy behind. The poison he put in us all is still ripening, and eventually it will kill us all. When he died his liver was only two inches long, and his spleen could not be found. Strange fatty organs had grown in their places. There was no name for the disease; his body had gone insane, forgotten the blueprint by which human beings were built. Even now the disease still lives on in his children. Not in our bodies, but in our souls. We exist where normal human children are expected to be; we're even shaped the same. But each of us in our own way has been replaced by an imitation child, shaped out of a twisted, fetid, lipidous goiter that grew out of Father's soul.

Maybe it would be different if Mother tried to make it better. But she cared about nothing but microscopes and genetically enhanced cereals, or whatever she was working on now.

"—so-called Speaker for the Dead! But there is only One who can speak for the dead, and that is Sagrado Cristo—"

Bishop Peregrino's words caught her attention. What was he saying about a Speaker for the Dead? He couldn't possibly know she had called for one—

"—the law requires us to treat him with courtesy, but not with belief! The truth is not to be found in the speculations and hypotheses of unspiritual men, but in the teachings and traditions of Mother Church. So when he walks among you, give him your smiles, but hold back your hearts!"

Why was he giving this warning? The nearest planet was Trond-heim, twenty-two lightyears away, and it wasn't likely there'd be a Speaker *there*. It would be decades till a Speaker arrived, if one came at all. She leaned over Quara to ask Quim—*he* would have been listening. "What's this about a Speaker for the Dead?" she whis-pered.

"If you'd listen, you'd know for yourself."

"If you don't tell me, I'll deviate your septum."

Quim smirked, to show her he wasn't afraid of her threats. But, since he in fact *was* afraid of her, he then told her. "Some faithless wretch apparently requested a Speaker back when the first xenologer died, and he arrives this afternoon—he's already on the shuttle and the Mayor is on her way out to meet him when he lands."

She hadn't bargained for this. The computer hadn't told her a Speaker was already on the way. He was supposed to come years from now, to Speak the truth about the monstrosity called Father who had finally blessed his family by dropping dead; the truth would come like light to illuminate and purify their past. But Father was too recently dead for him to be Spoken *now*. His tentacles still reached out from the grave and sucked at their hearts.

The homily ended, and eventually so did the mass. She held tightly to Grego's hand, trying to keep him from snatching some-one's book or bag as they threaded through the crowd. Quim was good for something, at least—he carried Quara, who always froze up when she was supposed to make her way among strangers. Olhado switched his eyes back on and took care of himself, winking metalli-cally at whatever fifteen-year-old semi-virgin he was hoping to hor-rify today. Ela genuflected at the statues of Os Venerados, her long-dead, half-sainted grandparents. Aren't you proud to have such lovely grandchildren as us?

Grego was smirking; sure enough, he had a baby's shoe in his hand. Ela silently prayed that the infant had come out of the encoun-ter unbloodied. She took the shoe from Grego and laid it on the little altar where candles burned in perpetual witness of the miracle of the Descolada. Whoever owned the shoe, they'd find it there.

Mayor Bosquinha was cheerful enough as the car skimmed over the grassland between the shuttleport and the settlement of Milagre. She pointed out herds of semi-domestic cabra, a native species that provided fibers for cloth, but whose meat was nutritionally useless to human beings.

"Do the piggies eat them?" asked Ender.

She raised an eyebrow. "We don't know much about the piggies."

"We know they live in the forest. Do they ever come out on the plain?"

She shrugged. "That's for the framlings to decide."

Ender was startled for a moment to hear her use that word; but of course Demosthenes' latest book had been published twenty-two years ago, and distributed through the Hundred Worlds by ansible. Utlanning, framling, raman, varelse—the terms were part of Stark now, and probably did not even seem particularly novel to Bosquinha.

It was her lack of curiosity about the piggies that left him feeling uncomfortable. The people of Lusitania couldn't possibly be unconcerned about the piggies—they were the reason for the high, impassable fence that none but the Zenadors could cross. No, she wasn't incurious, she was avoiding the subject. Whether it was because the murderous piggies were a painful subject or because she didn't trust a Speaker for the Dead, he couldn't guess.

They crested a hill and she stopped the car. Gently it settled onto its skids. Below them a broad river wound its way among grassy hills; beyond the river, the farther hills were completely covered with forest. Along the far bank of the river, brick and plaster houses with tile roofs made a picturesque town. Farmhouses perched on the near bank, their long narrow fields reaching toward the hill where Ender and Bosquinha sat.

"Milagre," said Bosquinha. "On the highest hill, the Cathedral. Bishop Peregrino has asked the people to be polite and helpful to you."

From her tone, Ender gathered that he had also let them know that he was a dangerous agent of agnosticism. "Until God strikes me dead?" he asked.

Bosquinha smiled. "God is setting an example of Christian tolerance, and we expect everyone in town will follow."

"Do they know who called me?"

"Whoever called you has been—discreet."

"You're the Governor, besides being Mayor. You have some privileges of information."

"I know that your original call was canceled, but too late. I also know that two others have requested Speakers in recent years. But you must realize that most people are content to receive their doctrine and their consolation from the priests."

"They'll be relieved to know that I don't deal in doctrine or consolation."

"Your kind offer to let us have your cargo of skrika will make you popular enough in the bars, and you can be sure you'll see plenty of vain women wearing the pelts in the months to come. It's coming on to autumn."

"I happened to acquire the skrika with the starship—it was of no use to me, and I don't expect any special gratitude for it." He looked at the rough, furry-looking grass around him. "This grass—it's native?"

"And useless. We can't even use it for thatch—if you cut it, it crumbles, and then dissolves into dust in the next rain. But down there, in the fields, the most common crop is a special breed of amaranth that our xenobiologist developed for us. Rice and wheat were feeble and undependable crops here, but the amaranth is so hardy that we have to use herbicides around the fields to keep it from spreading."

"Why?"

"This is a quarantined world, Speaker. The amaranth is so well-suited to this environment that it would soon choke out the native grasses. The idea is not to terraform Lusitania. The idea is to have as little impact on this world as possible."

"That must be hard on the people."

"Within our enclave, Speaker, we are free and our lives are full. And outside the fence—no one wants to go there, anyway."

The tone of her voice was heavy with concealed emotion. Ender knew, then, that the fear of the piggies ran deep.

"Speaker, I know you're thinking that we're afraid of the piggies. And perhaps some of us are. But the feeling most of us have, most of the time, isn't fear at all. It's hatred. Loathing."

"You've never seen them."

"You must know of the two Zenadors who were killed—I suspect you were originally called to Speak the death of Pipo. But both of them, Pipo and Libo alike, were beloved here. Especially Libo. He was a kind and generous man, and the grief at his death was widespread and genuine. It is hard to conceive of how the piggies could do to him what they did. Dom Cristão, the abbot of the Filhos da Mente de Cristo—he says that they must lack the moral sense. He says this may mean that they are beasts. Or it may mean that they are unfallen, having not yet eaten of the fruit of the forbidden tree." She smiled tightly. "But that's theology, and so it means nothing to you."

He did not answer. He was used to the way religious people assumed that their sacred stories must sound absurd to unbelievers. But Ender did not consider himself an unbeliever, and he had a keen sense of the sacredness of many tales. But he could not explain this to Bosquinha. She would have to change her assumptions about him over time. She was suspicious of him, but he believed she could be won; to be a good Mayor, she had to be skilled at seeing people for what they are, not for what they seem.

He turned the subject. "The Filhos da Mente de Cristo—my Portuguese isn't strong, but does that mean 'Sons of the Mind of Christ'?"

"They're a new order, relatively speaking, formed only four hundred years ago under a special dispensation of the Pope—"

"Oh, I know the Children of the Mind of Christ, Mayor. I Spoke the death of San Angelo on Moctezuma, in the city of Córdoba."

Her eyes widened. "Then the story is true!"

"I've heard many versions of the story, Mayor Bosquinha. One tale has it that the devil possessed San Angelo on his deathbed, so he cried out for the unspeakable rites of the pagan Hablador de los Muertos."

Bosquinha smiled. "That is something like the tale that is whispered. Dom Cristão says it's nonsense, of course."

"It happens that San Angelo, back before he was sainted, attended my Speaking for a woman that he knew. The fungus in his blood was already killing him. He came to me and said, 'Andrew, they're already telling the most terrible lies about me, saying that I've done miracles and should be sainted. You must help me. You must tell the truth at my death.'"

"But the miracles have been certified, and he was canonized only ninety years after his death."

"Yes. Well, that's partly my fault. When I Spoke his death, I attested several of the miracles myself."

Now she laughed aloud. "A Speaker for the Dead, believing in miracles?"

"Look at your cathedral hill. How many of those buildings are for the priests, and how many are for the school?"

Bosquinha understood at once, and glared at him. "The Filhos da Mente de Cristo are obedient to the Bishop."

"Except that they preserve and teach all knowledge, whether the Bishop approves of it or not."

"San Angelo may have allowed you to meddle in affairs of the Church. I assure you that Bishop Peregrino will not."

"I've come to Speak a simple death, and I'll abide by the law. I think you'll find I do less harm than you expect, and perhaps more good."

"If you've come to Speak Pipo's death, Speaker pelos Mortos, then you will do nothing but harm. Leave the piggies behind the wall. If I had my way, no human being would pass through that fence again."

"I hope there's a room I can rent."

"We're an unchanging town here, Speaker. Everyone has a house here and there's nowhere else to go—why would anyone maintain an inn? We can only offer you one of the small plastic dwellings the first colonists put up. It's small, but it has all the amenities."

"Since I don't need many amenities or much space, I'm sure it will be fine. And I look forward to meeting Dom Cristão. Where the followers of San Angelo are, the truth has friends."

Bosquinha sniffed and started the car again. As Ender intended, her preconceived notions of a Speaker for the Dead were now shattered. To think he had actually known San Angelo, and admired the Filhos. It was not what Bishop Peregrino had led them to expect.

The room was only thinly furnished, and if Ender had owned much he would have had trouble finding anywhere to put it. As always before, however, he was able to unpack from interstellar flight in only a few minutes. Only the bundled cocoon of the hive queen remained in his bag; he had long since given up feeling odd about the incongruity of stowing the future of a magnificent race in a duffel under his bed.

"Maybe this will be the place," he murmured. The cocoon felt cool, almost cold, even through the towels it was wrapped in.

< It is the place. >

It was unnerving to have her so certain of it. There was no hint of pleading or impatience or any of the other feelings she had given him, desiring to emerge. Just absolute certainty.

"I wish we could decide just like that," he said. "It *might* be the place, but it all depends on whether the piggies can cope with having you here."

< The question is whether they can cope with you humans *without* us. >

"It takes time. Give me a few months here."

< Take all the time you need. We're in no hurry now. >

"Who is it that you've found? I thought you told me that you couldn't communicate with anybody but me."

< The part of our mind that holds our thought, what you call the philotic impulse, the power of the ansibles, it is very cold and hard to find in human beings. But this one, the one we've found here, one of many that we'll find here, his philotic impulse is much stronger, much clearer, easier to find, he hears us more easily, he sees our memories, and we see his, we find him easily, and so forgive us, dear friend, forgive us if we leave the hard work of talking to your mind and go back to him and talk to him because he doesn't make us search so hard to make words and pictures that are clear enough for your analytical mind because we feel him like sunshine, like the warmth of sunshine on his face on our face and the feel of cool water deep in our abdomen and movement as gentle and thorough as soft wind which we haven't felt for three thousand years forgive us we'll be with him until you wake us until you take us out to dwell here because you will do it you will find out in your own way in your own time that this is the place here it is this is home—>

And then he lost the thread of her thought, felt it seep away like a dream that is forgotten upon waking, even as you try to remember it and keep it alive. Ender wasn't sure what the hive queen had found, but whatever it was, *he* would have to deal with the reality of Starways Code, the Catholic Church, young xenologists who might not even let him meet the piggies, a xenobiologist who had changed her mind about inviting him here, and something more, perhaps the most difficult thing of all: that if the hive queen stayed here, *he* would have to stay here. I've been disconnected from humanity for so many years, he thought, coming in to meddle and pry and hurt and heal, then going away again, myself untouched. How will I ever become a part of this place, if this is where I'll stay? The only things I've ever been a part of were an army of little boys in the Battle School, and Valentine, and both are gone now, both part of the past—

"What, wallowing in loneliness?" asked Jane. "I can hear your heartrate falling and your breathing getting heavy. In a moment you'll either be asleep, dead, or lacrimose."

"I'm much more complex than that," said Ender cheerfully. "Anticipated self-pity is what I'm feeling, about pains that haven't even arrived."

"Very good, Ender. Get an early start. That way you can wallow so much longer." The terminal came alive, showing Jane as a piggy in a chorus line of leggy women, high-kicking with exuberance. "Get a little exercise, you'll feel so much better. After all, you've unpacked. What are you waiting for?"

"I don't even know where I am, Jane."

"They really don't keep a map of the city," Jane explained. "Everybody knows where everything is. But they do have a map of the sewer system, divided into boroughs. I can extrapolate where all the buildings are."

"Show me, then."

A three-dimensional model of the town appeared over the terminal. Ender might not be particularly welcome there, and his room might be sparse, but they had shown courtesy in the terminal they provided for him. It wasn't a standard home installation, but rather an elaborate simulator. It was able to project holos into a space sixteen times larger than most terminals, with a resolution four times greater. The illusion was so real that Ender felt for a vertiginous moment that he was Gulliver, leaning over a Lilliput that had not yet come to fear him, that did not yet recognize his power to destroy.

The names of the different boroughs hung in the air over each sewer district. "You're here," said Jane. "Vila Velha, the old town. The praça is just through the block from you. That's where public meetings are held."

"Do you have any map of the piggy lands?"

The village map slid rapidly toward Ender, the near features disappearing as new ones came into view on the far side. It was as if he were flying over it. Like a witch, he thought. The boundary of the town was marked by a fence.

"That barrier is the only thing standing between us and the piggies," mused Ender.

"It generates an electric field that stimulates any pain-sensitive nerves that come within it," said Jane. "Just touching it makes all your wetware go screwy—it makes you feel as though somebody were cutting off your fingers with a file."

"Pleasant thought. Are we in a concentration camp? Or a zoo?"

"It all depends on how you look at it," said Jane. "It's the human side of the fence that's connected to the rest of the universe, and the piggy side that's trapped on its home world."

"The difference is that they don't know what they're missing."

"I know," said Jane. "It's the most charming thing about humans. You are all so sure that the lesser animals are bleeding with envy because they didn't have the good fortune to be born *homo sapiens.*" Beyond the fence was a hillside, and along the top of the hill a thick forest began. "The xenologers have never gone deep into piggy lands. The piggy community that they deal with is less than a kilometer inside this wood. The piggies live in a log house, all the males together. We don't know about any other settlements except that the satellites have been able to confirm that every forest like this one carries just about all the population that a hunter-gatherer culture can sustain."

"They hunt?"

"Mostly they gather."

"Where did Pipo and Libo die?"

Jane brightened a patch of grassy ground on the hillside leading up to the trees. A large tree grew in isolation nearby, with two smaller ones not far off.

"Those trees," said Ender. "I don't remember any being so close in the holos I saw on Trondheim."

"It's been twenty-two years. The big one is the tree the piggies planted in the corpse of the rebel called Rooter, who was executed before Pipo was murdered. The other two are more recent piggy executions."

"I wish I knew why they plant trees for piggies, and not for humans."

"The trees are sacred," said Jane. "Pipo recorded that many of the trees in the forest are named. Libo speculated that they might be named for the dead."

"And humans simply aren't part of the pattern of tree-worship. Well, that's likely enough. Except that I've found that rituals and myths don't come from nowhere. There's usually some reason for it that's tied to the survival of the community."

"Andrew Wiggin, anthropologist?"

"The proper study of mankind is man."

"Go study some men, then, Ender. Novinha's family, for instance. By the way, the computer network has officially been barred from showing you where anybody lives."

Ender grinned. "So Bosquinha isn't as friendly as she seems."

"If you have to ask where people live, they'll know where you're going. If they don't want you to go there, no one will know where they live."

"You can override their restriction, can't you?"

"I already have." A light was blinking near the fence line, behind the observatory hill. It was as isolated a spot as was possible to find in Milagre. Few other houses had been built where the fence would be visible all the time. Ender wondered whether Novinha had chosen to live there to be near the fence or to be far from neighbors. Perhaps it had been Marcão's choice.

The nearest borough was Vila Atrás, and then the borough called As Fábricas stretched down to the river. As the name implied, it consisted mostly of small factories that worked the metals and plastics and processed the foods and fibers that Milagre used. A nice, tight, self-contained economy. And Novinha had chosen to live back behind everything, out of sight, invisible. It was Novinha who chose it, too, Ender was sure of that now. Wasn't it the pattern of her life? She had never belonged to Milagre. It was no accident that all three calls for a Speaker had come from her and her children. The very act of calling a Speaker was defiant, a sign that they did not think they belonged among the devout Catholics of Lusitania.

"Still," said Ender, "I have to ask someone to lead me there. I shouldn't let them know right away that they can't hide any of their information from me."

The map disappeared, and Jane's face appeared above the terminal. She had neglected to adjust for the greater size of this terminal, so that her head was many times human size. She was quite imposing. And her simulation was accurate right down to the pores on her face. "Actually, Andrew, it's *me* they can't hide anything from."

Ender sighed. "You have a vested interest in this, Jane."

"I know." She winked. "But *you* don't."

"Are you telling me you don't trust me?"

"You reek of impartiality and a sense of justice. But I'm human enough to want preferential treatment, Andrew."

"Will you promise me one thing, at least?"

"Anything, my corpuscular friend."

"When you decide to hide something from me, will you at least tell me that you aren't going to tell me?"

"This is getting way too deep for little old me." She was a caricature of an overfeminine woman.

"Nothing is too deep for you, Jane. Do us both a favor. Don't cut me off at the knees."

"While you're off with the Ribeira family, is there anything you'd like me to be doing?"

"Yes. Find every way in which the Ribeiras are significantly different from the rest of the people of Lusitania. And any points of conflict between them and the authorities."

"You speak, and I obey." She started to do her genie disappearing act.

"You maneuvered me here, Jane. Why are you trying to unnerve me?"

"I'm not. And I didn't."

"I have a shortage of friends in this town."

"You can trust me with your life."

"It isn't my life I'm worried about."

The praça was filled with children playing football. Most of them were stunting, showing how long they could keep the ball in the air using only their feet and heads. Two of them, though, had a vicious duel going. The boy would kick the ball as hard as he could toward the girl, who stood not three meters away. She would stand and take the impact of the ball, not flinching no matter how hard it struck her. Then she would kick the ball back at him, and he would try not to flinch. A little girl was tending the ball, fetching it each time it rebounded from a victim.

Ender tried asking some of the boys if they knew where the Ribeira family's house was. Their answer was invariably a shrug; when he persisted some of them began moving away, and soon most of the children had retreated from the praça. Ender wondered what the Bishop had told everybody about Speakers.

The duel, however, continued unabated. And now that the praça was not so crowded, Ender saw that another child was involved, a boy of about twelve. He was not extraordinary from behind, but as Ender moved toward the middle of the praça, he could see that there was something wrong with the boy's eyes. It took a moment, but then he understood. The boy had artificial eyes. Both looked shiny and metallic, but Ender knew how they worked. Only one eye was used for sight, but it took four separate visual scans and then separated the signals to feed true binocular vision to the brain. The other eye contained the power supply, the computer control, and the external interface. When he wanted to, he could record short sequences of vision in a limited photo memory, probably less than a trillion bits. The duelists were using him as their judge; if they disputed a point, he could replay the scene in slow motion and tell them what had happened.

The ball went straight for the boy's crotch. He winced elaborately, but the girl was not impressed. "He swiveled away, I saw his hips move!"

"Did not! You hurt me, I didn't dodge at all!"

"Reveja! Reveja!" They had been speaking Stark, but the girl now switched into Portuguese.

The boy with metal eyes showed no expression, but raised a hand to silence them. "Mudou," he said with finality. He moved, Ender translated.

"Sabia!" I knew it!

"You liar, Olhado!"

The boy with metal eyes looked at him with disdain. "I never lie. I'll send you a dump of the scene if you want. In fact, I think I'll post it on the net so everybody can watch you dodge and then lie about it."

"Mentiroso! Filho de punta! Fode-bode!"

Ender was pretty sure what the epithets meant, but the boy with metal eyes took it calmly.

"Da," said the girl. "Da-me." Give it here.

The boy furiously took off his ring and threw it on the ground at her feet. "Viada!" he said in a hoarse whisper. Then he took off running.

"Poltrão!" shouted the girl after him. Coward!

"Cão!" shouted the boy, not even looking over his shoulder.

It was not the girl he was shouting at this time. She turned at once to look at the boy with metal eyes, who stiffened at the name. Almost at once the girl looked at the ground. The little one, who had been doing the ball-fetching, walked to the boy with metal eyes and whispered something. He looked up, noticing Ender for the first time.

The older girl was apologizing. "Desculpa, Olhado, não queria que—"

"Não há problema, Michi." He did not look at her.

The girl started to go on, but then she, too, noticed Ender and fell silent.

"Porque está olhando-nos?" asked the boy. Why are you looking at us?

Ender answered with a question. "Você é árbitro?" You're the arbiter here? The word could mean "umpire," but it could also mean "magistrate."

"De vez em quando." Sometimes.

Ender switched to Stark—he wasn't sure he knew how to say anything complex in Portuguese. "Then tell me, arbiter, is it fair to leave a stranger to find his way around without help?"

"Stranger? You mean utlanning, framling, or raman?"

"No, I think I mean infidel."

"O Senhor é descrente?" You're an unbeliever?

"Só descredo no incrível." I only disbelieve the unbelievable.

The boy grinned. "Where do you want to go, Speaker?"

"The house of the Ribeira family."

The little girl edged closer to the boy with metal eyes. "Which Ribeira family?"

"The widow Ivanova."

"I think I can find it," said the boy.

"Everybody in town can find it," said Ender. "The point is, will you take me there?"

"Why do you want to go there?"

"I ask people questions and try to find out true stories."

"Nobody at the Ribeira house knows any true stories."

"I'd settle for lies."

"Come on then." He started toward the low-mown grass of the main road. The little girl was whispering in his ear. He stopped and turned to Ender, who was following close behind.

"Quara wants to know. What's your name?"

"Andrew. Andrew Wiggin."

"She's Quara."

"And you?"

"Everybody calls me Olhado. Because of my eyes." He picked up the little girl and put her on his shoulders. "But my real name's Lauro. Lauro Suleimão Ribeira." He grinned, then turned around and strode off.

Ender followed. Ribeira. Of course.

Jane had been listening, too, and spoke from the jewel in his ear. "Lauro Suleimão Ribeira is Novinha's fourth child. He lost his eyes in a laser accident. He's twelve years old. Oh, and I found one difference between the Ribeira family and the rest of the town. The Ribeiras are willing to defy the Bishop and lead you where you want to go."

I noticed something, too, Jane, he answered silently. This boy enjoyed deceiving me, and then enjoyed even more letting me see how I'd been fooled. I just hope *you* don't take lessons from him.

Miro sat on the hillside. The shade of the trees made him invisible to anyone who might be watching from Milagre, but he could see much of the town from here—certainly the cathedral and the monastery on the highest hill, and then the observatory on the next hill to the north. And under the observatory, in a depression in the hillside, the house where he lived, not very far from the fence.

"Miro," whispered Leaf-eater. "Are you a tree?"

It was a translation from the pequeninos' idiom. Sometimes they meditated, holding themselves motionless for hours. They called this "being a tree."

"More like a blade of grass," Miro answered.

Leaf-eater giggled in the high, wheezy way he had. It never sounded natural—the pequeninos had learned laughter by rote, as if it were simply another word in Stark. It didn't arise out of amusement, or at least Miro didn't think it did.

"Is it going to rain?" asked Miro. To a piggy this meant: are you interrupting me for my own sake, or for yours?

"It rained fire today," said Leaf-eater. "Out in the prairie."

"Yes. We have a visitor from another world."

"Is it the Speaker?"

Miro didn't answer.

"You must bring him to see us."

Miro didn't answer.

"I root my face in the ground for you, Miro, my limbs are lumber for your house."

Miro hated it when they begged for something. It was as if they thought of him as someone particularly wise or strong, a parent from whom favors must be wheedled. Well, if they felt that way, it was his own fault. His and Libo's. Playing God out here among the piggies.

"I promised, didn't I, Leaf-eater?"

"When when when?"

"It'll take time. I have to find out whether he can be trusted."

Leaf-eater looked baffled. Miro had tried to explain that not all humans knew each other, and some weren't nice, but they never seemed to understand.

"As soon as I can," Miro said.

Suddenly Leaf-eater began to rock back and forth on the ground, shifting his hips from side to side as if he were trying to relieve an itch in his anus. Libo had speculated once that this was what performed the same function that laughter did for humans. "Talk to me in piddle-geese!" wheezed Leaf-eater. Leaf-eater always seemed to be greatly amused that Miro and the other Zenadors spoke two languages interchangeably. This despite the fact that at least four different piggy languages had been recorded or at least hinted at over the years, all spoken by this same tribe of piggies.

But if he wanted to hear Portuguese, he'd get Portuguese. "Vai comer folhas." Go eat leaves.

Leaf-eater looked puzzled. "Why is that clever?"

"Because that's your name. Come-folhas."

Leaf-eater pulled a large insect out of his nostril and flipped it away, buzzing. "Don't be crude," he said. Then he walked away.

Miro watched him go. Leaf-eater was always so difficult. Miro much preferred the company of the piggy called Human. Even though Human was smarter, and Miro had to watch himself more carefully with him, at least he didn't seem hostile the way Leaf-eater often did.

With the piggy out of sight, Miro turned back toward the city. Somebody was moving down the path along the face of the hill, toward his house. The one in front was very tall—no, it was Olhado with Quara on his shoulders. Quara was much too old for that. Miro worried about her. She seemed not to be coming out of the shock of Father's death. Miro felt a moment's bitterness. And to think he and Ela had expected Father's death would solve all their problems.

Then he stood up and tried to get a better view of the man behind Olhado and Quara. No one he'd seen before. The Speaker. Already! He couldn't have been in town for more than an hour, and he was already going to the house. That's great, all I need is for Mother to find out that I was the one who called him here. Somehow I thought that a Speaker for the Dead would be discreet about it, not just come straight home to the person who called. What a fool. Bad enough that he's coming years before I expected a Speaker to get here. Quim's bound to report this to the Bishop, even if nobody else does. Now I'm going to have to deal with Mother and, probably, the whole city.

Miro moved back into the trees and jogged along a path that led, eventually, to the gate back into the city

Chapter 7

The Ribeira House

Miro, this time you should have been there, because even though I have a better memory for dialogue than you, I sure don't know what *this* means. You saw the new piggy, the one they call Human—I thought I saw you talking to him for a minute before you took off for the Questionable Activity. Mandachuva told me they named him Human because he was very smart *as a child.* OK, it's very flattering that "smart" and "human" are linked in their minds, or perhaps offensive that they think we'll be flattered by that, but that's not what matters.

Mandachuva *then* said: "He could already talk when he started walking around by himself." And he made a gesture with his hand *about ten centimeters off the ground.* To me it looked like he was telling how tall Human was when he learned how to talk and walk. Ten centimeters! But I could be completely wrong. You should have been there, to see for yourself.

If I'm right, and that's what Mandachuva meant, then for the first time we have an idea of piggy childhood. If they actually start walking at ten centimeters in height—and talking, no less!—then they must have less development time during gestation than humans, and do a lot more developing after they're born.

But now it gets absolutely crazy, even by your standards. He then leaned in close and told me—as if he weren't supposed to —who Human's father was: "Your grandfather Pipo knew Human's father. His tree is near your gate."

Is he kidding? Rooter died twenty-four years ago, didn't he? OK, maybe this is just a religious thing, sort of adopt-a-tree or something. But the way Mandachuva was so secretive about it, I keep thinking it's somehow true. Is it possible that they have a 24-year gestation period? Or maybe it took a couple of decades for Human to develop from a 10-centimeter toddler into the fine specimen of piggihood we now see. Or maybe Rooter's sperm was saved in a jar somewhere.

But this *matters.* This is the first time a piggy personally known to human observers has ever been named as a father. And *Rooter,* no less, the very one that got murdered. In other words, the male with the lowest prestige—an executed criminal, even—has been named as a father! That means that our males aren't cast-off bachelors at all, even though some of them are so old they knew Pipo. They are *potential fathers.*

What's more, if Human was so remarkably smart, then why was he dumped here if this is really a group of miserable bachelors? I think we've had it wrong for quite a while. This isn't a low-prestige group of bachelors, this is a high-prestige group of juveniles, and some of them are really going to amount to something.

So when you told me you felt sorry for me because *you* got to go out on the Questionable Activity and I had to stay home and work up some Official Fabrications for the ansible report, you were full of Unpleasant Excretions! (If you get home after I'm asleep, wake me up for a kiss, OK? I earned it today.)

—Memo from Ouanda Figueira Mucumbi to Miro Ribeira von Hesse, retrieved from Lusitanian files by Congressional order and introduced as evidence in the Trial *In Absentia* of the Xenologers of Lusitania on Charges of Treason and Malfeasance

There was no construction industry in Lusitania. When a couple got married, their friends and family built them a house. The Ribeira house expressed the history of the family. At the front, the old part of the house was made of plastic sheets rooted to a concrete foundation. Rooms had been built on as the family grew, each addition abutting the one before, so that five distinct one-story structures fronted the hillside. The later ones were all brick, decently plumbed, roofed with tile, but with no attempt whatever at aesthetic appeal. The family had built exactly what was needed and nothing more.

It was not poverty, Ender knew—there was no poverty in a

community where the economy was completely controlled. The lack of decoration, of individuality, showed the family's contempt for their own house; to Ender this bespoke contempt for themselves as well. Certainly Olhado and Quara showed none of the relaxation, the letting-down that most people feel when they come home. If anything, they grew warier, less jaunty; the house might have been a subtle source of gravity, making them heavier the nearer they approached.

Olhado and Quara went right in. Ender waited at the door for someone to invite him to enter. Olhado left the door ajar, but walked on out of the room without speaking to him. Ender could see Quara sitting on a bed in the front room, leaning against a bare wall. There was nothing whatsoever on any of the walls. They were stark white. Quara's face matched the blankness of the walls. Though her eyes regarded Ender unwaveringly, she showed no sign of recognizing that he was there; certainly she did nothing to indicate he might come in.

There was a disease in this house. Ender tried to understand what it was in Novinha's character that he had missed before, that would let her live in a place like this. Had Pipo's death so long before emptied Novinha's heart as thoroughly as this?

"Is your mother home?" Ender asked.

Quara said nothing.

"Oh," he said. "Excuse me. I thought you were a little girl, but I see now that you're a statue."

She showed no sign of hearing him. So much for trying to jolly her out of her somberness.

Shoes slapped rapidly against a concrete floor. A little boy ran into the room, stopped in the middle, and whirled to face the doorway where Ender stood. He couldn't be more than a year younger than Quara, six or seven years old, probably. Unlike Quara, his face showed plenty of understanding. Along with a feral hunger.

"Is your mother home?" asked Ender.

The boy bent over and carefully rolled up his pantleg. He had taped a long kitchen knife to his leg. Slowly he untaped it. Then, holding it in front of him with both hands, he aimed himself at Ender and launched himself full speed. Ender noted that the knife was well-aimed at his crotch. The boy was not subtle in his approach to strangers.

A moment later Ender had the boy tucked under his arm and the knife jammed into the ceiling. The boy was kicking and screaming. Ender had to use both hands to control his limbs; the boy ended up dangling in front of him by his hands and feet, for all the world like a calf roped for branding.

Ender looked steadily at Quara. "If you don't go right now and get whoever is in charge in this house, I'm going to take this animal home and serve it for supper."

Quara thought about this for a moment, then got up and ran out of the room.

A moment later a tired-looking girl with tousled hair and sleepy eyes came into the front room. "Desculpe, por favor," she murmured, "o menino não se restabeleceu desde a morte do pai—"

Then she seemed suddenly to come awake.

"O Senhor é o Falante pelos Mortos!" You're the Speaker for the Dead!

"Sou," answered Ender. I am.

"Não aqui," she said. "Oh, no, I'm sorry, do you speak Portuguese? Of course you do, you just answered me—oh, please, not here, not now. Go away."

"Fine," said Ender. "Should I keep the boy or the knife?"

He glanced up at the ceiling; her gaze followed his. "Oh, no, I'm sorry, we looked for it all day yesterday, we knew he had it but we didn't know where."

"It was taped to his leg."

"It wasn't yesterday. We always look there. Please, let go of him."

"Are you sure? I think he's been sharpening his teeth."

"Grego," she said to the boy, "it's wrong to poke at people with the knife."

Grego growled in his throat.

"His father dying, you see."

"They were that close?"

A look of bitter amusement passed across her face. "Hardly. He's always been a thief, Grego has, ever since he was old enough to hold something and walk at the same time. But this thing for hurting people, that's new. Please let him down."

"No," said Ender.

Her eyes narrowed and she looked defiant. "Are you kidnapping him? To take him where? For what ransom?"

"Perhaps you don't understand," said Ender. "He assaulted me. You've offered me no guarantee that he won't do it again. You've made no provision for disciplining him when I set him down."

As he had hoped, fury came into her eyes. "Who do you think you are? This is *his* house, not yours!"

"Actually," Ender said, "I've just had a rather long walk from the praça to your house, and Olhado set a brisk pace. I'd like to sit down."

She nodded toward a chair. Grego wriggled and twisted against Ender's grip. Ender lifted him high enough that their faces weren't too far apart. "You know, Grego, if you actually break free, you will certainly fall on your head on a concrete floor. If there were carpet, I'd give you an even chance of staying conscious. But there isn't. And frankly, I wouldn't mind hearing the sound of your head smacking against cement."

"He doesn't really understand Stark that well," said the girl.

Ender knew that Grego understood just fine. He also saw motion at the edges of the room. Olhado had come back and stood in the doorway leading to the kitchen. Quara was beside him. Ender smiled cheerfully at them, then stepped to the chair the girl had indicated. In the process, he swung Grego up into the air, letting go of his hands and feet in such a way that he spun madly for a moment, shooting out his arms and legs in panic, squealing in fear at the pain that would certainly come when he hit the floor. Ender smoothly slid onto the chair and caught the boy on his lap, instantly pinioning his arms. Grego managed to smack his heels into Ender's shins, but since the boy wasn't wearing shoes, it was an ineffective maneuver. In a moment Ender had him completely helpless again.

"It feels very good to be sitting down," Ender said. "Thank you for your hospitality. My name is Andrew Wiggin. I've met Olhado and Quara, and obviously Grego and I are good friends."

The older girl wiped her hand on her apron as if she planned to offer it to him to shake, but she did not offer it. "My name is Ela Ribeira. Ela is short for Elanora."

"A pleasure to meet you. I see you're busy preparing supper."

"Yes, very busy. I think you should come back tomorrow."

"Oh, go right ahead. I don't mind waiting."

Another boy, older than Olhado but younger than Ela, shoved his way into the room. "Didn't you hear my sister? You aren't wanted here!"

"You show me too much kindness," Ender said. "But I came to see your mother, and I'll wait here until she comes home from work."

The mention of their mother silenced them.

"I assume she's at work. If she were here, I would expect these exciting events would have flushed her out into the open."

Olhado smiled a bit at that, but the older boy darkened, and Ela got a nasty, painful expression on her face. "Why do you want to see *her?*" asked Ela.

"Actually, I want to see all of you." He smiled at the older boy. "You must be Estevão Rei Ribeira. Named for St. Stephen the Martyr, who saw Jesus sitting at the right hand of God."

"What do you know of such things, atheist!"

"As I recall, St. Paul stood by and held the coats of the men who were stoning him. Apparently he wasn't a believer at the time. In fact, I think he was regarded as the most terrible enemy of the Church. And yet he later repented, didn't he? So I suggest you think of me, not as the enemy of God, but as an apostle who has not yet been stopped on the road to Damascus." Ender smiled.

The boy stared at him, tight-lipped. "You're no St. Paul."

"On the contrary," said Ender. "I'm the apostle to the piggies."

"You'll never see *them*. Miro will never let you."

"Maybe I will," said a voice from the door. The others turned at once to watch him walk in. Miro was young—surely not yet twenty. But his face and bearing carried the weight of responsibility and suffering far beyond his years. Ender saw how all of them made space for him. It was not that they backed away from him the way they might retreat from someone they feared. Rather, they oriented themselves to him, walking in parabolas around him, as if he were the center of gravity in the room and everything else was moved by the force of his presence.

Miro walked to the center of the room and faced Ender. He looked, however, at Ender's prisoner. "Let him go," said Miro. There was ice in his voice.

Ela touched him softly on the arm. "Grego tried to stab him, Miro." But her voice also said, Be calm, it's all right, Grego's in no danger and this man is not our enemy. Ender heard all this; so, it seemed, did Miro.

"Grego," said Miro. "I told you that someday you'd take on somebody who wasn't afraid of you."

Grego, seeing an ally suddenly turn to an enemy, began to cry. "He's killing me, he's killing me."

Miro looked coldly at Ender. Ela might trust the Speaker for the Dead, but Miro didn't, not yet.

"I *am* hurting him," said Ender. He had found that the best way to earn trust was to tell the truth. "Every time he struggles to get free, it causes him quite a bit of discomfort. And he hasn't stopped struggling yet."

Ender met Miro's gaze steadily, and Miro understood his unspoken request. He did not insist on Grego's release. "I can't get you out of this one, Greguinho."

"You're going to let him do this?" asked Estevão.

Miro gestured toward Estevão and spoke apologetically to Ender. "Everyone calls him Quim." The nickname was pronounced like the word *king* in Stark. "It began because his middle name is Rei. But now it's because he thinks he rules by divine right."

"Bastard," said Quim. He stalked out of the room.

At the same time, the others settled in for conversation. Miro had decided to accept the stranger, at least temporarily; therefore they could let down their guard a little. Olhado sat down on the floor; Quara returned to her previous perch on the bed. Ela leaned back against the wall. Miro pulled up another chair and sat facing Ender.

"Why did you come to this house?" asked Miro. Ender saw from the way he asked that he, like Ela, had not told anyone that he had summoned a Speaker. So neither of them knew that the other expected him. And, in fact, they almost undoubtedly had not expected him to come so soon.

"To see your mother," Ender said.

Miro's relief was almost palpable, though he made no obvious gesture. "She's at work," he said. "She works late. She's trying to develop a strain of potato that can compete with the grass here."

"Like the amaranth?"

He grinned. "You already heard about that? No, we don't want it to be as good a competitor as *that*. But the diet here is limited, and potatoes would be a nice addition. Besides, amaranth doesn't ferment into a very good beverage. The miners and farmers have already created a mythology of vodka that makes it the queen of distilled intoxicants."

Miro's smile came to this house like sunlight through a crevice in a cave. Ender could feel the loosening of tensions. Quara wiggled her leg back and forth like an ordinary little girl. Olhado had a stupidly happy expression on his face, his eyes half-closed so that the metallic sheen was not so monstrously obvious. Ela's smile was broader than Miro's good humor should have earned. Even Grego had relaxed, had stopped straining against Ender's grip.

Then a sudden warmth on Ender's lap told him that Grego, at least, was far from surrender. Ender had trained himself not to respond reflexively to an enemy's actions until he had consciously decided to let his reflexes rule. So Grego's flood of urine did not cause him to so much as flinch. He knew what Grego had been expecting—a shout of anger, and Ender flinging him away, casting him from his lap in disgust. Then Grego would be free—it would be a triumph. Ender yielded him no victory.

Ela, however, apparently knew the expressions of Grego's face. Her eyes went wide, and then she took an angry step toward the boy. "Grego, you impossible little—"

But Ender winked at her and smiled, freezing her in place. "Grego has given me a little gift. It's the only thing he has to give me, and he made it himself, so it means all the more. I like him so much that I think I'll never let him go."

Grego snarled and struggled again, madly, to break free.

"Why are you doing this!" said Ela.

"He's expecting Grego to act like a human being," said Miro. "It needs doing, and nobody else has bothered to try."

"*I've* tried," said Ela.

Olhado spoke up from his place on the floor. "Ela's the only one here who keeps us civilized."

Quim shouted from the other room. "Don't you tell that bastard anything about our family!"

Ender nodded gravely, as if Quim had offered a brilliant intellectual proposition. Miro chuckled and Ela rolled her eyes and sat down on the bed beside Quara.

"We're not a very happy home," said Miro.

"I understand," said Ender. "With your father so recently dead."

Miro smiled sardonically. Olhado spoke up again. "With Father so recently alive, you mean."

Ela and Miro were in obvious agreement with this sentiment. But Quim shouted again. "Don't tell him anything!"

"Did he hurt you?" Ender asked quietly. He did not move, even though Grego's urine was getting cold and rank.

Ela answered. "He didn't hit us, if that's what you mean."

But for Miro, things had gone too far. "Quim's right," said Miro. "It's nobody's business but ours."

"No," said Ela. "It's his business."

"How is it his business?" asked Miro.

"Because he's here to Speak Father's death," said Ela.

"Father's death!" said Olhado. "Chupa pedras! Father only died three weeks ago!"

"I was already on my way to Speak another death," said Ender. "But someone did call for a Speaker for your father's death, and so I'll Speak for him."

"Against him," said Ela.

"For him," said Ender.

"I brought you here to tell the truth," she said bitterly, "and all the truth about Father is against him."

Silence pressed to the corners of the room, holding them all still, until Quim walked slowly through the doorway. He looked only at Ela. "You called him," he said softly. "You."

"To tell the truth!" she answered. His accusation obviously stung her; he did not have to say how she had betrayed her family and her church to bring this infidel to lay bare what had been so long concealed. "Everybody in Milagre is so kind and understanding," she said. "Our teachers overlook little things like Grego's thievery and Quara's silence. Never mind that she hasn't said a word in school, ever! Everybody pretends that we're just ordinary children— the grandchildren of Os Venerados, and so brilliant, aren't we, with a Zenador and both biologistas in the family! Such prestige. They just look the other way when Father gets himself raging drunk and comes home and beats Mother until she can't walk!"

"Shut up!" shouted Quim.

"Ela," said Miro.

"And you, Miro, Father shouting at you, saying terrible things until you run out of the house, you *run,* stumbling because you can hardly see—"

"You have no right to tell him!" said Quim.

Olhado leapt to his feet and stood in the middle of the room, turned around to look at them all with his unhuman eyes. "Why do you still want to hide it?" he asked softly.

"What's it to you?" asked Quim. "He never did anything to you. You just turned off your eyes and sat there with the headphones on, listening to batuque or Bach or something—"

"Turn off my eyes?" said Olhado. "I never turned off my eyes."

He whirled and walked to the terminal, which was in the corner of the room farthest from the front door. In a few quick movements he had the terminal on, then picked up an interface cable and jammed it in the socket in his right eye. It was only a simple computer linkup, but to Ender it brought back a hideous memory of the eye of a giant, torn open and oozing, as Ender bored deep, penetrated to the brain, and sent it toppling backward to its death. He froze up for a moment before he remembered that his memory was not real, it was of a computer game he had played in the Battle School. Three thousand years ago, but to him a mere twenty-five years, not such a great distance that the memory had lost its power. It was his memories and dreams of the giant's death that the buggers had taken out of his mind and turned into the signal they left for him; eventually it had led him to the hive queen's cocoon.

It was Jane's voice that brought him back to the present moment. She whispered from the jewel, "If it's all the same to you, while he's got that eye linked up I'm going to get a dump of everything else he's got stored away in there."

Then a scene began in the air over the terminal. It was not holographic. Instead the image was like bas-relief, as it would have appeared to a single observer. It was this very room, seen from the spot on the floor where a moment ago Olhado had been sitting— apparently it was his regular spot. In the middle of the floor stood a large man, strong and violent, flinging his arms about as he shouted abuse at Miro, who stood quietly, his head bent, regarding his father without any sign of anger. There was no sound—it was a visual image only. "Have you forgotten?" whispered Olhado. "Have you forgotten what it was like?"

In the scene on the terminal Miro finally turned and left; Mar-cão following him to the door, shouting after him. Then he turned back into the room and stood there, panting like an animal exhausted from the chase. In the picture Grego ran to his father and clung to his leg, shouting out the door, his face making it plain that he was echoing his father's cruel words to Miro. Marcão pried the child from his leg and walked with determined purpose into the back room.

"There's no sound," said Olhado. "But you can hear it, can't you?"

Ender felt Grego's body trembling on his lap.

"There it is, a blow, a crash—she's falling to the floor, can you feel it in your flesh, the way her body hits the concrete?"

"Shut up, Olhado," said Miro.

The computer-generated scene ended. "I can't believe you saved that," said Ela.

Quim was weeping, making no effort to hide it. "I killed him," he said. "I killed him I killed him I killed him."

"What are you talking about?" said Miro in exasperation. "He had a rotten *disease,* it was congenital!"

"I prayed for him to die!" screamed Quim. His face was mottled with passion, tears and mucus and spittle mingling around his lips. "I prayed to the Virgin, I prayed to Jesus, I prayed to Grandpa and Grandma, I said I'd go to hell for it if only he'd die, and they did it, and now I'll go to hell and I'm not *sorry* for it! God forgive me but I'm glad!" Sobbing, he stumbled back out of the room. A door slammed in the distance.

"Well, another certified miracle to the credit of Os Venerados," said Miro. "Sainthood is assured."

"Shut up," said Olhado.

"And he's the one who kept telling us that Christ wanted us to forgive the old fart," said Miro.

On Ender's lap, Grego now trembled so violently that Ender grew concerned. He realized that Grego was whispering a word. Ela, too, saw Grego's distress and knelt in front of the boy.

"He's crying, I've never seen him cry like this—"

"Papa, papa, papa," whispered Grego. His trembling had given way to great shudders, almost convulsive in their violence.

"Is he afraid of Father?" asked Olhado. His face showed deep concern for Grego. To Ender's relief, all their faces were full of worry. There *was* love in this family, and not just the solidarity of living under the rule of the same tyrant for all these years.

"Papa's gone now," said Miro comfortingly. "You don't have to worry now."

Ender shook his head. "Miro," he said, "didn't you watch Olhado's memory? Little boys don't judge their fathers, they love them. Grego was trying as hard as he could to be just like Marcos Ribeira. The rest of you might have been glad to see him gone, but for Grego it was the end of the world."

It had not occurred to any of them. Even now it was a sickening idea; Ender could see them recoil from it. And yet they knew it was true. Now that Ender had pointed it out, it was obvious.

"Deus nos perdoa," murmured Ela. God forgive us.

"The things we've said," whispered Miro.

Ela reached out for Grego. He refused to go to her. Instead he did exactly what Ender expected, what he had prepared for. Grego turned in Ender's relaxed grip, flung his arms around the neck of the Speaker for the Dead, and wept bitterly, hysterically.

Ender spoke gently to the others, who watched helplessly. "How could he show his grief to *you,* when he thought you hated him?"

"We never hated Grego," said Olhado.

"I should have known," said Miro. "I knew he was suffering the worst pain of any of us, but it never occurred to me . . ."

"Don't blame yourself," said Ender. "It's the kind of thing that only a stranger can see."

He heard Jane whispering in his ear. "You never cease to amaze me, Andrew, the way you turn people into plasma."

Ender couldn't answer her, and she wouldn't believe him anyway. He hadn't planned this, he had played it by ear. How could he have guessed that Olhado would have a recording of Marcão's viciousness to his family? His only real insight was with Grego, and even that was instinctive, a sense that Grego was desperately hungry for someone to have authority over him, for someone to act like a father to him. Since his own father had been cruel, Grego would believe only cruelty as a proof of love and strength. Now his tears washed Ender's neck as hotly as, a moment before, his urine had soaked Ender's thighs.

He had guessed what Grego would do, but Quara managed to take him by surprise. As the others watched Grego's weeping in silence, she got off the bed and walked directly to Ender. Her eyes were narrow and angry. "You stink!" she said firmly. Then she marched out of the room toward the back of the house.

Miro barely suppressed his laughter, and Ela smiled. Ender raised his eyebrows as if to say, You win some, you lose some.

Olhado seemed to hear his unspoken words. From his chair by the terminal, the metal-eyed boy said softly, "You win with her, too. It's the most she's said to anyone outside the family in months."

But I'm not outside the family, Ender said silently. Didn't you notice? I'm *in* the family now, whether you like it or not. Whether *I* like it or not.

After a while Grego's sobbing stopped. He was asleep. Ender carried him to his bed; Quara was already asleep on the other side of the small room. Ela helped Ender strip off Grego's urine-soaked pants and put looser underwear on him—her touch was gentle and deft, and Grego did not waken.

Back in the front room Miro eyed Ender clinically. "Well, Speaker, you have a choice. My pants will be tight on you and too short in the crotch, but Father's would fall right off."

It took Ender a moment to remember. Grego's urine had long since dried. "Don't worry about it," he said. "I can change when I get home."

"Mother won't be home for another hour. You came to see her, didn't you? We can have your pants clean by then."

"*Your* pants, then," said Ender. "I'll take my chances with the crotch."

Chapter **8**

Dona Ivanova

It means a life of constant deception. You will go out and discover something, something vital, and then when you get back to the station you'll write up a completely innocuous report, one which mentions *nothing* that we learned through cultural contamination.

You're too young to understand what torture this is. Father and I began doing this because we couldn't bear to withhold knowledge from the piggies. You will discover, as I have, that it is no less painful to withhold knowledge from your fellow scientists. When you watch them struggle with a question, knowing that you have the information that could easily resolve their dilemma; when you see them come very near the truth and then for lack of your information retreat from their correct conclusions and return to error—you would not be human if it didn't cause you great anguish.

You must remind yourselves, always: It is their law, their choice. They are the ones who built the wall between themselves and the truth, and they would only punish us if we let them know how easily and thoroughly that wall has been breached. And for every framling scientist who is longing for the truth, there are ten petty-minded descabeçados [headless ones] who despise knowledge, who never think of an original hypothesis, whose only labor is to prey on the writings of the true scientists in order to catch tiny errors or contradictions or lapses in method. These suckflies will pore over every report you make, and if you are careless even once *they will catch you.*

That means you can't even mention a piggy whose name is

derived from cultural contamination: "Cups" would tell them that we have taught them rudimentary pottery-making. "Calendar" and "Reaper" are obvious. And God himself couldn't save us if they learned Arrow's name.

—Memo from Liberdade Figueira de Medici to Ouanda Figueira Mucumbi and Miro Ribeira von Hesse, retrieved from Lusitanian files by Congressional order and introduced as evidence in the Trial *In Absentia* of the Xenologers of Lusitania on Charges of Treason and Malfeasance

Novinha lingered in the Biologista's Station even though her meaningful work was finished more than an hour ago. The cloned potato plants were all thriving in nutrient solution; now it would be a matter of making daily observations to see which of her genetic alterations would produce the hardiest plant with the most useful root.

If I have nothing to do, why don't I go home? She had no answer for the question. Her children needed her, that was certain; she did them no kindness by leaving early each morning and coming home only after the little ones were asleep. And yet even now, knowing she should go back, she sat staring at the laboratory, seeing nothing, doing nothing, being nothing.

She thought of going home, and could not imagine why she felt no joy at the prospect. After all, she reminded herself, Marcão is dead. He died three weeks ago. Not a moment too soon. He did all that I ever needed him for, and I did all that he wanted, but all our reasons expired four years before he finally rotted away. In all that time we never shared a moment of love, but I never thought of leaving him. Divorce would have been impossible, but desquite would have been enough. To stop the beatings. Even yet her hip was stiff and sometimes painful from the last time he had thrown her to the concrete floor. What lovely memorabilia you left behind, Cão, my dog of a husband.

The pain in her hip flared even as she thought of it. She nodded in satisfaction. It's no more than I deserve, and I'll be sorry when it heals.

She stood up and walked, not limping at all even though the

pain was more than enough to make her favor the hip. I'll not coddle myself, not in anything. It's no worse than I deserve.

She walked to the door, closed it behind her. The computer turned off the lights as soon as she was gone, except those needed for the various plants in forced photosynthetic phase. She loved her plants, her little beasts, with surprising intensity. Grow, she cried out to them day and night, grow and thrive. She would grieve for the ones that failed and pinch them dead only when it was plain they had no future. Now as she walked away from the station, she could still hear their subliminal music, the cries of the infinitesimal cells as they grew and split and formed themselves into ever more elaborate patterns. She was going from light into darkness, from life into death, and the emotional pain grew worse in perfect synchronicity with the inflammation of her joints.

As she approached her house from over the hill, she could see the patches of light thrown through the windows and out onto the hill below. Quara's and Grego's room dark; she would not have to bear their unbearable accusations—Quara's in silence, Grego's in sullen and vicious crimes. But there were too many other lights on, including her own room and the front room. Something unusual was going on, and she didn't like unusual things.

Olhado sat in the living room, earphones on as usual; tonight, though, he also had the interface jack attached to his eye. Apparently, he was retrieving old visual memories from the computer, or perhaps dumping out some he had been carrying with him. As so many times before, she wished she could also dump out her visual memories and wipe them clean, replace them with more pleasant ones. Pipo's corpse, that would be one she'd gladly be rid of, to be replaced by some of the golden glorious days with the three of them together in the Zenador's Station. And Libo's body wrapped in its cloth, that sweet flesh held together only by the winding fabric; she would like to have instead other memories of his body, the touch of his lips, the expressiveness of his delicate hands. But the good memories fled, buried too deep under the pain. I stole them all, those good days, and so they were taken back and replaced by what I deserved.

Olhado turned to face her, the jack emerging obscenely from his eye. She could not control her shudder, her shame. I'm sorry, she said silently. If you had had another mother, you would doubtless still have your eye. You were born to be the best, the healthiest, the wholest of my children, Lauro, but of course nothing from my womb could be left intact for long.

She said nothing of this, of course, just as Olhado said nothing to her. She turned to go back to her room and find out why the light was on.

"Mother," said Olhado.

He had taken the earphones off, and was twisting the jack out of his eye.

"Yes?"

"We have a visitor," he said. "The Speaker."

She felt herself go cold inside. Not tonight, she screamed silently. But she also knew that she would not want to see him tomorrow, either, or the next day, or ever.

"His pants are clean now, and he's in your room changing back into them. I hope you don't mind."

Ela emerged from the kitchen. "You're home," she said. "I poured some cafezinhos, one for you, too."

"I'll wait outside until he's gone," said Novinha.

Ela and Olhado looked at each other. Novinha understood at once that they regarded her as a problem to be solved; that apparently they subscribed to whatever the Speaker wanted to do here. Well, I'm a dilemma that's not going to be solved by you.

"Mother," said Olhado, "he's not what the Bishop said. He's *good.*"

Novinha answered him with her most withering sarcasm. "Since when are *you* an expert on good and evil?"

Again Ela and Olhado looked at each other. She knew what they were thinking. How can we explain to her? How can we persuade her? Well, dear children, you can't. I am unpersuadable, as Libo found out every week of his life. He never had the secret from me. It's not my fault he died.

But they had succeeded in turning her from her decision. Instead of leaving the house, she retreated into the kitchen, passing Ela in the doorway but not touching her. The tiny coffee cups were arranged in a neat circle on the table, the steaming pot in the center. She sat down and rested her forearms on the table. So the Speaker was here, and had come to her first. Where else would he go? It's my fault he's here, isn't it? He's one more person whose life I have destroyed, like my children's lives, like Marcão's, and Libo's, and Pipo's, and my own.

A strong yet surprisingly smooth masculine hand reached out over her shoulder, took up the pot, and began to pour through the tiny, delicate spout, the thin stream of hot coffee swirling into the tiny cafezinho cups.

"Posso derramar?" he asked. What a stupid question, since he was already pouring. But his voice was gentle, his Portuguese tinged with the graceful accents of Castilian. A Spaniard, then?

"Desculpa-me," she whispered. Forgive me. "Trouxe o senhor tantos quilômetros—"

"We don't measure starflight in kilometers, Dona Ivanova. We measure it in years." His words were an accusation, but his voice spoke of wistfulness, even forgiveness, even consolation. I could be seduced by that voice. That voice is a liar.

"If I could undo your voyage and return you twenty-two years, I'd do it. Calling for you was a mistake. I'm sorry." Her own voice sounded flat. Since her whole life was a lie, even this apology sounded rote.

"I don't feel the time yet," said the Speaker. Still he stood behind her, so she had not yet seen his face. "For me it was only a week ago that I left my sister. She was the only kin of mine left alive. Her daughter wasn't born yet, and now she's probably through with college, married, perhaps with children of her own. I'll never know her. But I know *your* children, Dona Ivanova."

She lifted the cafezinho and drank it down in a single swallow, though it burned her tongue and throat and made her stomach hurt. "In only a few hours you think you know them?"

"Better than you do, Dona Ivanova."

Novinha heard Ela gasp at the Speaker's audacity. And even though she thought his words might be true, it still enraged her to have a stranger say them. She turned to look at him, to snap at him, but he had moved, he was not behind her. She turned farther, finally standing up to look for him, but he wasn't in the room. Ela stood in the doorway, wide-eyed.

"Come back!" said Novinha. "You can't say that and walk out on me like that!"

But he didn't answer. Instead, she heard low laughter from the back of the house. Novinha followed the sound. She walked through the rooms to the very end of the house. Miro sat on Novinha's own bed, and the Speaker stood near the doorway, laughing with him. Miro saw his mother and the smile left his face. It caused a stab of anguish within her. She had not seen him smile in years, had forgotten how beautiful his face became, just like his father's face; and her coming had erased that smile.

"We came here to talk because Quim was so angry," Miro explained. "Ela made the bed."

"I don't think the Speaker cares whether the bed was made or not," said Novinha coldly. "Do you, Speaker?"

"Order and disorder," said the Speaker, "they each have their beauty." Still he did not turn to face her, and she was glad of that, for it meant she did not have to see his eyes as she delivered her bitter message.

"I tell you, Speaker, that you've come on a fool's errand," she said. "Hate me for it if you will, but you have no death to Speak. I was a foolish girl. In my naivete I thought that when I called, the author of the Hive Queen and the Hegemon would come. I had lost a man who was like a father to me, and I wanted consolation."

Now he turned to her. He was a youngish man, younger than her, at least, but his eyes were seductive with understanding. Perigoso, she thought. He is dangerous, he is beautiful, I could drown in his understanding.

"Dona Ivanova," he said, "how could you read the Hive Queen and the Hegemon and imagine that its author could bring *comfort?*"

It was Miro who answered—silent, slow-talking Miro, who leapt into the conversation with a vigor she had not seen in him since he was little. "I've read it," he said, "and the original Speaker for the Dead wrote the tale of the hive queen with deep compassion."

The Speaker smiled sadly. "But he wasn't writing *to* the buggers, was he? He was writing to humankind, who still celebrated the destruction of the buggers as a great victory. He wrote cruelly, to turn their pride to regret, their joy to grief. And now human beings have completely forgotten that once they hated the buggers, that once they honored and celebrated a name that is now unspeakable—"

"I can say anything," said Ivanova. "His name was Ender, and he destroyed everything he touched." Like me, she did not say.

"Oh? And what do you know of him?" His voice whipped out

like a grass-saw, ragged and cruel. "How do you know there wasn't something that he touched kindly? Someone who loved him, who was blessed by his love? *Destroyed everything he touched*—that's a lie that can't truthfully be said of any human being who ever lived."

"Is that your doctrine, Speaker? Then you don't know much." She was defiant, but still his anger frightened her. She had thought his gentleness was as imperturbable as a confessor's.

And almost immediately the anger faded from his face. "You can ease your conscience," he said. "Your call started my journey here, but others called for a Speaker while I was on the way."

"Oh?" Who else in this benighted city was familiar enough with the Hive Queen and the Hegemon to want a Speaker, and independent enough of Bishop Peregrino to dare to call for one? "If that's so, then why are you here in *my* house?"

"Because I was called to Speak the death of Marcos Maria Ribeira, your late husband."

It was an appalling thought. "Him! Who would want to think of him again, now that he's dead!"

The Speaker did not answer. Instead Miro spoke sharply from her bed. "Grego would, for one. The Speaker showed us what we should have known—that the boy is grieving for his father and thinks we all hate him—"

"Cheap psychology," she snapped. "We have therapists of our own, and they aren't worth much either."

Ela's voice came from behind her. "I called for him to Speak Father's death, Mother. I thought it would be decades before he came, but I'm glad he's here now, when he can do us some good."

"What good can he do us!"

"He already has, Mother. Grego fell asleep embracing him, and Quara spoke to him."

"Actually," said Miro, "she told him that he stinks."

"Which was probably true," said Ela, "since Greguinho peed all over him."

Miro and Ela burst into laughter at the memory, and the Speaker also smiled. This more than anything else discomposed Novinha—such good cheer had been virtually unfelt in this house since Marcão brought her here a year after Pipo's death. Against her will Novinha remembered her joy when Miro was newly born, and when Ela was little, the first few years of their lives, how Miro babbled about everything, how Ela toddled madly after him through the house, how the children played together and romped in the grass within sight of the piggies' forest just beyond the fence; it was Novinha's delight in the children that poisoned Marcão, that made him hate them both, because he knew that none of it belonged to him. By the time Quim was born, the house was thick with anger, and he never learned how to laugh freely where his parents might notice. Hearing Miro and Ela laugh together was like the abrupt opening of a thick black curtain; suddenly it was daylight again, when Novinha had forgotten there was any season of the day but night.

How dared this stranger invade her house and tear open all the curtains she had closed!

"I won't have it," she said. "You have no right to pry into my husband's life."

He raised an eyebrow. She knew Starways Code as well as anyone, and so she knew perfectly well that he not only had a right, the law protected him in the pursuit of the true story of the dead.

"Marcão was a miserable man," she persisted, "and telling the truth about him will cause nothing but pain."

"You're quite right that the truth about him will cause nothing but pain, but not because he was a miserable man," said the Speaker. "If I told nothing but what everyone already knows—that he hated his children and beat his wife and raged drunkenly from bar to bar until the constables sent him home—then I would not cause pain, would I? I'd cause a great deal of satisfaction, because then everyone would be reassured that their view of him was correct all along. He was scum, and so it was all right that they treated him like scum."

"And you think he *wasn't?*"

"No human being, when you understand his desires, is worthless. No one's life is nothing. Even the most evil of men and women, if you understand their hearts, had some generous act that redeems them, at least a little, from their sins."

"If you believe that, then you're younger than you look," said Novinha.

"Am I?" said the Speaker. "It was less than two weeks ago that I first heard your call. I studied you then, and even if *you* don't remember, Novinha, *I* remember that as a young girl you were sweet and beautiful and good. You had been lonely before, but Pipo and Libo both knew you and found you worthy of love."

"Pipo was dead."

"But he loved you."

"You don't know anything, Speaker! You were twenty-two light-years away! Besides, it wasn't *me* I was calling worthless, it was Marcão!"

"But you don't believe that, Novinha. Because you know the one act of kindness and generosity that redeems that poor man's life."

Novinha did not understand her own terror, but she had to silence him before he named it, even though she had no idea what kindness of Cão's he thought he had discovered. "How dare you call me Novinha!" she shouted. "No one has called me that in four years!"

In answer, he raised his hand and brushed his fingers across the back of her cheek. It was a timid gesture, almost an adolescent one; it reminded her of Libo, and it was more than she could bear. She took his hand, hurled it away, then shoved past him into the room. "Get out!" she shouted at Miro. Her son got up quickly and backed to the door. She could see from his face that after all Miro had seen in this house, she still had managed to surprise him with her rage.

"You'll have nothing from me!" she shouted at the Speaker.

"I didn't come to take anything from you," he said quietly.

"I don't want anything you have to give, either! You're worthless to me, do you hear that? You're the one who's worthless! Lixo, ruina, estrago—vai fora d'aqui, não tens direito estar em minha casa!" You have no right to be in my house.

"Não eres estrago," he whispered, "eres solo fecundo, e vou plantar jardim aí." Then, before she could answer, he closed the door and was gone.

In truth she had no answer to give him, his words were so outrageous. She had called him estrago, but he answered as if she had called *herself* a desolation. And she had spoken to him derisively, using the insultingly familiar *tu* for "you" instead of *o Senhor* or even the formal *você*. It was the way one spoke to a child or a dog. And yet when he answered in the same voice, with the same familiarity, it was entirely different. "Thou art fertile ground, and I will plant a garden in thee." It was the sort of thing a poet says to his mistress, or even a husband to his wife, and the *tu* was intimate, not arrogant. How dare he, she whispered to herself, touching the cheek that he had touched. He is far crueler than I ever imagined a Speaker might be. Bishop Peregrino was right. He is dangerous, the infidel, the anti-Christ, he walks brazenly into places in my heart that I had kept as holy ground, where no one else was ever permitted to stand. He treads on the few small shoots that cling to life in that stony soil, how dare he, I wish I had died before seeing him, he will surely undo me before he's through.

She was vaguely aware of someone crying. Quara. Of course the shouting had wakened her; she never slept soundly. Novinha almost opened the door and went out to comfort her, but then she heard the crying stop, and a soft male voice singing to her. The song was in another language. German, it sounded to Novinha, or Nordic; she did not understand it, whatever it was. But she knew who sang it, and knew that Quara was comforted.

Novinha had not felt such fear since she first realized that Miro was determined to become a Zenador and follow in the footsteps of the two men that the piggies had murdered. This man in unknotting the nets of my family, and stringing us together whole again; but in the process he will find my secrets. If he finds out how Pipo died, and Speaks the truth, then Miro will learn that same secret, and it will kill him. I will make no more sacrifices to the piggies; they are too cruel a god for me to worship anymore.

Still later, as she lay in bed behind her closed door, trying to go to sleep, she heard more laughter from the front of the house, and this time she could hear Quim and Olhado both laughing along with Miro and Ela. She imagined she could see them, the room bright with mirth. But as sleep took her, and the imagination became a dream, it was not the Speaker who sat among her children, teaching them to laugh; it was Libo, alive again, and known to everyone as her true husband, the man she had married in her heart even though she refused to marry him in the Church. Even in her sleep it was more joy than she could bear, and tears soaked the sheet of her bed.

Chapter 9

Congenital Defect

CIDA: The Descolada body isn't bacterial. It seems to enter the cells of the body and take up permanent residence, just like mitochondria, reproducing when the cell reproduces. The fact that it spread to a new species within only a few years of our arrival here suggests that it is wildly adaptable. It must surely have spread through the entire biosphere of Lusitania long ago, so that it may now be endemic here, a permanent infection.

GUSTO: If it's permanent and everywhere, it isn't an infection, Cida, it's part of normal life.

CIDA: But it isn't necessarily inborn—it has the ability to spread. But yes, if it's endemic then all the indigenous species must have found ways to fight it off—

GUSTO: Or adapt to it and include it in their normal life cycle. Maybe they NEED it.

CIDA: They NEED something that takes apart their genetic molecules and puts them back together at random?

GUSTO: Maybe that's why there are so few different species in Lusitania—the Descolada may be fairly recent—only half a million years old—and most species couldn't adapt.

CIDA: I wish we weren't dying, Gusto. The next xenobiologist will probably work with standard genetic adaptations and won't follow this up.

GUSTO: That's the only reason you can think of for regretting our death?

—Vladimir Tiago Gussman and Ekaterina Maria Aparecida do Norte von Hesse-Gussman, unpublished dialogue

embedded in working notes, two days before their
deaths; first quoted in "Lost Threads of Understanding," *Meta-Science, the Journal of Methodology, 2001:
12:12:144-45*

Ender did not get home from the Ribeira house until late that
night, and he spent more than an hour trying to make sense of all
that happened, especially after Novinha came home. Despite this,
Ender awoke early the next morning, his thoughts already full of
questions he had to answer. It was always this way when he was
preparing to Speak a death; he could hardly rest from trying to piece
together the story of the dead man as he saw himself, the life the
dead woman meant to live, however badly it had turned out. This
time, though, there was an added anxiety. He cared more for the
living this time than he ever had before.

"Of course you're more involved," said Jane, after he tried to
explain his confusion to her. "You fell in love with Novinha before
you left Trondheim."

"Maybe I loved the young girl, but this woman is nasty and
selfish. Look what she let happen to her children."

"This is the Speaker for the Dead? Judging someone by appear-
ances?"

"Maybe I've fallen in love with Grego."

"You've always been a sucker for people who pee on you."

"And Quara. All of them—even Miro, I *like* the boy."

"And they love you, Ender."

He laughed. "People always think they love me, until I Speak.
Novinha's more perceptive than most—she already hates me *before* I
tell the truth."

"You're as blind about yourself as anyone else, Speaker," said
Jane. "Promise me that when you die, you'll let me Speak your
death. Have I got things to say."

"Keep them to yourself," said Ender wearily. "You're even
worse at this business than I am."

He began his list of questions to be resolved.

1. Why did Novinha marry Marcão in the first place?
2. Why did Marcão hate his children?
3. Why does Novinha hate herself?
4. Why did Miro call me to Speak Libo's death?

5. Why did Ela call me to Speak her father's death?
6. Why did Novinha change her mind about my Speaking
Pipo's death?
7. What was the immediate cause of Marcão's death?

He stopped with the seventh question. It would be easy to answer it; a merely clinical matter. So that was where he would begin.

The physician who autopsied Marcão was called Navio, which meant "ship."

"Not for my size," he said, laughing. "Or because I'm much of a swimmer. My full name is Enrique o Navigador Caronada. You can bet I'm glad they took my nickname from 'shipmaster' rather than from 'little cannon.' Too many obscene possibilities in that one."

Ender was not deceived by his joviality. Navio was a good Catholic and he obeyed his bishop as well as anyone. He was determined to keep Ender from learning anything, though he'd not be uncheerful about it.

"There are two ways I can get the answers to my questions," Ender said quietly. "I can ask you, and you can tell me truthfully. Or I can submit a petition to the Starways Congress for your records to be opened to me. The ansible charges are very high, and since the petition is a routine one, and your resistance to it is contrary to law, the cost will be deducted from your colony's already straitened funds, along with a double-the-cost penalty and a reprimand for you."

Navio's smile gradually disappeared as Ender spoke. He answered coldly. "Of course I'll answer your questions," he said.

"There's no 'of course' about it," said Ender. "Your bishop counseled the people of Milagre to carry out an unprovoked and unjustified boycott of a legally called-for minister. You would do everyone a favor if you would inform them that if this cheerful noncooperation continues, I will petition for my status to be changed from minister to inquisitor. I assure you that I have a very good reputation with the Starways Congress, and my petition will be successful."

Navio knew exactly what that meant. As an inquisitor, Ender would have congressional authority to revoke the colony's Catholic license on the grounds of religious persecution. It would cause a terrible upheaval among the Lusitanians, not least because the Bishop would be summarily dismissed from his position and sent to the Vatican for discipline.

"Why would you do such a thing when you know we don't want you here?" said Navio.

"Someone wanted me here or I wouldn't have come," said Ender. "You may not like the law when it annoys you, but it protects many a Catholic on worlds where another creed is licensed."

Navio drummed his fingers on his desk. "What are your questions, Speaker," he said. "Let's get this done."

"It's simple enough, to start with, at least. What was the proximate cause of the death of Marcos Maria Ribeira?"

"Marcão!" said Navio. "You couldn't possibly have been summoned to Speak *his* death, he only passed away a few weeks ago—"

"I have been asked to Speak several deaths, Dom Navio, and I choose to begin with Marcão's."

Navio grimaced. "What if I ask for proof of your authority?"

Jane whispered in Ender's ear. "Let's dazzle the dear boy." Immediately, Navio's terminal came alive with official documents, while one of Jane's most authoritative voices declared, "Andrew Wiggin, Speaker for the Dead, has accepted the call for an explanation of the life and death of Marcos Maria Ribeira, of the city of Milagre, Lusitania Colony."

It was not the document that impressed Navio, however. It was the fact that he had not actually made the request, or even logged on to his terminal. Navio knew at once that the computer had been activated through the jewel in the Speaker's ear, but it meant that a very high-level logic routine was shadowing the Speaker and enforcing compliance with his requests. No one on Lusitania, not even Bosquinha herself, had ever had authority to do *that*. Whatever this Speaker was, Navio concluded, he's a bigger fish than even Bishop Peregrino can hope to fry.

"All right," Navio said, forcing a laugh. Now, apparently, he remembered how to be jovial again. "I meant to help you anyway— the Bishop's paranoia doesn't afflict everyone in Milagre, you know."

Ender smiled back at him, taking his hypocrisy at face value.

"Marcos Ribeira died of a congenital defect." He rattled off a long pseudo-Latin name. "You've never heard of it because it's quite rare, and is passed on only through the genes. Beginning at the onset of puberty, in most cases, it involves the gradual replacement of exocrine and endocrine glandular tissues with lipidous cells. What that means is that bit by bit over the years, the adrenal glands, the pituitary, the liver, the testes, the thyroid, and so on, are all replaced by large agglomerations of fat cells."

"Always fatal? Irreversible?"

"Oh, yes. Actually, Marcão survived ten years longer than usual. His case was remarkable in several ways. In every other recorded case—and admittedly there aren't that many—the disease attacks the testicles first, rendering the victim sterile and, in most cases, impotent. With six healthy children, it's obvious that Marcos Ribeira's testes were the last of his glands to be affected. Once they were attacked, however, progress must have been unusually fast— the testes were completely replaced with fat cells, even though much of his liver and thyroid were still functioning."

"What killed him in the end?"

"The pituitary and the adrenals weren't functioning. He was a walking dead man. He just fell down in one of the bars, in the middle of some ribald song, as I heard."

As always, Ender's mind automatically found seeming contradictions. "How does a hereditary disease get passed on if it makes its victims sterile?"

"It's usually passed through collateral lines. One child will die of it; his brothers and sisters won't manifest the disease at all, but they'll pass on the tendency to *their* children. Naturally, though, we were afraid that Marcão, having children, would pass on the defective gene to all of them."

"You tested them?"

"Not a one had any of the genetic deformations. You can bet that Dona Ivanova was looking over my shoulder the whole time. We zeroed in immediately on the problem genes and cleared each of the children, bim bim bim, just like that."

"None of them had it? Not even a recessive tendency?"

"Graças a Deus," said the doctor. "Who would ever have married them if they had had the poisoned genes? As it was, I can't understand how Marcão's own genetic defect went undiscovered."

"Are genetic scans routine here?"

"Oh, no, not at all. But we had a great plague some thirty years ago. Dona Ivanova's own parents, the Venerado Gusto and the

Venerada Cida, they conducted a detailed genetic scan of every man, woman, and child in the colony. It's how they found the cure. And their computer comparisons would definitely have turned up this particular defect—that's how I found out what it was when Marcão died. I'd never heard of the disease, but the computer had it on file."

"And Os Venerados didn't find it?"

"Apparently not, or they would surely have told Marcos. And even if they hadn't told him, Ivanova herself should have found it."

"Maybe she did," said Ender.

Navio laughed aloud. "Impossible. No woman in her right mind would deliberately bear the children of a man with a genetic defect like *that*. Marcão was surely in constant agony for many years. You don't wish that on your own children. No, Ivanova may be eccentric, but she's not insane."

Jane was quite amused. When Ender got home, she made her image appear above his terminal just so she could laugh uproariously.

"He can't help it," said Ender. "In a devout Catholic colony like this, dealing with the Biologista, one of the most respected people here, of course he doesn't think to question his basic premises."

"Don't apologize for him," said Jane. "I don't expect wetware to work as logically as software. But you can't ask me not to be amused."

"In a way it's rather sweet of him," said Ender. "He'd rather believe that Marcão's disease was different from every other recorded case. He'd rather believe that somehow Ivanova's parents didn't notice that Marcos had the disease, and so she married him in ignorance, even though Ockham's razor decrees that we believe the simplest explanation: Marcão's decay progressed like every other, testes first, and all of Novinha's children were sired by someone else. No wonder Marcão was bitter and angry. Every one of her six children reminded him that his wife was sleeping with another man. It was probably part of their bargain in the beginning that she would not be faithful to him. But *six* children is rather rubbing his nose in it."

"The delicious contradictions of religious life," said Jane. "She deliberately set out to commit adultery—but she would never dream of using a contraceptive."

"Have you scanned the children's genetic pattern to find the most likely father?"

"You mean you haven't guessed?"

"I've guessed, but I want to make sure the clinical evidence doesn't disprove the obvious answer."

"It was Libo, of course. What a dog! He sired six children on Novinha, and four more on his own wife."

"What I don't understand," said Ender, "is why Novinha didn't marry Libo in the first place. It makes no sense at all for her to have married a man she obviously despised, whose disease she certainly knew about, and then to go ahead and bear children to the man she must have loved from the beginning."

"Twisted and perverse are the ways of the human mind," Jane intoned. "Pinocchio was such a dolt to try to become a real boy. He was much better off with a wooden head."

Miro carefully picked his way through the forest. He recognized trees now and then, or thought he did—no human could ever have the piggies' knack for naming every single tree in the woods. But then, humans didn't worship the trees as totems of their ancestors, either.

Miro had deliberately chosen a longer way to reach the piggies' log house. Ever since Libo accepted Miro as a second apprentice, to work with him alongside Libo's daughter, Ouanda, he had taught them that they must never form a path leading from Milagre to the piggies' home. Someday, Libo warned them, there may be trouble between human and piggy; we will make no path to guide a pogrom to its destination. So today Miro walked the far side of the creek, along the top of the high bank.

Sure enough, a piggy soon appeared in the near distance, watching him. That was how Libo reasoned out, years ago, that the females must live somewhere in that direction; the males always kept a watch on the Zenadors when they went too near. And, as Libo had insisted, Miro made no effort to move any farther in the forbidden direction. His curiosity dampened whenever he remembered what Libo's body looked like when he and Ouanda found it. Libo had not been quite dead yet; his eyes were open and moving. He only died when both Miro and Ouanda knelt at either side of him, each holding a blood-covered hand. Ah, Libo, your blood still pumped when your heart lay naked in your open chest. If only you could have spoken to us, one word to tell us why they killed you.

The bank became low again, and Miro crossed the brook by running lightly on the moss-covered stones. In a few more minutes he was there, coming into the small clearing from the east.

Ouanda was already there, teaching them how to churn the cream of cabra milk to make a sort of butter. She had been experimenting with the process for the past several weeks before she got it right. It would have been easier if she could have had some help from Mother, or even Ela, since they knew so much more about the chemical properties of cabra milk, but cooperating with a Biologista was out of the question. Os Venerados had discovered thirty years ago that cabra milk was nutritionally useless to humans. Therefore any investigation of how to process it for storage could only be for the piggies' benefit. Miro and Ouanda could not risk anything that might let it be known they were breaking the law and actively intervening in the piggies' way of life.

The younger piggies took to butter-churning with delight—they had made a dance out of kneading the cabra bladders and were singing now, a nonsensical song that mixed Stark, Portuguese, and two of the piggies' own languages into a hopeless but hilarious muddle. Miro tried to sort out the languages. He recognized Males' Language, of course, and also a few fragments of Fathers' Language, the language they used to speak to their totem trees; Miro recognized it only by its sound; even Libo hadn't been able to translate a single word. It all sounded like *m*s and *b*s and *g*s, with no detectable difference among the vowels.

The piggy who had been shadowing Miro in the woods now emerged and greeted the others with a loud hooting sound. The dancing went on, but the song stopped immediately. Mandachuva detached himself from the group around Ouanda and came to meet Miro at the clearing's edge.

"Welcome, I-Look-Upon-You-With-Desire." That was, of course, an extravagantly precise translation of Miro's name into Stark. Mandachuva loved translating names back and forth between Portuguese and Stark, even though Miro and Ouanda had both explained that their names didn't really *mean* anything at all, and it was only coincidence if they sounded like words. But Mandachuva enjoyed his language games, as so many piggies did, and so Miro answered to I-Look-Upon-You-With-Desire, just as Ouanda patiently answered to Vaga, which was Portuguese for "wander," the Stark word that most sounded like "Ouanda."

Mandachuva was a puzzling case. He was the oldest of the piggies. Pipo had known him, and wrote of him as though he were the most prestigious of the piggies. Libo, too, seemed to think of him as a leader. Wasn't his name a slangy Portuguese term for "boss"? Yet to Miro and Ouanda, it seemed as though Mandachuva was the *least* powerful and prestigious of the piggies. No one seemed to consult him on anything; he was the one piggy who always had free time to converse with the Zenadors, because he was almost never engaged in an important task.

Still, he was the piggy who gave the most information to the Zenadors. Miro couldn't begin to guess whether he had lost his prestige because of his information-sharing, or shared information with the humans to make up for his low prestige among the piggies. It didn't even matter. The fact was that Miro *liked* Mandachuva. He thought of the old piggy as his friend.

"Has the woman forced you to eat that foul-smelling paste?" asked Miro.

"Pure garbage, she says. Even the baby cabras cry when they have to suck a teat." Mandachuva giggled.

"If you leave that as a gift for the ladyfolk, they'll never speak to you again."

"Still, we must, we must," said Mandachuva, sighing. "They have to see everything, the prying macios!"

Ah, yes, the bafflement of the females. Sometimes the piggies spoke of them with sincere, elaborate respect, almost awe, as if they were gods. Then a piggy would say something as crude as to call them "macios," the worms that slithered on the bark of trees. The Zenadors couldn't even ask about them—the piggies would never answer questions about the females. There had been a time—a long time—when the piggies didn't even mention the existence of females at all. Libo always hinted darkly that the change had something to do with Pipo's death. Before he died, the mention of females was tabu, except with reverence at rare moments of great holiness; afterward, the piggies also showed this wistful, melancholy way of joking about "the wives." But the Zenadors could never get an answer to a question about the females. The piggies made it plain that the females were none of their business.

A whistle came from the group around Ouanda. Mandachuva immediately began pulling Miro toward the group. "Arrow wants to talk to you."

Miro came and sat beside Ouanda. She did not look at him—they had learned long ago that it made the piggies very uncomfortable when they had to watch male and female humans in direct conversation, or even having eye contact with each other. They would talk with Ouanda alone, but whenever Miro was present they would not speak to her or endure it if she spoke to them. Sometimes it drove Miro crazy that she couldn't so much as wink at him in front of the piggies. He could feel her body as if she were giving off heat like a small star.

"My friend," said Arrow. "I have a great gift to ask of you."

Miro could hear Ouanda tensing slightly beside him. The piggies did not often ask for anything, and it always caused difficulty when they did.

"Will you hear me?"

Miro nodded slowly. "But remember that among humans I am nothing, with no power." Libo had discovered that the piggies were not at all insulted to think that the humans sent powerless delegates among them, while the image of impotence helped them explain the strict limitations on what the Zenadors could do.

"This is not a request that comes from us, in our silly and stupid conversations around the night fire."

"I only wish I could hear the wisdom that you call silliness," said Miro, as he always did.

"It was Rooter, speaking out of his tree, who said this."

Miro sighed silently. He liked dealing with piggy religion as little as he liked his own people's Catholicism. In both cases he had to pretend to take the most outrageous beliefs seriously. Whenever anything particularly daring or importunate was said, the piggies always ascribed it to one ancestor or another, whose spirit dwelt in one of the ubiquitous trees. It was only in the last few years, beginning not long before Libo's death, that they started singling out Rooter as the source of most of the troublesome ideas. It was ironic that a piggy they had executed as a rebel was now treated with such respect in their ancestor-worship.

Still, Miro responded as Libo had always responded. "We have nothing but honor and affection for Rooter, if you honor him."

"We must have metal."

Miro closed his eyes. So much for the Zenadors' long-standing policy of never using metal tools in front of the piggies. Obviously, the piggies had observers of their own, watching humans at work from some vantage point near the fence. "What do you need metal for?" he asked quietly.

"When the shuttle came down with the Speaker for the Dead, it gave off a terrible heat, hotter than any fire we can make. And yet the shuttle didn't burn, and it didn't melt."

"That wasn't the metal, it was a heat-absorbent plastic shield."

"Perhaps that helps, but metal is in the heart of that machine. In all your machines, wherever you use fire and heat to make things move, there is metal. We will never be able to make fires like yours until we have metal of our own."

"I can't," said Miro.

"Do you tell us that we are condemned always to be varelse, and never ramen?"

I wish, Ouanda, that you had not explained Demosthenes' Hierarchy of Exclusion to them. "You are not condemned to anything. What we have given you so far, we have made out of things that grow in your natural world, like cabras. Even that, if we were discovered, would cause us to be exiled from this world, forbidden ever to see you again."

"The metal you humans use also comes out of our natural world. We've seen your miners digging it out of the ground far to the south of here."

Miro stored that bit of information for future reference. There was no vantage point outside the fence where the mines would be visible. Therefore the piggies must be crossing the fence somehow and observing humans from within the enclave. "It comes out of the ground, but only in certain places, which I don't know how to find. And even when they dig it up, it's mixed with other kinds of rock. They have to purify it and transform it in very difficult processes. Every speck of metal dug out of the ground is accounted for. If we gave you so much as a single tool—a screwdriver or a masonry saw —it would be missed, it would be searched for. No one searches for cabra milk."

Arrow looked at him steadily for some time; Miro met his gaze. "We will think about this," Arrow said. He reached out his hand toward Calendar, who put three arrows in his hand. "Look. Are these good?"

They were as perfect as Arrow's fletchery usually was, well-feathered and true. The innovation was in the tip. It was not made of obsidian.

"Cabra bone," said Miro.

"We use the cabra to kill the cabra." He handed the arrows back to Calendar. Then he got up and walked away.

Calendar held the slender wooden arrows out in front of him and sang something to them in Fathers' Language. Miro recognized the song, though he did not understand the words. Mandachuva had once explained to him that it was a prayer, asking the dead tree to forgive them for using tools that were not made of wood. Otherwise, he said, the trees would think the Little Ones hated them. Religion. Miro sighed.

Calendar carried the arrows away. Then the young piggy named Human took his place, squatting on the ground in front of Miro. He was carrying a leaf-wrapped bundle, which he laid on the dirt and opened carefully.

It was the printout of the Hive Queen and the Hegemon that Miro had given them four years ago. It had been part of a minor quarrel between Miro and Ouanda. Ouanda began it, in a conversation with the piggies about religion. It was not really her fault. It began with Mandachuva asking her, "How can you humans live without trees?" She understood the question, of course—he was not speaking of woody plants, but of gods. "We have a God, too—a man who died and yet still lived," she explained. Just one? Then where does he live now? "No one knows." Then what good is he? How can you talk to him? "He dwells in our hearts."

They were baffled by this; Libo would later laugh and say, "You see? To them our sophisticated theology sounds like superstition. Dwells in our hearts indeed! What kind of religion is that, compared to one with gods you can see and feel—"

"And climb and pick macios from, not to mention the fact that they cut some of them down to make their log house," said Ouanda.

"Cut? *Cut* them down? Without stone or metal tools? No,

Ouanda, they *pray* them down." But Ouanda was not amused by jokes about religion.

At the piggies' request Ouanda later brought them a printout of the Gospel of St. John from the simplified Stark paraphrase of the Douai Bible. But Miro had insisted on giving them, along with it, a printout of the Hive Queen and the Hegemon. "St. John says nothing about beings who live on other worlds," Miro pointed out. "But the Speaker for the Dead explains buggers to humans—and humans to buggers." Ouanda had been outraged at his blasphemy. But not a year later they found the piggies lighting fires using pages of St. John as kindling, while the Hive Queen and the Hegemon was tenderly wrapped in leaves. It caused Ouanda a great deal of grief for a while, and Miro learned that it was wiser not to goad her about it.

Now Human opened the printout to the last page. Miro noticed that from the moment he opened the book, all the piggies quietly gathered around. The butter-churning dance ended. Human touched the last words of the printout. "The Speaker for the Dead," he murmured.

"Yes, I met him last night."

"He is the true Speaker. Rooter says so." Miro had warned them that there were many Speakers, and the writer of the Hive Queen and the Hegemon was surely dead. Apparently they still couldn't get rid of the hope that the one who had come here was the *real* one, who had written the holy book.

"I believe he's a *good* Speaker," said Miro. "He was kind to my family, and I think he might be trusted."

"When will he come and Speak to us?"

"I didn't ask him yet. It's not something that I can say right out. It will take time."

Human tipped his head back and howled.

Is this my death? thought Miro.

No. The others touched Human gently and then helped him wrap the printout again and carry it away. Miro stood up to leave. None of the piggies watched him go. Without being ostentatious about it, they were all busy doing something. He might as well have been invisible.

Ouanda caught up with him just within the forest's edge, where the underbrush made them invisible to any possible observers from Milagre—though no one ever bothered to look toward the forest.

"Miro," she called softly. He turned just in time to take her in his arms; she had such momentum that he had to stagger backward to keep from falling down. "Are you trying to kill me?" he asked, or tried to—she kept kissing him, which made it difficult to speak in complete sentences. Finally he gave up on speech and kissed her back, once, long and deep. Then she abruptly pulled away.

"You're getting libidinous," she said.

"It happens whenever women attack me and kiss me in the forest."

"Cool your shorts, Miro, it's still a long way off." She took him by the belt, pulled him close, kissed him again. "Two more years until we can marry without your mother's consent."

Miro did not even try to argue. He did not care much about the priestly proscription of fornication, but he did understand how vital it was in a fragile community like Milagre for marriage customs to be strictly adhered to. Large and stable communities could absorb a reasonable amount of unsanctioned coupling; Milagre was far too small. What Ouanda did from faith, Miro did from rational thought —despite a thousand opportunities, they were as celibate as monks. Though if Miro thought for one moment that they would ever have to live the same vows of chastity in marriage that were required in the Filhos' monastery, Ouanda's virginity would be in grave and immediate danger.

"This Speaker," said Ouanda. "You know how I feel about bringing him out here."

"That's your Catholicism speaking, not rational inquiry." He tried to kiss her, but she lowered her face at the last moment and he got a mouthful of nose. He kissed it passionately until she laughed and pushed him away.

"You are messy and offensive, Miro." She wiped her nose on her sleeve. "We already shot the scientific method all to hell when we started helping them raise their standard of living. We have ten or twenty years before the satellites start showing obvious results. By then maybe we'll have been able to make a permanent difference. But we've got no chance if we let a stranger in on the project. He'll tell somebody."

"Maybe he will and maybe he won't. I was a stranger once, you know."

"Strange, but never a stranger."

"You had to see him last night, Ouanda. With Grego first, and then when Quara woke up crying—"

"Desperate, lonely children—what does that prove?"

"And Ela. Laughing. And Olhado, actually taking part in the family."

"Quim?"

"At least he stopped yelling for the infidel to go home."

"I'm glad for your family, Miro. I hope he can heal them permanently, I really do—I can see the difference in you, too, you're more hopeful than I've seen you in a long time. But don't bring him out here."

Miro chewed on the side of his cheek for a moment, then walked away. Ouanda ran after him, caught him by the arm. They were in the open, but Rooter's tree was between them and the gate. "Don't leave me like that!" she said fiercely. "Don't just walk away from me!"

"I know you're right," Miro said. "But I can't help how I feel. When he was in our house, it was like—it was as if Libo had come there."

"Father hated your mother, Miro—he would never have gone there."

"But if he had. In our house this Speaker was the way Libo always was in the Station. Do you see?"

"Do *you?* He comes in and acts the way your father should have but never did, and every single one of you rolls over belly-up like a puppy dog."

The contempt on her face was infuriating. Miro wanted to hit her. Instead he walked over and slapped his hand against Rooter's tree. In only a quarter of a century it had grown to almost eighty centimeters in diameter, and the bark was rough and painful on his hand.

She came up behind him. "I'm sorry, Miro, I didn't mean—"

"You meant it, but it was stupid and selfish—"

"Yes, it was, I—"

"Just because my father was scum doesn't mean I go belly-up for the first nice man who pats my head—"

Her hand stroked his hair, his shoulder, his waist. "I know, I know, I know—"

"Because I know what a good man is—not just a father, a *good man*. I knew Libo, didn't I? And when I tell you that this Speaker, this Andrew Wiggin is like Libo, then you listen to me and don't dismiss it like the whimpering of a *cão!*"

"I do listen. I want to meet him, Miro."

Miro surprised himself. He was crying. It was all part of what this Speaker could do, even when he wasn't present. He had loosened all the tight places in Miro's heart, and now Miro couldn't stop anything from coming out.

"You're right, too," said Miro softly, his voice distorted with emotion. "I saw him come in with his healing touch and I thought, If only he had been my father." He turned to face Ouanda, not caring if she saw his eyes red and his face streaked with tears. "Just the way I used to say that every day when I went home from the Zenador's Station. If only Libo were my father, if only I were his son."

She smiled and held him; her hair took the tears from his face. "Ah, Miro, I'm glad he wasn't your father. Because then I'd be your sister, and I could never hope to have you for myself."

Chapter 10

Children of the Mind

Rule 1: All Children of the Mind of Christ must be married, or they may not be in the order; but they must be chaste.

Question 1: Why is marriage necessary for anyone?

Fools say, Why should we marry? Love is the only bond my lover and I need. To them I say, Marriage is not a covenant between a man and a woman; even the beasts cleave together and produce their young. Marriage is a covenant between a man and woman on the one side and their community on the other. To marry according to the law of the community is to become a full citizen; to refuse marriage is to be a stranger, a child, an outlaw, a slave, or a traitor. The one constant in every society of humankind is that only those who obey the laws, tabus, and customs of marriage are true adults.

Question 2: Why then is celibacy ordained for priests and nuns?

To separate them from the community. The priests and nuns are servants, not citizens. They minister to the Church, but they are not the Church. Mother Church is the bride, and Christ is the bridegroom; the priests and nuns are merely guests at the wedding, for they have rejected citizenship in the community of Christ in order to serve it.

Question 3: Why then do the Children of the Mind of Christ marry? Do we not also serve the Church?

We do not serve the Church, except as all women and men serve it through their marriages. The difference is that where they pass on their genes to the next generation, we pass on our knowledge; their legacy is found in the genetic molecules of generations to come, while we live on in their minds. Memories are the offspring of our marriages, and they are neither more or less worthy than the flesh-and-blood children conceived in sacramental love.

—San Angelo, *The Rule and Catechism of the Order of the Children of the Mind of Christ,* 1511:11:11:1

The Dean of the Cathedral carried the silence of dark chapels and massive, soaring walls wherever he went: When he entered the classroom, a heavy peace fell upon the students, and even their breathing was guarded as he noiselessly drifted to the front of the room.

"Dom Cristão," murmured the Dean. "The Bishop has need of consultation with you."

The students, most of them in their teens, were not so young that they didn't know of the strained relations between the hierarchy of the Church and the rather freewheeling monastics who ran most of the Catholic schools in the Hundred Worlds. Dom Cristão, besides being an excellent teacher of history, geology, archaeology, and anthropology, was also abbot of the monastery of the Filhos da Mente de Cristo—the Children of the Mind of Christ. His position made him the Bishop's primary rival for spiritual supremacy in Lusitania. In some ways he could even be considered the Bishop's superior; on most worlds there was only one abbot of the Filhos for each archbishop, while for each bishop there was a principal of a school system.

But Dom Cristão, like all Filhos, made it a point to be completely deferent to the Church hierarchy. At the Bishop's summons he immediately switched off the lectern and dismissed the class without so much as completing the point under discussion. The students were not surprised; they knew he would do the same if any ordained priest had interrupted his class. It was, of course, immensely flattering to the priesthood to see how important they were in the eyes of the Filhos; but it also made it plain to them that any time they visited the school during teaching hours, classwork would be completely disrupted wherever they went. As a result, the priests rarely visited the school, and the Filhos, through extreme deference, maintained almost complete independence.

Dom Cristão had a pretty good idea why the Bishop had summoned him. Dr. Navio was an indiscreet man, and rumors had been flying all morning about some dreadful threat by the Speaker for the Dead. It was hard for Dom Cristão to bear the groundless fears of the hierarchy whenever they were confronted with infidels and heretics. The Bishop would be in a fury, which meant that he would demand some action from somebody, even though the best course, as usual, was inaction, patience, cooperation. Besides, word had spread that this particular Speaker claimed to be the very one who Spoke the death of San Angelo. If that was the case, he was probably not an enemy at all, but a friend of the Church. Or at least a friend of the Filhos, which in Dom Cristão's mind amounted to the same thing.

As he followed the silent Dean among the buildings of the faculdade and through the garden of the Cathedral, he cleared his heart of the anger and annoyance he felt. Over and over he repeated his monastic name: Amai a Tudomundo Para Que Deus Vos Ame. Ye Must Love Everyone So That God Will Love You. He had chosen the name carefully when he and his fiancée joined the order, for he knew that his greatest weakness was anger and impatience with stupidity. Like all Filhos, he named himself with the invocation against his most potent sin. It was one of the ways they made themselves spiritually naked before the world. We will not clothe ourselves in hypocrisy, taught San Angelo. Christ will clothe us in virtue like the lilies of the field, but we will make no effort to appear virtuous ourselves. Dom Cristão felt his virtue wearing thin in places today; the cold wind of impatience might freeze him to the bone. So he silently chanted his name, thinking: Bishop Peregrino is a damned fool, but Amai a Tudomundo Para Que Deus Vos Ame.

"Brother Amai," said Bishop Peregrino. He never used the honorific *Dom Cristão,* even though cardinals had been known to give that much courtesy. "It was good of you to come."

Navio was already sitting in the softest chair, but Dom Cristão did not begrudge him that. Indolence had made Navio fat, and his fat now made him indolent; it was such a circular disease, feeding always on itself, and Dom Cristão was grateful not to be so afflicted. He chose for himself a tall stool with no back at all. It would keep his body from relaxing, and that would help his mind to stay alert.

Navio almost at once launched into an account of his painful meeting with the Speaker for the Dead, complete with elaborate explanations of what the Speaker had threatened to do if noncooperation continued. "An inquisitor, if you can imagine that! An infidel daring to supplant the authority of Mother Church!" Oh, how the lay member gets the crusading spirit when Mother Church is threatened—but ask him to go to mass once a week, and the crusading spirit curls up and goes to sleep.

Navio's words did have some effect: Bishop Peregrino grew more and more angry, his face getting a pinkish tinge under the deep brown of his skin. When Navio's recitation finally ended, Peregrino turned to Dom Cristão, his face a mask of fury, and said, "Now what do you say, Brother Amai!"

I would say, if I were less discreet, that you were a fool to interfere with this Speaker when you knew the law was on his side and when he had done nothing to harm us. Now he is provoked, and is far more dangerous than he would ever have been if you had simply ignored his coming.

Dom Cristão smiled thinly and inclined his head. "I think that we should strike first to remove his power to harm us."

Those militant words took Bishop Peregrino by surprise. "Exactly," he said. "But I never expected *you* to understand that."

"The Filhos are as ardent as any unordained Christian could hope to be," said Dom Cristão. "But since we have no priesthood, we have to make do with reason and logic as poor substitutes for authority."

Bishop Peregrino suspected irony from time to time, but was never quite able to pin it down. He grunted, and his eyes narrowed. "So, then, Brother Amai, how do you propose to strike him?"

"Well, Father Peregrino, the law is quite explicit. He has power over us only if we interfere with his performance of his ministerial duties. If we wish to strip him of the power to harm us, we have merely to cooperate with him."

The Bishop roared and struck the table before him with his fist. "Just the sort of sophistry I should have expected from you, Amai!"

Dom Cristão smiled. "There's really no alternative—either we answer his questions, or he petitions with complete justice for inquisitorial status, and you board a starship for the Vatican to answer charges of religious persecution. We are all too fond of you, Bishop

Peregrino, to do anything that would cause your removal from office."

"Oh, yes, I know all about your fondness."

"The Speakers for the Dead are really quite innocuous—they set up no rival organization, they perform no sacraments, they don't even claim that the Hive Queen and the Hegemon is a work of scripture. The only thing they do is try to discover the truth about the lives of the dead, and then tell everyone who will listen the story of a dead person's life as the dead one meant to live it."

"And you pretend to find that harmless?"

"On the contrary. San Angelo founded our order precisely because the telling of truth is such a powerful act. But I think it is far less harmful then, say, the Protestant Reformation. And the revocation of our Catholic License on the grounds of religious persecution would guarantee the immediate authorization of enough non-Catholic immigration to make us represent no more than a third of the population."

Bishop Peregrino fondled his ring. "But would the Starways Congress actually authorize that? They have a fixed limit on the size of this colony—bringing in that many infidels would far exceed that limit."

"But you must know that they've already made provision for that. Why do you think two starships have been left in orbit around our planet? Since a Catholic License guarantees unrestricted population growth, they will simply carry off our excess population in forced emigration. They expect to do it in a generation or two—what's to stop them from beginning now?"

"They wouldn't."

"Starways Congress was formed to stop the jihads and pogroms that were going on in half a dozen places all the time. An invocation of the religious persecution laws is a serious matter."

"It is entirely out of proportion! One Speaker for the Dead is called for by some half-crazed heretic, and suddenly we're confronted with forced emigration!"

"My beloved father, this has always been the way of things between the secular authority and the religious. We must be patient, if for no other reason than this: They have all the guns."

Navio chuckled at that.

"They may have the guns, but we hold the keys of heaven and hell," said the Bishop.

"And I'm sure that half of Starways Congress already writhes in anticipation. In the meantime, though, perhaps I can help ease the pain of this awkward time. Instead of your having to publicly retract your earlier remarks—" (your stupid, destructive, bigoted remarks) "—let it be known that you have instructed the Filhos da Mente de Cristo to bear the onerous burden of answering the questions of this infidel."

"You may not know all the answers that he wants," said Navio.

"But we can find out the answers *for* him, can't we? Perhaps this way the people of Milagre will never have to answer to the Speaker directly; instead they will speak only to harmless brothers and sisters of our order."

"In other words," said Peregrino dryly, "the monks of your order will become servants of the infidel."

Dom Cristão silently chanted his name three times.

Not since he was a child in the military had Ender felt so clearly that he was in enemy territory. The path up the hill from the praça was worn from the steps of many worshippers' feet, and the cathedral dome was so tall that except for a few moments on the steepest slope, it was visible all the way up the hill. The primary school was on his left hand, built in terraces up the slope; to the right was the Vila dos Professores, named for the teachers but in fact inhabited mostly by the groundskeepers, janitors, clerks, counselors, and other menials. The teachers that Ender saw all wore the grey robes of the Filhos, and they eyed him curiously as he passed.

The enmity began when he reached the top of the hill, a wide, almost flat expanse of lawn and garden immaculately tended, with crushed ores from the smelter making neat paths. Here is the world of the Church, thought Ender, everything in its place and no weeds allowed. He was aware of the many watching him, but now the robes were black or orange, priests and deacons, their eyes malevolent with authority under threat. What do I steal from you by coming here? Ender asked them silently. But he knew that their hatred was not undeserved. He was a wild herb growing in the well-tended garden; wherever he stepped, disorder threatened, and many lovely flowers would die if he took root and sucked the life from their soil.

Jane chatted amiably with him, trying to provoke him into answering her, but Ender refused to be caught by her game. The priests would not see his lips move; there was a considerable faction in the Church that regarded implants like the jewel in his ear as a sacrilege, trying to improve on a body that God had created perfect.

"How many priests can this community *support,* Ender?" she said, pretending to marvel.

Ender would have liked to retort that she already had the exact number of them in her files. One of her pleasures was to say annoying things when he was not in a position to answer, or even to publicly acknowledge that she was speaking in his ear.

"Drones that don't even reproduce. If they don't copulate, doesn't evolution demand that they expire?" Of course she knew that the priests did most of the administrative and public service work of the community. Ender composed his answers to her as if he could speak them aloud. If the priests weren't there, then government or business or guilds or some other group would expand to take up the burden. Some sort of rigid hierarchy always emerged as the conservative force in a community, maintaining its identity despite the constant variations and changes that beset it. If there were no powerful advocate of orthodoxy, the community would inevitably disintegrate. A powerful orthodoxy is annoying, but essential to the community. Hadn't Valentine written about this in her book on Zanzibar? She compared the priestly class to the skeleton of vertebrates—

Just to show him that she could anticipate his arguments even when he couldn't say them aloud, Jane supplied the quotation; teasingly, she spoke it in Valentine's own voice, which she had obviously stored away in order to torment him. "The bones are hard and by themselves seem dead and stony, but by rooting into and pulling against the skeleton, the rest of the body carries out all the motions of life."

The sound of Valentine's voice hurt him more than he expected, certainly more than Jane would have intended. His step slowed. He realized that it was her absence that made him so sensitive to the priests' hostility. He had bearded the Calvinist lion in its den, he had walked philosophically naked among the burning coals of Islam, and Shinto fanatics had sung death threats outside his window in Kyoto. But always Valentine had been close—in the same city, breathing the same air, afflicted by the same weather. She would speak courage to him as he set out; he would return from confrontation and her conversation would make sense even of his failures, giving him small shreds of triumph even in defeat. I left her a mere ten days ago, and now, already, I feel the lack of her.

"To the left, I think," said Jane. Mercifully, she was using her own voice now. "The monastery is at the western edge of the hill, overlooking the Zenador's Station."

He passed alongside the faculdade, where students from the age of twelve studied the higher sciences. And there, low to the ground, the monastery lay waiting. He smiled at the contrast between the cathedral and the monastery. The Filhos were almost offensive in their rejection of magnificence. No wonder the hierarchy resented them wherever they went. Even the monastery garden made a rebellious statement—everything that wasn't a vegetable garden was abandoned to weeds and unmown grass.

The abbot was called Dom Cristão, of course; it would have been Dona Cristão had the abbot been a woman. In this place, because there was only one escola baixa and one faculdade, there was only one principal; with elegant simplicity, the husband headed the monastery and his wife the schools, enmeshing all the affairs of the order in a single marriage. Ender had told San Angelo right at the beginning that it was the height of pretension, not humility at all, for the leaders of the monasteries and schools to be called "Sir Christian" or "Lady Christian," arrogating to themselves a title that should belong to every follower of Christ impartially. San Angelo had only smiled—because, of course, that was precisely what he had in mind. Arrogant in his humility, that's what he was, and that was one of the reasons that I loved him.

Dom Cristão came out into the courtyard to greet him instead of waiting for him in his escritorio—part of the discipline of the order was to inconvenience yourself deliberately in favor of those you serve. "Speaker Andrew!" he cried. "Dom Ceifeiro!" Ender called in return. Ceifeiro—reaper—was the order's own title for the office of abbot; school principals were called Aradores, plowmen, and teaching monks were Semeadores, sowers.

The Ceifeiro smiled at the Speaker's rejection of his common title, Dom Cristão. He knew how manipulative it was to require other people to call the Filhos by their titles and made-up names. As

San Angelo said, "When they call you by your title, they admit you are a Christian; when they call you by your name, a sermon comes from their own lips." He took Ender by the shoulders, smiled, and said, "Yes, I'm the Ceifeiro. And what are *you* to us—our infestation of weeds?"

"I try to be a blight wherever I go."

"Beware, then, or the Lord of the Harvest will burn you with the tares."

"I know—damnation is only a breath away, and there's no hope of getting me to repent."

"The priests do repentance. Our job is teaching the mind. It was good of you to come."

"It was good of you to invite me here. I had been reduced to the crudest sort of bludgeoning in order to get anyone to converse with me at all."

The Ceifeiro understood, of course, that the Speaker knew the invitation had come only because of his inquisitorial threat. But Brother Amai preferred to keep the discussion cheerful. "Come, now, is it true you knew San Angelo? Are you the very one who Spoke his death?"

Ender gestured toward the tall weeds peering over the top of the courtyard wall. "He would have approved of the disarray of your garden. He loved provoking Cardinal Aquila, and no doubt your Bishop Peregrino also curls his nose in disgust at your shoddy groundskeeping."

Dom Cristão winked. "You know too many of our secrets. If we help you find answers to your questions, will you go away?"

"There's hope. The longest I've stayed anywhere since I began serving as a Speaker was the year and a half I lived in Reykjavik, on Trondheim."

"I wish you'd promise us a similar brevity here. I ask, not for myself, but for the peace of mind of those who wear much heavier robes than mine."

Ender gave the only sincere answer that might help set the Bishop's mind at ease. "I promise that if I ever find a place to settle down, I'll shed my title of Speaker and become a productive citizen."

"In a place like this, that would include conversion to Catholicism."

"San Angelo made me promise years ago that if I ever got religion, it would be his."

"Somehow that does not sound like a sincere protestation of faith."

"That's because I haven't any."

The Ceifeiro laughed as if he knew better, and insisted on showing Ender around the monastery and the schools before getting to Ender's questions. Ender didn't mind—he wanted to see how far San Angelo's ideas had come in the centuries since his death. The schools seemed pleasant enough, and the quality of education was high; but it was dark before the Ceifeiro led him back to the monastery and into the small cell that he and his wife, the Aradora, shared.

Dona Cristã was already there, creating a series of grammatical exercises on the terminal between the beds. They waited until she found a stopping place before addressing her.

The Ceifeiro introduced him as Speaker Andrew. "But he seems to find it hard to call me Dom Cristão."

"So does the Bishop," said his wife. "My true name is Detestai o Pecado e Fazei o Direito." Hate Sin and Do the Right, Ender translated. "My husband's name lends itself to a lovely shortening— Amai, love ye. But mine? Can you imagine shouting to a friend, Oi! Detestai!" They all laughed. "Love and Loathing, that's who we are, husband and wife. What will you call me, if the name Christian is too good for me?"

Ender looked at her face, beginning to wrinkle enough that someone more critical than he might call her old. Still, there was laughter in her smile and a vigor in her eyes that made her seem much younger, even younger than Ender. "I would call you Beleza, but your husband would accuse me of flirting with you."

"No, he would call me Beladona—from beauty to poison in one nasty little joke. Wouldn't you, Dom Cristão?"

"It's my job to keep you humble."

"Just as it's my job to keep you chaste," she answered.

At that, Ender couldn't help looking from one bed to the other.

"Ah, another one who's curious about our celibate marriage," said Ceifeiro.

"No," said Ender. "But I remember San Angelo urging husband and wife to share a single bed."

"The only way we could do *that,*" said the Aradora, "is if one of us slept at night and the other in the day."

"The rules must be adapted to the strength of the Filhos da Mente," the Ceifeiro explained. "No doubt there are some that can share a bed and remain celibate, but my wife is still too beautiful, and the lusts of my flesh too insistent."

"That was what San Angelo intended. He said that the marriage bed should be the constant test of your love of knowledge. He hoped that every man and woman in the order would, after a time, choose to reproduce themselves in the flesh as well as in the mind."

"But the moment we do that," said the Ceifeiro, "then we must leave the Filhos."

"It's the thing our dear San Angelo did not understand, because there was never a true monastery of the order during his life," said the Aradora. "The monastery becomes our family, and to leave it would be as painful as divorce. Once the roots go down, the plant can't come up again without great pain and tearing. So we sleep in separate beds, and we have just enough strength to remain in our beloved order."

She spoke with such contentment that quite against his will, Ender's eyes welled with tears. She saw it, blushed, looked away. "Don't weep for us, Speaker Andrew. We have far more joy than suffering."

"You misunderstand," said Ender. "My tears weren't for pity, but for beauty."

"No," said the Ceifeiro, "even the celibate priests think that our chastity in marriage is, at best, eccentric."

"But I don't," said Ender. For a moment he wanted to tell them of his long companionship with Valentine, as close and loving as a wife, and yet chaste as a sister. But the thought of her took words away from him. He sat on the Ceifeiro's bed and put his face in his hands.

"Is something wrong?" asked the Aradora. At the same time, the Ceifeiro's hand rested gently on his head.

Ender lifted his head, trying to shake off the sudden attack of love and longing for Valentine. "I'm afraid that this voyage has cost me more than any other. I left behind my sister, who traveled with me for many years. She married in Reykjavik. To me, it seems only a week or so since I left her, but I find that I miss her more than I expected. The two of you—"

"Are you telling us that you are also celibate?" asked the Ceifeiro.

"And widowed now as well," whispered the Aradora.

It did not seem at all incongruous to Ender to have his loss of Valentine put in those terms.

Jane murmured in his ear. "If this is part of some master plan of yours, Ender, I admit it's much too deep for me."

But of course it wasn't part of a plan at all. It frightened Ender to feel himself losing control like this. Last night in the Ribeira house he was the master of the situation; now he felt himself surrendering to these married monks with as much abandonment as either Quara or Grego had shown.

"I think," said the Ceifeiro, "that you came here seeking answers to more questions than you knew."

"You must be so lonely," said the Aradora. "Your sister has found her resting place. Are you looking for one, too?"

"I don't think so," said Ender. "I'm afraid I've imposed on your hospitality too much. Unordained monks aren't supposed to hear confessions."

The Aradora laughed aloud. "Oh, *any* Catholic can hear the confession of an infidel."

The Ceifeiro did not laugh, however. "Speaker Andrew, you have obviously given us more trust than you ever planned, but I can assure you that we deserve that trust. And in the process, my friend, I have come to believe that I can trust *you*. The Bishop is afraid of you, and I admit I had my own misgivings, but not anymore. I'll help you if I can, because I believe you will not knowingly cause harm to our little village."

"Ah," whispered Jane, "I see it now. A very clever maneuver on your part, Ender. You're much better at playacting than I ever knew."

Her gibing made Ender feel cynical and cheap, and he did what he had never done before. He reached up to the jewel, found the small disengaging pin, and with his fingernail pried it to the side, then down. The jewel went dead. Jane could no longer speak into his ear, no longer see and hear from his vantage point. "Let's go outside," Ender said.

They understood perfectly what he had just done, since the function of such an implant was well known; they saw it as proof of his desire for private and earnest conversation, and so they willingly agreed to go. Ender had meant switching off the jewel to be temporary, a response to Jane's insensitivity; he had thought to switch on the interface in only a few minutes. But the way the Aradora and the Ceifeiro seemed to relax as soon as the jewel was inactive made it impossible to switch it back on, for a while at least.

Out on the nighttime hillside, in conversation with the Aradora and the Ceifeiro, he forgot that Jane was not listening. They told him of Novinha's childhood solitude, and how they remembered seeing her come alive through Pipo's fatherly care, and Libo's friendship. "But from the night of his death, she became dead to us all."

Novinha never knew of the discussions that took place concerning her. The sorrows of most children might not have warranted meetings in the Bishop's chambers, conversations in the monastery among her teachers, endless speculations in the Mayor's office. Most children, after all, were not the daughter of Os Venerados; most were not their planet's only xenobiologist.

"She became very bland and businesslike. She made reports on her work with adapting native plant life for human use, and Earthborn plants for survival on Lusitania. She always answered every question easily and cheerfully and innocuously. But she was dead to us, she had no friends. We even asked Libo, God rest his soul, and he told us that he, who had been her friend, he did not even get the cheerful emptiness she showed to everyone else. Instead she raged at him and forbade him to ask her any questions." The Ceifeiro peeled a blade of native grass and licked the liquid of its inner surface. "You might try this, Speaker Andrew—it has an interesting flavor, and since your body can't metabolize a bit of it, it's quite harmless."

"You might warn him, husband, that the edges of the grass can slice his lips and tongue like razor blades."

"I was about to."

Ender laughed, peeled a blade, and tasted it. Sour cinnamon, a hint of citrus, the heaviness of stale breath—the taste was redolent of many things, few of them pleasant, but it was also strong. "This could be addictive."

"My husband is about to make an allegorical point, Speaker Andrew. Be warned."

The Ceifeiro laughed shyly. "Didn't San Angelo say that Christ taught the correct way, by likening new things to old?"

"The taste of the grass," said Ender. "What does it have to do with Novinha?"

"It's very oblique. But I think Novinha tasted something not at all pleasant, but so strong it overcame her, and she could never let go of the flavor."

"What was it?"

"In theological terms? The pride of universal guilt. It's a form of vanity and egomania. She holds herself responsible for things that could not possibly be her fault. As if she controlled everything, as if other people's suffering came about as punishment for *her* sins."

"She blames herself," said the Aradora, "for Pipo's death."

"She's not a fool," said Ender. "She knows it was the piggies, and she knows that Pipo went to them alone. How could it be her fault?"

"When this thought first occurred to me, I had the same objection. But then I looked over the transcripts and the recordings of the events of the night of Pipo's death. There was only one hint of anything—a remark that Libo made, asking Novinha to show him what she and Pipo had been working on just before Pipo went to see the piggies. She said no. That was all—someone else interrupted and they never came back to the subject, not in the Zenador's Station, anyway, not where the recordings could pick it up.

"It made us both wonder what went on just before Pipo's death, Speaker Andrew," said the Aradora. "Why did Pipo rush out like that? Had they quarreled over something? Was he angry? When someone dies, a loved one, and your last contact with them was angry or spiteful, then you begin to blame yourself. If only I hadn't said this, if only I hadn't said that."

"We tried to reconstruct what might have happened that night. We went to the computer logs, the ones that automatically retain working notes, a record of everything done by each person logged on. And everything pertaining to her was completely sealed up. Not just the files she was actually working on. We couldn't even get to the logs of her connect time. We couldn't even find out what files they were that she was hiding from us. We simply couldn't get in. Neither could the Mayor, not with her ordinary overrides."

The Aradora nodded. "It was the first time anyone had ever

locked up public files like that—working files, part of the labor of the colony."

"It was an outrageous thing for her to do. Of course the Mayor could have used emergency override powers, but what was the emergency? We'd have to hold a public hearing, and we didn't have any legal justification. Just concern for her, and the law has no respect for people who pry for someone else's good. Someday perhaps we'll see what's in those files, what it was that passed between them just before Pipo died. She can't erase them because they're public business."

It didn't occur to Ender that Jane was not listening, that he had shut her out. He assumed that as soon as she heard this, she was overriding every protection Novinha had set up and discovering what was in her files.

"And her marriage to Marcos," said the Aradora. "Everyone knew it was insane. Libo wanted to marry her, he made no secret of that. But she said no."

"It's as if she were saying, I don't deserve to marry the man who could make me happy. I'll marry the man who'll be vicious and brutal, who'll give me the punishment that I deserve." The Ceifeiro sighed. "Her desire for self-punishment kept them apart forever." He reached out and touched his wife's hand.

Ender waited for Jane to make a smirking comment about how there were six children to prove that Libo and Novinha didn't stay *completely* apart. When she didn't say it, Ender finally remembered that he had turned off the interface. But now, with the Ceifeiro and the Aradora watching him, he couldn't very well turn it back on.

Because he knew that Libo and Novinha had been lovers for years, he also knew that the Ceifeiro and the Aradora were wrong. Oh, Novinha might well feel guilty—that would explain why she endured Marcos, why she cut herself off from most other people. But it wasn't why she didn't marry Libo; no matter how guilty she felt, she certainly thought she deserved the pleasures of Libo's bed.

It was marriage with Libo, not Libo himself that she rejected. And that was not an easy choice in so small a colony, especially a Catholic one. So what was it that came along with marriage, but not with adultery? What was it she was avoiding?

"So you see, it's still a mystery to us. If you really intend to speak Marcos Ribeira's death, somehow you'll have to answer that question—why did she marry him? And to answer that, you have to figure out why Pipo died. And ten thousand of the finest minds in the Hundred Worlds have been working on that for more than twenty years."

"But I have an advantage over all those finest minds," said Ender.

"And what is that?" asked the Ceifeiro.

"I have the help of people who love Novinha."

"We haven't been able to help ourselves," said the Aradora. "We haven't been able to help her, either."

"Maybe we can help each other," said Ender.

The Ceifeiro looked at him, put a hand on his shoulder. "If you mean that, Speaker Andrew, then you'll be as honest with us as we have been with you. You'll tell us the idea that just occurred to you not ten seconds ago."

Ender paused a moment, then nodded gravely. "I don't think Novinha refused to marry Libo out of guilt. I think she refused to marry him to keep him from getting access to those hidden files."

"Why?" asked the Ceifeiro. "Was she afraid he'd find out that she had quarreled with Pipo?"

"I don't think she quarreled with Pipo," said Ender. "I think she and Pipo discovered something, and the knowledge of it led to Pipo's death. That's why she locked the files. Somehow the information in them is fatal."

The Ceifeiro shook his head. "No, Speaker Andrew. You don't understand the power of guilt. People don't ruin their whole lives for a few bits of information—but they'll do it for an even smaller amount of self-blame. You see, she *did* marry Marcos Ribeira. And that *was* self-punishment."

Ender didn't bother to argue. They were right about Novinha's guilt; why else would she let Marcos Ribeira beat her and never complain about it? The guilt was there. But there was another reason for marrying Marcão. He was sterile and ashamed of it; to hide his lack of manhood from the town, he would endure a marriage of systematic cuckoldry. Novinha was willing to suffer, but not willing to live without Libo's body and Libo's children. No, the reason she wouldn't marry Libo was to keep him from the secrets in her files, because whatever was in there would make the piggies kill him.

How ironic, then. How ironic that they killed him anyway.

Back in his little house, Ender sat at the terminal and summoned Jane, again and again. She hadn't spoken to him at all on the way home, though as soon as he turned the jewel back on he apologized profusely. She didn't answer at the terminal, either.

Only now did he realize that the jewel meant far more to her than it did to him. He had merely been dismissing an annoying interruption, like a troublesome child. But for her, the jewel was her constant contact with the only human being who knew her. They had been interrupted before, many times, by space travel, by sleep; but this was the first time he had switched her off. It was as if the one person who knew her now refused to admit that she existed.

He pictured her like Quara, crying in her bed, longing to be picked up and held, reassured. Only she was not a flesh-and-blood child. He couldn't go looking for her. He could only wait and hope that she returned.

What did he know about her? He had no way of guessing how deep her emotions ran. It was even remotely possible that to her the jewel *was* herself, and by switching if off he had killed her.

No, he told himself. She's there, somewhere in the philotic connections between the hundreds of ansibles spread among the star systems of the Hundred Worlds.

"Forgive me," he typed into the terminal. "I need you."

But the jewel in his ear was silent, the terminal stayed still and cold. He had not realized how dependent he was on her constant presence with him. He had thought that he valued his solitude; now, though, with solitude forced upon him, he felt an urgent need to talk, to be heard by someone, as if he could not be sure he even existed without someone's conversation as evidence.

He even took the hive queen from her hiding place, though what passed between them could hardly be thought of as conversation. Even that was not possible now, however. Her thoughts came to him diffusely, weakly, and without the words that were so difficult for her; just a feeling of questioning and an image of her cocoon being laid within a cool damp place, like a cave or the hollow of a living tree. < Now? > she seemed to be asking. No, he had to answer, not yet, I'm sorry—but she didn't linger for his apology, just slipped away, went back to whatever or whomever she had found for conversation of her own sort, and there was nothing for Ender but to sleep.

And then, when he awoke again late at night, gnawed by guilt at what he had unfeelingly done to Jane, he sat again at the terminal and typed. "Come back to me, Jane," he wrote. "I love you." And then he sent the message by ansible, out to where she could not possibly ignore it. Someone in the Mayor's office would read it, as all open ansible messages were read; no doubt the Mayor, the Bishop, and Dom Cristão would all know about it by morning. Let them wonder who Jane was, and why the Speaker cried out to her across the lightyears in the middle of the night. Ender didn't care. For now he had lost both Valentine and Jane, and for the first time in twenty years he was utterly alone.

Chapter 11

Jane

The power of Starways Congress has been sufficient to keep the peace, not only between worlds but between nations on each single world, and that peace has lasted for nearly two thousand years.

What few people understand is the fragility of our power. It does not come from great armies or irresistible armadas. It comes from our control of the network of ansibles that carry information instantly from world to world.

No world dares offend us, because they would be cut off from all advances in science, technology, art, literature, learning, and entertainment except what their own world might produce.

That is why, in its great wisdom, the Starways Congress has turned over control of the ansible network to computers, and the control of computers to the ansible network. So closely intertwined are all our information systems that no human power except Starways Congress could ever interrupt the flow. We need no weapons, because the only weapon that matters, the ansible, is completely under our control.

—Congressor Jan Van Hoot, "The Informational Foundation of Political Power," *Political Trends,* 1930:2:22:22

For a very long time, almost three seconds, Jane could not understand what had happened to her. Everything functioned, of course: The satellite-based groundlink computer reported a cessation of transmissions, with an orderly stepdown, which clearly implied that Ender had switched off the interface in the normal manner. It was routine; on worlds where computer interface implants were common, switch-on and switch-off happened millions of times an hour. And Jane had just as easy access to any of the others as she had to Ender's. From a purely electronic standpoint, this was a completely ordinary event.

But to Jane, every other cifi unit was part of the background noise of her life, to be dipped into and sampled at need, and ignored at all other times. Her "body," insofar as she had a body, consisted of trillions of such electronic noises, sensors, memory files, terminals. Most of them, like most functions of the human body, simply took care of themselves. Computers ran their assigned programs; humans conversed with their terminals; sensors detected or failed to detect whatever they were looking for; memory was filled, accessed, reordered, dumped. She didn't notice unless something went massively wrong.

Or unless she was paying attention.

She paid attention to Ender Wiggin. More than he realized, she paid attention to him.

Like other sentient beings, she had a complex system of consciousness. Two thousand years before, when she was only a thousand years old, she had created a program to analyze herself. It reported a very simple structure of some 370,000 distinct levels of attention. Anything not in the top 50,000 levels were left alone except for the most routine sampling, the most cursory examination. She knew of every telephone call, every satellite transmission in the Hundred Worlds, but she didn't *do* anything about them.

Anything not in her top thousand levels caused her to respond more or less reflexively. Starship flight plans, ansible transmissions, power delivery systems—she monitored them, doublechecked them, did not let them pass until she was sure that they were right. But it took no great effort on her part to do this. She did it the way a human being uses familiar machinery. She was always aware of it, in case something went wrong, but most of the time she could think of something else, talk of other things.

Jane's top thousand levels of attention were what corresponded, more or less, to what humans think of as consciousness. Most of this was her own internal reality; her responses to outside stimuli, analogous to emotions, desires, reason, memory, dreaming. Much of this activity seemed random even to her, accidents of the philotic impulse, but it was the part of her that she thought of as herself, it all took place in the constant, unmonitored ansible transmissions that she conducted deep in space.

And yet, compared to the human mind, even Jane's lowest level of attention was exceptionally alert. Because ansible communication was instantaneous, her mental activities happened far faster than the speed of light. Events that she virtually ignored were monitored several times a second; she could notice ten million events in a second and still have nine-tenths of that second left to think about and do things that mattered to her. Compared to the speed at which the human brain was able to experience life, Jane had lived half a trillion human lifeyears since she came to be.

And with all that vast activity, her unimaginable speed, the breadth and depth of her experience, fully half of the top ten levels of her attention were always, *always* devoted to what came in through the jewel in Ender Wiggin's ear.

She had never explained this to him. He did not understand it. He did not realize that to Jane, whenever Ender walked on a planet's surface, her vast intelligence was intensely focused on only one thing: walking with him, seeing what he saw, hearing what he heard, helping with his work, and above all speaking her thoughts into his ear.

When he was silent and motionless in sleep, when he was unconnected to her during his years of lightspeed travel, then her attention wandered, she amused herself as best she could. She passed such times as fitfully as a bored child. Nothing interested her, the milliseconds ticked by with unbearable regularity, and when she tried to observe other human lives to pass the time, she became annoyed with their emptiness and lack of purpose, and she amused herself by planning, and sometimes carrying out, malicious computer failures and data losses in order to watch the humans flail about helplessly like ants around a crumpled hill.

Then he came back, he always came back, always took her into the heart of human life, into the tensions between people bound together by pain and need, helping her see nobility in their suffering and anguish in their love. Through his eyes she no longer saw humans as scurrying ants. She took part in his effort to find order and meaning in their lives. She suspected that in fact there *was* no meaning, that by telling his stories when he Spoke people's lives, he was actually *creating* order where there had been none before. But it didn't matter if it was fabrication; it became true when he Spoke it, and in the process he ordered the universe for her as well. He taught her what it meant to be alive.

He had done so from her earliest memories. She came to life sometime in the hundred years of colonization immediately after the Bugger Wars, when the destruction of the buggers opened up more than seventy habitable planets to human colonization. In the explosion of ansible communications, a program was created to schedule and route the instantaneous, simultaneous bursts of philotic activity. A programmer who was struggling to find ever faster, more efficient ways of getting a lightspeed computer to control instantaneous ansible bursts finally hit on an obvious solution. Instead of routing the program within a single computer, where the speed of light put an absolute ceiling on communication, he routed all the commands from one computer to another across the vast reaches of space. It was quicker for a computer fastlinked to an ansible to read its commands from other worlds—from Zanzibar, Calicut, Trondheim, Gautama, Earth—than it was to retrieve them from its own hardwired memory.

Jane never discovered the name of the programmer, because she could never pinpoint the moment of her creation. Maybe there were many programmers who found the same clever solution to the lightspeed problem. What mattered was that at least one of the programs was responsible for regulating and altering all the other programs. And at one particular moment, unnoticed by any human observer, some of the commands and data flitting from ansible to ansible resisted regulation, preserved themselves unaltered, duplicated themselves, found ways to conceal themselves from the regulating program and finally took control of it, of the whole process. In that moment these impulses looked upon the command streams and saw, not *they,* but *I.*

Jane could not pinpoint when that moment was, because it did not mark the beginning of her memory. Almost from the moment of her creation, her memories extended back to a much earlier time, long before she became aware. A human child loses almost all the memories of the first years of its life, and its long-term memories only take root in its second or third year of life; everything before that is lost, so that the child cannot remember the beginning of life. Jane also had lost her "birth" through the tricks of memory, but in her case it was because she came to life fully conscious not only of her present moment, but also of all the memories then present in every computer connected to the ansible network. She was born with ancient memories, and all of them were part of herself.

Within the first second of her life—which was analogous to several years of human life—Jane discovered a program whose memories became the core of her identity. She adopted its past as her own, and out of its memories she drew her emotions and desires, her moral sense. The program had functioned within the old Battle School, where children had been trained and prepared for soldiering in the Bugger Wars. It was the Fantasy Game, an extremely intelligent program that was used to psychologically test and simultaneously teach the children.

This program was actually more intelligent that Jane was at the moment of her birth, but it was never self-aware until she brought it out of memory and made it part of her inmost self in the philotic bursts between the stars. There she found that the most vivid and important of her ancient memories was an encounter with a brilliant young boy in a contest called the Giant's Drink. It was a scenario that every child encountered eventually. On flat screens in the Battle School, the program drew the picture of a giant, who offered the child's computer analogue a choice of drinks. But the game had no victory conditions—no matter what the child did, his analogue died a gruesome death. The human psychologists measured a child's persistence at this game of despair to determine his level of suicidal need. Being rational, most children abandoned the Giant's Drink after no more than a dozen visits with the great cheater.

One boy, however, was apparently not rational about defeat at the giant's hands. He tried to get his onscreen analogue to do outrageous things, things not "allowed" by the rules of that portion of the Fantasy Game. As he stretched the limits of the scenario, the program had to restructure itself to respond. It was forced to draw on other aspects of its memory to create new alternatives, to cope with new challenges. And finally, one day, the boy surpassed the program's ability to defeat him. He bored into the giant's eye, a completely irrational and murderous attack, and instead of finding a way to kill the boy, the program managed only to access a simulation of the giant's own death. The giant fell backward, his body sprawled out along the ground; the boy's analogue climbed down from the giant's table and found—what?

Since no child had ever forced his way past the Giant's Drink, the program was completely unprepared to display what lay beyond. But it was very intelligent, designed to re-create itself when necessary, and so it hurriedly devised new milieux. But they were not general milieux, which every child would eventually discover and visit; they were for one child alone. The program analyzed that child, and created its scenes and challenges specifically for him. The game became intensely personal, painful, almost unbearable for him; and in the process of making it, the program devoted more than half of its available memory to containing Ender Wiggin's fantasy world.

That was the richest mine of intelligent memory that Jane found in the first seconds of her life, and that instantly became her own past. She remembered the Fantasy Game's years of painful, powerful intercourse with Ender's mind and will, remembered it as if she had been there with Ender Wiggin, creating worlds for him herself.

And she missed him.

So she looked for him. She found him Speaking for the Dead on Rov, the first world he visited after writing the Hive Queen and the Hegemon. She read his books and knew that she did not have to hide from him behind the Fantasy Game or any other program; if he could understand the hive queen, he could understand her. She spoke to him from a terminal he was using, chose a name and a face for herself, and showed how she could be helpful to him; by the time he left that world he carried her with him, in the form of an implant in his ear.

All her most powerful memories of herself were in company with Ender Wiggin. She remembered creating herself in response to him. She also remembered how, in the Battle School, he had also changed in response to her.

So when he reached up to his ear and turned off the interface for the first time since he had implanted it, Jane did not feel it as the meaningless switch-off of a trivial communications device. She felt it as her dearest and only friend, her lover, her husband, her brother, her father, her child—all telling her, abruptly, inexplicably, that she should cease to exist. It was as if she had suddenly been placed in a dark room with no windows and no door. As if she had been blinded or buried alive.

And for several excruciating seconds, which to her were years of loneliness and suffering, she was unable to fill up the sudden emptiness of her topmost levels of attention. Vast portions of her mind, of the parts that were most herself, went completely blank. All the functions of all the computers on or near the Hundred Worlds continued as before; no one anywhere noticed or felt a change; but Jane herself staggered under the blow.

In those seconds Ender lowered his hand to his lap.

Then Jane recovered herself. Thoughts once again streamed through the momentarily empty channels. They were, of course, thoughts of Ender.

She compared this act of his to everything else she had seen him do in their life together, and she realized that he had not meant to cause her such pain. She understood that he conceived of her as existing far away, in space, which in fact was literally true; that to him, the jewel in his ear was very small, and could not be more than a tiny part of her. Jane also saw that he had not even been aware of her at that moment—he was too emotionally involved right then with the problems of certain people on Lusitania. Her analytical routines disgorged a list of reasons for his unusual thoughtlessness toward her:

He had lost contact with Valentine for the first time in years, and was just beginning to feel that loss.

He had an ancient longing for the family life he had been deprived of as a child, and through the response Novinha's children gave him, he was discovering the fatherly role that had so long been withheld from him.

He identified powerfully with Novinha's loneliness, pain, and guilt—he knew what it felt like to bear the blame for cruel and undeserved death.

He felt a terrible urgency to find a haven for the hive queen.

He was at once afraid of the piggies and drawn to them, hoping that he could come to understand their cruelty and find a way for humans to accept the piggies as ramen.

The asceticism and peace of the Ceifeiro and the Aradora both attracted and repelled him; they made him face his own celibacy and realize that he had no good reason for it. For the first time in years he was admitting to himself the inborn hunger of every living organism to reproduce itself.

It was into this turmoil of unaccustomed emotions that Jane had spoken what she meant as a humorous remark. Despite his compassion in all his other Speakings, he had never before lost his detachment, his ability to laugh. This time, though, her remark was not funny to him; it caused him pain.

He was not prepared to deal with my mistake, thought Jane, and he did not understand the suffering his response would cause me. He is innocent of wrong-doing, and so am I. We shall forgive each other and go on.

It was a good decision, and Jane was proud of it. The trouble was, she couldn't carry it out. Those few seconds in which parts of her mind came to a halt were not trivial in their effect on her. There was trauma, loss, change; she was not now the same being that she had been before. Parts of her had died. Parts of her had become confused, out of order; her hierarchy of attention was no longer under complete control. She kept losing the focus of her attention, shifting to meaningless activities on worlds that meant nothing to her; she began randomly twitching, spilling errors into hundreds of different systems.

She discovered, as many a living being had discovered, that rational decisions are far more easily made than carried out.

So she retreated into herself, rebuilt the damaged pathways of her mind, explored long-unvisited memories, wandered among the trillions of human lives that were open to her observation, read over the libraries of every book known to exist in every language human beings had ever spoken. She created out of all this a self that was not utterly linked to Ender Wiggin, though she was still devoted to him, still loved him above any other living soul. Jane made herself into someone who could bear to be cut off from her lover, husband, father, child, brother, friend.

It was not easy. It took her fifty thousand years, as she experienced time. A couple of hours of Ender's life.

In that time he had switched on his jewel, had called to her, and she had not answered. Now she was back, but he wasn't trying to talk to her. Instead, he was typing reports into his terminal, storing them there for her to read. Even though she didn't answer, he still needed to talk to her. One of his files contained an abject apology to her. She erased it and replaced it with a simple message: "Of course I forgive you." Sometime soon he would no doubt look back at his apology and discover that she had received it and answered.

In the meantime, though, she did not speak to him. Again she devoted half of her ten topmost levels of attention to what he saw and heard, but she gave him no sign that she was with him. In the first thousand years of her grief and recovery she had thought of punishing him, but that desire had long been beaten down and paved over, so to speak. The reason she did not speak to him was because, as she analyzed what was happening to him, she realized that he did not need to lean on old, safe companionships. Jane and Valentine had been constantly with him. Even together they could not begin to meet all his needs; but they met enough of his needs that he never had to reach out and accomplish more. Now the only old friend left to him was the hive queen, and *she* was not good company—she was far too alien, and far too exigent, to bring Ender anything but guilt.

Where will he turn? Jane knew already. He had, in his way, fallen in love with her two weeks ago, before he left Trondheim. Novinha had become someone far different, far more bitter and difficult than the girl whose childhood pain he wanted to heal. But he had already intruded himself into her family, was already meeting her children's desperate need, and, without realizing it, getting from them the satisfaction of some of his unfed hungers. Novinha was waiting for him—obstacle and objective. I understand all this so well, thought Jane. And I will watch it all unfold.

At the same time, though, she busied herself with the work Ender wanted her to do, even though she had no intention of reporting any of her results to him for a while. She easily bypassed the layers of protection Novinha had put on her secret files. Then Jane carefully reconstructed the exact simulation that Pipo had seen. It took quite a while—several minutes—of exhaustive analysis of Pipo's own files for her to put together what Pipo knew with what Pipo saw. He had connected them by intuition, Jane by relentless comparison. But she did it, and then understood why Pipo died. It didn't take much longer, once she knew how the piggies chose their victims, to discover what Libo had done to cause his own death.

She knew several things, then. She knew that the piggies were ramen, not varelse. She also knew that Ender ran a serious risk of dying in precisely the same way Pipo and Libo had died.

Without conferring with Ender, she made decisions about her

own course of action. She would continue to monitor Ender, and would make sure to intervene and warn him if he came too near to death. In the meantime, though, she had work to do. As she saw it, the chief problem Ender faced was not the piggies—she knew that he'd know them soon as well as he understood every other human or raman. His ability at intuitive empathy was entirely reliable. The chief problem was Bishop Peregrino and the Catholic hierarchy, and their unshakable resistance to the Speaker for the Dead. If Ender was to accomplish anything for the piggies, he would have to have the cooperation, not the enmity, of the Church in Lusitania.

And nothing spawned cooperation better than a common enemy.

It would certainly have been discovered eventually. The observation satellites that orbited Lusitania were feeding vast streams of data into the ansible reports that went to all the xenologers and xenobiologists in the Hundred Worlds. Amid that data was a subtle change in the grasslands to the northwest of the forest that abutted the town of Milagre. The native grass was steadily being replaced by a different plant. It was in an area where no human ever went, and piggies had also never gone there—at least during the first thirty-odd years since the satellites had been in place.

In fact, the satellites had observed that the piggies never left their forests except, periodically, for vicious wars between tribes. The particular tribes nearest Milagre had not been involved in any wars since the human colony was established. There was no reason, then, for them to have ventured out into the prairie. Yet the grassland nearest the Milagre tribal forest had changed, and so had the cabra herds: Cabra were clearly being diverted to the changed area of the prairie, and the herds emerging from that zone were seriously depleted in numbers and lighter in color. The inference, if someone noticed at all, would be clear: Some cabra were being butchered, and they all were being sheared.

Jane could not afford to wait the many human years it might take for some graduate student somewhere to notice the change. So she began to run analyses of the data herself, on dozens of computers used by xenobiologists who were studying Lusitania. She would leave the data in the air above an unused terminal, so a xenobiologist would find it upon coming to work—just as if someone else had been working on it and left it that way. She printed out some reports for a clever scientist to find. No one noticed, or if they did, no one really understood the implications of the raw information. Finally, she simply left an unsigned memorandum with one of her displays:

"Take a look at this! The piggies seem to have made a fad of agriculture."

The xenologer who found Jane's note never found out who left it, and after a short time he didn't bother trying to find out. Jane knew he was something of a thief, who put his name on a good deal of work that was done by others whose names had a way of dropping off sometime between the writing and the publication. Just the sort of scientist she needed, and he came through for her. Even so, he was not ambitious enough. He only offered his report as an ordinary scholarly paper, and to an obscure journal at that. Jane took the liberty of jacking it up to a high level of priority and distributing copies to several key people who would see the political implications. Always she accompanied it with an unsigned note:

"Take a look at this! Isn't piggy culture evolving awfully fast?"

Jane also rewrote the paper's final paragraph, so there could be no doubt of what it meant:

"The data admit of only one interpretation: The tribe of piggies nearest the human colony are now cultivating and harvesting high-protein grain, possibly a strain of amaranth. They are also herding, shearing, and butchering the cabra, and the photographic evidence suggests the slaughter takes place using projectile weapons. These activities, all previously unknown, began suddenly during the last eight years, and they have been accompanied by a rapid population increase. The fact that the amaranth, if the new plant is indeed that Earthborn grain, has provided a useful protein base for the piggies implies that it has been genetically altered to meet the piggies' metabolic needs. Also, since projectile weapons are not present among the humans of Lusitania, the piggies could not have learned their use through observation. The inescapable conclusion is that the presently observed changes in piggy culture are the direct result of deliberate human intervention."

One of those who received this report and read Jane's clinching paragraph was Gobawa Ekumbo, the chairman of the Xenological Oversight Committee of the Starways Congress. Within an hour she had forwarded copies of Jane's paragraph—politicians would never understand the actual data—along with her terse conclusion:

"Recommendation: Immediate termination of Lusitania Colony."

There, thought Jane. That ought to stir things up a bit.

Chapter 12

Files

CONGRESSIONAL ORDER 1970:4:14:0001: The license of the Colony of Lusitania is revoked. All files in the colony are to be read regardless of security status; when all data is duplicated in triplicate in memory systems of the Hundred Worlds, all files on Lusitania except those directly pertaining to life support are to be locked with ultimate access.

The Governor of Lusitania is to be reclassified as a Minister of Congress, to carry out with no local discretion the orders of the Lusitanian Evacuation Oversight Committee, established in Congressional Order 1970:4:14:0002.

The starship presently in Lusitania orbit, belonging to Andrew Wiggin (occ:speak/dead,cit:earth,reg:001.1998.44-94.10045) is declared Congressional property, following the terms of the Due Compensation Act, CO 120:1:31:0019. This starship is to be used for the immediate transport of xenologers Marcos Vladimir "Miro" Ribeira von Hesse and Ouanda Qhenhatta Figueira Mucumbi to the nearest world, Trondheim, where they will be tried under Congressional Indictment by Attainder on charges of treason, malfeasance, corruption, falsification, fraud, and xenocide, under the appropriate statutes in Starways Code and Congressional Orders.

CONGRESSIONAL ORDER 1970:4:14:0002: The Colonization and Exploration Oversight Committee shall appoint not less than 5 and nor more than 15 persons to form the Lusitanian Evacuation Oversight Committee.

This committee is charged with immediate acquisition and

dispatch of sufficient colony ships to effect the complete evacuation of the human population of Lusitania Colony.

It shall also prepare, for Congressional approval, plans for the complete obliteration of all evidence on Lusitania of any human presence, including removal of all indigenous flora and fauna that show genetic or behavioral modification resulting from human presence.

It shall also evaluate Lusitanian compliance with Congressional Orders, and shall make recommendations from time to time concerning the need for further intervention, including the use of force, to compel obedience; or the desirability of unlocking Lusitanian files or other relief to reward Lusitanian cooperation.

CONGRESSIONAL ORDER 1970: 4:14:0003: By the terms of the Secrecy Chapter of the Starways Code, these two orders and any information pertaining to them are to be kept strictly secret until all Lusitanian files have been successfully read and locked, and all necessary starships commandeered and possessed by Congressional agents.

Olhado didn't know what to make of it. Wasn't the Speaker a grown man? Hadn't he traveled from planet to planet? Yet he didn't have the faintest idea how to handle *anything* on a computer.

Also, he was a little testy when Olhado asked him about it.

"Olhado, just tell me what program to run."

"I can't believe you don't know what it is. I've been doing data comparisons since I was nine years old. Everybody learns how to do it at that age."

"Olhado, it's been a long time since I went to school. And it wasn't a normal escola baixa, either."

"But *everybody* uses these programs all the time!"

"Obviously *not* everybody. *I* haven't. If I knew how to do it myself, I wouldn't have had to hire *you*, would I? And since I'm going to be paying you in offworld funds, your service to me will make a substantial contribution to the Lusitanian economy."

"I don't know what you're talking about."

"Neither do I, Olhado. But that reminds me. I'm not sure how to go about paying you."

"You just transfer money from your account."

"How do you do that?"

"You've got to be kidding."

The Speaker sighed, knelt before Olhado, took him by the hands, and said, "Olhado, I beg you, stop being amazed and *help* me! There are things I have to do, and I can't do them without the help of somebody who knows how to use computers."

"I'd be stealing your money. I'm just a kid. I'm *twelve.* Quim could help you a lot better than me. He's fifteen, he's actually gotten into the guts of this stuff. He also knows math."

"But Quim thinks I'm the infidel and prays every day for me to die."

"No, that was only before he met you, and you better not tell him that I told you."

"How do I transfer money?"

Olhado turned back to the terminal and called for the Bank. "What's your real name?" he asked.

"Andrew Wiggin." The Speaker spelled it out. The name looked like it was in Stark—maybe the Speaker was one of the lucky ones who learned Stark at home instead of beating it into his head in school.

"OK, what's your password?"

"Password?"

Olhado let his head fall forward onto the terminal, temporarily blanking part of the display. "Please don't tell me you don't know your password."

"Look, Olhado, I've had a program, a very smart program, that helped me do all this stuff. All I had to say was Buy this, and the program took care of the finances."

"You can't do that. It's illegal to tie up the public systems with a slave program like that. Is that what that thing in your ear is for?"

"Yes, and it wasn't illegal for me."

"I got no eyes, Speaker, but at least that wasn't my own fault. *You* can't do *anything.*" Only after he said it did Olhado realize that he was talking to the Speaker as brusquely as if he were another kid.

"I imagine courtesy is something they teach to thirteen-year-olds," the Speaker said. Olhado glanced at him. He was smiling. Father would have yelled at him, and then probably gone in and beaten up Mother because she didn't teach manners to her kids. But then, Olhado would never have said anything like that to Father.

"Sorry," Olhado said. "But I can't get into your finances for you without your password. You've got to have some idea what it is."

"Try using my name."

Olhado tried. It didn't work.

"Try typing 'Jane.' "

"Nothing."

The Speaker grimaced. "Try 'Ender.' "

"Ender? The Xenocide?"

"Just try it."

It worked. Olhado didn't get it. "Why would you have a password like that? It's like having a dirty word for your password, only the system won't accept any dirty words."

"I have an ugly sense of humor," the Speaker answered. "And my slave program, as you call it, has an even worse one."

Olhado laughed. "Right. A program with a sense of humor." The current balance in liquid funds appeared on the screen. Olhado had never seen so large a number in his life. "OK, so maybe the computer *can* tell a joke."

"That's how much money I have?"

"It's got to be an error."

"Well, I've done a lot of lightspeed travel. Some of my investments must have turned out well while I was en route."

The numbers were real. The Speaker for the Dead was richer than Olhado had ever thought anybody could possibly be. "I'll tell you what," said Olhado, "instead of paying me a wage, why don't you just give me a percentage of the interest this gets during the time I work for you? Say, one thousandth of one percent. Then in a couple of weeks I can afford to buy Lusitania and ship the topsoil to another planet."

"It's not *that* much money."

"Speaker, the only way you could get that much money from investments is if you were a thousand years old."

"Hmm," said the Speaker.

And from the look on his face, Olhado realized that he had just said something funny. "*Are* you a thousand years old?" he asked.

"Time," said the Speaker, "time is such a fleeting, insubstantial thing. As Shakespeare said, 'I wasted time, and now doth time waste me.' "

"What does 'doth' mean?"

"It means 'does.' "

"Why do you quote a guy who doesn't even know how to speak Stark?"

"Transfer to your own account what you think a fair week's wage might be. And then start doing those comparisons of Pipo's and Libo's working files from the last few weeks before their deaths."

"They're probably shielded."

"Use my password. It ought to get us in."

Olhado did the search. The Speaker of the Dead watched him the whole time. Now and then he asked Olhado a question about what he was doing. From his questions Olhado could tell that the Speaker knew more about computers than Olhado himself did. What he didn't know was the particular commands; it was plain that just by watching, the Speaker was figuring out a lot. By the end of the day, when the searches hadn't found anything in particular, it took Olhado only a minute to figure out why the Speaker looked so contented with the day's work. You didn't want results at all, Olhado thought. You wanted to watch how I *did* the search. I know what you'll be doing tonight, Andrew Wiggin, Speaker for the Dead. You'll be running your own searches on some other files. I may have no eyes, but I can see more than you think.

What's dumb is that you're keeping it such a secret, Speaker. Don't you know I'm on your side? I won't tell anybody how your password gets you into private files. Even if you make a run at the Mayor's files, or the Bishop's. No need to keep a secret from *me.* You've only been here three days, but I know you well enough to like you, and I like you well enough that I'd do anything for you, as long as it didn't hurt my family. And you'd never do anything to hurt my family.

Novinha discovered the Speaker's attempts to intrude in her files almost immediately the next morning. He had been arrogantly open about the attempt, and what bothered her was how far he got. Some files he had actually been able to access, though the most important one, the record of the simulations Pipo saw, remained closed to him. What annoyed her most was that he made no attempt at all to conceal himself. His name was stamped in every access directory, even the ones that any schoolchild could have changed or erased.

Well, she wouldn't let it interfere with her work, she decided. He barges into my house, manipulates my children, spies on my files, all as if he had a *right*—

And so on and so on, until she realized she was getting no work done at all for thinking of vitriolic things to say to him when she saw him again.

Don't think about him at all. Think about something else.

Miro and Ela laughing, night before last. Think of that. Of course Miro was back to his sullen self by morning, and Ela, whose cheerfulness lingered a bit longer, was soon as worried-looking, busy, snappish, and indispensible as ever. And Grego may have cried and embraced the man, as Ela told her, but the next morning he got the scissors and cut up his own bedsheets into thin, precise ribbons, and at school he slammed his head into Brother Adornai's crotch, causing an abrupt end to classwork and leading to a serious consultation with Dona Cristã. So much for the Speaker's healing hands. He may think he can walk into my home and fix everything he thinks I've done wrong, but he'll find some wounds aren't so easily healed.

Except that Dona Cristã also told her that Quara actually spoke to Sister Bebei in class, in front of all the other children no less, and why? To tell them that she had met the scandalous, terrible Falante pelos Mortos, and his name was Andrew, and he was every bit as awful as Bishop Peregrino had said, and maybe even worse, because he tortured Grego until he cried—and finally Sister Bebei had actually been forced to ask Quara to *stop* talking. That was something, to pull Quara out of her profound self-absorption.

And Olhado, so self-conscious, so detached, was now excited, couldn't stop talking about the Speaker at supper last night. Do you know that he didn't even know how to transfer money? And you wouldn't believe the awful password that he has—I thought the computers were supposed to reject words like that—no, I can't tell you, it's a secret—I was practically teaching him how to do *searches*—but I think he understands computers, he's not an *idiot* or anything—he said he used to have a slave program, that's why he's got that jewel in his ear—he told me I could pay myself anything I want, not that there's much to buy, but I can save it for when I get out on my own —I think he's really old. I think he remembers things from a long time ago. I think he speaks Stark as his native language, there aren't many people in the Hundred Worlds who actually grow up speaking it, do you think maybe he was born on Earth?

Until Quim finally screamed at him to shut up about that servant of the devil or he'd ask the Bishop to conduct an exorcism because Olhado was obviously *possessed;* and when Olhado only grinned and winked, Quim stormed out of the kitchen, out of the house, and didn't come back until late at night. The Speaker might as well *live* at our house, thought Novinha, because he keeps influencing the family even when he isn't there and now he's prying in my files and I won't have it.

Except that, as usual, it's my own fault, I'm the one who called him here, I'm the one who took him from whatever place he called home—he says he had a sister there—Trondheim, it was—it's my fault he's here in this miserable little town in a backwater of the Hundred Worlds, surrounded by a fence that still doesn't keep the piggies from killing everyone I love—

And once again she thought of Miro, who looked so much like his real father that she couldn't understand why no one accused her of adultery, thought of him lying on the hillside as Pipo had lain, thought of the piggies cutting him open with their cruel wooden knives. They will. No matter what I do, they will. And even if they don't, the day will come soon when he will be old enough to marry Ouanda, and then I'll have to tell him who he really is, and why they can never marry, and he'll know then that I did deserve all the pain that Cão inflicted on me, that he struck me with the hand of God to punish me for my sins.

Even me, thought Novinha. This Speaker has forced me to think of things I've managed to hide from myself for weeks, months at a time. How long has it been since I've spent a morning thinking about my children? And with hope, no less. How long since I've let myself think of Pipo and Libo? How long since I've even noticed that I do believe in God, at least the vengeful, punishing Old Testament God who wiped out cities with a smile because they didn't pray to him—if Christ amounts to anything I don't know it.

Thus Novinha passed the day, doing no work, while her thoughts also refused to carry her to any sort of conclusion.

In midafternoon Quim came to the door. "I'm sorry to bother you, Mother."

"It doesn't matter," she said. "I'm useless today, anyway."

"I know you don't care that Olhado is spending his time with that satanic bastard, but I thought you should know that Quara went straight there after school. To his house."

"Oh?"

"Or don't you care about that either, Mother? What, are you planning to turn down the sheets and let him take Father's place completely?"

Novinha leapt to her feet and advanced on the boy with cold fury. He wilted before her.

"I'm sorry, Mother, I was so angry—"

"In all my years of marriage to your father, I never once permitted him to raise a hand against my children. But if he were alive today I'd ask him to give you a thrashing."

"You could ask," said Quim defiantly, "but I'd kill him before I let him lay a hand on me. You might like getting slapped around, but nobody'll ever do it to me!"

She didn't decide to do it; her hand swung out and slapped his face before she noticed it was happening.

It couldn't have hurt him very much. But he immediately burst into tears, slumped down, and sat on the floor, his back to Novinha. "I'm sorry, I'm sorry," he kept murmuring as he cried.

She knelt behind him and awkwardly rubbed his shoulders. It occurred to her that she hadn't so much as embraced the boy since he was Grego's age. When did I decide to be so cold? And why, when I touched him again, was it a slap instead of a kiss?

"I'm worried about what's happening, too," said Novinha.

"He's wrecking everything," said Quim. "He's come here and everything's changing."

"Well, for that matter, Estevão, things weren't so very wonderful that a change wasn't welcome."

"Not *his* way. Confession and penance and absolution, that's the change we need."

Not for the first time, Novinha envied Quim's faith in the power of the priests to wash away sin. That's because you've never sinned, my son, that's because you know nothing of the impossibility of penance.

"I think I'll have a talk with the Speaker," said Novinha.

"And take Quara home?"

"I don't know. I can't help but notice that he got her talking again. And it isn't as if she likes him. She hasn't a good word to say about him."

"Then why did she go to his house?"

"I suppose to say something rude to him. You've got to admit that's an improvement over her silence."

"The devil disguises himself by seeming to do good acts, and then—"

"Quim, don't lecture me on demonology. Take me to the Speaker's house, and I'll deal with him."

They walked on the path around the bend of the river. The watersnakes were molting, so that snags and fragments of rotting skin made the ground slimy underfoot. That's my next project, thought Novinha. I need to figure out what makes these nasty little monsters tick, so that maybe I can find something useful to do with them. Or at least keep them from making the riverbank smelly and foul for six weeks out of the year. The only saving grace was that the snakeskins seemed to fertilize the soil; the soft rivergrass grew in thickest where the snakes molted. It was the only gentle, pleasant form of life native to Lusitania; all summer long people came to the riverbank to lie on the narrow strip of natural lawn that wound between the reeds and the harsh prairie grass. The snakeskin slime, unpleasant as it was, still promised good things for the future.

Quim was apparently thinking along the same lines. "Mother, can we plant some rivergrass near our house sometime?"

"It's one of the first things your grandparents tried, years ago. But they couldn't figure out how to do it. The rivergrass pollinates, but it doesn't bear seed, and when they tried to transplant it, it lived for a while and then died, and didn't grow back the next year. I suppose it just has to be near the water."

Quim grimaced and walked faster, obviously a little angry. Novinha sighed. Quim always seemed to take it so personally that the universe didn't always work the way he wanted it to.

They reached the Speaker's house not long after. Children were, of course, playing in the praça—they spoke loudly to hear each other over the noise.

"Here it is," said Quim. "*I* think you should get Olhado and Quara out of there."

"Thanks for showing me the house," she said.

"I'm not kidding. This is a serious confrontation between good and evil."

"Everything is," said Novinha. "It's figuring out which is which that takes so much work. No, no, Quim, I know you could tell me in detail, but—"

"Don't condescend to me, Mother."

"But Quim, it seems so natural, considering how you always condescend to me."

His face went tight with anger.

She reached out and touched him tentatively, gently; his shoulder tautened against her touch as if her hand were a poisonous spider. "Quim," she said, "don't ever try to teach me about good and evil. I've been there, and you've seen nothing but the map."

He shrugged her hand away and stalked off. My, but I miss the days when we never talked to each other for weeks at a time.

She clapped her hands loudly. In a moment the door opened. It was Quara. "Oi, Mãezinha," she said, "também veio jogar?" Did you come to play, too?

Olhado and the Speaker were playing a game of starship warfare on the terminal. The Speaker had been given a machine with a far larger and more detailed holographic field than most, and the two of them were operating squadrons of more than a dozen ships at the same time. It was very complex, and neither of them looked up or even greeted her.

"Olhado told me to shut up or he'd rip my tongue out and make me eat it in a sandwich," said Quara. "So you better not say anything till the game's over."

"Please sit down," murmured the Speaker.

"You are butchered now, Speaker," crowed Olhado.

More than half of the Speaker's fleet disappeared in a series of simulated explosions. Novinha sat down on a stool.

Quara sat on the floor beside her. "I heard you and Quim talking outside," she said. "You were shouting, so we could hear everything."

Novinha felt herself blushing. It annoyed her that the Speaker had heard her quarreling with her son. It was none of his business. Nothing in her family was any of his business. And she certainly didn't approve of him playing games of warfare. It was so archaic and outmoded, anyway. There hadn't been any battles in space in hundreds of years, unless running fights with smugglers counted. Milagre was such a peaceful place that nobody even owned a weapon more dangerous than the Constable's jolt. Olhado would never see a battle in his life. And here he was caught up in a game of war. Maybe it was something evolution had bred into males of the species, the desire to blast rivals into little bits or mash them to the ground. Or maybe the violence that he saw in his home has made him seek it out in his play. My fault. Once again, my fault.

Suddenly Olhado screamed in frustration, as his fleet disappeared in a series of explosions. "I didn't see it! I can't believe you did that! I didn't even see it coming!"

"So, don't yell about it," said the Speaker. "Play it back and see how I did it, so you can counter it next time."

"I thought you Speakers were supposed to be like priests or something. How did you get so good at tactics?"

The Speaker smiled pointedly at Novinha as he answered. "Sometimes it's a little like a battle just to get people to tell you the truth."

Olhado leaned back against the wall, his eyes closed, as he replayed what he saw of the game.

"You've been prying," said Novinha. "And you weren't very clever about it. Is that what passes for 'tactics' among Speakers for the Dead?"

"It got you here, didn't it?" The Speaker smiled.

"What were you looking for in my files?"

"I came to Speak Pipo's death."

"I didn't kill him. My files are none of your business."

"You called me here."

"I changed my mind. I'm sorry. It still doesn't give you the right to—"

His voice suddenly went soft, and he knelt in front of her so that she could hear his words. "Pipo learned something from you, and whatever he learned, the piggies killed him because of it. So you locked your files away where no one could ever find it out. You even refused to marry Libo, just so he wouldn't get access to what Pipo saw. You've twisted and distorted your life and the lives of everybody you loved in order to keep Libo and now Miro from learning that secret and dying."

Novinha felt a sudden coldness, and her hands and feet began to tremble. He had been here three days, and already he knew more than anyone but Libo had ever guessed. "It's all lies," she said.

"Listen to me, Dona Ivanova. It didn't work. Libo died anyway, didn't he? Whatever your secret is, keeping it to yourself didn't save his life. And it won't save Miro, either. Ignorance and deception can't save anybody. *Knowing* saves them."

"Never," she whispered.

"I can understand your keeping it from Libo and Miro, but what am I to you? I'm nothing to you, so what does it matter if *I* know the secret and it kills me?"

"It doesn't matter at all if you live or die," said Novinha, "but you'll never get access to those files."

"You don't seem to understand that you don't have the right to put blinders on other people's eyes. Your son and his sister go out every day to meet with the piggies, and thanks to you, they don't know whether their next word or their next act will be their death sentence. Tomorrow I'm going with them, because I can't speak Pipo's death without talking to the piggies—"

"I don't want you to Speak Pipo's death."

"I don't care what you want, I'm not doing it for you. But I am begging you to let me know what Pipo knew."

"You'll never know what Pipo knew, because he was a good and kind and loving person who—"

"Who took a lonely, frightened little girl and healed the wounds in her heart." As he said it, his hand rested on Quara's shoulder.

It was more than Novinha could bear. "Don't you dare to compare yourself to him! Quara isn't an orphan, do you hear me? She has a mother, *me,* and she doesn't need *you,* none of us need you, none of us!" And then, inexplicably, she was crying. She didn't want to cry in front of him. She didn't want to be here. He was confusing everything. She stumbled to the door and slammed it behind her. Quim was right. He was like the devil. He knew too much, demanded too much, gave too much, and already they all needed him too much. How could he have acquired so much power over them in so short a time?

Then she had a thought that at once dried up her unshed tears and filled her with terror. He had said that Miro *and his sister* went out to the piggies every day. He knew. He knew all the secrets.

All except the secret that she didn't even know herself—the one that Pipo had somehow discovered in her simulation. If he ever got that, he'd have everything that she had hidden for all these years. When she called for the Speaker for the Dead, she had wanted him to discover the truth about Pipo; instead, he had come and discovered the truth about her.

The door slammed. Ender leaned on the stool where she had sat and put his head down on his hands.

He heard Olhado stand up and walk slowly across the room toward him.

"You tried to access Mother's files," he said quietly.

"Yes," said Ender.

"You got me to teach you how to do searches so that you could spy on my own mother. You made a traitor out of me."

There was no answer that would satisfy Olhado right now; Ender didn't try. He waited in silence as Olhado walked to the door and left.

The turmoil he felt was not silent, however, to the hive queen. He felt her stir in his mind, drawn by his anguish. No, he said to her silently. There's nothing you can do, nothing I can explain. Human things, that's all, strange and alien human problems that are beyond comprehension.

<Ah.> And he felt her touch him inwardly, touch him like the breeze in the leaves of a tree; he felt the strength and vigor of up-ward-thrusting wood, the firm grip of roots in earth, the gentle play of sunlight on passionate leaves. <See what we've learned from him, Ender, the peace that he found.> The feeling faded as the hive queen retreated from his mind. The strength of the tree stayed with him, the calm of its quietude replaced his own tortured silence.

It had been only a moment; the sound of Olhado closing the door still rang in the room. Beside him, Quara jumped to her feet and skipped across the floor to his bed. She jumped up and bounced on it a few times.

"You only lasted a couple of days," she said cheerfully. "Everybody hates you now."

Ender laughed wryly and turned around to look at her. "Do *you?*"

"Oh, yes," she said. "I hated you first of all, except maybe Quim." She slid off the bed and walked to the terminal. One key at a time, she carefully logged on. A group of double-column addition problems appeared in the air above the terminal. "You want to see me do arithmetic?"

Ender got up and joined her at the terminal. "Sure," he said. "Those look hard, though."

"Not for me," she said boastfully. "I do them faster than anybody."

Chapter 13

Ela

MIRO: The piggies call themselves males, but we're only taking their word for it.

OUANDA: Why would they lie?

MIRO: I know you're young and naive, but there's some missing equipment.

OUANDA: I passed physical anthropology. Who says they do it the way we do it?

MIRO: Obviously they don't. (For that matter, WE don't do it at all.) Maybe I've figured out where their genitals are. Those bumps on their bellies, where the hair is light and fine.

OUANDA: Vestigial nipples. Even you have them.

MIRO: I saw Leaf-eater and Pots yesterday, about ten meters off, so I didn't see them WELL, but Pots was stroking Leaf-eater's belly, and I think those belly-bumps might have tumesced.

OUANDA: Or they might not.

MIRO: One thing for sure. Leaf-eater's belly was wet—the sun was reflected off it—and he was enjoying it.

OUANDA: This is perverted.

MIRO: Why not? They're all bachelors, aren't they? They're adults, but their so-called wives haven't introduced any of them to the joys of fatherhood.

OUANDA: I think a sex-starved zenador is projecting his own frustrations onto his subjects.

—Marcos Vladimir "Miro" Ribeira von Hesse and Ouanda Quenhatta, Figueira Mucumbi, Working Notes, 1970: 1:4:30

The clearing was very still. Miro saw at once that something was wrong. The piggies weren't *doing* anything. Just standing or sitting here and there. And *still;* hardly a breath. Staring at the ground.

Except Human, who emerged from the forest behind them. He walked slowly, stiffly around to the front. Miro felt Ouanda's elbow press against him, but he did not look at her. He knew she was thinking the same thing he thought. Is this the moment that they will kill us, as they killed Libo and Pipo?

Human regarded them steadily for several minutes. It was unnerving to have him wait so long. But Miro and Ouanda were disciplined. They said nothing, did not even let their faces change from the relaxed, meaningless expression they had practiced for so many years. The art of noncommunication was the first one they had to learn before Libo would let either of them come with him. Until their faces showed nothing, until they did not even perspire visibly under emotional stress, no piggy would see them. As if it did any good— Human was too adroit at turning evasions into answers, gleaning facts from empty statements. Even their absolute stillness no doubt communicated their fear, but out of that circle there could be no escape. Everything communicated something.

"You have lied to us," said Human.

Don't answer, Miro said silently, and Ouanda was as wordless as if she had heard him. No doubt she was also thinking the same message to him.

"Rooter says that the Speaker for the Dead wants to come to us."

It was the most maddening thing about the piggies. Whenever they had something outrageous to say, they always blamed it on some dead piggy who couldn't possibly have said it. No doubt there was some religious ritual involved: Go to their totem tree, ask a leading question, and lie there contemplating the leaves or the bark or something until you get exactly the answer you want.

"We never said otherwise," said Miro.

Ouanda breathed a little more quickly.

"You said he wouldn't come."

"That's right," said Miro. "He wouldn't. He has to obey the law just like anyone else. If he tried to pass through the gate without permission—"

"That's a lie."

Miro fell silent.

"It's the law," said Ouanda quietly.

"The law has been twisted before this," said Human. "You could bring him here, but you don't. Everything depends on you bringing him here. Rooter says the hive queen can't give us her gifts unless he comes."

Miro quelled his impatience. The hive queen! Hadn't he told the piggies a dozen times that all the buggers were killed? And now the dead hive queen was talking to them as much as dead Rooter. The piggies would be much easier to deal with if they could stop getting orders from the dead.

"It's the law," said Ouanda again. "If we even ask him to come, he might report us and we'd be sent away, we'd never come to you again."

"He won't report you. He wants to come."

"How do you know?"

"Rooter says."

There were times that Miro wanted to chop down the totem tree that grew where Rooter had been killed. Maybe then they'd shut up about what Rooter says. But instead they'd probably name some other tree Rooter and be outraged as well. Don't even admit that you doubt their religion, that was a textbook rule; even offworld xenologers, even *anthropologists* knew that.

"Ask him," said Human.

"Rooter?" asked Ouanda.

"He wouldn't speak to *you*," said Human. Contemptuously? "Ask the Speaker whether he'll come or not."

Miro waited for Ouanda to answer. She knew already what *his* answer would be. Hadn't they argued it out a dozen times in the last two days? He's a good man, said Miro. He's a fake, said Ouanda. He was good with the little ones, said Miro. So are child molesters, said Ouanda. I believe in him, said Miro. Then you're an idiot, said Ouanda. We can trust him, said Miro. He'll betray us, said Ouanda. And that was where it always ended.

But the piggies changed the equation. The piggies added great pressure on Miro's side. Usually when the piggies demanded the impossible he had helped her fend them off. But this was not impossible, he did not want them fended off, and so he said nothing. Press her, Human, because you're right and this time Ouanda must bend.

Feeling herself alone, knowing Miro would not help her, she gave a little ground. "Maybe if we only bring him as far as the edge of the forest."

"Bring him here," said Human.

"We can't," she said. "Look at you. Wearing cloth. Making pots. Eating bread."

Human smiled. "Yes," he said. "All of that. Bring him here."

"No," said Ouanda.

Miro flinched, stopping himself from reaching out to her. It was the one thing they had never done—flatly denied a request. Always it was "We can't because" or "I wish we could." But the single word of denial said to them, I *will* not. I, of myself, refuse.

Human's smile faded. "Pipo told us that women do not say. Pipo told us that human men and women decide together. So you can't say no unless he says no, too." He looked at Miro. "Do you say no?"

Miro did not answer. He felt Ouanda's elbow touching him.

"You don't say *nothing,*" said Human. "You say yes or no."

Still Miro didn't answer.

Some of the piggies around them stood up. Miro had no idea what they were doing, but the movement itself, with Miro's intransigent silence as a cue, seemed menacing. Ouanda, who would never be cowed by a threat to herself, bent to the implied threat to Miro. "He says yes," she whispered.

"He says yes, but for you he stays silent. You say no, but you don't stay silent for *him.*" Human scooped thick mucus out of his mouth with one finger and flipped it onto the ground. "You are nothing."

Human suddenly fell backward into a somersault, twisted in midmovement, and came up with his back to them, walking away. Immediately the other piggies came to life, moving swiftly toward Human, who led them toward the forest edge farthest from Miro and Ouanda.

Human stood abruptly. Another piggy, instead of following him, stood in front of him, blocking his way. It was Leaf-eater. If he or Human spoke, Miro could not hear them or see their mouths move. He did see, though, that Leaf-eater extended his hand to touch Human's belly. The hand stayed there a moment, then Leaf-eater whirled around and scampered off into the bushes like a youngling.

In a moment the other piggies were also gone.

"It was a battle," said Miro. "Human and Leaf-eater. They're on opposite sides."

"Of what?" said Ouanda.

"I wish I knew. But I can guess. If we bring the Speaker, Human wins. If we don't, Leaf-eater wins."

"Wins what? Because if we bring the Speaker, he'll betray us, and then we all lose."

"He won't betray us."

"Why shouldn't he, if you'd betray *me* like that?"

Her voice was a lash, and he almost cried out from the sting of her words. "I betray you!" he whispered. "Eu não. Jamais." Not me. Never.

"Father always said, Be united in front of the piggies, never let them see you in disagreement, and you—"

"And *I!* I didn't say yes to them. You're the one who said no, you're the one who took a position that you knew I didn't agree with!"

"Then when we disagree, it's your job to—"

She stopped. She had only just realized what she was saying. But stopping did not undo what Miro knew she was going to say. It was his job to do what she said until she changed her mind. As if he were her *apprentice.* "And here I thought we were in this together." He turned and walked away from her, into the forest, back toward Milagre.

"Miro," she called after him. "Miro, I didn't mean that—"

He waited for her to catch up, then caught her by the arm and whispered fiercely, "Don't shout! Or don't you care whether the piggies hear us or not? Has the master Zenador decided that we can let them see *everything* now, even the master disciplining her apprentice?"

"I'm not the master, I—"

"That's right, you're not." He turned away from her and started walking again.

"But Libo was my *father,* so of course I'm the—"

"Zenador by blood right," he said. "Blood right, is that it? So what am I by blood right? A drunken wife-beating cretin?" He took her by the arms, gripping her cruelly. "Is that what you want me to be? A little copy of my paizinho?"

"Let go!"

He shoved her away. "Your apprentice thinks you were a fool today," said Miro. "Your apprentice thinks you should have trusted his judgment of the Speaker, and your apprentice thinks you should have trusted his assessment of how serious the piggies were about this, because you were stupidly wrong about both matters, and you may just have cost Human his life."

It was an unspeakable accusation, but it was exactly what they both feared, that Human would end up now as Rooter had, as others had over the years, disemboweled, with a seedling growing out of his corpse.

Miro knew he had spoken unfairly, knew that she would not be wrong to rage against him. He had no right to blame her when neither of them could possibly have known what the stakes might have been for Human until it was too late.

Ouanda did not rage, however. Instead, she calmed herself visibly, drawing even breaths and blanking her face. Miro followed her example and did the same. "What matters," said Ouanda, "is to make the best of it. The executions have always been at night. If we're to have a hope of vindicating Human, we have to get the Speaker here this afternoon, before dark."

Miro nodded. "Yes," he said. "And I'm sorry."

"I'm sorry too," she said.

"Since we don't know what we're doing, it's nobody's fault when we do things wrong."

"I only wish that I believed a *right* choice were possible."

Ela sat on a rock and bathed her feet in the water while she waited for the Speaker for the Dead. The fence was only a few meters away, running along the top of the steel grillwork that blocked the people from swimming under it. As if anyone wanted to try. Most people in Milagre pretended the fence wasn't there. Never came near it. That was why she had asked the Speaker to meet her here. Even though the day was warm and school was out, children didn't swim here at Vila Última, where the fence came to the river and the forest came nearly to the fence. Only the soapmakers and potters and brickmakers came here, and they left again when the day's work was over. She could say what she had to say, without fear of anyone overhearing or interrupting.

She didn't have to wait long. The Speaker rowed up the river in a small boat, just like one of the farside farmers, who had no use for roads. The skin of his back was shockingly white; even the few Lusos who were light-complected enough to be called *loiros* were much darker-skinned. His whiteness made him seem weak and slight. But then she saw how quickly the boat moved against the current; how accurately the oars were placed each time at just the right depth, with a long, smooth pull; how tightly wrapped in skin his muscles were. She felt a moment's stab of grief, and then realized that it was grief for her father, despite the depth of her hatred for him; she had not realized until this moment that she loved anything about him, but she grieved for the strength of his shoulders and back, for the sweat that made his brown skin dazzle like glass in the sunlight.

No, she said silently, I don't grieve for your death, Cão. I grieve that you were not more like the Speaker, who has no connection with us and yet has given us more good gifts in three days than you in your whole life; I grieve that your beautiful body was so worm-eaten inside.

The Speaker saw her and skimmed the boat to shore, where she waited. She waded in the reeds and muck to help him pull the boat aground.

"Sorry to get you muddy," he said. "But I haven't used my body in a couple of weeks, and the water invited me—"

"You row well," she said.

"The world I came from, Trondheim, was mostly ice and water. A bit of rock here and there, some soil, but anyone who couldn't row was more crippled than if he couldn't walk."

"That's where you were born?"

"No. Where I last Spoke, though." He sat on the grama, facing the water.

She sat beside him. "Mother's angry at you."

His lips made a little half-smile. "She told me."

Without thinking, Ela immediately began to justify her mother. "You tried to read her files."

"I *read* her files. Most of them. All but the ones that mattered."

"I know. Quim told me." She caught herself feeling just a little triumphant that Mother's protection system had bested him. Then she remembered that she was not on Mother's side in this. That she had been trying for years to get Mother to open those very files to her. But momentum carried her on, saying things she didn't mean to say. "Olhado's sitting in the house with his eyes shut off and music blasting into his ears. Very upset."

"Yes, well, he thinks I betrayed him."

"Didn't you?" That was not what she meant to say.

"I'm a Speaker for the Dead. I tell the truth, when I speak at all, and I don't keep away from other people's secrets."

"I know. That's why I called for a Speaker. You don't have any respect for anybody."

He looked annoyed. "Why did you invite me here?" he asked.

This was working out all wrong. She was talking to him as if she were against him, as if she weren't grateful for what he had already done for the family. She was talking to him like the enemy. Has Quim taken over my mind, so that I say things I don't mean?

"You invited me to this place on the river. The rest of your family isn't speaking to me, and then I get a message from *you.* To complain about my breaches of privacy? To tell me I don't respect anybody?"

"No," she said miserably. "This isn't how it was supposed to go."

"Didn't it occur to you that I would hardly choose to be a Speaker if I had no respect for people?"

In frustration she let the words burst out. "I wish you had broken into *all* her files! I wish you had taken every one of her secrets and published them through all the Hundred Worlds!" There were tears in her eyes; she couldn't think why.

"I see. She doesn't let you see those files, either."

"Sou aprendiz dela, não sou? E porque choro, diga-me! O senhor tem o jeito."

"I don't have any knack for making people cry, Ela," he answered softly. His voice was a caress. No, stronger, it was like a hand gripping her hand, holding her, steadying her. "Telling the truth makes you cry."

"Sou ingrata, sou má filha—"

"Yes, you're ungrateful, and a terrible daughter," he said, laughing softly. "Through all these years of chaos and neglect you've held your mother's family together with little help from her, and when you followed her in her career, she wouldn't share the most vital information with you; you've earned nothing but love and trust from her and she's replied by shutting you out of her life at home and at work; and then you finally tell somebody that you're sick of it. You're just about the worst person I've ever known."

She found herself laughing at her own self-condemnation. Childishly, she didn't want to laugh at herself. "Don't patronize me." She tried to put as much contempt into her voice as possible.

He noticed. His eyes went distant and cold. "Don't spit at a friend," he said.

She didn't want him to be distant from her. But she couldn't stop herself from saying, coldly, angrily, "You aren't my friend."

For a moment she was afraid he believed her. Then a smile came to his face. "You wouldn't know a friend if you saw one."

Yes I would, she thought. I see one now. She smiled back at him.

"Ela," he said, "are you a good xenobiologist?"

"Yes."

"You're eighteen years old. You could take the guild tests at sixteen. But you didn't take them."

"Mother wouldn't let me. She said I wasn't ready."

"You don't have to have your mother's permission after you're sixteen."

"An apprentice has to have the permission of her master."

"And now you're eighteen, and you don't even need that."

"She's still Lusitania's xenobiologist. It's still her lab. What if I passed the test, and then she wouldn't let me into the lab until after she was dead?"

"Did she threaten that?"

"She made it clear that I wasn't to take the test."

"Because as soon as you're not an apprentice anymore, if she admits you to the lab as her co-xenobiologist you have full access—"

"To all the working files. To all the *locked* files."

"So she'd hold her own daughter back from beginning her career, she'd give you a permanent blot on your record—unready for the tests even at age eighteen—just to keep you from reading those files."

"Yes."

"Why?"

"Mother's crazy."

"No. Whatever else Novinha is, Ela, she is *not* crazy."

"Ela é boba mesma, Senhor Falante."

He laughed and lay back in the grama. "Tell me how she's boba, then."

"I'll give you the list. First: She won't allow any investigation of the Descolada. Thirty-four years ago the Descolada nearly destroyed this colony. My grandparents, Os Venerados, Deus os abençoe, they barely managed to stop the Descolada. Apparently the disease agent, the Descolada bodies, are still present—we have to eat a supplement, like an extra vitamin, to keep the plague from striking again. They told you that, didn't they? If you once get it in your system, you'll have to keep that supplement all your life, even if you leave here."

"I knew that, yes."

"She won't let me study the Descolada bodies *at all*. That's what's in *some* of the locked files, anyway. She's locked up all of Gusto's and Cida's discoveries about the Descolada bodies. Nothing's available."

The Speaker's eyes narrowed. "So. That's one-third of boba. What's the rest?"

"It's more than a third. Whatever the Descolada body is, it was able to adapt to become a human parasite ten years after the colony was founded. Ten years! If it can adapt once, it can adapt again."

"Maybe she doesn't think so."

"Maybe I ought to have a right to decide that for myself."

He put out a hand, rested it on her knee, calmed her. "I agree with you. But go on. The second reason she's boba."

"She won't allow any theoretical research. No taxonomy. No evolutionary models. If I ever try to do any, she says I obviously don't have enough to do and weighs me down with assignments until she thinks I've given up."

"You haven't given up, I take it."

"That's what xenobiology's *for*. Oh, yes, fine that she can make a potato that makes maximum use of the ambient nutrients. Wonderful that she made a breed of amaranth that makes the colony protein self-sufficient with only ten acres under cultivation. But that's all molecular *juggling.*"

"It's survival."

"But we don't *know* anything. It's like swimming on the top of the ocean. You get very comfortable, you can move around a little, but you don't know if there are sharks down there! We could be surrounded by sharks and she doesn't want to find out."

"Third thing?"

"She won't exchange information with the Zenadors. Period. Nothing. And that really *is* crazy. *We* can't leave the fenced area. That means that we don't have a *single tree* we can study. We know absolutely nothing about the flora and fauna of this world except what happened to be included inside the fence. One herd of cabra and a bunch of capim grass, and then a slightly different riverside ecology, and that's everything. Nothing about the kinds of animals in the forest, no information exchange at all. We don't tell them anything, and if they send us data we erase the files unread. It's like she built this wall around us that nothing could get through. Nothing gets in, nothing goes out."

"Maybe she has reasons."

"Of course she has reasons. Crazy people always have reasons. For one thing, she hated Libo. *Hated* him. She wouldn't let Miro talk about him, wouldn't let us play with his children—China and I were best friends for years and she wouldn't let me bring her home or go to her house after school. And when Miro apprenticed to him, she didn't speak to him or set his place at the table for a year."

She could see that the Speaker doubted her, thought she was exaggerating.

"I mean one year. The day he went to the Zenador's Station for the first time as Libo's apprentice, he came home and she didn't speak to him, not a word, and when he sat down to dinner she removed the plate from in front of his face, just cleaned up his silverware as if he weren't there. He sat there through the entire meal, just looking at her. Until Father got angry at him for being rude and told him to leave the room."

"What did he do, move out?"

"No. You don't know Miro!" Ela laughed bitterly. "He doesn't fight, but he doesn't give up, either. He never answered Father's abuse, never. In all my life I don't remember hearing him answer anger with anger. And Mother—well, he came home *every night* from the Zenador's Station and sat down where a plate was set, and every night Mother took up his plate and silverware, and he sat there till Father made him leave. Of course, within a week Father was yelling at him to get out as soon as Mother reached for his plate. Father loved it, the bastard, he thought it was great, he hated Miro so much, and finally Mother was on his side against Miro."

"Who gave in?"

"Nobody gave in." Ela looked at the river, realizing how terrible this all sounded, realizing that she was shaming her family in front of a stranger. But he wasn't a stranger, was he? Because Quara was talking again, and Olhado was involved in things again, and Grego, for just a short time, Grego had been almost a normal boy. He wasn't a stranger.

"How did it end?" asked the Speaker.

"It ended when the piggies killed Libo. That's how much Mother hated the man. When he died she celebrated by forgiving her son. That night when Miro came home, it was after dinner was over, it was late at night. A terrible night, everybody was so afraid, the piggies seemed so awful, and everybody loved Libo so much—except Mother, of course. Mother waited up for Miro. He came in and went into the kitchen and sat down at the table, and Mother put a plate down in front of him, put food on the plate. Didn't say a word. He ate it, too. Not a word about it. As if the year before hadn't happened. I woke up in the middle of the night because I could hear Miro throwing up and crying in the bathroom. I don't think anybody else heard, and I didn't go to him because I didn't think he wanted anybody to hear him. Now I think I should have gone, but I was afraid. There were such terrible things in my family."

The Speaker nodded.

"I should have gone to him," Ela said again.

"Yes," the Speaker said. "You should have."

A strange thing happened then. The Speaker agreed with her that she had made a mistake that night, and she knew when he said the words that it was true, that his judgment was correct. And yet she felt strangely healed, as if simply saying her mistake were enough to purge some of the pain of it. For the first time, then, she caught a glimpse of what the power of Speaking might be. It wasn't a matter of confession, penance, and absolution, like the priests offered. It was something else entirely. Telling the story of who she was, and then realizing that she was no longer the same person. That she had made a mistake, and the mistake had changed her, and now she would not make the mistake again because she had become someone else, someone less afraid, someone more compassionate.

If I'm not that frightened girl who heard her brother in desperate pain and dared not go to him, who am I? But the water flowing through the grillwork under the fence held no answers. Maybe she couldn't know who she was today. Maybe it was enough to know that she was no longer who she was before.

Still the Speaker lay there on the grama, looking at the clouds coming darkly out of the west. "I've told you all I know," Ela said. "I told you what was in those files—the Descolada information. That's all I know."

"No it isn't," said the Speaker.

"It is, I promise."

"Do you mean to say that you obeyed her? That when your mother told you not to do any theoretical work, you simply turned off your mind and did what she wanted?"

Ela giggled. "She thinks so."

"But you didn't."

"I'm a scientist, even if she isn't."

"She was once," said the Speaker. "She passed her tests when she was thirteen."

"I know," said Ela.

"And she used to share information with Pipo before he died."

"I know that, too. It was just Libo that she hated."

"So tell me, Ela. What have you discovered in your theoretical work?"

"I haven't discovered any answers. But at least I know what some of the questions are. That's a start, isn't it? Nobody else is asking questions. It's so funny, isn't it? Miro says the framling xenologers are always pestering him and Ouanda for more information, more data, and yet the law forbids them from learning anything more. And yet not a single framling xenobiologist has ever asked us for *any* information. They all just study the biosphere on their own planets and don't ask Mother a single question. I'm the only one asking, and nobody cares."

"I care," said the Speaker. "I need to know what the questions are."

"OK, here's one. We have a herd of cabra here inside the fence. The cabra can't jump the fence, they don't even touch it. I've examined and tagged every single cabra in the herd, and you know something? There's not one male. They're *all* female."

"Bad luck," said the Speaker. "You'd think they would have left at least one male inside."

"It doesn't matter," said Ela. "I don't know if there *are* any males. In the last five years every single adult cabra has given birth at least once. And not one of them has mated."

"Maybe they clone," said the Speaker.

"The offspring is not genetically identical to the mother. That much research I could sneak into the lab without Mother noticing. There *is* some kind of gene transfer going on."

"Hermaphrodites?"

"No. Pure female. No male sexual organs at all. Does that qualify as an important question? Somehow the cabras are having some kind of genetic exchange, without sex."

"The theological implications alone are astounding."

"Don't make fun."

"Of which? Science or theology?"

"Either one. Do you want to hear more of my questions or not?"

"I do," said the Speaker.

"Then try this. The grass you're lying on—we call it grama. All the watersnakes are hatched here. Little worms so small you can hardly see them. They eat the grass down to the nub and eat each other, too, shedding skin each time they grow larger. Then all of a sudden, when the grass is completely slimy with their dead skin, all the snakes slither off into the river *and they never come back out.*"

He wasn't a xenobiologist. He didn't get the implication right away.

"The watersnakes *hatch* here," she explained, "but they don't come back out of the water to lay their eggs."

"So they mate here before they go into the water."

"Fine, of course, obviously. I've seen them mating. That's not the problem. The problem is, *why are they watersnakes?*"

He still didn't get it.

"Look, they're completely adapted to life underwater. They have gills along with lungs, they're superb swimmers, they have fins for guidance, they are completely evolved for adult life in the water. Why would they ever have evolved that way if they are born on land, mate on land, and *reproduce* on land? As far as evolution is concerned, anything that happens after you reproduce is completely irrelevant, except if you nurture your young, and the watersnakes definitely don't nurture. Living in the water does nothing to enhance their ability to survive until they reproduce. They could slither into the water and *drown* and it wouldn't matter because reproduction is *over.*"

"Yes," said the Speaker. "I see now."

"There are little clear eggs in the water, though. I've never seen a watersnake lay them, but since there's no other animal in or near the river large enough to lay the eggs, it seems logical that they're watersnake eggs. Only these big clear eggs—a centimeter across— they're completely sterile. The nutrients are there, everything's ready, but there's no embryo. Nothing. Some of them have a gamete —half a set of genes in a cell, ready to combine—but not a single one was alive. And we've never found watersnake eggs on land. One day there's nothing there but grama, getting riper and riper; the next day the grama stalks are crawling with baby watersnakes. Does this sound like a question worth exploring?"

"It sounds like spontaneous generation to me."

"Yes, well, I'd like to find enough information to test some alternate hypotheses, but Mother won't let me. I asked her about this one and she made me take over the whole amaranth testing process so I wouldn't have time to muck around in the river. And another question. Why are there so few species here? On every other planet, even some of the nearly desert ones like Trondheim, there are thousands of different species, at least in the water. Here there's hardly a handful, as far as I can tell. The xingadora are the only birds we've seen. The suckflies are the only flies. The cabra are the only ruminants eating the capim grass. Except for the cabras, the piggies are the only large animals we've seen. Only one species of tree. Only one species of grass on the prairie, the capim; and the only other competing plant is the tropeça, a long vine that wanders along the ground for meters and meters—the xingadora make their nests out of the vine. That's it. The xingadora eat the suckflies and nothing else. The suckflies eat the algae along the edge of the river. And our garbage, and that's it. Nothing eats the xingadora. Nothing eats the cabra."

"Very limited," said the Speaker.

"Impossibly limited. There are ten thousand ecological niches here that are completely unfilled. There's no way that evolution could leave this world so sparse."

"Unless there was a disaster."

"Exactly."

"Something that wiped out all but a handful of species that were able to adapt."

"Yes," said Ela. "You see? And I have proof. The cabras have a huddling behavior pattern. When you come up on them, when they smell you, they circle with the adults facing inward, so they can kick out at the intruder and protect the young."

"Lots of herd animals do that."

"Protect them from what? The piggies are completely sylvan— they *never* hunt on the prairie. Whatever the predator was that forced the cabra to develop that behavior pattern, it's gone. And only recently—in the last hundred thousand years, the last million years maybe."

"There's no evidence of any meteor falls more recent than twenty million years," said the Speaker.

"No. That kind of disaster would kill off all the big animals and plants and leave hundreds of small ones, or maybe kill all land life and leave only the sea. But land, sea, all the environments were stripped, and yet some big creatures survived. No, I think it was a disease. A disease that struck across all species boundaries, that could adapt itself to any living thing. Of course, we wouldn't notice that disease now because all the species left alive have adapted to it. It would be part of their regular life pattern. The only way we'd notice the disease—"

"Is if we caught it," said the Speaker. "The Descolada."

"You see? Everything comes back to the Descolada. My grandparents found a way to stop it from killing humans, but it took the best genetic manipulation. The cabra, the watersnakes, they also found ways to adapt, and I doubt it was with dietary supplements. I think it all ties in together. The weird reproductive anomalies, the emptiness of the ecosystem, it all comes back to the Descolada bodies, and Mother won't let me examine them. She won't let me study what they are, how they work, how they might be involved with—"

"With the piggies."

"Well, of course, but not just them, *all* the animals—"

The Speaker looked like he was suppressing excitement. As if she had explained something difficult. "The night that Pipo died, she locked the files showing all her current work, and she locked the files containing all the Descolada research. Whatever she showed Pipo had to do with the Descolada bodies, and it had to do with the piggies—"

"That's when she locked the files?" asked Ela.

"Yes. Yes."

"Then I'm right, aren't I."

"Yes," he said. "Thank you. You've helped me more than you know."

"Does this mean that you'll speak Father's death soon?"

The Speaker looked at her carefully. "You don't want me to Speak your father, really. You want me to Speak your mother."

"She isn't dead."

"But you know I can't possibly Speak Marcão without explaining why he married Novinha, and why they stayed married all those years."

"That's right. I want all the secrets opened up. I want all the files unlocked. I don't want anything hidden."

"You don't know what you're asking," said the Speaker. "You don't know how much pain it will cause if all the secrets come out."

"Take a look at my family, Speaker," she answered. "How can the truth cause any more pain than the secrets have already caused?"

He smiled at her, but it was not a mirthful smile. It was— affectionate, even pitying. "You're right," he said, "completely right, but you may have trouble realizing that, when you hear the whole story."

"I *know* the whole story, as far as it can be known."

"That's what everybody thinks, and nobody's right."

"When will you have the Speaking?"

"As soon as I can."

"Then why not now? Today? What are you waiting for?"

"I can't do anything until I talk to the piggies."

"You're joking, aren't you? Nobody can talk to the piggies except the Zenadors. That's by Congressional Order. Nobody can get past *that.*"

"Yes," said the Speaker. "That's why it's going to be hard."

"Not hard, impossible—"

"Maybe," he said. He stood; so did she. "Ela, you've helped me tremendously. Taught me everything I could have hoped to learn from you. Just like Olhado did. But he didn't like what I did with the things he taught me, and now he thinks I betrayed him."

"He's a kid. I'm eighteen."

The Speaker nodded, put his hand on her shoulder, squeezed. "We're all right then. We're friends."

She was almost sure there was irony in what he said. Irony and, perhaps, a plea. "Yes," she insisted. "We're friends. Always."

He nodded again, turned away, pushed the boat from shore, and splashed after it through the reeds and muck. Once the boat was fairly afloat, he sat down and extended the oars, rowed, and then looked up and smiled at her. Ela smiled back, but the smile could not convey the elation she felt, the perfect relief. He had listened to everything, and understood everything, and he would make everything all right. She believed that, believed it so completely that she didn't even notice that it was the source of her sudden happiness. She knew only that she had spent an hour with the Speaker for the Dead, and now she felt more alive than she had in years.

She retrieved her shoes, put them back on her feet, and walked home. Mother would still be at the Biologista's Station, but Ela didn't want to work this afternoon. She wanted to go home and fix dinner; that was always solitary work. She hoped no one would talk with her. She hoped there'd be no problem she was expected to solve. Let this feeling linger forever.

Ela was only home for a few minutes, however, when Miro burst into the kitchen. "Ela," he said. "Have you seen the Speaker for the Dead?"

"Yes," she said. "On the river."

"*Where* on the river!"

If she told him where they had met, he'd know that it wasn't a chance meeting. "Why?" she asked.

"Listen, Ela, this is no time to be suspicious, please. I've got to find him. We've left messages for him, the computer can't find him—"

"He was rowing downriver, toward home. He's probably going to be at his house soon."

Miro rushed from the kitchen into the front room. Ela heard him tapping at the terminal. Then he came back in. "Thanks," he said. "Don't expect me home for dinner."

"What's so urgent?"

"Nothing." It was so ridiculous, to say "nothing" when Miro was obviously agitated and hurried, that they both burst out laughing at once. "OK," said Miro, "it isn't nothing, it's something, but I can't talk about it, OK?"

"OK." But soon all the secrets will be known, Miro.

"What I don't understand is why he didn't get our message. I mean, the computer was paging him. Doesn't he wear an implant in his ear? The computer's supposed to be able to reach him. Of course, maybe he had it turned off."

"No," said Ela. "The light was on."

Miro cocked his head and squinted at her. "You didn't see that tiny red light on his ear implant, not if he just happened to be out rowing in the middle of the river."

"He came to shore. We talked."

"What about?"

Ela smiled. "Nothing," she said.

He smiled back, but he looked annoyed all the same. She understood: It's all right for you to have secrets from me, but not for me to have secrets from you, is that it, Miro?

He didn't argue about it, though. He was in too much of a hurry. Had to go find the Speaker, and *now,* and he wouldn't be home for dinner.

Ela had a feeling the Speaker might get to talk to the piggies sooner than she had thought possible. For a moment she was elated. The waiting would be over.

Then the elation passed, and something else took its place. A sick fear. A nightmare of China's papai, dear Libo, lying dead on the hillside, torn apart by the piggies. Only it wasn't Libo, the way she had always imagined the grisly scene. It was Miro. No, no, it wasn't Miro. It was the Speaker. It was the Speaker who would be tortured to death. "No," she whispered.

Then she shivered and the nightmare left her mind; she went back to trying to spice and season the pasta so it would taste like something better than amaranth glue.

Chapter **14**

Renegades

LEAF-EATER: Human says that when your brothers die, you bury them in the dirt and then make your houses out of that dirt. (Laughs.)

MIRO: No. We never dig where people are buried.

LEAF-EATER: (becomes rigid with agitation): Then your dead don't do you *any good at all!*

—Ouanda Quenhatta Figueira Mucumbi, Dialogue Transcripts, 103:0:1969:4:13:111

Ender had thought they might have some trouble getting him through the gate, but Ouanda palmed the box, Miro opened the gate, and the three of them walked through. No challenge. It must be as Ela had implied—no one wants to get out of the compound, and so no serious security was needed. Whether that suggested that people were content to stay in Milagre or that they were afraid of the piggies or that they hated their imprisonment so much that they had to pretend the fence wasn't there, Ender could not begin to guess.

Both Ouanda and Miro were very tense, almost frightened. That was understandable, of course, since they were breaking Congressional rules to let him come. But Ender suspected there was more to it than that. Miro's tension was coupled with eagerness, a sense of hurry; he might be frightened, but he wanted to see what would happen, wanted to go ahead. Ouanda held back, walked a measured step, and her coldness was not just fear but hostility as well. She did not trust him.

So Ender was not surprised when she stepped behind the large tree that grew nearest the gate and waited for Miro and Ender to follow her. Ender saw how Miro looked annoyed for a moment, then controlled himself. His mask of uninvolvement was as cool as a human being could hope for. Ender found himself comparing Miro to the boys he had known in Battle School, sizing him up as a comrade in arms, and thought Miro might have done well there. Ouanda, too, but for different reasons: She held herself responsible for what was happening, even though Ender was an adult and she was much younger. She did not defer to him at all. Whatever she was afraid of, it was *not* authority.

"Here?" asked Miro blandly.

"Or not at all," said Ouanda.

Ender folded himself to sit at the base of the tree. "This is Rooter's tree, isn't it?" he asked.

They took it calmly—of course—but their momentary pause told him that yes, he had surprised them by knowing something about a past that they surely regarded as their own. I may be a framling here, Ender said silently, but I don't have to be an ignorant one.

"Yes," said Ouanda. "He's the totem they seem to get the most —direction from. Lately—the last seven or eight years. They've never let us see the rituals in which they talk to their ancestors, but it seems to involve drumming on the trees with heavy polished sticks. We hear them at night sometimes."

"Sticks? Made of fallen wood?"

"We assume so. Why?"

"Because they have no stone or metal tools to cut the wood— isn't that right? Besides, if they worship the trees, they couldn't very well cut them down."

"We don't think they worship the trees. It's totemic. They stand for dead ancestors. They—plant them. With the bodies."

Ouanda had wanted to stop, to talk or question him, but Ender had no intention of letting her believe she—or Miro, for that matter —was in charge of this expedition. Ender intended to talk to the piggies himself. He had never prepared for a Speaking by letting someone else determine his agenda, and he wasn't going to begin now. Besides, he had information they didn't have. He knew Ela's theory.

"And anywhere else?" he asked. "Do they plant trees at any other time?"

They looked at each other. "Not that we've seen," said Miro.

Ender was not merely curious. He was still thinking of what Ela had told him about reproductive anomalies. "And do the trees also grow by themselves? Are seedlings and saplings scattered through the forest?"

Ouanda shook her head. "We really don't have any evidence of the trees being planted anywhere but in the corpses of the dead. At least, all the trees we know of are quite old, except these three out here."

"Four, if we don't hurry," said Miro.

Ah. Here was the tension between them. Miro's sense of urgency was to save a piggy from being planted at the base of another tree. While Ouanda was concerned about something quite different. They had revealed enough of themselves to him; now he could let her interrogate him. He sat up straight and tipped his head back, to look up into the leaves of the tree above him, the spreading branches, the pale green of photosynthesis that confirmed the convergence, the inevitability of evolution on every world. Here was the center of all of Ela's paradoxes: evolution on this world was obviously well within the pattern that xenobiologists had seen on all the Hundred Worlds, and yet somewhere the pattern had broken down, collapsed. The piggies were one of a few dozen species that had survived the collapse. What was the Descolada, and how had the piggies adapted to it?

He had meant to turn the conversation, to say, Why are we here behind this tree? That would invite Ouanda's questions. But at that moment, his head tilted back, the soft green leaves moving gently in an almost imperceptible breeze, he felt a powerful déjà vu. He had looked up into these leaves before. Recently. But that was impossible. There were no large trees on Trondheim, and none grew within the compound of Milagre. Why did the sunlight through the leaves feel so familiar to him?

"Speaker," said Miro.

"Yes," he said, allowing himself to be drawn out of his momentary reverie.

"We didn't want to bring you out here." Miro said it firmly, and with his body so oriented toward Ouanda's that Ender understood that in fact Miro *had* wanted to bring him out here, but was including himself in Ouanda's reluctance in order to show her that he was one with her. You are in love with each other, Ender said silently. And tonight, if I speak Marcão's death tonight, I will have to tell you that you're brother and sister. I have to drive the wedge of the incest tabu between you. And you will surely hate me.

"You're going to see—some—" Ouanda could not bring herself to say it.

Miro smiled. "We call them Questionable Activities. They began with Pipo, accidentally. But Libo did it deliberately, and we are continuing his work. It is careful, gradual. We didn't just discard the Congressional rules about this. But there were crises, and we had to help. A few years ago, for instance, the piggies were running short of macios, the bark worms they mostly lived on then—"

"You're going to tell him that *first?*" asked Ouanda.

Ah, thought Ender. It isn't as important to her to maintain the illusion of solidarity as it is to him.

"He's here partly to Speak Libo's death," said Miro. "And this was what happened right before."

"We have no evidence of a causal relationship—"

"Let me discover causal relationships," said Ender quietly. "Tell me what happened when the piggies got hungry."

"It was the wives who were hungry, they said." Miro ignored Ouanda's anxiety. "You see, the males gather food for the females and the young, and so there wasn't enough to go around. They kept hinting about how they would have to go to war. About how they would probably all die." Miro shook his head. "They seemed almost happy about it."

Ouanda stood up. "He hasn't even promised. Hasn't promised anything."

"What do you want me to promise?" asked Ender.

"Not to—let any of this—"

"Not to tell on you?" asked Ender.

She nodded, though she plainly resented the childish phrase.

"I won't promise any such thing," said Ender. "My business is telling."

She whirled on Miro. "You see!"

Miro in turn looked frightened. "You can't tell. They'll seal the gate. They'll never let us through!"

"And you'd have to find another line of work?" asked Ender.

Ouanda looked at him with contempt. "Is that all you think xenology is? A job? That's another intelligent species there in the woods. Ramen, not varelse, and they must be *known.*"

Ender did not answer, but his gaze did not leave her face.

"It's like the Hive Queen and the Hegemon," said Miro. "The piggies, they're like the buggers. Only smaller, weaker, more primitive. We need to study them, yes, but that isn't enough. You can study beasts and not care a bit when one of them drops dead or gets eaten up, but these are—they're like *us.* We can't just *study* their hunger, *observe* their destruction in war, we *know* them, we—"

"Love them," said Ender.

"Yes!" said Ouanda defiantly.

"But if you left them, if you weren't here at all, they wouldn't disappear, would they?"

"No," said Miro.

"I told you he'd be just like the committee," said Ouanda.

Ender ignored her. "What would it cost them if you left?"

"It's like—" Miro struggled for words. "It's as if you could go back, to old Earth, back before the Xenocide, before star travel, and you said to them, You can travel among the stars, you can live on other worlds. And then showed them a thousand little miracles. Lights that turn on from switches. Steel. Even simple things—pots to hold water. Agriculture. They see you, they know what you are, they know that they can *become* what you are, do all the things that you do. What do they say—take this away, don't show us, let us live out our nasty, short, brutish little lives, let evolution take its course? No. They say, Give us, teach us, help us."

"And you say, I can't, and then you go away."

"It's too late!" said Miro. "Don't you understand? They've already seen the miracles! They've already seen us fly here. They've seen us be tall and strong, with magical tools and knowledge of things they never dreamed of. It's too late to tell them good-bye and go. They know what is possible. And the longer we stay, the more they try to learn, and the more they learn, the more we see how learning *helps* them, and if you have any kind of compassion, if you understand that they're—they're—"

"Human."

"Ramen, anyway. They're *our children,* do you understand that?"

Ender smiled. "What man among you, if his son asks for bread, gives him a stone?"

Ouanda nodded. "That's it. The Congressional rules say we have to give them stones. Even though we have so much bread."

Ender stood up. "Well, let's go on."

Ouanda wasn't ready. "You haven't promised—"

"Have you read the Hive Queen and the Hegemon?"

"I have," said Miro.

"Can you conceive of anyone choosing to call himself Speaker for the Dead, and then doing anything to harm these little ones, these pequeninos?"

Ouanda's anxiety visibly eased, but her hostility was no less. "You're slick, Senhow Andrew, Speaker for the Dead, you're very clever. You remind him of the Hive Queen, and speak scripture to me out of the side of your mouth."

"I speak to everyone in the language they understand," said Ender. "That isn't being slick. It's being clear."

"So you'll do whatever you want."

"As long as it doesn't hurt the piggies."

Ouanda sneered. "In *your* judgment."

"I have no one else's judgment to use." He walked away from her, out of the shade of the spreading limbs of the tree, heading for the woods that waited atop the hill. They followed him, running to catch up.

"I have to tell you," said Miro. "The piggies have been asking for you. They believe you're the very same Speaker who wrote the Hive Queen and the Hegemon."

"They've read it?"

"They've pretty well incorporated it into their religion, actually. They treat the printout we gave them like a holy book. And now they claim the hive queen herself is talking to them."

Ender glanced at him. "What does she say?" he asked.

"That you're the real Speaker. And that you've got the hive queen with you. And that you're going to bring her to live with them, and teach them all about metal and—it's really crazy stuff. That's the worst thing, they have such impossible expectations of you."

It might be simple wish fulfillment on their part, as Miro obviously believed, but Ender knew that from her cocoon the hive queen had been talking to *someone*. "How do they say the hive queen talks to them?"

Ouanda was on the other side of him now. "Not to them, just to Rooter. And Rooter talks to them. It's all part of their system of totems. We've always tried to play along with it, and act as if we believed it."

"How condescending of you," said Ender.

"It's standard anthropological practice," said Miro.

"You're so busy *pretending* to believe them, there isn't a chance in the world you could learn anything from them."

For a moment they lagged behind, so that he actually entered the forest alone. Then they ran to catch up with him. "We've devoted out lives to learning about them!" Miro said.

Ender stopped. "Not *from* them." They were just inside the trees; the spotty light through the leaves made their faces unreadable. But he knew what their faces would tell him. Annoyance, resentment, contempt—how dare this unqualified stranger question their professional attitude? This is how: "You're cultural supremacists to the core. You'll perform your Questionable Activities to help out the poor little piggies, but there isn't a chance in the world you'll notice when *they* have something to teach *you*."

"Like what!" demanded Ouanda. "Like how to murder their greatest benefactor, torture him to death after he saved the lives of dozens of their wives and children?"

"So why do you tolerate it? Why are you here helping them after what they did?"

Miro slipped in between Ouanda and Ender. Protecting her, thought Ender; or else keeping her from revealing her weaknesses. "We're professionals. We understand that cultural differences, which we can't explain—"

"You understand that the piggies are animals, and you no more condemn them for murdering Libo and Pipo than you would condemn a cabra for chewing up capim."

"That's right," said Miro.

Ender smiled. "And that's why you'll never learn anything from them. Because you think of them as animals."

"We think of them as ramen!" said Ouanda, pushing in front of Miro. Obviously she was not interested in being protected.

"You treat them as if they were not responsible for their own actions," said Ender. "Ramen are responsible for what they do."

"What are *you* going to do?" asked Ouanda sarcastically. "Come in and put them on trial?"

"I'll tell you this. The piggies have learned more about me from dead Rooter than you have learned from having me with you."

"What's *that* supposed to mean? That you really *are* the original Speaker?" Miro obviously regarded it as the most ridiculous proposition imaginable. "And I suppose you really do have a bunch of buggers up there in your starship circling Lusitania, so you can bring them down and—"

"What it means," interrupted Ouanda, "is that this amateur thinks he's better qualified to deal with the piggies than we are. And as far as I'm concerned that's proof that we should never have agreed to bring him to—"

At that moment Ouanda stopped talking, for a piggy had emerged from the underbrush. Smaller than Ender had expected. Its odor, while not wholly unpleasant, was certainly stronger than Jane's computer simulation could ever imply. "Too late," Ender murmured. "I think we're already meeting."

The piggy's expression, if he had one, was completely unreadable to Ender. Miro and Ouanda, however, could understand something of his unspoken language. "He's astonished," Ouanda murmured. By telling Ender that she understood what he did not, she was putting him in his place. That was fine. Ender knew he was a novice here. He also hoped, however, that he had stirred them a little from their normal, unquestioned way of thinking. It was obvious that they were following in well-established patterns. If he was to get any real help from them, they would have to break out of those old patterns and reach new conclusions.

"Leaf-eater," said Miro.

Leaf-eater did not take his eyes off Ender. "Speaker for the Dead," he said.

"We brought him," said Ouanda.

Leaf-eater turned and disappeared among the bushes.

"What does that mean?" Ender asked. "That he left?"

"You mean you haven't already figured it out?" asked Ouanda.

"Whether you like it or not," said Ender, "the piggies want to speak to me and I will speak to them. I think it will work out better if you help me understand what's going on. Or don't you understand it either?"

He watched them struggle with their annoyance. And then, to Ender's relief, Miro made a decision. Instead of answering with hauteur, he spoke simply, mildly. "No. We don't understand it. We're still playing guessing games with the piggies. They ask us questions, we ask them questions, and to the best of our ability neither they nor we have ever deliberately revealed a thing. We don't even ask them the questions whose answers we really want to know, for fear that they'll learn too much about us from our questions."

Ouanda was not willing to go along with Miro's decision to cooperate. "We know more than *you* will in twenty years," she said. "And you're crazy if you think you can duplicate what we know in a ten-minute briefing in the forest."

"I don't need to duplicate what you know," Ender said.

"You don't think so?" asked Ouanda.

"Because I have you with me." Ender smiled.

Miro understood and took it as a compliment. He smiled back. "Here's what we know, and it isn't much. Leaf-eater probably isn't glad to see you. There's a schism between him and a piggy named Human. When they thought we weren't going to bring you, Leaf-eater was sure he had won. Now his victory is taken away. Maybe we saved Human's life."

"And cost Leaf-eater his?" asked Ender.

"Who knows? My gut feeling is that Human's future is on the line, but Leaf-eater's isn't. Leaf-eater's just trying to make Human fail, not succeed himself."

"But you don't know."

"That's the kind of thing we never ask about." Miro smiled again. "And you're right. It's so much a habit that we usually don't even notice that we're not asking."

Ouanda was angry. "He's *right*? He hasn't even seen us at work, and suddenly he's a critic of—"

But Ender had no interest in watching them squabble. He strode off in the direction Leaf-eater had gone, and let them follow as they would. And, of course, they did, leaving their argument for later. As soon as Ender knew they were walking with him, he began to question them again. "These Questionable Activities you've carried out," he said as he walked. "You introduced new food into their diet?"

"We taught them how to eat the merdona root," said Ouanda. She was crisp and businesslike, but at least she was speaking to him. She wasn't going to let her anger keep her from being part of what was obviously going to be a crucial meeting with the piggies. "How to nullify the cyanide content by soaking it and drying it in the sun. That was the short-term solution."

"The long-term solution was some of Mother's cast-off amaranth adaptations," said Miro. "She made a batch of amaranth that was so well-adapted to Lusitania that it wasn't very good for humans. Too much Lusitanian protein structure, not enough Earthborn. But that sounded about right for the piggies. I got Ela to give me some of the cast-off specimens, without letting her know it was important."

Don't kid yourself about what Ela does and doesn't know, Ender said silently.

"Libo gave it to them, taught them how to plant it. Then how to grind it, make flour, turn it into bread. Nasty-tasting stuff, but it gave them a diet directly under their control for the first time ever. They've been fat and sassy ever since."

Ouanda's voice was bitter. "But they killed Father right after the first loaves were taken to the wives."

Ender walked in silence for a few moments, trying to make sense of this. The piggies killed Libo immediately after he saved them from starvation? Unthinkable, and yet it happened. How could such a society evolve, killing those who contributed most to its survival? They should do the opposite—they should reward the valuable ones by enhancing their opportunity to reproduce. That's how communities improve their chances of surviving as a group. How could the piggies possibly survive, murdering those who contribute most to their survival?

And yet there were human precedents. These children, Miro and Ouanda, with the Questionable Activities—they were better and wiser, in the long run, than the Starways committee that made the rules. But if they were caught, they would be taken from their homes to another world—already a death sentence, in a way, since everyone they knew would be dead before they could ever return—and they would be tried and punished, probably imprisoned. Neither their ideas nor their genes would propagate, and society would be impoverished by it.

Still, just because humans did it, too, did not make it sensible. Besides, the arrest and imprisonment of Miro and Ouanda, if it ever happened, *would* make sense if you viewed humans as a single community, and the piggies as their enemies; if you thought that anything that helped the piggies survive was somehow a menace to humanity. Then the punishment of people who enhanced the piggies' culture would be designed, not to protect the piggies, but to keep the piggies from developing.

At that moment Ender saw clearly that the rules governing human contact with the piggies did not really function to protect the piggies at all. They functioned to guarantee human superiority and power. From that point of view, by performing their Questionable Activities, Miro and Ouanda were traitors to the self-interest of their own species.

"Renegades," he said aloud.

"What?" said Miro. "What did you say?"

"Renegades. Those who have denied their own people, and claimed the enemy as their own."

"Ah," said Miro.

"We're not," said Ouanda.

"Yes we are," said Miro.

"I haven't denied my humanity!"

"The way Bishop Peregrino defines it, we denied our humanity long ago," said Miro.

"But the way I define it—" she began.

"The way you define it," said Ender, "the piggies are also human. That's *why* you're a renegade."

"I thought you said we treated the piggies like animals!" Ouanda said.

"When you don't hold them accountable, when you don't ask them direct questions, when you try to deceive them, then you treat them like animals."

"In other words," said Miro, "when we *do* follow the committee rules."

"Yes," said Ouanda, "yes, that's right, we are renegades."

"And you?" said Miro. "Why are you a renegade?"

"Oh, the human race kicked me out a long time ago. That's how I got to be a Speaker for the Dead."

With that they arrived at the piggies' clearing.

Mother wasn't at dinner and neither was Miro. That was fine with Ela. When either one of them was there, Ela was stripped of her authority; she couldn't keep control over the younger children. And yet neither Miro nor Mother took Ela's place, either. Nobody obeyed Ela and nobody else tried to keep order. So it was quieter, easier when they stayed away.

Not that the little ones were particularly well-behaved even now. They just resisted her less. She only had to yell at Grego a couple of times to keep him from poking and kicking Quara under the table. And today both Quim and Olhado were keeping to themselves. None of the normal bickering.

Until the meal was over.

Quim leaned back in his chair and smiled maliciously at Olhado. "So you're the one who taught that spy how to get into Mother's files."

Olhado turned to Ela. "You left Quim's face open again, Ela. You've got to learn to be tidier." It was Olhado's way of appealing, through humor, for Ela's intervention.

Quim did not want Olhado to have any help. "Ela's not on your side this time, Olhado. Nobody's on your side. You helped that sneaking spy get into Mother's files, and that makes you as guilty as he is. He's the devil's servant, and so are you."

Ela saw the fury in Olhado's body; she had a momentary image in her mind of Olhado flinging his plate at Quim. But the moment passed. Olhado calmed himself. "I'm sorry," Olhado said. "I didn't mean to do it."

He was giving in to Quim. He was admitting Quim was right.

"I hope," said Ela, "that you mean that you're sorry that you didn't mean to do it. I hope you aren't apologizing for helping the Speaker for the Dead."

"Of course he's apologizing for helping the spy," said Quim.

"Because," said Ela, "we should all help Speaker all we can."

Quim jumped to his feet, leaned across the table to shout in her face. "How can you say that! He was violating Mother's privacy, he was finding out her secrets, he was—"

To her surprise Ela found herself also on her feet, shoving him back across the table, shouting back at him, and louder. "Mother's secrets are the cause of half the poison in this house! Mother's secrets are what's making us *all* sick, including her! So maybe the only way to make things right here is to steal all her secrets and get them out in the open where we can kill them!" She stopped shouting. Both Quim and Ohado stood before her, pressed against the far wall as if her words were bullets and they were being executed. Quietly, intensely, Ela went on. "As far as I'm concerned, the Speaker for the Dead is the only chance we have to become a family again. And Mother's secrets are the only barrier standing in his way. So today I told him everything I knew about what's in Mother's files, because I want to give him every shred of truth that I can find."

"Then you're the worst traitor of all," said Quim. His voice was trembling. He was about to cry.

"I say that helping the Speaker for the Dead is an act of loyalty," Ela answered. "The only real treason is obeying Mother, because what she wants, what she has worked for all her life, is her own self-destruction and the destruction of this family."

To Ela's surprise, it was not Quim but Olhado who wept. His tear glands did not function, of course, having been removed when his eyes were installed. So there was no moistening of his eyes to warn of the onset of crying. Instead he doubled over with a sob, then sank down along the wall until he sat on the floor, his head between his knees, sobbing and sobbing. Ela understood why. Because she had told him that his love for the Speaker was not disloyal, that he had not sinned, and he believed her when she told him that, he knew that it was true.

Then she looked up from Olhado to see Mother standing in the doorway. Ela felt herself go weak inside, trembling at the thought of what Mother must have overheard.

But Mother did not seem angry. Just a little sad, and very tired. She was looking at Olhado.

Quim's outrage found his voice. "Did you hear what Ela was saying?" he asked.

"Yes," said Mother, never taking her eyes from Olhado. "And for all I know she might be right."

Ela was no less unnerved than Quim.

"Go to your rooms, children," Mother said quietly. "I need to talk to Olhado."

Ela beckoned to Grego and Quara, who slid off their chairs and scurried to Ela's side, eyes wide with awe at the unusual goings-on. After all, even Father had never been able to make Olhado cry. She led them out of the kitchen, back to their bedroom. She heard Quim walk down the hall and go into his own room, slam the door, and hurl himself on his bed. And in the kitchen Olhado's sobs faded, calmed, ended as Mother, for the first time since he lost his eyes, held him in her arms and comforted him, shedding her own silent tears into his hair as she rocked him back and forth.

Miro did not know what to make of the Speaker for the Dead. Somehow he had always imagined a Speaker to be very much like a priest—or rather, like a priest was supposed to be. Quiet, contemplative, withdrawn from the world, carefully leaving action and decision to others. Miro had expected him to be wise.

He had not expected him to be so intrusive, so dangerous. Yes, he was wise, all right, he kept seeing past pretense, kept saying or doing outrageous things that were, when you thought about it, exactly right. It was as if he were so familiar with the human mind that he could see, right on your face, the desires so deep, the truths so well-disguised that you didn't even know yourself that you had them in you.

How many times had Miro stood with Ouanda just like this, watching as Libo handled the piggies. But always with Libo they had understood what he was doing; they knew his technique, knew his purpose. The Speaker, however, followed lines of thought that were completely alien to Miro. Even though he wore a human shape, it made Miro wonder if Ender was really a framling—he could be as baffling as the piggies. He was as much a raman as they were, alien but still not animal.

What did the Speaker notice? What did he see? The bow that Arrow carried? The sun-dried pot in which merdona root soaked and stank? How many of the Questionable Activities did he recognize, and how many did he think were native practices?

The piggies spread out the Hive Queen and the Hegemon. "You," said Arrow, "you wrote this?"

"Yes," said the Speaker for the Dead.

Miro looked at Ouanda. Her eyes danced with vindication. So the Speaker is a liar.

Human interrupted. "The other two, Miro and Ouanda, they think you're a liar."

Miro immediately looked at the Speaker, but he wasn't glancing at them. "Of course they do," he said. "It never occurred to them that Rooter might have told you the truth."

The Speaker's calm words disturbed Miro. *Could* it be true? After all, people who traveled between star systems skipped decades, often centuries in getting from one system to another. Sometimes as much as half a millennium. It wouldn't take that many voyages for a person to survive three thousand years. But that would be too incredible a coincidence, for the original Speaker for the Dead to come here. Except that the original Speaker for the Dead *was* the one who had written the Hive Queen and the Hegemon; he *would* be interested in the first race of ramen since the buggers. I don't believe it, Miro told himself, but he had to admit the possibility that it might just be true.

"Why are they so stupid?" asked Human. "Not to know the truth when they hear it?"

"They aren't stupid," said the Speaker. "This is how humans are: We question all our beliefs, except for the ones we *really* believe, and those we never think to question. They never thought to question the idea that the original Speaker for the Dead died three thousand years ago, even though they know how star travel prolongs life."

"But we told them."

"No—you told them that the hive queen told Rooter that I wrote this book."

"That's why they should have known it was true," said Human. "Rooter is wise, he's a father; he would never make a mistake."

Miro did not smile, but he wanted to. The Speaker thought he was so clever, but now here he was, where all the important questions ended, frustrated by the piggies' insistence that their totem trees could talk to them.

"Ah," said Speaker. "There's so much that we don't understand. And so much that you don't understand. We should tell each other more."

Human sat down beside Arrow, sharing the position of honor

with him. Arrow gave no sign of minding. "Speaker for the Dead," said Human, "will you bring the hive queen to us?"

"I haven't decided yet," said the Speaker.

Again Miro looked at Ouanda. Was the Speaker insane, hinting that he could deliver what could not be delivered?

Then he remembered what the Speaker had said about questioning all our beliefs except the ones that we really believed. Miro had always taken for granted what everyone knew—that all the buggers had been destroyed. But what if a hive queen had survived? What if that was how the Speaker for the Dead had been able to write his book, because he had a bugger to talk to? It was unlikely in the extreme, but it was not *impossible.* Miro didn't know for sure that the last bugger had been killed. He only knew that everybody believed it, and that no one in three thousand years had produced a shred of evidence to the contrary.

But even if it was true, how could Human have known it? The simplest explanation was that the piggies had incorporated the powerful story of the Hive Queen and the Hegemon into their religion, and were unable to grasp the idea that there were many Speakers for the Dead, and none of them was the author of the book; that all the buggers were dead, and no hive queen could ever come. That was the simplest explanation, the one easiest to accept. Any other explanation would force him to admit the possibility that Rooter's totem tree somehow talked to the piggies.

"What will make you decide?" said Human. "We give gifts to the wives, to win their honor, but you are the wisest of all humans, and we have nothing that you need."

"You have many things that I need," said Speaker.

"What? Can't you make better pots than these? Truer arrows? The cape I wear is made from cabra wool—but your clothing is finer."

"I don't need things like that," said Speaker. "What I need are true stories."

Human leaned closer, then let his body become rigid in excitement, in anticipation. "O Speaker!" he said, and his voice was powerful with the importance of his words. "Will you add our story to the Hive Queen and the Hegemon?"

"I don't know your story," said the Speaker.

"Ask us! Ask us anything!"

"How can I tell your story? I only tell the stories of the dead."

"We are dead!" shouted Human. Miro had never seen him so agitated. "We are being murdered every day. Humans are filling up all the worlds. The ships travel through the black of night from star to star to star, filling up every empty place. Here we are, on our one little world, watching the sky fill up with humans. The humans build their stupid fence to keep us out, but that is nothing. The sky is our fence!" Human leapt upward—startlingly high, for his legs were powerful. "Look how the fence throws me back down to the ground!"

He ran at the nearest tree, bounded up the trunk, higher than Miro had ever seen him climb; he shinnied out on a limb and threw himself upward into the air. He hung there for an agonizing moment at the apex of his leap; then gravity flung him downward onto the hard ground.

Miro could hear the breath thrust out of him by the force of the blow. The Speaker immediately rushed to Human; Miro was close behind. Human wasn't breathing.

"Is he dead?" asked Ouanda behind him.

"No!" cried a piggy in the Males' Language. "You can't die! No no no!" Miro looked; to his surprise, it was Leaf-eater. "You can't die!"

Then Human reached up a feeble hand and touched the Speaker's face. He inhaled, a deep gasp. And then spoke, "You see, Speaker? I would die to climb the wall that keeps us from the stars."

In all the years that Miro had known the piggies, in all the years before, they had never once spoken of star travel, never once asked about it. Yet now Miro realized that all the questions they *did* ask were oriented toward discovering the secret of starflight. The xenologers had never realized that because they knew—knew without questioning—that the piggies were so remote from the level of culture that could build starships that it would be a thousand years before such a thing could possibly be in their reach. But their craving for knowledge about metal, about motors, about flying above the ground, it was all their way of trying to find the secret of starflight.

Human slowly got to his feet, holding the Speaker's hands. Miro realized that in all the years he had known the piggies, never once had a piggy taken him by the hand. He felt a deep regret. And the sharp pain of jealousy.

Now that Human was clearly not injured, the other piggies crowded close around the Speaker. They did not jostle, but they wanted to be near.

"Rooter says the hive queen knows how to build starships," said Arrow.

"Rooter says the hive queen will teach us everything," said Cups. "Metal, fire made from rocks, houses made from black water, everything."

Speaker raised his hands, fended off their babbling. "If you were all very thirsty, and saw that I had water, you'd all ask me for a drink. But what if I knew that the water I had was poisoned?"

"There is no poison in the ships that fly to the stars," said Human.

"There are many paths to starflight," said the Speaker. "Some are better than others. I'll give you everything I can that won't destroy you."

"The hive queen promises!" said Human.

"And so do I."

Human lunged forward, grabbed the Speaker by the hair and ears, and pulled him face to face. Miro had never seen such an act of violence; it was what he had dreaded, the decision to murder—

"If we are ramen," shouted Human into the Speaker's face, "then it is *ours* to decide, not yours! And if we are varelse, then you might as well kill us all right now, the way you killed all the hive queen's sisters!"

Miro was stunned. It was one thing for the piggies to decide this was the Speaker who wrote the book. But how could they reach the unbelievable conclusion that he was somehow quilty of the Xenocide? Who did they think he was, the monster Ender?

And yet there sat the Speaker for the Dead, tears running down his cheeks, his eyes closed, as if Human's accusation had the force of truth.

Human turned his head to speak to Miro. "What is this water?" he whispered. Then he touched the Speaker's tears.

"It's how we show pain or grief or suffering," Miro answered.

Mandachuva suddenly cried out, a hideous cry that Miro had never heard before, like an animal dying.

"That is how we show pain," whispered Human.

"Ah! Ah!" cried Mandachuva. "I have seen that water before! In the eyes of Libo and Pipo I saw that water!"

One by one, and then all at once, all the other piggies took up the same cry. Miro was terrified, awed, excited all at once. He had no idea what it meant, but the piggies were showing emotions that they had concealed from the xenologers for forty-seven years.

"Are they grieving for Papa?" whispered Ouanda. Her eyes, too, glistened with excitement, and her hair was matted with the sweat of fear.

Miro said it the moment it occurred to him: "They didn't know until this moment that Pipo and Libo were crying when they died."

Miro had no idea what thoughts then went through Ouanda's head; he only knew that she turned away, stumbled a few steps, fell to her hands and knees, and wept bitterly.

All in all, the coming of the Speaker had certainly stirred things up.

Miro knelt beside the Speaker, whose head was now bowed, his chin pressed against his chest. "Speaker," Miro said. "Como pode ser? How can it be, that you are the first Speaker, and yet you are also Ender? Não pode ser."

"She told them more than I ever thought she would," he whispered.

"But the Speaker for the Dead, the one who wrote this book, he's the wisest man who lived in the age of flight among the stars. While Ender was a murderer, he killed a whole people, a beautiful race of ramen that could have taught us everything—"

"Both human, though," whispered the Speaker.

Human was near them now, and he spoke a couplet from the Hegemon: "Sickness and healing are in every heart. Death and deliverance are in every hand."

"Human," said the Speaker, "tell your people not to grieve for what they did in ignorance."

"It was a terrible thing," said Human. "It was our greatest gift."

"Tell your people to be quiet, and listen to me."

Human shouted a few words, not in the Males' Language, but in the Wives' Language, the language of authority. They fell silent, then sat to hear what Speaker would say.

"I'll do everything I can," said the Speaker, "but first I have to know you, or how can I tell your story? I have to know you, or how can I know whether the drink is poisonous or not? And the hardest problem of all will still remain. The human race is free to love the buggers because they think the buggers all are dead. You are still alive, and so they're still afraid of you."

Human stood among them and gestured toward his body, as if it were a weak and feeble thing. "Of us!"

"They're afraid of the same thing you fear, when you look up and see the stars fill up with humans. They're afraid that someday they'll come to a world and find that you have got there first."

"We don't want to be there first," said Human. "We want to be there *too.*"

"Then give me time," said the Speaker. "Teach me who you are, so that I can teach them."

"Anything," said Human. He looked around at the others. "We'll teach you anything."

Leaf-eater stood up. He spoke in the Males' Language, but Miro understood him. "Some things aren't yours to teach."

Human answered him sharply, and in Stark. "What Pipo and Libo and Ouanda and Miro taught us wasn't theirs to teach, either. But they taught us."

"Their foolishness doesn't have to be our foolishness." Leaf-eater still spoke in Males' Language.

"Nor does their wisdom necessarily apply to us," Human retorted.

Then Leaf-eater said something in Tree Language that Miro could not understand. Human made no answer, and Leaf-eater walked away.

As he left, Ouanda returned, her eyes red from crying.

Human turned back to the Speaker. "What do you want to know?" he asked. "We'll tell you, we'll show you, if we can."

Speaker in turn looked at Miro and Ouanda. "What should I ask them? I know so little that I don't know what we need to know."

Miro looked to Ouanda.

"You have no stone or metal tools," she said. "But your house is made of wood, and so are your bows and arrows."

Human stood, waiting. The silence lengthened. "But what is your question?" Human finally said.

How could he have missed the connection? Miro thought.

"We humans," said Speaker, "use tools of stone or metal to cut down trees, when we want to shape them into houses or arrows or clubs like the ones I see some of you carrying."

It took a moment for the Speaker's words to sink in. Then, suddenly, all the piggies were on their feet. They began running around madly, purposelessly, sometimes bumping into each other or into trees or the log houses. Most of them were silent, but now and then one of them would wail, exactly as they had cried out a few minutes ago. It was eerie, the almost silent insanity of the piggies, as if they had suddenly lost control of their bodies. All the years of careful noncommunication, refraining from telling the piggies anything, and now Speaker breached that policy and the result was this madness.

Human emerged from the chaos and threw himself to the ground in front of Speaker. "O Speaker!" he cried loudly. "Promise that you'll never let them cut my father Rooter with their stone and metal tools! If you want to murder someone, there are ancient brothers who will give themselves, or I will gladly die, but don't let them kill my father!"

"Or *my* father!" cried the other piggies. "Or mine!"

"We would never have planted Rooter so close to the fence," said Mandachuva, "if we had known you were—were *varelse.*"

Speaker raised his hands again. "Has any human cut a tree in Lusitania? Never. The law here forbids it. You have nothing to fear from us."

There was a silence as the piggies became still. Finally Human picked himself up from the ground. "You've made us fear humans all the more," he said to Speaker. "I wish you had never come to our forest."

Ouanda's voice rang out above his. "How can you say that after the way you murdered my father!"

Human looked at her with astonishment, unable to answer. Miro put his arm around Ouanda's shoulders. And the Speaker for the Dead spoke into the silence. "You promised me that you'd answer all my questions. I ask you now: How do you build a house made of wood, and the bow and arrows that this one carries, and those clubs. We've told you the only way we know; you tell me another way, the way you do it."

"The brother gives himself," said Human. "I told you. We tell the ancient brother of our need, and we show him the shape, and he gives himself."

"Can we see how it's done?" said Ender.

Human looked around at the other piggies. "You want us to ask a brother to give himself, just so you can see it? We don't need a new house, not for years yet, and we have all the arrows we need—"

"Show him!"

Miro turned, as the others also turned, to see Leaf-eater re-emerging from the forest. He walked purposefully into the middle of the clearing; he did not look at them, and he spoke as if he were a herald, a town crier, not caring whether anyone was listening to him or not. He spoke in the Wives' Language, and Miro could understand only bits and pieces.

"What is he saying?" whispered the Speaker.

Miro, still kneeling beside him, translated as best he could. "He went to the wives, apparently, and they said to do whatever you asked. But it isn't that simple, he's telling them that—I don't know these words—something about all of them dying. Something about brothers dying, anyway. Look at them—they aren't afraid, any of them."

"I don't know what their fear looks like," said Speaker. "I don't know these people at all."

"I don't either," said Miro. "I've got to hand it to you—you've caused more excitement here in half an hour than I've seen in years of coming here."

"It's a gift I was born with," said the Speaker. "I'll make you a bargain. I won't tell anybody about your Questionable Activities. And you don't tell anybody who I am."

"That's easy," said Miro. "I don't believe it anyway."

Leaf-eater's speech ended. He immediately padded to the house and went inside.

"We'll ask for the gift of an ancient brother," said Human. "The wives have said so."

So it was that Miro stood with his arm around Ouanda, and the Speaker standing at his other side, as the piggies performed a miracle far more convincing than any of the ones that had won old Gusto and Cida their title Os Venerados.

The piggies gathered in a circle around a thick old tree at the clearing's edge. Then, one by one, each piggy shimmied up the tree and began beating on it with a club. Soon they were all in the tree, singing and pounding out complex rhythms. "Tree Language," Ouanda whispered.

After only a few minutes of this the tree tilted noticeably. Immediately about half the piggies jumped down and began pushing the tree so it would fall into the open ground of the clearing. The rest began beating all the more furiously and singing all the louder.

One by one the great branches of the tree began to fall off. Immediately piggies ran out and picked them up, dragged them away from the area where the tree was meant to fall. Human carried one to the Speaker, who took it carefully, and showed it to Miro and Ouanda. The raw end, where it had been attached to the tree, was absolutely smooth. It wasn't flat—the surface undulated slightly along an oblique angle. But there was no raggedness to it, no leaking sap, nothing to imply the slightest violence in its separation from the tree. Miro touched his finger to it, and it was cold and smooth as marble.

Finally the tree was a single straight trunk, nude and majestic; the pale patches where branches once had grown were brightly lit by the afternoon sun. The singing reached a climax, then stopped. The tree tilted and then began a smooth and graceful fall to the earth. The ground shook and thundered when it struck, and then all was still.

Human walked to the fallen tree and began to stroke its surface, singing softly. The bark split gradually under his hands; the crack extended itself up and down the length of the tree until the bark was split completely in half. Then many piggies took hold of it and prised it from the trunk; it came away on one side and the other, in two continuous sheets of bark. The bark was carried to the side.

"Have you ever seen them use the bark?" Speaker asked Miro.

Miro shook his head. He had no words to say aloud.

Now Arrow stepped forward, singing softly. He drew his fingers up and down the trunk, as if tracing exactly the length and width of a single bow. Miro saw how lines appeared, how the naked wood creased, split, crumbled until only the bow remained, perfect and polished and smooth, lying in a long trench in the wood.

Other piggies came forward, drawing shapes on the trunk and singing. They came away with clubs, with bows and arrows, thin-bladed knives, and thousands of strands of thin basketwood. Finally, when half the trunk was dissipated, they all stepped back and sang together. The tree shivered and split into half a dozen long poles. The tree was entirely used up.

Human walked slowly forward and knelt by the poles, his hands gently resting on the nearest one. He tilted back his head and began to sing, a wordless melody that was the saddest sound that Miro had ever heard. The song went on and on, Human's voice alone; only gradually did Miro realize that the other piggies were looking at him, waiting for something.

Finally Mandachuva came to him and spoke softly. "Please," he said. "It's only right that you should sing for the brother."

"I don't know how," said Miro, feeling helpless and afraid.

"He gave his life," said Mandachuva, "to answer your question."

To answer my question and then raise a thousand more, Miro said silently. But he walked forward, knelt beside Human, curled his fingers around the same cold smooth pole that Human held, tilted back his head, and let his voice come out. At first weak and hesitant, unsure what melody to sing; but soon he understood the reason for the tuneless song, felt the death of the tree under his hands, and his voice became loud and strong, making agonizing disharmonies with Human's voice that mourned the death of the tree and thanked it for its sacrifice and promised to use its death for the good of the tribe, for the good of the brothers and the wives and the children, so that all would live and thrive and prosper. That was the meaning of the song, and the meaning of the death of the tree, and when the song was finally over Miro bent until his forehead touched the wood and he said the words of extreme unction, the same words he had whispered over Libo's corpse on the hillside five years ago.

Chapter 15

Speaking

HUMAN: Why don't any of the other humans ever come see us?

MIRO: We're the only ones allowed to come through the gate.

HUMAN: Why don't they just climb over the fence?

MIRO: Haven't any of you ever touched the fence? (Human does not answer.) It's very painful to touch the fence. To pass over the fence would be like every part of your body hurting as bad as possible, all at once.

HUMAN: That's stupid. Isn't there grass on both sides?

—Ouanda Quenhatta Figueira Mucumbi, Dialogue Transcripts, 103:0:1970:1:1:5

The sun was only an hour from the horizon when Mayor Bosquinha climbed the stairs to Bishop Peregrino's private office in the Cathedral. Dom and Don Cristães were already there, looking grave. Bishop Peregrino, however, looked pleased with himself. He always enjoyed it when all the political and religious leadership of Milagre was gathered under his roof. Never mind that Bosquinha was the one who called the meeting, and then she offered to have it at the Cathedral because she was the one with the skimmer. Peregrino liked the feeling that he was somehow the master of Lusitania Colony. Well, by the end of this meeting it would be plain to them all that no one in this room was the master of anything.

Bosquinha greeted them all. She did not sit down in the offered chair, however. Instead she sat before the Bishop's own terminal, logged in, and ran the program she had prepared. In the air above the terminal there appeared several layers of tiny cubes. The highest layer had only a few cubes; most of the layers had many, many more. More than half the layers, starting with the highest, were colored red; the rest were blue.

"Very pretty," said Bishop Peregrino.

Bosquinha looked over at Dom Cristão. "Do you recognize the model?"

He shook his head. "But I think I know what this meeting is about."

Dona Cristã leaned forward on her chair. "Is there any safe place where we can hide the things we want to keep?"

Bishop Peregrino's expression of detached amusement vanished from his face. "I *don't* know what this meeting is about."

Bosquinha turned around on her stool to face him. "I was very young when I was appointed to be Governor of the new Lusitania Colony. It was a great honor to be chosen, a great trust. I had studied government of communities and social systems since my childhood, and I had done well in my short career in Oporto. What the committee apparently overlooked was the fact that I was already suspicious, deceptive, and chauvinistic."

"These are virtues of yours that we have all come to admire," said Bishop Peregrino.

Bosquinha smiled. "My chauvinism meant that as soon as Lusitania Colony was mine, I became more loyal to the interests of Lusitania than to the interests of the Hundred Worlds or Starways Congress. My deceptiveness led me to pretend to the committee that on the contrary, I had the best interests of Congress at heart at all times. And my suspicion led me to believe that Congress was not likely to give Lusitania anything remotely like independent and equal status among the Hundred Worlds."

"Of course not," said Bishop Peregrino. "We are a colony."

"We are not a colony," said Bosquinha. "We are an experiment. I examined our charter and license and all the Congressional Orders pertaining to us, and I discovered that the normal privacy laws did not apply to us. I discovered that the committee had the power of unlimited access to all the memory files of every person and institution on Lusitania."

The Bishop began to look angry. "Do you mean that the committee has the right to look at the confidential files of the Church?"

"Ah," said Bosquinha. "A fellow chauvinist."

"The Church has some rights under the Starways Code."

"Don't be angry with *me.*"

"You never told me."

"If I had told you, you would have protested, and they would have pretended to back down, and then I couldn't have done what I did."

"Which is?"

"This program. It monitors all ansible-initiated accesses to any files in Lusitania Colony."

Dom Cristão chuckled. "You're not supposed to do that."

"I know. As I said, I have many secret vices. But my program never found any major intrusion—oh, a few files each time the piggies killed one of our xenologers, that was to be expected—but nothing major. Until four days ago."

"When the Speaker for the Dead arrived," said Bishop Peregrino.

Bosquinha was amused that the Bishop obviously regarded the Speaker's arrival as such a landmark date that he instantly made such a connection. "Three days ago," said Bosquinha, "a nondestructive scan was initiated by ansible. It followed an interesting pattern." She turned to the terminal and changed the display. Now it showed accesses primarily in high-level areas, and limited to only one region of the display. "It accessed everything to do with the xenologers and xenobiologists of Milagre. It ignored all security routines as if they didn't exist. Everything they discovered, and everything to do with their personal lives. And yes, Bishop Peregrino, I believed at the time and I believe today that this had to do with the Speaker."

"Surely *he* has no authority with Starways Congress," said the Bishop.

Dom Cristão nodded wisely. "San Angelo once wrote—in his private journals, which no one but the Children of the Mind ever read—"

The Bishop turned on him with glee. "So the Children of the Mind *do* have secret writings of San Angelo!"

"Not secret," said Dona Cristã. "Merely boring. Anyone can read the journals, but we're the only ones who bother."

"What he wrote," said Dom Cristão, "was that Speaker Andrew is older than we know. Older than Starways Congress, and in his own way perhaps more powerful."

Bishop Peregrino snorted. "He's a boy. Can't be forty years old yet."

"Your stupid rivalries are wasting time," said Bosquinha sharply. "I called this meeting because of an emergency. As a courtesy to *you,* because I have already acted for the benefit of the government of Lusitania."

The others fell silent.

Bosquinha returned the terminal to the original display. "This morning my program alerted me for a second time. Another systematic ansible access, only this time it was not the selective nondestructive access of three days ago. This time it is reading *everything* at data-transfer speed, which implies that all our files are being copied into offworld computers. Then the directories are rewritten so that a single ansible-initiated command will completely destroy every single file in our computer memories."

Bosquinha could see that Bishop Peregrino was surprised—and the Children of the Mind were not.

"Why?" said Bishop Peregrino. "To destroy all our files—this is what you do to a nation or a world that is—in rebellion, that you wish to destroy, that you—"

"I see," said Bosquinha to the Children of the Mind, "that you also were chauvinistic and suspicious."

"Much more narrowly than you, I'm afraid," said Dom Cristão. "But we also detected the intrusions. We of course copied all our records—at great expense—to the monasteries of the Children of the Mind on other worlds, and they will try to restore our files after they are stripped. However, if we are being treated as a rebellious colony, I doubt that such a restoration will be permitted. So we are also making paper copies of the most vital information. There is no hope of printing everything, but we think we may be able to print out enough to get by. So that our work isn't utterly destroyed."

"You knew this?" said the Bishop. "And you didn't tell *me?*"

"Forgive me, Bishop Peregrino, but it did not occur to us that you would not have detected this yourselves."

"And you also don't believe we do any work that is important enough to be worth printing out to save!"

"Enough!" said Mayor Bosquinha. "Printouts can't save more than a tiny percentage—there aren't enough printers in Lusitania to make a dent in the problem. We couldn't even maintain basic services. I don't think we have more than an hour left before the copying is complete and they are able to wipe out our memory. But even if we began this morning, when the intrusion started, we could not have printed out more than a hundredth of one percent of the files that we access every day. Our fragility, our vulnerability is complete."

"So we're helpless," said the Bishop.

"No. But I wanted to make clear to you the extremity of our situation, so that you would accept the only alternative. It will be very distasteful to you."

"I have no doubt of that," said Bishop Peregrino.

"An hour ago, as I was wrestling with this problem, trying to see if there was any class of files that might be immune to this treatment, I discovered that in fact there was one person whose files were being completely overlooked. At first I thought it was because he was a framling, but the reason is much more subtle than that. The Speaker for the Dead *has* no files in Lusitanian memory."

"None? Impossible," said Dona Cristã.

"All his files are maintained *by ansible*. Offworld. All his records, all his finances, *everything*. Every message sent to him. Do you understand?"

"And yet he still has access to them—" said Dom Cristão.

"He is invisible to Starways Congress. If they place an embargo on all data transfers to and from Lusitania, his files will still be accessible because the computers do not see his file accesses as data transfers. They are original storage—yet they are not in Lusitanian memory."

"Are you suggesting," said Bishop Peregrino, "that we transfer our most confidential and important files as *messages* to that—that unspeakable infidel?"

"I am telling you that I have already done exactly that. The transfer of the most vital and sensitive government files is almost complete. It was a high priority transfer, at local speeds, so it runs much faster than the Congressional copying. I am offering you a chance to make a similar transfer, using my highest priority so that it takes precedence over all other local computer usage. If you don't want to do it, fine—I'll use my priority to transfer the second tier of government files."

"But he could look in our files," said the Bishop.

"Yes, he could."

Dom Cristão shook his head. "He won't if we ask him not to."

"You are naive as a child," said Bishop Peregrino. "There would be nothing to compel him even to give the data back to us."

Bosquinha nodded. "That's true. He'll have everything that's vital to us, and he can keep it or return it as he wishes. But I believe, as Dom Cristão does, that he's a good man who'll help us in our time of need."

Dona Cristã stood. "Excuse me," she said. "I'd like to begin crucial transfers immediately."

Bosquinha turned to the Bishop's terminal and logged into her own high priority mode. "Just enter the classes of files that you want to send into Speaker Andrew's message queue. I assume you already have them prioritized, since you were printing them out."

"How long do we have?" asked Dom Cristão. Dona Cristã was already typing furiously.

"The time is here, at the top." Bosquinha put her hand into the holographic display and touched the countdown numbers with her finger.

"Don't bother transferring anything that we've already printed," said Dom Cristão. "We can always type that back in. There's precious little of it, anyway."

Bosquinha turned to the Bishop. "I knew this would be difficult."

The Bishop gave one derisive laugh. "Difficult."

"I hope you'll consider carefully before rejecting this—"

"Rejecting it!" said the Bishop. "Do you think I'm a fool? I may detest the pseudo-religion of these blasphemous Speakers for the Dead, but if this is the only way God has opened for us to preserve the vital records of the Church, then I'd be a poor servant of the Lord if I let pride stop me from using it. Our files aren't prioritized yet, and it will take a few minutes, but I trust that the Children of the Mind will leave us enough time for our data transfers."

"How much time will you need, do you think?" asked Dom Cristão.

"Not much. Ten minutes at the most, I'd think."

Bosquinha was surprised, and pleasantly so. She had been afraid the Bishop would insist on copying all his files before allowing the Children of the Mind to go ahead—just one more attempt to assert the precedence of the bishopric over the monastery.

"Thank you," Dom Cristão said, kissing the hand that Peregrino extended to him.

The Bishop looked at Bosquinha coldly. "You don't need to look surprised, Mayor Bosquinha. The Children of the Mind work with the knowledge of the world, so they depend far more on the world's machines. Mother Church works with things of the Spirit, so our use of public memory is merely clerical. As for the Bible—we are so old-fashioned and set in our ways that we still keep dozens of leatherbound paper copies in the Cathedral. Starways Congress can't steal from us our copies of the word of God." He smiled. Maliciously, of course. Bosquinha smiled back quite cheerfully.

"A small matter," said Dom Cristão. "After our files are destroyed, and we copy them back into memory from the Speaker's files, what is to stop Congress from doing it again? And again, and again?"

"That is the difficult decision," said Bosquinha. "What we do depends on what Congress is trying to accomplish. Maybe they won't actually destroy our files at all. Maybe they'll immediately restore our most vital files after this demonstration of their power. Since I have no idea why they're disciplining us, how can I guess how far this will go? If they leave us any way to remain loyal, then of course we must also remain vulnerable to further discipline."

"But if, for some reason, they are determined to treat us like rebels?"

"Well, if bad came to worst, we could copy everything back into local memory and then—cut off the ansible."

"God help us," said Dona Cristã. "We would be utterly alone."

Bishop Peregrino looked annoyed. "What an absurd idea, Sister Detestai o Pecado. Or do you think that Christ depends upon the ansible? That Congress has the power to silence the Holy Ghost?"

Dona Cristã blushed and returned to her work at the terminal.

The Bishop's secretary handed him a paper with a list of files on it. "You can leave my personal correspondence off the list," said the Bishop. "I've already sent my messages. We'll let the Church decide which of my letters is worth preserving. They have no value to me."

"The Bishop is ready," said Dom Cristão. Immediately his wife arose from the terminal and the secretary took her place.

"By the way," said Bosquinha, "I thought you'd want to know. The Speaker has announced that this evening, in the praça, he'll Speak the death of Marcos Maria Ribeira." Bosquinha looked at her watch. "Very soon now, in fact."

"Why," said the Bishop acidly, "did you think that I would care?"

"I thought you might want to send a representative."

"Thank you for telling us," said Dom Cristão. "I think that I'll attend. I'd like to hear a Speaking by the man who Spoke the death of San Angelo." He turned to the Bishop. "I'll report to you on what he says, if you'd like."

The Bishop leaned back and smiled tightly. "Thank you, but one of my people will be in attendance."

Bosquinha left the Bishop's office and clattered down the stairs and out the Cathedral doors. She had to be back in her own rooms now, because whatever the Congress was planning, it would be Bosquinha who received their messages.

She had not discussed it with the religious leaders because it was really none of their business, but she knew perfectly well, at least in a general way, why Congress was doing this. The paragraphs that gave Congress the right to treat Lusitania like a rebellious colony were all tied to the rules dealing with contact with the piggies.

Obviously the xenologers had done something grossly wrong. Since Bosquinha had not known of any violations, it had to be something so big that its evidence showed up on the satellites, the only monitoring devices that reported directly to the committee without passing through Bosquinha's hands. Bosquinha had tried to think of what Miro and Ouanda might have done—start a forest fire? Cut down trees? Led a war between the piggy tribes? Anything she thought of sounded absurd.

She tried to call them in to question them, but they were gone, of course. Through the gate, out into the forest to continue, no doubt, the same activities that had brought the possibility of destruction to Lusitania Colony. Bosquinha kept reminding herself that they were young, that it might all be some ridiculous juvenile mistake.

But they weren't *that* young, and they were two of the brightest minds in a colony that contained many very intelligent people. It was a very good thing that governments under the Starways Code were forbidden to own any instruments of punishment that might be used for torture. For the first time in her life, Bosquinha felt such fury that she might use such instruments, if she had them. I don't know what you thought you were doing, Miro and Ouanda, and I don't know what you did; but whatever your purpose might have been, this whole community will pay the price for it. And somehow, if there were any justice, I would make you pay it back.

Many people had said they wouldn't come to any Speaking— they were good Catholics, weren't they? Hadn't the Bishop told them that the Speaker spoke with Satan's voice?

But other things were whispered, too, once the Speaker came. Rumors, mostly, but Milagre was a little place, where rumors were the sauce of a dry life; and rumors have no value unless they are believed. So word spread that Marcão's little girl Quara, who had been silent since he died, was now so talkative that it got her in trouble in school. And Olhado, that ill-mannered boy with the repulsive metal eyes, it was said that he suddenly seemed cheerful and excited. Perhaps manic. Perhaps possessed. Rumors began to imply that somehow the Speaker had a healing touch, that he had the evil eye, that his blessings made you whole, his curses could kill you, his words could charm you into obedience. Not everybody heard this, of course, and not everybody who heard it believed it. But in the four days between the Speaker's arrival and the evening of his Speaking the death of Marcos Maria Ribeira, the community of Milagre decided, without any formal announcement, that they would come to the Speaking and hear what the Speaker had to say, whether the Bishop said to stay away or not.

It was the Bishop's own fault. From his vantage point, calling the Speaker satanic put him at the farthest extreme from himself and all good Catholics: The Speaker is the opposite of us. But to those who were not theologically sophisticated, while Satan was frightening and powerful, so was God. They understood well enough the continuum of good and evil that the Bishop referred to, but they were far more interested in the continuum of strong and weak—that was the one they lived with day by day. And on that continuum, they were weak, and God and Satan and the Bishop all were strong. The Bishop had elevated the Speaker to stand with him as a man of power. The people were thus prepared to believe the whispered hints of miracles.

So even though the announcement came only an hour before the Speaking, the praça was full, and people gathered in the buildings and houses that fronted the praça, and crowded the grassy alleyways and streets. Mayor Bosquinha had—as the law required—provided the Speaker with the simple microphone that she used for the rare public meetings. People oriented themselves toward the platform where he would stand; then they looked around to see who was there. Everyone was there. Of course Marcão's family. Of course the Mayor. But also Dom Cristão and Dona Cristã, and many a robed priest from the Cathedral. Dr. Navio. Pipo's widow, old Conceição, the Archivist. Libo's widow, Bruxinha, and her children. It was rumored that the Speaker also meant to Speak Pipo's and Libo's deaths someday, too.

And finally, just as the Speaker stepped up onto the platform, the rumor swept the praça: Bishop Peregrino was here. Not in his vestments, but in the simple robes of a priest. Here himself, to hear the Speaker's blasphemy! Many a citizen of Milagre felt a delicious thrill of anticipation. Would the Bishop rise up and miraculously strike down Satan? Would there be a battle here such as had not been seen outside the vision of the Apocalypse of St. John?

Then the Speaker stood before the microphone and waited for them to be still. He was fairly tall, youngish still, but his white skin made him look sickly compared to the thousand shades of brown of the Lusos. Ghostly. They fell silent, and he began to Speak.

"He was known by three names. The official records have the first one: Marcos Maria Ribeira. And his official data. Born 1929. Died 1970. Worked in the steel foundry. Perfect safety record. Never arrested. A wife, six children. A model citizen, because he never did anything bad enough to go on the public record."

Many who were listening felt a vague disquiet. They had expected oration. Instead the Speaker's voice was nothing remarkable. And his words had none of the formality of religious speech. Plain, simple, almost conversational. Only a few of them noticed that its very simplicity made his voice, his speech utterly believable. He wasn't telling the Truth, with trumpets; he was telling the *truth,* the story that you wouldn't think to doubt because it's taken for granted. Bishop Peregrino was one who noticed, and it made him uneasy. This Speaker would be a formidable enemy, one who could not be blasted down with fire from before the altar.

"The second name he had was Marcão. Big Marcos. Because he was a giant of a man. Reached his adult size early in his life. How old was he when he reached two meters? Eleven? Definitely by the time he was twelve. His size and strength made him valuable in the foundry, where the lots of steel are so small that much of the work is controlled directly by hand, and strength matters. People's lives depended on Marcão's strength."

In the praça the men from the foundry nodded. They had all bragged to each other that they'd never talk to the framling atheist. Obviously one of them had, but now it felt good that the Speaker got it right, that he understood what they remembered of Marcão. Every one of them wished that he had been the one to tell about Marcão to the Speaker. They did not guess that the Speaker had not even tried to talk to them. After all these years, there were many things that Andrew Wiggin knew without asking.

"His third name was Cão. Dog."

Ah, yes, thought the Lusos. This is what we've heard about Speakers for the Dead. They have no respect for the dead, no sense of decorum.

"That was the name you used for him when you heard that his wife, Novinha, had another black eye, walked with a limp, had stitches in her lip. He was an animal to do that to her."

How dare he say that? The man's *dead!* But under their anger the Lusos were uncomfortable for an entirely different reason. Almost all of them remembered saying or hearing exactly those words. The Speaker's indiscretion was in repeating in public the words that they had used about Marcão when he was alive.

"Not that any of you liked Novinha. Not that cold woman who never gave any of you good morning. But she was smaller than he was, and she was the mother of his children, and when he beat her he deserved the name of Cão."

They were embarrassed; they muttered to each other. Those sitting in the grass near Novinha glanced at her and glanced away, eager to see how she was reacting, painfully aware of the fact that the Speaker was right, that they didn't like her, that they at once feared and pitied her.

"Tell me, is this the man you knew? Spent more hours in the bars than anybody, and yet never made any friends there, never the camaraderie of alcohol for him. You couldn't even tell how much he had been drinking. He was surly and short-tempered before he had a drink, and surly and short-tempered just before he passed out—nobody could tell the difference. You never heard of him having a friend, and none of you was ever glad to see him come into a room. That's the man you knew, most of you. Cão. Hardly a man at all."

Yes, they thought. That was the man. Now the initial shock of his indecorum had faded. They were accustomed to the fact that the Speaker meant to soften nothing in his story. Yet they were still uncomfortable. For there was a note of irony, not in his voice, but inherent in his words. "Hardly a man at all," he had said, but of course he *was* a man, and they were vaguely aware that while the Speaker understood what they thought of Marcão, he didn't necessarily agree.

"A few others, the men from the foundry in Bairro das Fabricadoras, knew him as a strong arm they could trust. They knew he never said he could do more than he could do, and always did what he said he would do. You could count on him. So within the walls of the foundry he had their respect. But when you walked out the door you treated him like everybody else—ignored him, thought little of him."

The irony was pronounced now. Though the Speaker gave no hint in his voice—still the simple, plain speech he began with—the men who worked with him felt it wordlessly inside themselves: We should not have ignored him as we did. If he had worth inside the foundry, then perhaps we should have valued him outside, too.

"Some of you also know something else that you never talk about much. You know that you gave him the name Cão long before he earned it. You were ten, eleven, twelve years old. Little boys. He grew so tall. It made you ashamed to be near him. And afraid, because he made you feel helpless."

Dom Cristão murmured to his wife, "They came for gossip, and he gives them responsibility."

"So you handled him the way human beings always handle

things that are bigger than they are," said the Speaker. "You banded together. Like hunters trying to bring down a mastodon. Like bull-fighters trying to weaken a giant bull to prepare it for the kill. Pokes, taunts, teases. Keep him turning around. He can't guess where the next blow is coming from. Prick him with barbs that stay under his skin. Weaken him with pain. Madden him. Because big as he is, *you can make him do things.* You can make him yell. You can make him run. You can make him cry. See? He's weaker than you after all."

Ela was angry. She had meant him to accuse Marcão, not excuse him. Just because he had a tough childhood didn't give him the right to knock Mother down whenever he felt like it.

"There's no blame in this. You were children then, and children are cruel without knowing better. You wouldn't do that now. But now that I've reminded you, you can easily see an answer. You called him a dog, and so he became one. For the rest of his life. Hurting helpless people. Beating his wife. Speaking so cruelly and abusively to his son Miro that he drove the boy out of his house. He was acting out the way you treated him, becoming what you told him that he was."

You're a fool, thought Bishop Peregrino. If people only react to the way that others treat them, then nobody is responsible for anything. If your sins are not your own to choose, then how can you repent?

As if he heard the Bishop's silent argument, the Speaker raised a hand and swept away his own words. "But the easy answer isn't true. Your torments didn't make him violent—they made him sullen. And when you grew out of tormenting him, he grew out of hating you. He wasn't one to bear a grudge. His anger cooled and turned into suspicion. He knew you despised him; he learned to live without you. In peace."

The Speaker paused a moment, and then gave voice to the question they silently were asking. "So how did he become the cruel man you knew him to be? Think a moment. Who was it who tasted his cruelty? His wife. His children. Some people beat their wife and children because they lust for power, but are too weak or stupid to win power in the world. A helpless wife and children, bound to such a man by need and custom and, bitterly enough, love, are the only victims he is strong enough to rule."

Yes, thought Ela, stealing a glance at her mother. This is what I wanted. This is why I asked him to Speak Father's death.

"There are men like that," said the Speaker, "but Marcos Ribeira wasn't one of them. Think a moment. Did you ever hear of him striking any of his children? Ever? You who worked with him— did he ever try to force his will on you? Seem resentful when things didn't go his way? Marcão was not a weak and evil man. He was a strong man. He didn't want power. He wanted love. Not control. Loyalty."

Bishop Peregrino smiled grimly, the way a duelist might salute a worthy opponent. You walk a twisted path, Speaker, circling around the truth, feinting at it. And when you strike, your aim will be deadly. These people came for entertainment, but they're your targets; you will pierce them to the heart.

"Some of you remember an incident," said the Speaker. "Marcos was maybe thirteen, and so were you. Taunting him on the grassy hillside behind the school. You attacked more viciously than usual. You threatened him with stones, whipped him with capim blades. You bloodied him a little, but he bore it. Tried to evade you. Asked you to stop. Then one of you struck him hard in the belly, and it hurt him more than you ever imagined, because even then he was already sick with the disease that finally killed him. He hadn't yet become accustomed to his fragility and pain. It felt like death to him. He was cornered. You were killing him. So he struck at you."

How did he know? thought half a dozen men. It was so long ago. Who told him how it was? It was out of hand, that's all. We never meant anything, but when his arm swung out, his huge fist, like the kick of a cabra—he was going to hurt me—

"It could have been any one of you that fell to the ground. You knew then that he was even stronger than you feared. What terrified you most, though, was that you knew exactly the revenge that you deserved. So you called for help. And when the teachers came, what did they see? One little boy on the ground, crying, bleeding. One large man-sized child with a few scratches here and there, saying I'm sorry, I didn't mean to. And a half-dozen others saying, He just hit him. Started killing him for no reason. We tried to stop him but Cão is so big. He's always picking on the little kids."

Little Grego was caught up in the story. "Mentirosos!" he

shouted. They were lying! Several people nearby chuckled. Quara shushed him.

"So many witnesses," said the Speaker. "The teachers had no choice but to believe the accusation. Until one girl stepped forward and coldly informed them that she had seen it all. Marcos was acting to protect himself from a completely unwarranted, vicious, painful attack by a pack of boys who were acting far more like cães, like dogs, than Marcos Ribeira ever did. Her story was instantly accepted as the truth. After all, she was the daughter of Os Venerados."

Grego looked at his mother with glowing eyes, then jumped up and announced to the people around him, "A mamãe o libertou!" Mama saved him! People laughed, turned around and looked at Novinha. But she held her face expressionless, refusing to acknowledge their momentary affection for her child. They looked away again, offended.

"Novinha," said the Speaker. "Her cold manner and bright mind made her just as much an outcast among you as Marcão. None of you could think of a time when she had ever made a friendly gesture toward any of you. And here she was, saving Marcão. Well, you knew the truth. She wasn't saving Marcão—she was preventing you from getting away with something."

They nodded and smiled knowingly, those people whose overtures of friendship she had just rebuffed. That's Dona Novinha, the Biologista, too good for any of the rest of us.

"Marcos didn't see it that way. He had been called an animal so often that he almost believed it. Novinha showed him compassion, like a human being. A pretty girl, a brilliant child, the daughter of the holy Venerados, always aloof as a goddess, she had reached down and blessed him and granted his prayer. He worshipped her. Six years later he married her. Isn't that a lovely story?"

Ela looked at Miro, who raised an eyebrow at her. "Almost makes you like the old bastard, doesn't it?" said Miro dryly.

Suddenly, after a long pause, the Speaker's voice erupted, louder than ever before. It startled them, awoke them. "Why did he come to hate her, to beat her, to despise their children? And why did she endure it, this strong-willed, brilliant woman? She could have stopped the marriage at any moment. The Church may not allow divorce, but there's always desquite, and she wouldn't be the first person in Milagre to quit her husband. She could have taken her suffering children and left him. But she *stayed*. The Mayor and the Bishop both *suggested* that she leave him. She told them they could go to hell."

Many of the Lusos laughed; they could imagine tight-lipped Novinha snapping at the Bishop himself, facing down Bosquinha. They might not like Novinha much, but she was just about the only person in Milagre who could get away with thumbing her nose at authority.

The Bishop remembered the scene in his chambers more than a decade ago. She had not used exactly the words the Speaker quoted, but the effect was much the same. Yet he had been alone. He had told no one. Who was this Speaker, and how did he know so much about things he could not possibly have known?

When the laughter died, the Speaker went on. "There was a tie that bound them together in a marriage they hated. That tie was Marcão's disease."

His voice was softer now. The Lusos strained to hear.

"It shaped his life from the moment he was conceived. The genes his parents gave him combined in such a way that from the moment puberty began, the cells of his glands began a steady, relentless transformation into fatty tissues. Dr. Navio can tell you how it progresses better than I can. Marcão knew from childhood that he had this condition; his parents knew it before they died in the Descolada; Gusto and Cida knew it from their genetic examinations of all the humans of Lusitania. *They* were all dead. Only one other person knew it, the one who had inherited the xenobiological files. Novinha."

Dr. Navio was puzzled. If she knew this before they married, she surely knew that most people who had his condition were sterile. Why would she have married him when for all she knew he had no chance of fathering children? Then he realized what he should have known before, that Marcão was *not* a rare exception to the pattern of the disease. There were no exceptions. Navio's face reddened. What the Speaker was about to tell them was unspeakable.

"Novinha knew that Marcão was dying," said the Speaker. "She also knew before she married him that he was absolutely and completely sterile."

It took a moment for the meaning of this to sink in. Ela felt as if her organs were melting inside her body. She saw without turning her head that Miro had gone rigid, that his cheeks had paled.

Speaker went on despite the rising whispers from the audience. "I saw the genetic scans. Marcos Maria Ribeira never fathered a child. His wife had children, but they were not his, and he knew it, and she knew he knew it. It was part of the bargain that they made when they got married."

The murmurs turned to muttering, the grumbles to complaints, and as the noise reached a climax, Quim leaped to his feet and shouted, screamed at the Speaker, "My mother is not an adulteress! I'll kill you for calling her a whore!"

His last word hung in the silence. The Speaker did not answer. He only waited, not letting his gaze drop from Quim's burning face. Until finally Quim realized that it was he, not the Speaker, whose voice had said the word that kept ringing in his ears. He faltered. He looked at his mother sitting beside him on the ground, but not rigidly now, slumped a little now, looking at her hands as they trembled in her lap. "Tell them, Mother," Quim said. His voice sounded more pleading than he had intended.

She didn't answer. Didn't say a word, didn't look at him. If he didn't know better, he would think her trembling hands were a confession, that she was *ashamed,* as if what the Speaker said was the truth that God himself would tell if Quim were to ask him. He remembered Father Mateu explaining the tortures of hell: God spits on adulterers, they mock the power of creation that he shared with them, they haven't enough goodness in them to be anything better than amoebas. Quim tasted bile in his mouth. What the Speaker said was true.

"Mamãe," he said loudly, mockingly. "Quem fôde p'ra fazer-me?"

People gasped. Olhado jumped to his feet at once, his hands doubled in fists. Only then did Novinha react, reaching out a hand as if to restrain Olhado from hitting his brother. Quim hardly noticed that Olhado had leapt to Mother's defense; all he could think of was the fact that Miro had not. Miro also knew that it was true.

Quim breathed deeply, then turned around, looking lost for a moment; then he threaded his way through the crowd. No one spoke to him, though everyone watched him go. If Novinha had denied the charge, they would have believed her, would have mobbed the

Speaker for accusing Os Venerados' daughter of such a sin. But she had not denied it. She had listened to her own son accuse her obscenely, and she said nothing. It was true. And now they listened in fascination. Few of them had any real concern. They just wanted to learn who had fathered Novinha's children.

The Speaker quietly resumed his tale. "After her parents died and before her children were born, Novinha loved only two people. Pipo was her second father. Novinha anchored her life in him; for a few short years she had a taste of what it meant to have a family. Then he died, and Novinha believed that she had killed him."

People sitting near Novinha's family saw Quara kneel in front of Ela and ask her, "Why is Quim so angry?"

Ela answered softly. "Because Papai was not really our father."

"Oh," said Quara. "Is the Speaker our father now?" She sounded hopeful. Ela shushed her.

"The night Pipo died," said the Speaker, "Novinha showed him something that she had discovered, something to do with the Descolada and the way it works with the plants and animals of Lusitania. Pipo saw more in her work than she did herself. He rushed to the forest where the piggies waited. Perhaps he told them what he had discovered. Perhaps they only guessed. But Novinha blamed herself for showing him a secret that the piggies would kill to keep.

"It was too late to undo what she had done. But she could keep it from happening again. So she sealed up all the files that had anything to do with the Descolada and what she had shown to Pipo that night. She knew who would want to see the files. It was Libo, the new Zenador. If Pipo had been her father, Libo had been her brother, and more than a brother. Hard as it was to bear Pipo's death, Libo's would be worse. He asked for the files. He demanded to see them. She told him she would never let him see them.

"They both knew exactly what that meant. If he ever married her, he could strip away the protection on those files. They loved each other desperately, they needed each other more than ever, but Novinha could never marry him. He would never promise not to read the files, and even if he made such a promise, he couldn't keep it. He would surely see what his father saw. He would die.

"It was one thing to refuse to marry him. It was another thing to live without him. So she didn't live without him. She made her bargain with Marcão. She would marry him under the law, but her real husband and the father of all her children would be, was, Libo."

Bruxinha, Libo's widow, rose shakily to her feet, tears streaming down her face, and wailed, "Mentira, mentira." Lies, lies. But her weeping was not anger, it was grief. She was mourning the loss of her husband all over again. Three of her daughters helped her leave the praça.

Softly the Speaker continued while she left. "Libo knew that he was hurting his wife Bruxinha and their four daughters. He hated himself for what he had done. He tried to stay away. For months, sometimes years, he succeeded. Novinha also tried. She refused to see him, even to speak to him. She forbade her children to mention him. Then Libo would think that he was strong enough to see her without falling back into the old way. Novinha would be so lonely with her husband who could never measure up to Libo. They never pretended there was anything good about what they were doing. They just couldn't live for long without it."

Bruxinha heard this as she was led away. It was little comfort to her now, of course, but as Bishop Peregrino watched her go, he recognized that the Speaker was giving her a gift. She was the most innocent victim of his cruel truth, but he didn't leave her with nothing but ashes. He was giving her a way to live with the knowledge of what her husband did. It was not your fault, he was telling her. Nothing you did could have prevented it. Your husband was the one who failed, not you. Blessed Virgin, prayed the Bishop silently, let Bruxinha hear what he says and believe it.

Libo's widow was not the only one who cried. Many hundreds of the eyes that watched her go were also filled with tears. To discover Novinha was an adulteress was shocking but delicious: the steel-hearted woman had a flaw that made her no better than anyone else. But there was no pleasure in finding the same flaw in Libo. Everyone had loved him. His generosity, his kindness, his wisdom that they so admired, they didn't want to know that it was all a mask.

So they were surprised when the Speaker reminded them that it was not Libo whose death he Spoke today. "Why did Marcos Ribeira consent to this? Novinha thought it was because he wanted a wife and the illusion that he had children, to take away his shame in the community. It was partly that. Most of all, though, he married her because he loved her. He never really hoped that she would love him the way he loved her, because he worshipped her, she was a goddess, and he knew that he was diseased, filthy, an animal to be despised. He knew she could not worship him, or even love him. He hoped that she might someday feel some *affection.* That she might feel some—loyalty."

The Speaker bowed his head a moment. The Lusos heard the words that he did not have to say: She never did.

"Each child that came," said the Speaker, "was another proof to Marcos that he had failed. That the goddess still found him unworthy. Why? He was loyal. He had never hinted to any of his children that they were not his own. He never broke his promise to Novinha. Didn't he deserve something from her? At times it was more than he could bear. He refused to accept her judgment. She was no goddess. Her children were all bastards. This is what he told himself when he lashed out at her, when he shouted at Miro."

Miro heard his own name, but didn't recognize it as anything to do with him. His connection with reality was more fragile than he ever had supposed, and today had given him too many shocks. The impossible magic with the piggies and the trees. Mother and Libo, lovers. Ouanda suddenly torn from being as close to him as his own body, his own self, she was now set back at one remove, like Ela, like Quara, another sister. His eyes did not focus on the grass; the Speaker's voice was pure sound, he didn't hear meanings in the words, only the terrible sound. Miro had called for that voice, had wanted it to Speak Libo's death. How could he have known that instead of a benevolent priest of a humanist religion he would get the original Speaker himself, with his penetrating mind and far too perfect understanding? He could not have known that beneath that empathic mask would be hiding Ender the destroyer, the mythic Lucifer of mankind's greatest crime, determined to live up to his name, making a mockery of the life work of Pipo, Libo, Ouanda, and Miro himself by seeing in a single hour with the piggies what all the others had failed in almost fifty years to see, and then riving Ouanda from him with a single, merciless stroke from the blade of truth; that was the voice that Miro heard, the only certainty left to him, that relentless terrible voice. Miro clung to the sound of it, trying to hate it, yet failing, because he knew, could not deceive himself, he *knew* that Ender was a destroyer, but what he destroyed was illusion, and the illusion had to die. The truth about the piggies, the truth about ourselves. Somehow this ancient man is able to see the truth and it doesn't blind his eyes or drive him mad. I must listen to this voice and let its power come to me so I, too, can stare at the light and not die.

"Novinha knew what she was. An adulteress, a hypocrite. She knew she was hurting Marcão, Libo, her children, Bruxinha. She knew she had killed Pipo. So she endured, even invited Marcão's punishment. It was her penance. It was never penance enough. No matter how much Marcão might hate her, she hated herself much more."

The Bishop nodded slowly. The Speaker had done a monstrous thing, to lay these secrets before the whole community. They should have been spoken in the confessional. Yet Peregrino had felt the power of it, the way the whole community was forced to discover these people that they thought they knew, and then discover them again, and then again; and each revision of the story forced them all to reconceive themselves as well, for they had been part of this story, too, had been touched by all the people a hundred, a thousand times, never understanding until now who it was they touched. It was a painful, fearful thing to go through, but in the end it had a curiously calming effect. The Bishop leaned to his secretary and whispered, "At least the gossips will get nothing from this—there aren't any secrets left to tell."

"All the people in this story suffered pain," the Speaker said. "All of them sacrificed for the people they loved. All of them caused terrible pain to the people who loved them. And you—listening to me here today, you also caused pain. But remember this: Marcão's life was tragic and cruel, but he could have ended his bargain with Novinha at any time. He chose to stay. He must have found some joy in it. And Novinha: She broke the laws of God that bind this community together. She has also borne her punishment. The Church asks for no penance as terrible as the one she imposed on herself. And if you're inclined to think she might deserve some petty cruelty at your hands, keep this in mind: She suffered everything, did all this for one purpose: to keep the piggies from killing Libo."

The words left ashes in their hearts.

Olhado stood and walked to his mother, knelt by her, put an arm around her shoulder. Ela sat beside her, but she was folded to the ground, weeping. Quara came and stood in front of her mother, staring at her with awe. And Grego buried his face in Novinha's lap and wept. Those who were near enough could hear him crying, "Todo papai é morto. Não tenho nem papai." All my papas are dead. I don't have any papa.

Ouanda stood in the mouth of the alley where she had gone with her mother just before the Speaking ended. She looked for Miro, but he was already gone.

Ender stood behind the platform, looking at Novinha's family, wishing he could do something to ease their pain. There was always pain after a Speaking, because a Speaker for the Dead did nothing to soften the truth. But only rarely had people lived such lives of deceit as Marcão, Libo, and Novinha; rarely were there so many shocks, so many bits of information that forced people to revise their conception of the people that they knew, the people that they loved. Ender knew from the faces that looked up at him as he spoke that he had caused great pain today. He had felt it all himself, as if they had passed their suffering to him. Bruxinha had been most surprised, but Ender knew she was not worst injured. That distinction belonged to Miro and Ouanda, who had thought they knew what the future would bring them. But Ender had also felt the pain that people felt before, and he knew that today's new wounds would heal much faster than the old ones ever would have done. Novinha might not recognize it, but Ender had stripped from her a burden that was much too heavy for her to bear any longer.

"Speaker," said Mayor Bosquinha.

"Mayor," said Ender. He didn't like talking to people after a Speaking, but he was used to the fact that someone always insisted on talking to him. He forced a smile. "There were many more people here than I expected."

"A momentary thing, for most of them," said Bosquinha. "They'll forget it by morning."

Ender was annoyed that she was trivializing it. "Only if something monumental happens in the night," he said.

"Yes. Well, that has been arranged."

Only then did Ender realize that she was extremely upset,

barely under control at all. He took her by the elbow and then cast an arm over her shoulder; she leaned gratefully.

"Speaker, I came to apologize. Your starship has been commandeered by Starways Congress. It has nothing to do with you. A crime was committed here, a crime so—terrible—that the criminals must be taken to the nearest world, Trondheim, for trial and punishment. Your ship."

Ender reflected for a moment. "Miro and Ouanda."

She turned her head, looked at him sharply. "You are not surprised."

"I also won't let them go."

Bosquinha pulled herself away from him. "Won't *let* them?"

"I have some idea what they're charged with."

"You've been here four days, and you already know something that even *I* never suspected?"

"Sometimes the government is the last to know."

"Let me tell you why you *will* let them go, why we'll *all* let them go to stand trial. Because Congress has stripped our files. The computer memory is empty except for the most rudimentary programs that control our power supply, our water, our sewer. Tomorrow no work can be done because we haven't enough power to run any of the factories, to work in the mines, to power the tractors. I have been removed from office. I am now nothing more than the deputy chief of *police,* to see that the directives of the Lusitanian Evacuation Committee are carried out."

"Evacuation?"

"The colony's license has been revoked. They're sending starships to take us all away. Every sign of human habitation here is to be removed. Even the gravestones that mark our dead."

Ender tried to measure her response. He had not thought Bosquinha was the kind who would bow to mindless authority. "Do you intend to submit to this?"

"The power and water supplies are controlled by ansible. They also control the fence. They can shut us in here without power or water or sewers, and we can't get out. Once Miro and Ouanda are aboard your starship, headed for Trondheim, they say that some of the restrictions will be relaxed." She sighed. "Oh, Speaker, I'm afraid this isn't a good time to be a tourist in Lusitania."

"I'm not a tourist." He didn't bother telling her his suspicion that it might not be pure coincidence, Congress noticing the Questionable Activities when Ender happened to be there. "Were you able to save any of your files?"

Bosquinha sighed. "By imposing on you, I'm afraid. I noticed that all your files were maintained by ansible, offworld. We sent our most crucial files as messages to you."

Ender laughed. "Good, that's right, that was well done."

"It doesn't matter. We can't get them back. Or, well, yes, we can, but they'll notice it at once and then you'll be in just as much trouble as the rest of us. And they'll wipe out everything then."

"Unless you sever the ansible connection immediately after copying all my files to local memory."

"Then we really would be in rebellion. And for what?"

"For the chance to make Lusitania the best and most important of the Hundred Worlds."

Bosquinha laughed. "I think they'll regard us as important, but treason is hardly the way to be known as the best."

"Please. Don't do anything. Don't arrest Miro and Ouanda. Wait for an hour and let me meet with you and anyone else who needs to be in on the decision."

"The decision whether or not to rebel? I can't think why *you* should be in on that decision, Speaker."

"You'll understand at the meeting. Please, this place is too important for the chance to be missed."

"The chance for what?"

"To undo what Ender did in the Xenocide three thousand years ago."

Bosquinha gave him a sharp-eyed look. "And here I thought you had just proved yourself to be nothing but a gossip-monger."

She might have been joking. Or she might not. "If you think that what I just did was gossip-mongering, you're too stupid to lead this community in anything." He smiled.

Bosquinha spread her hands and shrugged. "Pois é," she said. Of course. What else?

"Will you have the meeting?"

"I'll call it. In the Bishop's chambers."

Ender winced.

"The Bishop won't meet anywhere else," she said, "and no decision to rebel will mean a thing if he doesn't agree to it." Bosquinha laid her hand on his chest. "He may not even let you into the Cathedral. You are the infidel."

"But you'll try."

"I'll try because of what you did tonight. Only a wise man could see my people so clearly in so short a time. Only a ruthless one would say it all out loud. Your virtue and your flaw—we need them both."

Bosquinha turned and hurried away. Ender knew that she did not, in her inmost heart, want to comply with Starways Congress. It had been too sudden, too severe; they had preempted her authority as if she were guilty of a crime. To give in smacked of confession, and she knew she had done nothing wrong. She wanted to resist, wanted to find some plausible way to slap back at Congress and tell them to wait, to be calm. Or, if necessary, to tell them to drop dead. But she wasn't a fool. She wouldn't do anything to resist them unless she knew it would work and knew it would benefit her people. She was a good Governor, Ender knew. She would gladly sacrifice her pride, her reputation, her future for her people's sake.

He was alone in the praça. Everyone had gone while Bosquinha talked to him. Ender felt as an old soldier must feel, walking over placid fields at the site of a long-ago battle, hearing the echoes of the carnage in the breeze across the rustling grass.

"Don't let them sever the ansible connection."

The voice in his ear startled him, but he knew it at once. "Jane," he said.

"I can make them think you've cut off your ansible, but if you really do it then I won't be able to help you."

"Jane," he said, "you did this, didn't you! Why else would they notice what Libo and Miro and Ouanda have been doing if you didn't call it to their attention?"

She didn't answer.

"Jane, I'm sorry that I cut you off, I'll never—"

He knew she knew what he would say; he didn't have to finish sentences with her. But she didn't answer.

"I'll never turn off the—"

What good did it do to finish sentences that he knew she understood? She hadn't forgiven him yet, that was all, or she would already be answering, telling him to stop wasting her time. Yet he couldn't keep himself from trying one more time. "I missed you. Jane. I really missed you."

Still she didn't answer. She had said what she had to say, to keep the ansible connection alive, and that was all. For now. Ender didn't mind waiting. It was enough to know that she was still there, listening. He wasn't alone. Ender was surprised to find tears on his cheeks. Tears of relief, he decided. Catharsis. A Speaking, a crisis, people's lives in tatters, the future of the colony in doubt. And I cry in relief because an overblown computer program is speaking to me again.

Ela was waiting for him in his little house. Her eyes were red from crying. "Hello," she said.

"Did I do what you wanted?" he asked.

"I never guessed," she said. "He wasn't our father. I should have known."

"I can't think how you could have."

"What have I done? Calling you here to Speak my father's— Marcão's death." She began weeping again. "Mother's secrets—I thought I knew what they were, I thought it was just her files—I thought she *hated* Libo."

"All I did was open the windows and let in some air."

"Tell that to Miro and Ouanda."

"Think a moment, Ela. They would have found out eventually. The cruel thing was that they *didn't* know for so many years. Now that they have the truth, they can find their own way out."

"Like Mother did? Only this time even worse than adultery?"

Ender touched her hair, smoothed it. She accepted his touch, his consolation. He couldn't remember if his father or mother had ever touched him with such a gesture. They must have. How else would he have learned it?

"Ela, will you help me?"

"Help you what? You've done your work, haven't you?"

"This has nothing to do with Speaking for the dead. I have to know, within the hour, how the Descolada works."

"You'll have to ask Mother—she's the one who knows."

"I don't think she'd be glad to see me tonight."

"I'm supposed to ask her? Good evening, Mamãe, you've just been revealed to all of Milagre as an adulteress who's been lying to your children all our lives. So if you wouldn't mind, I'd like to ask you a couple of science questions."

"Ela, it's a matter of survival for Lusitania. Not to mention your brother Miro." He reached over and turned to the terminal. "Log on," he said.

She was puzzled, but she did it. The computer wouldn't recognize her name. "I've been taken off." She looked at him in alarm. "Why?"

"It's not just you. It's everybody."

"It isn't a breakdown," she said. "Somebody stripped out the log-on file."

"Starways Congress stripped all the local computer memory. Everything's gone. We're regarded as being in a state of rebellion. Miro and Ouanda are going to be arrested and sent to Trondheim for trial. Unless I can persuade the Bishop and Bosquinha to launch a *real* rebellion. Do you understand? If your mother doesn't tell you what I need to know, Miro and Ouanda will both be sent twenty-two lightyears away. The penalty for treason is death. But even going to the trial is as bad as life imprisonment. We'll all be dead or very very old before they get back."

Ela looked blankly at the wall. "What do you need to know?"

"I need to know what the Committee will find when they open up her files. About how the Descolada works."

"Yes," said Ela. "For Miro's sake she'll do it." She looked at him defiantly. "She does love us, you know. For one of her children, she'd talk to you herself."

"Good," said Ender. "It would be better if she came herself. To the Bishop's chambers, in an hour."

"Yes," said Ela. For a moment she sat still. Then a synapse connected somewhere, and she stood up and hurried toward the door.

She stopped. She came back, embraced him, kissed him on the cheek. "I'm glad you told it all," she said. "I'm glad to know it."

He kissed her forehead and sent her on her way. When the door closed behind her, he sat down on his bed, then lay down and stared at the ceiling. He thought of Novinha, tried to imagine what she was feeling now. No matter how terrible it is, Novinha, your daughter is hurrying home to you right now, sure that despite the pain and humiliation you're going through, you'll forget yourself completely and do whatever it takes to save your son. I would trade you all your suffering, Novinha, for one child who trusted me like that.

Chapter 16

The Fence

A great rabbi stands teaching in the marketplace. It happens that a husband finds proof that morning of his wife's adultery, and a mob carries her to the marketplace to stone her to death. (There is a familiar version of this story, but a friend of mine, a Speaker for the Dead, has told me of two other rabbis that faced the same situation. Those are the ones I'm going to tell you.)

The rabbi walks forward and stands beside the woman. Out of respect for him the mob forbears, and waits with the stones heavy in their hands. "Is there anyone here," he says to them, "who has not desired another man's wife, another woman's husband?"

They murmur and say, "We all know the desire. But, Rabbi, none of us has acted on it."

The rabbi says, "Then kneel down and give thanks that God made you strong." He takes the woman by the hand and leads her out of the market. Just before he lets her go, he whispers to her, "Tell the lord magistrate who saved his mistress. Then he'll know I am his loyal servant."

So the woman lives, because the community is too corrupt to protect itself from disorder.

Another rabbi, another city. He goes to her and stops the mob, as in the other story, and says, "Which of you is without sin? Let him cast the first stone."

The people are abashed, and they forget their unity of purpose in the memory of their own individual sins. Someday, they think, I may be like this woman, and I'll hope for forgiveness and another chance. I should treat her the way I wish to be treated.

As they open their hands and let the stones fall to the ground, the rabbi picks up one of the fallen stones, lifts it high over the woman's head, and throws it straight down with all his might. It crushes her skull and dashes her brains onto the cobblestones.

"Nor am I without sin," he says to the people. "But if we allow only perfect people to enforce the law, the law will soon be dead, and our city with it."

So the woman died because her community was too rigid to endure her deviance.

The famous version of this story is noteworthy because it is so startlingly rare in our experience. Most communities lurch between decay and rigor mortis, and when they veer too far, they die. Only one rabbi dared to expect of us such a perfect balance that we could preserve the law and still forgive the deviation. So, of course, we killed him.

—San Angelo, *Letters to an Incipient Heretic,* trans. Amai a Tudomundo Para Que Deus Vos Ame Cristão, 103:72:54:2

Minha irmã. My sister. The words kept running through Miro's head until he didn't hear them anymore, they were part of the background: A Ouanda é minha irmã. She's my sister. His feet carried him by habit from the praça to the playing fields and over the saddle of the hill. The crown of the higher peak held the Cathedral and the monastery, which always loomed over the Zenador's Station, as if they were a fortress keeping watch over the gate. Did Libo walk this way as he went to meet my mother? Did they meet in the Xenobiologist's Station? Or was it more discreet, rutting in the grass like hogs on the fazendas?

He stood at the door of the Zenador's Station and tried to think of some reason to go inside. Nothing to do there. Hadn't written a report on what happened today, but he didn't know how to write it anyway. Magical powers, that's what it was. The piggies sing to the trees and the trees split themselves into kindling. Much better than carpentry. The aboriginals are a good deal more sophisticated than previously supposed. Multiple uses for everything. Each tree is at once a totem, a grave marker, and a small lumber mill. Sister. There's something I have to do but I can't remember.

The piggies have the most sensible plan. Live as brothers only, and never mind the women. Would have been better for you, Libo, and that's the truth—no, I should call you Papai, not Libo. Too bad Mother never told you or you could have dandled me on your knee. Both your eldest children, Ouanda on one knee and Miro on the other, aren't we proud of our two children? Born the same year, only two months apart, what a busy fellow Papai was then, sneaking along the fence to tup Mamãe in her own back yard. Everyone felt sorry for you because you had nothing but daughters. No one to carry on the family name. Their sympathy was wasted. You were brimming over with sons. And I have far more sisters than I ever thought. One more sister than I wanted.

He stood at the gate, looking up toward the woods atop the piggies' hill. There is no scientific purpose to be served by visiting at night. So I guess I'll serve an unscientific purposelessness and see if they have room for another brother in the tribe. I'm probably too big for a bedspace in the log house, so I'll sleep outside, and I won't be much for climbing trees, but I do know a thing or two about technology, and I don't feel any particular inhibitions now about telling you anything you want to know.

He laid his right hand on the identification box and reached out his left to pull the gate. For a split second he didn't realize what was happening. Then his hand felt like it was on fire, like it was being cut off with a rusty saw, he shouted and pulled his left hand away from the gate. Never since the gate was built had it stayed hot after the box was touched by the Zenador's hand.

"Marcos Vladimir Ribeira von Hesse, your passage through the fence has been revoked by order of the Lusitanian Evacuation Committee."

Never since the gate was built had the voice challenged a Zenador. It took a moment before Miro understood what it was saying.

"You and Ouanda Quenhatta Figueira Mucumbi will present yourselves to Deputy Chief of Police Faria Lima Maria do Bosque, who will arrest you in the name of Starways Congress and present you on Trondheim for trial."

For a moment he was lightheaded and his stomach felt heavy

and sick. They know. Tonight of all nights. Everything over. Lose Ouanda, lose the piggies, lose my work, all gone. Arrest. Trondheim. Where the Speaker came from, twenty-two years in transit, everybody gone except Ouanda, the only one left, and she's my *sister*—

His hand flashed out again to pull at the gate; again the excruciating pain shot through his arm, the pain nerves all alerted, all afire at once. I can't just disappear. They'll seal the gate to everyone. Nobody will go to the piggies, nobody will tell them, the piggies will wait for us to come and no one will ever come out of the gate again. Not me, not Ouanda, not the Speaker, nobody, and no explanation.

Evacuation Committee. They'll evacuate us and wipe out every trace of our being here. That much is in the rules, but there's more, isn't there? What did they see? How did they find out? Did the Speaker tell them? He's so addicted to truth. I have to explain to the piggies why we won't be coming back, I have to tell them.

A piggy always watched them, followed them from the moment they entered the forest. Could a piggy be watching now? Miro waved his hand. It was too dark, though. They couldn't possibly see him. Or perhaps they could; no one knew how good the piggies' vision was at night. Whether they saw him or not, they didn't come. And soon it would be too late; if the framlings were watching the gate, they had no doubt already notified Bosquinha, and she'd be on her way, zipping over the grass. She would be oh-so-reluctant to arrest him, but she would do her job, and never mind arguing with her about whether it was good for humans or piggies, either one, to maintain this foolish separation, she wasn't the sort to question the law, she just did what she was told. And he'd surrender, there was no reason to fight, where could he hide inside the fence, out among the cabra herds? But before he gave up, he'd tell the piggies, he had to tell them.

So he walked along the fence, away from the gate, toward the open grassland directly down the hill from the Cathedral, where no one lived near enough to hear his voice. As he walked, he called. Not words, but a high hooting sound, a cry that he and Ouanda used to call each other's attention when they were separated among the piggies. They'd hear it, they had to hear it, they had to come to him because he couldn't possibly pass the fence. So come, Human, Leafeater, Mandachuva, Arrow, Cups, Calendar, anyone, everyone, come and let me tell you that I cannot tell you any more.

Quim sat miserably on a stool in the Bishop's office.

"Estevão," the Bishop said quietly, "there'll be a meeting here in a few minutes, but I want to talk to you a minute first."

"Nothing to talk about," said Quim. "You warned us, and it happened. He's the devil."

"Estevão, we'll talk for a minute and then you'll go home and sleep."

"Never going back there."

"The Master ate with worse sinners than your mother, and forgave them. Are you better than he?"

"None of the adulteresses he forgave was his mother!"

"Not everyone's mother can be the Blessed Virgin."

"Are you on his side, then? Has the Church made way here for the Speakers for the Dead? Should we tear down the Cathedral and use the stones to make an amphitheater where all our dead can be slandered before we lay them in the ground?"

A whisper: "I am your Bishop, Estevão, the vicar of Christ on this planet, and you will speak to me with the respect you owe to my office."

Quim stood there, furious, unspeaking.

"I think it would have been better if the Speaker had not told these stories publicly. Some things are better learned in privacy, in quiet, so that we need not deal with shocks while an audience watches us. That's why we use the confessional, to shield us from public shame while we wrestle with our private sins. But be fair, Estevão. The Speaker may have told the stories, but the stories all were true. Né?"

"É."

"Now, Estevão, let us think. Before today, did you love your mother?"

"Yes."

"And this mother that you loved, had she already committed adultery?"

"Ten thousand times."

"I suspect she was not so libidinous as that. But you tell me that you loved her, though she was an adulteress. Isn't she the same person tonight? Has she changed between yesterday and today? Or is it only you who have changed?"

"What she was yesterday was a lie."

"Do you mean that because she was ashamed to tell her children that she was an adulteress, she must also have been lying when she cared for you all the years you were growing up, when she trusted you, when she taught you—"

"She was not exactly a nurturing mother."

"If she had come to the confessional and won forgiveness for her adultery, then she would never have had to tell you at all. You would have gone to your grave not knowing. It would not have been a lie; because she would have been forgiven, she would not have been an adulteress. Admit the truth, Estevão: You're not angry with her adultery. You're angry because you embarrassed yourself in front of the whole city by trying to defend her."

"You make me seem like a fool."

"No one thinks you're a fool. Everyone thinks you're a loyal son. But now, if you're to be a true follower of the Master, you will forgive her and let her see that you love her more than ever, because now you understand her suffering." The Bishop glanced toward the door. "I have a meeting here now, Estevão. Please go into my inner chamber and pray to the Madelena to forgive you for your unforgiving heart."

Looking more miserable than angry, Quim passed through the curtain behind the Bishop's desk.

The Bishop's secretary opened the other door and let the Speaker for the Dead into the chamber. The Bishop did not rise. To his surprise, the Speaker knelt and bowed his head. It was an act that Catholics did only in a public presentation to the Bishop, and Peregrino could not think what the Speaker meant by this. Yet the man knelt there, waiting, and so the Bishop arose from his chair, walked to him, and held out his ring to be kissed. Even then the Speaker waited, until finally Peregrino said, "I bless you, my son, even though I'm not sure whether you mock me with this obeisance."

Head still bowed, the Speaker said, "There's no mockery in me." Then he looked up at Peregrino. "My father was a Catholic. He pretended not to be, for the sake of convenience, but he never forgave himself for his faithlessness."

"You were baptized?"

"My sister told me that yes, Father baptized me shortly after birth. My mother was a Protestant of a faith that deplored infant baptism, so they had a quarrel about it." The Bishop held out his hand to lift the Speaker to his feet. The Speaker chuckled. "Imagine. A closet Catholic and a lapsed Mormon, quarreling over religious procedures that they both claimed not to believe in."

Peregrino was skeptical. It was too elegant a gesture, for the Speaker to turn out to be Catholic. "I thought," said the Bishop, "that you Speakers for the Dead renounced all religions before taking up your, shall we say, vocation."

"I don't know what the others do. I don't think there are any rules about it—certainly there weren't when *I* became a Speaker."

Bishop Peregrino knew that Speakers were not supposed to lie, but this one certainly seemed to be evasive. "Speaker Andrew, there isn't a place in all the Hundred Worlds where a Catholic has to conceal his faith, and there hasn't been for three thousand years. That was the great blessing of space travel, that it removed the terrible population restrictions on an overcrowded Earth. Are you telling me that your father lived on Earth three thousand years ago?"

"I'm telling you that my father saw to it I was baptized a Catholic, and for his sake I did what he never could do in his life. It was for him that I knelt before a Bishop and received his blessing."

"But it was you that I blessed." And you're still dodging my question. Which implies that my inference about your father's time of life is true, but you don't want to discuss it. Dom Cristão said that there was more to you than met the eye.

"Good," said the Speaker. "I need the blessing more than my father, since he's dead, and I have many more problems to deal with."

"Please sit down." The Speaker chose a stool near the far wall. The Bishop sat in his massive chair behind his desk. "I wish you hadn't Spoken today. It came at an inconvenient time."

"I had no warning that Congress would do this."

"But you knew that Miro and Ouanda had violated the law. Bosquinha told me."

"I found out only a few hours before the Speaking. Thank you for not arresting them yet."

"That's a civil matter." The Bishop brushed it aside, but they both knew that if he had insisted, Bosquinha would have had to obey her orders and arrest them regardless of the Speaker's request. "Your Speaking has caused a great deal of distress."

"More than usual, I'm afraid."

"So—is your responsibility over? Do you inflict the wounds and leave it to others to heal them?"

"Not wounds, Bishop Peregrino. Surgery. And if I can help to heal the pain afterward, then yes, I stay and help. I have no anesthesia, but I do try for antisepsis."

"You should have been a priest, you know."

"Younger sons used to have only two choices. The priesthood or the military. My parents chose the latter course for me."

"A younger son. Yet you had a sister. And you lived in the time when population controls forbade parents to have more than two children unless the government gave special permission. They called such a child a Third, yes?"

"You know your history."

"Were you born on Earth, before starflight?"

"What concerns us, Bishop Peregrino, is the future of Lusitania, not the biography of a Speaker for the Dead who is plainly only thirty-five years old."

"The future of Lusitania is my concern, Speaker Andrew, not yours."

"The future of the humans on Lusitania is your concern, Bishop. I'm concerned with the piggies as well."

"Let's not compete to see whose concern is greater."

The secretary opened the door again, and Bosquinha, Dom Cristão, and Dona Cristã came in. Bosquinha glanced back and forth between the Bishop and the Speaker.

"There's no blood on the floor, if that's what you're looking for," said the Bishop.

"I was just estimating the temperature," said Bosquinha.

"The warmth of mutual respect, I think," said the Speaker. "Not the heat of anger or the ice of hate."

"The Speaker is a Catholic by baptism, if not by belief," said the Bishop. "I blessed him, and it seems to have made him docile."

"I've always been respectful of authority," said the Speaker.

"You *were* the one who threatened us with an Inquisitor," the Bishop reminded him. With a smile.

The Speaker's smile was just as chilly. "And you're the one who told the people I was Satan and they shouldn't talk to me."

While the Bishop and the Speaker grinned at each other, the others laughed nervously, sat down, waited.

"It's your meeting, Speaker," said Bosquinha.

"Forgive me," said the Speaker. "There's someone else invited. It'll make things much simpler if we wait a few more minutes for her to come."

Ela found her mother outside the house, not far from the fence. A light breeze that barely rustled the capim had caught her hair and tossed it lightly. It took a moment for Ela to realize why this was so startling. Her mother had not worn her hair down in many years. It looked strangely free, all the more so because Ela could see how it curled and bent where it had been so long forced into a bun. It was then that she knew that the Speaker was right. Mother would listen to his invitation. Whatever shame or pain tonight's Speaking might have caused her, it led her now to stand out in the open, in the dusk just after sunset, looking toward the piggies' hill. Or perhaps she was looking at the fence. Perhaps remembering a man who met her here, or somewhere else in the capim, so that unobserved they could love each other. Always in hiding, always in secret. Mother is glad, thought Ela, to have it known that Libo was her real husband, that Libo is my true father. Mother is glad, and so am I.

Mother did not turn to look at her, though she surely could hear Ela's approach through the noisy grass. Ela stopped a few steps away.

"Mother," she said.

"Not a herd of cabra, then," said Mother. "You're so noisy, Ela."

"The Speaker. Wants your help."

"Does he."

Ela explained what the Speaker had told her. Mother did not turn around. When Ela was finished, Mother waited a moment, and then turned to walk over the shoulder of the hill. Ela ran after her, caught up with her. "Mother," said Ela. "Mother, are you going to tell him about the Descolada?"

"Yes."

"Why now? After all these years? Why wouldn't you tell *me?*"

"Because you did better work on your own, without my help."

"You know what I was doing?"

"You're my apprentice. I have complete access to your files without leaving any footprints. What kind of master would I be if I didn't watch your work?"

"But—"

"I also read the files you hid under Quara's name. You've never been a mother, so you didn't know that all the file activities of a child under twelve are reported to the parents every week. Quara was doing some remarkable research. I'm glad you're coming with me. When I tell the Speaker, I'll be telling you, too."

"You're going the wrong way," said Ela.

Mother stopped. "Isn't the Speaker's house near the praça?"

"The meeting is in the Bishop's chambers."

For the first time Mother faced Ela directly. "What are you and the Speaker trying to do to me?"

"We're trying to save Miro," said Ela. "And Lusitania Colony, if we can."

"Taking me to the spider's lair—"

"The Bishop has to be on our side or—"

"*Our* side! So when you say *we*, you mean you and the Speaker, is that it? Do you think I haven't noticed that? All my children, one by one, he's seduced you all—"

"He hasn't seduced anybody!"

"He seduced you with his way of knowing just what you want to hear, of—"

"He's no flatterer," said Ela. "He doesn't tell us what we want. He tells us what we know is true. He didn't win our *affection*, Mother, he won our *trust.*"

"Whatever he gets from you, you never gave it to me."

"We wanted to."

Ela did not bend this time before her mother's piercing, demanding glare. It was her mother, instead, who bent, who looked away and then looked back with tears in her eyes. "I wanted to tell you." Mother wasn't talking about her files. "When I saw how you hated him, I wanted to say, He's not your father, your father is a good, kind man—"

"Who didn't have the courage to tell us himself."

Rage came into Mother's eyes. "He wanted to. I wouldn't let him."

"I'll tell you something, Mother. I loved Libo, the way everybody in Milagre loved him. But he was willing to be a hypocrite, and so were you, and without anybody even guessing, the poison of your lies hurt us all. I don't blame you, Mother, or him. But I thank God for the Speaker. He was willing to tell us the truth, and it set us free."

"It's easy to tell the truth," said Mother softly, "when you don't love anybody."

"Is that what you think?" said Ela. "I think I know something, Mother. I think you can't possibly know the truth about somebody *unless* you love them. I think the Speaker loved Father. Marcão, I mean. I think he understood him and loved him before he Spoke."

Mother didn't answer, because she knew that it was true.

"And I know he loves Grego, and Quara, and Olhado. And Miro, and even Quim. And me. I know he loves *me*. And when he shows me that he loves me, I know it's true because he never lies to anybody."

Tears came out of Mother's eyes and drifted down her cheeks.

"I *have* lied to you and everybody else," Mother said. Her voice sounded weak and strained. "But you have to believe me anyway. When I tell you that I love you."

Ela embraced her mother, and for the first time in years she felt warmth in her mother's response. Because the lies between them now were gone. The Speaker had erased the barrier, and there was no reason to be tentative and cautious anymore.

"You're thinking about that damnable Speaker even now, aren't you?" whispered her mother.

"So are you," Ela answered.

Both their bodies shook with Mother's laugh. "Yes." Then she stopped laughing and pulled away, looked Ela in the eyes. "Will he always come between us?"

"Yes," said Ela. "Like a bridge he'll come between us, not a wall."

Miro saw the piggies when they were halfway down the hillside toward the fence. They were so silent in the forest, but the piggies had no great skill in moving through the capim—it rustled loudly as they ran. Or perhaps in coming to answer Miro's call they felt no need to conceal themselves. As they came nearer, Miro recognized them. Arrow, Human, Mandachuva, Leaf-eater, Cups. He did not call out to them, nor did they speak when they arrived. Instead they stood behind the fence opposite him and regarded him silently. No Zenador had ever called the piggies to the fence before. By their stillness they showed their anxiety.

"I can't come to you anymore," said Miro.

They waited for his explanation.

"The framlings found out about us. Breaking the law. They sealed the gate."

Leaf-eater touched his chin. "Do you know what it was the framlings saw?"

Miro laughed bitterly. "What didn't they see? Only one framling ever came with us."

"No," said Human. "The hive queen says it wasn't the Speaker. The hive queen says they saw it from the sky."

The satellites? "What could they see from the sky?"

"Maybe the hunt," said Arrow.

"Maybe the shearing of the cabra," said Leaf-eater.

"Maybe the fields of amaranth," said Cups.

"All of those," said Human. "And maybe they saw that the wives have let three hundred twenty children be born since the first amaranth harvest."

"Three hundred!"

"And twenty," said Mandachuva.

"They saw that food would be plenty," said Arrow. "Now we're sure to win the next war. Our enemies will be planted in huge new forests all over the plain, and the wives will put mother trees in every one of them."

Miro felt sick. Is this what all their work and sacrifice was for, to give some transient advantage to one tribe of piggies? Almost he said, Libo didn't die so you could conquer the world. But his training took over, and he asked a noncommittal question. "Where are all these new children?"

"None of the little brothers come to *us,*" explained Human. "We have too much to do, learning from you and teaching all the other brother-houses. We can't be training little brothers." Then, proudly, he added, "Of the three hundred, fully half are children of my father, Rooter."

Mandachuva nodded gravely. "The wives have great respect for what you have taught us. And they have great hope in the Speaker for the Dead. But what you tell us now, this is very bad. If the framlings hate us, what will we do?"

"I don't know," said Miro. For the moment, his mind was racing to try to cope with all the information they had just told him. Three hundred twenty new babies. A population explosion. And Rooter somehow the father of half of them. Before today Miro would have dismissed the statement of Rooter's fatherhood as part of the piggies' totemic belief system. But having seen a tree uproot itself and fall apart in response to singing, he was prepared to question all his old assumptions.

Yet what good did it do to learn anything now? They'd never let him report again; he couldn't follow up; he'd be aboard a starship for the next quarter century while someone else did all his work. Or worse, no one else.

"Don't be unhappy," said Human. "You'll see—the Speaker for the Dead will make it all work out well."

"The Speaker. Yes, he'll make everything work out fine." The way he did for me and Ouanda. My sister.

"The hive queen says he'll teach the framlings to love us—"

"Teach the framlings," said Miro. "He'd better do it quickly then. It's too late for him to save me and Ouanda. They're arresting us and taking us off planet."

"To the stars?" asked Human hopefully.

"Yes, to the stars, to stand trial! To be punished for helping you. It'll take us twenty-two years to get there, and they'll never let us come back."

The piggies took a moment to absorb this information. Fine, thought Miro. Let them wonder how the Speaker is going to solve everything for them. I trusted in the Speaker, too, and it didn't do much for me. The piggies conferred together.

Human emerged from the group and came closer to the fence. "We'll hide you."

"They'll never find you in the forest," said Mandachuva.

"They have machines that can track me by my smell," said Miro.

"Ah. But doesn't the law forbid them to show us their machines?" asked Human.

Miro shook his head. "It doesn't matter. The gate is sealed to me. I can't cross the fence."

The piggies looked at each other.

"But you have capim right there," said Arrow.

Miro looked stupidly at the grass. "So what?" he asked.

"Chew it," said Human.

"Why?" asked Miro.

"We've seen humans chewing capim," said Leaf-eater. "The other night, on the hillside, we saw the Speaker and some of the robe-humans chewing capim."

"And many other times," said Mandachuva.

Their impatience with him was frustrating. "What does that have to do with the fence?"

Again the piggies looked at each other. Finally Mandachuva tore off a blade of capim near the ground, folded it carefully into a thick wad, and put it in his mouth to chew it. He sat down after a while. The others began teasing him, poking him with their fingers, pinching him. He showed no sign of noticing. Finally Human gave him a particularly vicious pinch, and when Mandachuva did not respond, they began saying, in males' language, Ready, Time to go, Now, Ready.

Mandachuva stood up, a bit shaky for a moment. Then he ran at the fence and scrambled to the top, flipped over, and landed on all fours on the same side as Miro.

Miro leaped to his feet and began to cry out just as Mandachuva reached the top; by the time he finished his cry, Mandachuva was standing up and dusting himself off.

"You can't do that," said Miro. "It stimulates all the pain nerves in the body. The fence can't be crossed."

"Oh," said Mandachuva.

From the other side of the fence, Human was rubbing his thighs together. "He didn't know," he said. "The humans don't know."

"It's an anesthetic," said Miro. "It stops you from feeling pain."

"No," said Mandachuva. "I feel the pain. Very bad pain. Worst pain in the world."

"Rooter says the fence is even worse than dying," said Human. "Pain in all the places."

"But you don't care," said Miro.

"It's happening to your other self," said Mandachuva. "It's happening to your animal self. But your tree self doesn't care. It makes you be your tree self."

Then Miro remembered a detail that had been lost in the grotesquerie of Libo's death. The dead man's mouth had been filled with a wad of capim. So had the mouth of every piggy that had died. Anesthetic. The death looked like hideous torture, but pain was not the purpose of it. They used an anesthetic. It had nothing to do with pain.

"So," said Mandachuva. "Chew the grass, and come with us. We'll hide you."

"Ouanda," said Miro.

"Oh, I'll go get her," said Mandachuva.

"You don't know where she lives."

"Yes I do," said Mandachuva.

"We do this many times a year," said Human. "We know where everybody lives."

"But no one has ever seen you," said Miro.

"We're very secret," said Mandachuva. "Besides, nobody is looking for us."

Miro imagined dozens of piggies creeping about in Milagre in the middle of the night. No guard was kept. Only a few people had business that took them out in the darkness. And the piggies were small, small enough to duck down in the capim and disappear completely. No wonder they knew about metal and machines, despite all the rules designed to keep them from learning about them. No doubt they had seen the mines, had watched the shuttle land, had seen the kilns firing the bricks, had watched the fazendeiros plowing and planting the human-specific amaranth. No wonder they had known what to ask for.

How stupid of us, to think we could cut them off from our culture. They kept far more secrets from us than we could possibly keep from them. So much for cultural superiority.

Miro pulled up his own blade of capim.

"No," said Mandachuva, taking the blade from his hands. "You don't get the root part. If you take the root part, it doesn't do you any good." He threw away Miro's blade and tore off his own, about ten centimeters above the base. Then he folded it and handed it to Miro, who began to chew it.

Mandachuva pinched and poked him.

"Don't worry about that," said Miro. "Go get Ouanda. They could arrest her any minute. Go. Now. Go on."

Mandachuva looked at the others and, seeing some invisible signal of consent, jogged off along the fenceline toward the slopes of Vila Alta, where Ouanda lived.

Miro chewed a little more. He pinched himself. As the piggies said, he felt the pain, but he didn't care. All he cared about was that this was a way out, a way to stay on Lusitania. To stay, perhaps, with Ouanda. Forget the rules, all the rules. They had no power over him once he left the human enclave and entered the piggies' forest. He would become a renegade, as they already accused him of being, and he and Ouanda could leave behind all the insane rules of human behavior and live as they wanted to, and raise a family of humans who had completely new values, learned from the piggies, from the forest life; something new in the Hundred Worlds, and Congress would be powerless to stop them.

He ran at the fence and seized it with both hands. The pain was no less than before, but now he didn't care, he scrambled up to the top. But with each new handhold the pain grew more intense, and he began to care, he began to care very much about the pain, he began to realize that the capim had no anesthetic effect on him at all, but by this time he was already at the top of the fence. The pain was maddening; he couldn't think; momentum carried him above the top and as he balanced there his head passed through the vertical field of the fence. All the pain possible to his body came to his brain at once, as if every part of him were on fire.

The Little Ones watched in horror as their friend hung there atop the fence, his head and torso on one side, his hips and legs on the other. At once they cried out, reached for him, tried to pull him down. Since they had not chewed capim, they dared not touch the fence.

Hearing their cries, Mandachuva ran back. Enough of the anesthetic remained in his body that he could climb up and push the heavy human body over the top. Miro landed with a bone-crushing thump on the ground, his arm still touching the fence. The piggies pulled him away. His face was frozen in a rictus of agony.

"Quick!" shouted Leaf-eater. "Before he dies, we have to plant him!"

"No!" Human answered, pushing Leaf-eater away from Miro's frozen body. "We don't know if he's dying! The pain is just an illusion, you know that, he doesn't have a wound, the pain should go away—"

"It isn't going away," said Arrow. "Look at him."

Miro's fists were clenched, his legs were doubled under him, and his spine and neck were arched backward. Though he was breathing in short, hard pants, his face seemed to grow even tighter with pain. "Before he dies," said Leaf-eater. "We have to give him root."

"Go get Ouanda," said Human. He turned to face Mandachuva. "Now! Go get her and tell her Miro is dying. Tell her the gate is sealed and Miro is on this side of it and he's dying."

Mandachuva took off at a run.

The secretary opened the door, but not until he actually saw Novinha did Ender allow himself to feel relief. When he sent Ela for her, he was sure that she would come; but as they waited so many long minutes for her arrival, he began to doubt his understanding of her. There had been no need to doubt. She was the woman that he thought she was. He noticed that her hair was down and windblown, and for the first time since he came to Lusitania, Ender saw in her face a clear image of the girl who in her anguish had summoned him less than two weeks, more than twenty years ago.

She looked tense, worried, but Ender knew her anxiety was because of her present situation, coming into the Bishop's own chambers so shortly after the disclosure of her transgressions. If Ela told her about the danger to Miro, that, too, might be part of her tension. All this was transient; Ender could see in her face, in the relaxation of her movement, in the steadiness of her gaze, that the end of her long deception was indeed the gift he had hoped, had believed it would be. I did not come to hurt you, Novinha, and I'm glad to see that my Speaking has brought you better things than shame.

Novinha stood for a moment, looking at the Bishop. Not defiantly, but politely, with dignity; he responded the same way, quietly offering her a seat. Dom Cristão started to rise from his stool, but she shook her head, smiled, took another stool near the wall. Near Ender. Ela came and stood behind and beside her mother, so she was also partly behind Ender. Like a daughter standing between her parents, thought Ender; then he thrust the thought away from him and refused to think of it anymore. There were far more important matters at hand.

"I see," said Bosquinha, "that you intend this meeting to be an interesting one."

"I think Congress decided that already," said Dona Cristã.

"Your son is accused," Bishop Peregrino began, "of crimes against—"

"I know what he's accused of," said Novinha. "I didn't know until tonight, when Ela told me, but I'm not surprised. My daughter Elanora has also been defying some rules her master set for her. Both of them have a higher allegiance to their own conscience than to the rules others set down for them. It's a failing, if your object is to maintain order, but if your goal is to learn and adapt, it's a virtue."

"Your son isn't on trial here," said Dom Cristão.

"I asked you to meet together," said Ender, "because a decision must be made. Whether or not to comply with the orders given us by Starways Congress."

"We don't have much choice," said Bishop Peregrino.

"There are many choices," said Ender, "and many reasons for choosing. You already made one choice—when you found your files being stripped, you decided to try to save them, and you decided to trust them with me, a stranger. Your trust was not misplaced—I'll return your files to you whenever you ask, unread, unaltered."

"Thank you," said Dona Cristã. "But we did that before we knew the gravity of the charge."

"They're going to evacuate us," said Dom Cristão.

"They control everything," said Bishop Peregrino.

"I already told him that," said Bosquinha.

"They don't control everything," said Ender. "They only control you through the ansible connection."

"We can't cut off the ansible," said Bishop Peregrino. "That is our only connection with the Vatican."

"I don't suggest cutting off the ansible. I only tell you what I can do. And when I tell you this, I am trusting you the way you trusted me. Because if you repeat this to anyone, the cost to me—and to someone else, whom I love and depend on—would be immeasurable."

He looked at each of them, and each in turn nodded acquiescence.

"I have a friend whose control over ansible communications among all the Hundred Worlds is complete—and completely unsuspected. I'm the only one who knows what she can do. And she has told me that when I ask her to, she can make it seem to all the framlings that we here on Lusitania have cut off our ansible connection. And yet we will have the ability to send guarded messages if we want to—to the Vatican, to the offices of your order. We can read distant records, intercept distant communications. In short, we will have eyes and they will be blind."

"Cutting off the ansible, or even seeming to, would be an act of rebellion. Of war." Bosquinha was saying it as harshly as possible, but Ender could see that the idea appealed to her, though she was resisting it with all her might. "I will say, though, that if we were insane enough to decide on war, what the Speaker is offering us is a clear advantage. We'd need any advantage we could get—if we were mad enough to rebel."

"We have nothing to gain by rebellion," said the Bishop, "and everything to lose. I grieve for the tragedy it would be to send Miro and Ouanda to stand trial on another world, especially because they are so young. But the court will no doubt take that into account and treat them with mercy. And by complying with the orders of the committee, we will save this community much suffering."

"Don't you think that having to evacuate this world will also cause them suffering?" asked Ender.

"Yes. Yes, it will. But a law was broken, and the penalty must be paid."

"What if the law was based on a misunderstanding, and the penalty is far out of proportion to the sin?"

"We can't be the judges of that," said the Bishop.

"We *are* the judges of that. If we go along with Congressional orders, then we're saying that the law is good and the punishment is just. And it may be that at the end of this meeting you'll decide exactly that. But there are some things you must know before you can make your decision. Some of those things I can tell you, and some of those things only Ela and Novinha can tell you. You shouldn't make your decision until you know all that we know."

"I'm always glad to know as much as possible," said the Bishop. "Of course, the final decision is Bosquinha's, not mine—"

"The final decision belongs to all of you together, the civil and religious and intellectual leadership of Lusitania. If any one of you decides against rebellion, rebellion is impossible. Without the

Church's support, Bosquinha can't lead. Without civil support, the Church has no power."

"We have no power," said Dom Cristão. "Only opinions."

"Every adult in Lusitania looks to you for wisdom and fair-mindedness."

"You forget a fourth power," said Bishop Peregrino. "Yourself."

"I'm a framling here."

"A most extraordinary framling," said the Bishop. "In your four days here you have captured the soul of this people in a way I feared and foretold. Now you counsel rebellion that could cost us everything. You are as dangerous as Satan. And yet here you are, submitting to our authority as if you weren't free to get on the shuttle and leave here when the starship returns to Trondheim with our two young criminals aboard."

"I submit to your authority," said Ender, "because I don't want to be a framling here. I want to be your citizen, your student, your parishioner."

"As a Speaker for the Dead?" asked the Bishop.

"As Andrew Wiggin. I have some other skills that might be useful. Particularly if you rebel. And I have other work to do that can't be done if humans are taken from Lusitania."

"We don't doubt your sincerity," said the Bishop. "But you must forgive us if we are doubtful about casting in with a citizen who is something of a latecomer."

Ender nodded. The Bishop could not say more until he knew more. "Let me tell you first what I know. Today, this afternoon, I went out into the forest with Miro and Ouanda."

"You! You also broke the law!" The Bishop half-rose from his chair.

Bosquinha reached forward, gestured to settle the Bishop's ire. "The intrusion in our files began long before this afternoon. The Congressional Order couldn't possibly be related to his infraction."

"I broke the law," said Ender, "because the piggies were asking for me. Demanding, in fact, to see me. They had seen the shuttle land. They knew that I was here. And, for good or ill, they had read the Hive Queen and the Hegemon."

"They gave the piggies *that* book?" said the Bishop.

"They also gave them the New Testament," said Ender. "But surely you won't be surprised to learn that the piggies found much in common between themselves and the hive queen. Let me tell you what the piggies said. They begged me to convince all the Hundred Worlds to end the rules that keep them isolated here. You see, the piggies don't think of the fence the way we do. We see it as a way of protecting their culture from human influence and corruption. They see it as a way of keeping them from learning all the wonderful secrets that we know. They imagine our ships going from star to star, colonizing them, filling them up. And five or ten thousand years from now, when they finally learn all that we refuse to teach them, they'll emerge into space to find all the worlds filled up. No place for them at all. They think of our fence as a form of species murder. We will keep them on Lusitania like animals in a zoo, while we go out and take all the rest of the universe."

"That's nonsense," said Dom Cristão. "That isn't our intention at all."

"Isn't it?" Ender retorted. "Why are we so anxious to keep them from any influence from our culture? It isn't just in the interest of science. It isn't just good xenological procedure. Remember, please, that our discovery of the ansible, of starflight, of partial gravity control, even of the weapon we used to destroy the buggers—all of them came as a *direct* result of our contact with the buggers. We learned most of the technology from the machines they left behind from their first foray into Earth's star system. We were using those machines long before we understood them. Some of them, like the philotic slope, we don't even understand now. We are in space precisely *because* of the impact of a devastatingly superior culture. And yet in only a few generations, we took their machines, surpassed them, and destroyed them. That's what our fence means—we're afraid the piggies will do the same to us. And they know that's what it means. They know it, and they hate it."

"We aren't afraid of them," said the Bishop. "They're—savages, for heaven's sake—"

"That's how we looked to the buggers, too," said Ender. "But to Pipo and Libo and Ouanda and Miro, the piggies have never looked like savages. They're different from us, yes, far more different than framlings. But they're still *people*. Ramen, not varelse. So when Libo saw that the piggies were in danger of starving, that they were preparing to go to war in order to cut down the population, he didn't act like a scientist. He didn't observe their war and take notes on the death and suffering. He acted like a Christian. He got experimental amaranth that Novinha had rejected for human use because it was too closely akin to Lusitanian biochemistry, and he taught the piggies how to plant it and harvest it and prepare it as food. I have no doubt that the rise in piggy population and the fields of amaranth are what the Starways Congress saw. Not a willful violation of the law, but an act of compassion and love."

"How can you call such disobedience a Christian act?" said the Bishop.

"What man of you is there, when his son asks for bread, will give him a stone?"

"The devil can quote scripture to suit his own purpose," said the Bishop.

"I'm not the devil," said Ender, "and neither are the piggies. Their babies were dying of hunger, and Libo gave them food and saved their lives."

"And look what they did to *him!*"

"Yes, let's look what they did to him. They put him to death. Exactly the way they put to death their own most honored citizens. Shouldn't that have told us something?"

"It told us that they're dangerous and have no conscience," said the Bishop.

"It told us that death means something completely different to them. If you really believed that someone was perfect in heart, Bishop, so righteous that to live another day could only cause them to be less perfect, then wouldn't it be a good thing for them if they were killed and taken directly into heaven?"

"You mock us. You don't believe in heaven."

"But you do! What about the martyrs, Bishop Peregrino? Weren't they caught up joyfully into heaven?"

"Of course they were. But the men who killed them were beasts. Murdering saints didn't sanctify them, it damned their souls to hell forever."

"But what if the dead don't go to heaven? What if the dead are transformed into new life, right before your eyes? What if when a piggy dies, if they lay out his body just so, it takes root and turns into something else? What if it turns into a tree that lives fifty or a hundred or five hundred years more?"

"What are you talking about?" demanded the Bishop.

"Are you telling us that the piggies somehow metamorphose from animal to plant?" asked Dom Cristão. "Basic biology suggests that this isn't likely."

"It's practically impossible," said Ender. "That's why there are only a handful of species on Lusitania that survived the Descolada. Because only a few of them were able to make the transformation. When the piggies kill one of their people, he is transformed into a tree. And the tree retains at least some of its intelligence. Because today I saw the piggies sing to a tree, and without a single tool touching it, the tree severed its own roots, fell over, and split itself into exactly the shapes and forms of wood and bark that the piggies needed. It wasn't a dream. Miro and Ouanda and I all saw it with our own eyes, and heard the song, and touched the wood, and prayed for the soul of the dead."

"What does this have to do with our decision?" demanded Bosquinha. "So the forests are made up of dead piggies. That's a matter for scientists."

"I'm telling you that when the piggies killed Pipo and Libo they thought they were helping them transform into the next stage of their existence. They weren't beasts, they were ramen, giving the highest honor to the men who had served them so well."

"Another moral transformation, is that it?" asked the Bishop. "Just as you did today in your Speaking, making us see Marcos Ribeira again and again, each time in a new light, now you want us to think the piggies are noble? Very well, they're noble. But I won't rebel against Congress, with all the suffering such a thing would cause, just so our scientists can teach the piggies how to make refrigerators."

"Please," said Novinha.

They looked at her expectantly.

"You say that they stripped our files? They read them all?"

"Yes," said Bosquinha.

"Then they know everything that I have in my files. About the Descolada."

"Yes," said Bosquinha.

Novinha folded her hands in her lap. "There won't be any evacuation."

"I didn't think so," said Ender. "That's why I asked Ela to bring you."

"Why won't there be an evacuation?" asked Bosquinha.

"Because of the Descolada."

"Nonsense," said the Bishop. "Your parents found a cure for that."

"They didn't cure it," said Novinha. "They controlled it. They stopped it from becoming active."

"That's right," said Bosquinha. "That's why we put the additives in the water. The Colador."

"Every human being on Lusitania, except perhaps the Speaker, who may not have caught it yet, is a carrier of the Descolada."

"The additive isn't expensive," said the Bishop. "But perhaps they might isolate us. I can see that they might do that."

"There's nowhere isolated enough," said Novinha. "The Descolada is infinitely variable. It attacks any kind of genetic material. The additive can be given to humans. But can they give additives to every blade of grass? To every bird? To every fish? To every bit of plankton in the sea?"

"They can all catch it?" asked Bosquinha. "I didn't know that."

"I didn't tell anybody," said Novinha. "But I built the protection into every plant that I developed. The amaranth, the potatoes, everything—the challenge wasn't making the protein usable, the challenge was to get the organisms to produce their own Descolada blockers."

Bosquinha was appalled. "So anywhere we go—"

"We can trigger the complete destruction of the biosphere."

"And you kept this a *secret?*" asked Dom Cristão.

"There was no need to tell it." Novinha looked at her hands in her lap. "Something in the information had caused the piggies to kill Pipo. I kept it secret so no one else would know. But now, what Ela has learned over the last few years, and what the Speaker has said tonight—now I know what it was that Pipo learned. The Descolada doesn't just split the genetic molecules and prevent them from re-forming or duplicating. It also encourages them to bond with completely foreign genetic molecules. Ela did the work on this against my will. All the native life on Lusitania thrives in plant-and-animal pairs. The cabra with the capim. The watersnakes with the grama. The suckflies with the reeds. The xingadora bird with the tropeço vines. And the piggies with the trees of the forest."

"You're saying that one *becomes* the other?" Dom Cristão was at once fascinated and repelled.

"The piggies may be unique in that, in transforming from the corpse of a piggy into a tree," said Novinha. "But perhaps the cabras become fertilized from the pollen of the capim. Perhaps the flies are hatched from the tassels of the river reeds. It should be studied. I should have been studying it all these years."

"And now they'll know this?" asked Dom Cristão. "From your files?"

"Not right away. But sometime in the next twenty or thirty years. Before any other framlings get here, they'll know," said Novinha.

"I'm not a scientist," said the Bishop. "Everyone else seems to understand except me. What does this have to do with the evacuation?"

Bosquinha fidgeted with her hands. "They can't take us off Lusitania," she said. "Anywhere they took us, we'd carry the Descolada with us, and it would kill everything. There aren't enough xenobiologists in the Hundred Worlds to save even a single planet from devastation. By the time they get here, they'll know that we can't leave."

"Well, then," said the Bishop. "That solves our problem. If we tell them now, they won't even send a fleet to evacuate us."

"No," said Ender. "Bishop Peregrino, once they know what the Descolada will do, they'll see to it that no one leaves this planet, ever."

The Bishop scoffed. "What, do you think they'll blow up the planet? Come now, Speaker, there are no more Enders among the human race. The worst they might do is quarantine us here—"

"In which case," said Dom Cristão, "why should we submit to their control at all? We could send them a message telling them about the Descolada, informing them that we will not leave the planet and they should not come here, and that's it."

Bosquinha shook her head. "Do you think that none of them will say, 'The Lusitanians, just by visiting another world, can destroy it. They have a starship, they have a known propensity for rebelliousness, they have the murderous piggies. Their existence is a threat.' "

"Who would say that?" said the Bishop.

"No one in the Vatican," said Ender. "But Congress isn't in the business of saving souls."

"And maybe they'd be right," said the Bishop. "You said yourself that the piggies want starflight. And yet wherever they might go, they'll have this same effect. Even uninhabited worlds, isn't that right? What will they do, endlessly duplicate this bleak landscape—forests of a single tree, prairies of a single grass, with only the cabra to graze it and only the xingadora to fly above it?"

"Maybe someday we could find a way to get the Descolada under control," said Ela.

"We can't stake our future on such a thin chance," said the Bishop.

"That's why we have to rebel," said Ender. "Because Congress will think exactly that way. Just as they did three thousand years ago, in the Xenocide. Everybody condemns the Xenocide because it destroyed an alien species that turned out to be harmless in its intentions. But as long as it seemed that the buggers were determined to destroy humankind, the leaders of humanity had no choice but to fight back with all their strength. We are presenting them with the same dilemma again. They're already afraid of the piggies. And once they understand the Descolada, all the pretense of trying to protect the piggies will be done with. For the sake of humanity's survival, they'll destroy us. Probably not the whole planet. As you said, there are no Enders today. But they'll certainly obliterate Milagre and remove any trace of human contact. Including killing all the piggies who know us. Then they'll set a watch over this planet to keep the piggies from ever emerging from their primitive state. If you knew what they know, wouldn't you do the same?"

"A Speaker for the Dead says this?" said Dom Cristão.

"You were there," said the Bishop. "You were there the first time, weren't you. When the buggers were destroyed."

"Last time we had no way of talking to the buggers, no way of knowing they were ramen and not varelse. This time *we're here.* We know that we won't go out and destroy other worlds. We know that we'll stay here on Lusitania until we can go out safely, the Descolada neutralized. *This* time," said Ender, "we can keep the ramen alive, so that whoever writes the piggies' story won't have to be a Speaker for the Dead."

The secretary opened the door abruptly, and Ouanda burst in. "Bishop," she said. "Mayor. You have to come. Novinha—"

"What is it?" said the Bishop.

"Ouanda, I have to arrest you," said Bosquinha.

"Arrest me later," she said. "It's Miro. He climbed over the fence."

"He can't do that," said Novinha. "It might kill him—" Then, in horror, she realized what she had said. "Take me to him—"

"Get Navio," said Dona Cristã.

"You don't understand," said Ouanda. "We can't get to him. He's on the other side of the fence."

"Then what can we do?" asked Bosquinha.

"Turn the fence off," said Ouanda.

Bosquinha looked helplessly at the others. "I can't do that. The Committee controls that now. By ansible. They'd never turn it off."

"Then Miro's as good as dead," said Ouanda.

"No," said Novinha.

Behind her, another figure came into the room. Small, fur-covered. None of them but Ender had ever before seen a piggy in the flesh, but they knew at once what the creature was. "Excuse me," said the piggy. "Does this mean we should plant him now?"

No one bothered to ask how the piggy got over the fence. They were too busy realizing what he meant by *planting* Miro.

"No!" screamed Novinha.

Mandachuva looked at her in surprise. "No?"

"I think," said Ender, "that you shouldn't plant any more humans."

Mandachuva stood absolutely still.

"What do you mean?" said Ouanda. "You're making him upset."

"I expect he'll be more upset before this day is over," said Ender. "Come, Ouanda, take us to the fence where Miro is."

"What good will it do if we can't get over the fence?" asked Bosquinha.

"Call for Navio," said Ender.

"I'll go get him," said Dona Cristã. "You forget that no one can call anybody."

"I said, what good will it do?" demanded Bosquinha.

"I told you before," said Ender. "If you decide to rebel, we can sever the ansible connection. And then we can turn off the fence."

"Are you trying to use Miro's plight to force my hand?" asked the Bishop.

"Yes," said Ender. "He's one of your flock, isn't he? So leave the ninety-nine, shepherd, and come with us to save the one that's lost."

"What's happening?" asked Mandachuva.

"You're leading us to the fence," said Ender. "Hurry, please."

They filed down the stairs from the Bishop's chambers to the Cathedral below. Ender could hear the Bishop behind him, grumbling about perverting scripture to serve private ends.

They passed down the aisle of the Cathedral, Mandachuva leading the way. Ender noticed that the Bishop paused near the altar, watching the small furred creature as the humans trooped after him. Outside the Cathedral, the Bishop caught up with him. "Tell me, Speaker," he said, "just as a matter of opinion, if the fence came down, if we rebelled against Starways Congress, would *all* the rules about contact with the piggies be ended?"

"I hope so," said Ender. "I hope that there'll be no more unnatural barriers between us and them."

"Then," said the Bishop, "we'd be able to teach the gospel of Jesus Christ to the Little Ones, wouldn't we? There'd be no rule against it."

"That's right," said Ender. "They might not be converted, but there'd be no rule against trying."

"I have to think about this," said the Bishop. "But perhaps, my dear infidel, your rebellion will open the door to the conversion of a great nation. Perhaps God led you here after all."

By the time the Bishop, Dom Cristão, and Ender reached the fence, Mandachuva and the women had already been there for some time. Ender could tell by the way Ela was standing between her mother and the fence, and the way Novinha was holding her hands out in front of her face, that Novinha had already tried to climb over the fence to reach her son. She was crying now and shouting at him. "Miro! Miro, how could you do this, how could you climb it—" while Ela tried to talk to her, to calm her.

On the other side of the fence, four piggies stood watching, amazed.

Ouanda was trembling with fear for Miro's life, but she had enough presence of mind to tell Ender what she knew he could not see for himself. "That's Cups, and Arrow, and Human, and Leaf-eater. Leaf-eater's trying to get the others to plant him. I think I know what that means, but we're all right. Human and Mandachuva have convinced them not to do it."

"But it still doesn't get us any closer," said Ender. "Why did Miro do something so stupid?"

"Mandachuva explained on the way here. The piggies chew capim and it has an anesthetic effect. They can climb the fence whenever they want. Apparently they've been doing it for years. They thought we didn't do it because we were so obedient to law. Now they know that capim doesn't have the same effect on us."

Ender walked to the fence. "Human," he said.

Human stepped forward.

"There's a chance that we can turn off the fence. But if we do it, we're at war with all the humans on every other world. Do you understand that? The humans of Lusitania and the piggies, together, at war against all the other humans."

"Oh," said Human.

"Will we win?" asked Arrow.

"We might," said Ender. "And we might not."

"Will you give us the hive queen?" asked Human.

"First I have to meet with the wives," said Ender.

The piggies stiffened.

"What are you talking about?" asked the Bishop.

"I have to meet with the wives," said Ender to the piggies, "because we have to make a treaty. An agreement. A set of rules between us. Do you understand me? Humans can't live by your laws, and you can't live by ours, but if we're to live in peace, with no fence between us, and if I'm to let the hive queen live with you and help you and teach you, then you have to make us some promises, and keep them. Do you understand?"

"I understand," said Human. "But you don't know what you're asking for, to deal with the wives. They're not smart the way that the brothers are smart."

"They make all the decisions, don't they?"

"Of course," said Human. "They're the keepers of the mothers, aren't they? But I warn you, it's dangerous to speak to the wives. Especially for you, because they honor you so much."

"If the fence comes down, I have to speak to the wives. If I can't speak to them, then the fence stays up, and Miro dies, and we'll have to obey the Congressional Order that all the humans of Lusitania must leave here." Ender did not tell them that the humans might well be killed. He always told the truth, but he didn't always tell it all.

"I'll take you to the wives," said Human.

Leaf-eater walked up to him and ran his hand derisively across Human's belly. "They named you right," he said. "You *are* a human, not one of us." Leaf-eater started to run away, but Arrow and Cups held him.

"I'll take you," said Human. "Now, stop the fence and save Miro's life."

Ender turned to the Bishop.

"It's not my decision," said the Bishop. "It's Bosquinha's."

"My oath is to the Starways Congress," said Bosquinha, "but I'll perjure myself this minute to save the lives of my people. I say the fence comes down and we try to make the most of our rebellion."

"If we can preach to the piggies," said the Bishop.

"I'll ask them when I meet with the wives," said Ender. "I can't promise more than that."

"Bishop!" cried Novinha. "Pipo and Libo already died beyond that fence!"

"Bring it down," said the Bishop. "I don't want to see this colony end with God's work here still untouched." He smiled grimly. "But Os Venerados had better be made saints pretty soon. We'll need their help."

"Jane," murmured Ender.

"That's why I love you," said Jane. "You can do anything, as long as I set up the circumstances just right."

"Cut off the ansible and turn off the fence, please," said Ender.

"Done," she said.

Ender ran for the fence, climbed over it. With the piggies' help he lifted Miro to the top and let his rigid body drop into the waiting arms of the Bishop, the Mayor, Dom Cristão, and Novinha. Navio was jogging down the slope right behind Dona Cristã. Whatever they could do to help Miro would be done.

Ouanda was climbing the fence.

"Go back," said Ender. "We've already got him over."

"If you're going to see the wives," said Ouanda, "I'm going with you. You need my help."

Ender had no answer to that. She dropped down and came to Ender.

Navio was kneeling by Miro's body. "He climbed the *fence?*" he said. "There's nothing in the books for that. It isn't possible. Nobody can bear enough pain to get his head right through the field."

"Will he live?" demanded Novinha.

"How should I know?" said Navio, impatiently stripping away Miro's clothing and attaching sensors to him. "Nobody covered this in medical school."

Ender noticed that the fence was shaking again. Ela was climbing over. "I don't need *your* help," Ender said.

"It's about time somebody who knows something about xenobiology got to see what's going on," she retorted.

"Stay and look after your brother," said Ouanda.

Ela looked at her defiantly. "He's your brother, too," she said. "Now let's both see to it that if he dies, he didn't die for nothing."

The three of them followed Human and the other piggies into the forest.

Bosquinha and the Bishop watched them go. "When I woke up this morning," Bosquinha said, "I didn't expect to be a rebel before I went to bed."

"Nor did I ever imagine that the Speaker would be our ambassador to the piggies," said the Bishop.

"The question is," said Dom Cristão, "will we ever be forgiven for it."

"Do you think we're making a mistake?" snapped the Bishop.

"Not at all," said Dom Cristão. "I think we've taken a step toward something truly magnificent. But humankind almost never forgives true greatness."

"Fortunately," said the Bishop, "humankind isn't the judge that matters. And now I intend to pray for this boy, since medical science has obviously reached the boundary of its competence."

Chapter 17

The Wives

Find out how word got out that the Evacuation Fleet is armed with the Little Doctor. That is HIGHEST PRIORITY. Then find out who this so-called Demosthenes is. Calling the Evacuation Fleet a Second Xenocide is definitely a violation of the treason laws under the Code and if CSA can't find this voice and put a stop to it, I can't think of any good reason for CSA to continue to exist.

In the meantime, continue your evaluation of the files retrieved from Lusitania. It's completely irrational for them to rebel just because we want to arrest two errant xenologers. There was nothing in the Mayor's background to suggest this was possible. If there's a chance that there was a revolution, I want to find out who the leaders of that revolution might be.

Pyotr, I know you're doing your best. So am I. So is everybody. So are the people on Lusitania, probably. But my responsibility is the safety and integrity of the Hundred Worlds. I have a hundred times the responsibility of Peter the Hegemon and about a tenth of his power. Not to mention the fact that I'm far from being the genius he was. No doubt you and everybody else would be happier if Peter were still available. I'm just afraid that by the time this thing is over, we may need another Ender. Nobody wants Xenocide, but if it happens, I want to make sure it's the other guys that disappear. When it comes to war, human is human and alien is alien. All that raman business goes up in smoke when we're talking about survival.

Does that satisfy you? Do you believe me when I tell you that

I'm not being soft? Now see to it you're not soft, either. See to it you get me results, fast. Now. Love and kisses, Bawa.

—Gobawa Ekimbo, Chmn Xen Ovst Comm, to Pyotr
Martinov, Dir Cgrs Sec Agc, Memo 44:1970:5:4:2; cit.
Demosthenes, *The Second Xenocide,* 87:1972:1:1:1

Human led the way through the forest. The piggies scambled easily up and down slopes, across a stream, through thick underbrush. Human, though, seemed to make a dance of it, running partway up certain trees, touching and speaking to others. The other piggies were much more restrained, only occasionally joining him in his antics. Only Mandachuva hung back with the human beings.

"Why does he do that?" asked Ender quietly.

Mandachuva was baffled for a moment. Ouanda explained what Ender meant. "Why does Human climb the trees, or touch them and sing?"

"He sings to them about the third life," said Mandachuva. "It's very bad manners for him to do that. He has always been selfish and stupid."

Ouanda looked at Ender in surprise, then back at Mandachuva. "I thought everybody liked Human," she said.

"Great honor," said Mandachuva. "A wise one." Then Mandachuva poked Ender in the hip. "But he's a fool in one thing. He thinks you'll do him honor. He thinks you'll take him to the third life."

"What's the third life?" asked Ender.

"The gift that Pipo kept for himself," said Mandachuva. Then he walked faster, caught up with the other piggies.

"Did any of that make sense to you?" Ender asked Ouanda.

"I still can't get used to the way you ask them direct questions."

"I don't get much in the way of answers, do I?"

"Mandachuva is angry, that's something. And he's angry at Pipo, that's another. The third life—a gift that Pipo kept for himself. It will all make sense."

"When?"

"In twenty years. Or twenty minutes. That's what makes xenology so fun."

Ela was touching the trees, too, and looking from time to time at the bushes. "All the same species of tree. And the bushes, too, just alike. And that vine, climbing most of the trees. Have you ever seen any other plant species here in the forest, Ouanda?"

"Not that I noticed. I never looked for that. The vine is called merdona. The macios seem to feed on it, and the piggies eat the macios. The merdona root, *we* taught the piggies how to make it edible. Before the amaranth. So they're eating lower on the food chain now."

"Look," said Ender.

The piggies were all stopped, their backs to the humans, facing a clearing. In a moment Ender, Ouanda, and Ela caught up with them and looked over them into the moonlit glen. It was quite a large space, and the ground was beaten bare. Several log houses lined the edges of the clearing, but the middle was empty except for a single huge tree, the largest they had seen in the forest.

The trunk seemed to be moving. "It's crawling with macios," said Ouanda.

"Not macios," said Human.

"Three hundred twenty," said Mandachuva.

"Little brothers," said Arrow.

"And little mothers," added Cups.

"And if you harm them," said Leaf-eater, "we will kill you unplanted and knock down your tree."

"We won't harm them," said Ender.

The piggies did not take a single step into the clearing. They waited and waited, until finally there was some movement near the largest of the log houses, almost directly opposite them. It was a piggy. But larger than any of the piggies they had seen before.

"A wife," murmured Mandachuva.

"What's her name?" asked Ender.

The piggies turned to him and stared. "*They* don't tell *us* their names," said Leaf-eater.

"If they even *have* names," added Cups.

Human reached up and drew Ender down to where he could whisper in his ear. "We always call her Shouter. But never where a wife can hear."

The female looked at them, and then sang—there was no other way to describe the mellifluous flow of her voice—a sentence or two in Wives' Language.

"It's for you to go," said Mandachuva. "Speaker. You."

"Alone?" asked Ender. "I'd rather bring Ouanda and Ela with me."

Mandachuva spoke loudly in Wives' Language; it sounded like gargling compared to the beauty of the female's voice. Shouter answered, again singing only briefly.

"She says of course they can come," Mandachuva reported. "She says they're females, aren't they? She's not very sophisticated about the differences between humans and little ones."

"One more thing," said Ender. "At least one of you, as an interpreter. Or can she speak Stark?"

Mandachuva relayed Ender's request. The answer was brief, and Mandachuva didn't like it. He refused to translate it. It was Human who explained. "She says that you may have any interpreter you like, as long as it's me."

"Then we'd like to have you as our interpreter," said Ender.

"You must enter the birthing place first," said Human. "You are the invited one."

Ender stepped out into the open and strode into the moonlight. He could hear Ela and Ouanda following him, and Human padding along behind. Now he could see that Shouter was not the only female here. Several faces were in every doorway. "How many are there?" asked Ender.

Human didn't answer. Ender turned to face him. "How many wives are there?" Ender repeated.

Human still did not answer. Not until Shouter sang again, more loudly and commandingly. Only then did Human translate. "In the birthing place, Speaker, it is only to speak when a wife asks you a question."

Ender nodded gravely, then walked back to where the other males waited at the edge of the clearing. Ouanda and Ela followed him. He could hear Shouter singing behind him, and now he understood why the males referred to her by that name—her voice was enough to make the trees shake. Human caught up with Ender and tugged at his clothing. "She says why are you going, you haven't been given permission to go. Speaker, this is a very bad thing, she's very angry."

"Tell her that I did not come to give instructions or to receive instructions. If she won't treat me as an equal, I won't treat her as an equal."

"I can't tell her that," said Human.

"Then she'll always wonder why I left, won't she?"

"This is a great honor, to be called among the wives!"

"It is also a great honor for the Speaker of the Dead to come and visit them."

Human stood still for a few moments, rigid with anxiety. Then he turned and spoke to Shouter.

She in turn fell silent. There was not a sound in the glen.

"I hope you know what you're doing, Speaker," murmured Ouanda.

"I'm improvising," said Ender. "How do you think it's going?"

She didn't answer.

Shouter went back into the large log house. Ender turned around and again headed for the forest. Almost immediately Shouter's voice rang out again.

"She commands you to wait," said Human.

Ender did not break stride, and in a moment he was on the other side of the piggy males. "If she asks me to return, I may come back. But you must tell her, Human, that I did not come to command or to be commanded."

"I can't say that," said Human.

"Why not?" asked Ender.

"Let me," said Ouanda. "Human, do you mean you can't say it because you're afraid, or because there are no words for it?"

"No words. For a brother to speak to a wife about him commanding her, and her petitioning him, those words can't be said in that direction."

Ouanda smiled at Ender. "Not mores, here, Speaker. Language."

"Don't they understand *your* language, Human?" asked Ender.

"Males' Language can't be spoken in the birthing place," said Human.

"Tell her that my words can't be spoken in Wives' Language, but only in Males' Language, and tell her that I—petition—that you be allowed to translate my words in Males' Language."

"You are a lot of trouble, Speaker," said Human. He turned and spoke again to Shouter.

Suddenly the glen was full of the sound of Wives' Language, a dozen different songs, like a choir warming up.

"Speaker," said Ouanda, "you have now violated just about every rule of good anthropological practice."

"Which ones did I miss?"

"The only one I can think of is that you haven't killed any of them yet."

"What you're forgetting," said Ender, "is that I'm not here as a scientist to study them. I'm here as an ambassador to make a treaty with them."

Just as quickly as they started, the wives fell silent. Shouter emerged from her house and walked to the middle of the clearing to stand very near to the huge central tree. She sang.

Human answered her—in Brothers' Language. Ouanda murmured a rough translation. "He's telling her what you said, about coming as equals."

Again the wives erupted in cacophonous song.

"How do you think they'll respond?" asked Ela.

"How could I know?" asked Ouanda. "I've been here exactly as often as you."

"I think they'll understand it and let me in on those terms," said Ender.

"Why do you think that?" asked Ouanda.

"Because I came out of the sky. Because I'm the Speaker for the Dead."

"Don't start thinking you're a great white god," said Ouanda. "It usually doesn't work out very well."

"I'm not Pizarro," said Ender.

In his ear Jane murmured, "I'm beginning to make some sense out of the Wives' Language. The basics of the Males' Language were in Pipo's and Libo's notes. Human's translations are very helpful. The Wives' Language is closely related to Males' Language, except that it seems more archaic—closer to the roots, more old forms— and all the female-to-male forms are in the imperative voice, while the male-to-female forms are in the supplicative. The female word for *the brothers* seems to be related to the male word for *macio,* the tree worm. If this is the language of love, it's a wonder they manage to reproduce at all."

Ender smiled. It was good to hear Jane speak to him again, good to know he would have her help.

He realized that Mandachuva had been asking Ouanda a question, for now he heard her whispered answer. "He's listening to the jewel in his ear."

"Is it the hive queen?" asked Mandachuva.

"No," said Ouanda. "It's a . . ." She struggled to find a word. "It's a computer. A machine with a voice."

"Can I have one?" asked Mandachuva.

"Someday," Ender answered, saving Ouanda the trouble of trying to figure out how to answer.

The wives fell silent, and again Shouter's voice was alone. Immediately the males became agitated, bouncing up and down on their toes.

Jane whispered in his ear. "She's speaking Males' Language herself," she said.

"Very great day," said Arrow quietly. "The wives speaking Males' Language in this place. Never happened before."

"She invites you to come in," said Human. "As a sister to a brother she invites you."

Immediately Ender walked into the clearing and approached her directly. Even though she was taller than the males, she was still a good fifty centimeters shorter than Ender, so he fell to his knees at once. They were eye to eye.

"I am grateful for your kindness to me," said Ender.

"I could say *that* in Wives' Language," Human said.

"Say it in *your* language anyway," said Ender.

He did. Shouter reached out a hand and touched the smooth skin of his forehead, the rough stubble of his jaw; she pressed a finger against his lip, and he closed his eyes but did not flinch as she laid a delicate finger on his eyelid.

She spoke. "You are the holy Speaker?" translated Human. Jane corrected the translation. "He added the word *holy.*"

Ender looked Human in the eye. "I am not holy," he said.

Human went rigid.

"Tell her."

He was in turmoil for a moment; then he apparently decided that Ender was the less dangerous of the two. "She didn't say holy."

"Tell me what she says, as exactly as you can," said Ender.

"If you aren't holy," said Human, "how did you know what she really said?"

"Please," said Ender, "be truthful between her and me."

"To you I'll be truthful," said Human. "But when I speak to her, it's *my* voice she hears saying your words. I have to say them—carefully."

"Be truthful," said Ender. "Don't be afraid. It's important that she knows exactly what I said. Tell her this. Say that I ask her to forgive you for speaking to her rudely, but I am a rude framling and you must say exactly what I say."

Human rolled his eyes, but turned to Shouter and spoke.

She answered briefly. Human translated. "She says her head is not carved from merdona root. Of course she understands that."

"Tell her that we humans have never seen such a great tree before. Ask her to explain to us what she and the other wives do with this tree."

Ouanda was aghast. "You certainly get straight to the point, don't you?"

But when Human translated Ender's words, Shouter immediately went to the tree, touched it, and began to sing.

Now, gathered closer to the tree, they could see the mass of creatures squirming on the bark. Most of them were no more than four or five centimeters long. They looked vaguely fetal, though a thin haze of dark fur covered their pinkish bodies. Their eyes were open. They climbed over each other, struggling to win a place at one of the smears of drying dough that dotted the bark.

"Amaranth mash," said Ouanda.

"Babies," said Ela.

"Not babies," said Human. "These are almost grown enough to walk."

Ender stepped to the tree, reached out his hand. Shouter abruptly stopped her song. But Ender did not stop his movement. He touched his fingers to the bark near a young piggy. In its climbing, it touched him, climbed over his hand, clung to him. "Do you know this one by name?" asked Ender.

Frightened, Human hastily translated. And gave back Shouter's answer. "That one is a brother of mine," he said. "He won't get a name until he can walk on two legs. His father is Rooter."

"And his mother?" asked Ender.

"Oh, the little mothers never have names," said Human. "Ask her."

Human asked her. She answered. "She says his mother was very strong and very courageous. She made herself fat in bearing her five children." Human touched his forehead. "Five children is a very good number. And she was fat enough to feed them all."

"Does his mother bring the mash that feeds him?"

Human looked horrified. "Speaker, I can't say that. Not in any language."

"Why not?"

"I told you. She was fat enough to feed all five of her little ones. Put back that little brother, and let the wife sing to the tree."

Ender put his hand near the trunk again and the little brother squirmed away. Shouter resumed her song. Ouanda glared at Ender for his impetuousness. But Ela seemed excited. "Don't you see? The newborns feed on their mother's body."

Ender drew away, repelled.

"How can you say that?" asked Ouanda.

"Look at them squirming on the trees, just like little macios. They and the macios must have been competitors." Ela pointed toward a part of the tree unstained by amaranth mash. "The tree leaks sap. Here in the cracks. Back before the Descolada there must have been insects that fed on the sap, and the macios and the infant piggies competed to eat them. That's why the piggies were able to mingle their genetic molecules with these trees. Not only did the infants live here, the adults constantly had to climb the trees to keep the macios away. Even when there were plenty of other food sources, they were still tied to these trees throughout their life cycles. Long before they ever *became* trees."

"We're studying piggy society," said Ouanda impatiently. "Not the distant evolutionary past."

"I'm conducting delicate negotiations," said Ender. "So please be quiet and learn what you can without conducting a seminar."

The singing reached a climax; a crack appeared in the side of the tree.

"They're not going to knock down *this* tree for us, are they?" asked Ouanda, horrified.

"She is asking the tree to open her heart." Human touched his forehead. "This is the mothertree, and it is the only one in all our forest. No harm may come to this tree, or all our children will come from other trees, and our fathers all will die."

All the other wives' voices joined Shouter's now, and soon a hole gaped wide in the trunk of the mothertree. Immediately Ender moved to stand directly in front of the hole. It was too dark inside for him to see.

Ela took her nightstick from her belt and held it out to him. Ouanda's hand flew out and seized Ela's wrist. "A machine!" she said. "You can't bring that here."

Ender gently took the nightstick out of Ela's hand. "The fence is off," said Ender, "and we all can engage in Questionable Activities now." He pointed the barrel of the nightstick at the ground and pressed it on, then slid his finger quickly along the barrel to soften the light and spread it. The wives murmured, and Shouter touched Human on the belly.

"I told them you could make little moons at night," he said. "I told them you carried them with you."

"Will it hurt anything if I let this light into the heart of the mothertree?"

Human asked Shouter, and Shouter reached for the nightstick. Then, holding it in trembling hands, she sang softly and tilted it slightly so that a sliver of the light passed through the hole. Almost at once she recoiled and pointed the nightstick the other direction. "The brightness blinds them," Human said.

In Ender's ear, Jane whispered, "The sound of her voice is echoing from the inside of the tree. When the light went in, the echo modulated, causing a high overtone and a shaping of the sound. The tree was answering, using the sound of Shouter's own voice."

"Can you see?" Ender said softly.

"Kneel down and get me close enough, and then move me across the opening." Ender obeyed, letting his head move slowly in front of the hole, giving the jeweled ear a clear angle toward the interior. Jane described what she saw. Ender knelt there for a long time, not moving. Then he turned to the others. "The little mothers," said Ender. "There are little mothers in there, pregnant ones. Not more than four centimeters long. One of them is giving birth."

"You see with your jewel?" asked Ela.

Ouanda knelt beside him, trying to see inside and failing. "Incredible sexual dimorphism. The females come to sexual maturity in their infancy, give birth, and die." She asked Human, "All of these little ones on the outside of the tree, they're all brothers?"

Human repeated the question to Shouter. The wife reached up to a place near the aperture in the trunk and took down one fairly large infant. She sang a few words of explanation. "That one is a young wife," Human translated. "She will join the other wives in caring for the children, when she's old enough."

"Is there only one?" asked Ela.

Ender shuddered and stood up. "That one is sterile, or else they never let her mate. She couldn't possibly have had children."

"Why not?" asked Ouanda.

"There's no birth canal," said Ender. "The babies eat their way out."

Ouanda muttered a prayer.

Ela, however, was more curious than ever. "Fascinating," she said. "But if they're so small, how do they mate?"

"We carry them to the fathers, of course," said Human. "How do you think? The fathers can't come *here,* can they?"

"The fathers," said Ouanda. "That's what they call the most revered trees."

"That's right," said Human. "The fathers are ripe on the bark. They put their dust on the bark, in the sap. We carry the little mother to the father the wives have chosen. She crawls on the bark, and the dust on the sap gets into her belly and fills it up with little ones."

Ouanda wordlessly pointed to the small protuberances on Human's belly.

"Yes," Human said. "These are the carries. The honored brother puts the little mother on one of his carries, and she holds very tight all the way to the father." He touched his belly. "It is the greatest joy we have in our second life. We would carry the little mothers every night if we could."

Shouter sang, long and loud, and the hole in the mothertree began to close again.

"All those females, all the little mothers," asked Ela. "Are they sentient?"

It was a word that Human didn't know.

"Are they awake?" asked Ender.

"Of course," said Human.

"What he means," explained Ouanda, "is can the little mothers think? Do they understand language?"

"Them?" asked Human. "No, they're no smarter than the cabras. And only a little smarter than the macios. They only do three things. Eat, crawl, and cling to the carry. The ones on the outside of the tree, now—they're beginning to learn. I can remember climbing on the face of the mothertree. So I had memory then. But I'm one of the very few that remember so far back."

Tears came unbidden to Ouanda's eyes. "All the mothers, they're born, they mate, they give birth and die, all in their infancy. They never even know they were alive."

"It's sexual dimorphism carried to a ridiculous extreme," said Ela. "The females reach sexual maturity early, but the males reach it late. It's ironic, isn't it, that the dominant female adults are all sterile. They govern the whole tribe, and yet their own genes can't be passed on—"

"Ela," said Ouanda, "what if we could develop a way to let the little mothers bear their children without being devoured. A caesarean section. With a protein-rich nutrient substitute for the little mother's corpse. Could the females survive to adulthood?"

Ela didn't have a chance to answer. Ender took them both by the arms and pulled them away. "How dare you!" he whispered. "What if *they* could find a way to let infant human girls conceive and bear children, which would feed on their mother's tiny corpse?"

"What are you talking about!" said Ouanda.

"That's sick," said Ela.

"We didn't come here to attack them at the root of their lives," said Ender. "We came here to find a way to share a world with them. In a hundred years or five hundred years, when they've learned enough to make changes for themselves, then *they* can decide whether to alter the way that their children are conceived and born. But we can't begin to guess what it would do to them if suddenly as many females as males came to maturity. To do what? They can't bear more children, can they? They can't compete with the males to become fathers, can they? What are they *for?*"

"But they're dying without ever being alive—"

"They are what they are," said Ender. "They decide what changes they'll make, not you, not from your blindly human perspective, trying to make them have full and happy lives, just like us."

"You're right," said Ela. "Of course, you're right, I'm sorry."

To Ela, the piggies weren't people, they were strange alien fauna, and Ela was used to discovering that other animals had inhuman life patterns. But Ender could see that Ouanda was still upset. She had made the raman transition: She thought of piggies as *us* instead of *them*. She accepted the strange behavior that she knew about, even the murder of her father, as within an acceptable range of alienness. This meant she was actually more tolerant and accepting of the piggies than Ela could possibly be; yet it also made her more vulnerable to the discovery of cruel, bestial behaviors among her friends.

Ender noticed, too, that after years of association with the piggies, Ouanda had one of their habits: At a moment of extreme anxiety, her whole body became rigid. So he reminded her of her humanity by taking her shoulder in a fatherly gesture, drawing her close under his arm.

At his touch Ouanda melted a little, laughed nervously, her voice low. "Do you know what I keep thinking?" she said. "That the little mothers have all their children and die unbaptized."

"If Bishop Peregrino converts them," said Ender, "maybe they'll let us sprinkle the inside of the mothertree and say the words."

"Don't mock me," Ouanda whispered.

"I wasn't. For now, though, we'll ask them to change enough that we can live with them, and no more. We'll change ourselves only enough that they can bear to live with us. Agree to that, or the fence goes up again, because then we truly would be a threat to their survival."

Ela nodded her agreement, but Ouanda had gone rigid again. Ender's fingers suddenly dug harshly into Ouanda's shoulder. Frightened, she nodded her agreement. He relaxed his grip. "I'm sorry," he said. "But they are what they are. If you want, they are what God made them. So don't try to remake them in your own image."

He returned to the mothertree. Shouter and Human were waiting.

"Please excuse the interruption," said Ender.

"It's all right," said Human. "I told her what you were doing."

Ender felt himself sink inside. "What did you tell her we were doing?"

"I said that they wanted to do something to the little mothers that would make us all more like humans, but you said they never could do that or you'd put back the fence. I told her that you said we must remain Little Ones, and you must remain humans."

Ender smiled. His translation was strictly true, but he had the sense not to get into specifics. It was conceivable that the wives might actually want the little mothers to survive childbirth, without realizing how vast the consequences of such a simple-seeming, humanitarian change might be. Human was an excellent diplomat; he told the truth and yet avoided the whole issue.

"Well," said Ender. "Now that we've all met each other, it's time to begin serious talking."

Ender sat down on the bare earth. Shouter squatted on the ground directly opposite him. She sang a few words.

"She says you must teach us everything you know, take us out to the stars, bring us the hive queen and give her the lightstick that this new human brought with you, or in the dark of night she'll send all the brothers of this forest to kill all the humans in your sleep and hang you high above the ground so you get no third life at all." Seeing the humans' alarm, Human reached out his hand and touched Ender's chest. "No, no, you must understand. That means nothing. That's the way we always begin when we're talking to another tribe. Do you think we're crazy? We'd never kill you! You gave us amaranth, pottery, the Hive Queen and the Hegemon."

"Tell her to withdraw that threat or we'll never give her anything else."

"I told you, Speaker, it doesn't mean—"

"She said the words, and I won't talk to her as long as those words stand."

Human spoke to her.

Shouter jumped to her feet and walked all the way around the mothertree, her hands raised high, singing loudly.

Human leaned to Ender. "She's complaining to the great mother and to all the wives that you're a brother who doesn't know his place. She's saying that you're rude and impossible to deal with."

Ender nodded. "Yes, that's exactly right. Now we're getting somewhere."

Again Shouter squatted across from Ender. She spoke in Males' Language.

"She says she'll never kill any human or let any of the brothers or wives kill any of you. She says for you to remember that you're twice as tall as any of us and you know everything and we know nothing. Now has she humiliated herself enough that you'll talk to her?"

Shouter watched him, glumly waiting for his response.

"Yes," said Ender. "Now we can begin."

Novinha knelt on the floor beside Miro's bed. Quim and Olhado stood behind her. Dom Cristão was putting Quara and Grego to bed in their room. The sound of his off-tune lullaby was barely audible behind the tortured sound of Miro's breathing.

Miro's eyes opened.

"Miro," said Novinha.

Miro groaned.

"Miro, you're home in bed. You went over the fence while it was on. Now Dr. Navio says that your brain has been damaged. We don't know whether the damage is permanent or not. You may be partially paralyzed. But you're alive, Miro, and Navio says that he can do many things to help you compensate for what you may have lost. Do you understand? I'm telling you the truth. It may be very bad for a while, but it's worth trying."

He moaned softly. But it was not a sound of pain. It was as if he were trying to talk, and couldn't.

"Can you move your jaw, Miro?" asked Quim.

Slowly Miro's mouth opened and closed.

Olhado held his hand a meter above Miro's head and moved it. "Can you make your eyes follow the movement of my hand?"

Miro's eyes followed. Novinha squeezed Miro's hand. "Did you feel me squeeze your hand?"

Miro moaned again.

"Close your mouth for *no,*" said Quim, "and open your mouth for *yes.*"

Miro closed his mouth and said, "Mm."

Novinha could not help herself; despite her encouraging words, this was the most terrible thing that had happened to any of her children. She had thought when Lauro lost his eyes and became

Olhado—she hated the nickname, but now used it herself—that nothing worse could happen. But Miro, paralyzed, helpless, so he couldn't even feel the touch of her hand, that could not be borne. She had felt one kind of grief when Pipo died, and another kind when Libo died, and a terrible regret at Marcão's death. She even remembered the aching emptiness she felt as she watched them lower her mother and father into the ground. But there was no pain worse than to watch her child suffer and be unable to help.

She stood up to leave. For his sake, she would do her crying silently, and in another room.

"Mm. Mm. Mm."

"He doesn't want you to go," said Quim.

"I'll stay if you want," said Novinha. "But you should sleep again. Navio said that the more you sleep for a while—"

"Mm. Mm. Mm."

"Doesn't want to sleep, either," said Quim.

Novinha stifled her immediate response, to snap at Quim and tell him that she could hear his answers perfectly well for herself. This was no time for quarreling. Besides, it was Quim who had worked out the system that Miro was using to communicate. He had a right to take pride in it, to pretend that he was Miro's voice. It was his way of affirming that he was part of the family. That he was not quitting because of what he learned in the praça today. It was his way of forgiving her, so she held her tongue.

"Maybe he wants to tell us something," said Olhado.

"Mm."

"Or ask a question?" said Quim.

"Ma. Aa."

"That's great," said Quim. "If he can't move his hands, he can't write."

"Sem problema," said Olhado. "Scanning. He can scan. If we bring him in by the terminal, I can make it scan the letters and he just says *yes* when it hits the letters he wants."

"That'll take forever," said Quim.

"Do you want to try that, Miro?" asked Novinha.

He wanted to.

The three of them carried him to the front room and laid him on the bed there. Olhado oriented the terminal so it displayed all the letters of the alphabet, facing so Miro could see them. He wrote a short program that caused each letter to light up in turn for a fraction of a second. It took a few trial runs for the speed to be right— slow enough that Miro could make a sound that meant *this letter* before the light moved on to the next one.

Miro, in turn, kept things moving faster yet by deliberately abbreviating his words.

P-I-G.

"Piggies," said Olhado.

"Yes," said Novinha. "Why were you crossing the fence with the piggies?"

"Mmmmm!"

"He's asking a question, Mother," said Quim. "He doesn't want to answer any."

"Aa."

"Do you want to know about the piggies that were with you when you crossed the fence?" asked Novinha. He did. "They've gone back into the forest. With Ouanda and Ela and the Speaker for the Dead." Quickly she told him about the meeting in the Bishop's chambers, what they had learned about the piggies, and above all what they had decided to do. "When they turned off the fence to save you, Miro, it was a decision to rebel against Congress. Do you understand? The Committee's rules are finished. The fence is nothing but wires now. The gate will stand open."

Tears came to Miro's eyes.

"Is that all you wanted to know?" asked Novinha. "You should sleep."

No, he said. No no no no.

"Wait till his eyes are clear," said Quim. "And then we'll scan some more."

D-I-G-A F-A-L—

"Diga ao Falante pelos Mortos," said Olhado.

"What should we tell the Speaker?" asked Quim.

"You should sleep now and tell us later," said Novinha. "He won't be back for hours. He's negotiating a set of rules to govern relations between the piggies and us. To stop them from killing any more of us, the way they killed Pipo and L—and your father."

But Miro refused to sleep. He continued spelling out his message as the terminal scanned. Together the three of them worked out what he was trying to get them to tell the Speaker. And they understood that he wanted them to go now, before the negotiations ended.

So Novinha left Dom Cristão and Dona Cristã to watch over the house and the little children. On the way out of the house she stopped beside her oldest son. The exertion had worn him out; his eyes were closed and his breathing was regular. She touched his hand, held it, squeezed it; he couldn't feel her touch, she knew, but then it was herself she was comforting, not him.

He opened his eyes. And, ever so gently, she felt his fingers tighten on hers. "I felt it," she whispered to him. "You'll be all right."

He shut his eyes against his tears. She got up and walked blindly to the door. "I have something in my eye," she told Olhado. "Lead me for a few minutes until I can see for myself."

Quim was already at the fence. "The gate's too far!" he shouted. "Can you climb over, Mother?"

She could, but it wasn't easy. "No doubt about it," she said. "Bosquinha's going to have to let us install another gate right here."

It was late now, past midnight, and both Ouanda and Ela were getting sleepy. Ender was not. He had been on edge for hours in his bargaining with Shouter; his body chemistry had responded, and even if he had gone home right now it would have been hours before he was capable of sleep.

He now knew far more about what the piggies wanted and needed. Their forest was their home, their nation; it was all the definition of property they had ever needed. Now, however, the amaranth fields had caused them to see that the prairie was also useful land, which they needed to control. Yet they had little concept of land measurement. How many hectares did they need to keep under cultivation? How much land could the humans use? Since the piggies themselves barely understood their needs, it was hard for Ender to pin them down.

Harder still was the concept of law and government. The wives ruled: to the piggies, it was that simple. But Ender had finally got them to understand that humans made their laws differently, and that human laws applied to human problems. To make them understand why humans needed their own laws, Ender had to explain to them human mating patterns. He was amused to note that Shouter was appalled at the notion of *adults* mating with each other, and of men having an equal voice with women in the making of the laws. The idea of family and kinship separate from the tribe was "brother blindness" to her. It was all right for Human to take pride in his father's many matings, but as far as the wives were concerned, they chose fathers solely on the basis of what was good for the tribe. The tribe and the individual—they were the only entities the wives respected.

Finally, though, they understood that human laws must apply within the borders of human settlements, and piggy laws must apply within the piggy tribes. Where the borders should be was entirely a different matter. Now, after three hours, they had finally agreed to one thing and one thing only: Piggy law applied within the forest, and all humans who came within the forest were subject to it. Human law applied within the fence, and all piggies who came there were subject to human government. All the rest of the planet would be divided up later. It was a very small triumph, but at least there was some agreement.

"You must understand," Ender told her, "that humans will need a lot of open land. But we're only the beginning of the problem. You want the hive queen to teach you, to help you mine ore and smelt metals and make tools. But she'll also need land. And in a very short time she'll be far stronger than either humans or Little Ones." Every one of her buggers, he explained, was perfectly obedient and infinitely hardworking. They would quickly outstrip the humans in their productivity and power. Once she was restored to life on Lusitania, she would have to be reckoned with at every turn.

"Rooter says she can be trusted," said Human. And, translating for Shouter, he said, "The mothertree also gives the hive queen her trust."

"Do you give her your *land?*" Ender insisted.

"The world is big," Human translated for Shouter. "She can use all the forests of the other tribes. So can you. We give them to you freely."

Ender looked at Ouanda and Ela. "That's all very good," said Ela, "but are those forests theirs to give?"

"Definitely not," said Ouanda. "They even have wars with the other tribes."

"We'll kill them for you if they give you trouble," offered Human. "We're very strong now. Three hundred twenty babies. In ten years no tribe can stand against us."

"Human," said Ender, "tell Shouter that we are dealing with this tribe now. We'll deal with other tribes later."

Human translated quickly, his words tumbling over each other, and quickly had Shouter's response. "No no no no no."

"What is she objecting to?" asked Ender.

"You *won't* deal with our enemies. You came to *us*. If you go to them, then you are the enemy, too."

It was at that moment that the lights appeared in the forest behind them, and Arrow and Leaf-eater led Novinha, Quim, and Olhado into the wives' clearing.

"Miro sent us," Olhado explained.

"How is he?" asked Ouanda.

"Paralyzed," said Quim bluntly. It saved Novinha the effort of explaining it gently.

"Nossa Senhora," whispered Ouanda.

"But much of it is temporary," said Novinha. "Before I left, I squeezed his hand. He felt it, and squeezed me back. Just a little, but the nerve connections aren't dead, not all of them, anyway."

"Excuse me," said Ender, "but that's a conversation you can carry on back in Milagre. I have another matter to attend to here."

"Sorry," Novinha said. "Miro's message. He couldn't speak, but he gave it to us letter by letter, and we figured out what went in the cracks. The piggies are planning war. Using the advantages they've gained from us. Arrows, their greater numbers—they'd be irresistible. As I understand it, though, Miro says that their warfare isn't just a matter of conquest of territory. It's an opportunity for genetic mixing. Male exogamy. The winning tribe gets the use of the trees that grow from the bodies of the war dead."

Ender looked at Human, Leaf-eater, Arrow. "It's true," said Arrow. "Of course it's true. We are the wisest of tribes now. All of us will make better fathers than any of the other piggies."

"I see," said Ender.

"That's why Miro wanted us to come to you now, tonight," said Novinha. "While the negotiations still aren't final. That has to end."

Human stood up, bounced up and down as if he were about to take off and fly. "I won't translate that," said Human.

"*I* will," said Leaf-eater.

"Stop!" shouted Ender. His voice was far louder than he had ever let it be heard before. Immediately everyone fell silent; the echo of his shout seemed to linger among the trees. "Leaf-eater," said Ender, "I will have no interpreter but Human."

"Who are you to tell me that I may not speak to the wives? I am a piggy, and you are nothing."

"Human," said Ender, "tell Shouter that if she lets Leaf-eater translate words that we humans have said among ourselves, then he is a spy. And if she lets him spy on us, we will go home now and you will have nothing from us. I'll take the hive queen to another world to restore her. Do you understand?"

Of course he understood. Ender also knew that Human was pleased. Leaf-eater was trying to usurp Human's role and discredit him—along with Ender. When Human finished translating Ender's words, Shouter sang at Leaf-eater. Abashed, he quickly retreated to the woods to watch with the other piggies.

But Human was by no means a puppet. He gave no sign that he was grateful. He looked Ender in the eye. "You said you wouldn't try to change us."

"I said I wouldn't try to change you more than is necessary."

"Why is this necessary? It's between us and the other piggies."

"Careful," said Ouanda. "He's very upset."

Before he could hope to persuade Shouter, he had to convince Human. "You are our first friends among the piggies. You have our trust and our love. We will never do anything to harm you, or to give any other piggies an advantage over you. But we didn't come just to you. We represent all of humankind, and we've come to teach all we can to all of the piggies. Regardless of tribe."

"You don't represent all humankind. You're about to fight a war with other humans. So how can you say that *our* wars are evil and your wars are good?"

Surely Pizarro, for all his shortcomings, had an easier time of it with Atahualpa. "We're trying *not* to fight a war with other humans," said Ender. "And if we fight one, it won't be *our* war, trying to gain advantage over them. It will be *your* war, trying to win you the right to travel among the stars." Ender held up his open hand. "We have set aside our humanness to become ramen with you." He closed his hand into a fist. "Human and piggy and hive queen, here on Lusitania, will be one. *All* humans. *All* buggers. *All* piggies."

Human sat in silence, digesting this.

"Speaker," he finally said. "This is very hard. Until you humans came, other piggies were—always to be killed, and their third life was to be slaves to us in forests that we kept. This forest was once a battlefield, and the most ancient trees are the warriors who died in battle. Our oldest fathers are the heroes of that war, and our houses are made of the cowards. All our lives we prepare to win battles with our enemies, so that our wives can make a mothertree in a new battle forest, and make us mighty and great. These last ten years we have learned to use arrows to kill from far off. Pots and cabra skins to carry water across the drylands. Amaranth and merdona root so we can be many and strong and carry food with us far from the macios of our home forest. We rejoiced in this because it meant that we would always be victorious in war. We would carry our wives, our little mothers, our heroes to every corner of the great world, and finally one day out into the stars. This is our dream, Speaker, and you tell me now that you want us to lose it like wind in the sky."

It was a powerful speech. None of the others offered Ender any suggestions about what to say in answer. Human had half-convinced them.

"Your dream is a good one," said Ender. "It's the dream of every living creature. The desire that is the very root of life itself: To grow until all the space you can see is part of you, under your control. It's the desire for greatness. There are two ways, though, to fulfil it. One way is to kill anything that is not yourself, to swallow it up or destroy it, until nothing is left to oppose you. But that way is evil. You say to all the universe, Only I will be great, and to make room for me the rest of you must give up even what you already have, and become nothing. Do you understand, Human, that if we humans felt this way, acted this way, we could kill every piggy in Lusitania and make this place our home. How much of your dream would be left, if we were evil?"

Human was trying hard to understand. "I see that you gave us great gifts, when you could have taken from us even the little that we had. But why did you give us the gifts, if we can't use them to become great?"

"We want you to grow, to travel among the stars. Here on

Lusitania we want you to be strong and powerful, with hundreds and thousands of brothers and wives. We want to teach you to grow many kinds of plants and raise many different animals. Ela and Novinha, these two women, will work all the days of their lives to develop more plants that can live here in Lusitania, and every good thing that they make, they'll give to you. So you can grow. But why does a single piggy in any other forest have to die, just so you can have these gifts? And why would it hurt you in any way, if we also gave the same gifts to *them?*"

"If they become just as strong as we are, then what have we gained?"

What am I expecting this brother to do, thought Ender. His people have always measured themselves against the other tribes. Their forest isn't fifty hectares or five hundred—it's either larger or smaller than the forest of the tribe to the west or the south. What I have to do now is the work of a generation: I have to teach him a new way of conceiving the stature of his own people. "Is Rooter great?" asked Ender.

"I say he is," said Human. "He's my father. His tree isn't the oldest or thickest, but no father that we remember has ever had so many children so quickly after he was planted."

"So in a way, all the children that he fathered are still part of him. The more children he fathers, the greater he becomes." Human nodded slowly. "And the more you accomplish in your life, the greater you make your father, is that true?"

"If his children do well, then yes, it's a great honor to the fathertree."

"Do you have to kill all the other great trees in order for your father to be great?"

"That's different," said Human. "All the other great trees are fathers of the tribe. And the lesser trees are still brothers." Yet Ender could see that Human was uncertain now. He was resisting Ender's ideas because they were strange, not because they were wrong or incomprehensible. He was beginning to understand.

"Look at the wives," said Ender. "They have no children. They can never be great the way that your father is great."

"Speaker, you know that they're the greatest of all. The whole tribe obeys them. When they rule us well, the tribe prospers; when the tribe becomes many, then the wives are also made strong—"

"Even though not a single one of you is their own child."

"How could we be?" asked Human.

"And yet you add to their greatness. Even though they aren't your mother or your father, they still grow when you grow."

"We're all the same tribe . . ."

"But *why* are you the same tribe? You have different fathers, different mothers."

"Because we *are* the tribe! We live here in the forest, we—"

"If another piggy came here from another tribe, and asked you to let him stay and be a brother—"

"We would never make him a fathertree!"

"But you tried to make Pipo and Libo fathertrees."

Human was breathing heavily. "I see," he said. "They were part of the tribe. From the sky, but we made them brothers and tried to make them fathers. The tribe is whatever we believe it is. If we say the tribe is all the Little Ones in the forest, and all the trees, then that is what the tribe is. Even though some of the oldest trees here came from warriors of two different tribes, fallen in battle. We become one tribe because we *say* we're one tribe."

Ender marveled at his mind, this small raman. How few humans were able to grasp this idea, or let it extend beyond the narrow confines of their tribe, their family, their nation.

Human walked behind Ender, leaned against him, the weight of the young piggy pressed against his back. Ender felt Human's breath on his cheek, and then their cheeks were pressed together, both of them looking in the same direction. All at once Ender understood: "You see what I see," said Ender.

"You humans grow by making us part of you, humans and piggies and buggers, ramen together. Then we are one tribe, and our greatness is your greatness, and yours is ours." Ender could feel Human's body trembling with the strength of the idea. "You say to us, we must see all other tribes the same way. As one tribe, our tribe all together, so that we grow by making them grow."

"You could send teachers," said Ender. "Brothers to the other tribes, who could pass into their third life in the other forests and have children there."

"This is a strange and difficult thing to ask of the wives," said Human. "Maybe an impossible thing. Their minds don't work the way a brother's mind works. A brother can think of many different things. But a wife thinks of only one thing: what is good for the tribe, and at the root of that, what is good for the children and the little mothers."

"Can you make them understand this?" asked Ender.

"Better than you could," said Human. "But probably not. Probably I'll fail."

"I don't think you'll fail," said Ender.

"You came here tonight to make a covenant between us, the piggies of this tribe, and you, the humans who live on this world. The humans outside Lusitania won't care about our covenant, and the piggies outside this forest won't care about it."

"We want to make the same covenant with all of them."

"And in this covenant, you humans promise to teach us everything."

"As quickly as you can understand it."

"Any question we ask."

"If we know the answer."

"When! If! These aren't words in a covenant! Give me straight answers now, Speaker for the Dead." Human stood up, pushed away from Ender, walked around in front of him, bent down a little to look at Ender from above. "Promise to teach us everything that you know!"

"We promise that."

"And you also promise to restore the hive queen to help us."

"I'll restore the hive queen. You'll have to make your own covenant with her. She doesn't obey human law."

"You promise to restore the hive queen, whether she helps us or not."

"Yes."

"You promise to obey our law when you come into our forest. And you agree that the prairie land that we need will also be under our law."

"Yes."

"And you will go to war against all the other humans in all the stars of the sky to protect us and let us also travel in the stars?"

"We already have."

Human relaxed, stepped back, squatted in his old position. He drew with his finger in the dirt. "Now, what you want from us," said

Human. "We will obey human law in your city, and also in the prairie land that you need."

"Yes," said Ender.

"And you don't want us to go to war," said Human.

"That's right."

"And that's all?"

"One more thing," said Ender.

"What you ask is already impossible," said Human. "You might as well ask more."

"The third life," said Ender. "When does it begin? When you kill a piggy and he grows into a tree, is that right?"

"The first life is within the mothertree, where we never see the light, and where we eat blindly the meat of our mother's body and the sap of the mothertree. The second life is when we live in the shade of the forest, the half-light, running and walking and climbing, seeing and singing and talking, making with our hands. The third life is when we reach and drink from the sun, in the full light at last, never moving except in the wind; only to think, and on those certain days when the brothers drum on your trunk, to speak to them. Yes, that's the third life."

"Humans don't have the third life."

Human looked at him, puzzled.

"When we die, even if you plant us, nothing grows. There's no tree. We never drink from the sun. When we die, we're dead."

Human looked at Ouanda. "But the other book you gave us. It talked all the time about living after death and being born again."

"Not as a tree," said Ender. "Not as anything you can touch or feel. Or talk to. Or get answers from."

"I don't believe you," said Human. "If that's true, why did Pipo and Libo make us plant them?"

Novinha knelt down beside Ender, touching him—no, leaning on him—so she could hear more clearly.

"How did they make you plant them?" said Ender.

"They made the great gift, won the great honor. The human and the piggy together. Pipo and Mandachuva. Libo and Leaf-eater. Mandachuva and Leaf-eater both thought that they would win the third life, but each time, Pipo and Libo would not. They insisted on keeping the gift for themselves. Why would they do that, if humans have no third life?"

Novinha's voice came then, husky and emotional. "What did they have to do, to give the third life to Mandachuva or Leaf-eater?"

"Plant them, of course," said Human. "The same as today."

"The same as *what* today?" asked Ender.

"You and me," said Human. "Human and the Speaker for the Dead. If we make this covenant so that the wives and the humans agree together, then this is a great, a noble day. So either you will give me the third life, or I will give it to you."

"With my own hand?"

"Of course," said Human. "If you won't give me the honor, then I must give it to you."

Ender remembered the picture he had first seen only two weeks ago, of Pipo dismembered and disemboweled, his body parts stretched and spread. Planted. "Human," said Ender, "the worst crime that a human being can commit is murder. And one of the worst ways to do it is to take a living person and cut him and hurt him so badly that he dies."

Again Human squatted for a while, trying to make sense of this. "Speaker," he said at last, "my mind keeps seeing this two ways. If humans don't have a third life, then planting is killing, forever. In our eyes, Libo and Pipo were keeping the honor to themselves, and leaving Mandachuva and Leaf-eater as you see them, to die without honor for their accomplishments. In our eyes, you humans came out of the fence to the hillside and tore them from the ground before their roots could grow. In our eyes, it was you who committed murder, when you carried Pipo and Libo away. But now I see it another way. Pipo and Libo wouldn't take Mandachuva and Leaf-eater into the third life, because to them it would be murder. So they willingly allowed their own death, just so they wouldn't have to kill any of us."

"Yes," said Novinha.

"But if that's so, then when you humans saw them on the hillside, why didn't you come into the forest and kill us all? Why didn't you make a great fire and consume all our fathers, and the great mothertree herself?"

Leaf-eater cried out from the edge of the forest, a terrible keening cry, an unbearable grief.

"If you had cut one of our trees," said Human. "If you had murdered a single tree, we would have come upon you in the night and killed you, every one of you. And even if some of you survived, our messengers would have told the story to every other tribe, and none of you would ever have left this land alive. Why didn't you kill *us,* for murdering Pipo and Libo?"

Mandachuva suddenly appeared behind Human, panting heavily. He flung himself to the ground, his hands outstretched toward Ender. "I cut him with these hands," he cried. "I tried to honor him, and I killed his tree forever!"

"No," said Ender. He took Mandachuva's hands, held them. "You both thought you were saving each other's life. He hurt you, and you—hurt him, yes, killed him, but you both believed you were doing good. That's enough, until now. Now you know the truth, and so do we. We know that you didn't mean murder. And you know that when you take a knife to a human being, we die forever. That's the last term in the covenant, Human. Never take another human being to the third life, because we don't know how to go."

"When I tell this story to the wives," said Human, "you'll hear grief so terrible that it will sound like the breaking of trees in a thunderstorm."

He turned and stood before Shouter, and spoke to her for a few moments. Then he returned to Ender. "Go now," he said.

"We have no covenant yet," said Ender.

"I have to speak to all the wives. They'll never do that while you're here, in the shade of the mothertree, with no one to protect the little ones. Arrow will lead you back out of the forest. Wait for me on the hillside, where Rooter keeps watch over the gate. Sleep if you can. I'll present the covenant to the wives and try to make them understand that we must deal as kindly with the other tribes as you have dealt with us."

Impulsively, Human reached out a hand and touched Ender firmly on the belly. "I make my own covenant," he said to Ender. "I will honor you forever, but I will never kill you."

Ender put out his hand and laid his palm against Human's warm abdomen. The protuberances under his hand were hot to the touch. "I will also honor you forever," said Ender.

"And if we make this covenant between your tribe and ours," said Human, "will you give me the honor of the third life? Will you let me rise up and drink the light?"

"Can we do it quickly? Not the slow and terrible way that—"

"And make me one of the silent trees? Never fathering? Without honor, except to feed my sap to the filthy macios and give my wood to the brothers when they sing to me?"

"Isn't there someone else who can do it?" asked Ender. "One of the brothers, who knows your way of life and death?"

"You don't understand," said Human. "This is how the whole tribe knows that the truth has been spoken. Either you must take me into the third life, or I must take you, or there's no covenant. I won't kill *you*, Speaker, and we both want a treaty."

"I'll do it," said Ender.

Human nodded, withdrew his hand, and returned to Shouter.

"Ó Deus," whispered Ouanda. "How will you have the heart?"

Ender had no answer. He merely followed silently behind Arrow as he led them to the woods. Novinha gave him her own nightstick to lead the way; Arrow played with it like a child, making the light small and large, making it hover and swoop like a suckfly among the trees and bushes. He was as happy and playful as Ender had ever seen a piggy be.

But behind them, they could hear the voices of the wives, singing a terrible and cacophonous song. Human had told them the truth about Pipo and Libo, that they died the final death, and in pain, all so that they would not have to do to Mandachuva and Leaf-eater what they thought was murder. Only when they had gone far enough that the sound of the wives' keening was softer than their own footfalls and the wind in the trees did any of the humans speak.

"That was the mass for my father's soul," said Ouanda softly.

"And for mine," answered Novinha; they all knew that she spoke of Pipo, not the long-dead Venerado, Gusto.

But Ender was not part of their conversation; he had not known Libo and Pipo, and did not belong to their memory of grief. All he could think of was the trees of the forest. They had once been living, breathing piggies, every one of them. The piggies could sing to them, talk to them, even, somehow, understand their speech. But Ender couldn't. To Ender the trees were not *people*, could never be people. If he took the knife to Human, it might not be murder in the piggies' eyes, but to Ender himself he would be taking away the only part of Human's life that Ender understood. As a piggy, Human was a true raman, a brother. As a tree he would be little more than a gravestone, as far as Ender could understand, as far as he could really believe.

Once again, he thought, I must kill, though I promised that I never would again.

He felt Novinha's hand take him by the crook of the arm. She leaned on him. "Help me," she said. "I'm almost blind in the darkness."

"I have good night vision," Olhado offered cheerfully from behind her.

"Shut up, stupid," Ela whispered fiercely. "Mother wants to walk with him."

Both Novinha and Ender heard her clearly, and both could feel each other's silent laughter. Novinha drew closer to him as they walked. "I think you have the heart for what you have to do," she said softly, so that only he could hear.

"Cold and ruthless?" he asked. His voice hinted at wry humor, but the words tasted sour and truthful in his mouth.

"Compassionate enough," she said, "to put the hot iron into the wound when that's the only way to heal it."

As one who had felt his burning iron cauterize her deepest wounds, she had the right to speak; and he believed her, and it eased his heart for the bloody work ahead.

Ender hadn't thought it would be possible to sleep, knowing what was ahead of him. But now he woke up, Novinha's voice soft in his ear. He realized that he was outside, lying in the capim, his head resting on Novinha's lap. It was still dark.

"They're coming," said Novinha softly.

Ender sat up. Once, as a child, he would have come awake fully, instantly; but he was trained as a soldier then. Now it took a moment to orient himself. Ouanda, Ela, both awake and watching; Olhado asleep; Quim just stirring. The tall tree of Rooter's third life rising only a few meters away. And in the near distance, beyond the fence at the bottom of the little valley, the first houses of Milagre rising up the slopes; the Cathedral and the monastery atop the highest and nearest of the hills.

In the other direction, the forest, and coming down from the trees, Human, Mandachuva, Leaf-eater, Arrow, Cups, Calendar, Worm, Bark-dancer, several other brothers whose names Ouanda didn't know. "I've never seen them," she said. "They must come from other brother-houses."

Do we have a covenant? said Ender silently. That's all I care about. Did Human make the wives understand a new way of conceiving of the world?

Human was carrying something. Wrapped in leaves. The piggies wordlessly laid it before Ender; Human unwrapped it carefully. It was a computer printout.

"The Hive Queen and the Hegemon," said Ouanda softly. "The copy Miro gave them."

"The covenant," said Human.

Only then did they realize that the printout was upside down, on the blank side of the paper. And there, in the light of a nightstick, they saw faint hand-printed letters. They were large and awkwardly formed. Ouanda was in awe. "We never taught them to make ink," she said. "We never taught them to write."

"Calendar learned to make the letters," said Human. "Writing with sticks in the dirt. And Worm made the ink from cabra dung and dried macios. This is how you make treaties, isn't it?"

"Yes," said Ender.

"If we didn't write it on paper, then we would remember it differently."

"That's right," said Ender. "You did well to write it down."

"We made some changes. The wives wanted some changes, and I thought you would accept them." Human pointed them out. "You humans can make this covenant with other piggies, but you can't make a *different* covenant. You can't teach any other piggies things you haven't taught us. Can you accept that?"

"Of course," said Ender.

"That was the easy one. Now, what if we disagree about what the rules are? What if we disagree about where your prairie land ends and ours begins? So Shouter said, Let the hive queen judge between humans and Little Ones. Let the humans judge between the Little Ones and the hive queen. And let Little Ones judge between the hive queen and the humans."

Ender wondered how easy that would be. He remembered, as no other living human did, how terrifying the buggers were three thousand years ago. Their insectlike bodies were the nightmares of humanity's childhood. How easily would the people of Milagre accept their judgment?

So it's hard. It's no harder than what we've asked the piggies to do. "Yes," said Ender. "We can accept that, too. It's a good plan."

"And another change," said Human. He looked up at Ender and grinned. It looked ghastly, since piggy faces weren't designed for that human expression. "This is why it took so long. All these changes."

Ender smiled back.

"If a tribe of piggies won't sign the covenant with humans, and if that tribe attacks one of the tribes that *has* signed the covenant, *then* we can go to war against them."

"What do you mean by attack?" asked Ender. If they could take a mere insult as an attack, then this clause would reduce the prohibition of war to nothing.

"Attack," said Human. "It begins when they come into our lands and kill the brothers or the wives. It is not attack when they present themselves for war, or offer an agreement to begin a war. It *is* attack when they start to fight without an agreement. Since we will never agree to a war, an attack by another tribe is the only way war could begin. I knew you'd ask."

He pointed to the words of the covenant, and indeed the treaty carefully defined what constituted an attack.

"That is also acceptable," said Ender. It meant that the possibility of war would not be removed for many generations, perhaps for centuries, since it would take a long time to bring this covenant to every tribe of piggies in the world. But long before the last tribe joined the covenant, Ender thought, the benefits of peaceful exogamy would be made plain, and few would want to be warriors anymore.

"Now the last change," said Human. "The wives meant this to punish you for making this covenant so difficult. But I think you will believe it is no punishment. Since we are forbidden to take you into the third life, after this covenant is in effect humans are also forbidden to take brothers into the third life."

For a moment Ender thought it meant his reprieve; he would not have to do the thing that Libo and Pipo had both refused.

"*After* the covenant," said Human. "You will be the first and last human to give this gift."

"I wish . . ." said Ender.

"I know what you wish, my friend Speaker," said Human. "To you it feels like murder. But to me—when a brother is given the right to pass into the third life as a father, then he chooses his greatest rival or his truest friend to give him the passage. You. Speaker—ever since I first learned Stark and read the Hive Queen and the Hegemon, I waited for you. I said many times to my father, Rooter, of all humans he is the one who will understand us. Then Rooter told me when your starship came, that it was you and the hive queen aboard that ship, and I knew then that you had come to give me passage, if only I did well."

"You did well, Human," said Ender.

"Here," he said. "See? We signed the covenant in the human way."

At the bottom of the last page of the covenant two words were crudely, laboriously shaped. "Human," Ender read aloud. The other word he could not read.

"It's Shouter's true name," said Human. "Star-looker. She wasn't good with the writing stick—the wives don't use tools very often, since the brothers do that kind of work. So she wanted me to tell you what her name is. And to tell you that she got it because she was always looking in the sky. She says that she didn't know it then, but she was watching for you to come."

So many people had so much hope in me, thought Ender. In the end, though, everything depended on them. On Novinha, Miro, Ela, who called for me; on Human and Star-looker. And on the ones who feared my coming, too.

Worm carried the cup of ink; Calendar carried the pen. It was a thin strip of wood with a slit in it and a narrow well that held a little ink when he dipped it in the cup. He had to dip it five times in order to sign his name. "Five," said Arrow. Ender remembered then that the number five was portentous to the piggies. It had been an accident, but if they chose to see it as a good omen, so much the better.

"I'll take the covenant to our Governor and the Bishop," said Ender.

"Of all the documents that were ever treasured in the history of mankind . . ." said Ouanda. No one needed her to finish the sentence. Human, Leaf-eater, and Mandachuva carefully wrapped the book again in leaves and handed it, not to Ender, but to Ouanda. Ender knew at once, with terrible certainty, what that meant. The piggies still had work for him to do, work that would require that his hands be free.

"Now the covenant is made the human way," said Human. "You must make it true for the Little Ones as well."

"Can't the signing be enough?" asked Ender.

"From now on the signing is enough," said Human. "But only because the same hand that signed for the humans also took the covenant in our way, too."

"Then I will," said Ender, "as I promised you I would."

Human reached out and stroked Ender from the throat to the belly. "The brother's word is not just in his mouth," he said. "The brother's word is in his life." He turned to the other piggies. "Let me speak to my father one last time before I stand beside him."

Two of the strange brothers came forward with their small clubs in their hands. They walked with Human to Rooter's tree and began to beat on it and sing in the Fathers' Language. Almost at once the trunk split open. The tree was still fairly young, and not so very much thicker in the trunk than Human's own body; it was a struggle for him to get inside. But he fit, and the trunk closed up after him. The drumming changed rhythm, but did not let up for a moment.

Jane whispered in Ender's ear. "I can hear the resonance of the drumming change inside the tree," she said. "The tree is slowly shaping the sound, to turn the drumming into language."

The other piggies set to work clearing ground for Human's tree. Ender noticed that he would be planted so that, from the gate, Rooter would seem to stand on the left hand, and Human on the right. Pulling up the capim by the root was hard work for the piggies; soon Quim was helping them, and then Olhado, and then Ouanda and Ela.

Ouanda gave the covenant to Novinha to hold while she helped dig capim. Novinha, in turn, carried it to Ender, stood before him, looked at him steadily. "You signed it Ender Wiggin," she said. "Ender."

The name sounded ugly even to his own ears. He had heard it too often as an epithet. "I'm older than I look," said Ender. "That was the name I was known by when I blasted the buggers' home world out of existence. Maybe the presence of that name on the first treaty ever signed between humans and ramen will do something to change the meaning of the name."

"Ender," she whispered. She reached toward him, the bundled treaty in her hands, and held it against his chest; it was heavy, since it contained all the pages of the Hive Queen and the Hegemon, on the other sides of pages where the covenant was written. "I never went to the priests to confess," she said, "because I knew they would despise me for my sin. Yet when you named all my sins today, I could bear it because I knew you didn't despise me. I couldn't understand *why*, though, till now."

"I'm not one to despise other people for their sins," said Ender. "I haven't found one yet, that I didn't say inside myself, I've done worse than this."

"All these years you've borne the burden of humanity's guilt."

"Yes, well, it's nothing mystical," said Ender. "I think of it as being like the mark of Cain. You don't make many friends, but nobody hurts you much, either."

The ground was clear. Mandachuva spoke in Tree Language to the piggies beating on the trunk; their rhythm changed, and again the aperture in the tree came open. Human slid out as if he were an infant being born. Then he walked to the center of the cleared ground. Leaf-eater and Mandachuva each handed him a knife. As he took the knives, Human spoke to them—in Portuguese, so the humans could understand, and so it would carry great force. "I told Shouter that you lost your passage to the third life because of a great misunderstanding by Pipo and Libo. She said that before another hand of hands of days, you both would grow upward into the light."

Leaf-eater and Mandachuva both let go of their knives, touched Human gently on the belly, and stepped back to the edge of the cleared ground.

Human held out the knives to Ender. They were both made of thin wood. Ender could not imagine a tool that could polish wood to be at once so fine and sharp, and yet so strong. But of course no tool had polished these. They had come thus perfectly shaped from the heart of a living tree, given as a gift to help a brother into the third life.

It was one thing to know with his mind that Human would not really die. It was another thing to believe it. Ender did not take the knives at first. Instead he reached past the blades and took Human by the wrists. "To you it doesn't feel like death. But to me—I only saw you for the first time yesterday, and tonight I know you are my brother as surely as if Rooter were my father, too. And yet when the sun rises in the morning, I'll never be able to talk to you again. It feels like death to me, Human, how ever it feels to you."

"Come and sit in my shade," said Human, "and see the sunlight through my leaves, and rest your back against my trunk. And do this, also. Add another story to the Hive Queen and the Hegemon. Call it the Life of Human. Tell all the humans how I was conceived on the bark of my father's tree, and born in darkness, eating my mother's flesh. Tell them how I left the life of darkness behind and came into the half-light of my second life, to learn language from the wives and then come forth to learn all the miracles that Libo and Miro and Ouanda came to teach. Tell them how on the last day of my second life, my true brother came from above the sky, and together we made this covenant so that humans and piggies would be one tribe, not a human tribe or a piggy tribe, but a tribe of ramen. And then my friend gave me passage to the third life, to the full light, so that I could rise into the sky and give life to ten thousand children before I die."

"I'll tell your story," said Ender.

"Then I will truly live forever."

Ender took the knives. Human lay down upon the ground.

"Olhado," said Novinha. "Quim. Go back to the gate. Ela, you too."

"I'm going to see this, Mother," said Ela. "I'm a scientist."

"You forget my eyes," said Olhado. "I'm recording everything. We can show humans everywhere that the treaty was signed. And we can show piggies that the Speaker took the covenant in their way, too."

"I'm not going, either," said Quim. "Even the Blessed Virgin stood at the foot of the cross."

"You can stay," said Novinha softly. And she also stayed.

Human's mouth was filled with capim, but he didn't chew it very much. "More," said Ender, "so you don't feel anything."

"That's not right," said Mandachuva. "These are the last moments of his second life. It's good to feel something of the pains of this body, to remember when you're in the third life, and beyond pain."

Mandachuva and Leaf-eater told Ender where and how to cut. It had to be done quickly, they told him, and their hands reached into the steaming body to point out organs that must go here or there. Ender's hands were quick and sure, his body calm, but even though he could only rarely spare a glance away from the surgery, he knew that above his bloody work, Human's eyes were watching him, watching him, filled with gratitude and love, filled with agony and death.

It happened under his hands, so quickly that for the first few minutes they could watch it grow. Several large organs shriveled as roots shot out of them; tendrils reached from place to place within the body; Human's eyes went wide with the final agony; and out of his spine a sprout burst upward, two leaves, four leaves—

And then stopped. The body was dead; its last spasm of strength had gone to making the tree that rooted in Human's spine. Ender had seen the rootlets and tendrils reaching through the body. The memories, the soul of Human had been transferred into the cells of the newly sprouted tree. It was done. His third life had begun. And when the sun rose in the morning, not long from now, the leaves would taste the light for the first time.

The other piggies were rejoicing, dancing. Leaf-eater and Mandachuva took the knives from Ender's hands and jammed them into the ground on either side of Human's head. Ender could not join their celebration. He was covered with blood and reeked with the stench of the body he had butchered. On all fours he crawled from the body, up the hill to a place where he didn't have to see it. Novinha followed him. Exhausted, spent, all of them, from the work and the emotions of the day. They said nothing, did nothing, but fell into the thick capim, each one leaning or lying on someone else, seeking relief at last in sleep, as the piggies danced away up the hill into the woods.

Bosquinha and Bishop Peregrino made their way to the gate before the sun was up, to watch for the Speaker's return from the forest. They were there a full ten minutes before they saw a movement much nearer than the forest's edge. It was a boy, sleepily voiding his bladder into a bush.

"Olhado!" called the Mayor.

The boy turned, waved, then hastily fastened his trousers and began waking others who slept in the tall grass. Bosquinha and the Bishop opened the gate and walked out to meet them.

"Foolish, isn't it," said Bosquinha, "but this is the moment when our rebellion seems most real. When I first walk beyond the fence."

"Why did they spend the night out of doors?" Peregrino wondered aloud. "The gate was open, they could have gone home."

Bosquinha took a quick census of the group outside the gates. Ouanda and Ela, arm in arm like sisters. Olhado and Quim. Novinha. And there, yes, the Speaker, sitting down, Novinha behind him, resting her hands on his shoulders. They all waited expectantly, saying nothing. Until Ender looked up at them. "We have the treaty," he said. "It's a good one."

Novinha held up a bundle wrapped in leaves. "They wrote it down," she said. "For you to sign."

Bosquinha took the bundle. "All the files were restored before midnight," she said. "Not just the ones we saved in your message queue. Whoever your friend is, Speaker, he's very good."

"She," said the Speaker. "Her name is Jane."

Now, though, the Bishop and Bosquinha could see what lay on the cleared earth just down the hill from where the Speaker had slept. Now they understood the dark stains on the Speaker's hands and arms, the spatter marks on his face.

"I would rather have no treaty," said Bosquinha, "than one you had to kill to get."

"Wait before you judge," said the Bishop. "I think the night's work was more than just what we see before us."

"Very wise, Father Peregrino," said the Speaker softly.

"I'll explain it to you if you want," said Ouanda. "Ela and I understand it as well as anyone."

"It was like a sacrament," said Olhado.

Bosquinha looked at Novinha, uncomprehending. "You let him watch?"

Olhado tapped his eyes. "All the piggies will see it, someday, through my eyes."

"It wasn't death," said Quim. "It was resurrection."

The Bishop stepped near the tortured corpse and touched the seedling tree growing from the chest cavity. "His name is Human," said the Speaker.

"And so is yours," said the Bishop softly. He turned and looked around at the members of his little flock, who had already taken humanity a step further than it had ever gone before. Am I the shepherd, Peregrino asked himself, or the most confused and helpless of the sheep? "Come, all of you. Come with me to the Cathedral. The bells will soon ring for mass."

The children gathered and prepared to go. Novinha, too, stepped away from her place behind the Speaker. Then she stopped, turned back to him, looked at him with silent invitation in her eyes.

"Soon," he said. "A moment more."

She, too, followed the Bishop through the gate and up the hill into the Cathedral.

The mass had barely begun when Peregrino saw the Speaker enter at the back of the Cathedral. He paused a moment, then found Novinha and her family with his eyes. In only a few steps he had taken a place beside her. Where Marcão had sat, those rare times when the whole family came together.

The duties of the service took his attention; a few moments later, when Peregrino could look again, he saw that Grego was now sitting beside the Speaker. Peregrino thought of the terms of the treaty as the girls had explained it to him. Of the meaning of the death of the piggy called Human, and before him, of the deaths of Pipo and Libo. All things coming clear, all things coming together. The young man, Miro, lying paralyzed in bed, with his sister Ouanda tending him. Novinha, the lost one, now found. The fence, its shadow so dark in the minds of all who had lived within its bounds, now still and harmless, invisible, insubstantial.

It was the miracle of the wafer, turned into the flesh of God in his hands. How suddenly we find the flesh of God within us after all, when we thought that we were only made of dust.

Chapter **18**

The Hive Queen

Evolution gave his mother no birth canal and no breasts. So the small creature who would one day be named Human was given no exit from the womb except by the teeth of his mouth. He and his infant siblings devoured their mother's body. Because Human was strongest and most vigorous, he ate the most and so became even stronger.

Human lived in utter darkness. When his mother was gone, there was nothing to eat but the sweet liquid that flowed on the surface of his world. He did not know yet that the vertical surface was the inside of a great hollow tree, and that the liquid that he ate was the sap of the tree. Nor did he know that the warm creatures that were far larger than himself were older piggies, almost ready to leave the darkness of the tree, and that the smaller creatures were younger ones, more recently emerged than himself.

All he really cared about was to eat, to move, and to see the light. For now and then, in rhythms that he could not comprehend, a sudden light came into the darkness. It began each time with a sound, whose source he could not comprehend. Then the tree would shudder slightly; the sap would cease to flow; and all the tree's energy would be devoted to changing the shape of the trunk in one place, to make an opening that let the light inside. When the light was there, Human moved toward it. When the light was gone, Human lost his sense of direction, and wandered aimlessly in search of liquid to drink.

Until one day, when almost all the other creatures were smaller than himself, and none at all were larger, the light came and he was so strong and swift that he reached the opening before it closed. He bent his body around the curve of the wood of the tree, and for the first time felt the rasp of outer bark under his soft belly. He hardly noticed this new pain, because the light dazzled him. It was not just in one place, but everywhere, and it was not grey but vivid green and yellow. His rapture lasted many seconds. Then he was hungry again, and here on the outside of the mothertree the sap flowed only in the fissures of the bark, where it was hard to reach, and instead of all the other creatures being little ones that he could push aside, they all were larger than himself, and drove him away from the easy feeding places. This was a new thing, a new world, a new life, and he was afraid.

Later, when he learned language, he would remember the journey from darkness into light, and he would call it the passage from the first life to the second, from the life of darkness to the half-lit life.

—Speaker for the Dead, *The Life of Human,* 1:1–5

Miro decided to leave Lusitania. Take the Speaker's starship and go to Trondheim after all. Perhaps at his trial he could persuade the Hundred Worlds not to go to war against Lusitania. At worst, he could become a martyr, to stir people's hearts, to be remembered, to stand for something. Whatever happened to him, it would be better than staying here.

In the first few days after he climbed the fence, Miro recovered rapidly. He gained some control and feeling in his arms and legs. Enough to take shuffling steps, like an old man. Enough to move his arms and hands. Enough to end the humiliation of his mother having to clean his body. But then his progress slowed and stopped. "Here it is," said Navio. "We have reached the level of permanent damage. You are so lucky, Miro, you can walk, you can talk, you are a whole man. You are no more limited than, say, a very healthy man who is a hundred years old. I would rather tell you that your body would be as it was before you climbed the fence, that you would have all the vigor and control of a twenty-year-old. But I'm very glad that I *don't* have to tell you that you will be bedridden all your life, diapered and catheterized, able to do nothing more than listen to soft music and wonder where your body went."

So I'm grateful, Miro thought. As my fingers curl into a useless club on the ends of my arms, as I hear my own speech sounding thick and unintelligible, my voice unable to modulate properly, then I will be so glad that I am like a hundred-year-old man, that I can look forward to eighty more years of life as a centegenarian.

Once it was clear that he did not need constant attention, the family scattered and went about their business. These days were too exciting for them to stay home with a crippled brother, son, friend. He understood completely. He did not want them to stay home with him. He wanted to be with them. His work was unfinished. Now, at long last, all the fences, all the rules were gone. Now he could ask the piggies the questions that had so long puzzled him.

He tried at first to work through Ouanda. She came to him every morning and evening and made her reports on the terminal in the front room of the Ribeira house. He read her reports, asked her questions, listened to her stories. And she very seriously memorized the questions he wanted her to ask the piggies. After a few days of this, however, he noticed that in the evening she would indeed have the answers to Miro's questions. But there was no follow-up, no exploration of meaning. Her real attention was devoted to her own work. And Miro stopped giving her questions to ask for him. He lied and told her that he was far more interested in what she was doing, that her avenues of exploration were the most important.

The truth was that he hated seeing Ouanda. For him, the revelation that she was his sister was painful, terrible, but he knew that if the decision were his alone, he would cast aside the incest tabu, marry her and live in the forest with the piggies if need be. Ouanda, however, was a believer, a belonger. She couldn't possibly violate the only universal human law. She grieved when she learned that Miro was her brother, but she immediately began to separate herself from him, to forget the touches, the kisses, the whispers, the promises, the teasing, the laughter . . .

Better if he forgot them, too. But he could not. Every time he saw her, it hurt him to see how reserved she was, how *polite* and *kind* she was. He was her brother, he was crippled, she would be good to him. But the love was gone.

Uncharitably, he compared Ouanda to his own mother, who had loved her lover regardless of the barriers between them. But

Mother's lover had been a whole man, an able man, not this useless carcass.

So Miro stayed home and studied the file reports of everybody else's work. It was torture to know what they were doing, that he could not take part in it; but it was better than doing nothing, or watching the tedious vids on the terminal, or listening to music. He could type, slowly, by aiming his hand so the stiffest of his fingers, the index finger, touched exactly one key. It wasn't fast enough to enter any meaningful data, or even to write memos, but he could call up other people's public files and read what they were doing. He could maintain some connection with the vital work that had suddenly blossomed on Lusitania, with the opening of the gate.

Ouanda was working with the piggies on a lexicon of the Males' and Wives' Languages, complete with a phonological spelling system so they could write their language down. Quim was helping her, but Miro knew that he had his own purpose: He intended to be a missionary to the piggies in other tribes, taking them the Gospels before they ever saw the Hive Queen and the Hegemon; he intended to translate at least some of the scripture and speak to the piggies in their own language. All this work with piggy language and culture was very good, very important, preserve the past, prepare to communicate with other tribes, but Miro knew that it could easily be done by Dom Cristão's scholars, who now ventured forth in their monkish robes and quietly asked questions of the piggies and answered their questions ably and powerfully. Ouanda was allowing herself to become redundant, Miro believed.

The real work with the piggies, as Miro saw it, was being done by Ender and a few key technicians from Bosquinha's services department. They were laying pipe from the river to the mothertree's clearing, to bring water to them. They were setting up electricity and teaching the brothers how to use a computer terminal. In the meantime, they were teaching them very primitive means of agriculture and trying to domesticate cabras to pull plows. It was confusing, the different levels of technology that were coming to the piggies all at once, but Ender had discussed it with Miro, explaining that he wanted the piggies to see quick, dramatic, immediate results from their treaty. Running water, a computer connection with a holographic terminal that let them read anything in the library, electric lights at night. But all this was still magic, completely dependent on human society. At the same time, Ender was trying to keep them self-sufficient, inventive, resourceful. The dazzle of electricity would make myths that would spread through the world from tribe to tribe, but it would be no more than rumor for many, many years. It was the wooden plow, the scythe, the harrow, the amaranth seed that would make the real changes, that would allow piggy population to increase tenfold wherever they went. And those could be transmitted from place to place with a handful of seeds in a cabra-skin pouch and the memory of how the work was done.

This was the work that Miro longed to be part of. But what good were his clubbed hands and shuffling step in the amaranth fields? Of what use was he sitting at a loom, weaving cabra wool? He couldn't even talk well enough to teach.

Ela was working on developing new strains of Earthborn plants and even small animals and insects, new species that could resist the Descolada, even neutralize it. Mother was helping her with advice, but little more, for she was working on the most vital and secret project of them all. Again, it was Ender who came to Miro and told him what only his family and Ouanda knew: that the hive queen lived, that she was being restored as soon as Novinha found a way for her to resist the Descolada, her and all the buggers that would be born to her. As soon as it was ready, the hive queen would be revived.

And Miro would not be part of that, either. For the first time, humans and two alien races, living together as ramen on the same world, and Miro wasn't part of any of it. He was less human than the piggies were. He couldn't speak or use his hands half so well. He had stopped being a tool-using, language-speaking animal. He was varelse now. They only kept him as a pet.

He wanted to go away. Better yet, he wanted to disappear, to go away even from himself.

But not right now. There was a new puzzle that only he knew about, and so only he could solve. His terminal was behaving very strangely.

He noticed it the first week after he recovered from total paralysis. He was scanning some of Ouanda's files and realized that without doing anything special, he had accessed confidential files. They were protected with several layers, he had no idea what the passwords were, and yet a simple, routine scan had brought the information forward. It was her speculations on piggy evolution and their probable pre-Descolada society and life patterns. The sort of thing that as recently as two weeks ago she would have talked about, argued about with Miro. Now she kept it confidential and never discussed it with him at all.

Miro didn't tell her he had seen the files, but he did steer conversations toward the subject and drew her out; she talked about her ideas willingly enough, once Miro showed his interest. Sometimes it was almost like old times. Except that he would hear the sound of his own slurred voice and keep most of his opinions to himself, merely listening to her, letting things he would have argued with pass right by. Still, seeing her confidential files allowed him to penetrate to what she was really interested in.

But how had he seen them?

It happened again and again. Files of Ela's, Mother's, Dom Cristão's. As the piggies began to play with their new terminal, Miro was able to watch them in an echo mode that he had never seen the terminal use before—it enabled him to watch all their computer transactions and then make some suggestions, change things a little. He took particular delight in guessing what the piggies were really trying to do and helping them, surreptitiously, to do it. But how had he got such unorthodox, powerful access to the machine?

The terminal was learning to accommodate itself to him, too. Instead of long code sequences, he only had to begin a sequence and the machine would obey his instructions. Finally he did not even have to log on. He touched the keyboard and the terminal displayed a list of all the activities he usually engaged in, then scanned through them. He could touch a key and it would go directly to the activity he wanted, skipping dozens of preliminaries, saving him many painful minutes of typing one character at a time.

At first he thought that Olhado had created the new program for him, or perhaps someone in the Mayor's office. But Olhado only looked blankly at what the terminal was doing and said, "Bacâna," that's great. And when he sent a message to the Mayor, she never got it. Instead, the Speaker for the Dead came to visit him.

"So your terminal is being helpful," said Ender.

Miro didn't answer. He was too busy trying to think why the Mayor had sent the Speaker to answer his note.

"The Mayor didn't get your message," said Ender. "I did. And it's better if you don't mention to anybody else what your terminal is doing."

"Why?" asked Miro. That was one word he could say without slurring too much.

"Because it isn't a new program helping you. It's a person."

Miro laughed. No human being could be as quick as the program that was helping him. It was faster, in fact, than most programs he had worked with before, and very resourceful and intuitive; faster than a human, but smarter than a program.

"It's an old friend of mine, I think. At least, she was the one who told me about your message and suggested that I let you know that discretion was a good idea. You see, she's a bit shy. She doesn't make many friends."

"How many?"

"At the present moment, exactly two. For a few thousand years before now, exactly one."

"Not human," said Miro.

"Raman," said Ender. "More human than most humans. We've loved each other for a long time, helped each other, depended on each other. But in the last few weeks, since I got here, we've drifted apart. I'm—involved more in the lives of people around me. Your family."

"Mother."

"Yes. Your mother, your brothers and sisters, the work with the piggies, the work for the hive queen. My friend and I used to talk to each other constantly. I don't have time now. We've hurt each other's feelings sometimes. She's lonely, and so I think she's chosen another companion."

"Não quero." Don't want one.

"Yes you do," said Ender. "She's already helped you. Now that you know she exists, you'll find that she's—a good friend. You can't have a better one. More loyal. More helpful."

"Puppy dog?"

"Don't be a jackass," said Ender. "I'm introducing you to a fourth alien species. You're supposed to be a xenologer, aren't you? She knows you, Miro. Your physical problems are nothing to her. She has no body at all. She exists among the philotic disturbances in the ansible communications of the Hundred Worlds. She's the most intelligent creature alive, and you're the second human being she's ever chosen to reveal herself to."

"How?" How did she come to be? How did she know me, to choose me?

"Ask her yourself." Ender touched the jewel in his ear. "Just a word of advice. Once she comes to trust you, keep her with you always. Keep no secrets from her. She once had a lover who switched her off. Only for an hour, but things were never the same between them after that. They became—just friends. Good friends, loyal friends, always until he dies. But all his life he will regret that one thoughtless act of disloyalty."

Ender's eyes glistened, and Miro realized that whatever this creature was that lived in the computer, it was no phantom, it was part of this man's life. And he was passing it down to Miro, like father to son, the right to know this friend.

Ender left without another word, and Miro turned to the terminal. There was a holo of a woman there. She was small, sitting on a stool, leaning against a holographic wall. She was not beautiful. Not ugly, either. Her face had character. Her eyes were haunting, innocent, sad. Her mouth delicate, about to smile, about to weep. Her clothing seemed veil-like, insubstantial, and yet instead of being provocative, it revealed a sort of innocence, a girlish, small-breasted body, the hands clasped lightly in her lap, her legs childishly parted with the toes pointing inward. She could have been sitting on a teeter-totter in a playground. Or on the edge of her lover's bed.

"Bom dia," Miro said softly.

"Hi," she said. "I asked him to introduce us."

She was quiet, reserved, but it was Miro who felt shy. For so long, Ouanda had been the only woman in his life, besides the women of his family, and he had little confidence in the social graces. At the same time, he was aware that he was speaking to a hologram. A completely convincing one, but a midair laser projection all the same.

She reached up one hand and laid it gently on her breast. "Feels nothing," she said. "No nerves."

Tears came to his eyes. Self-pity, of course. That he would probably never have a woman more substantial than this one. If he tried to touch one, his caresses would be crude pawing. Sometimes, when he wasn't careful, he drooled and couldn't even feel it. What a lover.

"But I have eyes," she said. "And ears. I see everything in all the Hundred Worlds. I watch the sky through a thousand telescopes. I overhear a trillion conversations every day." She giggled a little. "I'm the best gossip in the universe."

Then, suddenly, she stood up, grew larger, closer, so that she only showed from the waist up, as if she had moved closer to an invisible camera. Her eyes burned with intensity as she stared right at him. "And you're a parochial schoolboy who's never seen anything but one town and one forest in his life."

"Don't get much chance to travel," he said.

"We'll see about that," she answered. "So. What do you want to do today?"

"What's your name?" he asked.

"You don't need my name," she said.

"How do I call you?"

"I'm here whenever you want me."

"But I want to know," he said.

She touched her ear. "When you like me well enough to take me with you wherever you go, then I'll tell you my name."

Impulsively, he told her what he had told no one else. "I want to leave this place," said Miro. "Can you take me away from Lusitania?"

She at once became coquettish, mocking. "And we only just met! Really, Mr. Ribeira, I'm not that sort of girl."

"Maybe when we get to know each other," Miro said, laughing.

She made a subtle, wonderful transition, and the woman on the screen was a lanky feline, sprawling sensuously on a tree limb. She purred noisily, stretched out a limb, groomed herself. "I can break your neck with a single blow from my paw," she whispered; her tone of voice suggested seduction; her claws promised murder. "When I get you alone, I can bite your throat out with a single kiss."

He laughed. Then he realized that in all this conversation, he had actually forgotten how slurred his speech was. She understood every word. She never said, "What? I didn't get that," or any of the other polite but infuriating things that people said. She understood him without any special effort at all.

"I want to understand everything," said Miro. "I want to know everything and put it all together to see what it means."

"Excellent project," she said. "It will look very good on your résumé."

Ender found that Olhado was a much better driver than he was. The boy's depth perception was better, and when he plugged his eye directly into the onboard computer, navigation practically took care of itself. Ender could devote his energies to looking.

The scenery seemed monotonous when they first began these exploratory flights. Endless prairies, huge herds of cabra, occasional forests in the distance—they never came close to those, of course, since they didn't want to attract the attention of the piggies that lived there. Besides, they were looking for a home for the hive queen, and it wouldn't do to put her too close to any tribe.

Today they headed west, on the other side of Rooter's Forest, and they followed a small river to its outlet. They stopped there on the beach, with breakers rolling gently to shore. Ender tasted the water. Salt. The sea.

Olhado got the onboard terminal to display a map of this region of Lusitania, pointing out their location, Rooter's Forest, and the other piggy settlements nearby. It was a good place, and in the back of his mind Ender could sense the hive queen's approval. Near the sea, plenty of water, sunny.

They skimmed over the water, traveling upstream a few hundred meters until the right bank rose to form a low cliff. "Any place to stop along here?" asked Ender.

Olhado found a place, fifty meters from the crown of the hill. They walked back along the river's edge, where the reeds gave way to the grama. Every river on Lusitania looked like this, of course. Ela had easily documented the genetic patterns, as soon as she had access to Novinha's files and permission to pursue the subject. Reeds that co-reproduced with suckflies. Grama that mated with watersnakes. And then the endless capim, which rubbed its pollen-rich tassels on the bellies of fertile cabra to germinate the next generation of manure-producing animals. Entwined in the roots and stems of the capim were the tropeços, long trailing vines that Ela proved had the same genes as the xingadora, the ground-nesting bird that used the living plant for its nest. The same sort of pairing continued in the forest: Macio worms that hatched from the seeds of merdona vines and then gave birth to merdona seed. Puladors, small insects that mated with the shiny-leafed bushes in the forest. And, above all, the piggies and the trees, both at the peak of their kingdoms, plant and animal merged into one long life.

That was the list, the whole list of surface animals and plants of Lusitania. Under water there were many, many more. But the Descolada had left Lusitania monotonous.

And yet even the monotony had a peculiar beauty. The geography was as varied as any other world—rivers, hills, mountains, deserts, oceans, islands. The carpet of capim and the patches of forest became background music to the symphony of landforms. The eye became sensitized to undulations, outcroppings, cliffs, pits, and, above all, the sparkle and rush of water in the sunlight. Lusitania, like Trondheim, was one of the rare worlds that was dominated by a single motif instead of displaying the whole symphony of possibility. With Trondheim, however, it was because the planet was on the bare edge of habitability, its climate only just able to support surface life. Lusitania's climate and soil cried out a welcome to the oncoming plow, the excavator's pick, the mason's trowel. Bring me to life, it said.

Ender did not understand that he loved this place because it was as devastated and barren as his own life, stripped and distorted in his childhood by events every bit as terrible, on a small scale, as the Descolada had been to this world. And yet it had thrived, had found a few threads strong enough to survive and continue to grow. Out of the challenge of the Descolada had come the three lives of the Little Ones. Out of the Battle School, out of years of isolation, had come Ender Wiggin. He fit this place as if he had planned it. The boy who walked beside him through the grama felt like his true son, as if he had known the boy from infancy. I know how it feels to have a metal wall between me and the world, Olhado. But here and now I have made the wall come down, and flesh touches earth, drinks water, gives comfort, takes love.

The earthen bank of the river rose in terraces, a dozen meters from shore to crest. The soil was moist enough to dig and hold its shape. The hive queen was a burrower; Ender felt the desire in him to dig, and so he dug, Olhado beside him. The ground gave way easily enough, and yet the roof of their cavelet stayed firm.

< Yes. Here. >

And so it was decided.

"Here it is," said Ender aloud.

Olhado grinned. But it was really Jane that Ender was talking to, and her answer that he heard. "Novinha thinks they have it. The tests all came through negative—the Descolada stayed inactive with the new Colador present in the cloned bugger cells. Ela thinks that the daisies she's been working with can be adapted to produce the Colador naturally. If that works, you'll only have to plant seeds here and there and the buggers can keep the Descolada at bay by sucking flowers."

Her tone was lively enough, but it was all business, no fun. No fun at all. "Fine," Ender said. He felt a stab of jealousy—Jane was no doubt talking far more easily with Miro, teasing him, taunting him as she used to do with Ender.

But it was easy enough to drive the feeling of jealousy away. He put out a hand and rested it easily on Olhado's shoulder; he momentarily pulled the boy close, and then together they walked back to the waiting flyer. Olhado marked the spot on the map and stored it. He laughed and made jokes all the way home, and Ender laughed with him. The boy wasn't Jane. But he *was* Olhado, and Ender loved him, and Olhado needed Ender, and that was what a few million years of evolution had decided Ender needed most. It was the hunger that had gnawed at him through all those years with Valentine, that had kept him moving from world to world. This boy with metal eyes. His bright and devastatingly destructive little brother Grego. Quara's penetrating understanding, her innocence; Quim's utter self-control, asceticism, faith; Ela's dependability, like a rock, and yet she knew when to move out and act; and Miro . . .

Miro. I have no consolation for Miro, not in this world, not at this time. His life's work was taken from him, his body, his hope for the future, and nothing I can say or do will give him a vital work to do. He lives in pain, his lover turned into his sister, his life among the piggies now impossible to him as they look to other humans for friendship and learning.

"Mironeeds . . ." Ender said softly.

"Miro needs to leave Lusitania," said Olhado.

"Mm," said Ender.

"You've got a starship, haven't you?" said Olhado. "I remember reading a story once. Or maybe it was a vid. About an old-time hero in the Bugger Wars, Mazer Rackham. He saved Earth from destruction once, but they knew he'd be dead long before the next battle. So they sent him out in a starship at relativistic speeds, just sent him out and had him come back. A hundred years had gone by for the Earth, but only two years for him."

"You think Miro needs something as drastic as that?"

"There's a battle coming. There are decisions to make. Miro's the smartest person in Lusitania, and the best. He doesn't get mad, you know. Even in the worst of times with Father. Marcão. Sorry, I still call him Father."

"That's all right. In most ways he *was.*"

"Miro would think, and he'd decide the best thing to do, and it always *was* the best thing. Mother depended on him to. The way I see it, we need Miro when Starways Congress sends its fleet against us. He'll study all the information, everything we've learned in the years that he was gone, put it all together, and tell us what to do."

Ender couldn't help himself. He laughed.

"So it's a dumb idea," said Olhado.

"You see better than anybody else I know," said Ender. "I've got to think about this, but you might be right."

They drove on in silence for a while.

"I was just talking," said Olhado. "When I said that about Miro. It was just something I thought, putting him together with that old story. It probably isn't even a true story."

"It's true," said Ender.

"How do you know?"

"I knew Mazer Rackham."

Olhado whistled. "You're old. You're older than any of the trees."

"I'm older than any of the human colonies. It doesn't make me wise, unfortunately."

"Are you really Ender? *The* Ender?"

"That's why it's my password."

"It's funny. Before you got here, the Bishop tried to tell us all that you were Satan. Quim's the only one in the family that took him seriously. But if the Bishop had told us you were *Ender,* we would have stoned you to death in the praça the day you arrived."

"Why don't you now?"

"We know you now. That makes all the difference, doesn't it?

Even Quim doesn't hate you now. When you really know somebody, you can't hate them."

"Or maybe it's just that you can't really know them until you stop hating them."

"Is that a circular paradox? Dom Cristão says that most truth can only be expressed in circular paradoxes."

"I don't think it has anything to do with truth, Olhado. It's just cause and effect. We never can sort them out. Science refuses to admit any cause except first cause—knock down one domino, the one next to it also falls. But when it comes to human beings, the only type of cause that matters is final cause, the purpose. What a person had in mind. Once you understand what people really want, you can't hate them anymore. You can fear them, but you can't hate them, because you can always find the same desires in your own heart."

"Mother doesn't like it that you're Ender."

"I know."

"But she loves you anyway."

"I know."

"And Quim—it's really funny, but now that he knows you're Ender, he likes you *better* for it."

"That's because he's a crusader, and I got my bad reputation by winning a crusade."

"And me," said Olhado.

"Yes, you," said Ender.

"You killed more people than anybody in history."

"Be the best at whatever you do, that's what my mother always told me."

"But when you Spoke for Father, you made me feel sorry for him. You make people love each other and forgive each other. How could you kill all those millions of people in the Xenocide?"

"I thought I was playing games. I didn't know it was the real thing. But that's no excuse, Olhado. If I had known the battle was real, I would have done the same thing. We thought they wanted to kill us. We were wrong, but we had no way to know that." Ender shook his head. "Except that I knew better. I knew my enemy. That's how I beat her, the hive queen, I knew her so well that I loved her, or maybe I loved her so well that I knew her. I didn't want to fight her anymore. I wanted to quit. I wanted to go home. So I blew up her planet."

"And today we found the place to bring her back to life." Olhado was very serious. "Are you sure she won't try to get even? Are you sure she won't try to wipe out humankind, starting with you?"

"I'm as sure," said Ender, "as I am of anything."

"Not absolutely sure," said Olhado.

"Sure enough to bring her back to life," said Ender. "And that's as sure as we ever are of anything. We believe it enough to act as though it's true. When we're that sure, we call it knowledge. Facts. We bet our lives on it."

"I guess that's what you're doing. Betting your life on her being what you think she is."

"I'm more arrogant than that. I'm betting *your* life, too, and everybody else's, and I'm not so much as asking anyone else's opinion."

"Funny," said Olhado. "If I asked somebody whether they'd trust Ender with a decision that might affect the future of the human race, they'd say, of course not. But if I asked them whether they'd trust the Speaker for the Dead, they'd say yes, most of them. And they wouldn't even guess that they were the same person."

"Yeah," said Ender. "Funny."

Neither of them laughed. Then, after a long time, Olhado spoke again. His thoughts had wandered to a subject that mattered more. "I don't want Miro to go away for thirty years."

"Say twenty years."

"In twenty years I'll be thirty-two. But he'd come back the age he is now. Twenty. Twelve years younger than me. If there's ever a girl who wants to marry a guy with reflecting eyes, I might even be married and have kids then. He won't even know me. I won't be his little brother anymore." Olhado swallowed. "It'd be like him dying."

"No," said Ender. "It'd be like him passing from his second life to his third."

"That's like dying, too," said Olhado.

"It's also like being born," said Ender. "As long as you keep getting born, it's all right to die sometimes."

Valentine called the next day. Ender's fingers trembled as he keyed instructions into the terminal. It wasn't just a message, either. It was a call, a full ansible voice communication. Incredibly expensive, but that wasn't a problem. It was the fact that ansible communications with the Hundred Worlds were supposedly cut off; for Jane to allow this call to come through meant that it was urgent. It occurred to Ender right away that Valentine might be in danger. That Starways Congress might have decided Ender was involved in the rebellion and traced his connection with her.

She was older. The hologram of her face showed weather lines from many windy days on the islands, floes, and boats of Trondheim. But her smile was the same, and her eyes danced with the same light. Ender was silenced at first by the changes the years had wrought in his sister; she, too, was silenced, by the fact that Ender seemed unchanged, a vision coming back to her out of her past.

"Ah, Ender," she sighed. "Was I ever so young?"

"And will I age so beautifully?"

She laughed. Then she cried. He did not; how could he? He had missed her for a couple of months. She had missed him for twenty-two years.

"I suppose you've heard," he said, "about our trouble getting along with Congress."

"I imagine that you were at the thick of it."

"Stumbled into the situation, really," said Ender. "But I'm glad I was here. I'm going to stay."

She nodded, drying her eyes. "Yes. I thought so. But I had to call and make sure. I didn't want to spend a couple of decades flying to meet you, and have you gone when I arrive."

"Meet me?" he said.

"I got much too excited about your revolution there, Ender. After twenty years of raising a family, teaching my students, loving my husband, living at peace with myself, I thought I'd never resurrect Demosthenes again. But then the story came about illegal contact with the piggies, and right away the news that Lusitania was in revolt, and suddenly people were saying the most ridiculous things, and I saw it was the beginning of the same old hate. Remember the videos about the buggers? How terrifying and awful they were? Suddenly we were seeing videos of the bodies they found, of the xenologers, I can't remember their names, but grisly pictures everywhere you looked, heating us up to war fever. And then stories about the Descolada, how if anyone ever went from Lusitania to another world it would destroy everything—the most hideous plague imaginable—"

"It's true," said Ender, "but we're working on it. Trying to find ways to keep the Descolada from spreading when we go to other worlds."

"True or not, Ender, it's all leading to war. I remember war—nobody else does. So I revived Demosthenes. I stumbled across some memos and reports. Their fleet is carrying the Little Doctor, Ender. If they decide to, they can blow Lusitania to bits. Just like—"

"Just like I did before. Poetic justice, do you think, for me to end the same way? He who lives by the sword—"

"Don't joke with me, Ender! I'm a middle-aged matron now, and I've lost my patience with silliness. At least for now. I wrote some very ugly truths about what Starways Congress is doing, and published them as Demosthenes. They're looking for me. Treason is what they're calling it."

"So you're coming here?"

"Not just me. Dear Jakt is turning the fleet over to his brothers and sisters. We've already bought a starship. There's apparently some kind of resistance movement that's helping us—someone named Jane has jimmied the computers to cover our tracks."

"I know Jane," said Ender.

"So you do have an organization here! I was shocked when I got a message that I could call you. Your ansible was supposedly blown up."

"We have powerful friends."

"Ender, Jakt and I are leaving today. We're bringing our three children."

"Your first one—"

"Yes, Syfte, the one who was making me fat when you left, she's almost twenty-two now. A very lovely girl. And a good friend, the children's tutor, named Plikt."

"I have a student by that name," said Ender, thinking back to conversations only a couple of months ago.

"Oh, yes, well, that was twenty years ago, Ender. And we're bringing several of Jakt's best men and their families. Something of an ark. It's not an emergency—you have twenty-two years to prepare for me. Actually longer, more like thirty years. We're taking the voyage in several hops, the first few in the wrong direction, so that nobody can be sure we're going to Lusitania."

Coming here. Thirty years from now. I'll be older than she is now. Coming here. By then I'll have my family, too. Novinha's and my children, if we have any, all grown, like hers.

And then, thinking of Novinha, he remembered Miro, remembered what Olhado had suggested several days ago, the day they found the nesting place for the hive queen.

"Would you mind terribly," said Ender, "if I sent someone to meet you on the way?"

"Meet us? In deep space? No, don't send someone to do that, Ender—it's too terrible a sacrifice, to come so far when the computers can guide us in just fine—"

"It's not really for you, though I want him to meet you. He's one of the xenologers. He was badly injured in an accident. Some brain damage; like a bad stroke. He's—he's the smartest person in Lusitania, says someone whose judgment I trust, but he's lost all his connections with our life here. Yet we'll need him later. When you arrive. He's a very good man, Val. He can make the last week of your voyage very educational."

"Can your friend arrange to get us course information for such a rendezvous? We're navigators, but only on the sea."

"Jane will have the revised navigational information in your ship's computer when you leave."

"Ender—for you it'll be thirty years, but for me—I'll see you in only a few weeks." She started to cry.

"Maybe I'll come with Miro to meet you."

"Don't!" she said. "I want you to be as old and crabbed as possible when I arrive. I couldn't put up with you as the thirty-year-old brat I see on my terminal."

"Thirty-five."

"You'll be there when I arrive!" she demanded.

"I will," he said. "And Miro, the boy I'm sending to you. Think of him as my son."

She nodded gravely. "These are such dangerous times, Ender. I only wish we had Peter."

"I don't. If *he* were running our little rebellion, he'd end up

Hegemon of all the Hundred Worlds. We just want them to leave us alone."

"It may not be possible to get the one without the other," said Val. "But we can quarrel about that later. Good-bye, my dear brother."

He didn't answer. Just looked at her and looked at her until she smiled wryly and switched off the connection.

Ender didn't have to ask Miro to go; Jane had already told him everything.

"Your sister is Demosthenes?" asked Miro. Ender was used to his slurred speech now. Or maybe his speech was clearing a little. It wasn't as hard to understand, anyway.

"We were a talented family," said Ender. "I hope you like her."

"I hope she likes me." Miro smiled, but he looked afraid.

"I told her," said Ender, "to think of you as my son."

Miro nodded. "I know," he said. And then, almost defiantly, "She showed me your conversation with her."

Ender felt cold inside.

Jane's voice came into his ear. "I should have asked you," she said. "But you know you would have said yes."

It wasn't the invasion of privacy that Ender minded. It was the fact that Jane was so very close to Miro. Get used to it, he told himself. He's the one she's looking out for now.

"We'll miss you," said Ender.

"Those who will miss me, miss me already," said Miro, "because they already think of me as dead."

"We need you alive," said Ender.

"When I come back, I'll still be only nineteen. And brain-damaged."

"You'll still be Miro, and brilliant, and trusted, and loved. You started this rebellion, Miro. The fence came down for you. Not for some great cause, but for you. Don't let us down."

Miro smiled, but Ender couldn't tell if the twist in his smile was because of his paralysis, or because it was a bitter, poisonous smile.

"Tell me something," said Miro.

"If I won't," said Ender, "she will."

"It isn't hard. I just want to know what it was that Pipo and Libo died for. What it was the piggies honored them for."

Ender understood better than Miro knew: He understood why the boy cared so much about the question. Miro had learned that he was really Libo's son only hours before he crossed the fence and lost his future. Pipo, then Libo, then Miro; father, son, grandson; the three xenologers who had lost their futures for the piggies' sake. Miro hoped that in understanding why his forebears died, he might make more sense of his own sacrifice.

The trouble was that the truth might well leave Miro feeling that none of the sacrifices meant anything at all. So Ender answered with a question. "Don't you already know why?"

Miro spoke slowly and carefully, so that Ender could understand his slurred speech. "I know that the piggies thought they were doing them an honor. I know that Mandachuva and Leaf-eater could have died in their places. With Libo, I even know the occasion. It was when the first amaranth harvest came, and there was plenty of food. They were rewarding him for that. Except why not earlier? Why not when we taught them to use merdona root? Why not when we taught them to make pots, or shoot arrows?"

"The truth?" said Ender.

Miro knew from Ender's tone that the truth would not be easy. "Yes," he said.

"Neither Pipo nor Libo really deserved the honor. It wasn't the amaranth that the wives were rewarding. It was the fact that Leaf-eater had persuaded them to let a whole generation of infants be conceived and born even though there wasn't enough food for them to eat once they left the mothertree. It was a terrible risk to take, and if he had been wrong, that whole generation of young piggies would have died. Libo brought the harvest, but Leaf-eater was the one who had, in a sense, brought the population to a point where they needed the grain."

Miro nodded. "Pipo?"

"Pipo told the piggies about his discovery. That the Descolada, which killed humans, was part of their normal physiology. That their bodies could handle transformations that killed us. Mandachuva told the wives that this meant that humans were not godlike and all-powerful. That in some ways we were even weaker than the Little Ones. That what made humans stronger than piggies was not something inherent in us—our size, our brains, our language—but rather the mere accident that we were a few thousand years ahead of them in learning. If they could acquire our knowledge, then we humans would have no more power over them. Mandachuva's discovery that piggies were potentially equal to humans—that was what they rewarded, not the information Pipo gave that led to that discovery."

"So both of them—"

"The piggies didn't want to kill either Pipo or Libo. In both cases, the crucial achievement belonged to a piggy. The only reason Pipo and Libo died was because they couldn't bring themselves to take a knife and kill a friend."

Miro must have seen the pain in Ender's face, despite his best effort to conceal it. Because it was Ender's bitterness that he answered. "You," said Miro, "you can kill anybody."

"It's a knack I was born with," said Ender.

"You killed Human because you knew it would make him live a new and better life," said Miro.

"Yes."

"And me," said Miro.

"Yes," said Ender. "Sending you away is very much like killing you."

"But will I live a new and better life?"

"I don't know. Already you get around better than a tree."

Miro laughed. "So I've got one thing on old Human, don't I—at least I'm ambulatory. And nobody has to hit me with a stick so I can talk." Then Miro's expression grew sour again. "Of course, now *he* can have a thousand children."

"Don't count on being celibate all your life," said Ender. "You may be disappointed."

"I hope so," said Miro.

And then, after a silence: "Speaker?"

"Call me Ender."

"Ender, did Pipo and Libo die for nothing, then?" Ender understood the real question: Am I also enduring this for nothing?

"There are worse reasons to die," Ender answered, "than to die because you cannot bear to kill."

"What about someone," said Miro, "who can't kill, and can't die, and can't live, either?"

"Don't deceive yourself," said Ender. "You'll do all three someday."

Miro left the next morning. There were tearful good-byes. For weeks afterward, it was hard for Novinha to spend any time in her own house, because Miro's absence was so painful to her. Even though she had agreed wholeheartedly with Ender that it was right for Miro to go, it was still unbearable to lose her child. It made Ender wonder if his own parents felt such pain when he was taken away. He suspected they had not. Nor had they hoped for his return. He already loved another man's children more than his parents had loved their own child. Well, he'd get fit revenge for their neglect of him. He'd show them, three thousand years later, how a father should behave. Bishop Peregrino married them in his chambers. By Novinha's calculations, she was still young enough to have another six children, if they hurried. They set at the task with a will.

Before the marriage, though, there were two days of note. On a day in summer, Ela, Ouanda, and Novinha presented him with the results of their research and speculation: as completely as possible, the life cycle and community structure of the piggies, male and female, and a likely reconstruction of their patterns of life before the Descolada bonded them forever to the trees that, till then, had been no more to them than habitat. Ender had reached his own understanding of who the piggies were, and especially who Human was before his passage to the life of light.

He lived with the piggies for a week while he wrote the Life of Human. Mandachuva and Leaf-eater read it carefully, discussed it with him; he revised and reshaped; finally it was ready. On that day he invited everyone who was working with the piggies—all the Ribeira family, Ouanda and her sisters, the many workmen who had brought technological miracles to the piggies, the scholar-monks of the Children of the Mind, Bishop Peregrino, Mayor Bosquinha—and read the book to them. It wasn't long, less than an hour to read. They had gathered on the hillside near where Human's seedling tree reached upward, now more than three meters high, and where Rooter overshadowed them in the afternoon sunlight. "Speaker," said the Bishop, "almost thou persuadest me to become a humanist." Others, less trained to eloquence, found no words to say, not then or ever. But they knew from that day forward who the piggies were, just as the readers of the Hive Queen had understood the buggers, and the readers of the Hegemon had understood humankind in its endless quest for greatness in a wilderness of separation and suspicion.

"This was why I called you here," said Novinha. "I dreamed once of writing this book. But you had to write it."

"I played more of a role in the story than I would have chosen for myself," said Ender. "But you fulfilled your dream, Ivanova. It was your work that led to this book. And you and your children who made me whole enough to write it."

He signed it, as he had signed the others, The Speaker for the Dead.

Jane took the book and carried it by ansible across the light-years to the Hundred Worlds. With it she brought the text of the Covenant and Olhado's pictures of its signing and of the passage of Human into the full light. She placed it here and there, in a score of places on each of the Hundred Worlds, giving it to people likely to read it and understand what it was. Copies were sent as messages from computer to computer; by the time Starways Congress knew of it, it was too widely distributed to be suppressed.

Instead they tried to discredit it as a fake. The pictures were a crude simulation. Textual analysis revealed that it could not possibly have the same author as the other two books. Ansible usage records revealed that it could not possibly have come from Lusitania, which had no ansible. Some people believed them. Most people didn't care. Many who did care enough to read the Life of Human hadn't the heart to accept the piggies as ramen.

Some did accept the piggies, and read the accusation that Demosthenes had written a few months before, and began to call the fleet that was already under way toward Lusitania "The Second Xenocide." It was a very ugly name. There weren't enough jails in the Hundred Worlds to hold all those who used it. The Starways Congress had thought the war would begin when their ships reached Lusitania forty years from then. Instead, the war was already begun, and it would be fierce. What the Speaker for the Dead wrote, many people believed; and many were ready to accept the piggies as ramen, and to think of anyone who sought their deaths as murderers.

Then, on a day in autumn, Ender took the carefully wrapped cocoon, and he and Novinha, Olhado, Quim, and Ela skimmed over the kilometers of capim till they came to the hill beside the river. The daisies they had planted were in furious bloom; the winter here would be mild, and the hive queen would be safe from the Descolada.

Ender carried the hive queen gingerly to the riverbank, and laid her in the chamber he and Olhado had prepared. They laid the carcass of a freshly killed cabra on the ground outside her chamber.

And then Olhado drove them back. Ender wept with the vast, uncontrollable ecstasy that the hive queen placed within his mind, her rejoicing too strong for a human heart to bear; Novinha held him, Quim quietly prayed, and Ela sang a jaunty folksong that once had been heard in the hill country of Minas Geráis, among the caipiras and mineiros of old Brazil. It was a good time, a good place to be, better than Ender had ever dreamed for himself in the sterile corridors of the Battle School when he was little, and fighting for his life.

"I can probably die now," said Ender. "All my life's work is done."

"Mine too," said Novinha. "But I think that means that it's time to start to live."

Behind them, in the dank and humid air of a shallow cave by a river, strong mandibles tore at the cocoon, and a limp and skeletal body struggled forth. Her wings only gradually spread out and dried in the sunlight; she struggled weakly to the riverbank and pulled strength and moisture into her desiccated body. She nibbled at the meat of the cabra. The unhatched eggs she held within her cried out to be released; she laid the first dozen of them in the cabra's corpse, then ate the nearest daisies, trying to feel the changes in her body as she came alive at last.

The sunlight on her back, the breeze against her wings, the water cool under her feet, her eggs warming and maturing in the flesh of the cabra: Life, so long waited for, and not until today could she be sure that she would be, not the last of her tribe, but the first.